KICKING THE AIR

KICKING THE AIR

Graham Ison

This first world edition published in Great Britain 2005 by
SEVERN HOUSE PUBLISHERS LTD of
9–15 High Street, Sutton, Surrey SM1 1DF.
This first world edition published in the USA 2005 by
SEVERN HOUSE PUBLISHERS INC of
595 Madison Avenue, New York, N.Y. 10022.

British Library Cataloguing in Publication Data

Ison, Graham
    Kicking the air
    1.   Brock, Detective Inspector (Fictitious character) - Fiction
    2.   Poole, Detective Sergeant (Fictitious character) - Fiction
    3.   Murder - Investigation - England - London - Fiction
    4.   Police - England - London - Fiction
    5.   Detective and mystery stories
    I.   Title
    823.9'14 [F]

    ISBN 0-7278-6217-0

Typeset by Palimpsest Book Production Ltd.,
Polmont, Stirlingshire, Scotland.
Printed and bound in Great Britain by
MPG Books Ltd., Bodmin, Cornwall.

One

Nine o'clock on Wednesday evening.

'I think we'll call it a day, Dave,' I said to my sergeant.

We'd been making our brains hurt trying to put together a report for the Crown Prosecution Service on a guy we'd arrested for murder, a task often more difficult than solving the murder itself.

That's when the call came in.

The car we normally used had a sticker from Transport Branch on the windscreen declaring the vehicle unroadworthy due to a transmission problem, whatever the hell that meant. Why not fix it instcad of going about plastering little notices on the damned thing? We both muttered oaths and took a cab for the half mile or so to Waterloo Bridge from our office at Curtis Green.

Not many people – including, believe it or not, the police – know that Curtis Green is tucked away behind Richmond Terrace Mews, just off Whitehall, and long, long ago was part of New Scotland Yard. Before the Yard got overcrowded and was shifted to Victoria, that is. Unhappily, however, the new headquarters is similarly overcrowded, and is also called New Scotland Yard, a decision that confuses those tourists who rely on outdated guide books, and who trot down Whitehall in search of it.

But even fewer people – and that still includes the police – know that Curtis Green houses Serious Crime Group West and that it has the responsibility for investigating all major crimes from there to Hillingdon.

Well, nearly.

1

Just for the record, that responsibility excludes what is known – daringly for the now terrifyingly politically correct Metropolitan Police – as 'black-on-black' crime, which is dealt with by something called Operation Trident. The onus of investigating serious sexual crimes falls on Project Sapphire. Oh, and there's something called Operation Emerald that looks after witnesses and victims.

And there are probably one or two other 'specialist' squads that I have yet to come across.

What's left is down to poor bloody sharp-end coppers like me. And Dave Poole, my black sergeant bag-carrier. Why he hasn't been snapped up by Operation Trident is a mystery, but he reckons that if he stays in the shadows they won't be able to see him. Dave has a quirky sense of humour, which is why he sometimes refers to himself as Colour-Sergeant Poole.

Come to think of it, there are so many specialist squads at the Yard now, it's a wonder that there's anything left for the Serious Crime Group to deal with at all. I've even heard there's a squad that spends all its time – well, Monday to Friday, nine to five – dreaming up new code words for new squads. But that might just be a malicious rumour put about by those who do the real work, few of us though there are these days. Nevertheless, I think I must have gone wrong somewhere to finish up where I am. I know of one superintendent with twenty years' service who, after his two years of 'foot' duty – which he did in a car – has been ensconced in a nice, warm office ever since.

However, enough of this philosophizing. As it turned out, we needn't have rushed. When we got to Waterloo police station there was just a body bag – with a body in it – on the landing stage.

In case you're wondering where a landing stage fits into all this, Waterloo is London's only floating police station and is manned by what used to be called Thames Division. Until, that is, it was renamed the Marine Support Unit by the afore-mentioned 'new names and total confusion squad' at Scotland Yard.

The victim had been found floating in the river by the obser-vant crew of a police launch. They are always observant in

2

such matters because they get a bonus for recovering bodies from the murky waters of the Thames.

As it is beneath the dignity of the Water Rats – as river coppers are known to us of the elite – to hang about guarding a dead body, two police officers had been summoned from Charing Cross police station to ensure, presumably, that it didn't fall into the hands of a latter-day Burke and Hare.

One of the officers, I subsequently discovered, was 'learning beats', which means that she had just emerged from that forcing establishment they call the Hendon Training School, doubtless still starry-eyed and intent on working for a safer London. Good luck. She was a girl with a blonde ponytail that reached her shoulder blades, silly bitch. She clearly had yet to discover that some yob would seize it and swing her round like a rag doll at the first punch-up in which she got involved.

Her male companion – optimistically styled a 'tutor constable' – was chatting to an unsavoury youth in what used to be called plain clothes, although there was nothing plain about his ensemble. I assumed, and later discovered, that he was a CID officer, God help us.

Dave immediately set about asking questions of this trio in the hope that they might have something useful to tell us. A vain quest.

In the meantime, I unzipped the body bag sufficient to study the victim's face. She was a young brunette – about twenty-five, I reckoned – and pretty, and there was something that looked like a bootlace tight around her neck.

'Find out anything?' I asked when Dave returned.

'The clown in fancy dress claims to be a CID officer from Charing Cross police station, guv.'

'How fascinating.' I beckoned to this vision to join us. 'And what's your part in this drama?' I asked.

'The DI sent me down to liaise, sir.' Preening himself slightly, the youth announced that he was a detective constable.

'So liaise, my son. What, for instance, d'you know about this?' I asked, waving at the body.

'Er, nothing, sir.'

'I see. Well, now that you've played a significant part in

this investigation, you may as well go back to the nick and do some work.'

Somewhat relieved, I imagine, the DC scurried away.

'According to the "feet" ' – Dave gestured at the two PCs – 'the river police spotted the body just opposite the Houses of Parliament.'

'She's not an MP, I suppose?' I asked hopefully.

'Doubt it,' said Dave, glancing down at the girl's face. 'She's too good-looking.'

'Pity. Which side?'

'Which side?'

'Which side of the river,' I repeated patiently. 'If the body was nearer the Lambeth side than the Westminster side, it'd be down to SCG South.'

'I don't think the commander will let us get away with that, guv,' said Dave thoughtfully. 'After all, it's on our side now.'

I didn't think we'd get away with it either. But I should mention that the commander, a life-long Uniform Branch wally, had – in the twilight of his career – been turned into a paper detective by someone in the Human Resources Branch at Commissioner's Office, as we of the cognoscenti call Scotland Yard. Unfortunately for me and my colleagues, the commander had a misplaced notion that the more murders his officers investigated, the greater would be the glory reflecting upon him. And would doubtless culminate in the award of the Queen's Police Medal for Distinguished Service, or something even more prestigious. Naïve fool! The only award I'd ever received was my Woodman's Badge when I was a Boy Scout. Apart, that is, from my Police Long Service and Good Conduct Medal, which the governor handed me one day when I happened to be passing his office.

'Has someone sent for the pathologist and the rest of the circus?' I enquired, looking round.

'I have.' Dave had clearly been busy on his mobile. 'The crime-scene examiners are on their way, guv, and so's Henry.'

Henry Mortlock, an exponent of black humour that rivalled that of most detectives, was the Home Office pathologist who always managed to turn up for my dead bodies. Perhaps he enjoys my company. On the other hand, it may just be that that's how the roster works out.

And, as if on cue, Henry arrived.

'Well, Harry, we meet again.' Mortlock rubbed his hands together and looked at the woman's face. After a moment's contemplation he undid the body bag fully. 'Hmm!' he said, and for a few moments gazed at the naked body. 'Well, there's not much I can do here. No good taking her temperature.'

'I suppose not,' I said. 'She doesn't look as though she's sickening for anything. Not any more.'

As usual Henry ignored my flippancy. I think he thought he had the monopoly on smart remarks. 'Get it to the mortuary, Harry, there's a good chap.' He stood up and hummed a few bars from Mozart's *Figaro*.

There wasn't much I could do either. The absence of clothing would make identification that much more difficult, and I had a nagging suspicion that it would be some time before we found out who she was. But, unusually for me, I had a bit of luck there.

Two of the scientific lot's white vans arrived on the road just above the police station. After a short delay, during which time I imagined that the technicians of murder were donning their white overalls, Linda Mitchell, the chief crime-scene examiner, appeared on the landing stage.

She looked down at our body. 'I understand she was pulled out of the river, Mr Brock?'

'Yes,' I said. 'That's why she's wet.'

'In that case, photographing the victim is about all we can do on site,' said Linda. She too had a tendency to ignore my smart remarks.

'And fingerprints,' I suggested.

'Of course,' said Linda, and shot me a withering glance that implied I was doubting her professional competence.

Meanwhile, Dave was busy making telephone calls to God knows who, arranging for the removal of the body to Henry Mortlock's butchery.

I went into the front office of the nick. 'I'm DCI Brock, Serious Crime Group West,' I said to the station officer, a weary sergeant who looked as though he wished he were ten

5

years older and thus eligible for a pension. 'Where's the boat's crew that found this body, Skip?' I cocked a thumb towards the door.

'Back on patrol, sir.' The sergeant's expression suggested that I'd just made a fatuous enquiry.

'Did they, by any chance, happen to mention the ligature around the victim's neck when they brought her ashore?' I didn't try to disguise my sarcasm.

'Yes, sir, they did mention that. That's why we called Wapping.'

'What's Wapping got to do with anything?' I asked. This was obviously going to be a tortuous conversation. 'That's the headquarters of the OCU, sir.' The sergeant pronounced it 'ock-you'.

'The what?' I knew what he meant, but I hate acronyms. Along with all the other things I hate about today's Metropolitan Police.

'The operational command unit, sir,' said the sergeant slowly, and in such a way that implied he was treating with an idiot.

'And?'

'They said to refer it to CX. That's Charing Cross nick, sir. Er, police station.'

'I see. So the boat's crew, well knowing that this was a suspicious death, decided not to wait for me, and went back on patrol. Got that right, have I?'

'They got a shout, sir,' said the sergeant, playing his trump. 'Bit of a punch-up on a gin palace, down near Blackfriars Bridge.' He turned to his computer screen. 'All quiet on arrival. They're on their way back as I speak, sir.'

'Obviously a priority,' I muttered, and walked out of the office just as a launch was tying up. A sergeant and a constable stepped lightly on to the landing stage.

I introduced myself and Dave. 'What's the SP?' I asked. SP is a piece of verbal shorthand that the police have culled from the racing fraternity and means 'starting price', but when a policeman uses it he means 'What's the story?'

'We were patrolling upstream, sir,' said the sergeant, 'when we spotted the floater just abeam the Houses of Parliament.

6

Taffy' – he nodded towards his PC – 'got her inboard, but she was already dead.'

'Probably because of the ligature round her neck,' observed Dave mildly.

'Given the tide at this time of year, Skip, where could she have gone in?' I asked.

'Ah, that's a good question, sir.' The sergeant took off his cap and scratched at his thinning hair. 'And I can't answer it until I know *when* she went in.'

'Thanks a lot. You've been a great help. DS Poole will take brief statements from you both.'

And then everything happened at once. Henry Mortlock went, the crime-scene white-suits left, the body was removed and the boat's crew continued their patrol, no doubt to sort out a few more revellers who were polluting the environment with their drunken carousing.

Thursday morning. An unidentified murder victim, no idea what to do next and the commander poking about in the incident room. What more could one ask?

'What d'you think, Mr Brock?' enquired the commander.

'I'm waiting for the result of a search of fingerprint records, sir,' I said. 'Until we know who the victim is, we're a bit stuck.'

A bit stuck! We haven't got a bloody clue. Literally.

'Mmm! Yes, I suppose so. Er, any thoughts on the cause of death?' This despite the fact that Linda Mitchell's team had already produced blown-up photographs of the dead woman, including a close-up of the ligature around the girl's neck. All of which had been posted on a notice board by the ever-efficient Detective Sergeant Colin Wilberforce, the incident-room manager.

'At a rough guess, sir,' I ventured, with just a hint of irony, 'strangled with a ligature.' I pointed at the close-up with my pen. 'That ligature. But, of course, we'll have to wait until Henry's finished.' I glanced at my watch. 'I'm just about to leave for the post-mortem.'

'Who's Henry?' The commander knew fine who I was talking about.

7

'Dr Mortlock, sir. The Home Office pathologist,' I said.

'I see.' The commander wrinkled his nose. He always treated highly qualified medical practitioners with some deference, and would never dream of referring to them by their first name. Perhaps he feared that one of them would one day declare him unfit for further service. Then he wouldn't know what the hell to do with himself.

Henry Mortlock was always at his best when he was conducting a post-mortem. Attired in all-over white – tunic, trousers and rubber boots – he was lovingly sorting through his collection of ghoulish instruments when I arrived.

'Ah, Harry, you've got here. Now I can begin.'

After some consideration, he selected a scalpel and opened up the body from throat to pubis to the accompaniment of his very own hummed version of some obscure symphony. Well, it was obscure to me.

It took an hour of incision, muttering and the occasional operatic aria before Henry declared himself reasonably satisfied. He was never more than *reasonably* satisfied. 'I'll let you have my report, Harry,' he said, 'but on the face of it, my professional opinion is that this young woman died as a result of strangulation with a ligature and was dead before she entered the water.'

What a coincidence. I'd more or less worked that out for myself.

'There's some post-mortem grazing on the woman's back,' Henry continued, 'and I'm of the view that she'd been dead less than twenty-four hours when your fishermen dredged her up. Oh, and she'd indulged in sexual intercourse – probably consensual – shortly before dying. I've obtained a sample from the victim's vagina. Might be a good idea to send it for DNA analysis.'

'That *is* a good idea, Henry,' I said, but my sarcasm escaped this eminent pathologist.

All I had to do now was find the guy who'd had it off with her. He might be the murderer, but knowing my luck, maybe not.

* * *

8

Dave and I grabbed a quick bite to eat and then hastened back to Curtis Green in time for Colin Wilberforce to announce that a piece of good news had flooded in. The woman's fingerprints were on record and we now had a name: Patricia Hunter.

'What's her form, Colin?' If she was on record she must have been convicted of a crime within the past seven years. Otherwise a compassionate government would have declared it to be a 'spent' conviction and rubbed it out. Bit like the victim herself.

'One previous five years ago for shoplifting in Oxford Street, sir. Fined three hundred pounds plus costs. Her antecedents show her to have been an actress at the time.' Colin looked up and grinned. We both knew what that was a euphemism for. 'And they also show that her fine was paid by a guy called Bruce Phillips. There's no address for him.'

'Have you got an address for the woman?' I asked.

'According to this' – Colin waved the printout –'she was living at nineteen Saxony Street, Chelsea, sir. But, as I said, that was five years ago.'

'Age?'

Colin had no need to refer to the woman's record again. 'She'd've been twenty-six now, sir,' he said promptly, having already worked it out.

I glanced at the clock: half past two. 'Know where Saxony Street, Chelsea, is, Dave?'

'Not offhand, guv, but no doubt I'll find it,' said Dave with a sigh.

Saxony Street was not far from Chelsea Embankment, which, given that Patricia Hunter had been found floating in the river, was interesting. But probably irrelevant.

We introduced ourselves to a svelte brunette of indeterminate age who told us her name was Clare Barker.

Once seated in her plush sitting room, we explained that we were trying to trace any friends or relatives of Patricia Hunter who had, according to our records, lived at 19 Saxony Street five years previously.

'Is she a missing person?' asked Mrs Barker.

'Not any more,' said Dave.

9

'Oh!' That seemed to mystify Mrs Barker momentarily. 'Well, my husband and I bought this house about two years ago,' she said. 'The previous owners had converted it into three flats, but we changed it back and refurbished it, and now we occupy the whole house.'

'So the name Patricia Hunter doesn't mean anything to you?'

'No, I'm sorry. I've no idea where you'd find her now.'

'We *have* found her,' said Dave. 'Floating in the river.'

'Oh, my goodness!' Mrs Barker looked shocked and put a hand to her mouth. 'Was it an accident?'

'We don't think so,' I said. 'She'd been strangled.' That'll give the Chelsea set something to chatter about, I thought.

'How dreadful,' was Mrs Barker's further contribution to the conversation.

'Can you tell me who you bought the house from?' I asked hopefully. The death of Patricia Hunter was already showing signs of developing into a complex investigation. But little did I know then that it was going to get considerably more complex before we found the woman's killer.

'I'll ask my husband.' Mrs Barker rose from her chair. 'He's in the study and he dealt with all of that,' she added over her shoulder as she glided gracefully from the room.

A few moments later she reappeared followed by a man in a Paisley shirt and chinos. 'I'm Sandy Barker,' he said. 'How can I help you? Clare mentioned something about a murder,' he added with a frown.

I repeated what we knew and what we wanted to know.

'As Clare told you, we bought the house about two years ago.' Barker handed me a business card. 'That's the estate agent who handled the sale – they're in the King's Road – and the people we bought the house from were called Mason. I think that was their name.' He glanced at his wife and she nodded.

'Any idea where these Masons moved to?' I asked, hoping to short-circuit a visit to the estate agent.

'No, sorry,' said Barker.

'Does the name Bruce Phillips mean anything to you?'

'No, sorry,' said Barker again.

Oh well, it was worth a try.

* * *

10

'There's nothing we can do until the morning, Dave,' I said as we drove back to Curtis Green. 'We may as well have an early night while we've still got the chance.'

Not that Dave ever minded working late. His gorgeous wife Madeleine was a principal ballet dancer, and rarely got home before midnight.

As for my girlfriend Sarah Dawson, a scientist at the Metropolitan Forensic Science Laboratory, she's grown accustomed to the bizarre hours I work. I think she even believes me now when I tell her I've been working late at the office.

Two

The ligature had been sent to the forensic science laboratory, and I decided to go there myself. For two reasons. Firstly to see Sarah and, secondly, to see if I could hurry up the analysis of the ligature. Which *also* meant seeing Sarah, because she is the rope, yarn, string and miscellaneous ligatures expert. I do love combining business with pleasure.

Sarah is thirty-one and gorgeous. She has long black hair, long legs and an hour-glass figure. But now, perched on a stool at her bench, she was in her professional mode, emphasized by the white lab coat she was wearing, and the heavy black-framed glasses.

'I thought you'd be here sooner or later, Harry,' she said.

'So, what can you tell me, darling?'

'About what?' Sarah didn't smile, just appraised me rather severely over her glasses. I got the disturbing feeling that she didn't want to see me today. Perhaps it was just that she was rather busy.

'The ligature.'

'Ah, the ligature.' Sarah swung round on her stool, revealing a black nylon-clad knee. 'You can have all the scientific mumbo-jumbo if you want it, Harry, but it's some form of thin electrical flex, and it was tied in a running slipknot.'

'A running slipknot, eh? Were you a Girl Guide?' I asked.

'Yes, as a matter of fact, I was.'

'You never told me about that.'

'There are a lot of things you don't know about me,' said Sarah. But, despite the banter, I detected something tense

12

about her this afternoon. And her enigmatic comment was to prove truer than I knew.

'It was obviously tied at the back of the neck then,' I mused. 'There was no knot visible from the front when I examined the body.'

'That would be right,' said Sarah. 'The CSEs said it was tied at the back.'

'What sort of electrical wire was it?'

'Fairly standard, I should think.' Sarah smiled. 'But finding out's your job, Harry. You're the detective. I've no idea where it came from. And there's one more thing which is bound to excite you.'

'Apart from what usually excites me, you mean?'

'There was the slightest trace of greasepaint on the piece of wire,' she said, making no attempt to match my badinage.

'That's interesting. The victim, Patricia Hunter, was an actress.'

'That should be easy then. There are only about fifty theatres in London.'

That sort of sarcasm was alien to Sarah's character and I wondered what had ruffled her feathers. I found out almost immediately.

'Thanks.' I started towards the door, but Sarah stopped me.

'Harry.' She turned back to her bench and toyed with a pair of callipers.

'What is it?'

It was some seconds before she answered, but then she faced me once again. 'I've resigned from the lab,' she said as she took off her glasses.

'Resigned? But what are you going to do? You've got a brilliant career ahead of you and—'

Sarah held up a hand. 'I'm moving to Poole in Dorset, Harry,' she said simply.

'Christ, that must be a hundred miles away,' I said. I was completely taken aback by her bald statement. 'But why? I thought that we – you and I – were going to make something of this relationship.'

Tears welled up in her eyes. 'It can't be helped, Harry. My father's seriously ill and my mother can't cope. They're both in their late sixties and . . .' She paused for a moment. 'I don't

13

think my father will last too long. It's one of those things that can't be helped,' she said again. 'I wish to God there was some other way.'

'But I thought your parents lived in Cornwall. Helston if I remember correctly.'

'They did, but they got fed up with Cornish winters. I persuaded them to move to Dorset. There's a flat in their new house that I'm going to occupy . . . for a while anyway.'

'For a while?' I didn't like the sound of any of this. 'But what about your sister? Can't she do anything to help out?' Sarah's sister Margaret lived in Staines with her carping little husband David, an air-traffic controller at Heathrow, and their two kids.

'There's no way she can get to Poole on a regular basis, not with David's job and everything. The best that he could do would be to get a transfer to the air-traffic control centre at Swanwick, but that's still fifty miles away, and even so, Margaret's never been one for worrying about our parents too much. And she's got a job and the children to ferry back and forth to school.'

'But what about us?' I asked. I was at the beginning of a tricky murder investigation that I suspected would go on and on, and the last thing I wanted was the sudden departure of my girlfriend. Call it selfish if you like, but I'd nurtured high hopes that we would get married. Now, however, Sarah had suddenly announced that she was moving over a hundred miles away. The implication was that I might never see her again.

'Why don't we have dinner tonight?' I said. 'See if we can't sort something out.'

Sarah shook her head. 'Are you seriously suggesting that you'll have time for dinner with all you've got on your plate, Harry?' She obviously hadn't intended the remark to be funny and neither of us laughed.

Suddenly the awful truth dawned on me: she was trying to let me down lightly. 'Have you met someone else, Sarah?' I asked, hoping to God I was wrong.

The tears began again, and she nodded as she fumbled for a tissue from the box on her bench. 'I'm sorry, Harry.' There was a pause. 'But my father really is ill and I do have to go

14

there to look after him. I wasn't making that up.' She paused again. 'But yes, I have been seeing someone, and we're getting married.'

'Do I know this guy?' I asked lamely.

She shook her head. 'No, he's in the army.'

'Oh, not again.' Her previous fiancé, Captain Peter Hunt, had been killed a few years ago during some footling exercise on Salisbury Plain and I didn't think she'd ever recovered from it. But now . . . 'How did you meet?'

'At Bovingdon Camp. That's in Dorset too.'

'I know. I was quite good at geography.' I tried to keep the sarcasm out of my voice, but failed miserably.

'Last April, I had to go down there to do some work for which the military police hadn't the resources. I stayed overnight in one of their messes and this major took me in to dinner. It just went on from there. I'm truly sorry, Harry.'

'You mean he's a military policeman?' I briefly considered making some trite remark about jumping out of the frying pan into the fire, but thought better of it.

'No, he just happened to be there. He's in the Hussars and he lives in the mess.' Sarah paused. 'I won't invite you to the wedding, Harry. It wouldn't be fair.'

'I hope you'll be very happy, Sarah,' I said and turned on my heel. I was too choked to say anything else.

'You're looking decidedly fed up with life, guv,' said Dave, when I got back to the office.

'Yeah, well, a complex murder is not exactly designed to cheer you up, Dave,' I said, deciding against telling him about my break-up with Sarah. At least, not yet. I knew that very soon he would come up with another invitation to see Madeleine performing in a ballet. Time enough then. I suppose I still nurtured a vain hope that it would all come right again, and that the bold Hussar was an infatuation that would go away as quickly as it had arrived to disrupt our bliss.

Fortunately I was likely to be heavily engrossed in the murder I was investigating, with little time, I hoped, to feel sorry for myself. Having finally divorced my wife Helga and moved to a flat in Surbiton, everything had been going swimmingly: Sarah and I had really hit it off. And then this.

I couldn't blame her really, try as I might; there's no contest between a detective facing danger at all hours – her view, not mine – and an army officer in a swish uniform who'd take her to glittering balls, point-to-point meetings and polo matches. Well, that's the way I saw the army. I just hoped, for Sarah's sake, that he didn't end up in Iraq or some such God-awful place. I don't think she could stand losing another soldier.

'Let's find something to eat, Dave,' I said.

Detective Constable Nicola Chance had been busy in my absence. During the morning, she'd visited the estate agent who'd handled the sale and purchase of the house in which the Barkers now lived at Chelsea. The vendors were indeed called Mason, as the Barkers had said, and they lived in Putney. Well, that was a relief. They could have moved to Scotland, I suppose.

But my optimism was short-lived. Nicola had already telephoned them and although they confirmed that Patricia Hunter had rented a flat at 19 Saxony Street, she had left some four years ago and they had no idea where she'd gone. But, they had told Nicola, a man by the name of Bruce Phillips had shared the accommodation with Patricia.

And Bruce Phillips was the guy who'd paid her shoplifting fine.

As if that wasn't enough, the result of the DNA database search had come back: there was no match with the seminal fluid found in Patricia Hunter's body.

But there was one glimmer of useful information in the report from the forensic science laboratory. Fibres had been found in the hair of the dead woman. And tests were being carried out at the laboratory to see if the possible origin of those fibres could be narrowed down.

I sent for Detective Inspector Frank Mead, the former Flying Squad officer in charge of the legwork team that made all the enquiries I didn't have time to make.

'We know that Patricia Hunter was calling herself an actress

16

five years ago, Frank,' I began, 'and with any luck she may still be one.'

'If she was one in the first place, Harry,' said Frank. He also knew that 'actress' was often how call girls described themselves. That's when they weren't calling themselves 'models', of course.

I told him about the slight trace of greasepaint that Sarah had found on the ligature with which the girl had been murdered. 'So it's possible that the body *is* that of an actress,' I said.

'Or a prostitute,' said Frank, refusing to give up.

'Exactly so, but we've got to start with the obvious.'

'Like a check on all the theatres in London,' Frank said with a sigh.

'There's only about fifty of them,' I said with similar irony to that used by Sarah only that morning but which, now, seemed like ages ago. 'And get someone to check the toms' register, too. If she was on the game, we might be able to trace someone who knew her. Or has missed her.'

'Right.' Frank had been making notes as I spoke. 'Anything else?'

'Not at the moment.' I told him about the fibres found in the woman's hair. 'There is one thing puzzling me though. Henry Mortlock said that the body had post-mortem grazing on the back.'

'Given that she finished up in the river,' said Frank, looking up from his pocket book, 'she could have been pushed over a bridge. That might have caused the grazing.'

'That's what I was thinking. Get someone to have a word with Thames Division' – I couldn't be bothered with this Marine Support Unit business – 'and see if anyone there can hazard a guess as to where the body might have gone into the river.'

'I thought you'd asked them already.'

'I spoke to them on Wednesday, but we didn't know how long the victim had been dead then. With any luck we'll finish up with a fairly short stretch of the river and not many bridges. And if the grazing was caused by a concrete coping, we can rule out those with metal guard rails, like Waterloo Bridge, Albert Bridge, Tower Bridge and one or two others. At least,

17

I think they've got metal rails. But get someone to check it anyway. With any luck we can reduce it to two or three bridges. That at least might give us a starting point. If this girl really was pushed off a bridge, that is. It's a shot in the dark, I know, but right now we're clutching at straws.'

'I don't see any straws at all, guv,' said Dave and paused. 'But what about dentists?'

'What d'you mean by dentists, Dave? You got a dental problem?'

'Not me, her.'

With exaggerated patience, an unusual trait in my make-up, I said, 'Would you mind explaining that?'

'Why don't we get an odontologist to make a chart of the victim's teeth and send it round to dentists. Might just be that she's had some treatment recently and her dentist could give us a current address.'

'D'you know how many dentists there are in London, Dave?' I asked.

'Got a better idea, sir?' Dave always called me 'sir' when I asked what he regarded as a stupid question.

I had to admit that I couldn't come up with anything that was more feasible than Dave's suggestion. I turned to Frank Mead. 'Does the job still have its own tame dentist, or at least a consultant on its books?'

'I don't know, Harry, but I'll find out. We might get lucky.'

'We need to get something,' I said gloomily.

'I'll get the team started on the theatres, then,' said Frank. 'You never know, we might get *really* lucky.'

'That'll be the day, guv,' said Dave.

Until we started to get the results of the enquiries that had been put in tow, and the outcome of the scientific analyses, there was little point in working over the weekend.

But by Monday, things had begun to happen.

A report from the lab had partially identified the fibre found in the victim's hair. Although it later turned out to be a bum steer, the examining scientist was of the opinion that the fibre was likely to have come from the floor covering in a Ford, Bedford or Renault van.

18

I tried not to get too excited by this shred of information, but it did point to the possibility that the victim's body had been transported from wherever she had been killed to where she had been pitched into the river.

But then she would have been, wouldn't she? I didn't somehow see a guy carrying the body of a dead nude woman through the streets. Oh, I don't know though: these days anything goes. If he had the unlikely misfortune to meet a patrolling constable he'd probably claim to be taking her to a fancy-dress ball at a nudist colony.

There was only one problem: there were thousands of Ford, Bedford and Renault vans in and around London. And we still didn't know which bridge the woman had been thrown from, assuming we had guessed right that the grazing was caused by a bridge coping anyway.

Later on the Monday, Frank Mead reported that a chart of Patricia Hunter's teeth had been prepared and forwarded to the General Dental Council in Wimpole Street for circulation.

Three

It was at about three o'clock on Monday afternoon that I got the phone call from a DI at Charing Cross.

'I understand you're dealing with the Patricia Hunter job, guv'nor,' he said.

'Yes, I am.'

'Ah!' There was a distinct pause. 'I've just been doing a bit of checking up . . .'

'Congratulations.'

'I've been on annual leave for a few days, you see.'

'Go on.' I was beginning to get disturbing vibes about this phone call.

'Well, not to put too fine a point on it, guv, there's been a bit of a cock-up.'

'I'm glad nothing's changed in the job,' I said. 'So?'

'This Patricia Hunter was reported missing here last Friday.' The Charing Cross DI sounded unhappy about all this and, as the tale unfolded, it proved that he was entitled to be. 'The clown who took the details forgot to enter it on the PNC. It was only this morning that I heard someone mentioning it. I found the idiot who took the report and put a squib up his arse.'

'Oh, good!' It wasn't the DI's fault. In fact, he had been the one who'd spotted the error. Every report of a missing person should be entered on the Police National Computer database. Someone had indeed cocked up.

'Who was the informant?' I asked.

'A Miss Gail Sutton.'

'Address?'

'She's got a bedsit at thirty-seven Griffin Street – it's off Kingsway somewhere – and she's currently appearing in a musical called . . .' There was a rustling of paper and I visualized the DI fervently riffling through his notes. 'Yeah, got it. *Scatterbrain* at the Granville.'

'What time will she be there?' This was pure laziness on my part, although I preferred to regard it as economic use of the commissioner's time, the Granville Theatre being closer to my office than Kingsway.

'Hang on a minute.' There were further rustlings. 'Monday to Thursday she gets in at about seven. In the evening that is. Fridays about four and Saturdays at two. Sorry about all this, guv.'

'So will my commander be,' I said, determined not to afford the collective staff of Charing Cross police station too much comfort.

The stage-door keeper at the Granville was seventy at least, either that or he'd had a hard life, and sported a ragged, nicotine-stained walrus moustache.

'Yus?' He looked up from the racing page of that morning's edition of the *Sun* and peered at me through finger-marked, pebble-lensed, vintage spectacles.

'We're police officers,' I said, indicating Dave as I did so. 'We want to see a Miss Gail Sutton.'

'I'll bet you do, guv'nor,' said the stage-door keeper with a cackle. 'Everyone does. Bit of all right, she is. A real beauty. I'll see if I can get hold of her.' He chuckled again. 'Everyone wants to get hold of *her*, and who's to blame 'em, eh?' He moved a mug of tea to one side, ran his finger down a list and made a telephone call. 'She's a smasher,' he added as he waited for an answer.

'I think I get the picture,' I said.

The stage-door keeper hadn't exaggerated. The blonde who appeared some minutes later was tall – probably about five-ten, even without her high heels – and wore a feathered head-dress that added a good ten inches to her already impressive height. And she was indeed a beauty.

Beneath her open robe was a figure-hugging basque in red

and gold satin above a pair of very long legs that were encased in sheer black nylon.

'I'm Gail Sutton. How can I help you?' she asked in cultured tones, casting an appraising glance at Dave.

'We're police officers, Miss Sutton. Is there somewhere we can talk in private?' There was now a constant stream of chattering people passing through the stage door.

Without a word the girl led us down a short flight of stone steps and into an unused dressing room that was not much larger than a cupboard.

'What's this about?' she asked, turning to face us.

'Patricia Hunter,' I said.

'Oh, at last. I was beginning to wonder if the police were in the slightest bit interested in her disappearance.'

'I'm Detective Chief Inspector Brock of the Serious Crime Group,' I began. 'I'm afraid that Miss Hunter is dead.'

'Oh my God, no!' The girl sat down heavily on a hard wooden chair, the only seat in the small room, and crossed her legs. Outside there was a burst of laughter as more people – members of the cast, I presumed – traipsed down the steps.

'When did you last see her, Miss Sutton?' I asked, having explained the circumstances in which Patricia Hunter's body had been found.

'You don't happen to have a cigarette, do you?' The girl was obviously distressed by the news we had just given her. 'And I wish you'd call me Gail.'

I gave her a Marlboro, and Dave produced his cigarette lighter with all the panache of an unctuous head waiter.

'Thanks.' Gail blew a plume of smoke into the air and dispersed it with a wave of her hand. 'I saw Patricia at about eleven o'clock last Monday evening, after we'd finished the show, but she didn't turn up for either the Tuesday or Wednesday performances. I had a word with Charlie—'

'Charlie?' queried Dave.

'Charlie's the stage-door keeper,' said Gail, 'but he hadn't heard from her. I wondered if she'd been taken ill or something. Anyway, when she didn't turn up for the Thursday-evening performance, I began to get really worried, so I went up to her place—'

'Where is that?' asked Dave.

'Coping Road, Islington. Number thirty-four,' said Gail. 'Anyway, her landlady hadn't seen anything of her either and was a bit worried. So I popped into Charing Cross police station and reported her missing. You see, no one in the theatre had heard from her, and there was no answer when I rang her mobile.' Somewhere outside, a bell rang. 'Ah, overture and beginners,' she said. 'I'm on in ten minutes.'

'What part d'you play?' asked Dave.

Gail gave a scornful laugh. 'I'm in the chorus line, darling,' she said. 'And quite frankly at thirty-five I'm getting a bit too old for it. A show every night, Monday to Thursday, and two on Fridays and Saturdays. Wears a girl out, I can tell you,' she added, forcing a smile in Dave's direction.

'Yeah, I know,' said Dave. 'My wife's a dancer.'

'Really? What's she in?'

'The Royal Ballet,' said Dave.

'Oh, a classical dancer.' There was a hint of envy in the way Gail said it. 'I wanted to go into the ballet, but they said I was too tall. So here I am hoofing it for a living in this silly costume.'

'It's a very nice costume,' said Dave, making that comment an excuse for appraising the girl's legs once more.

'Look, Gail,' I said, interrupting this cosy little chat, 'we really need to talk to you at some length, and now doesn't seem to be the right moment. When can you spare us some time?'

'Could you make it tomorrow morning at about eleven? Would that be OK?'

'Certainly,' I said. 'And I understand you live at thirty-seven Griffin Street.'

'It's only a bedsit,' said Gail, confirming what the Charing Cross DI had told me. 'I go home at the weekends . . . what's left of them. I live in Kingston.'

'With your husband?'

Gail gave me a long, penetrating look before replying to what was blatantly an unnecessary question. 'Not any more,' she said disdainfully. 'We divorced about three years ago.' She stood up. 'If you'll excuse me, the show must go on.' Pausing at the door, she said, 'Why don't you come in and see it? Charlie will fix you up with a couple of seats. There are plenty to spare.'

'I'd love to,' I said, 'but unfortunately we don't have the time. We've a murder to investigate.'

Dave and I went straight from the Granville to the address that Gail Sutton had given us for our murder victim.

The landlady was a businesslike woman named Mrs Parsons. She was about fifty, and clearly didn't much like the look of us. Until we told her who we were and why we were there.

'Aren't you supposed to have a warrant to search someone's room?' Mrs Parsons posed the question hesitantly when we asked if we could have a look round Patricia Hunter's bedsit.

But Dave knew how to deal with such half-hearted obstruction. 'Not when the occupant's dead,' he said.

'*Dead?* Holy Mary, Mother of God!' Mrs Parsons crossed herself. 'When did this happen?'

'Her body was found in the river last Wednesday evening, Mrs Parsons,' I said. 'She'd been murdered.'

'Oh the poor dear child.' Mrs Parsons's mild Irish accent became a little more pronounced.

At a guess the wallpaper in Patricia Hunter's sparsely furnished room must have been at least ten years old, and was peeling in places, mainly from the damp that was seeping through the walls. The room looked very much as though it was only used for sleeping during the working week. I'm not too familiar with theatrical lodgings, but I imagined it to be fairly typical.

'Found anything, Dave?' I asked, by which I meant anything that was likely to reveal more about Patricia Hunter than we already knew. Which was precious little.

'A notebook with addresses in it, a building-society passbook and some corres, guv.'

'Corres' is police shorthand for any form of correspondence, and these days, I suppose, anything stored on a computer.

'What does it tell us, Dave?'

'The passbook's got about eighteen grand in it, and all the

letters are from a couple called Mum and Dad. Probably her parents,' he added with a smirk.

'We'll make a detective of you yet,' I said. 'Where do her parents live?'

'Wimbledon,' said Dave. 'And that's the address in the pass-book, too.'

'Eighteen thousand pounds is a lot to have in the bank,' I mused. 'She doesn't get paid that well, surely.'

'Perhaps she's a bit more than a chorus girl,' said Dave.

'Yeah, quite possibly.' Perhaps Frank Mead had been right after all, and she had been a prostitute, if only part-time.

'There's something else,' said Dave, still thumbing through the book he'd found. 'This guy Bruce Phillips has popped up again. There's an address for him here: nine Petersfield Street, Fulham. Flat twelve.'

'I'm looking forward to meeting Mr Phillips,' I said. 'I've a feeling he may be able to assist us in our enquiries.' I glanced at my watch. 'But right now we'd better go and tell Patricia Hunter's parents.' It was not a task I relished, even after upwards of twenty-four years in the job. Her name had been deliberately withheld from the press until we'd found her family, but now we were going to have to break the news to them. Turning back to the landlady, I asked, 'How long had Miss Hunter lived here?'

'It must be a couple of months now,' said Mrs Parsons. 'She was in *Scatterbrain* at the Granville, you know. We get a lot of theatricals here, and I'm glad to have them. They're never any trouble. Too tired, most of the time, poor dears.'

'Did she ever mention a man called Bruce Phillips?'

'Not to me, but like I said, she'd only been here a few months. We hardly had time to chat, what with the hours she worked.'

'Did she have any callers?'

'Not that I know of.'

'D'you know if she went anywhere last weekend?' I asked.

'Well, she didn't stay here, that's for sure. She left for the theatre on Saturday afternoon and I didn't see her again until the Monday morning.'

'Any idea where she went, Mrs Parsons?'

'I think she said she'd been to Brighton, but I don't know where. She mentioned something about having connections down there.'

'There's a Brighton address in this book of hers, guv,' said Dave. 'Number sixteen Fenwick Road. Well, I imagine it's the address where she stayed. Mr and Mrs Hunter, it says here.' And he tapped the little book.

'I wonder if they're relatives. Either that or they're Patricia Hunter's parents and have moved recently.'

'It'd have to be very recent,' said Dave. 'One of the letters from "Mum and Dad" is dated last month.'

'Even so, Dave, it looks as though we're due a trip to Brighton.'

'Can't we get the local law to do it, guv? After all, it might be a blow-out.'

I gave that some thought, but not for long. 'Good idea. We could go traipsing down there and find they're out. Get Colin Wilberforce to ring the Brighton police and ask them to make an appointment for us to see Mr and Mrs Hunter tomorrow afternoon.'

'Right, guv,' said Dave, and pulled out his mobile.

I turned to Patricia Hunter's landlady. 'Thank you for you help, Mrs Parsons. We may have to see you again, of course. However, in the meantime I'd like to have some of my other officers come here to do a proper search of her room and her belongings, probably first thing tomorrow morning. Will that be all right?'

'Yes, of course.' Mrs Parsons shook her head sadly. 'I still can't believe it,' she said.

Given that the letters Dave had found in Patricia Hunter's room were dated only a matter of weeks ago, it seemed likely that her parents were living in Wimbledon rather than Brighton. So we went there first, even though it was now quite late in the day, but it was the sort of unpalatable duty that could not be delayed.

Having arranged to meet a family liaison officer at Wimbledon police station, the three of us made our way to the Hunters' house. According to the electoral roll, they were called Robert and Daphne.

26

'Do you have a daughter called Patricia, Mr Hunter?' I asked, once we were settled in their front room.

'Yes, we do,' said Hunter, a worried expression already on his face. 'What's happened?' But he and his wife knew instinctively why we were there.

'I'm afraid I've got some bad news for you,' I said.

There is no easy or sympathetic way to tell people that their daughter has been murdered, but I did it as quickly and as tactfully as possible.

It's not as if I didn't know how they felt. I shall never forget the day the governor called me into his office to tell me that my four-year-old son Robert had drowned in a neighbour's pond while Helga was at work. And that was the start of the long-drawn-out dispute between Helga and me that had led, eventually, to our divorce.

Daphne Hunter had burst into tears at the news of her daughter's death and was still sobbing uncontrollably. I was glad that the liaison officer was a woman. They're much better than men at coping with that sort of thing.

The FLO took Mrs Hunter upstairs to her bedroom and then went into the kitchen to make tea. It's the copper's universal panacea: if in doubt, make some tea.

But I still had to find out what had happened to Patricia. Beyond what we knew already, that is. Which wasn't a great deal.

'Mr Hunter, can you tell me if your daughter had any boyfriends?' I asked, once he was alone with Dave and me.

'Quite a few, I should imagine.' Hunter had maintained a stoic reserve at the news of his daughter's death. 'She was an attractive girl.'

'What did she do for a living?' I knew that Patricia had been in *Scatterbrain* at the time of her death, but I wondered whether she had pursued another career prior to taking up dancing.

There was a long pause before Hunter answered. 'She was a dancer, Mr Brock. It wasn't a choice of career I approved of, and neither did my wife. We might be old-fashioned, but the theatre seems to me to be a sordid world, and the idea of our daughter being mixed up with those people did worry us.

We weren't very keen on her living in Islington, either, but she said it was all that she could afford. You see, Trisha wanted to earn enough to put herself through university. She was a very bright kid at school, got A-levels and all that sort of thing. But I'm a fire-fighter, and even though the missus works on the check-out at a local supermarket, there's still not enough money to pay for higher education. She was determined though, and said she didn't mind what she did if it meant that she could get a degree. She wanted to be a solicitor.'

'It looks as though she was getting near her goal,' I said. 'Her bank book had eighteen thousand pounds in it.'

'Good God!' said Hunter. 'I had no idea. The theatre obviously pays better than I thought.'

'D'you know where she was working . . . as a dancer?' I knew, but I wondered if he did.

'No, I'm afraid not, not exactly. It was a West End theatre. At least that's what she told us. We asked if we could come and see the show she was in, but she said it wouldn't be worth it.' Hunter gave a bleak smile. 'She said she was in the back row of the chorus and we wouldn't even see her.' He paused. 'I must admit it made me wonder.'

'Wonder what, Mr Hunter?'

'If she was in the theatre at all.'

'When was this?'

'About a year ago, I think.'

'Have you any idea how long she had been on the stage?'

'About five years, I think, but she never said much about it on the rare occasions we saw her. Always changed the subject, if you know what I mean.'

'How long ago did Patricia leave home, Mr Hunter?'

'It must be all of six years now.'

'Do you happen to know the names of any of her boyfriends?'

'I think she mentioned some chap in one of her letters,' said Hunter. 'I'll see if I can find it.' He stood up and left the room with the slow shambling walk of a man bowed down with grief.

He returned a few moments later, clutching a piece of blue notepaper. 'His name was Bruce Phillips,' he said, 'but she didn't say much more about him than that she'd met him. Daphne – that's the wife – said she thought it sounded serious. You know what women are, always hoping for a wedding so they can buy a new hat. We wrote and asked when we could meet him, but Trisha never replied.'

'Did she mention his address, or how long she'd known him?' I asked.

'No,' said Hunter, 'just the name.'

'One last question. Does the address sixteen Fenwick Road, Brighton, mean anything to you?'

Robert Hunter shook his head immediately. 'Not a thing,' he said. 'Should it?'

'It was listed in your daughter's address book with the names Mr and Mrs Hunter against it.' I looked up. 'Not relatives, then?'

'Not as far as I know,' said Hunter.

And that was it. All that our interview with Patricia Hunter's father had achieved was to muddy the waters a little more than they were muddied already.

The reply from the Brighton police was waiting for me when I arrived at the office the following morning. There was no Mr and Mrs Hunter living at 16 Fenwick Road, nor had there been for at least the last four years. The address was that of a boarding house that catered for holiday visitors and was run by a couple called Richards.

'I suppose we'll have to go down there at some time,' I said.

'Thought we might,' said Dave. 'Nothing like a day at the seaside to cheer us up.'

'Yes, but first we've an appointment with Gail Sutton.'

Gail Sutton's room was small but very tidy. The bed was one of those contraptions that folds up against the wall, and there was an armchair, a dressing table and a television set. And precious little else.

This morning, the chorus girl was dressed in jeans and a tee shirt. 'Excuse my bare feet,' she said, 'but hoofing in a pair of heels isn't good for them. I like to let them out occasionally.' She pulled down the bed and invited us to sit on it. 'Sorry about the accommodation, but it's really only somewhere to sleep when I've finished at the theatre. As I said, I live in Kingston.'

'I live in Surbiton,' I said.

'Oh, whereabouts?'

We exchanged addresses and then got down to business.

'We think that Patricia may have had some connection with Brighton. Did she ever mention Brighton in conversation?'

'No, I don't remember her doing so.'

'D'you know if she had any men friends, Gail?'

'Not that I know of. Of course, we all get the usual pushy lechers who hang around the stage door in dirty raincoats, but a few choice Anglo-Saxon words usually sees them off.' She laughed at the thought. 'And more often than not there's a policeman there at turning-out time to see we're all right.'

'I'll bet there is,' I said. *And to hell with crime.* 'But I was thinking more of a regular boyfriend that Patricia might have had. Did she, for example, ever mention a man called Bruce Phillips?' The guy who had paid Patricia's shoplifting fine five years ago – and had been described to her parents as a boyfriend – was still intriguing me, but relationships tend to come and to go. As I knew only too well. 'Lives in Fulham.'

Gail shook her head slowly. 'I don't recall her mentioning anyone of that name,' she said, 'but perhaps . . .'

'Perhaps what?'

'Over the last couple of weeks she's been shooting off straight after the show.'

'D'you think she was meeting somebody?'

'Possibly, but if she was, she was unusually secretive about it. Normally we talk about boyfriends with each other. All the girls do.' Gail shot me an amused glance. 'I suppose you men are the same about girlfriends.'

'When we've got girlfriends to talk *about*,' I said somewhat wistfully.

Dave looked sideways at me, a quizzical expression on his face; I'd have to tell him about Sarah's departure soon, I supposed. But Gail was on it immediately.

'You're not married, then?'

30

'No, divorced. But to get back to Patricia, you've no idea who this was she may have been meeting?'

'No, I'm sorry. I'd love to be able to help. She was my closest friend.'

'Does that mean you knew her before this show started then?'

'Oh no, but one tends to make friends quickly in this game,' said Gail. 'And lose them just as quickly,' she added, a sad expression on her face.

'What sort of girl was Patricia?' I asked.

Gail didn't hesitate. 'She was a super girl. There were times when I thought she was too innocent to be in the theatre. Very homely sort of kid. Always talking about her parents. In fact she used to visit them quite often.'

That, however, did not accord with what Patricia Hunter's father had said. He had talked of 'the rare occasions when we saw her'.

That our victim was supposedly a homely, parent-loving girl certainly didn't fool Dave. He looked up from his pocket book. 'Was Patricia bisexual, Gail?' he asked.

Gail stared at him in surprise. 'Why on earth should you think that?'

'I don't think it, I'm just asking the question.'

'I'd put money on her being straight,' said Gail, but it was obvious that the possibility had never occurred to her.

I knew why Dave had posed the question: he was wondering if Patricia Hunter had been having an affair with another woman. If so, that might have explained her secretiveness. And if that was the case, she might have been murdered by that other woman. Lesbian murders were not unknown in the annals of crime.

Four

It had gone half past three that afternoon by the time we reached 16 Fenwick Road, Brighton. There was a neon sign over the door, which read 'The Golden Riviera Guest House'.

'Bloody hell!' said Dave. 'Talk about delusions of grandeur.'

John Richards – he ran the place with his wife Barbara, he told us – was a dapper little man in his forties, with a pencil-line moustache and a fold-over hairstyle. He looked as though he'd have been more at home running a hairdressing salon than a boarding house.

'As a matter of fact, we had the police here yesterday,' he announced when we'd told him who we were.

'I know,' I said, 'that's why we're here.' I explained how his establishment featured in our enquiry, and asked if the names Mr and Mrs Hunter, Patricia Hunter or Bruce Phillips meant anything to him.

Richards shook his head. 'As I told the police yesterday, I've never heard of any of them,' he said, as he conducted us into what he described as the lounge, where, at one end, he had created a small bar. It was fussily done: a large mirror behind spirit bottles in optics, coloured glasses on shelves illuminated by spotlights and a flashing neon sign that read 'Every Hour is Happy Hour'. 'Care for a drink, gents?'

'No thanks. Did any young women stay here over the last two or three weeks, Mr Richards?' I asked, bearing in mind that Gail Sutton told us that Patricia Hunter had been secretive about her movements during that time. 'This one would have been about twenty-six. A good-looking brunette.'

'We've had quite a few girls like that staying here,' said

32

Richards, 'but usually with their husbands . . . or partners, I suppose I should say. Must be politically correct these days,' he added with an embarrassed laugh.

'This would have been between late on a Saturday and first thing on a Monday. And very likely last Saturday.'

Richards shook his head. 'We only take bookings Saturday to Saturday,' he said. 'One-nighters will usually go to a hotel. Either on the seafront or somewhere in town. There's plenty to choose from.'

'What about young men staying here on their own?'

'Been one or two. I think they come down here from the Smoke intent on picking up a girl in one of the nightclubs, but I tend to discourage bookings from their sort. Nothing but trouble. They're either peddling drugs or they come in late, pissed out of their brains.'

'I'd like to have a look at your register,' said Dave, opening his pocket book and waggling his pen in anticipation. 'Or is it all on a computer?'

'God, no. I can't cope with those things. Won't keep you a minute.' Seconds later Richards reappeared with a large book.

'You've had three or four single men staying here over the past couple of months,' Dave said accusingly, as he glanced up.

'I told you that. But at the end of the day, we're in this business to make money, you know, and as I said just now, we tend not to encourage singles. They always expect a discount for single-room occupancy.'

Dave scribbled down the names that interested him and then looked up. 'How long have you been here, Mr Richards?'

'About four years now, I suppose. I used to run a newsagent's business in Balham, but I got sick and tired of getting up at four in the morning. And then there were the complaints from people whose papers hadn't been delivered. Half the time the bloody wholesaler's delivery would turn up after the kids who did the paper rounds had gone off, and I finished up having to do it myself. I tell you, there was no fun in it, so me and the missus decided to come down here and set up this place. She was born just along the coast, in Hove.'

'Has it always been a guest house?'

'No, it was a private house when we bought it. Cost us a packet to set it up, but now that we've recouped what we laid out we're into profit.'

'And who were the people you bought it from?' I asked.

Richards furrowed his brow. 'Webster, I think.'

'Not a Mr and Mrs Hunter?'

'No, definitely not. Like I said, the name doesn't mean anything to me. I'm sure it was Webster. A retired bank manager or something of the sort. Went to live in Yorkshire. He was about seventy then, so he's probably dead now. He said something about being browned off with what he called the refugees on social security who were taking over the town.'

First thing next morning, I held a conference with Frank Mead and Dave to mull over what we'd learned so far. It wasn't much.

'The Marine Support Unit wasn't much help, Harry,' said Frank. 'They took a rough guess that Patricia Hunter probably went into the river around Hammersmith, and that she was carried downstream by the current.'

'Can't they be more specific than that?' I asked.

'The problem,' Frank continued, 'is that we know roughly when she died, but not when she went into the river. If you want my opinion, we can forget Hammersmith. It's too iffy.'

'Henry Mortlock reckoned that Patricia Hunter had been dead less than twenty-four hours,' I mused. 'I suppose it's possible that the murderer had her hidden away somewhere before he dumped her.'

'You said that Gail Sutton last saw her at eleven o'clock on Monday evening,' volunteered Frank. 'So the murderer couldn't have had her stacked up for long.'

'*Quot homines, tot sententiae*,' said Dave quietly.

'What the hell does that mean, Poole?' demanded Frank. He was always irritated by Dave's occasional Latin quotations.

'So many men, so many opinions, guv,' Dave answered.

'Bloody university tossers,' muttered Frank.

Dave Poole had graduated in English at London University,

a fact I'd only discovered a year after he'd joined the Serious Crime Group. His grandfather, a doctor, had come over from Jamaica in the fifties and had practised in Bethnal Green. Dave's father, an accountant, had put Dave through university and had been disappointed that his son had become a copper and thus, as Dave himself put it, the black sheep of the family. But I wasn't at all sorry. Dave was one of the best sergeants I'd ever had working with me.

'Anyone else worth following up in the address book you found at Patricia Hunter's place at Coping Road, Dave?' I asked.

'There's Bruce Phillips, the guy who paid Patricia Hunter's shoplifting fine, guv,' said Dave. 'Seems to be popping up everywhere, that guy. And there are one or two others, but it wasn't an index book, just a notebook. So the names and addresses were probably entered in chronological order.'

'Phillips didn't by any chance feature in Richards's register, did he?' I asked.

'What, he of the Golden Riviera Guest House?' asked Dave with a smirk. 'No, guv. The three most recent names in that – for what they're worth – were Craig Pearce, Rikki Thompson and Sam Johnson.'

'I suppose this Sam Johnson didn't stay there with a bloke called Boswell, by any chance?' Frank asked sarcastically, determined to get back at Dave for flaunting his knowledge of Latin.

'Not to my knowledge, sir,' said Dave with a straight face. 'I've put them all on the PNC, guv,' he continued, turning to me, 'but a Bruce Phillips came up. The Australians tried to extradite him for fraud a few years back.'

'What happened?'

'He did a runner. Not been seen since apparently.'

'Frank, perhaps you'd get someone to make enquiries at this Phillips's place in . . . where was it, Dave?'

'Number nine Petersfield Street, Fulham. Flat twelve,' replied Dave promptly.

Frank scribbled down the address. 'Good as done,' he said. 'D'you want him brought in? If he's still there, which is extremely unlikely.'

'Not yet. Hang on, though. Dave and I'll do Petersfield Street. You take the three that were listed in the guest-house register at Brighton. Colin Wilberforce has got the addresses in the incident room.'

'Whereabouts are these addresses?' asked Frank.

'One of them is in London, guv,' said Dave, 'one's in Chichester and the other's in Slough.'

'Thanks a bundle,' said Frank.

'I should get the local law to do the ones in Chichester and Slough, Frank,' I said. 'I doubt that they're involved, but if any of them do turn out to be a bit tasty, I'll have a go at them myself.' I glanced at my watch. 'And now, Dave, we'll go and have a chat with the manager of the Granville.'

In my experience, managers of West End theatres are usually rather pompous individuals who parade about in evening dress in the foyer smiling at the patrons just as they are arriving. But disappearing the moment there is a complaint. About the service in the crush bar, the austerity of the seating, the cost of the programmes or the exorbitant price of the ice cream. However, in the case of the Granville, I couldn't have been more wrong.

The woman into whose office Dave and I were shown was about fifty, with immaculate, slightly greying hair, and a smart two-piece suit in navy blue.

'I was hoping to speak to the manager,' I said, unwisely as it turned out. Chauvinist that I am, I assumed that the woman was the manager's secretary.

'I *am* the manager. Elizabeth Price. And you are?'

'Detective Chief Inspector Harry Brock of Scotland Yard, and this is DS Poole, Mrs Price. It is *Mrs* Price, is it?'

'It is indeed. Please sit down. May I offer you some coffee?'

'Thank you.'

Elizabeth Price crossed to a side table. 'I presume you've come about Patricia Hunter.' She spoke over her shoulder as she busied herself pouring coffee from a jug that stood on a heated stand. 'I understand that you were here the day before yesterday and talked about her to another of the chorus girls, Gail Sutton. A tragedy. I'm told she was a good dancer, that girl.' She placed two cups of coffee on our side of the desk and sat down behind it.

'Do you happen to know where her parents live?' I asked. Having already spoken to the Hunters, I knew where they lived, but I was hoping to resolve the apparent enigma of the Mr and Mrs Hunter of Fenwick Road, Brighton, who Patricia had recorded in her address book.

'No, I'm afraid not.' Mrs Price absently stirred her coffee. 'To be perfectly honest, Mr Brock, these girls come and go. The producers of shows like *Scatterbrain* hire the theatre and come with the complete package. We have no part in arranging casting or anything like that.' She paused. 'I could try the producer for you to see if he knows anything about her, but somehow I doubt it.'

'Thank you. That would be helpful.'

While Mrs Price made a telephone call, I gazed around at the framed posters with which the walls were adorned. There had been some well-known shows at the theatre over the years and some well-known actors and actresses in them.

After a short conversation, Mrs Price replaced the receiver. 'I'm sorry, Mr Brock, but he has no idea. To be frank with you, chorus girls are two a penny, and when the producers want a line-up they advertise in *The Stage* and hold auditions. The queue usually stretches halfway down the road outside. Most of the time they don't know the names of the dancers they hire. And even if they do, the girls have probably assumed stage names. If you've been christened Vera Higginbottom, for example, you're unlikely to see it up in lights. These girls all want to be stars, but most of them never make it.'

'No, I suppose not,' I said, digesting this piece of harsh realism.

'Are there any vans here?' Dave asked suddenly.

I knew why he was asking, but Mrs Price looked puzzled by the question.

'Vans? D'you mean the sort that are used for shifting scenery?'

'Any sort.'

'No, there aren't. Moving scenery is the responsibility of the people who put on the show. There are companies

37

that specialize in that sort of thing and when a show closes the producers arrange movement of the scenery. Why, is it important?'

'It could be,' said Dave, not wishing to give too much away.

'And the way this show's going, they'll be turning up to take the scenery away very soon.'

'Is it closing then?'

'Looks like it,' said Mrs Price phlegmatically. 'It's just not getting bums on seats, what with the constant terrorist threat.' She glanced at an old theatre bill advertising a Second World War show entitled *The Yanks Are Coming*, and smiled. 'Contrary to the old song, the Yanks *aren't* coming, not any more. I'll give it another week.'

'We'll have to get a move on then,' said Dave. 'Does your chief electrician happen to be about this morning?'

Mrs Price was clearly having difficulty in following Dave's constantly changing line of questioning, but didn't ask why he wanted to know. Presumably she believed that we knew what we were doing. A refreshing change from the usual armchair detectives who thought they knew more about our job than we did. *And sometimes they did, but we never admitted it.*

'I'll see,' she said, and made another phone call.

A few minutes later the chief electrician appeared in the office. He was wearing a blue boiler suit and his glasses were held together with a piece of sticking plaster across the bridge. 'You wanted me, Mrs Price?'

'Yes, Jim, these gentlemen are from the police. They're making enquiries about Patricia Hunter, the girl who was murdered.' Mrs Price indicated the electrician with a wave of her hand. 'This is Jim Rugg,' she said, turning to me.

Rugg nodded in our direction. 'So how can I help, gents? Terrible business.'

I wasn't sure whether he meant the business Dave and I were in, or the murder of the chorus girl.

Dave opened his briefcase and withdrew a clear plastic bag containing the ligature with which Patricia Hunter had been strangled. 'Have a look at that, Mr Rugg.'

The electrician took the bag and stared closely at the contents. 'What about it?' he asked, looking up.

38

'Is that sort of wire ever used in the theatre?'

'Could be. It looks like the cable we use for the lighting circuits. There's miles of the stuff running all over the theatre.'

'D'you have a lot of it?'

'We've got drums of it. I keep it in my storeroom. Why, d'you want some?' Rugg asked with a grin.

'Yes, please. Half a metre should do.'

'Half a metre? What you wiring up, then? Half a metre won't get you far.'

'I'm not wiring anything up, Mr Rugg,' said Dave, taking back the exhibit. 'We need it for comparison.'

'Oh, right. I'll nip and get you some.'

'I'll come with you, if I may,' said Dave, and followed the electrician from the room.

'Why on earth does your sergeant need some of that wire, Mr Brock?' asked Mrs Price, surprised yet again by Dave's apparently unrelated demands. Perhaps being in the theatrical business, she thought that all policemen should be as staid and courtly as the principal character in Priestley's *An Inspector Calls*.

'The piece that Sergeant Poole showed Mr Rugg was the wire that Patricia Hunter was strangled with,' I said.

'Good God!' Elizabeth Price gave an involuntary shudder. 'But I thought she was drowned.'

'No. She was certainly found in the river, but she was already dead by the time she went in. As a matter of interest, would your electrician ever have anything to do with grease-paint?'

Mrs Price laughed. 'I doubt it. The electricians are very scathing about the acting profession – it's a trade union thing, I think – and the less they have to do with them the better. But to answer your question, no electrician would have any legitimate reason for having anything to do with greasepaint.' She paused. 'I suppose it's possible they might get some on their hands if they were called to replace a bulb in one of the dressing rooms . . . something like that. But it would be accidental. I presume you have a reason for asking.'

39

'Yes, I do,' I said, without enlightening the theatre manager any further. But I didn't need to.

'Does that mean you have grounds to suspect an electrician of having something to do with that poor girl's death?'

'Not at all,' I said. I thought it unnecessary to tell her that, right now, I was considering it as a possibility. And on the meagre evidence we had so far, a very strong possibility.

'Get your length of flex, Dave?' I asked on the way back to Curtis Green.

'Yes, guv, and it certainly looks like the piece that was round Patricia Hunter's neck. But on the down side, Jim Rugg told me that we'd probably find the same stuff in every theatre in the country. Incidentally, the electrician's storeroom is not kept locked. Anyone could walk in there. I also learned that he's got three assistants working with him at the Granville.'

None of which was a pleasing result. Even in the unlikely event that we found the drum from which our piece of flex had come, we'd only get a mechanical fit if it had been cut directly from what was left.

'Did Rugg know Patricia Hunter?'

'No. He's seen the chorus, obviously – he reckoned there were about twenty or so of them – but says he never had anything to do with them. And, as far as he knew, neither did any of his assistants. He did have occasion to change a few light bulbs around the mirrors in their changing room last week, though. Reckoned it was full of half-naked birds at the time. Some people have all the luck.'

'Nevertheless, I'll get one of Mr Mead's team to have a word with his assistants,' I said. 'In the meantime, grab someone to take your bit of flex across to the lab.'

'Is Sarah dealing with that, guv?'

'Yes.'

Dave paused for a moment or two, as though debating whether to put his next question. 'Is there something wrong between you and Sarah, guv? I mean, if it's none of my business, tell me to belt up.'

'We've split,' I said.

'Sorry to hear that,' said Dave. But that was all he said. The

CID is a graveyard of broken marriages and abandoned partnerships.

'The commander wants a word, sir,' said Colin Wilberforce the moment we entered the incident room. I suppose one day the confusing-names squad will change it to 'occurrence room' in the interests of accuracy.

'What about, did he say?'

'No, sir.'

The commander was seated behind his desk. But, there again, where else would he be?

'You wanted me, sir?'

'Ah, Mr Brock . . .'

The commander always called me 'Mr Brock' rather than 'Harry', in case, I suppose, I returned the compliment by using his first name. He couldn't have handled that.

'What progress are you making in the Hunter death, Mr Brock?' The commander never called a murder a murder until the jury said it was. After all, it might turn out to be manslaughter. Bit meticulous is the commander. He leaned back in his executive chair and linked his fingers across the waistcoat he invariably wore, winter and summer. I think the waistcoat's a status thing. 'The assistant commissioner was asking,' he added, as though he had no personal interest in the investigation.

I told him that we'd positively identified the dead girl and found out where she'd been living. I also mentioned that she'd been associated with a Bruce Phillips, a fugitive from Australian justice.

'There's an extradition warrant out for him, sir.'

'Why's he not been arrested then, Mr Brock?' asked the commander, as though it was my fault that Phillips was still at large.

'When the Extradition Unit went to knock him off, sir, he'd done a runner.'

The commander frowned at that. 'You mean he'd absconded?'

'Yes, sir,' I said, and only just stopped myself from adding, 'That as well.' The commander's a bit short on humour.

To finish up with, I told him about our visit to the Granville, and threw in a bit of unintelligible mumbo-jumbo about the flex with which Patricia Hunter had been strangled. 'Enquiries are continuing, sir,' I said unnecessarily.

'Yes, good, good.' The commander nodded as though what I had just told him made sense.

Well, it had, of course, but not necessarily to him.

'I'll keep you posted, sir.'

'Of course,' said the commander, in a way that suggested I would be unwise not to do so.

Five

Colin Wilberforce appeared in the doorway of my office. 'Excuse me, sir.'

'Yes, what is it, Colin?'

'While you were with the commander, sir,' he said, 'a Mrs Price rang from the Granville Theatre. She's got some information for you if you'd care to ring back.'

Elizabeth Price certainly had got some information. The first, and comparatively unimportant piece of news, was that *Scatterbrain* was closing on Friday. She sounded almost pleased that her prediction had been correct. The second, and far more useful snippet, was that a man named Peter Crawford had telephoned the theatre enquiring after Patricia Hunter, who, he had said, was his girlfriend.

'What did you say to him, Mrs Price?' I asked.

'I'm afraid I lied. I said that I wasn't responsible for the cast and didn't know the name anyway. I felt a bit guilty at not telling him what had happened, but I didn't want to break the news that his girlfriend was dead, not over the phone. So I took his telephone number and said I'd get someone to call. Did I do the right thing, Mr Brock?'

'You did absolutely the right thing, Mrs Price, and thank you very much. I'll get in touch with him straight away.'

Colin did a subscriber check on Peter Crawford's telephone number, and within minutes came up with the address where he lived.

Peter Crawford's apartment at Burgundy Court, a modern block of flats in Davos Street, Chelsea – not far from Saxony

43

Street where Patricia Hunter had once lived – must have cost an arm and a leg. From which I deduced that Crawford was worth a bob or two. Or he was a villain. But then I'm a cynic.

The suave Crawford was dressed in shirt, slacks and shoes that, judging from their cut and quality, could not possibly have come from a high-street chain store. Inclining his head in bafflement when we introduced ourselves, he invited us into a tastefully furnished sitting room.

'May I offer you gentlemen a drink?'

'No thank you.'

'Do take a seat, then,' said Crawford, indicating a Chesterfield with a sweep of his hand, 'and tell me how I can help you.'

'It's about Patricia Hunter,' I said.

'How did you know that she and I—?'

'The manager of the Granville phoned me to say that you'd been making enquiries about her, Mr Crawford.'

'Well, that's true, but how does that involve the police?' As Crawford realized how it might possibly have involved us, his expression changed dramatically. 'Oh, God, you don't mean something's happened to her, do you?' It was what, in the theatre, is called a bravura performance. *Perhaps he was an actor. And used greasepaint. And was, therefore, a suspect.*

'I'm afraid so,' I said. 'A week ago, her body was recovered from the Thames. She'd been strangled.'

'But I didn't see anything about that in *The Times*.'

'Her name's not yet been released to the media,' I said.

For a few moments Crawford remained silent, his head forward, chin on chest. Then he made a strange comment. 'I don't think I've ever known anyone who was murdered,' he said.

'How long had you known Miss Hunter?' I asked.

'Only about six or seven weeks, I suppose.'

'And how did you meet?'

There was a moment's hesitation, and then: 'I went to see the show – *Scatterbrain* – and noticed her in the front row of the chorus. I went to see it twice more after that, and then I sent her an invitation to have dinner with me. Bit old-fashioned these days, I suppose, and I didn't think she'd accept. But she did.' Crawford managed a wry smile, and I wondered if he was one of the stage-door, raincoated, pushy lechers that Gail Sutton had mentioned. 'We went out a few times, not that it was easy with the hours she worked, but we did manage the occasional lunch.'

'And a weekend or two in Brighton?' asked Dave, raising an eyebrow as he took out his pocket book.

Crawford glanced sharply at Dave. Not a hostile glance, but not a friendly one either. 'How did you know that?'

'I didn't,' said Dave, 'but we know that Miss Hunter went down there a few times.'

We didn't know that, of course, but I think it was a safe assumption.

'Yes, as a matter of fact, we did go to Brighton two or three times.'

'And where did you stay?'

'The Grand. It's the big hotel on the front.'

'Yes, I know where it is,' said Dave, hiding his disappointment that Crawford hadn't stayed at the Golden Riviera Guest House.

But looking around Crawford's apartment, that came as no surprise. I couldn't visualize him staying at John Richards's crummy boarding house in Fenwick Road, not with the money he'd so obviously got. And that led to my next question.

'What's your profession, Mr Crawford?'

'Advertising.' Crawford snapped out the answer, almost as if he resented what to him must have seemed like intrusive questioning.

It certainly explained his wealth. He must have been in one of those advertising agencies that charges telephone numbers just to change a company logo. As I've said many times before, I'm in the wrong business.

'Did she ever mention someone called Bruce Phillips?' I asked.

'No,' said Crawford. 'Who's he?'

'I've no idea. Just a name that came up in the course of our

45

enquiries,' I said, and paused. 'When did you last see Miss Hunter?'

Crawford thought about that. 'The weekend before last,' he said eventually.

'And you've had no contact since then?'

'No, but not for the want of trying.'

'Meaning?'

'I tried ringing her mobile. From about Wednesday of last week, I suppose. But there was never any answer, even though I left messages on her voicemail or whatever it's called. Now I know why.'

'Was there some reason why you didn't call at the theatre after the show? Or at her address? I presume you knew where she lived.'

'Yes, of course I did,' said Crawford. 'But I was out of town.'

'Where exactly?'

'Look, is all this really necessary?' Crawford spread his hands and assumed an apologetic expression. It was almost as though he thought we were wasting *our* time rather than his.

'Yes it is, Mr Crawford,' I said. 'I am dealing with the murder of Miss Hunter, and it's necessary for me to ask questions.'

'Yes, of course. I'm sorry. I should have realized. Well, it so happens that I was in Edinburgh, and I can give you the address of the company with whom I was discussing a television advertising campaign. I'm sure the young lady I saw up there would be happy to confirm what I've just told you. And that's why I was ringing Patricia on her mobile, rather than trying to see her in person.'

Frank Mead had not been wasting his time. By the time Dave and I got back to Curtis Green at nine o'clock, he'd already checked two of the three names that appeared in the register of the Golden Riviera Guest House at Brighton.

Local police had confirmed that both Sam Johnson and Rikki Thompson had copper-bottomed alibis that covered them for the period between which Patricia Hunter was last seen alive, and when her body had been found in the Thames. But it appeared that the Londoner, Craig Pearce, had furnished a false home address when he went to Brighton. Certainly the occupants of 117 Minerva Road, Tooting, had never heard of him. Frank had promptly put Pearce's name on the Police National Computer.

Someone who gave a false address always aroused my interest. The reason could usually be traced back to one of two things: a woman or a crime. In this case it could well be both.

However, given the lateness of the hour – as we say in the trade – that could wait another day.

But one should never say things like that.

'Craig Pearce has been nicked, guv,' said Colin Wilberforce, the moment I stepped into the incident room.

'Christ, are you a bloody mind-reader, Colin?'

Colin smiled. 'Wish I was, sir,' he said. 'Anyway, a crowd of yobs was indulging in a bit of a punch-up on a bus in Whitehall, and as luck would have it, there was an area car coming round from Parliament Square. The crew got stuck in but there were only two of them against about ten yobs. The upshot was that most of the tearaways scarpered, but our lads managed to lay hands on Pearce. He's in Charing Cross nick awaiting your pleasure.'

In my early days in the job, I once had an inspector who reckoned that a police station ought to be like a bank: tranquil. It's as well that he didn't live long enough to see Charing Cross nick this evening.

Among the twenty or so prisoners in the custody suite there was the usual collection of drunks – male *and* female – a couple of low-life layabouts whose profession was the sale of cannabis and other assorted narcotics, and a Bosnian refugee who'd been duffed up simply because he was a Bosnian refugee – that's what he'd told the constable who'd arrested him anyway – and whose blood had made a mess of his Pierre Cardin shirt and his expensive suede jacket. But the officer who'd arrested him was charging him with assault on police. So whose blood was it? Not my problem.

47

I fought my way through this amorphous mass to the accompaniment of muttered protests from the few whose native language was English and who thought I was jumping the queue.

A harassed custody sergeant – custody sergeants always look harassed – glanced up. 'Help you?' he asked wearily.

'Detective Chief Inspector Brock, SCG West,' I said, 'and this is DS Poole,' I added, indicating Dave with a jerk of my thumb.

'Yes, sir?'

'I need to talk to a prisoner called Craig Pearce. Nicked in Whitehall. Punch-up on a bus.'

'Yes, sir. Charged with assault and making an affray with persons not in custody. He's banged up in Cell Three. I'll get the gaoler to bring him up.' The custody sergeant put down his pen and bellowed for someone he called GH.

I should explain that GH is the job's internal code for the police station at Hackney, and I wondered what a Hackney officer was doing at Charing Cross, some six miles distant from his home turf. However, when the officer appeared, it was clear why he was called GH: he was suffering from a nasty affliction of acne . . . as in 'Ackney. But that's copper's black humour for you.

Craig Pearce was an unsavoury-looking youth with iron-mongery adorning his earlobes, his nose, his tongue, his lower lip and probably other parts of his anatomy that, mercifully, were not currently on display. His head had been shaved to leave a four-inch-wide strip of greasy black hair that culmi-nated in a ponytail. In his position I'd've sued my barber with all the certainty of a successful outcome and substantial damages. It is, however, a widely held belief among such human detritus that the further away from courts of law they can stay, the healthier they will remain.

Patricia Hunter had been a pretty brunette and I wondered what the hell she'd seen in this gorilla. If, in fact, she'd seen him at all. He certainly didn't stand comparison with the urbane Peter Crawford whose apartment we'd left an hour ago.

'You were arrested on a bus in Whitehall having been

48

involved in a disturbance,' I began, just to test the water.

'Nothing to do with me,' said Pearce, rehearsing the villain's standard reflex response to any accusation of crime. Had his solicitor been present, he would have said something trite like, 'My client has a complete answer to the charge.'

'Frankly, I couldn't care less,' I said. 'Such minor matters are of no interest to me.'

'You see, Mr Pearce,' chipped in Dave, 'my guv'nor wants to talk to you about a murder.'

'*Do what?*' Pearce sat up straight with all the alacrity of someone who has just received a substantial electric shock up his arse. He stared, mesmerized, at Dave. 'I ain't done no murder. It was just a bit of a bundle on a bus. The driver was giving us lip, see. Not showing respeck.' I was pleased to see that Dave's intervention had introduced a measure of alarm into Pearce's response. 'I want a brief.'

'Why?' I asked.

''Cos I never done it, that's why.'

'Never did what?'

'I never done no murder.'

Dave frowned at Pearce's use of a double negative.

'Then you won't be needing a mouthpiece, will you?' I said.

The logic of that appeared to elude Craig Pearce.

'Well, I, er . . .'

'How long have you known Patricia Hunter?'

'Never heard of her.'

'How about the Golden Riviera Guest House at Brighton?'

'What about it?'

'You stayed there some time ago.'

'Free country, innit?' said Pearce, clearly labouring under an age-old delusion.

'Miss Hunter was an actress who stayed there.' There was no proof that she had, but the address had been in her little book. 'So what were you doing in Brighton?'

'Having a weekend down there, wer'n I? Done a few clubs an' that.'

'When you say you did a few clubs, do you mean you robbed them?'

'Leave it out.'

Dave leaned across the table, his face very close to Pearce's. 'Where were you on the eleventh and twelfth of June?'

A smile spread across Craig Pearce's face. 'In the nick.'

'*What?*' Dave sat back and surveyed the prisoner.

'I was in the Scrubs doing three months for GBH. Mind you, it was a fit-up. Just like this job you're trying to put on me now.'

Which turned out to be true – not the fit-up, of course – and just goes to show that a suspect's criminal record should be examined *before* you waste your time interrogating him.

We went back to Curtis Green and booked off. But not before I'd sent a message to the Lothian and Borders Police asking them to check Peter Crawford's alibi with the company he claimed to have visited in Edinburgh.

The police in Edinburgh had been highly efficient. By half past nine the following morning they had informed us that Crawford had indeed visited the advertising manager of the firm he'd mentioned. But he had been with her *only on Monday*, leaving in good time to catch the 6 o'clock flight to London. If he had been so minded.

Colin turned to his computer and played a brief scherzo on the keys. 'That means that he could have arrived at Heathrow as early as ten past seven, sir,' he said.

'Which would have given him plenty of time to murder Patricia Hunter, guv,' said Dave, as he peeled a banana. His wife Madeleine had told him that bananas were good for him. 'And that puts him well in the frame.'

'Thanks a lot, Dave,' I said, 'but I don't somehow see a wealthy advertising executive murdering an actress.'

'Funnier things have happened, guv,' said Dave, pointedly waving his banana skin in the air before dropping it into a wastepaper basket. I suppose I should have read some symbolism into the little charade of the banana skin.

'Yes . . .' I mused. 'I think it's time we spoke to Crawford again, Dave,' I said. I was suspicious about the discrepancy between what he'd told us concerning his absence from London – or at least what he'd implied – and what we'd learned from the police in Edinburgh.

50

'He's there, guv.' Dave had done his usual telephone trick: ringing Crawford and apologizing for having dialled a wrong number. In that way we wouldn't have a wasted journey, nor would we alert him to our impending visit.

Although it was only just past six o'clock when we arrived at Peter Crawford's flat, he was attired in a beautifully-cut dinner jacket when he answered the door.

'Oh, it's you.'

'Yes, Mr Crawford, it's us,' I said. 'We need to have a few words with you.'

'I don't have very long.' Crawford drew back the cuff of his shirt and glanced at his gold Rolex watch. 'I'm due to attend a dinner in the West End very shortly. At the Dorchester, as a matter of fact. It's an advertising convention. May pick up a bit of business.'

Crawford didn't look as though he needed to pick up any more business. He appeared to be doing all right as he was. Certainly if the quality and cut of his dinner jacket was anything to go by.

'It shouldn't take long,' I said.

'That's all right, then. You'd better come in.'

'You told us that you were in Edinburgh during the week commencing Monday the tenth of June, Mr Crawford,' I began.

'That's correct.'

'And where did you stay?'

'I, er . . .'

'Let me try something else. How *long* were you in Edinburgh?'

'The whole week. Monday until Friday.'

'So where did you stay?'

If Crawford was starting to get rattled by my persistent questioning, he didn't show it. 'Does this have something to do with Patricia Hunter's death?' he asked patiently.

'It's what we call a process of elimination, Mr Crawford.'

But now he did begin to get a little annoyed. 'Really?' It was a sarcastic response. 'Well, I don't see that where I stayed has anything to do with your so-called process of elimination.'

51

I adopted an attitude of infinite patience, something that always surprised Dave. 'I am naturally suspicious of anyone who declines to tell me where they were at the time of a murder, Mr Crawford. Particularly when that person claims to have been a friend of the victim.'

There was a distinct pause while, I imagine, Crawford 'considered his position'.

'I was staying with my wife.'

'So, you had a girlfriend in London and a wife in Scotland?'

'I wouldn't be the first man to have a mistress,' said Crawford, glancing at his watch again. 'Look, Chief Inspector, I really do have to go.'

'Of course you do, sir. If you just tell me where it was that you stayed with your wife, I'll leave you in peace.'

'But why d'you want to know?'

'Because we have checked with the company you visited and they told us that you were with them for just one day: Monday the tenth of June. If you'd told me that in the first place, I wouldn't have had to come and waste your time again. Or mine.'

Crawford sat down, suddenly. For a moment or two he gazed at the floor, his hands linked between his knees. Then he looked up.

'My wife is a few years older than me, Chief Inspector. She's been suffering from Alzheimer's disease for a while now, and she's in a secure home. I visit her whenever I can, but it's largely a waste of time. She doesn't seem to know who I am any more, or what I'm talking about.'

'I see. And where is this home, Mr Crawford?'

'Edinburgh.' Crawford rose to his feet and walked across to a side table upon which stood a telephone. He scribbled a few lines on a sheet of paper he took from a pad and handed it to me. 'That's the address of the home,' he said. 'I stayed in our house in Edinburgh from Monday night to Friday morning of that week. The address of that's on there too.' He gestured at the piece of paper.

'How old is your wife?' I asked.

'Forty-five.'

'A little young to have Alzheimer's disease, isn't she?'

Crawford raised his head, a suspicion of weariness on his face as if he'd been obliged to explain this many times. 'I can see you know little about the disease,' he said. 'I can assure you that age is no bar to contracting it. And it doesn't matter how intelligent the victim is. My wife had a very high IQ.'

Six

'I suppose it's understandable that he didn't want to admit to having a mistress while his wife was in a secure home in Edinburgh suffering from some incurable disease, Dave,' I said, as we left Crawford's apartment.

'So what are we going to do about it, guv?'

'Ask the Edinburgh police to check on his story. Get Colin to phone them when we get back.'

'He's a bit dodgy, if you ask me.' Dave was always prepared to see the worst in people, particularly those who seemed to make a lot of money out of doing very little. I suppose he's been working with me for too long.

'If he was in the frame, Dave, he'd've made sure he'd got a cast-iron alibi, all sewn up neat and tidy. Not something as woolly as his story was.'

'Yeah, maybe.' Dave was always reluctant to believe what anyone said, especially if they were as supercilious and well-heeled as Crawford. 'So where are we going now?' he asked as he started the engine and slammed the gear lever into drive.

Even though Crawford had told us that he was Patricia Hunter's boyfriend, it didn't necessarily mean he was her *only* boyfriend. And there was still the shadowy Bruce Phillips to track down. Not that I expected easily to find a man who was on the run from the Australian courts.

'Petersfield Street, Fulham, Dave. See what we can learn about Phillips.'

Number 9 Petersfield Street, Fulham, was a block of fairly new luxury service flats. And according to the array of bell pushes next to the intercom there were twelve apartments. But the label for flat 12 no longer bore the names of either Hunter or Phillips. If it ever had. At random, and because I'm inherently lazy, I picked flat 1 on the ground floor. The label said it was occupied by someone called Mace.

The woman who answered the door was in her forties and wearing jeans, a tee shirt and an apron. She examined us suspiciously – Dave Poole in particular – but the look changed to one of curiosity when we told her who we were. And who we were looking for.

'Bruce Phillips?' For a moment or two the woman savoured the name, eventually shaking her head. 'No one of that name here, love,' she said. 'Not as far as I know.'

'Do you happen to know if there's *ever* been anyone of that name here?' I asked. 'We were told that he was living in flat twelve.'

'No, love, sorry. I've never heard of him.'

I played a hunch and tried another tack. 'Do you know if there were any theatricals living here at any time, Mrs Mace? It is *Mrs* Mace, is it?'

'Yes. Toni Mace. It's short for Antonia, but I never really liked the name. That's life, though, isn't it? Your parents give you a name and you're stuck with it.'

'Yes, it's a problem,' I agreed. I'd been stuck with the name Harold, but never used it. 'I asked about theatricals, Mrs Mace.'

'Do call me Toni, love, and you'd better come in. Don't mind the kitchen, do you?' she asked as she led us into an expensively fitted kitchen in which there was a state-of-the-art cooker and an American-style refrigerator. 'Cup of tea? I've just made one.'

'Thank you.' Dave and I sat down on high stools along a breakfast bar. 'I was asking about theatricals,' I said once again.

'Come to think of it, there was a nice young girl here for about a year after we moved in, and I'm sure she was in number twelve. It was one of the top flats anyway, and there's only two on each floor. She could have been an actress, I suppose. Trouble is, we don't see very much of each other here, what with the lift and everything. It's only if you happen to be going out when they're coming in – or vice versa – that you bump into the other people living here.'

'You didn't know her name, I suppose?' I asked hopefully.

'No,' said Toni. 'We do tend to keep ourselves to ourselves.'

'Can you describe this girl?' Dave asked.

'Early twenties, I should think. Brunette. Nice-looking girl. I certainly envied her the figure she had,' she added wistfully. 'She must have been at least a thirty-eight D-cup, and she had a tiny waist and gorgeous legs. Often wore a miniskirt, and so would I have done if I'd had her body.'

The description certainly sounded like Patricia Hunter, but could also have fitted a thousand other women. 'D'you happen to know when she moved out?' I asked.

'No, love, sorry.' Mrs Mace paused for a second or two. 'Come to think of it, though, it could have been a year ago. It must have been that long since I last saw her.' She put mugs of tea in front of us. 'There you are.' She pulled a packet of cigarettes from her apron pocket and lit one. As an afterthought, she offered the packet to Dave and me.

'Did you ever see her with a man?'

'Only the once, and that must have been well over a year ago. Big hunk of a guy.' Toni Mace glanced at Dave. 'About your build, I should think, but with blond hair. Wouldn't have been surprised if he dyed it. Some men are so vain, aren't they?'

'Did you ever speak to this girl?' I asked.

'No more than half a dozen words at most, I should think. And that was only once or twice, just to say hello, or talk about the weather. Funny that, isn't it, the way people always talk about the weather when they can't think of anything else to say?'

'And you've no idea what she did for a living, Mrs Mace?'

'It's Toni, love,' she reminded me as she waved her cigarette smoke towards an extractor fan. 'No, d'you know I never thought to ask. But like I said, she could have been in the theatre. Or a model.' Then, as an apparent afterthought, she asked, 'Why are you interested in her? Has she done something wrong?'

'No, she was murdered. On the eleventh or twelfth of this month.'

'Well I never,' said Toni. 'You never know what's going to happen, do you?'

'One other thing,' said Dave. 'Are these flats owned or rented?'

'We bought ours. Well, us and the building society,' said Toni with a laugh. 'But some are rentals. We've seen all sorts of different people come and go since we've been here. Trouble is, we sometimes get a noisy lot. They don't care who they disturb, and I wouldn't like to see what they do to the flats they rent. Just don't seem to care these days, some young people, what with their noisy parties and God knows what else that they get up to. I can tell you, I've smelled cannabis in the hall on more than one occasion. We've had a go at the ground landlords about it from time to time, but they don't seem to care so long as they get their money.'

'Who are the ground landlords?' I asked.

Toni Mace rummaged about in a drawer next to the cooker and produced a bill. 'That's them,' she said. 'Anyway, that's who we pay our ground rent and maintenance to.'

Dave took a note of the details, and we thanked Toni for the tea.

'D'you think your husband might be able to tell us anything, Toni?' I asked.

'He's dead, love. Died last year. Cancer, it was. Still, his life insurance took care of the mortgage, otherwise I wouldn't still be here.'

We took the lift to the top floor and tried number 12 first, the flat that Patricia Hunter had apparently shared with Bruce Phillips, if the entry in her notebook was true.

But we fared no better there. The woman who answered the door had only just moved in and had never heard of anyone called Patricia Hunter or Bruce Phillips.

The door of number 11 was eventually opened by a white youth whose arm was around a half-naked black girl whose hair was braided into dreadlocks. Both were giggling, and each of them was openly smoking a joint.

The giggling stopped when we mentioned the magic word

57

'police' and a murder, but as they'd only rented the place a week ago they were unable to take us any nearer finding Phillips.

Dave was all for pursuing the drugs offences, but as we had neither the time nor a warrant, and the government didn't give a toss anyway, we left it. Even these days, murder takes precedence over narcotics. Just.

The next morning, I rang the ground landlord's agent. But he added very little to what we knew already. As far as he could tell from his files, a Bruce Phillips had rented flat 12 – 'Before it was decided to sell them all off,' he volunteered – and had paid the rent regularly. The lease had been terminated at the end of May last year and he didn't know where Phillips had gone. There had never been any complaints about him that the agent was aware of, and he had no idea whether Phillips had shared the accommodation with a woman. And judging by his tired response to my questions, the agent couldn't have cared less if he had done. I floated the name of Patricia Hunter, but that drew a blank as well.

I now considered the enigma that was facing me. The address of the Golden Riviera Guest House had been found in Patricia Hunter's address book, but she had no apparent connection with it. However, we had confirmed that the Petersfield Street address of Bruce Phillips that had been in her book was correct. And presumably Patricia Hunter had lived there with him prior to moving to 34 Coping Road, Islington. But Toni Mace had never heard of Phillips. My problem was going to be finding him, because suddenly he had become a front-runner for Patricia's murder.

Frank Mead dropped into the office. While Dave and I had been amusing ourselves talking to Toni Mace in Fulham, he'd been busy. One of his detective sergeants had interviewed the assistant electricians at the Granville Theatre, but none of them had even known Patricia Hunter, at least not by name. The officer had also obtained their dates of birth from the obliging Mrs Price, and had searched their names in Criminal Records Office, or whatever it's called these days. But nothing.

'I think we'll have to go further back in Patricia Hunter's address book than we've been already,' I said, clutching at straws and tossing them in Frank's direction. 'There's got to be a connection somewhere. Talk to the guys whose names have been crossed out, Frank.'

'Edward Archer and Nick Lloyd, guv,' said Dave, without even having to think about it. 'Addresses are in the incident room.'

I took Saturday off and left Frank Mead in charge on the strict understanding that he was to call me if anything cropped up that couldn't wait until Monday.

It was no fun being single again. The freedom it brings is offset by having to do everything oneself. If you wanted morning tea, that is. And I couldn't get under way without tea. I had a wonderfully cheerful lady cleaner who came in and 'did' twice a week, so I was able to avoid things like dusting, polishing and vacuuming.

Maybe I should have gone to work after all. But not wanting to sit in my flat alone, watching daytime television, I decided to go into Kingston and catch up on some essential shopping. Like shirts, all but one of which were in the washing machine.

I didn't recognize her at first. Probably because she was wearing sunglasses. I'd noticed her, of course: I tend always to notice tall, shapely blondes. She was wearing jeans – the sort that makes it look as though she'd been poured into them – a sloppy sweater and a baseball cap with her long hair tucked through the gap at the back.

'It's Mr Brock, isn't it?'

'Yes.'

'It's Gail. Gail Sutton.' She laughed and waved a hand in front of my face in a parody of testing my vision.

'Sorry, I was miles away.' *What a brilliant liar I am!* 'How are you?'

'Unemployed.'

'Yes, I heard that *Scatterbrain* had closed, but I thought you called it "resting" in your profession.'

Gail laughed. 'Self-delusion knows no bounds in the theatrical world,' she said. 'Call it what you like, but the money stopped at eleven o'clock last night.'

'I'd better buy you a cup of coffee, then,' I said. 'Now that you're penniless.'

'Are you any nearer finding out who murdered Patricia?' asked Gail, once we were settled in a nearby coffee shop with cups of coffee-flavoured froth in front of us.

'No, but we have found her parents. They live in Wimbledon.'

'Oh God!' Gail paused, cup in mid-air. 'I'll bet they were upset.'

'Of course they were,' I said rather tersely, but then apologized. 'I'm sorry, but we get hardened to tragedies of that sort in my business.'

Gail shuddered, and I suspected it was from the thought that the psychopath who'd killed Patricia Hunter was still at large. She took a packet of cigarettes from her bag and offered it to me.

I paused briefly and then took one. I'd been trying to give up for ages. Ever since I was at school in fact, when a master caught me having a quick drag behind the bike sheds and told me a horror story about his brother dying from tobacco-induced lung cancer. But I'd never been able to summon the willpower. And Dave was no help.

'D'you think you'll catch him, Mr Brock?'

'It's Harry, and yes I do. No doubt about it.'

My God! Did I just say that?

I glanced at my watch. 'D'you fancy a spot of lunch? I hate to see starving actresses on the streets. Begging's a big problem in London now.'

Gail hesitated and then smiled. 'Well, I er . . .'

'I'm going to eat somewhere anyway,' I said, 'and I hate eating alone.'

'OK, thanks.'

We found a decent pub and spent a few minutes studying the bar menu.

'Red or white?' I asked.

'Neither, thanks,' she said. 'I've got to drive later on.'

We took our food and a couple of soft drinks out to a terrace

60

facing the river, and settled at a vacant bench beneath a sun canopy. For a few minutes we watched the river traffic of small motor boats crewed by weekend sailors accompanied by middle-aged, overweight women stretched out on cabin roofs, and wearing bikinis in the vain belief that they could get away with it.

'You told me the other day that you're divorced.'

'Yes, and so are you, aren't you?' Gail glanced at me and took a sip of her diet cola.

'Yes, I am,' I said, and left it at that, hoping for some inexplicable reason that she wouldn't probe further.

'So, you're on your own now?'

It was understandable, I suppose, that Gail wanted to be under no illusions about my precise marital status. I guessed that she'd had some unhappy experiences with men who'd turned out to be married. Something I imagined to be the fate of an attractive chorus girl.

'Yes, I'm afraid so.' I didn't think it was a good idea to mention that I had broken up with my long-standing girlfriend only a week ago. 'What about you?'

'The hours of work in the theatre are not exactly conducive to finding a partner.' It was a sour comment and for a moment Gail looked sad. 'Hoofing it every night, and twice on Fridays and Saturdays, doesn't leave much time for socializing.'

'No, I suppose not.' It looked as though this banal conversation was going to continue, so I decided to explore more deeply. 'What happened to your husband?'

Gail shot me one of those looks that said it's none of your damned business, and for a moment or two I thought she wasn't going to answer. But she did. Eventually. 'I was in a revival of Coward's *Private Lives* at Richmond – this was about four years ago – and I went down with some bug. I took some paracetamol, lumbered my understudy and came home early. Surprise, surprise, I found him in bed – *our bed!* – with some nude dancer he'd picked up. Well, she was nude then, anyway,' she added with a wry smile.

'What did he do, your husband?'

'Took off with a flea in his ear, and so did his bedmate. We divorced nine months later.'

61

I laughed. 'No, I meant what was his profession?'

Gail laughed too. 'Oh, he was a director. That's how I met him. Directing a musical I was in.'

'Just now you said you were in *Private Lives*. Does that mean you're really an actress? Rather than a dancer.'

'I was then, but in this game you have to take what you can get. Fortunately, I was trained as a dancer so I've always got that to fall back on.'

'What are you going to do now?'

'Go home and do some washing and ironing.'

'No, I meant what are you going to do about a job?'

'Oh, I'll find something. Sweet-talk my agent and scour the pages of *The Stage*, I suppose. That's the usual thing. I hope I can find something that lasts a bit longer than *Scatterbrain*.'

'Will you try for an acting part? I should think that's less strenuous than dancing,' I said, as we left the pub.

Gail smiled. 'If I can persuade someone to give me an audition,' she said, but she didn't sound too sanguine about the prospect.

'It's a pity I don't know any casting agents,' I said, smiling. Well, I did know one, but he was doing life in Parkhurst prison. And he hadn't been any good at it anyway. After a suitable pause, I took a chance. 'How about having dinner with me tonight?' I'd said it without thinking and immediately wondered whether it was a good idea.

'No, Harry. Sorry.'

Obviously not a good idea. 'Just a thought,' I said.

'Oh, I'd've loved to have dinner with you, but I'm committed for this evening.'

I might have known it. Despite what she'd said about the difficulty of establishing relationships, a stunningly attractive girl like Gail was bound to have an admirer. Or two.

But I was wrong.

'I'm visiting my parents this weekend. Driving up this afternoon, as a matter of fact. They haven't seen much of me lately, mainly because they live in Nottingham, and it's quite a hike up there. But another time, eh?' She ferreted about in her handbag, took out a pen and a small notebook. She scribbled a few lines, tore out the page and handed it to me. 'That's my Kingston phone number,' she said.

We parted outside the pub and I spent a few seconds watching her walk away. And wondering if this could be the start of something more lasting than my relationship with Sarah Dawson.

Seven

On Monday morning we received confirmation from a dentist in Ewell that Patricia Hunter *was* Patricia Hunter, according to her teeth anyway. We'd asked the General Dental Council to circularize the practitioners in London and the Home Counties first, rather than waste their time, and ours, in sending her records all over the country. Although we had identified her before seeking the help of the dental profession, it did provide us with another address for her.

'According to this dentist, sir,' – Colin Wilberforce tapped the printout – 'Patricia Hunter had lived in Epsom at the date of her last treatment, which was some six years ago.'

'Well, I hope he's right,' I said, 'I don't want to waste any more time. Get on to Linda Mitchell, tell her that Dave and I are going to this Epsom address now, and she's to stand by at Epsom police station in case we need her. I'll want fingerprints lifted from the address to make sure it tallies with the body we've got in the mortuary.'

'It's in the Surrey Police area, sir,' cautioned Colin.

'I know it is, Colin, and if they want to get all territorial about it and investigate my murder, they can have it with pleasure. But until then, I'll use our own resources.'

Colin grinned. 'I thought you'd say that, sir.'

'But you'd better send the Surrey lot a message saying that we'll be on their patch.'

'Right, sir.' Colin made a note on his pad.

'Where's Dave?'

'I'm here, guv,' said Dave, entering the incident room with a tray of coffee.

64

'Good. We're going to Epsom.'

'We've missed the Derby, guv,' said Dave.

'Yes, I'm Eleanor Hunter,' said the woman who'd answered the door. She was a plain woman. Her hair, greying slightly, was severely cut in a short, mannish crop, and she wore trousers and a baggy sweater.

'Are you Patricia's sister?' I asked, after telling her, as sympathetically as I could, that Patricia was dead.

'I am, but she didn't live here any more. We didn't get on.'

'Did she ever visit a dentist in Ewell, Miss Hunter?' I asked, doing my belt-and-braces routine.

'Yes, I believe she did, but that was a long time ago.'

'And presumably she lived here at that time.'

'For a while,' said Patricia's sister, 'but she left about five years ago.'

'I'd like to have some of my people examine the room she lived in. You see, we need to check it for fingerprints in order to make sure that it is Patricia that was found.' That wasn't the reason, of course. I wanted to see if there were any fingerprints of someone else. Someone else who might have murdered her. Even so, I didn't hold out much hope, not after five years.

'Do whatever you have to. It's upstairs, first on the right.'

Dave went into the street and called up Linda Mitchell on his mobile.

'What happened to Patricia?' asked Eleanor.

It struck me as rather strange that Patricia's sister had waited so long to pose that question.

I explained, as briefly as possible, the circumstances in which the body of Patricia Hunter had been found.

'I'm not surprised,' said Eleanor coldly. 'I warned her that the life she was leading would end in tragedy, but she wouldn't listen.'

'How old was she, Miss Hunter?'

'She'd've been twenty-six now. She was five years younger than me.'

Really? You look more than thirty-one to me.

'What was this lifestyle of hers that you disapproved of?'

'She was in the theatre. Dancing half-naked was contrary to all the Christian principles of our church. Our late parents brought us up in the Methodist faith and that sort of thing was frowned upon.'

'Your *late* parents?' Dave and I had been speaking to Patricia Hunter's parents only last Friday in Wimbledon. Strange that. The Hunters hadn't mentioned that they had another daughter. There was clearly something amiss here, but I wasn't going to raise it at this point. Not until I'd found out more about Eleanor Hunter. So I let her continue.

'Our father died of cancer at quite an early age, and our mother committed suicide shortly afterwards.' Eleanor Hunter spoke in matter-of-fact tones, with no trace of sadness as she recounted a story that I knew damned well was a pack of lies. And I wondered why she was lying. But I wasn't going to challenge her account. Not until I'd checked with a few independent sources. 'I was left to look after Patricia, but she insisted on the theatre as a career and I'm afraid we fell out over it. There was nothing I could do to dissuade her. She was of age, after all. I told her to leave.'

'Did your sister ever talk of any men friends, Miss Hunter?'

'Certainly not,' said Eleanor vehemently. 'She never discussed her private life with me, and I wouldn't have wanted to hear anyway. These stage women lead a dissolute life, you know.' It was obvious that the Christian principles which Eleanor so fervently espoused did not include one of sisterly love.

There was a knock at the door and Dave admitted the crime-scene examiners.

The room that Patricia Hunter had occupied had been cleaned and there was no trace of any of the girl's possessions. But to my surprise, Linda's people did manage to lift one or two fingerprints. And after they had taken a set of elimination prints from Eleanor Hunter we left.

At two o'clock that afternoon I was told that the fingerprints Linda Mitchell had found were those of Patricia Hunter and her sister Eleanor.

Eleanor Hunter had told us very little. She didn't know where Patricia had been living and she didn't know the names of any of the shows she had been appearing in. And what was more, she didn't seem to care about the fate of her sister. But that she had claimed their parents were dead was a bizarre twist.

I set young John Appleby the task of arranging for an urgent search of the General Register Office in Southport to check on the dates of birth of Patricia and Eleanor Hunter. It was possible that, despite Eleanor's claim that Patricia was her sister, they weren't related. Hunter was, after all, a fairly common name. But why should she do it? More to the point, why should she lie about the fate of their parents?

What was important now was to discover what Patricia Hunter had been doing before she joined the chorus line in *Scatterbrain*. We had traced some of the addresses where she had lived, all of which were in the Greater London area, but she could as easily have been with some second-rate repertory company in Sheffield, Truro or Glasgow for some of the time since leaving Epsom. If she had been in the theatre at all before appearing at the Granville. But she'd been found in the Thames at Westminster, and that gave me the probably fallacious hope that it was in London that she'd met the man, if it was a man, who had killed her. And the address in Brighton was still puzzling me.

What I needed now was a photograph of her. Her callous sister Eleanor had told us that she had no pictures of Patricia – which may or may not have been true – and I asked Frank Mead to arrange for searches of the Passport Office, and the Driver and Vehicle Licensing Agency at Swansea.

I was not interested in whether Patricia had been abroad or whether she could drive a car, but putting a post-mortem photograph in the newspapers or on television is counter-productive on two counts. Firstly, it is rarely a good likeness, and secondly, it alerts the killer to the fact that we've found the subject's dead body. However, a passport photograph, accompanied by a brief report saying that she is missing from home, would merely indicate that we don't know where she is. That was the theory, anyway.

Frank, as usual, came up with the goods.

After telling Patricia's parents what we proposed to do, I rang the Head of News at the Yard's Public Affairs Directorate

67

and asked him to arrange publication of the photograph in the London press and on local television stations.

It was about two o'clock the following afternoon when Colin took the phone call.

'A woman called Candy Simpson just rang, sir,' he said. 'She'd seen Patricia Hunter's photograph in the paper. She says she's not missing at all,' he added with a wry grin.

'That's true,' said Dave. 'We know where she is: in the mortuary.' But as he often says, he has a black sense of humour.

'Where is this woman, Colin? Do we have an address?' I asked.

'Another actress, sir,' said Colin with a sly smile as he handed me the message. 'She's got digs in Pender Street, Paddington, but she's appearing in a play at the Alhambra in Holborn. She'll be there from about six o'clock.'

The theatre advertised a play called *The Birthday Party*, and Candy Simpson's name was listed well down among the cast. In fact, it only just made it. The stage-door keeper made a phone call and then showed us to a tiny dressing room with a star on the door. For what that was worth.

The actress, quite unembarrassed at wearing nothing but a G-string, was seated at a dressing table. I reckoned she was in her twenties.

'I hope you don't mind me carrying on, darlings,' she said, talking to our reflections in a mirror around which was a battery of lights, 'but it always takes me ages to get ready.'

'Not at all, Miss Simpson. You carry on.'

'I suppose you want to know where Patricia's gone,' she said, leaning closer to the mirror as she examined the mascara she had just put on.

'We've already found her.'

'Oh, that's good.' Candy Simpson carefully applied lipstick and puckered her lips before pressing them gently with a tissue. 'So you don't really need to talk to me at all, then. But as you're here you may as well sit down.' Without diverting her gaze from the mirror, she indicated a worn sofa with a theatrical flourish of her hand.

'I'm sorry to have to tell you that Patricia Hunter's dead.'

Abandoning all thoughts of preparing for her imminent appearance in *The Birthday Party*, Candy swung round on her chair, her face registering shock. 'Oh no! But the piece in the paper only said that she was missing.'

'It was deliberately misleading,' I said, 'because we didn't want to let her killer know that we'd found her body.'

'*Her killer?*'

'Yes, she was murdered.'

'How awful. When did this happen?'

'Her body was found in the Thames at Westminster, a week ago last Wednesday. She'd been strangled.'

Candy gave a convulsive shudder. 'I was her understudy, you see. Not that it's a great part, but it was a start. I play the maid and I have to come in and say, "Dinner is served, My Lord." Twice. I suppose you could say she did me a good turn really.'

I wondered why a maid with only one line to speak should have required an understudy. I'd've thought that, in an emergency, anyone could have taken it on. Even one of the usherettes.

'Patricia Hunter was in *Scatterbrain* at the Granville up until her death,' I said.

'What?' Candy stared at me in disbelief. 'I never knew that,' she said.

'So how did you come to get her part?'

'It must have been about three months ago,' said Candy, her concentration now fully on me. 'I thought she'd done what she said she was going to do.'

'And what was that?'

'She'd met this man. Jeremy, he was called.'

'Did you meet him?'

'No, but Patricia was ecstatic about him. A wonderful guy, she said he was.'

'What d'you know about him?'

'Only what Patricia told me. She said he'd got a studio flat in Docklands and a villa in the South of France at a place called . . .' Candy paused. 'Yes, it was in St Raphaël, or just outside, I think she said. Apparently she and Jeremy

69

were going to get married and move there permanently. She kept on about it. Her idea was to walk out of the play one night without telling anybody and never come back. And that's what I thought she'd done. She was always promising to do it if she ever won the lottery. And I thought she had. Sort of.'

'How long had she known this man, Miss Simpson?'

'I don't really know, but I got the impression that she'd only recently met him. At least, she didn't start talking about him until about a fortnight before she left. I warned her about the risk of getting married so quickly and I told her that she ought to get to know him first.' Candy spread her hands. 'I mean, how can you decide a thing like that when you've only known a guy for a fortnight? But it was probably the money. You know, the sports car, the flat in London and the villa in France. I think he turned her head with all his talk of spending cloudless days soaking up the sun on a French Riviera beach.'

'What was this man's surname?'

'I'm sorry, I don't know. She never told me. I don't think it was a secret, but I never thought to ask.'

'A flat in Docklands, you say? D'you know where?'

'No. Sorry,' said Candy again, and paused. 'D'you think he was the one who murdered her?'

'I don't know, Miss Simpson, but obviously I'll have to talk to him.'

'When did Miss Hunter manage to see this man?' asked Dave. He'd once told me about the problems he'd had when he was courting Madeleine; having a girlfriend who worked most evenings in the theatre made socializing difficult. 'I assume you're on stage every night Monday to Saturday.'

'*And* matinees on Wednesday and Saturday, darling,' said Candy ruefully. Turning briefly to the dressing table, she picked up her watch and glanced at it. 'I think they spent most lunch times together, but it is very difficult. Unless we're resting, of course.' She forced a smile. 'God knows why we do it. It's certainly not the money. The theatre's nothing short of slavery, you know.' She stood up, donned a bra, a short black dress and a frilly cap before tying on a white apron.

70

'Did Patricia ever go to this flat of Jeremy's?' I asked. 'Or to his place in France?'

'Not that I know of. If she did, she never mentioned it. But I'm pretty sure she didn't go. She was so bubbling over with it all that I'm certain she couldn't have kept it to herself. Mind you, she did shoot off every night, straight after her second entrance.'

'Have you any idea what this guy Jeremy did for a living?' Dave asked.

'No, she never said anything about that. Actually, I thought, from what she said, that he was so rich he didn't have to work.'

'So it's possible that he was spinning her a yarn, and she just believed everything he told her?' I said, taking back the questioning.

Candy nodded slowly. 'I imagine so. Poor little kid. Fancy getting taken in with a story like that.'

'It happens, Miss Simpson,' I said.

'One other thing,' said Dave. 'D'you know where Patricia lived?'

'Yes. She had a flat in Courtney Street. It's just round the corner from here. Number sixty-four, I think.'

Yet another address to be checked out. A last thought occurred to me. 'Did Patricia Hunter ever mention a man called Bruce Phillips?' I asked.

Candy Simpson considered the question for a moment or two. 'No, I don't think so,' she said eventually. 'In fact, I'm sure she didn't.' She took a last look in the mirror and adjusted the frilly cap.

There was a loud knock at the door as we stood up to leave, and a voice shouted, 'Five minutes, Candy!'

'Think there's anything to be read into Riviera, guv?' asked Dave next morning. 'We've got the Golden Riviera Guest House in Brighton, and the Côte d'Azur in the South of France where Jeremy – whoever he is – promised to take Patricia.'

'You're having me on, Dave,' I said. 'If this guy's got as much money as he claimed to have, I don't see him putting up at Richards's boarding house in Brighton. And even if he wasn't rich, he'd have splashed out just to make an impression.'

'D'you know what I think, guv?' said Dave, ferreting about in his shabby nylon briefcase and eventually producing a banana.

'Enlighten me, Dave.'

'I think that Patricia Hunter was a lying little bitch. All this chat about some guy turning up and promising to marry her and cart her off to the South of France is a load of bullshit. I reckon that she was up to something and just didn't want anyone else to know what it was.'

'Yeah, it all sounded too good to be true. One thing's certain, though. If we find Jeremy, and his DNA matches the seminal fluid found in Patricia Hunter's body, I reckon we've got our man.'

'So long as he's got a Ford, Renault or Bedford van,' said Dave, peeling his banana.

'All of which gives me an idea,' I mused. 'But we're going to need more men.'

'Amen to that.'

'I know the body was found at just after eight o'clock on the Wednesday evening, and Henry Mortlock estimated that she'd been dead about twenty-four hours, but common sense tells me that this guy disposed of her during the night. Only a maniac would dump a body in the river in broad daylight.'

'Only a maniac goes about murdering people,' observed Dave laconically.

'And that means that he probably has a legitimate reason for driving a van in the middle of the night,' I continued – ignoring, as I usually did, Dave's dry aside – 'and lives close to the Thames between, say, Hammersmith and Westminster.'

'That's a bloody great "if", guv,' said Dave. 'And a hell of a lot of houses to visit.'

I stood up and put on my jacket. 'I suppose I'll have to see the commander and plead for help.'

'Good luck,' said Dave, 'but why?'

'I think the only thing we can do is to arrange for police

72

to stop all Ford, Bedford and Renault vans operating during the night in that area.'

Dave dropped his banana skin into the wastepaper bin. 'What a very good idea, sir,' he said.

Somewhat hesitantly, I tapped on the commander's door.

'Hello, Harry.'

I was surprised to see, not the commander, but Detective Chief Superintendent Alan Cleaver sitting in the boss's chair.

'I was looking for the commander, guv,' I said.

'On leave, Harry. On a whim he decided to take Mrs Commander off to Paris for a long weekend. I'm acting. What can I do for you?'

I explained, as succinctly as possible, my progress in the murder I was investigating, and my thoughts about setting up roadblocks to check on vans.

'Jesus!' said a surprised Cleaver. 'I didn't realize how complicated that job had become. Just bring me up to speed, will you?'

'Yes, sir. The river police recovered Patricia Hunter from the Thames at Westminster on the twelfth of June, but it's beginning to look as though she was a dark horse. She had various addresses, a sister who didn't give a damn about the girl's welfare, and who told us her parents were dead, despite our having interviewed them two days previously. And then there's a boyfriend called Bruce Phillips who we've yet to trace, mainly, I think, because it's likely he's identical with a Bruce Phillips who's on the run from an Australian extradition warrant. And then there's some mysterious guy called Jeremy. According to another witness, he had promised to spirit our victim away to the south of France for a life of luxury. She was an actress by the way.'

'A bit of a puzzle,' said Cleaver, as usual understating the case.

'And some,' I said. 'All we really know so far is that she'd indulged in sexual intercourse shortly before her death, but there's no match for the semen in the DNA database. The CSEs also found fibres in the woman's hair that appear to come from the matting in a Ford, Renault or Bedford van.

73

And there were some unidentified particles in grazing on her body.'

'And the commander's not given you any extra men?'

'Not one, guv,' I said, sitting down in the commander's plush armchair.

'Right. First of all, more officers.' Cleaver started to make notes on a pad as he spoke. 'And we'll arrange to have Territorial Support Groups doing checks throughout the night.' He glanced at his watch. 'If you can list the areas where you want this done, I'll get on to the Area DACs and set it up for tonight. That OK with you?'

'That'd be fine, guv,' I said.

'Good.' Cleaver leaned back in his chair.

Dave looked up despondently as I entered my office. 'Don't tell me,' he said. 'The answer's no.'

'The answer's yes,' I said.

'Blimey, how d'you swing that, guv?'

'Mr Cleaver's acting commander,' I said. 'He didn't even blink. Now all we've got to do is work out where we want these stops done.'

'I've done it,' said Dave, handing me a sheet of paper. 'And while you've been twisting the guv'nor's arm, I've been thinking.'

'You be careful, Dave,' I said. 'Carry on like that and you might get promoted.'

'It doesn't work that way according to what I've heard,' muttered Dave, and tossed me a cigarette. 'But there is one thing. What about the mysterious Bruce Phillips?'

'What about him?'

'Well, we haven't found him yet. He's not only listed in Patricia Hunter's address book, but when we checked that address, it turned out to be where she had lived herself at one time. What's more, her father reckoned that she mentioned him in a letter as being a boyfriend.'

'But how the hell do we track him down, Dave?'

'There's a fortune-teller who turns up at the fair on Clapham Common every year,' said Dave drily. 'Incidentally, while you were having an audience with the acting commander, I rang

Richards at the Golden Riviera Guest House and got him to go through his books. No couple called Jeremy and Patricia stayed there during the last year.'

'Thanks, Dave. Somehow I didn't think they would have done.'

'So, d'you reckon that this Jeremy and the missing Bruce Phillips could be one and the same?'

I shrugged. 'It's a possibility, Dave.'

Eight

'We've got an answer from the Edinburgh police, sir,' said Colin Wilberforce, appearing in the doorway of my office.

'What do they have to say?'

'First of all they made enquiries at the address in Colinton – it's a suburb of Edinburgh – that Crawford said was his house, but there was no one there. However, the next-door neighbours claimed to have seen a car on his drive a couple of times between Tuesday and Friday of the week he said he was there, but they couldn't remember exactly when. One neighbour mentioned that he'd told them he was visiting someone in a local hospital.'

'Hospital? I thought it was a secure home. That's what Crawford said.'

'Yes, but the local police checked it out, sir, and it's an expensive nursing home that caters for rich people with mental problems. The door's kept locked and visitors are admitted by whoever's on duty at the time. The police up there say that Crawford visited a few times during the week, but they don't know how often. The home doesn't keep a log and so long as a visitor's *bona fide*, they let him in.'

'That rules him out, then,' I said. 'I don't suppose these neighbours of his noted the car number, did they?'

'No, sir. They didn't even know the make.'

'Incidentally, Colin, have we had any follow-up on the grazing found on the victim's back?'

'Yes, sir.' Colin shuffled through the sheaf of papers he was carrying. 'Linda Mitchell's team checked those bridges that have concrete balustrades and there's no match.'

76

'No match? Well, that blows that theory out of the water.'

'It seems that they recovered some minute specks of dust or concrete from the grazing on the body – something like that – but it doesn't correspond with anything on the bridges they checked. Linda's hazarded a guess that they might have come from the floor of a garage or storeroom. There was also a slight trace of a substance that could be motor oil. The lab's doing further checks now.'

'Interesting. Perhaps she was strangled in a garage somewhere, conveyed in a van, and then dumped.'

'Or,' said Dave, 'she was conveyed in a van that had traces of this dust and oil in it.'

As usual, Dave had found fault with my all-too-easy assumption.

On Thursday morning, I found Colin Wilberforce at his desk sorting through a pile of report sheets.

'What have you got there, Colin?' I asked.

'Results of the TSG's stop-and-search operation last night, sir.'

'Any good?'

Colin grinned. 'Matter of opinion,' he said. 'Altogether the TSG units stopped some thirty-seven Ford, Renault and Bedford vans. All the drivers appeared to have a legitimate reason for driving about in the middle of the night. There were electricians, computer repair men, postmen, night-delivery guys and office-cleaning people. Oh, and a few plumbers.'

'Got the plumbers' telephone numbers?' asked Dave.

'D'you fancy a plumber for this topping then, Dave?' asked Colin.

'No,' said Dave, 'but there's something wrong with my bloody drains.'

Colin Wilberforce had reduced the bundle of reports of the TSG 'stops' to what he called a computerized database – whatever the hell that meant – but the results were disappointing. There was not a single driver whose name was Jeremy. Or, for that matter, Bruce Phillips either. But that was no surprise. Not that any of it meant much: the man with whom Patricia Hunter had been so besotted may not have given her his real name. And if he was indeed her murderer, who would blame him? Apart from which, if he was as rich as Candy Simpson said Patricia Hunter had told her he was, he wouldn't be driving about in a van in the middle of the night. Unless . . .

'Only one thing for it, Frank,' I said to DI Mead. 'Every one of these people has to be checked out. Find out where they were on the nights of the murders and see if they had anything to do with theatres or were even regular theatre-goers.'

Frank was busy making notes. 'I'll run them through Criminal Records Office too,' he said, glancing up from his pocket book. He couldn't be bothered either with the constant name changes with which the job seems to be beset these days.

I don't know why he bothered to say that: a CRO search is standard procedure. Perhaps it was his way of telling me not to try teaching my grandmother to suck eggs.

I grinned and held up my hands in an attitude of surrender. 'Yeah, OK, Frank.' I turned to Dave. 'Dave, see if the lab has had second thoughts about the fibres found on the victim. It's possible that they've refined their conclusions to exclude some makes of van.'

'Right, guv.' Dave tapped his teeth with his pen. 'Of course, what would be really helpful right now would be to have another murder that took place last night. Then we could double-check Mr Mead's list of van drivers. Never know, might get a match.'

'Shut up, Poole,' said Frank.

I was still puzzling over how we could track down the mysterious Bruce Phillips. The London telephone directory was no help: there were hundreds of people called Phillips, and only a very stupid fugitive would publish his name in a telephone directory. I just hoped that something would turn up to point me in the right direction.

And it did, sooner than I'd expected. Nearly.

'Later this afternoon, we'll take a look at Patricia Hunter's flat in Courtney Street, Dave.'

'Yeah, sure. By the way, Appleby got the results of the

search of the General Register Office at Southport. There's no trace of an Eleanor Hunter being born thirty-one years ago. But the people up there did confirm Robert and Daphne Hunter as Patricia's parents.'

'In that case, we'll talk to Eleanor again. Right now. I wonder what the hell's she's playing at.'

We drove to Epsom, determined to unravel the mystery of Eleanor Hunter and what she'd told us about the 'death' of her parents.

'When we were here last, Miss Hunter, you told us that your parents had died some years ago.'

'That's correct.'

'In that case, how d'you explain the fact that I spoke to them last Friday?'

For some moments, Eleanor Hunter remained silent.

'Miss Hunter?'

When eventually she spoke there was disdain in her voice. 'I don't see that any of this is your business,' she said.

'Perhaps you'll let me be the judge of that,' I said.

There was a further silence before the woman spoke again. 'We had a relationship,' she said curtly.

'Who did?'

'Patricia and me.'

'What sort of relationship?' I asked, having deduced from Eleanor Hunter's masculine appearance what form that relationship would have taken.

'A lesbian relationship,' Eleanor said defiantly, raising her chin slightly and staring me in the eye. 'And then Patricia ruined it all. She found some man and went off with him. After all I'd done for her too. I'd looked after that girl, doted on her. I loved her. And how did she repay me? She went with a man.' The expression on her face was one of bitter hatred, and I wondered if we'd just found another suspect for Patricia Hunter's murder.

'So this story you told my chief inspector about the death of her parents was all nonsense, was it?' asked Dave.

'I said *our* parents. But it was my parents who'd died.'

'Why did you tell me that they were Patricia's parents then?'

79

'I don't know. I just said it on the spur of the moment,' said Eleanor, her eyes glittering.

'You do appreciate, I hope, that obstructing the police in a murder enquiry is a very serious matter.' But as I said it, I had a nasty thought that Eleanor may just enjoy a few months in the women's prison at Holloway. Not that I anticipated the Crown Prosecution Service stirring themselves sufficiently to bring a case against her.

'I don't care,' said Eleanor. 'That bitch deserved everything she got. I told her that no good would come of associating with men. They always let you down, and it looks as though one of them killed her. Well, serve her right, I say.'

'And is your name Hunter?'

'No, it's Carson.'

'Why did you change it to Hunter?'

'I didn't. I adopted it. Despite what you may think, neighbours still look down their noses at two women living together and sharing a bed, so we pretended to be sisters.' For no good reason, Eleanor laughed. 'The neighbours are a terrible trial,' she said. 'Got nothing better to do than mind other people's business.'

'You have wasted a great deal of my time,' I said sternly. 'And time is of the essence in a murder enquiry.'

'That's your problem,' said Eleanor, still refusing to be cowed by my earlier threat.

'What was the name of this man that Patricia went off with, Miss Carson?'

'I've no idea.'

'I think you have.'

There was a long pause before Eleanor Carson spoke again. 'It was someone called Bruce Phillips,' she said. 'The silly little bitch said she was going to marry him,' she added, and scoffed at the thought.

I couldn't work out whether Patricia Hunter's former lover was acting out of spite – it certainly seemed that way – but for the moment I decided to leave it. Apart from logging her in the back of my mind as a suspect.

'Go via Epsom nick, Dave,' I said as we drove away from Eleanor Carson's house. 'You never know, we might learn something there.'

80

The station officer at Epsom, a grizzled, grey-haired sergeant, laughed outright when we mentioned Eleanor's name.

'Mad as a hatter, sir,' he said. 'On average we get called there by her neighbours about once a month. The last time was at two o'clock on a Sunday morning. Dear Eleanor was standing in her back garden, stark naked, holding a paraffin lamp aloft and singing hymns at the top of her voice. It seems that "Onward Christian Soldiers" was her favourite. She really ought to be sectioned. Not that we haven't tried,' he added with a sigh.

'I don't wonder Patricia cleared off,' said Dave.

We drove direct from Epsom police station to Holborn.

Number 64 Courtney Street, Holborn, was an old Victorian house that had been converted into flats. Next to the front door was the usual entryphone system, but no names were posted alongside the bell pushes and the door was open anyway. So much for security.

There was a table in the entrance hall on which was a pile of letters. I sorted through it but it was only junk mail for someone called James Meredith who resided in Flat 2.

I rang the bell of the ground-floor flat.

The man who answered the door inspected us closely. I suppose that, in common with most Central London residents, he had been plagued by market researchers and door-to-door salespersons flogging anything from religion to subscriptions for magazines that were destined to go bankrupt before you'd received all the copies you'd paid for. Or even the first one.

'Yes?' he said in a tired voice, and adopted the stance of a man fully prepared to throw us into the street the moment we mentioned money, or suggested that the Lord was his salvation. Or worse still, both.

'I understand a woman called Patricia Hunter lived here . . .' I began.

'Not any more,' said the man, and started to close the door.

Dave put a hand against it and pushed. 'Police,' he said.

The door opened again. 'So?'

'We are investigating Patricia Hunter's murder,' I said.

'Bloody hell!' The man opened the door wide and stared

at us, slack-jawed. 'When did that happen then?' There was the slightest trace of an accent, East-European maybe, possibly Polish at a guess. So what? We're all in the European Union now.

'Perhaps we should come in, Mr, er . . . ?'

'Lang, Erik Lang,' he said. Which may or may not have been his real name. 'Erik with a K.'

'When did you last see Miss Hunter?' I asked as we followed him into a cluttered sitting-room-cum-office.

Lang thought about that before answering. 'When she moved out,' he said. 'That must have been a couple of months ago, I suppose.'

'Did you know her well?'

'Not really. We'd exchange a few words if we met in the hall, or when she came in to pay the rent. Nothing more. We tend to keep ourselves to ourselves here.' Just what Toni Mace had said. Strange how one can live in a crowded city and never really get to know anyone else.

'I take it that you're the landlord.'

'Yes.'

'And do you actually own the property?'

'Yes, I do, but what's that got to do with—?'

'When did she move in, Mr Lang?'

I think Lang grasped that I didn't intend to be messed about. 'Just a tick,' he said and crossed to the window sill. Picking up a cashbook of some sort, he thumbed through a couple of pages. 'Just before last Christmas.'

'And was the tenancy in her name?' asked Dave, his pocket book already out.

'Yes, er . . . well, no. I don't know.'

'Well, which is it: yes, no, or don't know?' asked Dave in the manner of someone conducting a public opinion poll.

Lang paused, presumably because he was contravening some part of the various Rent Acts, the Finance Act, the plethora of VAT regulations or one of the multifarious European Union regulations that these days emanate from Brussels. And was wondering whether we were about to do him for it. *I should care, when I've a murder to clear up.*

'There was nothing formal. No written agreement or

anything like that. It was a man who rang up first off. He said he was arranging a flat for his girlfriend. He mentioned something about her being in show business and didn't have the time to look around. But she was the one who paid the rent.'

'And his name?' demanded Dave.

'Ah, you've got me there,' said Lang.

'It is important, if you can remember, Mr Lang,' I said.

'Oh, just a minute. Come to think of it, I do have it here somewhere.' Lang pulled down the flap of a bureau and took out a desk diary. 'Yes, here we are. He rang to make an appointment and I jotted his name down.'

'And what was his name?' Dave asked with a sigh of impatience.

'Bruce Phillips,' said Lang.

'Did he leave a contact number, by any chance?' Dave gave no indication that the name was of vital importance. 'Or an address?' he added hopefully.

'No,' said Lang. 'I never thought to ask him.'

'And did he actually come here?' I asked.

'No. He said he was making the appointment for Miss Hunter, and it was her that turned up.'

'Did you ever see a man going up to her flat, Mr Lang?' asked Dave.

'No.'

'Who's occupying the flat now?' I asked.

'No one. I had a man in there for two weeks, but he moved out again the day before yesterday.'

'It's empty then?'

'Yes.'

'I'd like to have a look round.'

'Sure. I'll get the key.'

To say that it was small would be exaggerating: a bed, a tiny kitchen area, and a shower, all squeezed into a converted loft space. In places the slant of the roof made it difficult to stand upright. Unless you were about four-feet-two tall. I was not surprised that the last tenant had stayed for only a couple of weeks. It made me wonder what had brought Patricia Hunter from the comparative luxury of the flat at Petersfield Street to something that was little more than a flop.

Dave and I spent a few fruitless minutes looking round, but there was nothing of interest to us, and certainly nothing that would advance our investigation.

As we returned to the ground floor to give the key back to Lang, I noticed that James Meredith's junk mail had vanished from the hall table. Good, he was in. With any luck, he'd have been nosier than the landlord.

And he had.

We told Meredith who we were and he almost dragged us into his flat. Perhaps the poor guy was lonely or just adored policemen. The first I could believe; the second I doubted. 'Come in,' he said warmly, 'and join me in a drink.' Brooking no refusal, he produced a bottle of whisky and three glasses from a tall cupboard fashioned from some exotic tropical wood. 'It's nice, isn't it?' he said, running his hand lovingly over the carved surface. 'It's ethnic.'

I didn't bother to point out that everything was ethnic to a greater or lesser degree, and hoped that Dave wouldn't come out with one of his thumbnail lectures on the misuse of the English language.

'I've had a bloody awful day at the office,' Meredith continued, handing Dave and me a glass of Scotch, 'so I thought to myself, sod it, and knocked off early. Still, nothing to what you chaps have to put up with, I imagine,' he added ruefully.

'What do you do in this office of yours?' Dave asked.

'I'm an accountant,' said Meredith, looking even more apologetic. 'Bloody computers all day long.'

'Patricia Hunter,' I said before Dave could make one of his sarcastic comments about accountants.

'Girl who used to live upstairs, you mean? Moved out a while back. I was sorry to see her go.'

'I'm afraid Miss Hunter's been murdered, Mr Meredith,' I said. 'That's why we're here.'

A look of stunned disbelief appeared on Meredith's face. 'Oh God, surely not!' He shook his head like a boxer who'd just received a debilitating uppercut, took a sip of whisky and remained silent for some moments. 'Christ! You just don't know what's around the corner, do you?' he said eventually.

'She was some looker, that girl. She was an actress, you know. Not surprising really. Like I said, she was a good-looking girl.'

I'd seen some quite ugly actresses over the years, but didn't think it was worth mentioning.

'How well did you get to know her?'

'I think it's fair to say I got to know her very well.' Meredith grinned and drained his whisky. 'As a matter of fact, I chatted her up shortly after she arrived and we hit it off straight away. She came down here for a drink from time to time, and I took her out to dinner on the few occasions she wasn't working. It wasn't all that easy, you see, what with her being on the stage and working late. Sometimes she was so tired that she'd stay overnight at the theatre. Apparently they've got bedrooms there, so she said. But I don't know much about the theatre.'

Dave shot me a glance that said it was bloody obvious Meredith didn't know anything about the theatre. But Dave did, and he knew that what Patricia Hunter had told our helpful accountant was nonsense. The nights she claimed to have been staying at the Granville, or wherever, were more than likely spent in a client's bed.

'But it was getting serious,' the naïve Meredith went on. 'After she'd been here for about four months, I made a tentative suggestion that she should move in with me, never thinking that she'd say yes. But she jumped at it, and we agreed to shift her stuff down to my flat on the following Sunday.' He let out a sigh of exasperation. 'And that's when it all went pear-shaped.'

'What happened?' I asked.

Meredith stood up and poured himself another whisky. 'Another one?' he asked, pointing at our glasses.

'No thanks.'

'Well, I met her in the hall on the Friday morning and she was with this guy,' Meredith continued. 'I didn't have a clue who he was. I thought maybe he was someone from the theatre who'd come by to collect something. You know, like a script.' Dave glanced at the ceiling. 'Anyway, I said something like "Hello, darling" and asked her if she was all set for Sunday's move, but she cut me dead. Never said a word.'

85

'Did you speak to her about it later?'

'Too right,' said Meredith. 'I went up to her flat and asked her what the hell it was all about.'

'And what did she say?'

'Well, for a start she didn't let me in, and she said she didn't want to talk about it. I asked her if she'd met someone else, but she said no. I just got a complete blank. And she couldn't close the door fast enough. As a matter of fact she seemed frightened even to be talking to me. And the very next day she moved out.'

'Did she tell you where she was going? Or leave a phone number?'

'No, nothing. I never saw her again. In fact, I didn't even know she'd gone. I went upstairs to her flat but there was no answer. I had a word with Erik Lang and he said she'd gone, vamoosed, but he didn't know where.'

'What sort of impression did you get of this man you saw, Mr Meredith?' I asked. 'Did the two of them look as though they were well acquainted?'

'Hard to say really. I only saw him that one time and that was very brief.'

'What did he look like, this guy?' Dave asked, pocket book and pen once more at the ready.

Meredith looked out of the window, as if trying to visualize the man he'd seen with Patricia Hunter. 'About five-ten or eleven, I suppose. Heavily built.' He glanced at Dave. 'Bit like you except that he had blond hair. That's about it really.'

'Did he speak with an Australian accent?' Dave asked.

'I don't know. He didn't say anything, just glowered. Why? D'you think an Australian killed her?'

Dave ignored Meredith's query and glanced at me. 'E-fit, guv?'

'What?' Given that Dave had graduated in English at London University, I often wished he'd get into the habit of speaking the language he'd spent three years studying.

'I think it may be a good idea if we got Mr Meredith to create a computer-aided likeness of the man he saw with Miss Hunter . . . sir.'

'Why the hell didn't you say so?' I said. 'Good idea.' I

turned to Meredith. 'Would you be prepared to come to a nearby police station and have a go at making up a picture of the man you saw?'

'Sure. When?'

'How about now?' I gave Dave a questioning look. 'What d'you reckon, Dave?'

'Got the car outside. Let's do it.'

But after a session lasting over an hour, aided by a very patient E-fit operator, the image that Meredith finally produced could have fitted a thousand men. Oh well, it was worth a try.

Nine

'This man Phillips is beginning to annoy me, Dave,' I said, over a pint in the Red Lion in Whitehall. 'There wasn't a Bruce Phillips on that list of stops the TSG did last night, was there?'

'Come on, guv, you know there wasn't. You checked it.'

'I was hoping I might have missed it,' I said gloomily, 'but he wouldn't have been on the list, not with the luck we've been having with this damned enquiry. And if he's still about, he's almost bound to have changed his name by now.'

'I doubt it,' said Dave. 'It strikes me he's an arrogant bastard. He must know he's wanted on an extradition warrant, but he still goes around using his own name. It pops up all over the place. Everywhere we look.' He ordered two more pints before continuing his theorizing. 'And I reckon he must have known Patricia Hunter for some time, guv.'

'Yeah, that's bugging me too. When was it that Eleanor Carson said Patricia left her for Bruce Phillips?'

'Five years ago, if we can believe anything that Eleanor told us, particularly after what that skipper at Epsom said about her. But Patricia could have known him even longer. We don't know when she put his name in her address book, but her old man said she'd mentioned Phillips in a recent letter as a boyfriend, *and* he rented the flat for her at Courtney Street.' Pausing long enough to give me a cigarette, Dave added, 'I suppose we could do the rounds of the theatres with that E-fit that Meredith did.'

'What, fifty-odd theatres and at least two hundred people, cast and staff, in each? Waste of time, Dave. Anyway, I doubt that he got it anything like our man. Just trying to be helpful. And can you imagine the result? It would be a whole load of "maybes" followed by hours of fruitless legwork.' I had long been of the opinion that E-fits were successful in a ratio of about one to every thousand.

'Yeah, I suppose you're right, guv.' Dave stared dolefully into his beer as though hopeful of finding the answer there. 'But what about the business of her going away with this Jeremy guy?'

'I've got reservations about that too, Dave. I think she was just spinning Candy Simpson a line. Like you said, boasting she'd got a rich boyfriend when Candy hadn't. Go home, Dave. We've done enough for one day.'

'And we haven't achieved a damned thing,' said Dave gloomily.

'Buy you a drink, gents?' said a voice.

I turned. Standing behind me was an odious creep known universally as Fat Danny, crime reporter of the worst tabloid in Fleet Street. And that, believe me, is an accolade for which there is much competition. Danny was overweight, and his pudding face was permanently greasy. And he had a tendency to wave his podgy little hands about the whole time he was talking. He had a reputation – envied by several other crime reporters – for being able not only to sniff out the most salacious of crimes, but also to track down the officers investigating it. Not that that was difficult, given that the Red Lion was the nearest pub to Curtis Green.

'Sure, Danny, we'll take a couple of pints of best off you.'

'So, Mr Brock, how's the Patricia Hunter job going?' asked Danny once he'd got a round in.

'Nowhere right now,' I said.

'But you must have some leads, surely?'

'One or two, but none that I can tell you about.'

'Your secret's safe with me, Mr Brock, you know that.'

'You given up journalism to become a Trappist monk then?' put in Dave.

'You know what I mean, Mr Brock,' said Danny, ignoring Dave and tapping the side of his nose with a forefinger. 'Non-attributable and all that. But a little bird told me that you had teams of uniforms out last night stopping vans. That something to do with this Hunter job, was it?'

'Maybe.'

'It's a good story. Glamorous showgirl brutally murdered and found floating in the river right opposite the Houses of Parliament. It's what front pages were made for. And a bit of publicity wouldn't do you any harm. Might even get you promoted. Oh, come on, Mr Brock, give me a break.'

'OK. We think the body of Patricia Hunter was conveyed in a van from where she was murdered to where she was dumped in the river.'

'And whereabouts *was* she dumped?' asked Danny optimistically.

'If you can tell me that, Danny, I'll make sure you get a letter of thanks signed personally by the commissioner.'

'Terrific, but seriously, haven't you got any suspects lined up?'

'Not one, Danny.'

'Leave it out, Mr Brock, I've got to write something.'

'Try your resignation,' said Dave.

It's one of life's paradoxes that even when you tell a journalist the truth, he still doesn't believe you.

It was almost seven o'clock. Having checked with Gavin Creasey, the night-duty incident-room sergeant, that there was nothing demanding my immediate attention, I went into my office and rang Gail Sutton.

'Hello?' The voice was hesitant and didn't sound like the chorus girl I'd met at the Granville and with whom I'd later had lunch in Kingston. I wondered if she shared her house with another girl.

'Is Gail there, please?'

'Who's that?'

'Harry Brock.'

'Oh, Harry, it's you.' There was relief in her voice, and I suddenly realized that the death of her friend, and her own association with the same theatre, might well have caused a woman living alone to feel vulnerable and not a little scared.

'I've got an idea.'

90

'What's that?'

'How about you jump on a train at Surbiton and come to Waterloo? It's only sixteen minutes. I'll meet you and take you to dinner. *And* I'll take you home afterwards. How about it?'

'That would be wonderful, Harry. Where are we going?'

'I know this great restaurant that does a wonderful steak and kidney pudding,' I said.

There was a distinct pause, and then, 'Have you ever noticed my figure, Harry?' Gail asked.

I laughed. 'What sort of question's that, for God's sake? Of course I've noticed it.'

'Well, it doesn't stay like that on a diet of steak and kidney pudding. I'm not in the running for playing one of the Ugly Sisters yet.'

'This place does fish as well, or whatever takes your fancy.'

'That's all right, then.'

'Have you got a mobile?'

'Yes, of course.'

'Right. Once you're on the train give me a ring and I'll be there to meet you.' And I gave her the number of my own mobile.

The concourse at Waterloo station was still thronged with bustling crowds of workers on their way home, even though it was nearing eight o'clock. Several trains that had stopped at Surbiton were due to arrive about now and I positioned myself near the indicator board in an attempt to spot Gail.

For a moment or two my attention was riveted on an elegant blonde in a silver-grey trouser suit gliding between the mass of self-centred travellers – a mass that, nevertheless, seemed automatically to part as she neared them – when suddenly I realized that it *was* Gail.

'Hi! Hope you haven't been waiting long.'

'No, I only just got here,' I lied and took her arm, convincing myself that this was a necessary precaution against her being knocked down by the panic-stricken runners obsessed with catching a train that had probably already left. 'You look great.'

'Gawd bless yer, sir,' she chided in bantering, mock-Cockney tones that ably demonstrated the range of her acting ability. 'Where are we going?'

'You'll see,' I said, steering her towards the taxi rank outside the station.

When we arrived at Rules Restaurant in Maiden Lane, the cab driver, his eyes on Gail but talking to me, said, 'Enjoy your game, guv'nor.'

'What's this about a game?' Gail asked, giving me a suspicious glance as the taxi pulled away. 'What did he mean by that?'

I laughed. 'Nothing sinister,' I said. 'This restaurant specializes in game. You know, venison, pheasant, quail. That sort of thing.'

'Oh, that's all right then,' said Gail, flashing me a sexy smile.

As the restaurant manager conducted us to our table, an inordinate number of male eyes seemed to lose interest in their food, and a man on the far side of the ornate room gave Gail a discreet wave. He probably hoped that I wouldn't notice. But I did. Jealousy was already beginning to set in.

'An admirer of yours?' I asked.

'One of many,' she replied airily with a wave of her hand. 'A starving chorus girl can't afford to turn down free meals.'

I was sufficient of a cynic to wonder what she had offered in return. 'Have you found another job yet?' I asked, once I had ordered a carafe of white wine as a preamble to studying the menu.

'To tell you the truth, I haven't been looking. Anyway it was only last Friday that *Scatterbrain* closed. So I'm resting for a bit. Literally, I mean, rather than in the theatrical sense.'

I assumed that the fear of what she believed to be a psychopath with a taste for murdering showgirls, and who was running loose in the capital, had played some part in Gail's decision to steer clear of the stage for a while.

And as if confirming that view, she asked, once again, 'Are you any nearer to discovering who killed Patricia yet, Harry?'

'No, I'm afraid not. But we have found out that she lived

at three different addresses recently. And she had a boyfriend called Peter Crawford, one called Bruce Phillips and another called Jeremy. Did she ever mention any of them?'

'I'm sorry, no. Patricia never mentioned boyfriends. Just a minute though.' Gail paused to take a sip of wine. 'Jeremy. Yes, come to think of it, she did mention a Jeremy.'

'Surname?' I prompted.

'Payne. That was it. Jeremy Payne. Funny that. You can know someone for quite a while and never find out much about them. Not that that seems to be a problem for you,' she continued with a smile. 'You've already found out that I've been divorced for three years, and why. But I don't know a thing about you.' She gave me a questioning glance.

'All right, you've got me,' I said, and laughed. I went on to tell her about meeting Helga Büchner, a German physiotherapist at Westminster Hospital who had treated me professionally – at first anyway – after I'd been involved in a ruckus with a crowd of yobs in Whitehall. I'd been a young uniformed PC at the time and Helga and I had embarked on a whirlwind romance. Two months later we were married. The cynics at the nick, the women police in particular, had scoffed and said it wouldn't last, and they were right: it didn't. Mind you, sixteen years of marriage isn't bad by today's batting average. Looking back, the only thing I really got out of it was to have learned fluent German. And that was in the interests of interpreting the snide asides about me that habitually passed between Helga and her harridan of a mother.

'How long ago?' asked Gail. She touched the arm of a passing waiter. 'D'you think you could get me a bottle of still water, darling?' she purred. 'Evian, or something of the sort.'

'Of course, madam.' The waiter was clearly besotted by his gorgeous customer, and scurried away to do her bidding.

'How long ago what?' I asked.

'How long ago was the divorce?'

'Oh, about a year, but it had started to fall apart well before that. Helga insisted on carrying on working, even after Robert was born.'

Gail raised her eyebrows. 'Oh, you've got a son, have you?'

She didn't sound too happy at that. Perhaps her plans for the future were working more rapidly than were mine.

'Not any more. He was drowned in a friend's pond. Helga had left him with her while she went to work. He was only four.'

There were no words of condolence from Gail, she just nodded. Her devoted waiter arrived with a bottle of water and, briefly touching his hand, she gave him a captivating smile and mouthed a word of thanks. Looking at me again, and picking her words with obvious care, she said, 'That, I should think, is enough to destroy any marriage.'

That suited me. I couldn't stand false sentiment, and, in any event, the accident had happened years ago.

'What about you? Are you happy working in the theatre?'

'Are you happy in the police force?' she countered.

'It's what I do,' I said. 'I'm stuck with it, and I wouldn't know what else to do.'

'Exactly,' said Gail, somewhat ambiguously.

'Did Patricia ever mention anything about sixteen Fenwick Road, Brighton?'

She looked a little surprised at the sudden change in subject. 'Not that I can recall. Is it important?'

'It may be,' I said.

Gail considered my question for a moment or two longer. 'No, definitely not. Why?'

'It's a bit strange really. That Brighton address was in her address book together with the names of a Mr and Mrs Hunter, but when we went there it turned out to be a boarding house. The guy who runs the place had never heard of Patricia. Anyway, as I told you, we tracked down her parents to an address in Wimbledon.'

'Perhaps she got the Brighton address wrong. Did you try the houses on either side?'

Don't you just love it when a rank amateur tells you how to do your job? And gets it right.

'No,' I said thoughtfully. 'Have you ever considered the police as a career?'

Gail laughed. 'I don't like the uniform. Mind you, if ever I'm forced into doing strippagrams, I might learn to like it.'

94

'I don't like the uniform either,' I said, trying to force from my mind the vision of Gail performing a strippagram routine. 'That's why I became a detective.'

The first course arrived, and we reverted to discussing mundane matters.

'Have you always been in the theatre, Gail?'

'Yes. Eighteen years now. My parents wanted me to be a doctor, but I'm afraid that wasn't my scene. I left school at sixteen and did a year at dance school. I'd always had this heady ambition to be an actress, but I had to start in the chorus before I was able to land a few walk-on parts. After that I managed to get some speaking roles – even got one or two television parts – but now I'm back hoofing again. Or was. Still, you have to take what you can get.'

'Are you happy with your lot?' I asked.

'Case of having to be really. It's nowhere near as glamorous a profession as some people think. And on top of everything else, I've a suspicion that my ex put the bubble in for me. I certainly had a longish run of unsuccessful auditions after we split. Bit spiteful was Gerald.'

'Are your parents still alive?'

'You know they are. Don't you remember me telling you that I was going to see them last Saturday? They live in Nottingham.' Gail sounded as though she was beginning to doubt my abilities as a detective. 'My father's a property developer. Done very well, too, which is why I don't have to worry much about working. I'm an only child and he dotes on me. *And* he sends me an allowance when I'm "resting". Anyway, I got the house out of the divorce settlement, so I'm coping quite well.'

In other words, mind your own business.

And I did. For the rest of the meal we talked pleasantries.

'Would you like something else?' I asked when Gail's adoring waiter returned to hover with the dessert menu.

'No thanks, just coffee. I can't afford to put on weight.'

The man who had been seated on the other side of the restaurant waved as he left.

Gail waved back. ''Bye, darling,' she said loudly, and a few heads turned. Her admirer looked as though he wished he'd crept out. Particularly as I waved too.

95

'This guy Jeremy Payne,' I said, reverting to our previous conversation. 'Did Patricia say anything about him?'

'Only that he was very rich.'

'Nothing about where he lived?'

'No.'

'Did she mention a flat in Docklands or a villa in the South of France?'

'No, she certainly didn't.' Gail laughed. 'If she had I'd've had him off her. Men like that are few and far between.'

I know she'd laughed, but her comment was not exactly encouraging to a detective chief inspector for whom promotion was a distant and probably vain hope.

We travelled back to Surbiton together, and I saw her to the door of her house in Kingston. It was a three-storied townhouse tucked away in a quiet little mews, and I wondered if Gail's property developer father had bought it for his daughter and her ex-husband as a wedding present.

'Thank you for dinner, Harry,' she said. 'I really did enjoy it.' And holding both of my hands in hers, gave me a chaste kiss on the cheek. Just like my mother used to when she sent me off to school.

There wasn't much to cheer me up on Friday morning.

'What about the fibres, Dave? Have we got anything back on that?'

'Ah, the fibres, yes,' said Dave, and flicked back through his 'action' book. 'I rang the lab and the guy I spoke to agreed that on closer analysis, the fibres could only have come from a Ford van, rather than a Bedford or a Renault.'

'Hooray!' I said sarcastically. 'Progress at last.' I glanced at my watch. 'Time for the morning briefing.'

The incident room was crowded, not only with my own team, but with the additional officers that the acting commander had managed to steal from somewhere.

'I'll just run over the story so far,' I began. 'We've got a dead woman: Patricia Hunter, found in the Thames opposite the Houses of Parliament.' I indicated the photograph of the victim with a wave of the hand. 'We found an address book at the flat she lived in last – that's the one at Coping Road,

Islington – but I think we can safely discount the names and addresses that we found in it, with the exception of Bruce Phillips.'

'Who's he, guv'nor?' asked a sergeant from among the ranks of Cleaver's reinforcements.

'Apart from fancying him for this job, he's wanted by the Australian police for fraud, if it's the same Phillips. There's an Interpol red-corner circular out for him, but when proceedings were started at Bow Street, he disappeared,' I said.

'Don't blame him, guv'nor,' said a voice in the audience.

'According to Patricia's little book,' I continued, 'he had an address in Petersfield Street, Fulham, an address that she probably shared with Phillips. But he'd long gone when we checked there, and none of the present residents had heard of him. He did however arrange the viewing of a flat on Patricia Hunter's behalf at sixty-four Courtney Street, Holborn, and she'd lived there for about six months before moving on to her last address at Coping Road, Islington.' I nodded towards Dave. 'DS Poole will fill you in on a few other details.'

'A guy called Meredith, one of Patricia's neighbours at Courtney Street, saw a man who could have been Phillips,' Dave began, 'but we're not sure it was him. However, Meredith was almost certainly screwing Miss Hunter on a regular basis and she'd agreed to move into his flat. However he was stupid enough to mention it to her when he met her in the hall with this mystery man. The next thing that happened was – abracadabra – she'd moved out and left no forwarding address.'

'Any ideas as to why, Skip?' asked a DC.

'The inference is that she was scared stiff of the guy Meredith saw her with,' said Dave. 'We got Meredith to do an E-fit but it's worse than useless. And just to complicate the whole business, when we interviewed Patricia Hunter's parents in Wimbledon, her old man said she'd written saying that Bruce Phillips was her boyfriend. But again, he hadn't seen Phillips in the flesh. And finally, we tracked down someone at an Epsom address who purported to be Patricia's sister, a woman called Eleanor Hunter. She told us that her parents – and therefore Patricia's – had both died some years ago, despite the fact that we'd interviewed them only two days previously. But that's turned out to be a bum steer. Patricia and Eleanor, whose real name is Carson, were having a lesbian relationship before Patricia took off in favour of a man who she told Eleanor was called Bruce Phillips. However, we later learned from the police at Epsom that Eleanor's a screwball with a predilection for singing hymns in the nude in her back garden at two in the morning. There, that's simple enough for you, isn't it? I may ask questions later.'

'What about the Brighton address that Patricia Hunter had in her book?' asked a woman detective.

'We drew a blank there,' said Dave. 'It turned out to be the Golden Riviera Guest House, run by a couple called Richards. They'd never heard of Mr and Mrs Hunter, Patricia Hunter or Bruce Phillips.'

'Which reminds me,' I said, remembering what Gail Sutton had suggested. 'Frank, get someone to ask the Brighton police to check a few of the houses on either side of sixteen Fenwick Road. It's just possible that Patricia Hunter wrote down the wrong house number.'

Frank nodded as he wrote on his clipboard. 'Leave it to me, I'll get someone to do it.'

'Just to summarize the rest of it,' I continued, 'the victim was a chorus girl. She had recently indulged in sexual intercourse but the lab couldn't match the semen to their DNA database. And the ligature used to strangle the Hunter girl was possibly from a type of electrical cable used in the theatre.'

'Theatre as in song and dance, not as in surgical operations,' said Dave in an aside, and got a laugh.

'And finally,' I said, 'the grazing on her body revealed traces of dust and oil that may be linked to the floor of a garage somewhere. And the fibres found in the dead woman's hair indicated that she might have been transported in a Ford van. The night before last, the TSG did a number of stops in the central London area, but we're no further forward . . . at this stage.' I glanced at Frank Mead.

'Still checking them out, Harry. Let you know the results ASAP.'

'Don't forget this guy Jeremy,' Dave whispered.

'Ah yes. We think his name's Jeremy Payne. An actress at

the Alhambra theatre – her name's Candy Simpson – told us that Patricia Hunter had said that she was going to marry a guy called Jeremy who'd promised to whisk her off to a life of luxury in the south of France. This guy apparently told Patricia he had pots of money, a flat in Docklands and a villa in St Raphaël.'

One of the women detectives scoffed. 'Stupid little cow,' she muttered.

'About three months before her body was found,' I continued, 'she walked out of the play she was then appearing in, apparently to depart for ever.'

'Well, she got that right,' said the same woman detective.

'The priorities are, therefore, to find Bruce Phillips and to get any more information we can on this mysterious, and ostensibly monied, guy called Jeremy Payne. Any questions?'

There were no questions.

It was getting on for lunch time when Tom Challis, one of Frank Mead's sergeants, came into my office.

'Got a moment, guv?'

'What's on your mind, Tom?'

Challis handed me a small slip of paper. 'A receipt, guv. Found in Patricia Hunter's room at Coping Road.'

'What about it?' I asked. Apart from the fact that it had been screwed up and then smoothed out again, it looked like any other credit-card receipt.

'It goes out to a shop in Jermyn Street, and it's for a man's shirt. A fifty-five-quid shirt, at that.'

'Well, I suppose it's possible that Patricia Hunter bought it for a boyfriend, Tom.'

Challis shook his head. 'No she didn't, guv. I've checked with the credit-card company, and the account's in the name of a Geoffrey Forman of thirteen Ridgely Road, Barnes. Thought it was worth a mention.'

'Indeed it was, Tom. Where exactly was this receipt found?'

'In her dressing-table drawer along with all her other bits and pieces. You'll notice it had been screwed up. Maybe he dropped it and she put it away in case it was important.'

'It is,' I said, 'and he probably doesn't know he's lost it.'

99

This was beginning to look like the first break we'd had since the whole enquiry had started with the recovery of Patricia Hunter's body from the Thames. 'I suppose the credit-card people didn't tell you what this guy Forman did for a living, Tom, did they?'

'No, guv, and I didn't think to ask. I can get back to them, if you like. But from what I've learned over the years, they don't keep their records up to date, not so far as occupation is concerned anyway. Usually people don't bother to notify of a change of job, not unless it's likely to improve their credit rating. Incidentally, I ran him through CRO, but there's nothing on him. Not on the details we've got so far, anyway. The only Geoffrey Forman I found was a forty-five-year-old East End villain currently doing a handful for a blagging.'

'Well, there's only one thing for it. Dave and I will pay Mr Forman a visit. Is Dave in the incident room?'

'Yes, guv.'

'Good. Ask him to come in.'

Dave sauntered into my office a few minutes later. 'Tom Challis has been shooting his mouth off that he's just solved this job for us, guv,' he said. Challis was the type of brash detective who didn't appeal to Dave.

I laughed. 'He might just have done,' I said, and repeated to Dave what Challis had told me. 'Tom Challis might just have hit on the solution.'

Dave frowned. 'I shouldn't hold your breath, guv,' he said.

And he was right to be cynical. Over the years, detectives have many promising leads that, after hours of painstaking and time-consuming enquiries, turn out to be useless. But we had to try. After all, right now there was nothing else.

Ten

Given that most people in the world seem to knock off at about three on a Friday afternoon – coppers excepted, of course – I decided that Dave and I would make for Barnes.

Number 13 Ridgely Road was a large detached house, the type that estate agents were once fond of describing as a suburban villa. *And it was no more than half a mile from the River Thames.* But I've been excited by coincidences of that sort too often in the past to get excited now.

The woman who answered the door was an elegant brunette who, I guessed, was about thirty. Her hair was straight to just below shoulder length, and she was wearing a low-cut cream-silk dress and high heels.

'Yes?' The glance was one of interest rather than the concern with which two strange men on the doorstep are usually greeted.

'Mrs Forman?'

'No.'

Well, that was a good start. Will nothing go right with this damned enquiry?

'I understood that Mr Geoffrey Forman lived here,' I said. 'We're police officers.'

'Oh!' The woman glanced briefly beyond my right shoulder at the Alfa Romeo parked in front of her house. Perhaps she thought our visit was to do with some traffic offence. 'How do I know you're policemen?' she asked with an apologetic smile.

Wise woman. Dave and I produced our warrant cards and she seemed satisfied.

'I'm Donna Lodge,' she said. 'Geoff's my partner, but he's not here at the moment. In fact he's abroad on business.'

'I see.' That was unfortunate, to say the least. 'Can you tell me when he's likely to be back?'

'Not exactly. He travels a lot, you see.' As an apparent afterthought, Donna invited us into the front room of the house. 'May I ask what it's about?' With a gesture of her hand, she indicated that we should sit down, and then seated herself in an armchair opposite us, crossing her legs and carefully arranging the skirt of her dress. A woman perfectly at ease.

This is always the tricky part of any investigation. If I mentioned the receipt that had been found in Patricia Hunter's room – the one that DS Challis had traced to Forman – Donna Lodge might just blow a gasket. And, for an encore, collapse in a fit of the vapours. And ask her partner some very searching questions when eventually he walked through the door.

But I could do without all that. I smiled, disarmingly I hoped, and embarked on the sort of bewildering mumbo-jumbo intended to disguise the true reasons for my enquiry. If Forman was the murderer, the last thing I wanted was his partner warning him that the police were taking an active interest in a dead actress called Patricia Hunter.

'It's a rather complicated case, Ms Lodge, and I won't weary you with the finer details. That said, it's quite likely, at the end of the day, that it'll all come to nothing. But we have to go through the motions, so to speak.' I then launched into the standard fallback lie. 'However, in short, a business card with Mr Forman's name and address on it was found at the scene of an office-breaking where a number of computers were stolen. But the police are obliged to eliminate all the innocent parties. Of which, I'm sure, he is one.' There was a flaw in this little piece of fiction however: a business card would have had a business address on it, not a home address. I just hoped that Forman's partner wouldn't notice.

'What my chief inspector means, Ms Lodge,' said Dave, contributing to the smokescreen, 'is that in the unlikely event that we have enough to warrant sending a report to the Crown

Prosecution Service, they'll ask all sorts of silly questions, like why didn't you check out that address, and if we don't have the answers, the whole thing gets delayed while we go out and do what we should have done in the first place. Even so, I don't think it'll come to anything.'

'I see.'

But judging from the bemused expression on Ms Lodge's face, she didn't see at all. And that suited me fine.

'Have you any idea when he may return?' I asked again, but in such an offhand way that it gave the impression that I didn't care very much.

'Not really, no. As I said just now, he travels a great deal, and at the moment he's in Germany. In Düsseldorf, as a matter of fact.'

'Mmm!' I nodded sagely. 'What does he travel in exactly?'

Beside me, my English-language purist of a sergeant gave a discreet cough. Had I posed the question to him in that form, he would have said 'an aeroplane', and added 'sir'. But Ms Lodge knew what I meant.

'It's something to do with computers. I don't understand a thing about them. Half the time I haven't a clue what he's talking about when he does come home.'

'I know how you feel. The world of computers is a mystery to me as well,' I said with a smile. 'But that would probably explain it. No doubt he visits offices all the time, and it would be natural for them to have his name and address.' I dug myself in a bit deeper, but I thought I'd mention it before Ms Lodge did. Or worse, Mr Forman. 'That's strange though. Presumably he has an office somewhere, and the card would have had that address on it rather than this one.'

'Not necessarily. He works from home, you see.'

'Ah, that would explain it,' I said, breathing a sigh of relief. I stood up and produced one of my own cards, hoping that she was unaware that the Serious Crime Group didn't investigate tuppenny-ha'penny office-breakings. 'It'll probably be a waste of his time and mine, but perhaps you'd ask him to give me a ring when he does get home, Ms Lodge. There's no rush,' I added, praying that Mr Forman would not take that proviso too literally. If this guy was Patricia Hunter's killer, the sooner we got hold of him the better, just in case he was thinking of striking again.

Donna Lodge took the card and examined it. 'Yes, of course,' she said, 'but I've no idea when that will be.'

'Does he have a mobile phone?' asked Dave casually.

'I think so, but I don't know what the number is. Geoff's very particular about not using it while he's driving. It's this new law, you know.' Donna paused. 'But then you would know, wouldn't you?' she said with another apologetic smile.

There was little point in mentioning that the law was far from new. But if he was our murderer – and *was* tempted to strike again – he wouldn't want to get pulled by our traffic brethren for using his mobile if he'd got a body in the boot. Smart fellow.

And so we had to leave it there. Being an inveterate collector of such things, Dave took a note of the Alfa Romeo's index number, and we returned to Curtis Green.

Dave wandered into my office with two cups of coffee. 'A rep doesn't work at the weekends,' he said thoughtfully. 'I wouldn't mind betting Forman's over the side, probably with some gorgeous German bird in Düsseldorf,' he added, and nicked one of my cigarettes.

I resisted the temptation to expound on the dangers of becoming involved with German women, gorgeous or otherwise. 'Well, unless there's some innocent explanation for one of his receipts being in Patricia Hunter's room, Dave, I think it's safe to assume that he's screwing around. And if he's in the habit of taking out actresses—'

'In more ways than one,' observed Dave drily. 'But a lot of married guys have it off with other birds. They don't necessarily top 'em though.'

'I suppose we'll just have to wait for him to come home to roost,' was my only contribution.

'If he does,' muttered Dave gloomily. 'There's a bit of toot there, you know, guv,' he continued. 'That house must be worth at least three-quarters of a million, and the Alfa Romeo – which incidentally is registered in Donna Lodge's name –

is only a year old. As for the dress she was wearing, well, Madeleine would die for it.'

'There must be more money in flogging computers than I thought,' I said.

'If he is actually selling them, guv. He may be one of those consultants who goes around advising firms on computer systems. And charging them the earth for telling them to buy expensive installations that they don't really need. And then getting a kickback from the computer company that supplies them.'

'On the other hand, maybe it's Donna who's got the money,' I said.

'In which case, he'd be raving mad to push his luck by having it off with another bird. But there again, Madeleine's always telling me that men are complete idiots. She reckons the average male spends more time on buying a new car than he does on picking a wife.'

'Sounds to me as though your Madeleine's a shrewd woman, Dave.'

'You can say that again,' said Dave, and rapidly changed the subject. 'So what's next, guv?'

'If Donna owns the Alfa Romeo, Geoffrey Forman must have a car of his own. See if the DVLA at Swansea can come up with anything.'

Dave made a note and then glanced up. 'He's probably got a company car,' he said. 'And that'll be in the company's name. Or even a leasing company.'

'You're such a comfort to me, Dave,' I said, 'but Donna Lodge said he works from home.'

'Still might be working for someone else,' Dave said. 'Incidentally, I had a look at one of the job's Ford vans this morning.'

'What the hell's that got to do with the price of fish?'

'There's no floor covering in the back. It's just bare metal.'

'So what, Dave? Could be that some cost-cutting bean counter at the Yard is saving us some money by ordering vans without carpet.'

'I don't think so, but if that's the case, the lab boys might have given us a bum steer, and the fibres found on our victim came from somewhere else.'

105

'You'd better check that out, Dave,' I said. If he was right, and the lab was wrong, it might have given us a better chance of narrowing down our list of suspects. But if the fibres didn't come from a Ford van, we'd wasted our time, and that of the TSGs that did the night-time stops in Central London last Wednesday. Nevertheless, I was still absolutely certain that the body of our victim must have been moved by night.

Any thoughts of an early night, a forlorn hope anyway in a murder enquiry, were shattered by Frank Mead's arrival in my office.

'I've just had an interesting conversation with a DI on the Sussex Vice Squad in Lewes, Harry.'

'Why Lewes?'

'They cover the whole county but work out of HQ, which is at Lewes, and my query about sixteen Fenwick Road eventually filtered through to them.'

I sat up and took notice. 'Yes, go on.'

'As we know, sixteen Fenwick Road meant nothing to the Sussex lads or to us, but *sixty-one* Fenwick Road rang a bell with the Vice Squad down there.'

'Is that a coincidence or a mistake, or d'you think Patricia Hunter deliberately transposed the numbers in her address book, Frank?'

'Or it's nothing to do with her at all,' said Frank. 'However, about three months ago the Vice Squad received some information that sixty-one Fenwick Road was a wholesale knocking shop. They kept obo for about a fortnight, during which time they clocked a number of women entering the premises, usually in the late morning or early afternoon. These women were not seen to leave again until much later, well gone midnight in most cases, and sometimes even the following day. But it was the clientele that interested our Sussex brethren.'

'In what way?' I asked.

'They all appeared to be well-heeled. The boys and girls down there collected car numbers and checked them out. There were one or two from the Brighton area, but most of the punters came down from London or the leafy suburbs

106

thereof, some even in chauffeur-driven cars, would you believe.'

'Did they spin this knocking shop, guv?' asked Dave.

'With a vengeance, and on a night when the place was heaving. They found a load of kinky gear, naked guys tied up and getting whipped by naked birds and all sorts of other perversions apparently. What's more, the DI who I spoke to reckoned that a few of the punters were in *Who's Who*.'

'Oh dear!' said Dave. 'I'll bet a few hours of fun there will have cost 'em a fortune.'

'It did,' said Frank. 'But apparently they could afford it.'

'So what's the bottom line?' I asked.

'The place was shut down, obviously,' said Frank, 'and the *madame* who was running the place was done for keeping a brothel and living on the immoral earnings, *et cetera, et cetera*. But the local law were pretty sure that she was just a front put up to take the flak, and that there was someone else behind it: a Mister Big. Probably from the Smoke. They made exhaustive enquiries but, needless to say, no one was talking.

'That said, however, one of the girls let slip to one of the women officers that an Australian occasionally came down, threw his weight about and enjoyed a freebie whenever he wanted it with whoever he wanted. And this tom reckoned he ran the show. But someone obviously got to her, because, when it came to making a written statement, she clammed up and said she must have been misquoted.'

'I think we could hazard a guess as to who the Australian was, guv,' said Dave, and, deciding it was time to consume an orange, plucked one from his briefcase.

'But no mention of Phillips or Patricia Hunter,' I said. 'Or, for that matter, a Jeremy Payne?'

'No, but the Vice Squad only found four women in the place when they raided it.'

'Only four?'

'Yeah. Apparently there was a secret room that didn't get turned over because they didn't know it was there, not until it was too late. Most of the other girls – the Vice lads reckoned there were six working there at any one time, and ten

107

on Fridays and Saturdays – shot in there and laid low until the Old Bill had gone.' Frank laughed. 'Unfortunately the aforementioned well-heeled punters didn't know this room existed. As a result the trouserless ones were obliged to assist police with their enquiries, until later being released without charge.'

'How very unfortunate,' I murmured.

'Of the four toms who were captured, only one, a girl called Barbara Clark, lived in London,' said Frank. 'At fifteen Westacre Close, Wandsworth. The other three were local. But all of good quality, so I was told.'

'Well, there goes our Friday evening,' I said, glancing at Dave. 'It's too much of a coincidence that Patricia Hunter had sixteen Fenwick Road in her address book, and that the Sussex Old Bill turned over number sixty-one as a brothel. *And* that there's word of an Australian being bandied about. Did the Vice Squad down there collect the names of these punters, Frank?'

'Makes interesting reading,' said Frank, handing me a list. 'A Crown Court judge, a clergyman—'

'Presumably he was in the missionary position when they found him,' said Dave quietly.

'And half a dozen assorted entrepreneurs,' continued Frank, ignoring Dave's aside. 'Apparently one of the punters was heard complaining to the madam that it was supposed to be a discreet set-up. Didn't help much though, she was in handcuffs at the time; the job's not hers.' He gave a short, cynical laugh.

I ran my eye down the list. 'There are only three of these who live in London: the judge, the clergyman and one of the businessmen. And given that Patricia Hunter was found floating in the Thames at Westminster, we may as well start with them.'

'Definitely a good idea to have a go at the judge,' said Dave. 'Never know when we might need an iffy warrant at some time in the future.'

'You're nothing if not an opportunist, Dave,' I said. 'But why not? He sits in London. But he can wait a bit. First we'll see Ms Clark.'

* * *

108

It was a small, modern town house in a part of Wandsworth that undoubtedly attracted high property prices and, therefore, proved that the sex business must be profitable. Very profitable. But then I always knew that.

I rang the bell, even though the chances of finding a prostitute at home on a Friday evening – or any other evening for that matter – are remote. But this particular evening we were in luck. Which made a change.

'Miss Clark?' I enquired when a young woman opened the door an inch or two on the chain.

'Have you got an appointment?' asked the girl, her expression registering surprise that there were two of us.

'Didn't know we needed one,' said Dave, displaying his warrant card.

'Oh, bloody hell!' The girl closed the door sufficient to disconnect the chain and then opened it fully. 'You'd better come in, I suppose,' she said with a sigh, and led the way upstairs to a comfortably furnished sitting room.

She was a good-looking girl in her twenties, well-dressed, her hair neatly arranged, her make-up discreet. In fact one would not immediately have taken her for a prostitute. Perhaps the Sussex Vice Squad had got it wrong and Miss Clark had been in the Fenwick Road brothel merely to provide ancillary services as a manicurist. There again, maybe not.

'I'm told that you were one of the prostitutes found at sixty-one Fenwick Road, Brighton, when it was raided by police about two months ago, Miss Clark.' I saw no reason to pussy-foot about.

'And of what possible interest is that to you? What I do for a living occasionally interests the police, and may be frowned upon by our virtuous society, except for those members of it who take advantage of my body, of course. But it's not an offence because in my case there's no soliciting involved.'

'I am aware of that, Miss Clark,' I said. I had to admit to being somewhat taken aback by Barbara Clark's confidence. She may have been a prostitute, but she was well spoken, appeared to be well educated and was conversant with the law affecting her 'profession'.

'In that case, what is it you want?' She drew back the sleeve of her jacket and glanced at the gold watch adorning her wrist. 'I do have an appointment shortly,' she said, 'and I don't like to keep my clients waiting.'

Time to bring this rather superior young lady down to earth, I thought.

'I am investigating the murder of a woman called Patricia Hunter,' I said. 'No doubt you've read about it in the paper.'

'Oh!' Barbara Clark sat down, rather suddenly.

'I can see that the name means something to you.'

'Yes, it does. I knew her.'

'And what about Bruce Phillips?'

'Who?' Despite the girl's implied denial, it was obvious that the name had had some effect upon her. She tensed visibly and glanced away from me. Reaching across to an occasional table, she took a cigarette from an open packet, lit it and drew on it heavily enough to make the tip glow fiercely.

'I think you do, Miss Clark,' I continued. 'And I want to talk to him because I think he knew Patricia Hunter. And I'm hoping that you may be able to help me find him.'

Barbara looked up at me, but the confidence had ebbed and there was now a very frightened young girl bunched up in the armchair. 'I don't know anything about him,' she said in less than convincing tones.

'But you knew Patricia Hunter, you said.'

'Yes.' The reply came out in a whisper.

'How did you meet her?'

'We were both working in Brighton, at Fenwick Road. We'd usually meet up here and drive down together.'

'In your car?'

'Yes, in my car.'

'How often was this?'

'Twice a week. Wednesdays and Saturdays. Other girls worked other shifts, so there was a service from three in the afternoon to three in the morning.'

'Why travel all the way to Brighton twice a week? Is the London end of your profession that overcrowded now?'

'For the money, of course.' The woman's response was

dismissive, as though her reasoning was quite logical. 'The set-up down there provided an anything-goes service, and we girls were paid two thousand pounds for a twelve-hour shift. That was four K a week . . . tax-free.'

I did a quick bit of mental arithmetic. If that was the going rate for the Fenwick Road working girls, the punters must have been forking out small fortunes.

'When did you last see Patricia Hunter, Barbara?' By now Dave and I had sat down on the sofa facing the woman.

She stubbed out her half-finished cigarette and screwed it hard into the ashtray, almost as if it had offended her.

'I last saw her about two months ago when the fuzz busted the place in Brighton. I was unlucky. When your lot came charging in, I was upstairs with some slob of a clergyman on top of me and couldn't move. But Patricia told me afterwards that she'd been on the ground floor. She was riding her guy, so she was able to dismount and escape to the bolthole. Then she waited until the fuss was over and the captains and the kings had departed. But I haven't seen her since then. I don't know where she went.'

'D'you know the name of the guy who was having it off with Patricia?' I asked.

'I don't even know the name of the clergyman who was screwing me,' said Barbara. 'Names were never used unless one of the johns asked for a private meeting at his home or a hotel somewhere, then he'd give us his phone number.'

'Did any of them make an arrangement of that sort with Patricia?'

'Not as far as I know, no.'

'What the hell's a girl like you doing tomming?' asked Dave, slowly shaking his head.

'Earning money,' said Barbara. 'I've got a degree in business studies, but the best job I could get when I came down from university was clerking in a building society. It would have taken forever to pay off my student loan on the wages they offered. I can earn more in a night now than I would have done in a month there.' Her explanation was delivered in matter-of-fact tones, and she didn't seem at all embarrassed at explaining her economic strategy. And that, it

111

seemed, was the rationale that had dictated her choice of career.

'Bruce Phillips,' I said, just when Barbara Clark thought I'd forgotten about him.

'I know nothing about any Bruce Phillips,' she said again. But the mere mention of his name had clearly unnerved her and her hand shook as she reached for another cigarette.

'Let's not play games, Barbara. When Fenwick Road was raided, one of the girls told a policewoman that an Australian guy would turn up there from time to time and take his pick of the girls. Were you the girl who told the policewoman that?'

'No.'

'Were you one of the girls that this mysterious Australian fancied?' asked Dave.

'Might have been, I suppose.'

'Does that mean he had the pleasure of your services?'

'He might have done,' said Barbara. 'You tend not to look at faces in my job. It's usually a case of bang-bang and thank you ma'am. Some of the johns were quite old guys and five minutes was a bloody marathon for them.'

'Is that another way of saying you can't give us a description of this Australian?' Dave asked. 'Or won't.'

'Precisely so,' said Barbara.

'Have you seen him again?' I persisted, sensing that she knew who we were talking about. 'Here in London for instance?'

'No. And I'm not sure that I've entertained an Aussie anyway. I'm not very good at accents. I did have a South African doctor once. That any help?'

'This is serious, Barbara,' I said, and decided to show my hand. 'It's quite possible that this Bruce Phillips, who is an Australian, murdered Patricia Hunter, and it's imperative that we find him soon.'

'Before he takes it into his head to murder any of the other girls who work for him,' said Dave casually.

Barbara looked at me, then at Dave, and then back at me. 'That sounds like a very good reason for keeping my mouth shut, doesn't it, guys? Even if I knew the man. Which I don't.'

112

But she couldn't disguise the fact that her face had drained of colour.

'Why did he beat you up?' asked Dave suddenly.

The question coming out of context caught Barbara off guard. 'How did you know that?' she blurted out, before realizing that she'd been tricked by an experienced detective well-versed in interrogation techniques.

'So you do know this Australian after all,' I said.

Barbara Clark parried my accusation with an explanation. 'I suppose it was my fault really. One of my clients at Brighton really hurt me quite badly – a bloody sadist he was – so I grabbed his balls and twisted until he screamed. That put him off his stroke.' Barbara's demure appearance and cultured tones conflicted strangely with her description of the revenge she had meted out to her assailant. 'I was out of order really. After all, that's what I was there for. Anyway he complained to the woman running the place. She told this Australian and he slapped me around. Said this john had paid good money to do whatever he wanted to do to me.'

'How long were you off work after that?' Dave asked.

'A couple of weeks,' said Barbara miserably.

'And was this shadowy Australian who beat you up called Bruce Phillips by any chance?'

'I don't know.'

'Or Geoffrey Forman?'

'I've never heard of anyone called Geoffrey Forman.'

It appeared that Barbara Clark was still too terrified to admit that the Australian was Phillips. But I was sure she knew that he was. I tried another tack.

'Since the Brighton caper came to an end, you've been working in London, haven't you?'

'Yes.'

'And Bruce Phillips is your pimp, isn't he?'

'I don't know what you mean.'

'I'm sure a girl like you doesn't hang around Shepherd Market, Barbara, so you must get your bookings somewhere. And I don't somehow see you advertising in telephone boxes.'

113

'I don't know how it happens, but I get phone calls from time to time telling me to go to some john's apartment, or a hotel.' The girl was struggling now, desperately trying to avoid revealing the identity of a man who obviously put her in fear, but at once digging herself in deeper each time she opened her mouth.

'So how d'you get paid, Barbara?' Dave asked.

There was a moment's hesitation and then the girl said, 'I take credit cards.'

'And how d'you pay your pimp?'

'I don't know what you're talking about. I've said too much already and I'm not saying any more.'

'We found Patricia Hunter's address book. In it was written: Mr and Mrs Hunter, sixteen Fenwick Road. Any idea what that was all about?'

'Yes. Patricia told me that she could never remember addresses and wrote it down in case she ever had to go down there on her own. She switched the house number round and wrote her parents' name against it.' For the first time since we'd arrived at her house, the elegant young tom smiled. 'She couldn't very well write "the cathouse where I work" next to it, could she?'

Rather than drink in a Wandsworth pub, we drove back to Curtis Green, parked the car and strolled along to the Red Lion.

'What d'you reckon, Dave?' I asked, once the essential business of buying the beer had been accomplished.

'She's scared out of her wits, guv. I'm surprised that she said as much as she did. It looks very much as though Phillips is her pimp, which means she wasn't telling the truth about getting paid by credit card.'

'No, I reckon Phillips gets the payment and then takes his cut before paying the girl. But how and where does he do it, I wonder?'

'I don't think he'd be daft enough to use a bank account,' said Dave, taking the top off his beer. 'Too easy to trace.'

'If we ever lay hands on him,' I said, 'and can prove he murdered Patricia Hunter, he won't be too worried about living

114

on the immoral earnings. But the business about Patricia writing down the Fenwick Road address perhaps explains why there were other addresses in her book. Each time she got a booking she jotted it down in case she forgot.'

'Evenin', gents,' said the unmistakeable voice of Fat Danny.

'Bugger off,' said Dave.

Eleven

By Monday morning, Dave had all the answers to the queries about the fibres, but those answers were not particularly helpful. In fact, they proved to be downright *unhelpful*, even though they were the result of an innocent mistake.

'It seems I was right, guv,' he began. 'I had another word with the lab and they were full of apologies.'

'You mean they've cocked it up,' I said and sat down in one of the chairs in the incident room ready to be depressed.

'Apparently they gave the analysis of the fibres to some keen young scientist just out of university to cut his teeth on,' Dave continued. 'It seems he made a comparison with a stock control sample at the lab . . . and got it wrong.'

'Bloody marvellous,' I said. 'So what's the answer?'

'They had a senior scientist go over the evidence again and he said that the fibres came from a rug or carpet, not one that would be found in a van.'

'I don't know whether that's a help or not,' I mused.

'And,' Dave continued, intent on further depressing me, 'it would appear to be a fairly common sort.'

'Would be,' I said, the depression beginning to take root. 'So what are they doing about it?'

'They're doing a rush job to see if they can narrow it down.'

'I should bloody well hope so,' I said.

'Is there a problem, Mr Brock?'

Just what I needed. The commander back from his sojourn in the French capital and desperate to interfere.

'Did you have a good time in Paris, sir?' I asked.

The commander frowned. 'How did you know I'd gone to Paris?' he asked suspiciously.

'I'm a detective, sir,' I said.

From the expression on his face, the commander didn't much care for that smart remark. 'You mentioned a problem, I believe, Mr Brock.'

I explained about the laboratory's inaccurate identification of the fibres.

The commander frowned again. 'That's just not good enough,' he said crossly. 'I'll speak to the director about it. Here we are dealing with a complex murder and they get amateurs doing the work.'

Well, he should know all about amateurs interfering in murder enquiries.

'Yes, sir,' I said.

'It looks very much to me as though they're not maximizing focused deployment,' the commander mumbled, selecting a bit of meaningless jargon from his ragbag of Police College psychobabble. He muttered a few more unintelligible phrases and finally took sanctuary in his office.

'The DVLA came up with a BMW registered to Geoffrey Forman at the Barnes address, guv,' said Dave, once normality had been restored to the office. 'Colin's put it on the PNC. Oh, and by the way, Tom Challis got back to the credit-card people. They've got Forman down as a consultant, which covers a multitude of sins, but they have no record of which company he worked for. Of course, he may be in business on his own account.'

'And that doesn't vary much from what we were told by Donna Lodge,' I said. 'Assuming she was telling us the truth.'

'It was you who sort of suggested that he was a computer consultant, guv, and she might just have gone along with it. Could hardly say he was running a brothel, could she?'

Dave was right, of course, but I was not prepared to admit it. Fortunately, Dave changed the subject.

'It was in Patricia Hunter's Coping Road room that the receipt was found, wasn't it, guv?' he asked.

'Yes.'

'I wonder if she ever mentioned Geoffrey Forman to that

gorgeous bird we chatted up at the Granville. Gail Sutton, wasn't it? Some figure.'

I let it go. Dave didn't know that I was actively pursuing the delectable Gail. 'We didn't know about a guy called Geoffrey Forman when I spoke to her last,' I said, 'but I'll mention it to her. In fact, I'll pop in and see her on my way home tonight. She doesn't live far from me.'

Dave gave me a long, hard stare. 'Yeah, good thinking, guv,' he said eventually, and grinned.

'And this morning, we might just put the same question to Patricia Hunter's landlady at Coping Road . . .' I paused to ferret around among the papers on my desk, searching for the name.

'Mrs Parsons,' said Dave.

'That's the one. It's possible that Patricia Hunter mentioned him to her.'

'If he's our man,' said Dave. 'I wonder if he's also known as Bruce Phillips,' he added, echoing what I'd been thinking for some time.

I swung round in my chair and asked Colin Wilberforce if Geoffrey Forman had telephoned over the weekend.

'No, sir,' said Colin, which came as no surprise.

'I'm beginning to think nasty thoughts about this Forman guy, Dave,' I said.

'And the elegant Donna Lodge isn't all that she'd like you to think, either, guv,' said Dave.

'Oh?'

'She was convicted of shoplifting in Oxford Street five years ago.' Dave paused, presumably for effect. 'And guess who paid her fine.'

'Not Bruce Phillips?'

'Got it in one,' said Dave. 'The same guy who paid Patricia Hunter's fine.'

'Why didn't that show up on the CRO search you did on Friday?' I knew that if it had been there, Dave would have spotted it. 'Wasn't it on her antecedents?' I guessed that some sloppy DC had skimped on his paperwork.

'No, but this morning I had a word with a pal of mine on the Extradition Unit in SO6. He'd got more details than are recorded in CRO.'

'And presumably this pal of yours still doesn't know where Bruce Phillips is.'

'No, guv,' said Dave and chuckled. 'But he said to let him know if we found him, and he'd be grateful.'

'I'll bet he would,' I said. 'Incidentally, what exactly do the Australian police want this guy for?'

'Long-firm fraud. The usual thing: he set up shop after shop, ordered loads of gear that he paid for in cash until they trusted him with credit. Then he put in a few more orders, slowly increasing the amount of the order and then did a flit with the goods. Without paying for the last order. Apparently he went from state to state. Took a long time for them to catch up with him and each time they did, he'd gone. That's when the Commonwealth Police took an interest in him.'

'When was all this, Dave?'

'The Australians reckon he was at it for about a year to eighteen months, but he disappeared off their screens about six years ago.'

'So it wasn't very long after he arrived here from Australia that Patricia Hunter and Donna Lodge were both done for shoplifting. Both were nicked at about the same time, and each time Phillips paid their fines. Sounds like he was running a hoist ring.'

'I reckon,' said Dave.

'And is he an Australian national?'

'Yes, born in Sydney.'

'One thing's for sure, Dave,' I said. 'We'll need to have another word or two with Ms Lodge, but first we'll have another chat with Mrs Parsons about Patricia Hunter.'

'She'd sometimes sit in the kitchen and have a cup of tea with me,' said Mrs Parsons, 'but I never heard her say anything about boyfriends. I don't think she had much time for that sort of thing.'

'Did a man ever call here for her?' I asked. 'I know I asked you before, but . . .'

'I wasn't thinking straight that first evening you came round, Mr Brock, what with the shock of poor Pat's death and all,' said Mrs Parsons, 'but now you come to mention it, there was

119

one occasion. He didn't call here, he came in with her, and they went straight up to her room.'

'And you didn't mind that?' I asked.

'Why should I, dear?' said Mrs Parsons. 'If they're going to get up to naughties they might as well do it here.'

Which was a very refreshing outlook, and certainly one that differed sharply from the attitude of section-house sergeants and the harridans in charge of nurses' homes when I was courting Helga. Believe me, St James's Park can be very cold at times.

'D'you remember what he looked like, this man?' asked Dave.

'Very ordinary as I recollect. I do remember that he was wearing jeans and a tatty old sweater though, and I thought Patricia deserved better than a scruff like him. She was always well turned out, that poor girl.'

'How tall was he?' persisted Dave, determined to get as much as he could from the late Patricia Hunter's landlady.

'About your height, dear. What are you, about six foot?'

'Yes.' Dave wrote that snippet of information in his pocket book. 'What colour was his hair?'

'Brown, I think. Or it might have been fair. I don't really remember.'

'Moustache, beard?'

'I don't think so. Maybe. No, I'm not sure.'

Dave gave up on trying to get a decent description. 'Were they carrying anything?'

I wondered why Dave asked that, but then I recalled that the receipt found in Patricia's room had been for a man's shirt and was in Geoffrey Forman's name.

'Yes, they had a few carrier bags with them. I think Pat said something about their having been shopping in the West End that morning. It was a Saturday.'

Shopping, eh? Perhaps shop*lifting* would have been a better description.

'How did you come to see them, Mrs Parsons?' I asked.

'I wasn't being nosey,' the landlady replied defensively.

I smiled and held up a hand. 'I was hoping you *were*,' I said. 'I'm trying to find this poor girl's killer.'

That placated the woman. 'As a matter of fact, I was putting the empty milk bottles out on the step. If you forget, you suddenly find you've got a dozen of them cluttering up the kitchen.'

'It's a problem,' I agreed, even though I bought my milk from the supermarket. And often forgot. I've quite got used to black tea. 'So that's when you saw them, was it?'

'Yes. Just as I opened the front door, Pat was on the step looking in her handbag for her key.'

'Did she introduce this man to you?'

'No. She just said something like "Hello, Mrs P", and went on upstairs.' A sudden frightening thought occurred to Mrs Parsons. 'Glory be, you don't think it was him who murdered her, do you?' she asked, putting a hand to her mouth.

'Right now, Mrs Parsons,' I said, 'I don't know who killed her.'

'Did this man speak at all?' asked Dave, joining in again. He was obviously hoping for confirmation of an Australian accent.

'No, he just smiled, and the two of them went on upstairs. He stayed for about an hour and then went again.'

I didn't ask Mrs Parsons how she knew when he'd gone. I presumed she was putting out more milk bottles.

Donna Lodge did not seem at all surprised to see us again.

'I'm afraid Geoffrey still hasn't come home,' she said with yet another of her apologetic smiles. 'But he did ring me over the weekend. He said that he'll probably be away for another week.' Barefooted, she was attired in a pair of ragged-ended denim shorts and a tee-shirt, and her hair was gathered back into a ponytail.

'As a matter of fact, it's you we've come to see, Ms Lodge,' I said.

'Oh, well, I don't know how I can help you, but you'd better come in.'

'Bruce Phillips,' I said, adopting a full frontal approach once we had been shown, somewhat reluctantly I suspected, into the sitting room.

Donna Lodge's expression didn't change at all, unless you

counted the raised eyebrow of puzzlement that suddenly greeted the Australian's name. 'Who?'

'Bruce Phillips. Does that name mean anything to you, Ms Lodge?'

'No, I can't say that it does. Is this something to do with the burglary you mentioned when you were here the other day?'

'No.'

'Well, what then?'

'When you were convicted of shoplifting four years ago, Bruce Phillips paid your fine, Ms Lodge.' I sat back and waited for the reaction to my no-frills accusation.

'That was all a terrible mistake. I'd picked up some underwear from one department and then wandered around the shop to where the dresses were. But I didn't find anything I liked. I walked out of the shop, completely forgetting that I'd still got the underwear in my hand. I tried to explain that it was a lapse of memory, but they didn't believe me, and neither did the magistrate. I was fined four hundred pounds.'

The magistrate must have been hellishly benevolent that morning, because her version of what had happened didn't accord with the record of her conviction. According to the arresting officers, she'd been found in possession of considerably more than just underwear. Like the two expensive dresses, the three sets of silk underwear and a bikini. And it was all in a bag strapped around her waist under her coat so that she looked as though she was pregnant. It was an old hoister's trick. 'And Bruce Phillips paid the fine,' I said.

'Certainly not. I paid it myself. I told you just now, I've never heard of a Bruce Phillips.' Donna began to assume the attitude of the wronged innocent. 'Look, if this doesn't have anything to do with the burglary you came about the other day, why are you asking all these questions about my unfortunate mistake?'

'Because we are interested in finding Bruce Phillips in connection with another matter,' said Dave. 'According to our records, he is shown as having paid your fine. We thought, therefore, that you might be able to tell us where he was.'

It wasn't on her records of course, and it was just possible that Dave's mate in the Extradition Unit had got it wrong.

'I'll say it again,' Donna said crossly, 'I've never heard of him, so I'm unlikely to be able to tell you where he is, am I?'

'In that case, I'm sorry to have bothered you, Ms Lodge. There's obviously been some mistake.' I decided that to mention Patricia Hunter's name would not be a good idea. At least, not at this stage. 'Perhaps you'd get Mr Forman to telephone me as soon as he gets back.'

'Certainly, but I've no idea when that will be.'

'I'm sure she's involved somehow, guv,' said Dave as we drove away from Ridgely Road and made for Curtis Green.

'And sufficiently well briefed, probably by Phillips, to be one jump ahead of us all the time,' I said. 'I reckon that Geoffrey Forman and Donna Lodge could be in this together. It's possible that they both knew Patricia Hunter and something gave them cause to murder her. But God knows what, or how we're going to prove it.'

'And I wouldn't be at all surprised if Forman and Bruce Phillips weren't one and the same,' Dave said for about the tenth time. 'I'd love to hear what she's saying to him on the phone right now. What's the chance of getting an intercept put on?'

'We'd never get the Home Secretary to sign a warrant to tap her phone, Dave, not on the evidence we've got so far.'

'No, I suppose not.' Dave braked sharply and cursed an errant cyclist who appeared to think that traffic law didn't apply to him. 'An obo then?'

'We don't have the manpower for an observation,' I said. 'We're supposed to solve murders single-handed these days, or hadn't you heard?'

I decided it was time to have a chat about Bruce Phillips with Dave's pal on the Extradition Unit.

'Yes, we've got a photograph of him, guv. For what it's worth.' The detective sergeant dealing with Phillips's case was called Don Lacey. 'D'you want a copy?'

'Yes, please. What was the last address you had for this guy?'

Lacey poked about in a filing cabinet and produced both the photograph and a docket. 'He was living at flat twelve, nine Petersfield Street, Fulham, guv, but when we went there to nick him he'd done a runner.'

'Who did you speak to there?' I asked. I glanced at the blurred head-and-shoulders photograph of Phillips that looked as though it had been taken by a surveillance team. It was the face of a man who I guessed to be in his late twenties or early thirties, and who had long hair, a bushy beard and heavy horn-rimmed spectacles. All of which was no bloody help at all. I'd seen dozens of men who looked like him in the custody suite of a police station. Usually after a drugs raid.

Lacey thumbed through his file. 'A woman called Donna Lodge,' he said. 'But she told us that Phillips had left a couple of days previously and she didn't know where he'd gone. And we haven't seen hair nor hide of him since.'

'Well, I'm buggered,' I said. 'We've just left her and she denied all knowledge of Bruce Phillips. She was convincing enough to make me wonder whether there'd been a cock-up with the paperwork.'

'Don't blame her,' said Lacey. 'Where was this?'

'Number thirteen Ridgely Road, Barnes,' said Dave.

Lacey made a note on his file.

'Where did this photograph come from?' I asked.

'Australian police. He's forty years old now,' said Lacey, and gave me Phillips's date of birth. 'They admitted that it's a bit of an old photograph, and probably wasn't a very good likeness even then, if you can see any likeness at all. It's a racing certainty that he's changed his appearance since it was taken.'

'Did you make any enquiries elsewhere at the Petersfield Street flats, Don?'

'We had a chat with the neighbours at number eleven – it's just across the hall from number twelve – but they hadn't seen anything of Phillips for a week or so. In fact, they didn't even know his name. So it might not have been him anyway. I showed them the photograph, but they couldn't ID him from it. Not surprising really. The only man they'd regularly seen coming out of flat twelve was clean-shaven and apparently with twenty-twenty vision.' Lacey paused to give an expressive shrug. 'Something else that was interesting though, those same neighbours reckoned that they'd seen other men calling at the flat from time to time. Sometimes in the afternoon, sometimes in the evening.'

'Was there any mention of a woman called Patricia Hunter at that flat?'

'No, guv. I was told that there was another woman living there, a blonde who more or less fits the description of the Hunter girl, apart from the hair colour, which doesn't mean a thing. But she wasn't there when we busted the place. And Donna Lodge claimed that she was there on her own, and had been since Phillips left. Patricia Hunter's name didn't mean anything to me until Dave told me you were investigating her murder. D'you reckon she was mixed up with this Phillips guy?'

'I'm bloody sure of it. We knew that Bruce Phillips had paid Patricia Hunter's shoplifting fine, but it was you telling Dave that he'd also paid Donna Lodge's fine that linked the three of them together.' And I went on to tell Lacey about the receipt in Forman's name that had been found at Patricia Hunter's last address.

'Sounds as though Phillips was running a hoisting ring, guv. You know, a professional shoplifting scam.'

'Yes, I do know what a hoisting ring is,' I said, somewhat tersely, 'but that doesn't explain the comings and goings of men at the flat. Unless they were part of his ring. Or were fencing the property stolen by his girls.'

Lacey laughed. 'I reckon it was a high-class knocking shop. I passed the details over to the uniform branch, but by the time they got around to it, Donna had gone as well. We checked back but the flat was occupied by someone else. There was no forwarding address and when we made enquiries of the post office, there was no redirection order either. But from what you say, we now know where Donna Lodge is, and maybe Bruce Phillips isn't far away.'

125

'Don't put money on it, Skip,' I said. And that proved to be right.

'Harry! What are you doing here?' asked Gail when I arrived at her house.

'I wondered if you fancied a drink. There's a reasonably decent pub not far from here.'

'Why don't you come in and have one here?'

'Thanks,' I said and followed her upstairs to a sitting room on the first floor that ran the full width of the house, a house not unlike the one in which Barbara Clark lived at Wandsworth. There were two brown leather sofas facing each other with a low coffee table between them. An expensive hi-fi stood in one corner and a wide-screen television in another.

'You seem to be doing all right for a struggling, out-of-work chorus girl,' I said.

'I get by,' said Gail. 'Whisky, gin, vodka, brandy?' She stood with her hand hovering over a selection of bottles on a sofa table.

'Whisky would be fine, thanks.'

'Ice or water?'

'Neither, thanks.'

She handed me a crystal tumbler containing a good inch of Scotch, and poured a gin and tonic for herself. 'Excuse me while I get myself some ice.' She returned from the kitchen and sat on the sofa opposite the one in which I was sitting. Raising her glass in brief salute, she asked, 'And to what do I owe the pleasure of this visit, Harry?'

'I wondered if Patricia Hunter had ever mentioned a computer consultant called Geoffrey Forman,' I said. 'Lives in Barnes.'

'No, she never spoke to me about any of her boyfriends, apart from Jeremy Payne, but as I said the other day, the name Geoffrey doesn't mean anything. Why?'

'We found a receipt in her room. It was on this guy's credit-card account.'

Gail shook her head. 'No, sorry, Harry. Doesn't ring any bells. Still, it's nice to see you.'

I decided against telling Gail about Patricia Hunter's other career in the Brighton brothel – at least, not yet – and for the next hour, we chatted about all sorts of mundane things until, eventually, I glanced at my watch and stood up.

'Well, I must be going,' I said.

'I suppose so,' said Gail.

Oh well, better luck next time, Brock.

Twelve

'I suppose we'll have to go back and see Donna Lodge again, guv,' said Dave.

'Yes, but I've a shrewd suspicion that we may just find the cupboard's bare,' I said, repeating, more or less, what I'd told DS Lacey the previous day. 'If only we'd known that your mate had been to Petersfield Street and spoken to Donna Lodge, we'd've had more to front her with.'

'How about a search warrant and spin the drum, guv?' said Dave.

I looked doubtful. 'Maybe,' I said, 'but I wouldn't mind betting that we'd find nothing. It might come to that though.'

'D'you think there *is* a tie-up between Patricia Hunter's murder and Phillips, Forman and Lodge?' asked Dave. 'Or even the mysterious Jeremy Payne?'

'I don't know, but Forman's certainly got some questions to answer when we find him.'

'But if he's really Phillips, he may be back in Oz already,' said Dave.

'In that case, we'll do the obvious,' I said. 'Colin, ring Steve Granger at the Australian High Commission and ask him if he's going to be in this morning, because I need to see him urgently.'

Colin Wilberforce swung round and grabbed the phone. 'Yes, sir.'

'Yes, I remember this one, Harry,' said Inspector Steve Granger, the Australian Commonwealth Police officer who was seconded to his country's High Commission, 'but once your chaps said he'd shot through, we put the file on the back burner. Have you got some more info on this no-hoper then?'

I told Granger of our particular interest in Phillips and asked whether it was possible that he was now back in Australia.

'Wouldn't be at all surprised. I think if I knew you guys were after me, Harry, I'd shoot through too. But of course he couldn't possibly have got past the airport controls without your guys picking him up, could he?' Granger laughed.

'That was a low blow, Steve,' I said. We both knew that arresting a wanted villain at the airport was a hit-and-miss affair. Both here and in Australia. The irony was that if you nicked one, you'd miss the next one because you were too busy doing the paperwork on the first one.

The Aussie copper laughed again and made a phone call. After a few minutes of exchanging insults with the police officer he was talking to, presumably at the headquarters of the Commonwealth Police, he replaced the receiver. 'It's half past seven in the evening in Canberra,' he said. 'The duty inspector doesn't know anything about Phillips, but he'll leave a message for the bunco squad and they'll let me know.' He paused. 'D'you really think this guy's mixed up in this murder then?'

I shrugged. 'I don't know, Steve, but when we do get hold of him, he's certainly got some questions to answer. Apart from the extradition, I mean.'

'I've had a thought, Dave,' I said, as we left Australia House in the Strand.

'Good heavens, sir,' said Dave.

'It's just possible that this Jeremy Payne guy visited the theatre, and that's where he first met Patricia Hunter. Or at least saw her.'

'How does that help, guv?'

'If he made a booking, the theatre might just have a record of it.'

'The Alhambra's not far from here.'

We grabbed a taxi and ten minutes later were being shown into the manager's office.

129

'How can I help you, gentlemen?' The manager was called Stroud.

I explained about the murder of Patricia Hunter and Stroud made the usual sympathetic noises before adding, 'Yes, I remember her. She was in the play that's running now.'

'We're interested in tracing a man who befriended her, Mr Stroud, and it's possible that he reserved a seat for the show.'

'Name?' Stroud put on a pair of horn-rimmed glasses and looked important.

'Jeremy Payne.'

'One moment.' Stroud reached for the telephone and tapped out a number. He relayed the name and waited. 'They'll ring me back,' he said.

For the next few minutes we engaged in desultory conversation. The phone rang.

'Stroud.' The manager listened and made a few notes on his notepad. 'It seems he was a regular customer,' he said as he replaced the receiver. 'But I can't give you an address for Mr Payne. All I have is a credit-card number. But it seems he saw the play about three or four times.'

'Thank you for your assistance, Mr Stroud,' I said. I knew that with a credit-card number we stood a good chance of tracing Jeremy Payne.

We found a sandwich shop for a quick 'on the hoof' lunch, and made our way to Barnes.

There was no answer at 13 Ridgely Road, and no sign of Donna Lodge's Alfa Romeo.

The best we could extract from anyone was a next-door neighbour's opinion that our quarry had gone away. 'I just happened to notice her putting suitcases in her car this morning,' said the woman. I got the impression that she would *just happen* to notice everything her neighbours did. Thank God!

'Have you seen Mr Forman lately?' I asked.

'Mr Forman?'

'He's the man who lives with Ms Lodge.'

'*Lives* with? Good heavens, you mean they're not married?'

That revelation clearly put Forman's neighbour on our side, for what good it did. 'No, I haven't seen him lately.'

Dave produced the photograph of Phillips that we'd obtained from Lacey. 'Is this Mr Forman?' he asked.

The neighbour studied the poor print and then shook her head, 'Oh no,' she said. 'Mr Forman doesn't have a beard and he doesn't wear glasses.'

'We blew it, Dave,' I said as we drove away from Ridgely Road. 'It was all right when we spun her that fanny about Forman and the office-breaking, but the minute we mentioned Phillips, she made the connection and took off.'

'So what do we do now, guv?' asked Dave.

'Time we started pulling in some favours from a few snouts,' I said, without much hope of finding anyone in the criminal underworld who knew the whereabouts of Bruce Phillips. Or who would be prepared to share that information with us if they did know. Those who populate the shadowy fringes of West End villainy are reluctant to inform on killers, just in case they get topped themselves for opening their mouths.

When we returned to Curtis Green, I gave Frank Mead the job of sending out the members of his team to make enquiries around the West End to see if any of their informants had heard anything of Bruce Phillips. Although I had no great expectation that they would come up with anything, I was wrong.

However, there were other things to do.

'I think we may just catch that naughty judge who was caught with his trousers down at Brighton, Dave,' I said, and reached for the phone. 'Before he packs it in for the day.'

It wasn't difficult to track down the court at which the judge was presiding, and I rang to make an appointment.

'His Honour usually rises at four thirty,' said the judge's adenoidal clerk. 'But he won't be going home. He's dining at his inn of court this evening.'

I glanced at my watch. 'I should be able to make it by then,' I said.

'May I tell His Honour what it's about? Of course, if it's a warrant—'

'No, it's not. You may tell the judge that I'm investigating a serious criminal matter and I think he may be able to assist me in my enquiries.' I didn't deem it politic to mention that, when it came to it, I might just need a warrant *for* the judge, not from him.

The judge, a youngish fellow – probably in his late forties – had abandoned his wig, gown and jacket and was sitting in his shirtsleeves smoking a pipe.

'My clerk tells me that I may be able to help you with some criminal matter, Chief Inspector,' he said after I had introduced myself and Dave. 'I must say I'm intrigued.'

'Fenwick Road, Brighton, sir. Number sixty-one to be precise.'

'Oh Christ!' said the judge and leaned forward, a concerned look on his face. 'What about it?'

'I understand that you have visited the establishment in the past and were there the night it was raided by police. That would have been just over two months ago.'

'Yes, I was there.' The judge sat back and spent several seconds fiddling with his pipe before he got around to relighting it. I assumed that he was giving himself time to think. 'I take it, Chief Inspector,' he continued, raising an eyebrow, 'that none of this will be made public?' It sounded more like a threat than a question.

'I see no reason why it should, sir.'

'So how can I help you?'

'Did you ever engage the services of a young lady called Patricia Hunter?'

'No, I don't think so.'

Dave produced the photograph of Patricia and handed it to the judge.

'That's her, sir.'

The judge examined the print carefully. 'Ah yes, I do remember her,' the judge said. 'That's the girl who called herself Dolores. She and I were, um . . .'

'Were engaged in intimate conversation, sir?'

'Exactly.' His Honour placed the photograph in the centre of his desk and once more leaned back in his chair. 'Don't

132

tell me that those idiots in Brighton are thinking of launching a prosecution, surely.'

'I doubt it, sir,' I said. 'Apart from the woman who ran the place, and who was prosecuted for keeping a brothel' – the judge winced at my accurate description – 'I don't see that either the prostitutes or their clients have committed any offences.'

'Quite so, Chief Inspector, quite so. I was just about to say the same thing myself.' The judge adopted an air of bewilderment. The sort of expression I imagine he assumed when counsel embarked on a line of questioning that was leading nowhere. 'But what is your interest? I take it that you're Metropolitan officers.'

'We are indeed, sir, and my interest is that I am investigating the murder of that young lady.' I gestured at the photograph on the judge's desk.

'Hell's bells and buckets of blood!' exclaimed the judge. 'When was this?'

'Her body was recovered from the Thames opposite the Houses of Parliament at about eight o'clock during the evening of Wednesday the twelfth of June this year.'

'Thank God for that.'

'I beg your pardon, sir?' It seemed an extraordinarily inapposite statement for him to make.

'Don't misunderstand me, Chief Inspector.' The judge smiled and ran a hand over his desktop. 'I didn't mean to sound callous. It's most regrettable when a young woman like that meets an untimely end. No, what I meant was that I was in St Malo, in Brittany. Sailed across in my boat, d'you see? On Friday the thirty-first of May. Stayed there for three weeks.'

'With your wife, sir?' asked Dave.

'Er, yes. With my wife, Sergeant.'

'While you were at Fenwick Road, sir, did you by any chance come across an Australian?' I asked. 'Or, for that matter, hear anyone talking about such a person?'

'Not that I recall. Why?'

'We believe that an Australian named Bruce Phillips was behind the Fenwick Road set-up.'

'And you think he may be connected with this girl's murder?'

133

'That I don't know, sir, but there is an extradition warrant out for his arrest. He's wanted in Australia for long-firm fraud.'

The judge looked a little sick and paused for a moment or two, doubtless considering the implications not only of having been caught out visiting a brothel, but now learning that it may have been owned by a wanted criminal. 'Well, I wish you luck, Chief Inspector.' He stood up, signalling an end to our interview. But as we reached the door, he spoke again. 'Perhaps you'd afford me the courtesy of advising me when you've arrested this man, Chief Inspector.'

'If you wish, sir.'

'Good. In the circumstances it would be most improper if he were to be arraigned before me. I'm sure you understand.'

'Oh, I do indeed, sir,' I said, and smiled.

We left the judge to enjoy dinner at his inn of court, if he still had an appetite.

'What d'you reckon, guv?' asked Dave. 'He seems kosher enough.'

'You know me, Dave, I never trust anyone. Particularly lawyers. If his yacht was tied up in St Malo for three weeks, the harbour master there will have noted it. And no doubt the French customs will have known it was there too. We'll check. Just in case he's telling lies.'

'Wouldn't be the first time a judge has done that,' said Dave.

We drove south of the river and eventually found the rectory where our fornicating clergyman lived. 'I suppose this clergyman is the one who prevented Barbara Clark from escaping to the bolthole,' I said as I rang the doorbell.

The door was answered by a woman who announced that she was the clergyman's wife. Which made her husband an *adulterous* fornicating clergyman.

We were shown into the study and were joined shortly afterwards by a man of about forty wearing, unsurprisingly, a clerical collar. But that jarred somewhat with the cricket sweater and jeans.

'Sorry to keep you,' he said. 'I've been gardening.'

134

I suppose the clerical collar was so that the weeds would know he was a man of the cloth.

'I'm Detective Chief Inspector Brock of New Scotland Yard,' I began, 'and this is—'

But I got no further.

'A young man in trouble?' said the clergyman, beaming benevolently at Dave.

'Not at the moment,' I said. 'He's my assistant, Detective Sergeant Poole.'

'Ah!' The parson took off his spectacles and polished them with his handkerchief before replacing them carefully. 'Do sit down, gentlemen.'

'Just because I'm black, doesn't necessarily make me a villain,' said Dave with a beatific smile. He was accustomed to being typecast, but never let anyone get away with it.

'No, quite so. How may I help you then?'

'I understand that you're familiar with sixty-one Fenwick Road, Brighton, padre?' I said.

The clergyman adjusted his glasses and glanced at each of us in turn before returning his gaze to me. 'I'm not sure that I know that address. I don't often have time to get to the seaside. Being a busy rector doesn't give one a great deal of time for holidays. Is it a boarding house?'

'More of a bawdy house,' said Dave, 'and when the Sussex Vice Squad raided it about two months ago, one of the names they took was yours.'

'Oh dear!'

'And one of the other names they took was that of Barbara Clark, a prostitute known to be working there. We were told by the Sussex Police that you and she were *each* unfrocked at the time and were—'

The clergyman held up a hand. 'I know, I know,' he said, 'and ever since that awful night I've prayed for forgiveness.'

'That's all right, then,' said Dave.

'Our interest is in this young woman,' I said, as Dave, right on cue, handed the parson the photograph of Patricia Hunter. 'She was also a prostitute working at sixty-one Fenwick Road the night of the police raid. Have you ever seen her before, or had sexual relations with her?'

135

'No.' It had taken the clergyman but a brief glance to disavow any knowledge of the girl known in Brighton, and elsewhere, as Dolores. 'Why d'you ask?'

'Because she's been murdered.'

The clergyman closed his eyes and intertwined his fingers in an attitude of supplication. 'Oh the poor dear child,' he intoned in sepulchral tones.

We asked the usual questions, but our errant parson knew nothing of any Australians, had never heard the name Bruce Phillips, and further assured us that he would never sin again.

It was nearing eight o'clock by the time we drew into the Hampstead road where Tim Oliver lived. 'I'm getting heartily sick of this, Dave,' I said.

'Never know, guv, this might be the one,' said Dave hopefully. But I don't think he believed it any more than I did. But you've got to try.

It was a large house and as we arrived, a green Bentley saloon pulled on to the drive. A liveried chauffeur jumped out and opened the rear door of the car.

'Mr Oliver?' I asked as the well-fed and well-dressed man reached his front door.

'Yes?' Oliver stared nervously at Dave, as though fearing he was about to be robbed. As Dave often said, he tended to have that effect on people.

'We're police officers, sir. We'd like to have a word with you.'

'Oh? What about?' Oliver put his key in the door, opened it and shouted, 'I'm home, darling.'

'Fenwick Road, Brighton.'

'Oh, that.' Oliver embraced a woman dressed in a green jumper and a tweed skirt. 'Hello, darling.'

'You're early,' said the woman, and glanced at Dave and me. 'Oh no, you haven't brought more of your people for dinner, Tim. It's really too bad. Why didn't you ring me?'

'They're not stopping, dear. Just a couple of policemen wanting to talk to me.'

'Oh, that's all right then. I'll leave you to it.'

Oliver conducted us into a wood-panelled study. There was

a desk, a couple of leather armchairs and the obligatory computer set on a custom-built workstation in the corner of the room. Next to it were copies of the *Daily Telegraph* and the *Financial Times*.

'Have a pew,' he said, pointing at the armchairs. 'Now, what's all this about Fenwick Road?' he asked, seating himself behind the desk. 'Care for a drink?'

'No thanks.'

Oliver reached across to a small table and transferred a whisky decanter and a glass to his desk. He poured himself a substantial measure, and took a sip. 'Fire away.'

'Dolores,' I said.

Oliver grinned. 'Ah, Dolores, yes. Good-looking girl, that one.'

'How well did you know her, Mr Oliver?'

'Only carnally, old boy. But why the questions?'

'She was murdered on or about the twelfth of June.'

'Christ! Really?' Oliver took another gulp of whisky.

'When did you last see her?'

Oliver laughed. 'I thought they only asked that in second-rate television shows. Well now, let me see.' He paused. 'A couple of times after the Brighton fiasco, I suppose.'

'Where?'

'West End hotels. Can't remember the names of them, but I could look it up on my credit-card account.'

This man was an enigma. He had a wife who was well preserved for her age, which was probably about fifty, but here he was talking quite openly about his trysts with a prostitute.

'Doesn't your wife mind?' I asked.

'Not a bit, old boy.' Oliver lowered his voice. 'Well, that said, of course, she doesn't know, but I think she may suspect. You know what women are like, never miss a trick. But I don't think she'd care very much even if she did find out. All that sort of thing's over between us. If ever she happened across one of the bills, I'd tell her it wasn't me. Probably spin her some yarn about an arrangement I'd made – and paid for – for some of our visiting Japanese clients. And in a few cases that would be true. The old Japs love to get their leg over when they're in England, you know.'

'Is this the woman you knew as Dolores?' Dave asked as he handed over the print.

Oliver glanced at it. 'Yes, that's her. What a bloody waste. Murdered you say?'

'Yes. Her real name was Patricia Hunter. Did you know that?'

Oliver shook his head. 'No, she was only ever known as Dolores to me.' He returned the print. 'As a matter of fact, she was the girl I was having it off with when your chaps busted in. Dolores was on top of me at the time, but she leaped off and ran. God knows where she went, but when the chief copper got us all lined up and started taking names and addresses, she wasn't anywhere to be seen. I'm afraid the Brighton boys in blue quite ruined a jolly good evening. No sense of humour, that's their problem. And I didn't get my money back either.'

'Bruce Phillips?'

'Who?'

'An Australian,' I said. 'The police in Sussex believe he was the man who was really running the place down there.'

'Don't know the name, old boy, but there was certainly an Australian knocking about when the law came steaming in. But I don't know where he went. He wasn't in the line-up of us naughty boys.'

That was interesting. Barbara Clark had vehemently denied the presence of a mysterious Australian at Fenwick Road the night of the police raid, but it was clear from her demeanour that she would have been too terrified to mention him even if he had been there. She'd certainly done her best to avoid knowing anything about him, apart from mentioning that a man who could have been him had given her a beating. On the other hand, that may have been a coincidence; she may not have seen Phillips. But even if Patricia Hunter had told Barbara Clark that he'd been in the bolthole after the raid was over, she didn't repeat it. However, on her previous form, she may have been too scared to tell us even that much.

'These meetings with Dolores in West End hotels, Mr Oliver. How did you make the arrangements to meet her?'

'About a week before the Brighton raid, I asked her if she

was open to a bit of private business, and she jumped at it,' said Oliver. 'And I was pleased too. It worked out much cheaper without a middleman. Not that I minded forking out, but you've got to shop around, haven't you?'

'What time of the day did these meetings take place?'

'The afternoons, of course. I know what I said about my wife not being concerned, but there's no need to antagonize her, eh what?'

'How did you pay Dolores, Mr Oliver?'

'She took credit cards, old boy. Had this wonderful little portable machine in her briefcase. And she was very careful to get her money before we started the fun and games. Shrewd little cookie, that one.'

'Any idea of the name of the payee, Mr Oliver?'

'Not a clue. I know what I said about madam' – he cocked a thumb in the general direction of where he imagined his wife to be – 'but I always shred my bills as soon as I've paid them. To tell you the truth, I never noticed what her account was called.'

'Do you have any connection with the theatre, Mr Oliver?'

'Go there occasionally. The lady wife enjoys the odd evening out, you know.'

'That wasn't quite what I meant,' I said. 'Have you ever been involved in the management or production side?'

'Good God no. Much too risky. Unless you happen to be Andrew Lloyd Webber, of course.'

'Amateur dramatics, then?'

Oliver laughed. 'You must be joking. It's as much as I can do to stand up and say something at the AGM of my company.'

'And what does your company do, Mr Oliver?'

'Import and export. Why?'

I countered his question with one of my own. 'Where were you between the tenth and twelfth of June, Mr Oliver?'

Oliver laughed again. 'You've been watching too much TV, old boy. Now, where was I between those dates?' He glanced at the ceiling for a moment and then looked down again. 'I don't know. If you care to give my secretary a ring at my office sometime, she'll have a look in my diary. But I can't remember offhand.'

And that, I thought, would give you adequate time to make a few false entries.

But, I wondered, could it be that this man was Patricia Hunter's killer? He was rich, confident, and a womanizer. Perhaps we'd been misled into thinking that the Australian fugitive was the one who'd murdered the prostitute known as Dolores, when all along . . .

Thirteen

Dave and I returned to Curtis Green and mulled over what we had learned. Which wasn't very much. The judge and the clergyman were non-starters in my book, although I still intended to check the judge's story about being in Brittany at the time Patricia Hunter was murdered. But even so, a Crown Court judge? Be reasonable. Although, there again . . .

Tim Oliver however was a different ball game altogether. For a start he was much too glib and much too open about his sessions with the murdered Patricia Hunter. And he had skilfully avoided giving me a direct answer to my question concerning his whereabouts when she had been murdered.

The other aspect, of course, was that Oliver was undoubtedly affluent. All the trappings were there: a magnificent house, a chauffeur-driven Bentley, and if he had any more suits like the one he was wearing, his tailor must be a rich man too. But if his wife learned of his shenanigans with a prostitute, despite Oliver claiming that she didn't care, she might just take it into her head to seek a divorce. And that could cost him a lot of money. It was possible, therefore, that Patricia Hunter might have been blackmailing him. And blackmail is a very good motive for murder.

Suddenly Mr Tim Oliver had risen to a point very close to the top of my list of suspects.

The next morning, Colin Wilberforce announced that he'd had a call from the Australian High Commission.

'Inspector Granger said that an email from Canberra came in during the night, sir. The Commonwealth Police have no knowledge of Bruce Phillips returning to Australia. But according to this' – he gestured with the printout – 'they say it doesn't mean he hasn't. And they pointed out that Australia is a big place, sir,' he added with a grin.

'Very helpful,' I said. 'Just look how long it took them to find Ned Kelly.'

Just before eleven, Nicola Chance, a vivacious Spanish-speaking detective constable who could charm the birds off the trees, bounced into my office. Despite her slender build, she knew how to take care of herself.

There was a story that when she was still in uniform, on duty in Trafalgar Square on a New Year's Eve, a drunken sailor had approached her and asked for a date. But he'd made the terrible mistake of grabbing hold of her and trying to give her a kiss. In a blur of judo movements the sailor had described a parabola through the air and finished up with a broken arm. I'd often wondered how he'd explained that injury to his shipmates in Portsmouth, when eventually he arrived back there. The beak had weighed him off for assault on police and, given that he was technically absent without leave by then, directed he be handed over to the shore patrol.

'I think I've got something, sir,' she said.

'Not measles, is it?'

'No, sir.' Nicola smiled. She'd been on the team long enough to have grown accustomed to my sense of humour. 'Last evening I dropped into the Kookaburra. It's a nightclub in—'

'It's also an Australian laughing jackass,' I said. 'I suppose I should read something into that.'

Nicola smiled again. 'Well, it's certainly frequented by the Australian community. I got talking to one of the hostesses, a girl called Lisa, who knows Bruce Phillips. And she reckoned she'd seen him in the club quite recently.'

'How recently is quite recently?'

'A week ago, sir. Wednesday the twenty-sixth to be exact.'

'How did she come to know him, Nicola?'

'She used to work for him apparently.'

'What, as a tom?' I was sure now that Phillips was the

Australian whose involvement in the Fenwick Road brothel Barbara Clark had been at pains to deny.

'No, she was part of his hoisting gang. She said that he had about four or five girls, of which she was one, working the Oxford Street, Regent Street and Knightsbridge shops. It was quite a sophisticated operation by all accounts.'

'Any idea why they packed it in? Presuming they have, of course.'

'According to Lisa, the shoplifting squads at West End Central, Marylebone and Kensington nicks got wise to what was happening and homed in on them enough to make it an unhealthy pursuit. So Phillips's little team moved out of Central London. They had a brief fling at the Bluewater Centre, the big shopping complex at Greenhithe in Kent, but they were chased out of there and tried their hand at Brent Cross. It seems that the job's intelligence system worked well though, and the local police in those places had been warned that they were coming.'

'Did this Lisa of yours say whether she'd spoken to Phillips, Nicola?'

'Only briefly. He asked her if she wanted to work for him again.'

'Doing what?' I asked, but I'd guessed.

Nicola smiled again. 'He offered to set her up in a flat so that she could provide a "service" for carefully selected, affluent clients.'

'I don't suppose he told her where this place was.'

'No, sir, but Lisa told him to get lost. She said he was a nasty bastard and wouldn't shrink from beating them up if they stepped out of line. She didn't want anything else to do with him. End of story.'

'Had she seen him in there before? Recently, I mean.'

'She said not, sir, but that doesn't mean he isn't a frequent visitor. Lisa doesn't work every night and he could've been in at times when she wasn't on duty.'

'Was she ever done for shoplifting?'

'Yes, twice, sir. And each time Phillips paid her fine. But Lisa said that the last time she was up before the beak, she was threatened with imprisonment if she offended again.'

143

'So she decided to go on the game as a safer option, I suppose.'

'What, being a hostess in a nightclub, sir? Perish the thought.' Nicola gave me a mock frown. 'But she did mention that two of the other girls on his little scam carried on working for him. As high-class call girls.'

'Any names?'

'Yes, sir, Donna Lodge and Patricia Hunter.'

But, surprise, surprise, that was no surprise.

I rang Granger at Australia House. 'You can tell your guys to stop looking for Bruce Phillips, Steve,' I said. 'He was sighted in London a week ago.'

'No worries,' said Granger. 'Let me know when you've baled him up,' he added with a chuckle, 'and we'll have what's left.'

The news that Phillips was still in London created as many problems as it solved. It was now crucial that we find him. In my book, his association with the 'actress' Patricia Hunter, and his reputation for using violence, put him in the front rank of suspects for her murder. And despite Donna Lodge's neighbour's certainty that the photograph of the bearded, bespectacled Phillips that we'd shown her was not the clean-shaven, keen-sighted Geoffrey Forman, I still wondered if they were one and the same.

I sent for Frank Mead.

'Frank, I've got a lousy assignment for a couple of your guys, ideally a man and a woman.' I was joking, of course. It was the sort of assignment that every detective loves.

'Yeah, go on, Harry.'

'Nicola Chance has got a snout at the Kookaburra night-club called Lisa, a hostess. And Lisa saw Bruce Phillips in there a week ago. Get a couple of our people to sit around in the place until he shows up. I'll get Nicola to brief Lisa to point him out if he turns up.'

'And if he does?' asked Frank.

'Tell them to nick him. He's wanted for extradition. And with any luck the murder of Patricia Hunter.' But then I had second thoughts. 'On the other hand, it might be better if they housed him. He's too smart a bastard to hold his hands up to murder, so we'll need the sort of evidence that may be found at wherever he's living now. But whatever happens, tell them not to lose him.'

'Right, Harry.' Mead paused at the door. 'By the way, all the checks on the stops the TSG did the other night were blowouts.'

'Of course they were, Frank,' I said.

I sent for DS Challis and told him to get back to Forman's credit-card company and find out where and when he'd been using his plastic since buying a shirt, the receipt for which had been found in Patricia Hunter's bedsit at Coping Road. And if he'd recently notified them of a change of address. I was hoping that he'd used his card in the Kookaburra Club on the night that Nicola's informant saw Phillips there.

That's the beauty of this modern world in which we live: it's very difficult to do anything without leaving a trail.

Mind you, if Forman was as cunning as I was beginning to believe he was, there was no telling what devious steps he might have taken to avoid being tracked down.

It didn't take long. One quick phone call and Challis was back with the answers.

'The company still has Forman's Barnes address shown for him, guv,' said Challis, 'and he's got a variable direct debit with his bank so that the account is settled every month.'

'So he doesn't have to go home to check his credit-card bill,' I mused.

'Since buying his shirt, Forman's visited a couple of restaurants in London . . .' Challis looked up and grinned. 'They were top-line restaurants and the amounts involved seem to indicate that he wasn't dining alone. And on the twenty-sixth of June, guv, he spent fifty-odd quid in the Kookaburra Club in—'

'Got the bastard,' I said, hitting the top of my desk with the flat of my hand. And instantly regretting it: it hurt. 'That's the same night that Nicola Chance's snout saw Phillips in the K Club. I'm bloody sure that Forman is Phillips.'

145

'Beginning to look that way, guv,' said Challis.

'Any record of Forman having used his card in Germany recently, Tom? Düsseldorf in particular.'

Challis looked down at his notes. 'No, sir, nothing.'

'If Forman's the womanizer I think he is, he couldn't possibly go to Germany without spending a few Euros, especially in a nightclub,' I said. 'Of which, in Düsseldorf, there are many.'

'Looks like he didn't go, guv,' said Challis, who was fully conversant with the twists and turns of the case.

'Well, if Phillips is Forman, we know that he didn't.' And then something else occurred to me. 'Do a check with the passport office, Tom, and see if Forman's got a passport.'

'If Forman is Phillips, he might have done a *Day of the Jackal* job,' said Challis, referring to the scam whereby villains had been known to obtain a passport in the name of a dead child who would have been about their age had they lived.

'I don't think so, Tom. I seem to recall something about them having put a stop to that.' Mind you, it takes years to put a brake on the lumbering Home Office administrative machine. And Phillips wouldn't have used his Australian passport in case he got picked up at a port or airport because there was an extradition warrant out for him. 'Incidentally, Tom, while you're in the credit-card mood, see what you can do with this.' I gave him the details of Jeremy Payne's credit card, which we had obtained from the manager of the Alhambra. I had far from excluded Patricia Hunter's rich boyfriend from my enquiries.

Having armed DCs John Appleby and Sheila Armitage with the Australian police photograph of Phillips, for what good that was likely to be, Frank Mead had detailed them to mount the observation at the Kookaburra Club. But I had no great hope that it would produce a result. Despite what Lisa had told Nicola Chance about not wanting anything else to do with Phillips, there was always the possibility that she'd lied. For all we knew, she could have been on the phone to him the moment Nicola left the club.

The two officers had also been given a copy of Donna

146

Lodge's criminal-record photograph on the off-chance that she might show up at the club too. But perhaps I was relying too much on my hunch that Forman and Phillips were one and the same, stronger though that hunch was becoming by the hour.

I considered again Dave's suggestion of obtaining a warrant to search 13 Ridgely Road, Barnes, but I doubted that I could convince a district judge that there was enough evidence to justify it. Yet. After all, I didn't *know* that Forman was Phillips, even though I strongly suspected it. But perhaps that would be enough.

At five o'clock, Dave swanned into my office, a conspiratorial expression on his face.

'I've got some freebies, guv. Madeleine's dancing in *Les Sylphides* tonight. I wondered if you and—' He broke off. 'Ah, I'd forgotten. Sorry.'

'Keep it to yourself, Dave, but I've been seeing Gail Sutton recently.'

Dave grinned. 'Good for you, guv. Well, if you and she fancy a bit of culture tonight, the offer's there.'

'Yeah, why not? I'll give her a bell.'

'OK, guv, let me know. Kick-off's seven thirty at the Royal Opera House.'

Once Dave had left my office, I rang Gail. 'Dave Poole's got some free tickets for *Les Sylphides* tonight,' I said. 'D'you fancy seeing it?'

There was a lengthy pause while, I imagine, Gail was working out how to let me down lightly.

'Harry, I work in the theatre, and to be honest, the last thing I want to do right now is to get togged up, travel to London and *go* to the theatre. D'you mind awfully if I say no?'

'Sorry,' I said, 'never gave it a thought. How about dinner then, locally somewhere?'

There was another pause. Then, 'I've got a better idea. Why don't you come round here and I'll cook you dinner?'

'You're on,' I said. 'What time?'

'As soon as you can make it.'

*　　*　　*

147

I got to Gail's house at about eight thirty. She was holding a bottle of champagne when she opened her front door.

'I never open champagne when there's a man around to do it for me,' she said, handing me the bottle before leading the way upstairs to the living room.

'I take it you often open it yourself then,' I quipped.

She gave me a playful punch. 'Hardly ever,' she said.

Living on my own, I tended either to eat out or grab a take-away. Neither of which did me much good. And when I attempted to cook something for myself it was usually a disaster. Consequently, to have someone prepare a home-cooked meal for me was a real luxury.

We started with smoked salmon, a dill sauce and brown bread. Then came chicken breasts on pasta with a tarragon sauce and green salad. All of which was accompanied by a splendid bottle of Pinot Grigio.

'Would you like some cheese, Harry?' Gail asked. 'I don't eat puddings and I haven't got anything in.'

I shook my head. 'No thanks, that was absolutely superb. You must have done a crash dive on the supermarket to get all that in.' It would have taken me about a week's planning to produce a meal of the sort she had just served. Not that I would have tried.

'No, I had it all in,' said Gail, 'except for the wine. Would you like a brandy?'

'That would be good.'

'It's on the side table in the sitting room. Help yourself and I'll make some coffee.'

Over coffee and brandy we talked about things we had done, some interesting, some dull, and places we had visited and the holidays we had enjoyed. In my case, not many. When I was married to Helga, our holidays consisted of visiting her parents in Cologne. Not to be recommended. They were boring little people and they'd never forgiven Helga for marrying me. On two counts: I was English *and* a copper.

'Good God!' I said, glancing at my watch. 'It's almost midnight. I must be going.'

'Do you have to?' asked Gail.

*   *   *

148

The next morning, a downcast DC Appleby reported that he and Sheila Armitage had spent the evening in the Kookaburra Club. 'You're not looking too happy, John.' I said. 'Didn't you have any joy?'

'Yes and no, sir,' said Appleby. 'We spotted Phillips—'

'How? He's not still sporting a beard and glasses, surely?'

'No, sir, but when he came in, Lisa, one of the hostesses, said, "Hello, Bruce." He was quite angry about it and told her to keep her voice down and never to use his name.'

'Why are you so fed up then?'

'We lost him, sir.' Appleby looked even more miserable. 'When he left the club, Sheila Armitage and I followed him, but I reckon he's on the alert for surveillance all the time. He walked casually down the street, stopping occasionally to look in shop windows. But the minute he spotted a taxi, he hailed it and jumped in. There wasn't another cab in sight, otherwise we'd've had a go at following him.'

'Did these windows he looked in have glass that was at an angle to the footway?' asked Dave. 'The sort of shops that have a deeply recessed doorway?'

Appleby thought about that for a moment or two. 'Yes, come to think of it, they did, Skip.'

It was the oldest trick in the book: stopping ostensibly to look in shop windows but using the glass as a mirror to see if you're being followed. 'Don't worry, John,' I said. I was disappointed, naturally, but the young DCs had done their best. 'He'll come again. D'you think he sussed you?'

'I'm pretty sure he didn't, sir.'

'Good. Well, get back there again tonight and see if you have better luck.'

'There was one other thing, sir. Donna Lodge was there. Sheila ID'd her from the CRO photograph. But we didn't try to house her, because Mr Mead said you were more interested in finding out where Phillips was going.'

'Was she indeed?' I was not so much surprised as pleased. 'Don't worry about that, but did she and Phillips make contact?'

'Only briefly, sir. Donna came in some time after Phillips and sat on a stool at the bar. When Phillips went up to order a drink, he slid an envelope to her. He never said anything,

149

just slid the envelope along the bar and then walked away and sat down with his drink.'

'Did she open the envelope, John?'

'No, sir. She folded it in half and put it in her handbag. Then she finished her drink and left.'

'Looks as though she's still on the game,' I mused.

'She didn't pick up anyone in the club, sir,' said Appleby defensively, presumably wondering if he'd missed something he shouldn't have missed.

'I'm not surprised. I don't think that's her scene. I reckon she's at the top end of the market. Phillips is probably pimping for her, collecting the money and paying her at the club. If Donna turns up when you go back tonight, follow her rather than Phillips. If he *is* pimping for her, he'll come again.'

Despite what Appleby had said, it looked very much as though Phillips had sussed him and Sheila Armitage as being in the job, and had taken evasive action. After all, he was, according to the Australian police, an accomplished villain. On the other hand, he might have been the sort of hardened criminal who employed counter-surveillance tactics *all* the time. Just in case. That too would account for his not talking to Donna Lodge, even though she claimed they were living together. If, of course, Phillips was Forman.

And from what DS Lacey of the Extradition Unit had said about questioning Donna Lodge when he called at Petersfield Street, it was obvious that she must have warned him of our interest. Particularly after we'd paid her a second visit in Barnes. And that must have been why she'd done a flit. What interested me now was to find out where she'd been living since leaving Ridgely Road. And that, I hoped, would be discovered by Appleby and Armitage.

'One other thing, John. Donna Lodge owns an Alfa Romeo. When you get back to the incident room, ask Sergeant Wilberforce to have the number put on the PNC. I'm particularly interested to find out if it's parked up anywhere.'

I brought Frank Mead up to speed on what Appleby had learned the previous evening, and for a moment he sat in thoughtful silence.

'When I was on the Flying Squad, Harry,' he said eventually, 'there was an Australian sergeant called Ebdon.'

'What about him?' I asked.

'It's not a him, it's a her,' said Frank. 'Kate Ebdon. She came to the Squad from Leman Street in the East End. Some years ago now. She's got flame-red hair and usually dresses in a man's shirt and jeans.'

'She's not butch, is she?'

Frank laughed. 'No way. And there are several guys on the Squad who could testify to that. But more to the point, she's Australian.'

'So what are you suggesting?'

'If we could borrow her, she may just be able to get alongside Phillips in the Kookaburra Club, being an Australian, I mean. You never know, it may just short-circuit our enquiry.'

'Well, right now we could use any help we can get. I'll have a word with the governor of the Flying Squad.'

'I hope you know what you're doing, Harry,' said the operational head of the Squad when I rang him and explained why I wanted to borrow his Australian sergeant. And he laughed.

'Why d'you say that, guv?'

'She's a bloody firebrand, that one. Mind you, if you don't mind her hitting your suspect, she should be all right.'

'She'll fit in, guv.' I crossed my fingers and asked if I could borrow her.

At two o'clock that afternoon, Detective Sergeant Kate Ebdon reported for duty. A shapely thirty-five-year-old, she was dressed, as Frank had said she would be, in jeans and a man's white shirt. And her long red hair was tied back with a green velvet ribbon.

'I understand I'm to be attached to you for a while, guv'nor,' she said, gazing around my tiny office before plonking herself, uninvited, in the sole armchair.

'We've got a problem, Kate,' I began, and went on to tell her the situation with Phillips. 'By the way, this is DS Dave Poole,' I added, indicating Dave.

Kate Ebdon afforded Dave a quick smile. 'G'day, mate,'

she said. I got the impression she was hamming up her Australian accent, probably because her boss had told her why I wanted her assistance.

'If you can get to know this Phillips, it may help us to tie him in with this murder of Patricia Hunter,' I continued. 'But you'll have to tread carefully. If he makes an admission of murder, which is most unlikely, bear in mind that he may not repeat it once he's in custody and under caution. And a one-to-one confession to someone he doesn't know is a police officer won't count for anything.' I was well aware that cases had foundered in the past where an admission had been made under similar circumstances.

'Yeah, that'd be right,' said Kate with a humourless laugh. 'Protect the villain and to hell with the victim. That's the name of the game,' she added, expressing a view of the law common among coppers.

'What I want you to do, if you can, is to find out as much as you can about his background,' I continued. 'Where he's living, who he's running with. Well, I don't have to tell you. It's more of an intelligence-gathering exercise.'

'Where's he from, guv?' Kate seemed a bit put out that I didn't want her to feel his collar.

'Sydney. At least according to the Australian High Commission.'

'That's a bit of luck,' said Kate. 'So am I. Who d'you talk to at Australia House?'

'Inspector Granger.'

'Oh, right. Steve's a mate of mine. OK if I have another word with him and get all the info? If he's getting his stuff from Canberra, it's probably years out of date.' It was obvious that Kate had no very high opinion of the Commonwealth Police.

'We've got all they have on record, but he's promised to let me have anything else that turns up.'

Kate nodded. 'Right,' she said. 'I was having a chat with the skipper in the incident room—'

'Colin Wilberforce.'

'Yeah, that's the guy. He was telling me there's an extradition warrant out for Phillips. If he's showing up at the Kookaburra

Club, why don't we just nick him?'

'It's not that simple,' I said. 'We could have him away any time we liked – now we know he's in the UK – but he's a professional villain and he's not going to cough to a murder. If we arrest him, he'll be sent back to Australia and our murder will be left on the books. We've got to get more evidence against him if we don't want that to happen.'

'So the idea is for me to hang around the K Club and get to know him, right?'

'Yes. D'you know where the K Club is?'

'Sure. Been in there a few times. It's where a lot of the Aussie expats hang out.'

'I should warn you, though. We think he's running a stable of toms. Don't get recruited.'

Kate let out a raucous laugh. 'No probs, guv. He'll get a knee in his balls if he tries to come on to me.'

And even after so short an acquaintance with Detective Sergeant Ebdon, I was in no doubt about that.

Fourteen

The next morning, DC Appleby reported to my office at about nine o'clock.

'Last night was a blowout, sir. Neither Phillips nor Donna Lodge showed up at the K Club.'

'In that case, John, leave it until next Wednesday. It could be that he only turns up once a week for the specific purpose of paying Donna.'

'But he might have other girls working for him, sir, and he wouldn't take the risk of paying them all on the same night.'

I pondered that proposition; Appleby could be right. 'It's possible, John, but I'm putting another officer in there in the meantime. I don't want Phillips to get used to seeing you.'

Appleby looked somewhat crestfallen at that, as though I'd somehow impugned his professional ability.

'Nothing personal, John,' I said, 'but I've borrowed a sergeant from the Flying Squad. She's Australian, and the idea is for her to get alongside Phillips, if that's who he is, and see if she can gain his confidence.'

'Is that the red-haired girl in the incident room, sir?'

'Yes, it is, John, and tread warily. She might be tempted to have a nice young man like you for breakfast.'

Appleby frowned. 'But I'm married, sir,' he said.

'So you are,' I said thoughtfully, 'but I'm not sure that would make any difference to Sergeant Ebdon.'

'Now that we know Forman met Donna in the K Club, guv,' said Dave, after a worried Appleby had left the office, 'I reckon we've got grounds for searching his Ridgely Road address in Barnes.'

'Maybe.' But I was still unsure.

'It stands to reason,' Dave persisted. 'When this guy came into the K Club, Lisa, the so-called hostess, called him Bruce and he got all arsey about it. And the same night Forman puts fifty-odd pounds on his credit card. All in the K Club. That's too much of a coincidence.'

'Most people have a computer these days,' I said.

'Are you changing the subject?' asked Dave, tossing me a cigarette.

'No, but it may be a good idea to get a circuit judge's warrant. I wouldn't like to find something incriminating on their computer – if they've got one – only to have it ruled out as inadmissible in court.'

'Oh, we're going to court now, are we, sir?' enquired Dave sarcastically.

'I hope so, but if this guy keeps personal records on a computer – like his bank details, for example – it could turn out to be evidence.' I was floundering a bit here, but the moguls at the Crown Prosecution Service can get all bitchy if you don't get it absolutely right. To say nothing of assorted judges and barristers.

'On the other hand,' commented Dave, 'we might just find our friend Phillips there.'

'We should be so lucky.'

The circuit judge at Middlesex Crown Court had studied my 'information' with a measure of scepticism, but after a few steps of legal tap-dancing on my part, and the fact that Phillips was wanted for extradition, he finally, and somewhat reluctantly I suspect, granted me a search warrant.

'When are we going to do this, guv?' Dave asked as we left the court.

'As soon as we can assemble Linda Mitchell and her team of crime-scene examiners,' I said. 'I'd like to go in and out without either Forman or Donna Lodge knowing that we've been there.'

'Can't do that, guv. Section sixteen of the Police and

Criminal Evidence Act says that if there's no one there, you've got to leave a copy of the search warrant in a prominent place.'

'Define "prominent", Dave,' I said. That had him.

Apart from a mellifluous version of the Westminster chimes, there was no response when I rang the doorbell of 13 Ridgely Road, Barnes. And that suited me fine.

One of Linda Mitchell's CSEs spent a few moments working on the lock and we were in.

A quick tour of the house confirmed what I had suspected. Since last Tuesday, the day that Donna Lodge had departed, according to her nosey neighbour, the place appeared not to have been lived in. Whatever other failings Donna Lodge may have had, slovenliness was not among them: she had left the house in pristine condition. The bed was made, the kitchen spotless and devoid of dirty crockery, and the cushions had been plumped up on the sofa and armchairs in the sitting room. It was almost as if she and Forman had no intention of returning.

But they had left a computer in the study.

'Do we know whether this house is owned or rented by Donna, Dave?' I asked. In view of the basics, like furniture, it had all the marks of a rented property.

'No, we don't, guv, and it takes a hell of a lot of phone calls to find out. The local council are no help: they just send the council-tax demand to whoever's occupying the place. We could try a Land Registry search, but that would take forever and a day. And what would it tell us anyway?'

'It might tell us if they were coming back. We could try the helpful neighbour.'

'I'd put money on them never coming near the place again,' said Dave. 'Looks like we frightened them off.'

I had to agree with Dave. It had been a mistake to turn up here last Monday asking questions about Bruce Phillips.

'D'you want to have a go at the computer in the study, Dave?' I suggested.

'One of Linda's guys is a computer expert, guv. It'd be better if we let him play with it.'

The CSE who knew about computers was called Dennis. 'You wanted me, Mr Brock?'

156

'Yes, Dennis, see what you can do with the computer. Dave tells me that it'll probably need a password, so I'm not holding out too much hope.'

Dennis scoffed. 'Passwords only stop amateurs getting in,' he said scornfully.

We followed him into the study. He sat down in front of the computer and gazed at it briefly. Interlinking his fingers and stretching them like a pianist about to play Rachmaninov's Third, he began. It didn't take long.

'There's the first one that might be of interest.' Dennis sat back with a satisfied expression on his face. 'Have a look.' He leaned sideways so that I could see the email on the screen: *Donna – meet Nick Lloyd tonight at his h/a eight p.m. for an all-nighter.* It was timed at 1610 hours on Tuesday the second of July, but was unsigned.

But we knew from having called at Ridgely Road at one o'clock on that day that Donna had already left. Poor old Nick Lloyd must have spent the evening watching television. And waiting. And hoping.

'Lloyd was one of the names in Patricia Hunter's address book, guv,' Dave said mildly.

'Bloody hell, so it was,' I said. 'That email says that Donna was supposed to meet him at his home address. Where is it?'

Dave thumbed through his pocket book. 'Tanley Road, Richmond, guv.' He looked up. 'Mr Mead checked it out. This Lloyd guy said he'd never heard of Patricia Hunter, had no idea how his name had got into her address book, and had a rock-solid alibi for the night of her murder.'

'So he's a liar,' I said.

'I wonder if Edward Archer was also one of Donna's clients,' said Dave. 'His address was in Patricia's little book too.'

But before I had time to comment on that, Dennis gave a shout of triumph. 'This you'll like,' he said. 'I've found a website.' He felt it necessary to explain, which was just as well; I hadn't a clue what he was talking about. 'I switched to the internet and it's been programmed to go straight to this . . .'

The website was an advertisement for prostitutes. And among ten photographs of naked women in provocative poses was one of Donna Lodge. Alongside her picture was the name Fleur and details of her vital statistics.

'Fleur, eh? Looks like her leaves have fallen off,' commented Dave in an aside. 'But a nice little stable of fillies nevertheless.' He looked closer at the screen. 'And guess whose picture is called Kimberley, guv.' He looked up and grinned. 'Judging by this, I'd've said she was more than a thirty-six B-cup.'

I looked at the nude Dave was pointing at. It was Barbara Clark. 'So she did know who Forman was,' I said.

'Bloody tramps,' said Linda, who had joined our little group of professional voyeurs. It was the only time I'd heard her swear.

'How do they make contact, Dennis?' I asked.

'There's an email address, Mr Brock, but I'll put money on it going out to a web-based mail account.'

'Meaning?' I hate all this computer-speak.

'It means that the email address goes out to the guy who makes the arrangements for these girls. He can pick up the messages from any computer in the world, so he could even be in another country. Then he'll relay the message to the chosen girl and off she'll go.' Dennis turned in his chair and gave a lascivious grin.

I was now damned sure that Phillips was on the other end of that email address, and we knew he *was* in the country. However, the website had been kept up to date and there was no photograph of Patricia Hunter, alias Dolores. Assuming, of course, that she had been posted on the website in the first place.

'It could mean that Nick Lloyd was innocent . . .' I began. Dave scoffed. 'Innocent' was not a word he used very much. 'When Mr Mead saw him, he denied all knowledge of Patricia Hunter,' I continued, 'but he might have got some reaction if he'd known, at the time, that her trade name was Dolores, like Donna Lodge calls herself Fleur and Barbara Clark is Kimberley. It was the judge who first told us that the Hunter girl was Dolores.'

Linda Mitchell's team lifted a few fingerprints from various parts of the house, but our cursory search revealed nothing else of interest. The wardrobe was devoid of clothing and there was nothing of a personal nature. It confirmed my original thought: that Donna Lodge had gone for good. But where, I wondered?

And it was me who'd shot himself in the foot by alerting her to our interest in Phillips.

But, in a sense, so had Phillips himself. If he was the man with the email address. And I was sure he was. One thing was certain: he would be furious if he ever found out that Donna Lodge had been stupid enough to abandon the computer with all that valuable information on it. And given what we'd learned about his mercurial temperament, that might well have put her life in danger. It behoved us to find him as soon as possible. But he was proving to be a devious bastard and it wasn't going to be easy.

We took the computer with us. We'd got what we wanted, and the recently departed occupants knew we were interested in them, so it didn't matter if they found out that we'd searched the house. If they ever came back.

I scrounged a piece of Sellotape from Linda and used it to stick a copy of the search warrant to the mirror in the hall. 'That prominent enough for you, Dave?'

'Yes, sir.'

'What sort of place does this Nick Lloyd live in, Frank?' I asked DI Mead when we'd returned to Curtis Green and I'd explained the story so far.

'It's a block of service flats,' said Frank, and after a moment, seeking recall from the ceiling, added, 'Number six, Mayberry Court, Tanley Road, Richmond.'

'Tell me about him.'

'Single guy about thirty-five, give or take. Works in the City, something to do with high finance. Spends all day shuffling huge amounts of money around the world apparently. Drives a Ferrari. Said he'd never heard of Patricia Hunter and was at a party the night of her murder. Not that I mentioned the murder, just talked about a missing person. I checked out his story and there were about fifty witnesses to say he was there. In Chichester.'

'What, a party on a Tuesday?' I said.

'So what?' rejoined Frank. 'They don't give a toss, these guys. They've got so much money that by the time they're forty, they're burned out and retire, poor dears. Beats coppering, that's for sure.'

From what Frank had told me, finding Nick Lloyd at home was going to be a hit-and-miss affair. I tossed a coin and determined that Dave and I would pay him a visit tomorrow evening, Saturday. Well, it was as good a day as any other.

In the meantime, I decided it was time to take Gail Sutton out for a meal. A small return for the meal she had prepared for me. And what had followed.

It was a quiet little restaurant that I hadn't explored before. And it was within walking distance of where both Gail and I lived, which was an advantage. It meant I could have a drink. Contrary to popular opinion, there is nothing the Black Rats – as the traffic police are known – like better than to get a positive breathalyser reading from a CID officer.

'Have you caught him yet?' asked Gail before I'd even had time to study the menu. She seemed more obsessed with the progress of my enquiry than did the commander.

'Not yet,' I said, 'but we're getting closer.' Well, I had to say something. That or appear to be totally incompetent. I was now certain that Geoffrey Forman was Bruce Phillips and was running a team of prostitutes, but whether he'd murdered Patricia Hunter was still something to be resolved. And if he had, why? I decided to float the idea.

'D'you think that Patricia may have been a call-girl, Gail?' I asked, knowing full well that she had been a very active call-girl. I broke my bread roll and reached for the butter rather than make eye contact.

I was expecting either confirmation or outraged denial, but to my surprise Gail's response was measured.

'I suppose it's possible, darling,' she said mildly. 'When showgirls are out of work, they'll turn to anything to make ends meet.' She raised an eyebrow and looked directly at me. 'But if you're thinking what I think you're thinking, forget it. I'm not one of them.' Then she laughed.

160

'The thought never crossed my mind,' I said.

'What makes you think she might have been?' Gail asked, putting down her menu and shooting a captivating smile at a passing waiter.

The waiter was there in an instant. 'Are you ready to order, madam?' he enquired.

'Well, what makes you think she *might* have been a call-girl?' Gail asked again, once the wearisome business of ordering our meal was out of the way. I hate deciding what to eat, and usually go for the same tried and tested dishes.

'Actually, I know she was,' I said, and told her what we'd learned about Patricia Hunter's activities at the Fenwick Road 'health farm for tired businessmen', as the Sussex Vice Squad had described it. 'That and a bit of shoplifting.'

'Shoplifting?' Curiously, that seemed to have shocked Gail more than learning that her friend had been on the game.

'Yes. We think she was part of a professional shoplifting ring some years ago. Run by an Australian called Bruce Phillips.'

'You mentioned him before,' Gail said. 'Didn't you ask me if Patricia had ever talked about him?'

'Yes, I did, and we're still looking for him,' I commented, taking the first bite of a rather good terrine that had arrived in record time. It definitely improves the service if you take a good-looking girl out to dinner. 'He's wanted in Australia for a number of offences.'

'And do you think he might have murdered Patricia?'

'It's a possibility I'm considering,' I said, but decided against telling Gail exactly why I thought so.

'What a damned silly thing for her to have got involved in.'

I wasn't sure whether Gail meant prostitution or shoplifting. 'It happens,' I said.

'She was a good dancer, that girl, and she was young enough to have got on well in the profession. What a waste.'

Yesterday afternoon, Tom Challis had obtained details of Jeremy Payne's home address from the credit-card company. It was in a not very salubrious part of Stockwell. That in itself did not sound like the residence of someone who claimed to have a flat in Docklands and a villa in St Raphaël, and who drove a sports car. Nevertheless Dave and I went there. That's what police work's all about.

The woman who answered the door was clearly in the middle of doing housework. She wore an apron and had a duster in one hand.

'Yes, what is it?'

'We're police officers, madam,' I said. 'Does a Jeremy Payne live here?'

'Yes, but he's not here at the moment. Is it something to do with the van?'

'Oh, he has a van, does he?' I clutched at that passing straw with alacrity.

'Well, he doesn't own it. He drives it for the firm he works for.' As an apparent afterthought, the woman opened the door wide. 'You'd better come in, I suppose.'

We were conducted into a shabby front room. An upright vacuum cleaner stood in the centre of the carpet and we'd obviously interrupted the woman's hoovering.

'Are you Mrs Payne?' I asked.

'Yes. What's this all about, Officer?'

'And Jeremy's your son, is he?'

'Yes. Is he in some sort of trouble?' Mrs Payne looked concerned. 'It's not drugs, is it?'

'No. Tell me, Mrs Payne, does your son go to the theatre much?'

'Oh yes. He loves the theatre. He hopes to become an actor one day. He's very keen on amateur dramatics. As a matter of fact he's in a show tonight. It's called *Kiss Me Kate*.'

This was beginning to sound very promising. First we learn that Jeremy Payne drives a van, and then we find that he's into amateur dramatics. And amateur dramatics means access to greasepaint. I took it a stage further.

'Does Jeremy ever go to France, Mrs Payne?'

'Yes, as a matter of fact he went there last year for a holiday.'

'Whereabouts, d'you know?'

'It was in the south somewhere.' But then the protective mother came to life. 'Look, d'you mind telling me what this is all about?'

'We think he may be able to assist us,' I said smoothly. 'We believe he may have witnessed an incident that we're investigating. At the Granville Theatre.'

A sudden look of fear crossed the woman's face. 'Does that mean he'll have to go to court? I wouldn't like that. You know what happens to people who give evidence against criminals. They usually end up getting petrol poured through their letterbox.'

So much for the commissioner's claim that public confidence in the police had improved.

'Oh, I shouldn't think so, not for one moment,' I said. *Unless I charge him with Patricia Hunter's murder, that is.* 'Have you any idea when he'll be home, Mrs Payne?'

'Not until late tonight. He's working this morning and then he'll go straight to the hall where they're doing the musical. He helps to set things up, you see.'

Armed with the address of the venue for the latest amateur production of *Kiss Me Kate*, Dave and I arrived there at about three o'clock.

'I'm looking for Jeremy Payne,' I said to a passing 'actress'.

'So am I, darling,' said this vision. 'He should've been here an hour ago. It's too bad. People say they're coming here to help and then they don't turn up.'

'Does that often happen?' asked Dave.

'Not with him,' said the girl thoughtfully. 'Come to think of it, he's always here.'

'Does he have a mobile phone?' Dave asked.

The girl looked at Dave as though he'd just emerged from the Ark. 'Doesn't everyone, darling?' she asked, and wandered off shouting for someone called Damien.

'We've done it again, Dave,' I said. 'I'll put money on his mother having alerted him.'

'He'll come, guv,' said Dave, more in hope than in certainty.

All of a sudden, Jeremy Payne had come to the head of the queue of Patricia Hunter's possible murderers.

Despite my initial doubts, Nick Lloyd was at home on the Saturday evening, which was a bonus. But it was some time

163

before he answered the door. When he did so, he was attired in a shirt, unbuttoned at the cuffs, and a pair of jeans. And he was barefooted and his hair was ruffled.

'Yes?' There was something insufferably superior about the way the City trader uttered that single word.

'We're police officers, Mr Lloyd. We'd like a word.'

'Well, I'm afraid it's not convenient right now. I'm entertaining.' Lloyd cast a scathing glance at Dave and began to close the door.

'We can do it here or at Richmond police station,' I said, gently pushing the door open again. 'Please yourself.' Although it is not an offence to engage the services of a prostitute in the confines of one's own home, it is certainly a crime to murder her. Anywhere. That Patricia Hunter had recorded Lloyd's name and address, coupled with the fact that he had booked Donna Lodge for an 'all-nighter' was good enough for me to regard him as a suspect.

'What the hell are you talking about?' demanded Lloyd, his original hostility beginning to wane quite sharply. He opened the door wide and stepped back. 'If it's about the Ferrari, I've sold it,' he said. 'I'm sick and tired of getting pulled by you people simply because I've got an expensive car. It's just bloody envy, I suppose.'

Lloyd led us into a sitting room that was furnished in somewhat bizarre taste, but nonetheless one in which no expense had been spared. He closed the door and turned to us with an expression of intolerance on his face. 'Well, what's this all about?' he demanded. 'And it'd better be good because my next phone call will be to my solicitor.'

'Why? Have you done something wrong?' asked Dave with a masterful portrayal of innocence on his face.

'No, it'll be to initiate a complaint of police harassment,' snapped Lloyd. 'This is the second time I've had you people here asking intrusive questions about my private life.'

'And it may not be the last,' said Dave mildly, 'unless you give us the answers we are looking for.'

We sat down uninvited.

'Patricia Hunter,' I said.

Lloyd had remained standing, presumably to give himself

some ascendancy over us mere policemen. 'I told that other copper that I know nothing about any Patricia Hunter. I've never heard of the damned woman. So perhaps you'd better begin by telling me what the hell it is you want.'

'I don't know if the other officer explained our interest—'

'He said she was missing and mentioned something about my name and address being found in some book of hers,' said Lloyd before I was able to go any further. 'Well, I know damn-all about it. Or her.'

'The reason for our interest,' I continued, 'is that Patricia Hunter was murdered.'

'Christ, he never told me that,' said Lloyd, and at last sat down opposite us. He paused for a moment or two and then added, 'Well, it's nothing to do with me. I don't know the damned woman.'

'Did Fleur turn up last Tuesday?' enquired Dave.

'Fleur? What Fleur?' Lloyd posed the question in an offhand way, but it had obviously struck home.

'The Fleur you ordered off the Internet. She's a prostitute, and quite an expensive one I should think.' Dave was beginning to enjoy himself.

'Now look here—'

'Before we go any further,' I said, 'have a look at this.' I handed him a photograph of Patricia Hunter. 'And be very careful what you say, Mr Lloyd, because, as I told you, I'm investigating this girl's murder.'

'Oh God!' Lloyd stared at the print of the dead showgirl as if mesmerized. 'It's Dolores.'

'Tell me about her,' I said.

Lloyd returned the photograph. 'I saw her a couple of times.'

'Let's not pussyfoot about, Mr Lloyd,' said Dave. 'She's a prostitute and you engaged her services via the Internet. And at the beginning of the week you also put in a request for Fleur on the same Internet site.'

'There's nothing wrong in that.' Lloyd spoke sharply. 'What I do with my money is my business.'

'But when the woman Dolores is murdered, Mr Lloyd, it becomes my business,' I said.

'Good God Almighty, I didn't kill her,' said Lloyd. There

165

was desperation in his voice now, probably at the thought that we might not believe him.

'Convince me.'

'It's true. I did arrange for her to come here on two occasions and—'

'When?'

'I'll need to look in my diary.' Lloyd reached across to a leather jacket that was draped over the back of his armchair and withdrew a small leather-bound book. He thumbed through it until he found the appropriate page. 'She came here on the first of June and again on the eighth.'

'What time did she get here?' Dave asked.

Lloyd looked a little puzzled by the question. 'It was about midnight, I suppose.'

'Is that the time you asked her to come?'

'No, as a matter of fact, I'd rather have seen her earlier, but I assumed she had another appointment. Why?'

'No reason,' said Dave. But it was likely that her late arrival was because she'd only just left the theatre. Busy girl, combining business with business.

'Was there any reason why you didn't order her again?' persisted Dave.

'I like a change.' There was a return of Lloyd's superior attitude with that statement.

'So you decided to screw Fleur instead. Had her before, had you?'

I could see that Lloyd was not much impressed by Dave's earthiness. I suppose he didn't like to have what he thought of as an adventure, or even a romantic tryst, reduced to the sort of basic language that Dave occasionally revelled in.

'Yes, twice. Now look, I'm getting fed up with this. I told that other copper that I was at a party in Chichester on the date he mentioned, and there were dozens of people who saw me there. But I didn't know this girl had been murdered.'

'You didn't see her picture in the paper?' I asked.

'There was nothing about it in the *Financial Times*,' said Lloyd scathingly.

'And did Dolores spend all night with you on those two occasions?' I asked, ignoring his attempt at lofty disdain.

'Yes, she did. So what?'

'Tell me how this Internet thing works,' said Dave. 'What is it, whore-dot-com, or something like that?' He was playing with Lloyd now; we'd got the Internet address from the computer at Barnes.

Lloyd fell back against the cushions of his armchair, visibly deflated. 'There's an email address on the website,' he said quietly. 'You send a message to it asking for the services of one of the girls whose pictures are on the website. You pay by credit card and she turns up. You can either hire her by the hour, or opt for an all-night session.'

'Must cost a packet,' commented Dave.

'So what,' said Lloyd defiantly. 'It's what I flog my guts out for. So I can enjoy myself. And it's not illegal.'

'Not for you, it's not,' said Dave, 'but it is for the guy who runs it. And very shortly we'll be arresting him. You say you paid by credit card . . .'

'Yes, I did.'

'D'you have your credit-card statement?'

'Yes, why?'

'Would you tell me the name of the account to which your payment went?'

Lloyd knew the answer without referring to his statement. 'It was Grind, Isle of Man.'

'Hilarious,' said Dave, and laughed. But the reality behind the irony was that we both knew tracking down a credit-card account based in the Isle of Man was fraught with difficulties. And that meant that any chance of finding the names of other clients was almost certainly stillborn.

Our conversation was interrupted by the door to the sitting room crashing back against the wall. 'If you want to turn this into an all-night screw, ducky, it'll cost you a monkey more than you've paid already,' said a raucous cockney voice. 'Up front.'

All three of us turned.

On the threshold of the room stood a girl wrapped in what I presumed was one of Lloyd's shirts. And nothing else. Her long blonde hair tumbled around her shoulders and she stood, one leg in front of the other, with her hands on her hips, her breasts thrust forward so that her pert nipples showed through the thin material. She didn't seem at all alarmed at seeing Dave and me, and I imagined that, with the innate perspicacity of her trade, she knew that we were Old Bill. And couldn't have cared less. Her coarseness was certainly a marked change from Donna Lodge's sophistication, but perhaps Lloyd liked a bit of rough for a change.

Dave withdrew the printout of Forman's website from his pocket, studied it briefly and then glanced at the girl in the doorway. 'You must be Domino,' he said.

'So what, darling?' Domino pouted at Dave.

'We may have to speak to you again, Mr Lloyd,' I said, as Dave and I stood up to leave.

'I hope the Skoda runs better than your Ferrari,' said Dave.

'*Skoda*?' screeched Domino as we reached the front door. 'You never said you drove a bleedin' Skoda.' Perhaps she thought that his performance would be similarly diminished. Despite what they may say, even prostitutes prefer a good performer.

'What d'you think, guv?' asked Dave as we drove away from Mayberry Court.

'I think we wasted our time, Dave.'

'Yeah, but it was good fun, wasn't it?'

'But it's about to get better,' I said. 'I get the distinct impression that Domino's not going to be there that long. I think we'll hang about and have a chat with her when she emerges.'

Dave reversed back to the space where we'd parked originally and switched off the engine.

Fifteen

It was about half an hour later that Domino emerged from Nick Lloyd's flat. She was dressed in tight-fitting black leather trousers, and a black, sleeveless, high-necked, crop-top. A leather bag was slung across one shoulder.

And she didn't look happy.

Whether it was Dave's throwaway suggestion that Lloyd now drove a Skoda, or whether Lloyd had been so disconcerted by our visit that he had gone off the idea of forking out an extra five hundred pounds for an 'all-nighter' didn't really matter.

Dave crossed the pavement and confronted her.

'My guv'nor would like a word with you, Domino. Why don't you step into our office?' he said, opening the rear door of the car.

'What the hell's this all about?' Domino's response was truculent, but she got in.

'Bruce Phillips,' I said, once the girl had settled herself in the centre of the back seat.

'I don't know no Bruce Phillips,' said Domino.

'Really? He's the guy who fixes up your appointments and then pays you. Having taken a hefty whack for himself, of course. In other words he's your pimp.'

'No he ain't.'

'Well, who is, then?'

Domino looked from me to Dave and back again. 'Dunno what you're talking about,' she said.

'When did you last see Patricia Hunter?' asked Dave.

'Never heard of her.'

169

Dave showed her the photograph.

'That's Dolores,' said Domino without hesitation.

'And did she work for Phillips too?' I asked.

'I told you, I never heard of him.'

'I don't think you realize just how serious this is, Domino,' I said. 'Patricia Hunter – Dolores – has been murdered. The police fished her body out of the river over three weeks ago.'

'Christ!' said Domino. 'I never knew that.'

'It was in all the papers.'

'Don't never read 'em, do I?'

'Not even the *Financial Times*?' asked Dave impishly.

'Do what?'

'Did you ever meet Dolores?' I asked.

'Nah, course not. We all work alone, see. Because—' Domino stopped suddenly, presumably realizing that she was about to compromise the pimp she worked for.

'Because your pimp keeps you all separate in the vain hope that he won't get done for living on immoral earnings. Is that it?'

'Yeah, summat like that,' mumbled Domino.

'Have you got another job, Domino?' asked Dave.

The girl gave Dave an arch look. 'Do a bit of temping,' she said.

Dave laughed. 'Yeah, I can see that,' he said, 'but have you got another job?'

'In an office, dimbo,' said Domino cheekily.

It was a good question. Dave was obviously thinking that if all Phillips's girls had another job, he could claim that he wasn't living on their immoral earnings. That could explain why Patricia Hunter was working as a chorus girl. But such elaborate precautions wouldn't wash with a judge.

'Who is your pimp, then?' I repeated.

'You must be bloody joking, mister.' In common with most prostitutes, Domino was reluctant to reveal the name of her 'minder', especially to the police. Such treachery could have unpleasant results. Even fatal ones.

'You might be next,' said Dave mildly, as if reading the young tom's thoughts.

'You don't mean . . . ?' For a few seconds, Domino reflected on the implication of Dave's comment. ''Ere, this ain't going no further, is it?' she asked, leaning forward, a hopeful expression on her face.

'Your secret's safe with me,' I lied.

'Forman. Geoffrey Forman,' said the girl.

'And how does the system work, Domino? Incidentally, I'm not going to keep calling you Domino. What's your real name?'

There was a further hesitation before Domino replied. 'Marlene West,' she said eventually.

'So, how does it work, Marlene?'

'Geoff's got a website and we advertise on it. Any john what wants a good screw orders one of us by sending Geoff an email. We've all got laptops or mobiles and Geoff sends us an email or a text message telling us where to go and when.'

'And how does he pay you?' asked Dave, although we both knew the answer to that. Or thought we did.

'We meet him in the Kookaburra Club and he gives us our money. I have to go there at five o'clock Tuesday evenings. If I miss the five o'clock slot on a Tuesday, I have to wait another week. He's very particular about that.'

'I'll bet he is,' I said. 'And where does this Geoffrey Forman live?'

'Haven't a clue, darling,' said Domino, giving me a cheeky smile.

'And where do you live, Marlene?' Dave asked.

'What d'you want to know that for?'

'In case you get a visit,' Dave said ominously.

Marlene misunderstood Dave, as he had meant her to. She thought he was concerned with her safety, whereas he was hoping Phillips might turn up there one day. It was a forlorn hope, but we had to try everything in the book if we were going to amass enough evidence to convict this elusive Australian of murder. Assuming he had committed the murder, that is. However, I was not losing sight of the fact that our recent enquiries had also put Jeremy Payne firmly in the frame.

And so Payne's name had been added to the police national computer along with the others in whom we were interested.

Marlene gave us her address but, I suspect, not without

171

some misgivings, misgivings confirmed by her final utterance.

'You ain't never seen me. Right, copper?'

'Doesn't look like we're any further forward, guv,' said Dave as Marlene West alias Domino sashayed off into the night.

Linda Mitchell's report on the fingerprints found at Barnes was on my desk on Monday morning. Fortunately, the Australian police had included a set of Phillips's dabs in their request for his extradition. And they tallied with one of the sets found at 13 Ridgely Road. The other prints, unsurprisingly, were those of Donna Lodge. But that's all there was: just two sets of prints.

'Either Phillips *is* Forman, or Donna Lodge has some explaining to do as to why we found Phillips's prints at Barnes,' I said to Dave.

'It's got to be him,' said Dave. 'We know they were shacked up together at Petersfield Street. At least, Don Lacey was sure they had been when he went chasing Phillips with an extradition warrant.'

But further debate was cut short by the arrival of Kate Ebdon.

'G'day, guv,' she said brightly. 'He was there.'

'Who was where?'

'Phillips. I spent the evening in the K Club and he turned up at about half nine.'

'Did you get to talk to him, Kate?'

'Sure. He bought me a drink and we got chatting.'

'Did he say anything interesting though?' I asked.

'Not really, no. We talked about Down Under and the places we both knew in Sydney. But I'd only been chatting to him for about half an hour when he offered me a job.'

'What sort of job?' I asked, a smile on my face.

'He said it was a position – he emphasized the word "position" – where a good-looking sheila like me could make a lot of money.' Kate smirked at the recollection.

'What did you say to that?' I asked.

'I told him to go screw himself. But he just laughed. Anyway, when I got around to asking him what he did for a living, he clammed up. There was one interesting thing though: about ten o'clock some girl turned up and sat at the bar. Phillips walked across and gave her an envelope. She finished her drink and pissed off. Neither of them said a word.'

'Did you ask him about it?'

'Too right. He said it was his ex and he was paying her alimony. Well, that was obviously a load of bullshit, but I didn't press it.'

'What did she look like, this girl?' I asked.

'Why don't we get Kate to have a look at the website, guv?' said Dave.

'Good idea,' I said, and the three of us adjourned to the incident room, where Colin Wilberforce had set up the computer we'd seized from Barnes.

'That's her,' said Kate, pointing to a dark-haired girl whose 'stage name' was listed as Petal. 'Ah! She was there too,' she added, pointing to the photograph of Fleur. 'Funny that, though. She came in, saw Phillips talking to me and buggered off a bit smartish.'

'That,' I said, 'is Donna Lodge.' I explained about the raid on the Barnes house. 'And that's where we got this computer.'

'Looks as though Donna had to go without her fee on Saturday, guv,' said Dave. 'But in view of what Domino said about sticking to a day and time, I reckon Donna must be more important than just one of his girls. I reckon she's his second-in-command, and meets him whenever she feels like it.'

'I think I've made a decision, Dave,' I said.

'Blimey, sir, be careful.'

'I think it's time we nicked Donna Lodge and found out what she's got to say for herself.'

'When do we do that?'

'*We* don't, Dave. I'm not going to dignify a tom with being arrested by a detective chief inspector. I'll let Appleby do it. Get him in if he's there.'

'What d'you want me to do, guv?' asked Kate.

'Carry on as usual. I'll be interested in Phillips's reaction to one of his star players getting knocked off. If he mentions it.'

'Sir?' Appleby appeared in the office doorway.

'Come in, John. I've got a job for you and Sheila Armitage.'

'Yes, sir?'

'I want Donna Lodge arrested. But don't do it in the K Club. Wait until she leaves and nick her in the street.'

'Yes, sir.' Appleby grinned, presumably at the thought he was about to do something positive.

It was at eight o'clock that evening when the call came in.

'I've got John Appleby on the line, sir,' said Gavin Creasey, the night-duty incident-room sergeant. 'He's arrested Donna Lodge.'

'Where's he taken her?'

'West End Central nick, sir.'

'Put him through.' I grabbed the phone. 'Well done, John. DS Poole and I will be there shortly. What was her reaction?'

There was a pause while, I imagined, Appleby selected the right words to describe Donna's response. 'Well, sir, after a few profanities on her part, she seemed to be somewhat put out.'

I laughed. 'That sounds about right,' I said. 'Did she, by any chance, meet Phillips in the club?'

'Yes, sir. It was the usual routine except that Donna Lodge was there first this evening. She was sitting at the bar, as usual, when Phillips came in, and handed her an envelope. She left straight away, and we arrested her outside.'

'What did Phillips do . . . after he'd paid her?'

'Went and sat down at DS Ebdon's table, sir.'

It was an entirely different Donna Lodge from the one we'd interviewed at Barnes. Immaculately dressed in a black, two-piece suit with a white jabot, black tights and spike heels, she was reclining in a chair in the interview room, smoking a cigarette, despite the no smoking sign. But we had more important things to discuss than that.

'What the hell is this all about?' she demanded when Dave and I entered the room. 'I want a lawyer.'

'Where's Bruce Phillips living, Ms Lodge?' I asked, by way of an opener.

'I don't know how many times I have to say this, but I don't know anyone called Bruce Phillips.'

174

'Really?' I made a pretence of riffling through the file I'd brought with me. 'Apart from paying your shoplifting fine, you've met him several times in the Kookaburra Club. This evening included. And when you were brought to this station and searched, you were found to have an envelope containing a thousand pounds. An envelope that Phillips had handed you only minutes before you were arrested.'

'What have you got in *your* wallet?' Donna asked sarcastically. 'Have I been arrested for possessing a thousand pounds?'

'Why did Phillips give you that money?'

'I keep telling you that I don't know a Phillips. The man who gave me that money was Geoffrey Forman. As I told you when you came to Barnes, he's my partner and, strange though it may seem, he gives me housekeeping from time to time.'

I couldn't help laughing. 'Good try,' I said. 'So you meet up in the Kookaburra Club so that he can hand you your housekeeping money? Funny that. Most people give their partners the housekeeping money at home.' What she didn't realize, or perhaps didn't care about, was that she had just confirmed that Forman *was* Phillips. 'When did he get back from Düsseldorf then?' I asked.

But Donna greeted that question with stony silence.

'We searched your house at Barnes, Ms Lodge,' said Dave, 'after you'd done a runner, and we found a computer on which was a website advertising the services of prostitutes. On that website was a rather revealing photograph of you, beside which was the name Fleur and some numbers: thirty-eight, twenty-six, thirty-six, if I remember correctly. The website also gave an email address through which clients could obtain your undivided attention for as long as they were prepared to pay for it.'

Donna said nothing, but was obviously shaken by what we knew and, probably, the sudden realization that she'd been foolish enough to leave the computer behind when she fled. And, no doubt, she was wondering what Phillips would say when he found out.

'By the way,' Dave continued, 'Nick Lloyd is not best pleased with you. He sent an email asking for you to turn a trick for him last Tuesday night.'

'I don't know what you're talking about,' said Donna, 'and I want to phone a friend.'

'Why?' I asked.

'To tell him I've been arrested, of course.'

'Have you got a mobile?'

'Of course I have, but that sergeant at the desk took it off me when I was brought in here.'

'Get the lady a phone, Dave,' I said.

A couple of minutes later, Dave returned with a phone and plugged it into a socket. 'There you are,' he said. 'Dial nine for an outside line.'

'I'm entitled to make the call in private,' snapped Donna.

'No you're not,' said Dave. 'That only applies to a discussion with your legal representative.'

Donna shot Dave a scathing glance and tapped out a number. 'Hello, it's me. I've been arrested . . . West End Central . . . I don't know why . . . Yes, all right.' She replaced the receiver and sat back in her chair, a smug expression on her face, before lighting another cigarette. 'And don't bother trying to trace it,' she said. 'It was to a pay-as-you-go mobile. And now perhaps you'll tell me what you're going to charge me with. It certainly won't be prostitution, because I don't solicit in a public place.'

'You should have become a lawyer,' Dave observed mildly.

'Which reminds me,' said Donna. 'I asked for a solicitor.'

'You won't be needing one,' I said. 'You're not being charged with anything. You're free to go.'

Donna sat bolt upright. 'Then what the bloody hell did you bring me in here for?' she demanded with a flash of temper that had not been apparent before.

'On suspicion of harbouring a fleeing felon,' said Dave, conjuring up an impressive bit of legalistic jargon that was more eloquent than accurate.

'Oh? And who might that be?' asked Donna and laughed.

It was time to bring this mouthy tom down to earth. And time to play the next hand.

'We are looking for Bruce Phillips in connection with the

murder of Patricia Hunter, whose body was found in the Thames on Wednesday the twelfth of June,' I said.

I could see that Donna Lodge had paled, even beneath her make-up. There was a moment's hesitation before she recovered herself. 'I've not heard of either of them,' she said, but there was little conviction in her protestation of ignorance.

'That's all right then,' I said. 'Because anyone withholding information about Bruce Phillips is likely to find themselves standing beside him in the dock at the Old Bailey.' Not that I thought there was much chance of that.

The moment Donna Lodge had left the police station, I rang Kate Ebdon's mobile, but the result was disappointing.

'He left about twenty minutes ago, guv,' she said.

'So he didn't get a call on his mobile *before* he left.'

'No, guv.'

And so we were no further forward. My elaborate plan to arrest Donna, despite there being nothing with which to charge her, had come to nought.

But I still had Plan B up my sleeve. I'd arranged for her to be followed, the moment she left the nick, by some of the officers whom Alan Cleaver, the commander's deputy, had lent me. I reckoned that my last statement would have thrown Donna into a panic, and that she wouldn't be able to resist telling Phillips, as soon as possible, what we had wanted from her.

But as it turned out, I was wrong about that too.

Dennis, the CSE who was a dab hand at computers, was unable to offer any further assistance either. His report confirmed what he had said last Friday at Barnes: the email address on the website could be picked up anywhere in the world. I rang him and asked him to explain what Donna had said about a pay-as-you-go mobile phone being untraceable.

'She was quite right, Mr Brock. Any one of the shops that specializes in mobile phones will sell you a pay-as-you-go phone. They'll allocate you a number and away you go. You top it up, so to speak, by purchasing talk time from just about anywhere. Even supermarkets, these days.'

'I get the impression, Dennis, that you're telling me that I'll have a hard job tracing this guy.'

'I reckon so, Mr Brock. For a start you don't know where he might have bought it, so you can't find out the number, and even if you were lucky to get the number, the guy might have bought it second-hand anyway. It's virtually impossible to trace it. Even if you'd done a one-four-seven-one after Donna Lodge had finished her call from the nick, you'd only have got a number, but trying to track down who owns it . . .' Dennis gave an expressive shrug. 'Well, forget it.'

'Thanks, Dennis,' I said, trying to keep the disappointment out of my voice.

'No joy, guv?' asked Dave.

'No. This bugger's too clever by half, Dave.'

'I think we'd more or less come to that conclusion,' said Dave.

The mistake I'd made – one of many I'd made in this damned enquiry – was to assume that Donna Lodge would leave the police station and get a taxi to wherever it was that she was living now. But she didn't. She walked back to the Kookaburra Club, went past it and got into her own car. And the cab that the surveillance officers had managed to hire was no match for the Alfa Romeo. That one of the following officers had evidence of at least three counts of reckless driving and one of ignoring a red traffic light, before they lost her completely, did little to help. Oh well!

'I think we'll do the Barnes address again, Dave,' I said, more out of desperation than anything constructive.

'I doubt that Phillips will have gone back there, guv,' said Dave.

'So do I, Dave, but when we found the computer, we thought we'd got all the answers. I'm not sure that we searched thoroughly enough.'

'We could bugger him up completely, guv,' said Dave, peeling yet another banana.

'In what way?'

'How about ordering up Phillips's entire collection of birds for the same night in different parts of London and then knock 'em off.'

'What for? They're not committing any offence. Do it if you like, but you can use your credit card. Sure as hell I'm not using mine.'

'Ah,' said Dave, 'I never thought of that.' He seemed as gloomy as me about the whole business.

'It's not a bad idea, even so, Dave. We might try calling up say, Petal, and seeing if she can shed any light on Phillips's whereabouts.' However, it didn't take long for me to abandon that brainwave. 'On second thoughts it'd probably make the commander's eyes water if I claimed that on expenses. And I doubt that Petal would say any more than Kimberley, Domino or Fleur. I think we'll scrub it.'

On Tuesday morning, we returned to 13 Ridgely Road with another warrant, and Linda and a couple of her CSEs. Our last warrant was still stuck to the hall mirror, from which, detective that I am, I deduced that no one had returned since last we were there.

'What are we looking for, guv?' asked Dave.

'Everything and anything,' I said. 'But in unlikely places. The sort of places we didn't look in before.'

It took an hour. And then Linda appeared flourishing a piece of paper.

'Donald thinks he's found something that might be useful, Mr Brock,' she said, handing me the slip. 'It was tucked in behind a tea caddy in one of the kitchen cabinets.'

'What is it?'

'It's a request for information from the local council.'

I studied the drab official form. It noted that Geoffrey Forman had rented a lock-up garage at the rear of a block of flats in Breda Gardens, Barnes. It went on to ask whether Forman was responsible for paying council tax on the premises, or if this liability would fall upon the owner of the said garage.

'Where the hell's Breda Gardens?' I asked of no one in particular.

'No idea,' said Dave. And neither had anyone else.

'Well someone find out for God's sake,' I said, somewhat brusquely.

Dave rang the local nick on his mobile. 'Just round the corner from here, guv,' he said, cancelling the call.

The council form had specified that the owner of the lock-up garage was a Mr Thomas of 6 Delilah Court. We promptly visited 6 Delilah Court. But Mr Thomas appeared not to be there. Well, he wouldn't be, would he? But his wife was.

'Oh yes,' she said. 'My husband rented that to Mr Forman about two months ago.'

I was ill-disposed to explain specifically why the garage was of interest to us, but told Mrs Thomas that, in pursuance of a serious criminal matter, we would be obliged to look inside it.

Mrs Thomas demurred at that. 'Well, I don't know,' she said. 'You see, Mr Forman – he's a very nice man incidentally – wanted it to keep furniture in. And as we've got another garage, we were quite happy to let him have it.'

'I can get a search warrant, Mrs Thomas,' I explained, 'but it would make my job much easier if we were able just to have a quick look in there.'

'Oh well, I suppose it'll be all right.' And with that somewhat grudging authority, Mrs Thomas closed the door.

'Don't know why we bothered,' muttered Dave.

Donald, the CSE who'd found the form, removed the padlock in a trice. There was none of Geoffrey Forman's furniture inside the garage, but there was what proved to be an extremely telling piece of evidence: a Ford van.

And that was only the start.

'I think you'd better get the rest of your team up here, Linda,' I said.

But Linda Mitchell was already busy on her mobile.

180

Sixteen

The garage was fitted with shelving on which were a few half-empty paint pots and an old golf club. Three or four lengths of curtain rail had been abandoned in a corner at the far end, next to a dartboard with a single dart in it, and a piece of carpet. Slung from the rafters was a twelve-foot length of blueish fibreglass that I presumed was a boat mast. All of which, I imagined, was a legacy from Mr Thomas. With the exception, I hoped, of the carpet.

After a cursory inspection of the Ford van, Linda suggested that it should be removed to the forensic science laboratory for a detailed examination.

Dave, in the meantime, had been busy on his mobile. 'The van's registered to a Robert Peel of thirteen Ridgely Road, Barnes, guv.'

'The saucy bastard's taking the piss,' I said. Robert Peel was the founder of the Metropolitan Police. But it did explain why, when checks had been made with the DVLA, they told us that the only vehicle registered to Geoffrey Forman was a BMW.

After several further calls, Dave managed to impose upon the Transport Branch – which is probably called something else now, courtesy of the Funny Names Squad – to send a flatbed truck to collect the Ford. But not before he'd thrown in the commander's name to emphasize the urgency. Transport Branch obviously hadn't met the commander, otherwise it would have had no effect. But it appeared to work in this case.

An hour later, the truck arrived. The crew alighted, sucked through its collective teeth, muttered something about Health and Safety, and was finally imposed upon to winch the Ford van on to its vehicle.

The removal of the van revealed the existence of an inspection pit. But this was no ordinary inspection pit. Once the cover had been removed, we were treated to the sight of a steel safe against the wall at one end of the pit. It was fitted with both key and combination locks, and alongside it was a coil of thin electrical flex.

'Well now, ain't that interesting,' said Dave, and, turning to Linda, he asked, 'Reckon your blokes can banjo that peter?' It was one of his rare excursions into the criminal vernacular. For banjo read 'break into', and for peter read 'safe'.

'I hope so,' said Linda, and jumped into the inspection pit for a closer look at the safe.

'There's only one problem,' I said. 'We don't know that it's Forman's safe. It might belong to Mr Thomas.'

'Ah, good point, guv,' said Dave.

'Which means,' I continued, 'that we'll have to get hold of the said Mr Thomas before we can go any further.'

Leaving the CSEs to guard our find, Dave and I returned to 6 Delilah Court and spoke, once more, to Mrs Thomas.

'We have searched the garage your husband rented to Mr Forman,' I began, 'and we found a safe in the inspection pit.'

'Really?' Mrs Thomas did not seem too excited about this. Certainly not as excited as we were.

'Do you know if it belongs to your husband?'

'No.'

'No, it doesn't, or no, you don't know?'

'I don't know,' said Mrs Thomas, and then, caution dawning at last, she asked, 'Anyway, how do I know you're policemen?'

And to think of all the money the police waste on crime prevention and the equally useless Neighbourhood Watch scheme. I showed her my warrant card but, as she'd probably never seen one before, it didn't count for much. Nevertheless, she seemed satisfied.

'Can you tell me how we can get hold of your husband, Mrs Thomas?' I asked with great patience. 'It is rather urgent.'

'He's upstairs. He works from home.'

Dave glanced skywards, but otherwise restrained himself from making one of his usual acerbic comments.

'Perhaps we could have a word with him,' I said, still exercising great patience.

Mrs Thomas pondered the request. 'I'll see if he's available,' she said, after due consideration. 'He doesn't care to be interrupted when he's working.'

'Maybe if you were to tell him we're investigating a murder, he could spare us a moment or two,' I said, at last deciding that there was no reason to keep the purpose of our enquiries a secret any longer.

'Oh my goodness!' said Mrs Thomas and disappeared, leaving us standing on the doorstep.

Mr Thomas was a small, bald-headed man with unfashionable glasses and a toothbrush moustache.

'Can I help you?' he asked in the nasal manner one expects of a shop assistant in a gents' outfitters, but rarely finds these days.

'We have reason to believe that Mr Forman may be able to assist us in connection with a murder,' I said. There was little point in disguising our interest in the errant Mr Forman. In the unlikely event that Thomas told Forman, I now believed he wouldn't be telling him something he didn't already know.

'I see,' said Thomas, displaying no change in either his expression or his tone of voice. 'Perhaps you'd better come in.'

At last!

'We have searched the garage you rented to him,' I continued, once we were in the Thomases' sitting room, a sitting room overburdened with bric-à-brac and what I took to be family photographs in silver frames, including, prominently, one of a young man in cap and gown clutching a scroll, 'and we discovered a safe installed in the inspection pit.'

'Really?' Thomas raised his eyebrows.

'Is it your safe, Mr Thomas?'

'No.'

'Were you aware that it was there?' I asked, struggling on.

'No.'

'So I can safely assume it's Mr Forman's, I suppose.'

183

'Well, I don't know about that,' said Thomas, obviously cautious in assigning ownership of the safe, 'but it's not mine.'

'Thank you, Mr Thomas,' said Dave. 'You've been most helpful.'

We returned to the garage.

'I've had a good look at it, Mr Brock,' said Linda, 'and we're going to have to open it in situ. It seems to be bolted to the floor or the wall, and we'll only be able to get at the bolts once it's open.'

'Can you do it?' I asked.

'Not immediately. I'll have to send for a lance cutter, and that'll take time.'

'How much time?'

'About an hour.'

I glanced at my watch. It was midday. 'We'll send for the cavalry and get some lunch,' I said. 'Ring the local nick, Dave, and get some uniforms round here to mind the place.'

Two PCs eventually arrived and were instructed to stand guard on the garage until we returned.

At one o'clock, following a rushed bite to eat at a local pub, we returned to the garage to find the cutting team waiting for us.

It took them about twenty minutes to remove the door to the safe, but it proved to be well worth the wait.

Inside we found a handbag containing all the usual things that a woman's handbag usually contains: cosmetics, a key, a few tissues and a purse. But it also contained a credit card and a bank card. *And each bore the name of Patricia Hunter.*

'He'll have a job explaining that away,' observed Dave drily. 'I wonder why he hung on to them.'

'There are some murderers who like to keep mementoes, Dave,' I said, 'but God knows why. It usually does for them in the end.'

'So what's next, guv? Round to the Kookaburra Club and knock him off?'

'He won't be there, will he, Dave?' I said.

'There is another thing, guv,' said Dave.

'Which is?'

'Forman might also be Jeremy Payne, and the Robert Peel

in whose name the van is registered may be his employer. His mother said he was a van driver.'

'D'you know, Dave,' I said, 'you have a happy knack of fouling up the simplest of enquiries.'

'Just a thought, sir,' said Dave.

'Yeah, but Payne lives in Stockwell. He's unlikely to park his van here in Barnes.'

'Unless the firm he works for is in Barnes, guv,' said Dave, determined, as ever, to have the last word.

But even if Dave's theory turned out to be correct, I realized, too late, that we'd gone about this enquiry all wrong. It had been a mistake to interview Donna Lodge at Barnes before we'd spoken to Dave's mate on the Extradition Unit, and then to have compounded that error by arresting her in the vain hope that she might point the finger at Forman, alias Phillips, for Patricia Hunter's murder. All we'd actually succeeded in doing was to warn Phillips of our interest.

And on top of everything else, Jeremy Payne appeared to have done a runner.

The trouble with criminal investigation is that you never know these things in advance. Making decisions is very easy with hindsight.

But of one thing I was certain: Phillips would never show his face in the K Club again. But we had to try.

Domino was due to show up at five o'clock that evening to collect her pay. Dave lay in wait with Kate Ebdon, but the coarse cockney whore with the prosaic name of Marlene West didn't appear. Nor did Phillips.

For the next five days, teams of officers kept observation outside the Kookaburra Club. On the inside, DS Kate Ebdon and DCs Appleby and Armitage sat around spending some of the commissioner's money, but achieving nothing else. DC Nicola Chance spoke to Lisa, the hostess who had first alerted us to Phillips's presence, but she claimed not to have seen him since the night Appleby and Armitage had arrested Donna Lodge. And Donna Lodge didn't show up either.

Although I was certain that Phillips was not going to return to the K Club, I decided to let the observation run until first

185

thing on Monday morning. There was little doubt in my mind that he'd changed his centre of operations or, at least, changed the venue he'd used for paying his prostitutes.

But in the meantime, I tried one last throw. Dave and I visited the expensive block of service flats in Islington where Marlene West, alias Domino, had told us she rented an apartment. Perhaps she could be persuaded to tell us what the new payment arrangements were.

But according to a neighbour, Miss West had left at nine o'clock on Sunday morning. *Twelve hours after we'd talked to her outside Nick Lloyd's apartment.* The helpful neighbour further volunteered the information that a man had arrived to help Miss West shift her belongings.

'You didn't happen to notice the number of the car, I suppose?' I asked hopefully. 'Or the make?'

'It was a blue one.'

We didn't bother to ask for a description: we knew bloody well who it would have been. Bruce Phillips was turning out to be a master of damage limitation. And it seemed that he frightened Domino more than we did.

No sooner had we returned to Curtis Green from Islington than we were off again.

'I've just had a call from Brixton nick, sir,' said Colin Wilberforce. 'About ten minutes ago a Mrs Payne walked in with her son Jeremy. According to the station officer, she practically had him in a hammerlock-and-bar.'

Mrs Payne and her son, guarded by a uniformed constable, a rare sight indeed, were in an interview room at Brixton police station.

'I've brought him here because you want to talk to him,' said Mrs Payne. 'He only came home this morning. I don't know where he'd been, and I suppose it was my fault telephoning him to tell him that you'd called at the house. But I told him it's no good running away from the police because they'll always find you.'

Oh, such faith.

'Thank you, Mrs Payne,' I said. 'I'll interview him on his own, if you don't mind.'

'But—'

'How old is your son, Mrs Payne?'

'He'll be twenty-six next birthday.'

'In that case the law does not require the attendance of an adult.' I turned to the PC. 'Perhaps you'd take Mrs Payne for a cup of tea,' I said.

Jeremy Payne was a good-looking lad in a weak sort of way, and I could quite understand why he had aspirations for the acting profession. Doubtless his friends had told him that, with his looks, he ought to 'go on the stage'. *Oh well!*

'I know what this is about,' said Payne before I had a chance to say anything. 'It's about Patricia Hunter, isn't it? I saw in the paper that she'd been murdered.'

'Yes, it is. So why did you run away?'

'I thought you must have known what I'd done.'

Heavens above, it can't be this easy.

I toyed with the idea of cautioning this young man, but decided that if he had murdered Patricia Hunter, he would undoubtedly repeat his confession if, later, I *did* caution him. In the coppering game, one develops an instinct for assessing character.

'So what *did* you do?'

'I told her I wanted to marry her.'

'And did you want to marry her?'

'I wouldn't have minded, but I knew she wouldn't want to marry a van driver from Stockwell, so I pretended I was something else.'

'Such as?'

'I told her I had a swish flat in Docklands and a place in the South of France.'

'Where in the South of France?' asked Dave.

There was a moment's hesitation. 'St Raphaël. I knew the place, see, because I went there for a holiday last year. It was only a package holiday, but it meant I could sound quite knowledgeable.' Payne's accent had become more sophisticated during the telling of this tale, and I could understand that he was probably quite good as an amateur thespian. It certainly appeared that he'd fooled Patricia Hunter with his acting.

'And you told her you had a Ferrari, too,' commented Dave.

'No, a Porsche,' said Payne, as though the technical details of his lie were important. 'But I haven't.'

'Where were you between the tenth and twelfth of June, Mr Payne?'

Jeremy consulted a small diary. 'On stage,' he said, somewhat loftily.

'What, all day?'

'No, of course not. I was working during the day and went straight from there to the hall where we were doing *Cabaret*.'

'Bit ambitious for an amateur company, wasn't it?' suggested Dave.

'We're really very good,' said Jeremy, preening himself slightly, 'even if I do say so myself.'

'Is there anyone who can verify that?'

'Well, I was delivering all day. I work for an electrical wholesaler. You can ask my boss. And as far as the evenings are concerned, you could check with Lorraine.'

'Lorraine who?' Dave took out his pen and opened his pocket book.

'Can't remember. Martin, I think, but she played Sally Bowles. She's very good. I played Emcee.'

'And after the show, you took her to bed, did you?' asked Dave, making a shrewd guess.

Payne blushed. 'How did you know that?' he demanded.

'I guessed,' said Dave. 'What tales did you tell *her*?'

'Well, I er—'

'Don't bother,' said Dave with a grin. 'And what's more, the only reason you spun this fanny to Patricia Hunter was so that you could get her into bed, wasn't it? You knew bloody well that you couldn't keep up the pretence, because once she found out the truth she'd've been off like a long dog.'

'You can go, Mr Payne, once we've taken your fingerprints,' I said, 'and I advise you not to tell stories of that sort to any more prostitutes, because their minders have a reputation for turning nasty with people who bullshit in order to get a freebie.'

'She wasn't a prostitute,' exclaimed Payne angrily, 'she was an actress.'

'Oh dear!' said Dave, 'you do have a lot to learn, Mr Payne. But take it from me, Patricia Hunter was a professional whore.'

However, the possibility of Payne's involvement in the death of Patricia Hunter was ruled out by the report from the forensic science lab that was waiting for me when Dave and I returned to the office.

The traces of oil and particles found on the garage floor matched those that had been found in the grazing on Patricia Hunter's back. And the fibres found in the dead showgirl's hair tallied with those taken from the piece of carpet that had been in a corner of the garage. The coil of electrical flex had been examined and the scientist who had taken Sarah Dawson's place at the laboratory was convinced that the ligature used to strangle Patricia Hunter matched it. Significantly, it also revealed traces of greasepaint.

But the best bit of all was that Phillips's fingerprints had been found *inside* the safe. *And on Patricia Hunter's credit card.* And they didn't tally with the set we'd taken from Jeremy Payne.

'Got him, the careless bastard,' I said.

'All we've got to do now is find him,' said Dave, selecting a large orange from his canvas briefcase. 'What about the van, guv?'

The Ford van had revealed traces – albeit minute, but that was good enough – of the same carpet fibres that had been found in Patricia Hunter's hair, and satisfied me that Phillips had used it to convey her dead body wrapped in the carpet we'd found, to wherever he had pitched her into the river. And given that the crucial evidence had been found at Barnes, it's likely that he had driven less than half a mile to do it.

I hate a waiting game and to fill in the time I decided to deal with some of the loose ends that inevitably crop up in a murder enquiry. And given that we now knew that Phillips masqueraded as Forman, it was also possible that he had assumed other identities. There again, either Tim Oliver or Edward Archer could have been the murderer. The weary business of elimination went on.

Both the St Malo harbourmaster and the French customs had confirmed the presence of the judge's yacht during the crucial period. And although the harbourmaster had seen a man and a woman on deck from time to time, he was unable to confirm that it was the judge.

Tim Oliver, however, was a different ball game. To start with, his secretary told us, somewhat sniffily, that Mr Oliver had certainly been at a business conference in Birmingham, which, happily for him, had lasted from Monday the tenth of June to Wednesday the twelfth. But, when we told her that we would check – because this was a murder enquiry – she eventually admitted that he hadn't been in Birmingham at all. He had spent the relevant period in a hotel in Winchester, and most of it in bed. *With her.* Oh well!

Frank Mead had made several attempts to see Edward Archer, another of the names in Patricia Hunter's address book, but Archer had not been at home on the occasions Frank had called at Wilmslow Gardens, Stockwell. However, he had verified, from what we call local enquiries, that that was where he lived. I decided to pay him a visit.

And he wasn't at home this time, either.

The man who answered the door was about forty, tall and well built, with a completely shaven head and an earring in his left ear. 'Ted Archer? No, mate. He's away at the moment. Who wants to know?'

Could it be a coincidence that this man spoke with an Australian accent?

'We're police officers,' I said, producing my warrant card.

'What again? You're the third or fourth lot of coppers we've had round here. Christ, what's he done? Ted's as straight as a die.'

'Is Mr Archer, by any chance, an Australian?' I asked.

'Yeah, we both are. Why d'you ask?'

I was suddenly possessed of a gut feeling that we should have tracked down Edward Archer much earlier in this investigation. Was he Phillips alias Forman in yet another guise? 'I think it would be better if we came in and had a chat, Mr, er . . . ?'

'Palmer. Ned Palmer. Yeah, sure, come in.' He nodded in Dave's direction. 'He a copper an' all?'

'Yes,' said Dave. 'Life's full of little surprises, isn't it?'

'Have you any idea where Mr Archer is?' I asked, once we were settled in the living room.

'Not a clue, mate. Last time I rang him on his mobile, he was in India. Least, that's where he said he was, but he could've been anywhere, I suppose.'

'Yes,' I said, not without a measure of misgiving. 'What exactly does Mr Archer do for a living, Mr Palmer?'

'Christ, mate, call me Ned. That's us: Ted and Ned.' Palmer gave a throaty laugh. 'We've never been ones to stand on ceremony. Now then, let me think: what *does* Ted do?' Palmer gazed up at the ceiling. 'He's something in the City. God knows what and God knows where, but he's always off round the world somewhere.'

'When did you last see him?'

'Must have been a week ago, but he was in and out like a bloody rocket. Trouble is, I work all hours, and sometimes we don't see each other for weeks on end.'

'What do *you* do, then?' asked Dave.

'I hope you blokes don't mind me asking, but what the hell's this all about? Has Ted got himself into some sort of bother? It's not an immigration thing, surely? I mean, we've both got work permits and God knows how many other bits of paper.'

'We think Mr Archer may be able to assist us with enquiries we're making regarding a murder, Ned,' said Dave.

Even though Palmer had asked us to call him Ned, he seemed somehow disconcerted that Dave had done so. Or perhaps it was mention of a murder. His next utterance proved it. '*A murder!* Bloody hell. Ted's had nothing to do with any murder, for Christ's sake.' For a moment or two, he stared at the floor, shaking his head.

'My sergeant asked what *you* do for a living,' I said.

Palmer was obviously taken aback by the realization that Archer might be able to help us solve a murder or, worse, might have committed one. 'Me?' He looked up. 'I'm a deep-sea diver. I've been working off the Isles of Scilly lately. Sometimes I don't get home for a week at a time. Sometimes it's months. Matter of fact, you were lucky to catch me now.'

191

'D'you know the Kookaburra Club?' Dave asked.

'Yeah, sure I know it,' said Palmer. 'Go for a drink there sometimes. Not that often though. It's usually full of bloody Aussies.' And he laughed.

'And Mr Archer? Does he go there too?'

'Yeah, I think so. Now you mention it, we've been there together a couple of times.' Palmer paused. 'Is that where this murder happened?'

'No.' Now it was my turn to pause. 'D'you know if Mr Archer ever used a website to engage the services of a prostitute?'

Palmer laughed outright. 'Yeah, sure he did. It's not illegal, is it? Is this what this is all about?'

'Did *you* ever use such a website?'

'Yeah. Why?'

Dave produced the computer printout on which Fleur, Domino and Kimberley, among others, appeared. 'D'you recognize any of these women, Mr Palmer?' he asked.

After a few moments' scrutiny, the Australian pointed to a black girl who traded under the name of Ebony. 'Had her a couple of times. She's great. I'd recommend her to anyone.' Rather pointedly, Palmer glanced at Dave.

'D'you happen to know if Mr Archer ever engaged a girl known as Dolores?'

'Damned if I know, mate. I know he had Ebony once or twice, but you'll have to ask him about the others.'

'How about this girl, then?' Dave asked, showing Palmer the photograph of Patricia Hunter.

'Don't know her. Who's she?'

'She's the one who was murdered. That's Dolores.'

'Christ, what sick bastard would want to croak a pretty kid like that?'

'That's what I'm trying to find out, Ned,' I said. 'Have you any idea when Mr Archer will be back home?'

'No, mate, sorry. The first I usually know of it is when he comes crashing through the door. He's a noisy bastard is Ted.'

'How long have you been in England?' I asked.

'About a year.'

'And Mr Archer?'

'A lot longer than that. About six or seven years, I suppose.'

'And where in Australia does Mr Archer come from?'

'Sydney,' said Palmer without hesitation.

'When were you last in Brighton, Ned?' asked Dave with a suddenness designed to catch Palmer on the hop.

'Brighton? Now let me see. Must have been about seven or eight years ago.'

'But you said just now that you'd only been in England a year.'

'That's right, mate. I'm talking about the Brighton in South Australia. I was born in Gleneig, not far from Adelaide. Brighton's the next town of any size south of there.'

Dave and I returned to Curtis Green with a feeling of foreboding. Was Archer really Phillips? He came from Sydney, had been in the country about the same length of time as Phillips, and had had dealings with the prostitutes in Phillips's stable. But we only had Palmer's word for it that Archer had engaged their services. For all we knew, he could be running them. After all, Palmer had admitted that he hardly ever saw the bloke. And they'd both frequented the Kookaburra Club.

We had to find Archer as soon as we could. And that wasn't going to be easy, because I had a nasty feeling that Palmer was not telling us the truth. If he'd been living in the same house as Archer for a year, how come he didn't know exactly where Archer worked? Unless Archer didn't want him to know. On the other hand, I'd come to the conclusion that Palmer wasn't the brightest of individuals. But, as every policeman finds out sooner or later, appearances and first impressions can be deceptive.

Seventeen

By now, I had done a number of things that policemen always do.

Some time ago, Phillips's name had been entered on the Police National Computer as being wanted for extradition, and I'd now added the information that I wished to question him in connection with the murder of Patricia Hunter, and for good measure included the name of Edward Archer as a possible alias. In addition to listing the BMW registered in Forman's name, I also included details of Donna Lodge's Alfa Romeo, with instructions that she was to be detained in connection with the same matter.

I was not surprised that it was Donna Lodge who was found first.

It was four o'clock on that Monday afternoon that Dave and I once again came face to face with the prostitute known to her clients as Fleur.

A traffic car patrolling the Notting Hill area had spotted her driving sedately along Holland Park Avenue, and had given her a pull, as the Black Rats are wont to say, and promptly arrested her. She was now in Notting Hill nick.

'I want to know why I was arrested by two common policemen,' she began. 'And if you're going to talk about Bruce Phillips again, I'll tell you what—'

'Save your breath,' I said. 'Bruce Phillips and Geoffrey Forman are one and the same, as we now know and you've known all along. Last Tuesday we found a lock-up garage at the rear of a block of flats in Breda Gardens, Barnes. That garage had been rented by Phillips in the name of Forman. When the garage was searched, we found a safe containing various items of property belonging to Patricia Hunter, also known as Dolores.'

'I don't believe it,' protested Donna. 'You're making it up.' But judging by the speed with which the blood had drained from her face, she had been shocked at how much we had discovered.

'The interesting piece of paper that led us first to find and then to search that garage,' I continued, 'was found in the kitchen cabinet at thirteen Ridgely Road, Barnes. Your kitchen cabinet, Ms Lodge.'

'I didn't know anything about that. Nothing at all.'

'In that case, you will appreciate how important it is for us to find Bruce Phillips as quickly as possible. By the way, we also found a Ford van in that garage.'

'Really?' Donna lit another cigarette.

'Registered in the name of Robert Peel.'

'I know nothing about it. And I don't know anything about any Robert Peel.'

Which confirmed all that I'd read about the school history syllabus having gone to pot in recent years.

'I suppose that was Geoffrey's doing,' continued Donna. 'He must have put that name on the form, or whatever it is one does.' All the fight had gone out of Donna now. 'I knew that he was wanted in Australia for something,' she said quietly, thus confirming to my satisfaction, yet again, that Forman was Phillips, 'but he told me it was all a mistake. Something to do with outstanding debts. I'm sure he wouldn't have killed anyone.'

'Where is he, Ms Lodge?' I persisted, certain that she knew the answer.

'I don't know,' protested Donna. 'I honestly don't know.'

'After you were arrested by my officers last Monday and I interviewed you at West End Central police station, you telephoned Phillips and told him what had happened to you. And that led him to panic because he knew that if the police had found *you* it wouldn't be long before we found *him*.'

'I admit that I phoned *Geoffrey*.' Donna put emphasis on

195

the name, apparently still intent on denying that Forman was Phillips.

'Furthermore, we've learned' – actually it was an assumption – 'that he has ceased to use the Kookaburra Club as a venue for paying you girls what you earn from prostitution. So where do you have to go now to collect your pay?'

'We don't. He rang me, and I suppose he rang the other girls, to say that in future he would send the money by post.'

'What, cash?'

'Of course not. By cheque.'

'Do you have one of those cheques?'

By way of a reply, Donna withdrew a cheque from her handbag. It was for a thousand pounds drawn on a well-known high street bank. *And signed by Robert Peel.* I handed it to Dave, who took a note of the details before returning it to Donna. But we both knew that we wouldn't find the mythical Robert Peel at the address the bank had for him. Even if we managed to persuade the bank to reveal it. But I did wonder why Donna had parted with the cheque so easily. It was only later on that I discovered why.

'Where are you living now?'

'In a hotel in the West End, just for the time being, but I'm going back to Barnes.'

'Not today you're not,' I said.

'Why?' asked Donna. 'What's going to happen now?'

'You will be detained here pending further enquiries, Ms Lodge. I'm by no means satisfied that you were not involved in the murder of Patricia Hunter and the disposal of her body.'

At that point Donna Lodge broke down completely. Great sobs wracked her body and she ferreted about in her handbag for a tissue. By the time she recovered and looked up, she was an absolute mess: eyes red-rimmed, mascara running down her cheeks and her hair – previously well coifed – disarranged. But despite the compelling histrionics, I was convinced that she was play-acting.

'If I tell you all I know, will that help me?'

I glanced at Dave. He knew what I wanted him to do, and

he knew I could never remember the words of the caution. And I'd lost my little card with it all on.

He switched on the tape recorder, told it what it needed to know and began. 'Donna Lodge, you do not have to say anything, but it may harm your defence if you do not mention when questioned something which you later rely on in court. Anything you do say may be given in evidence.' And after a pause, he added, 'You are entitled to the services of a solicitor if you wish to have one present.'

'No, I don't.' Donna shook her head and, after a lengthy pause, added, 'I suppose that in a sense it was Patricia's own fault really.'

Well that was hardly original. Strange how the victim always seems to be responsible for his or her own demise. At least in the eyes of the killer.

'Go on,' I said.

'It was after she was arrested for shoplifting. Patricia wanted no more to do with it because the magistrate remanded her on bail for reports and said he was considering a custodial sentence. He said he knew it was a hoisting ring. Well, Patricia went into a blind panic, but Bruce told her not to worry, that worse things happen at sea, or something trite like that. Then he was stupid enough to tell her that he was wanted in Australia and that he'd take care of her. He knew how to avoid going to prison, he said, and he'd make sure she didn't go either.'

'But she was fined,' I said.

Donna smiled. 'I know, but Bruce told her that if she got done for prostitution, she'd go to prison just the same, which was nonsense, of course. That's why he told her to keep moving from one address to another. Patricia was a devious little bitch though,' she continued, 'and she threatened to tell the police where he was if he didn't pay her double for getting laid. It was blackmail really.'

'Which is why Phillips kept moving as well, I suppose,' I commented, but Donna didn't respond to that.

'And that wasn't all,' Donna continued. 'To begin with, he did pay her extra, but that wasn't good enough for her. She wanted to marry him, the silly little cow. Well, Bruce wasn't up for that.'

197

'So he killed her?'

'I didn't know that. In fact, I still can't believe it. All I do know is that she disappeared. I thought that he'd paid for her to go to the South of France. Just to get her out of the way. That's what Patricia said he'd told her anyway.'

Funny how the South of France kept cropping up in this enquiry.

'Three years ago, you and she shared a flat at Petersfield Street, Fulham, where you ran a call-girl service. Where was Phillips then?'

'He'd gone back to Australia. He'd heard somehow that he was wanted there, so he decided to lie low for a while. But a year later he was back.'

'Are you saying that he went back to Australia, knowing that he was wanted there?' I was beginning to think that Phillips wasn't so clever after all, or that Donna was still not telling the whole truth. Or didn't know what the truth was.

Donna shrugged. 'I don't know why he went. Perhaps he didn't go at all. All I do know is that he disappeared for a while. He said he'd been to Australia, but I don't really know where he went.'

That sounded more like it. It would have been crass stupidity for him to return to the very country that wanted him for several counts of long-firm fraud. And Phillips wasn't stupid. The likelihood was that he had taken refuge elsewhere in the United Kingdom. Created a new identity for himself perhaps, but he wouldn't have dared risk attempting to leave the country, even less entering Australia.

'But then he came back?'

'Yes, but he decided that the shoplifting game was too dangerous. That's when he set up the website for us. There were about ten of us girls altogether and he took our photographs in the nude' – Donna gave a coy little smile – 'and gave us names like Fleur and Domino and Dolores, and set up what he said was a foolproof way of getting business for us without getting into trouble himself.'

'And you've no idea where he is now?'

'No, honestly.'

198

'But you do now admit that Geoffrey Forman and Bruce Phillips are one and the same.'

'Yes,' said Donna softly.

'To your knowledge, did Phillips ever use the name Archer, Edward Archer?'

'No, I've never heard that name.'

Which might have been the truth. There was no telling with this woman.

'When did you last see Patricia Hunter, Ms Lodge?'

Donna gave a convulsive sob, maybe at the thought that the man she'd been living with could be a ruthless killer. There again, it may have been the thought that she too could finish up in prison. 'About six or seven weeks ago, I suppose.'

'And where was that?'

'Bruce and I were having a drink in the Kookaburra Club when she came in to collect her money. Bruce usually handed the girls an envelope and they left, but she started a row at the bar, shouting and screaming at him. By the time she eventually left, Bruce was in a furious temper.'

'Did he say why?'

'Yes, he told me that she was trying to put the arm on him again and he wasn't having any of it. He was really steamed up about her. I told him to forget it, but he said that if she did what she'd threatened to do, which was to tell the police, he'd finish up behind bars in Australia.'

'Did he say anything else?'

'He said that she'd have to be stopped, but I didn't think he meant he was going to kill her. I still can't believe that he would have done.'

'Why was she working as a chorus girl in *Scatterbrain*?' asked Dave.

'She'd always said that she wanted to go on the stage. She reckoned she was fed up with being screwed every night for peanuts. I don't know where she got that idea. We only turned a trick three times a week at the most, and got five hundred a time for it. And that was after Bruce took his cut.'

'What was so special about you that Phillips allowed you to live with him?' I asked.

There was a long pause and then Donna flashed me a superior smile. 'We're married,' she said, and lit another cigarette. 'So you can forget any ideas about me giving evidence against him.'

Terrific! The icing on the cake. If she really *was* married to Phillips, she would be neither competent nor compellable to give evidence against him. Damn and blast the bloody woman!

And she'd known it all along, the smug bitch. That's why she'd told us all she knew. But even then, I thought that she'd only been telling us half-truths. And when we analysed it, she'd really told us little that we didn't know already.

But why had we not found a trace of that marriage when the usual checks were made at the General Register Office at Southport?

'Where were you married?' I asked in a voice that even I thought was remarkably restrained.

'Scotland,' said Donna.

Which, of course, explained it.

'But even though you're married, he still sends you out to get screwed three times a week.'

'I enjoy my work,' said Donna.

It was nigh on eight o'clock by the time a frustrated Dave and I returned to Curtis Green. I was on the point of abandoning the day and going down to the Red Lion for a drink when Gavin Creasey, the night-duty incident-room sergeant, rang through to my office.

'I just got a phone call from the station officer at Brixton, sir.'

'Not Mrs Payne again, surely?'

'No, sir.' Creasey sounded somewhat puzzled, but he wasn't as conversant with the twists and turns of the enquiry as the rest of us, and Payne's name probably didn't ring any bells with him. 'The sergeant there said that an Edward Archer walked into the nick about ten minutes ago. Apparently he thinks you want to talk to him. The station officer said he checked the PNC and you've got Archer flagged up.'

'Too bloody right, I have, Gavin. Get back on to Brixton

nick and tell them under no circumstances to let this guy go until I get there. I don't care if they put him in a straightjacket and bung him in a cell, but they're to hang on to him. Got it?'

'Yes, sir,' said Gavin.

'My mate Ned Palmer reckons you've been looking for me,' said Archer. 'What's the problem? Ned said something about a murder.' He shook his head in apparent bewilderment. 'I don't know anything about any murder.'

Was this guy a great actor, or what?

Dave produced the photograph of Patricia Hunter. 'Did you know this woman?' he asked.

'That's Dolores,' said Archer without any hesitation. 'Ned told me she's the one who was killed.'

Archer was about the same age as Phillips, and could have been him. At least from the rather vague descriptions that we'd been given by the various people who'd claimed to have seen him. Or thought they had.

'How did you meet her?' I asked, not prepared to believe what Ned Palmer had told me.

Archer ran his hand round his chin and grinned inanely. 'Found her on a website. She's a prossy.'

'Yes, I know that. How many times did you meet up with her?'

'About three, I reckon. She was pretty bloody good for a pommy sheila.'

'Where did this take place?'

Archer thought about that for a moment. 'A couple of times down my place in Stockwell, when Ned was at work, like, and once at some flat in Fulham. Petersfield Street, it was. I remembered that because I've got a mate called Peter Field back in Oz.'

'When was this?'

'What, at Petersfield Street? About a year back.'

'Anyone else there at the time?'

Archer laughed. 'You joking? No, mate, it was a one-to-one. Mind you, I wouldn't have minded a threesome. Never thought of it really.'

201

'And the last time you saw Dolores?'

'Must have been six months ago, I reckon. To tell you the truth, I couldn't afford her any more.'

'Bruce Phillips,' said Dave suddenly.

'Who?' The name seemed to have no effect on Archer.

'Bruce Phillips is an Australian from Sydney.'

'Really? I'm from Sydney too.'

'Have you ever heard of him?' Dave asked.

'No. Should I have done? Damn near every other Australian's called Bruce.'

'He frequents the Kookaburra Club. I understand you occasionally go there,' I said.

'Been there a few times, yes. Never heard of him though. What does he do?'

'He runs the team of prostitutes on the website that you use.'

'Is that a fact?' Archer shook his head. 'No, never heard of him.'

'What do you do, Mr Archer. For a living, I mean.'

'I'm a courier. Carry diamonds and important documents all over the place. It doesn't pay much, but I get to see some good places.' Archer laughed. 'Get to meet some pretty exotic sheilas, too.'

'And where were you the week beginning Monday the tenth of June?'

Archer reached down and picked up his briefcase. Extracting an A4 diary, he riffled through its pages until he found the entry he wanted. 'Week beginning the tenth of June,' he murmured. 'Yeah, got it. On that Monday, I took off for Lagos, Nigeria . . .' He looked up. 'That's a godforsaken place, I can tell you. Not a decent hotel anywhere. And the bloody beer's warm,' he added in final condemnation. Glancing down at his diary again, he said, 'And I got back here on Thursday the thirteenth, having gone via Kenya with a pile of securities that weighed a ton. Finished up back here in London on the Friday of that week. Here, see for yourself.' And he handed over his diary.

I looked at the entries and, as far as I could tell, they appeared to be genuine. Nevertheless, I asked the name of the firm he

202

worked for. He gave me a business card and invited me to check with his boss.

I did, and Archer was telling the truth.

Another one off the list.

Eighteen

In my book, we now had enough evidence to charge Bruce Phillips with the murder of Patricia Hunter, and possibly even enough to convince the sceptical Crown Prosecution Service to take him to trial. But all of that remained academic until we actually laid hands on the man.

But Phillips was a crafty bastard, and I suspected it would be some time before I had the pleasure of taking him into custody.

Although we still had Donna Lodge banged up in Notting Hill nick, I knew that the law wouldn't allow me to keep her there indefinitely, and there just wasn't the evidence to charge her with anything relating to the Hunter murder. But I was hoping to hang on to her long enough for me to arrest Phillips before she was able to tell him how much we knew and, for that matter, how much she had told us. If he learned of that, he might just kill her. These days you don't get any more porridge for two murders than you do for one. In any case, he would certainly become even more elusive than he was now. If that were possible.

But we'd have to move fast. Even with a superintendent giving the OK for an extension, she'd have to be released by four o'clock on Wednesday morning. Realistically that gave us only tomorrow to catch up with Phillips.

Late on Monday evening, I rang Inspector Steve Granger at home and told him the story so far. He laughed. 'Bad luck, mate,' he said.

Undaunted, I continued. 'Steve, any chance you could get back to Canberra and ask them to send everything they've got on Phillips, whether it seems relevant or not? It's pretty urgent.'

'No probs, mate,' was Granger's confident reply.

Halfway through the following morning, Colin Wilberforce stuck his head round my door. 'Mr Granger at Australia House has got the information you wanted, sir,' he said. 'He suggested you meet him for lunch at the usual restaurant at one o'clock.'

'Splendid,' I said, as ready as ever to take a lunch off our generous colonial friends.

What I didn't know was that the kaleidoscope was about to be shaken again.

The Australian Government, in common with the United States and one or two others, believed in encouraging the police officers attached to their respective missions to entertain their British counterparts in the hope that they might obtain some useful intelligence, *without giving too much in exchange*.

The plan was cocked up a bit because the British took a similar view: that the intelligence flow should be incoming rather than outgoing.

The result was something of a cagey stalemate until sufficient mutual confidence had been engendered between the individuals concerned. And then they swapped information quite freely and enjoyed eating at the expense of their respective governments. And laughing up their sleeves while doing it. Metaphorically, of course.

As a result, the restaurant where Steve Granger and I usually met was one of the better-class eating establishments in the West End.

Steve was already there, and there was a large malt whisky waiting for me, but it was not until the meal was over that he produced a slim file from the briefcase at his feet.

'This is just about everything that we've got on this guy, Harry. He's got a few previous convictions. Minor stuff really: a bit of thieving, selling cannabis at rock festivals when he was a youngster, that sort of thing. But then, as I said the last time we talked about him, he got into long-firm fraud. In every bloody state in Australia. Cunning bastard.'

205

'How come he never got captured then, Steve?' I asked.

'I suppose he'd worked out that if he moved from state to state it would take our fragmented policing system ages to catch up with him. And he was right. It wasn't until the Commonwealth Police started putting things together that they were able to build a case. But by then the galah had taken off.' Steve broke off to order brandy. 'Each time he reneged on the payments for his last order, he'd shoot through to a different part of the country. He pulled his first scam in Sydney and promptly moved to the Northern Territory. After he'd pulled a couple of strokes there – in Darwin of all places – he opened up in Perth. From there he went to Rockhampton, out east in Queensland, and then to Adelaide.' He passed the file across the table. 'It's all there, Harry. Take it and digest it at your leisure.'

I took the file and flicked it open to the first page. 'Now that's interesting,' I said.

'What is?' Steve took a sip of his cognac and leaned forward, his arms on the table.

I pointed to the scrap of information in the Australian file that had attracted my interest and explained why I thought it could be relevant.

But Steve Granger was an experienced detective, and the coppering game varies very little from one country to another. 'I reckon that's a bit tenuous, mate,' he said. 'A hell of a lot of women who were born there were given that name. Although I say it myself, Aussies can be an unimaginative crowd when it comes to things like that.'

It was but a scintilla of suspicion, but it had to be followed up.

'Any progress, Mr Brock?' The commander drifted into the incident room, polishing his glasses with his colourful pocket handkerchief.

'I'm thinking of going to Edinburgh, sir.'

'Really? Why?' The commander replaced his glasses and peered at me closely. 'Holiday? I've heard that the area around the Kyle of Lochalsh is very pleasant at this time of year.'

'No, sir, business.' I explained the reasons, not that they

206

sounded too convincing, and certainly not to our tame, paper detective.

'But is that really necessary? Just because Phillips was married to the Lodge woman up there makes your assumption seem rather tenuous in my eyes.' As always the commander was thinking of the expense, cost-conscious *apparatchik* that he was.

'It will have been worthwhile if it means the arrest of Phillips, sir.'

'Mmm, I suppose so. But make sure you use one of those budget airlines.' And with that throwaway line, the commander retreated to preside over his paper empire. One of the DCs had once suggested that he had a black belt in origami. I gave the DC a bollocking; you can't have junior officers going about slagging off commanders.

Donna Lodge had been released from custody at four o'clock on Tuesday afternoon, there being nothing with which I could charge her. I'd floated the idea of assisting an offender, but the Crown Prosecution Service would have none of it.

On Wednesday morning, we arrived at Edinburgh Airport and were met by a detective inspector of the Lothian and Borders Police who introduced himself as Charlie Nicholas. And he was an Englishman.

'What the hell's an Englishman doing up here?' I asked.

'I was in the navy at Faslane,' said Nicholas. 'Married a local girl and when I'd finished my time I joined the job.' He grinned. 'Beats coppering in the Smoke,' he added. 'Anyway, what are you after?'

'An Australian called Bruce Phillips,' I said, and went on to explain our interest, and the reason Dave and I had come to Scotland.

'I know a bit about that,' said Nicholas. 'It was one of my blokes who did the original enquiry for you.'

We drove into the heart of Edinburgh and straight to the private nursing home that was now at the centre of my investigation.

A pretty young matron – she didn't look old enough to be a nurse, let alone a matron – introduced herself as Connie McLachlan and told us that she was in charge.

'I don't know how much you know about Alzheimer's disease,' she began, 'but I doubt that you'll get much out of this lady. Some days, she's quite lucid, but on others, she makes no sense at all. I don't know exactly what you want to ask her, but her short-term memory isn't very good. With this complaint, it's the one that goes first, and half the time she can't remember what you said to her five minutes ago. Her long-term memory's usually all right though. At the moment.'

'How often does her husband come to see her?' I asked.

Connie McLachlan gave me a questioning look. 'She doesn't have a husband,' she said. 'At least, not as far as I know. But her son comes to see her occasionally. Peter Crawford, that is.'

I was suddenly possessed of that feeling that detectives get when they're sure a solution is imminent. And that what I had thought when Steve Granger had showed me Phillips's file was about to be confirmed. 'How old is Mrs Crawford, Matron?'

'We have her down as sixty-five – anyway, that's what her son told us when he brought her in – but she could be older.'

'And how long ago was she admitted?'

The matron paused, calculating. 'It must be three or four years ago, I suppose. I can look it up for you if you want.'

'No, that's good enough. May we see her?'

The matron smiled. 'Aye, you can if you wish, but as I said, I doubt that she'll know what you're talking about.'

I decided that it would be detrimental to my professional standing to admit that, right now, I didn't know what I was talking about either. Crawford had been adamant that it was his wife who was here, not his mother. Admittedly he'd told us that at forty-five she was a little older than he was, but the fact that the hospital authorities believed her to be at least twenty years older than that merely served to heighten my suspicion of Peter Crawford.

Even so, we may have been wasting our time. Perhaps Alzheimer's disease accelerated the ageing process. I didn't know enough about it to offer an opinion. A sketchy first-aid course when I'd joined the job, coupled with what I'd picked up attending post-mortems, did little to expand my knowledge of medicine.

When we entered the airy, sunny room, Mrs Crawford was sitting in an armchair watching television and sipping a drink from a plastic beaker. Even though she was seated, I could see that she was probably a tall big-boned woman.

'Alicia, these gentlemen have come all the way from London to talk to you,' said Connie McLachlan.

The confused old lady gazed at us and smiled a vague smile. 'Oh, how nice,' she said. 'I don't get many visitors.'

'Mrs Crawford—' I began, but got no further. The woman's mood changed instantly, and she hurled the beaker at the television, leaving a trail of liquid across the carpet.

'Now, now, Alicia,' said the matron gently, 'there's no need for that. These gentlemen are friends.'

'I've told you before, my name's not Crawford. It's Phillips. Why does everyone call me Crawford? It's not my name.' Alicia began rocking backwards and forwards in her chair, hammering the armrests with clenched fists. 'It's not my name. Not my name!' she shouted.

Connie McLachlan turned to us with a sympathetic expression on her face. 'I don't know what it is,' she said, 'but she's always going off like that the minute anyone calls her Mrs Crawford. I'm sorry, I should have warned you. I doubt whether she'll answer any questions now. It'll take some time to calm her down.'

'It's all right, Matron,' I said. 'Believe it or not, she's told me all I wanted to know.' I glanced at Alicia Phillips. 'Were you born in Alice Springs?' I asked.

'How did you know that?' growled Alicia, and glanced around as though seeking a missile to throw at me.

The mistake I'd made was to ask the Edinburgh police to check whether Peter Crawford had visited Alicia Crawford without telling them he'd told us she was his wife. If the Scottish officers had known that and had informed me that she was Crawford's mother, we might have resolved this enquiry a damned sight sooner. How easy it is to be wise after the event. But at least the commander would be satisfied that the expense of our trip to Scotland had been justified.

'What are you going to do now, Harry?' asked DI Nicholas.

'D'you know this house that Crawford claims to own and where he said he'd stayed, Charlie? It's in a place called Colinton.' And I gave him the full address.

'Soon find it,' said Nicholas. 'It's about six miles out of the city. Want to stop off for lunch on the way?'

Crawford's house, the sort of stone dwelling typical of Scottish architecture, was set back from the road sufficient to allow two cars to be parked on the drive. And two cars were there. Nearest the house was a BMW – we knew from Dave's check with the DVLA that it was Forman's – and behind it was Donna Lodge's Alfa Romeo.

'Blimey!' murmured Dave. 'That's a bit of luck.'

If the owners of those two cars were in the house, it was good luck indeed. And about time, too.

The three of us, DI Nicholas, Dave and me, walked up the drive, but Dave and I stood to one side of the door, out of sight.

'This is what I want you to say . . .' I whispered to Charlie Nicholas, and gave him brief instructions.

'Good afternoon, madam,' said Nicholas when the door was opened. 'I'm a police officer. Is Mr Crawford at home? It's about his mother.'

All right, so it was a dirty trick, but not as dirty as murdering a prostitute. Prostitutes have rights, too.

'I'll get him for you,' said the familiar cultured voice of Donna Lodge, or more correctly Donna Phillips. We had established from the Scottish General Register Office that she and Phillips had indeed been married in Edinburgh a year ago.

Dave and I moved into view as Crawford appeared in the doorway. We were probably the last people he expected to see on his doorstep, and there was a stunned look on his face as he recognized us and realized that we knew who he was and why we wanted him.

Then he turned and ran back up the hall. But he didn't run fast enough. Shoving past me and the Edinburgh DI, Dave sped after Crawford and laid him low with a flying tackle that would have brought the crowd to their feet at Twickenham.

210

'Peter Crawford, also known as Bruce Phillips, you are wanted on a warrant of extradition issued by the Bow Street magistrate in respect of offences alleged to have been committed by you in Australia,' I said when Dave had dragged our quarry upright again and handcuffed him.

It didn't sound much of a finale to all the convolutions of the murder enquiry that had brought us, eventually, to the door of a very ordinary house on the outskirts of Edinburgh, but it was enough.

'You can't arrest me in Scotland,' said Phillips smugly. 'You don't have the authority.' The very English tones in which he'd spoken when we'd interviewed him in Chelsea had now given way to an Australian accent, but it hadn't affected his knowledge of British law.

'I'm not arresting you,' I said. 'Allow me to introduce Detective Inspector Nicholas of the Lothian and Borders Police. He will arrest you.'

By the time we were ready to leave, Charlie Nicholas had summoned a police van crewed by two burly constables to take us to the airport.

'If you want to borrow these lads to accompany you to London, Harry, you're more than welcome,' said Charlie.

'Thanks,' I said, 'but I reckon Dave and I can take care of him. You could telephone my office though, and ask them to send an escort to meet us at Heathrow.'

It was seven o'clock that evening before we'd lodged Phillips in the cells at Charing Cross police station but, tired though we both were, the Police and Criminal Evidence Act clock had started ticking and there was no time to waste. Not that I intended to waste any on Phillips. From what we'd learned of him, he was a devious bastard. And his opening statement in the interview room proved it.

'I won't fight extradition, mate,' he said. 'You can put me on a plane for Sydney first thing tomorrow morning.'

'It'll be a bloody long time before you see Sydney again . . . *mate*,' said Dave.

Phillips gave Dave the sort of scathing glance that he probably afforded Aborigines who had the audacity to live in their

211

own country. 'I'm talking to the organ grinder, not the monkey,' he said.

But black policemen live with that sort of racist insult all their professional lives. And probably their social lives too. Dave just laughed, switched on the tape recorder and cautioned Phillips once again. You can't be too careful when there are lawyers lurking in the wings waiting to catch us out in even the most trifling of mistakes.

'Bruce Phillips, I shall shortly charge you with the murder of Patricia Hunter on or about the twelfth of June this year,' I began.

'Is that right? And what makes you think I'm Bruce Phillips?'

'Donna told me,' I said, and had the satisfaction of seeing a dark look of hatred spread across Phillips's face. 'And your mother.'

'You leave my mother out of this!' snapped Phillips.

'The one thing that puzzles me,' I said, 'is why you contacted the Granville Theatre after you'd murdered Patricia Hunter.'

'I didn't murder her,' Phillips sneered. 'She was my girl-friend and I was worried about her.'

Like hell he was. Phillips, in the guise of Crawford, had made that call in an attempt to mislead us into believing that he was a concerned and innocent party. I had to admit that it had been a pretty cunning ploy, but he would have many years in prison, I hoped, to reflect that that call had been the beginning of a train of events that had eventually caused his downfall. A downfall that was aided by the overconfidence that led him to believe he could outwit the police, by his carelessness in leaving a credit-card receipt on the floor of Patricia Hunter's room at Coping Road, and the irresistible urge of many murderers like him to keep a memento of their victim.

But best of all was the fatal error of leaving his fingerprints on the *inside* of the safe we'd found in the garage, and on the dead girl's credit card. And that's how we knew for certain that Crawford was Phillips, because the first thing we'd done on arrival at Charing Cross police station was to have him fingerprinted. And those prints also tallied with the ones the

Australian Commonwealth Police had sent us with their request for Phillips's extradition. Clever that, ain't it?

And the Crown Prosecution Service went for it too, without demur. I suppose there's a first for everything.

On the Thursday I charged Bruce Phillips with the wilful murder of Patricia Hunter, took him to court and got an eight-day lay down. The next time he surfaced it would be in front of a circuit judge. But the real fun would begin quite a while after that.

And along with the rest of Fleet Street, Fat Danny had plastered it all over the front page of the disreputable tabloid that he dignified with the term newspaper.

The following evening, I took Gail Sutton out to dinner at Rules, my favourite restaurant. And it was she who brought up the arrest of Phillips.

'You got your man, then, Harry.'

'You make me sound like a Canadian Mountie,' I said.

'I read all about it in this morning's paper. And I saw a shot of you on television.'

Gail was certainly much more cheerful this evening than she had been in the month or so since I'd first met her, and I can only imagine that it was because Patricia Hunter's murderer – although that had yet to be proved to the satisfaction of the court – was now in custody.

We finished our meal and stepped out into Maiden Lane. I looked up and down for a taxi to take us to Waterloo, but in vain. We walked along to the corner of Southampton Street, but fared no better there.

'You know, Harry, there's something I've always wanted to do,' said Gail.

'And what's that?'

She took hold of my arm and steered me towards the Strand. 'Stay the night at the Savoy Hotel.'

There was still some unfinished business that had yet to be resolved. The following week we flew to Edinburgh once again and met up with Charlie Nicholas.

The advertising manager of the company Crawford claimed

213

to have visited on the Monday that Patricia Hunter was murdered, was an attractive, willowy redhead with a typically Scottish complexion. She introduced herself as Morag Wilson, and was all bright-eyed and bushy-tailed. Until we told her who we were and why we were there.

'Mrs Wilson, I understand that a Peter Crawford visited you on the tenth of June last in connection with a television advertising project.'

'That's right.' Mrs Wilson beamed at us.

'Really?'

'Yes, really.'

'That's interesting. Because we have charged Peter Crawford, who is actually an Australian called Bruce Phillips, with the murder in London on that date, of a young woman named Patricia Hunter. And he will shortly appear at the Old Bailey.'

Morag Wilson blanched and began to shake, and gripped the arms of her chair so hard that her knuckles showed white.

'I don't believe it,' she said in a whisper.

'Why did you provide him with a false alibi? And before you answer, you'd better listen to what Detective Inspector Nicholas here has to say to you.'

Charlie Nicholas reeled off the caution and began to make notes in his pocket book.

'He told me that some men were after him and if I could say he was up here, it'd be all right. He said it was something to do with a gambling debt.'

That was obviously rubbish, unless you counted us as the men who were after him.

'What is your relationship with Crawford?' Nicholas asked. Thanks to the vagaries of British law, the prosecution of the case against Morag Wilson would be in his hands.

There was a lengthy pause before Morag Wilson replied. 'We're lovers,' she said.

'And presumably, therefore, you'll have done anything he asked you?' Nicholas said.

'Yes,' she whispered. 'But if I'd known that he was a murderer—'

Nicholas held up his hand. 'Don't bother to say any more,

Mrs Wilson. The matter will be reported to the Procurator-Fiscal and I have to tell you that legal proceedings for assisting an offender may well follow.'

And with that we left Morag Wilson in tears, doubtless wondering, like many others, why the hell she had ever become involved with the smooth-talking man known variously as Peter Crawford, Geoffrey Forman and Bruce Phillips.

Phillips's trial took place at the Old Bailey some months later. With all the money he had acquired from his nefarious activities, Phillips, as was to be expected, had briefed one of the bar's leading Queen's Counsel.

But even so eminent a silk was unable to do much to counter the mass of evidence we had built against his client. Not that he didn't try, but then that was what he was being paid for.

When my turn came to be cross-examined, Phillips's QC rose languidly from his seat on the front bench, hitched his gown back on to his left shoulder and regarded me – for a few silent moments – with all the hubris that his class, education and social standing could muster.

'Chief Inspector, I understand that you arrested my client in Scotland—'

'No, sir.'

Momentarily disconcerted, the QC glanced down at his brief, an elegant, well-manicured finger flicking through the pages until he found what he wanted. 'But Mr Phillips was arrested in Colinton, near Edinburgh, was he not?' He affected an air of amusement designed to indicate that he'd caught me out.

'Yes, sir, he was arrested in Scotland, but not by me.'

'But you were there, were you not?'

'Yes, sir.' I do enjoy a bit of legal fencing.

'So, what you are saying is that you did *not* arrest him. Is that correct?' The silk glanced across at the jury box, his expression implying that he'd got this dim policeman on the spit and was about to roast him.

'That is correct, sir, yes.'

With a theatrical gesture that may have fooled the jury, but

215

didn't fool me – and certainly didn't impress the judge – the QC moved his spectacles down an inch and stared at me over the top of them. 'Then who did arrest my client?' he asked, with just the hint of exasperation.

'Detective Inspector Nicholas of the Lothian and Borders Police, sir.'

'But why should a Scottish officer have arrested him, pray? After all, you were the officer investigating the alleged murder with which my client stands indicted, are you not?'

'Detective Inspector Nicholas had the authority, sir, and as I was not in physical possession of the warrant, I did not. But he was not arresting your client on a charge of murder, he was executing a warrant of arrest on behalf of the Australian Government. Your client is wanted for extradition to that country.'

Gotcha! And it hurt. Visibly.

With a convincing display of outrage, Phillips's counsel turned to the judge. 'My Lady, that is irrelevant to the case before the court, and I must ask that the chief inspector be directed—'

'If you don't want answers, don't ask questions,' said the judge dismissively.

And so it went on, the QC nitpicking at trivia in an attempt to discredit police evidence, but it failed. Even without a confession from Phillips, the circumstantial evidence was so overwhelming that the jury took slightly less than an hour to convict him.

The judge sentenced him to life imprisonment and announced that the count of living on immoral earnings would remain on file, a pronouncement that didn't seem to worry Phillips too much.

Some weeks later, the Lord Chief Justice placed a tariff of twenty years minimum on the life sentence. I wasn't there to see Phillips's reaction, but I imagine he wasn't too chuffed about it.

After the trial, I rang Steve Granger at Australia House.

'I guess you'll have to wait about twenty years to get Phillips back,' I said. 'He's just gone down for life.'

'No worries, mate,' said Granger. 'We don't mind you paying for his board and lodging.'

'Your lot learned to play rugby yet?' I countered.

Because the prosecution of Morag Wilson depended upon the outcome of Phillips's trial, it was not until a week after his appeal had been disallowed that she appeared before the Edinburgh sheriff's court.

However, we were not obliged to travel north again to give evidence, as the case against her was now in the hands of DI Nicholas. Morag Wilson pleaded not guilty, but it did her little good. Once Charlie Nicholas produced the certificate of Phillips's conviction and gave details of Morag Wilson's admission, the fifteen members of the jury found her guilty within thirty minutes.

The Scottish courts, like their English counterparts, take a dim view of people who assist offenders, particularly when those offenders are murderers. She was sentenced to a year's imprisonment, but she didn't complete it.

Six weeks later she was found hanged in her cell at Inverness prison.

But the whole Phillips thing still irritated me.

'We never did find out who she'd had it off with just before her death, Dave, because Phillips's DNA didn't match the seminal fluid that was found in Patricia Hunter's body,' I said when we were having a pint in the Red Lion not long after the trials of both Phillips and Morag Wilson.

'So what?' said Dave. 'It's all water under the bridge. Waterloo Bridge.'

'Or why there was greasepaint on the wire with which Phillips strangled Patricia Hunter. Neither he nor Donna Lodge had ever had any direct contact with the theatre.'

But that's police work for you. Real police work, I mean. It's not like the police 'soaps' that abound on television where the scriptwriter insists on tying up *all* the loose ends.

'Never mind, guv,' said Dave, as he got another round in.

'What's more,' I said, determined to beat myself up, 'you've had a lesson in how to make a cock-up of investigating a murder. To think I alerted Phillips by mentioning him to Donna Lodge before we knew that he was also Forman. If I hadn't done that, we might have captured him much sooner. And if only we'd known that Alicia Crawford was Peter Crawford's mother, not his wife, we might have homed in on him before we did, and saved ourselves a lot of time.'

'Yeah, but we got lucky, guv, and that's all that matters. We got a result,' said Dave. 'What's more, you met Gail Sutton.'

'Yes, Dave,' I said thoughtfully, 'there is that.'

Acts of Regeneration

Acts of Regeneration

Allegory and Archetype in the Works of Norman Mailer

Robert J. Begiebing

University of Missouri Press

Columbia & London, 1980

Copyright © 1980 by
The Curators of the University of Missouri
University of Missouri Press, Columbia, Missouri 65211
Library of Congress Catalog Card Number 80-50416
Printed and bound in the United States of America

Library of Congress Cataloging in Publication Data

Begiebing, Robert J. 1946–
  Acts of Regeneration.

  Bibliography: p.204
  Includes index.
  1. Mailer, Norman—Allegory and symbolism.
I. Title.
PS3525.A4152Z594   813'.52   80–50416
ISBN 0-8262-0310-8

For permissions, see p. 209

*For Linda
and Brie*

Acknowledgments

I wish to give special thanks to Gary Lindberg who read the entire manuscript with extraordinary thoroughness and competence and whose wise advice informs this book. I also want to thank Philip Nicoloff and Andy Merton for their time and encouragement. William Woodward and Paul Brockelman offered excellent advice in the areas of psychology and philosophy, respectively, and gave me the humane reassurance necessary to complete my work. The University of New Hampshire generously granted me a fellowship for the summer of 1976 and for the academic year of 1977 that provided me with the freedom essential to write the major portion of this book and to do justice to its subject.

I also thank Linda, my wife, for her secretarial labors with the manuscript and for putting up with my absence—sometimes physical, sometimes mental—while I worked on this book.

One final note of thanks to Robert Lucid who, through his kindness and support from afar, helped me more than he probably realizes.

R. J. B.
Manchester, New Hampshire
July 1980

Contents

Acts of Regeneration

1

Introduction

The modern mind has forgotten those old truths that speak of the death of the old man and of the making of a new one, of spiritual rebirth and similar old-fashioned "mystical absurdities." My patient, being a scientist of today, was more than once seized by panic when he realized how much he was gripped by such thoughts. He was afraid of becoming insane, whereas the man of two thousand years ago would have welcomed such dreams and rejoiced in the hope of a magical rebirth and renewal of life. But our modern attitude looks back proudly upon the mists of superstition and of medieval or primitive credulity and entirely forgets that it carries the whole living past in its lower stories of the skyscraper of rational consciousness. Without the lower stories our mind is suspended in mid air. No wonder that it gets nervous. The true history of the mind is not preserved in learned volumes but in the living mental organism of everyone.

— Carl Jung, *Psychology and Religion*

One of Norman Mailer's widely known statements, which appears in *Advertisements for Myself*, is that his purpose as a writer is to create "a revolution in the consciousness of our time." When we understand what Mailer means by revolutionary consciousness, we can approach his work in a way that cuts through much of the critical and popular controversy about him. The first purpose of this study, then, will be to define Mailer's revolutionary consciousness by discovering how it operates in his work. In general, the consciousness Mailer and his heroes seek would integrate conscious and unconscious life, awaken metaphorical vision, and regenerate the resources of divine energy in human beings. I shall call this consciousness *heroic consciousness*. Mailer's principal theme is the struggle of Life against Death in the contemporary world. It is his conviction that the survival and growth of humanity and the victory of Life depend upon our capacity to attain heroic consciousness. We will see how Mailer consistently expresses his theme through the allegorical mode, and how he embodies acts of regeneration in universal patterns of the quest for rebirth.

Mailer sees the conflict between the positivistic perception and the metaphorical perception of existence as at the heart of the struggle between Life and Death. In particular, Mailer argues, twentieth-century man's *use* of science and technology has built "a wall across the route of metaphor." Though the purpose of true

1

science is to *reveal* nature, the purpose of our science is to *convert* nature. Our science, to Mailer, is therefore "incarcerated" by its own arrogance and deadened by its liquidation of metaphor. The mere piling up of laboratory methodology and the use of technology to separate humanity from nature or to control nature itself destroy the deepest experiences of mankind, which originate in metaphor.[1]

> That is, in fact, the unendurable demand of the middle of this century, to restore the metaphor, and thereby displace the scientist from his center. . . . The scientist will describe the structure and list the properties of the molecule . . . but the scientist will not look at the metaphorical meaning of the physical structure. . . . He will not ponder what biological or spiritual experience is suggested by the formal structure of the molecule, for metaphor is not to the present interest of science. It is instead the desire of science to be able to find the cause of cancer in some virus: a virus—you may count on it—which will be without metaphor. You see, that will then be equal to saying that the heart of the disease of all diseases is empty of meaning, that cancer is caused by a specific virus which has no character or quality, and is in fact void of philosophy and bereft of metaphysics. . . . a future to life depends on creating forms of an intensity which will capture the complexity of modern experience and dignify it, illumine . . . its danger . . . the discovery of new meaning may live in ambush at the center of a primitive fire. (pp. 310–11)

Mailer contrasts intuitive perceptions and a primitive knowledge of life with what he calls generally "totalitarianism." On the one hand are those deeply felt experiences of mankind that are unconscious, spiritual, telepathic, and primitive. The writer must try to tap such experiences by boldly exploring the mystery of his own life and of the life around him. He explores the mystery of himself by adventuring into "the jungle of his unconscious." With the lessons of this inward journey he explores the world around him and tries to glimpse the outer "reality . . . unconsciously, telepathetically," and metaphorically. The writer does not explore mystery to categorize its elements or to convert or manipulate it. His explorations increase his understanding of what is and what can be. The primitive truth Mailer seeks is the nature of our world's spiritual ecology and economy; he wants to know how the individual and humanity can best live and grow as a part of something larger than itself. Musing on Frazer's *The Golden Bough*, Mailer considers the primordial and spiritual field of force in which we live, and he believes that there is some exchange, some communication of forces and totem relation between all life—men, trees, grain, insects, and animals.[2]

1. *Cannibals and Christians* (hereafter cited as *CC*), pp. 307–9. Unless otherwise indicated, all citations are to works by Norman Mailer.
2. *CC*, pp. 108, 211, 274. See also *Of a Fire on the Moon* (hereafter cited as *Fire*),

On the other hand is "cancer" or totalitarianism, which Mailer calls the disease of our time. By totalitarianism Mailer refers generally to that tendency in the modern world to regiment and pacify life, to homogenize diversity and individuality, and to stifle dissent and change. Whatever cuts off humanity from its roots and from its instincts is also totalitarian. In his fiction and nonfiction, Mailer associates institutions, persons, or forces with totalitarianism by their intentions, functions, and effects in the world. Mailer's central metaphor for totalitarianism is the Devil, or Death; his central metaphor for the intuitive, instinctual life is God, or Life.[3]

In his fiction and nonfiction, Mailer's heroes participate in the battle between Life and Death and engage in a quest to find the roots of life and to embody what Mailer calls "It." In *Advertisements for Myself*, he associates It with Lawrence's "blood," Hemingway's "Good," Shaw's life force, the Yoga's *prana*, and divine energy.[4] The quest of Mailer's narrator-heroes is founded upon the author's perception of transcendent forces operating in the human being and the phenomenal world. In 1975 Mailer summed up his convictions about the struggle between Life and Death forces and about the necessary quest for life force after reading *Bantu Philosophy* in preparation for writing *The Fight*. These convictions generate the theme and pattern of Mailer's whole canon.

> For he discovered that the instinctive philosophy of African tribesmen happened to be close to his own. Bantu philosophy . . . saw humans as forces, not beings. Without putting it into words, he had always believed that. . . . By such logic, men and women were more than the parts of themselves, which is to say more than the result of their heredity and experience. A man was not only what he contained, not only his desires, his memory and his personality, but also the forces that came to inhabit him at any moment from all things living and dead. So a man was not only himself but the karma of all generations past that still lived in him, not only a human with his own psyche but also a part of the

pp. 468–69. Mailer makes the same point about the "telepathic power of things" in *The Faith of Graffiti*, no pagination; photographs by Mervyn Kurlansky and Jon Naar.

3. See *CC*, pp. 238–39, for the more complete discussion of totalitarianism. See also *The Presidential Papers* (hereafter cited as *PP*), pp. 6–7. My use of the phrase "Life against Death" derives from those words and that theme as they arise in Mailer's work, not from Norman O. Brown's *Life against Death*. I avoid parallels between Brown's work and Mailer's because I believe the two writers are on antithetical paths in one significant way. In his early work, Brown is a thoroughgoing Freudian. My psychological emphasis is Jungian. Though both Freud and Jung are seminal figures in modern psychoanalysis, Mailer himself has disparaged the reductionist and materialistic tendencies in Freudianism (just as Brown has done in his more recent work) in favor of Jung and transcendental existentialism.

4. *Advertisements for Myself* (hereafter cited as *Ads*), p. 351.

resonance, sympathetic or unsympathetic, of every root and
thing . . . about him. He would take his balance, his quivering place,
in a field of all the forces of the living and dead. . . . One did one's best
to live in the pull of those forces in such a way as to increase one's own
force. . . . but the beginning of wisdom was to enrich oneself, enrich
the *muntu* which was the amount of life in oneself, the size of the
human being in oneself.[5]

Mailer's work since *The Naked and the Dead* is a series of explorations into the forces operating in our lives. No writer has been more
aware of the limits of programmatic realism for expressing his
perceptions of these forces. In a speech to the Modern Language
Association, he argues that both the realistic and aristocratic impulses in American letters have failed to "ignite the nation's consciousness of itself." In our century, movies, the mass media, and
television fill the gap left by this failure with a meretricious, commercial art that disproportionately shapes the consciousness of the
people. In the process, Mailer believes the deepest, most unrecover-
able human experiences have been lost. For Mailer the tragedy is
that our survival depends upon mankind's deepest experiences. To
recover such experience, Mailer prescribes "robust art."

Such art would be existential in theme; it would depict, for
example, a hero who must face his own being by defying chaos,
testing his courage, and creating a self on his own terms rather than
on the terms of a society that seems absurd. But Mailer's existentialism assumes metaphysical proportions. Indeed, the pattern
most consistently emerging from his work, as he describes it, is a
reflection of his obsession with how God exists. Is He essential or
existential? Is He all-powerful or an "embattled existential creature
who may succeed or fail in His vision" like the rest of us (*CC*, p. 214)?
A robust art must also be "hearty" and "savage"; that is, it would
depict a protagonist's struggle to reach somehow what is fundamental and primitive in his or her humanity. Robust art, Mailer argues,
must also give definition to its subject, depict precise if extreme
experience, and help to "protect the world from its dissolution in
compromise, lack of focus, and entropy," all of which characterize
the "plague" or disease of "progressive formlessness" in our time. In
the modern world the dream is the vehicle of our deepest experiences, and one vehicle for robust art, therefore, is the dream novel.
By dream, Mailer does not mean simple Freudian wish fulfillment
but a "theatrical review" in which we test, with a surrealistic
intensity, our capacity to meet the shocks and ambushes of the
waking world that affect our conscious and unconscious life. As his
career developed through 1968, Mailer placed more and more em-

5. *The Fight*, pp. 38–39.

phasis on the dream, which he calls "the country cousin" of the novel.[6]

Mailer frankly considers his role as novelist to be that of spiritual missioner and embattled therapist or exorcist in the modern world. He has argued that the new frontier for the American novel lies in the attack upon the "dead forts" of the spirit and the collective cowardice that have entrapped humanity since World War II (*CC*, p. 130). Mailer is on a metaphysical errand as well as an existential one. He has tried to gain some of the complexity and power of expression that the oldest dreamers had. In examining medieval visionary allegory, Paul Piehler echoes Mailer's own description of the positivist's usurpation of the dreamer in the modern world: "the external troubles of modern society are no longer felt as sufficiently complex and overwhelming to require resort to visions; instead they are dealt with by purely external authorities on rational principles. Priest and prophet have given way to bureaucrat and politician."[7]

When we consider that Mailer's themes focus on the battle between Life and Death, when we see that the dream is the foundation of his concept of robust art, when we understand that Mailer's concern over the survival of the human race urges him to write books that are intended to generate action, it should not be improbable that Mailer writes allegorically. Yet it is precisely the question of the mode of Mailer's art that split his early critics into two camps— his detractors, the realists, and his defenders, those who began to see other strengths and goals beyond realism in his novels during the late sixties.

It is in his recourse to the dream, to perceptions generally termed *visionary*, and to the allegorical mode that Mailer's work is to be distinguished from realism as well as from the fabulism (the conscious or mechanical appropriation of specific parables, epics, or myths) associated with many of his American contemporaries.[8] Yet the problem remains that if the criticism of the late sixties and early seventies has suggested an approach to Mailer, it has not been definitive, and it has abused the very terminology and tradition that criticism of Mailer most needs to clarify. In fact, the misconceptions

6. I am summarizing Mailer's discussion of robust art in *CC*, pp. 101–3, 214, and in *Existential Errands: Twenty-Six Pieces Selected by the Author from the Body of All His Writings*, pp. 111–12, 122.

7. Paul Piehler, *The Visionary Landscape*, p. 4.

8. Such recent critics as Robert Merrill are still missing the distinction between conscious fabulism and visionary allegory. Merrill concludes that Mailer's *An American Dream* and *Why Are We in Vietnam?* are failures of fabulation. Merrill compares Mailer's "fables" unfavorably to Nabokov's, Pynchon's, and Barth's modern fables. But Mailer's works fail as fables only because Mailer is not a fabulist but an archetypal allegorist. See Robert Merrill's *Norman Mailer* (Boston: Twayne, 1978), especially p. 85.

about allegory are so widespread that the term must be defined in any study of its use. I intend to do so specifically as I go along, but some general qualities of allegory need emphasis at the outset. We need a substantial conception of the allegorical mode in the face of loose usage, misconception, and bias. Three studies are particularly useful in clarifying what allegory is: Edwin Honig's *Dark Conceit*, Angus Fletcher's *Allegory: The Theory of a Symbolic Mode*, and Paul Piehler's *The Visionary Landscape*.

Allegory, which excludes no literary genre, is viable in all times because it seeks to fulfill what Fletcher has called "major social and spiritual needs." The fulfillment of such needs is precisely Mailer's purpose. The problem of understanding allegory arises from the simple fact that modern criticism is still swayed by the nineteenth-century aesthetic that separated symbolic literature from the allegorical. The creators of this aesthetic, notably Coleridge, argued that in allegory the symbols are disembodied from "real" people and events and become mere simulacra in a moral lesson. But the structure of true allegory is neither preconceived nor totally opposed to the realistic, pragmatic approach to life. Fletcher has stressed that allegory is rarely a "pure modality," and Honig has said that a pure modality would "neglect the moral qualifications that make experience meaningful" as much as programmatic realism.[9]

What we may need most is a distinction between allegories. When I refer to *rational allegory*, I mean allegory that separates from the mode its ancient function of representing a spiritual world through the details of the phenomenal world, as allegory in the eighteenth century tended to separate the spiritual world from the phenomenal. The appeal of rational allegory, therefore, lies solely in the direct translatability of all the allegorical material and in the writer's display of rational ingenuity and wit. When I refer to *true allegory*, I mean allegory that reunites the spiritual and phenomenal worlds. Such allegories portray mankind's direct encounter with spiritual powers and with an inner, visionary world largely through the details of the phenomenal world.[10] This second definition is crucial to Mailer's work because Mailer tries to regenerate our primitive capacity to perceive spiritual truths by restoring a lost spiritual dimension to our internal lives and our external world. True allegory subsumes rational allegory. In true allegory the conscious and symbolic functions of mind operate simultaneously, creating an indivisible, organic whole. By symbolic I mean the prerational and the

---

9. Edwin Honig, *Dark Conceit*, p. 180. Angus Fletcher, *Allegory: The Theory of a Symbolic Mode*, pp. 312–13. Future references are parenthetical.

10. This distinction is based on Piehler's distinction between "allegory proper" and "allegory as genre." See *Landscape*, pp. 10–12, 45.

intuitive elements of allegory that are, as Piehler has pointed out, expressed through "ancient and profound images," the emotional impact of which is strong but not entirely explicable in rational terms. As Piehler suggests, we can best understand these images "in terms of their development from the mythological imagery of Western culture," or, I would add, in terms of what we now recognize as archetypal patterns and images.

I will base my discussion of archetypal images on the work of Jung for several reasons. Like Jung, Mailer is interested in the unconscious as a primitive source of psychic truth and a potential source of psychic integration or wholeness. Both Mailer and Jung believe that the self (the total personality) has both somatic and mental bases, and that psychic phenomena are rooted not only in body and mind and not only in conscious and unconscious mind, but in the personal and transpersonal psyche. Both, for example, stress the influence of collective human experience upon the psychic experiences of individuals. Further, in examining relationships between structure and theme, an analysis of archetypal imagery helps us to understand a work's symbolic design. In allegory, structure and theme are especially close. Jung's work represents the original and most comprehensive system of archetypal imagery. Moreover, Jung's explanations of the impulses behind psychic images can, when appropriate, illuminate ramifications in a work we would otherwise miss. It is significant, for instance, that Mailer's conception of the crisis in modern consciousness is close to Jung's conception of the spiritual crisis in modern humanity, just as Mailer's view of the modern crisis is close to the view of such post-Jungians as Joseph Campbell and Erich Neumann, whose works will also help us to understand the patterns in Mailer's work.

On the other hand we do not know how familiar Mailer is with Jung, although in a rare reference to Jung in the 1960s, Mailer points out that he is an "existential psychologist." I myself doubt that Mailer is as closely familiar with Jung as he is with those psychologists he mentions frequently: Freud (with little sympathy), Wilhelm Reich, and Robert Lidner. Though of course we can assume any writer in midcentury is aware of Jung, and though we know the modern writer has much mythical material available to him as a part of his cultural inheritance, Mailer's intellectual coincidence with Jung appears to be more accidental than studied. And there are at least three other reasons to suggest that Mailer's symbolic and archetypal imagery is more authentic (or visionary) than it is mechanically borrowed.

First, after *The Naked and the Dead*, Mailer began to emphasize the unconscious elements of his work, just as he continually disparaged the reductive, mechanical appropriation of psychological theory in some of his contemporaries. Mailer admits that in writing *The Naked and the Dead* he thought in terms of symbols, forms, allegorical (or rational) structures, and classical myths and that he could barely write a sentence without convincing himself it was on five levels. But as soon as he jettisons such "lower academic literary apparatus" in favor of simple writing without "a formal thought" in his conscious mind, he starts writing what I believe to be true (or archetypal) allegory, though he gives every reason to believe he is unaware of it.[11] In the *Paris Review* interview in 1964, Mailer again describes his mode of working in *Barbary Shore* as possession by "some intelligence" that (questions of the book's quality aside) demonstrated to him that he had "no conscious control of it; if I hadn't heard about the unconscious I would have had to postulate one to explain the phenomenon." He divides the book into conscious (political) and unconscious (sexual and psychotic) themes and levels.[12]

Second, if Mailer is aware of the unconscious themes and images in his books, he does not, however, like to analyze them himself, as he made clear when a young professor probed him on the issue during the march on the Pentagon. Mailer's "regard . . . for the power of symbols suspected a discussion of their nature was next to defacing them."[13] In an interview with Laura Adams for *Partisan Review*, Mailer insists his books must rest on the "realistic content before their metaphorical content can be sustained." But he goes on to define his "realism" itself not as the "ordinary" realism but as the realism of extreme experience, just as he argues that the meta-phorical-realistic level is not mere "fantasy" but "psychic reality."[14] In short, Mailer is aware of the role of his unconscious in his work but is unable and unwilling to define that role specifically, which is

11. Mailer's statements here appear in *Existential Errands*, p. 102. In 1948, Mailer suggested what kind of rational "allegorical" element he has in mind in *Naked* when he claimed the book to be not simply realistic but a "symbolic" and "composite" view of the Pacific war. Mount Anaka, for example, was to represent for the men who challenged her "death and man's creative urge, fate, man's desire to conquer the elements—all kinds of things that you never dream of separating and stating so badly." See *Current Biography, 1948*, ed. Anna Rothe (New York: H. W. Wilson, 1948), p. 410. But no emphasis on the rational symbolism of *Naked* completely discounts a strongly derivative naturalism.

12. *Paris Review* 8:31 (1964): 35, 40.

13. *The Armies of the Night*, p. 69.

14. Laura Adams, "Existential Aesthetics: An Interview with Norman Mailer," pp. 200–201. This distinction is confusing, and Mailer, defensive about his symbolism, is probably trying to suggest something such as he did in *CC* when he said that there is "no clear boundary between experience and imagination," p. 211. At any rate, since *Armies* his comments on and use of the dream elements in his work have been gradually tempered by a caution that suggests a movement toward strengthening the realistic element in his work.

probably as it should be. Analysis is the job of the critic. And Mailer's reticence is in fact typical of a tendency in post-eighteenth-century allegorists, as Honig points out. The modern allegorist is a symbolist in retreat from any view of his art that would identify his work with a "predetermined moral or aesthetic schema." He or she also retreats from any "irresponsible eclecticism" in art and from any scientific or psychological theories that would make art seem to serve the social causes and programs of others. The modern allegorist is caught between defending his own art and assaulting all art that seems to falsify, or to distort by simplifying, the complex nature of mankind's life and destiny. Melville, Honig's first example, denied any allegorical content or intention in *Moby Dick* until Nathaniel and Sophia Hawthorne brought Melville to an understanding of allegory that led him to accept the "part-&-parcel allegoricalness of the whole."[15]

Third, in Mailer's work, the archetypal patterns and images emerge gradually over the years; they do not spring fully developed, as we would expect they might were they merely lifted out of Jung. But whether we approach Mailer with a penchant for the rational and mechanical or the prerational and spontaneous, the analysis of the archetypal patterns either way reveals coherences, meanings, designs, and themes explicable only in terms of the archetypal imagery itself. Such imagery by its nature appeals to the whole person, not just to conscious self, and that appeal to the whole is fundamental to Mailer's approach to his readers and to the extension of consciousness.

It would be useful at this point to define four general qualities of allegory based upon the work of Honig, Fletcher, and Piehler. These four qualities are important to this study of Mailer's own allegories. The general theoretical points I will make here are illustrated in detail in the three studies of allegory cited. The first quality of allegories is that they are dominated by their themes. We could say that realism is the fiction of sense experience and allegory is the fiction of ideas, but it would be more accurate to say that in allegory, the dominant idea controls sense experience, imagery, and action. Sense experience in turn reveals idea. The theme, or the ideal as Honig calls it, is the central concept the whole work "proves or fulfills." Since the ideal is typically rooted in the metaphysical impulse of the writer, allegory is not only art, but art constantly moving toward religion and philosophy.

Both Honig and Fletcher emphasize that allegorical theme is

15. Honig's examples here are Kafka, Joyce, Faulkner, and Mann. Honig points out similar attitudes toward the "allegorical" in their work on the part of Poe and Henry James. See *Dark Conceit*, pp. 51–52, 193–95.

typically reducible to an essential, theological dualism, which may, as Honig believes, arise from the polarized nature of the human mind itself. As the narrative progresses, the essential polarities are dramatized in conflict. The specific identities of persons as well as objects and events grow out of the larger oppositional relationships. The persons, objects, and events represent, in microcosm, polarities and conflicts that are macrocosmic. A person or thing is literally itself, but it is also a part, a finite manifestation, of an infinite polarity. The reader is increasingly aware that he is in a world of concentrated purpose. This concentration is one element of allegory that gives it the characteristics of a dream, or what Honig calls the "Dream Artifice."

But the reader or critic often assumes that the connection between dominant ideal and the narrative specifics is mechanical. The central argument of *Dark Conceit* is that the ideal is identified with and revealed through an organic design and purpose. The purposes and meanings of persons and things must be amplified and grow naturally out of each action in the narrative, extending in the narrative process the original identities of persons and things to as "many clusters of meaning as the traffic of the dominant ideal will bear" (Honig, p. 114). We must distinguish, therefore, between mere moralizing and symbolizing a philosophic view. In symbolizing, the fiction and the allegory are simultaneous and integrated, not separated, creations. It is this integration of the literal and the symbolic visions of reality that gives allegory its self-contained creative authority.

A second quality of allegory is that allegorical characters, which may range from the most hollow type-character to a most realistic or dynamic character, tend to act according to what Fletcher calls the principle of "daemonic agency." Characters act as if they were possessed by some larger force, idea, or habit. As main characters align themselves as agents or synecdoches fitting into the dualistic pattern, they generate subcharacters, or doubles, who react with or against them. In the daemonic world, the limits of freedom are narrow, and as we might expect, only the more heroic, powerful characters are able to alter their progress toward one element of the dualism or the other, that is, toward good or evil, Life or Death. In Mailer, for example, we will see that the stasis of a character is precisely what defines his or her defeat and the hero's danger.

This allegorical hero, whether he represents the values of the dominant culture or represents alienation or autonomy from a culture, typically undergoes the ordeal of a quest, the goal of which may be unknown to the hero. His quest is an archetypal quest for greater life, energy, movement, and self-realization, and the quest is typically initiated by some threshold symbol that suggests the thematic center of the allegory and serves as an emblem of narrative and symbolic coherence—Dante's dark forest, Bunyan's "Den" and "man clothed in rags," Melville's Spouter Inn and Peter Coffin signs, or Hawthorne's wild rosebush beside a prison door. The hero's quest progresses in a concentrated, dreamlike world where "every experience has greater possible value than the hero himself can detect." The hero will depend on others to help him understand the quest's meaning, and he will face the choice between misleading or helpful guides (see Honig, pp. 70–74, 78). Whether we recognize the allegorical hero by such physical signs as a talisman, some burden, or some peculiarity of appearance, he is always a person about to undergo some rite of passage or ordeal that will test his capacity to be a bearer of new consciousness. Since the chief purpose of Mailer's writings is to stimulate a new consciousness, it is important to see the heroes in his work as moving toward this goal.

A third quality of allegory is equally important to any consideration of Mailer's allegories because it is relevant to a central criticism against his work: it is realistically improbable. But in allegory, plausibility of action depends on criteria other than mere verisimilitude or Aristotelian mimesis. Allegory may depend upon verisimilitude, but it often depends on other principles of causation and unity: magic, telepathy, ritualistic necessity, daemonic agency, or the generation of subcharacters and doubles. If the characters do not interact plausibly or according to probability, they still act with, as Fletcher puts it, "a certain logical necessity."

A fourth quality of allegory is symbolic action, by which I mean the structure allegories are likely to take. Fletcher divides the structural possibilities into progress and battle. Progress may be simply a physical quest in which the hero leaves one "home" to journey to another. Or, the journey may be an introspective one through the self, or as in Mailer's case, the physical journey may clearly represent an inward journey. The goal of the journey is self-knowledge. All that the journey requires to represent progress is forward motion toward some goal. To the extent that the hero is a daemonic agent, he has no choice but to stay on his quest (see Fletcher, pp. 150–57).

Battle gives allegory its peculiar dialectical structure. This structure is represented by the ancient gigantomachia—the battle between Titans for control of the world—of Hesiod; or, it is represented by psychomachia—the psychologized "fight for mansoul" typified by the "debate" and the "dialogue," as in Mailer's earliest allegories, or by actual violence symbolizing ideological warfare. Progress often merges with battle in a single allegory. But Fletcher maintains one distinction between the two. Progress assumes "manifestly a ritual form," a sequence of equal steps in one principal direction. Battle, on the other hand, has the effect of symmetry and balance. For whereas ritual implies "a continual unfolding, a moving sequence," symmetry implies stasis, or conflict caught in "a given moment of time." The conflict of battle can be symmetrically repeated within a work so that we see each side's ideological arguments presented more or less equally, as they are in *Barbary Shore* (see Fletcher, pp. 157–59). As Honig points out, the dream, allegory, and heroic mythology all share these four allegorical qualities (pp. 68–72, 173–74).

We saw that Mailer admitted to a mechanical use of narrative levels and symbols in *The Naked and the Dead.* He has also admitted, and numerous critics have echoed, his debt to such realists as Dos Passos and Farrell in his first published novel. But our concern here will be with the quite different direction of Mailer's work after *Naked*, with Mailer's departure from naturalism, with his explorations into his own unconscious, and with his conscious and unconscious allegorical techniques. In the following chapters, beginning with *Barbary Shore*, we will look at each major work with a specificity seldom applied. We will approach allegory with a view to surmounting both prejudice against the allegorical tradition and misconceptions about Mailer's use of the mode. Mailer writes books in which the material world is given transcendent meaning. He tries to create narratives that are no longer "void of philosophy and bereft of metaphysics," that engage the writer and reader in the exploration of the unconscious, and that confront the reader with an intensity that Mailer believes may restore reality to metaphor and a future to life.

2

Barbary Shore

The Ewe of Africa bring offerings to their chopping knives . . . and other tools, and recognize spirits called *trō* in hollow trees, in springs, in nests of termites. "The moment," says J. Speith . . . "in which an object or its striking characteristics enters into any remarkable relationship with human spirit and life, whether this is agreeable or repellent, is the birth hour of the *trō* for the consciousness of the Ewe." —Wayne Shumaker, *Literature and the Irrational*

After his success with the derivative naturalism of *The Naked and the Dead*, Mailer searched for a new subject and mode. He felt he had exhausted the experiences of his first twenty-four years in his first novel; yet he also felt he had to prove to himself and to everyone else that he was capable of something new.[1] What he discovers in writing *Barbary Shore* (1951) is the allegorical mode. We might expect that a writer's experiment with something new would have its weaknesses, and *Barbary Shore* has several. It is for one thing too pure a use of the mode. The reader is kept at too great a distance from the characters. The dream artifice is so obvious as to appear arbitrary. And just when the novel reaches its greatest potential for movement and growth, it is consumed by an ideological debate and, as Mailer put it, ultimately collapses "into a chapter of political speech" (*Ads*, p. 94).

On the other hand, in *Cannibals and Christians*, Mailer describes *Barbary Shore* as his most imaginative novel. This novel comes least from external experience and most from internal impulses.[2] Mailer tried to fit what he called his sense of "unreality" after writing *Naked* "into a drastic vision, an introduction of the brave to the horrible, a dream, a nightmare which would belong to others and yet be my own." Mailer acknowledges that this experiment in imagination was a failure because he tried for something beyond his reach, but he also assesses accurately the importance of *Barbary* in the evolution of his work. "Much of my later writing cannot be

---

1. See *Advertisements for Myself* (hereafter cited as *Ads*), pp. 92–93. Future references are parenthetical. Unless otherwise indicated, all citations are to works by Norman Mailer.

2. *Cannibals and Christians*, p. 211.

13

understood without a glimpse of the odd shadow and theme-maddened light *Barbary Shore* casts before it" (*Ads*, p. 94).

The critics' failure to examine the imaginative energy in *Barbary Shore* has caused a false critical emphasis. Beginning with Norman Podhoretz, critics tend not to rise above the artificiality of the novel's political allegory. Criticism has stifled *Barbary* with a series of rational, diagrammatic schemes such as John Stark's: Hollingsworth is Capitalist State, Lannie and Lovett are Trotskyism, McLeod is Bolshevism, Guinevere is the Masses—all of which, Stark assures us, add up to "a capsule history of the Left."[3] But the novel is much more than its political allegory. Between 1949 and 1955 Mailer came to see "that politics as politics interests me less . . . than politics as a part of everything else in life" (*Ads*, p. 271). So while he was discovering the allegorical mode, Mailer was also moving away from his interest in political machinery and ideology and moving toward his explorations of ultimate values, toward Good and Evil. His breaking away from the Progressive party in 1949 and writing *Barbary Shore* were two acts that reflect this movement.

The political allegory in *Barbary* is a metaphor for something larger. This novel is Mailer's first definite expression of his metaphysical preoccupations; it begins his continuously expanding vision of the forces at work in our lives. It is partially Mailer's own fault that the cumulative effect of the novel's political terminology obscures its larger theme for the critics.[4] At this stage Mailer is not completely

3. John Stark, "*Barbary Shore*: The Basis of Mailer's Best Work," *MFS*, pp. 403–4.
4. Early and late this is true. The novel's reception in 1951 started a view of *Barbary Shore* it has never quite recovered from. Maxwell Geismar called it a novel of the "political issues of our time" expressing the theme that a normal sex life is impossible until "the neurosis of history has been reconciled." Though he thought the novel worked well "symbolically," Geismar felt it was still a mistake. One wonders what he meant by "symbolically." To him Guinevere is a slut, Monina a "parody of a Hollywood starlet," Lannie the "ostensible" heroine. See "Frustrations, Neuroses, and History," *Saturday Review*, pp. 15–16. Irving Howe, in "Some Political Novels," *Nation*, p. 568, says this "bad" novel can be read as a "political allegory" but that the "weird collection of disembodied voices" fails to draw our interest. He ends by charging *Barbary Shore* with an unimpressive political message, which is, in the "long run," too negative, dogmatic, and untrue. Charles Rolo liked the novel better and considered it a "remarkable advance" in imaginative coloring and in style over *The Naked and the Dead*. Yet he felt the parts far more impressive than the whole, regretting that the novel never achieved "the coherence of a political parable." He also disliked the "fuzzy political nihilism" of Mailer's plague-on-both-your-houses attitude. See "A House in Brooklyn," *Atlantic*, pp. 82–83. Such recent critics as Jean Radford, Philip Bufithis, and Robert Merrill echo similar views. In *Norman Mailer: A Critical Study*, p. 51, Jean Radford considers *Barbary Shore* a political allegory in which Lovett and Lannie represent the modern split in political consciousness. Philip Bufithis, in *Norman Mailer* (New York: Frederick Ungar, 1978), p. 34, calls the novel a "political commentary on the state of the world." In *Norman Mailer*, Robert Merrill dismisses *Barbary* as an "Orwellian political novel" and a "rigid allegory," see p. 66.

clear about how he will express the difference between political or historical fact and the metaphorical ramifications of that fact. But surely *Barbary* demonstrates its author's consciousness of politics as metaphor rather than politics as merely politics. The conflict between FBI agent Hollingsworth and Marxist theoretician McLeod, which is the fundamental conflict in the book, is a metaphor for the conflict between just this limited vision of things and events as facts in themselves (Hollingsworth's "realism" as McLeod calls it) and that "metaphysical" vision that sees the metaphorical meaning of things or events (McLeod's "context"). What confuses, what is unfortunate, is that Mailer, through McLeod, uses such political terminology as *socialist culture* or *revolutionary socialism* to identify what McLeod also calls "metaphysical" vision. We shall see that by such terminology McLeod does not mean any dogmatic ideology and still less any political or legislative machinery. He means a consciousness that perceives the connections between things, people, and actions, and between parts and wholes. Mailer's imprecise use of terminology suggests his own inability to use politics effectively as metaphor during this important transitional period in the early fifties.

If the misplaced critical emphasis on *Barbary Shore* is more understandable than it is admirable, we can still best comprehend the novel by examining the imaginative energy of its art. For all of its weaknesses as an experiment in allegory, *Barbary* is artistically consistent and compact. Its strengths lie not in its political, rational allegory, but in its true allegory. This novel has the coherence of a fully symbolic process. Every detail has a purpose; every character and image fit, with striking congruity, into the larger pattern and theme. This becomes clear as the characters are marshaled, through the images they project, on the side of either Life or Death. Mailer expresses his theme of Life against Death through a peculiarly allegorical technique. The important thing about this theme and technique is that they establish a pattern, a central line of organization and structure, that, with variations, becomes the pattern of Mailer's future work. In its largest outlines, this pattern is an archetype of rebirth.

Mikey Lovett is the narrator-hero. Wounded, amnestic, he represents the innocent, potential consciousness that will grow, and from which self-realization will increase. What he witnesses generates his growth.

> Probably I was in the war. There is the mark of a wound behind my ear, an oblong of *unfertile flesh* where no hair grows. It is covered over now, and may be *disguised* by even the clumsiest barber, but no barber can hide the scar on my back. For that a tailor is more in order.

> When I stare into the mirror I am returned a face doubtless more handsome than the original, but the straight nose, the modelled chin, and the smooth cheeks are only evidence of a stranger's art. It does not matter how often I decide the brown hair and gray eyes must have always been my own; there is nothing I can recognize, not even my age . . . but thanks to whoever tended me, a young man without a wrinkle in his skin stands for a *portrait* in the mirror (my italics).[5]

Lovett is at this point a hollow young man who "had no past and was therefore without a future"; he is unable to understand or see relationships between the people he meets, feeling "like an adolescent first entering the adult world where everyone is strange and individual." He has "so disconnected" himself from the world that he has "everything to discover." This loss of identity shames him. He is determined to hide his loss and to "masquerade like anyone else," indeed like every other character in the novel, while he waits for some "sign" that will return his past and future, his identity, to him.

At the end of Chapter 1, this narrator introduces us to one of his fantasies; this fantasy begins the dreamlike perspective of the novel and serves as a threshold symbol of the journey that is to come. Lovett sees a "traveller," a plump middle-aged man who returns from a "long trip" and is in a hurry to get home. He cannot read the newspaper on his "peaceful" and "weary" ride through the city in his cab. Suddenly he discovers the cab has taken the wrong route, but he dares not disturb the driver. He can only watch "his city" pass by the windows. Though it is his city, he has never seen these streets, the "architecture is strange," the people "dressed in unfamiliar clothing," a sign "printed in an alphabet he cannot read." To quiet his horror, the man tells himself this is only a dream, but Lovett, the dreamer, calls out to the man that he is wrong, that this is no dream but the real city and that his cab is history. Then "the image shatters." Immediately Lovett tells us that "what has been fanciful is now concrete." "Now" is that future from which he writes to us; it is a time in which buildings have electric circuits that no longer function and people are compelled to fourteen hours labor each day (p. 56).

Much in the first third of the novel reinforces the dream quality of the narrative that Lovett's fantasy of the traveler initiates. This dream artifice makes us continually refer the events and vision of the novel to Lovett's state of mind. His mind is fragmented between reality and fantasy; he has great difficulty telling whether his fantasies, "voyages" as he calls them, reflect real or mythical events. Some he senses are "false shores," such as his fantasy of sleeping with Guinevere and being disturbed by a stranger who enters the

---

5. *Barbary Shore*, p. 3. Future references are parenthetical.

bedroom from "the threshold" to menace him (p. 58). But even such "false shores" portend future events. The stranger, for example, turns out to be McLeod (p. 83). The technical function of the fantasies is to sustain the blur of unconsciousness throughout the novel and to emphasize the ambiguous possibility that the novel's world and characters are products of Lovett's dreaming mind. Indeed, the journey that began as a dream will end as one. Lovett, at the novel's end, tosses at night on his bed as all the dramatis personae dance before him. "Each of them passed before me, magnified, exaggerated, conducting a monologue to which I was audience. . . . So they danced. . . . Had I conducted dialogues with them through the night?" (pp. 289–90). The fantasies also give Lovett a kind of protean identity in this fanciful, fluctuating world while he searches for a real identity: he can be and is warrior, lover, labor-camp victim, all-American youth, or revolutionary.

As Lovett introduces his six main characters, we come to see that a particular kind of drama is taking place. In this drama characters reveal themselves to be "agents" whose conflicts are less interpersonal struggles than battles between the larger forces that compete to shape the modern world. What Mailer invigorates by such a drama is the primitive force of allegory as embodied, for example, in the medieval dream vision. With *Barbary Shore*, Mailer initiates a series of allegories in which a central consciousness registers and responds to, and to varying degrees participates in, the debates and battles of what Paul Piehler in *The Visionary Landscape* calls *potentiae*. The visionary's quest is for some principle of authority by which his life may be regulated. The *potentiae* represent spiritual forces of good and evil; their dialogues and battles are offered to the reader for "spiritual participation," so that readers may avail themselves of the processes of "healing and transcendence."

When we consider Mailer's later allegories, it becomes increasingly important to understand that the *potentiae* of allegory generally embody, as Piehler puts it, the power of mythical figures, or archetypes, as well as "the prosaic accuracy of abstract terms." The dialogues between *potentiae* and between the narrator-hero and the *potentiae* intellectualize processes "otherwise embodied in myth and ritual." *Barbary Shore* typifies the pattern of the visionary dialogue. The dreamer is "profoundly disturbed by some spiritual crisis." His cry for help brings on the dream, which has a mysterious impact; it also summons the beneficent *potentiae* who act as spiritual authorities and guides. The guides—a nature goddess or wise old sage, for example—are connected to the cosmic imagery of the allegory itself. The resolution of the dreamer's crisis is often achieved by "raising him to a higher spiritual state." The basic psychological strategy is to overcome evil forces by identifying, analyzing, and confronting them with healing forces so that they may be "repudiated and destroyed."[6]

Throughout the first nineteen chapters of *Barbary*, Lovett gradually identifies the representatives of good and evil forces who are polarized by the images they project. Images of onanism, sexual perversity, mechanism, stasis, literalness of vision, and lack of sympathy or love express the alliance of Death. Leroy Hollingsworth projects the central image of Death and is the force or influence toward which the dead and dying gravitate.

It is a mark of Lovett's potential that he soon discovers a crack in Hollingsworth's facade, and a mark of Lovett's fortune that Hollingsworth reveals his true nature shortly thereafter in Chapter 13. After Chapter 13, Lovett has less and less difficulty seeing the nature of the other figures as they cluster about Hollingsworth and reject McLeod. McLeod, the novel's center of wisdom and life, provides the narrator-hero with his first clue to Hollingsworth's nature: "He's got a mind like a garbage pail." Yet even at their first meeting, Lovett senses a vague insidiousness about Hollingsworth. His disordered room seems visited by "violence" rather than "sloth." His movements begin to seem like empty "gestures"; his "hir-hir-hir" of laughter has "no real merriment" but sounds like "the mechanical laughter in a canned radio program, the fans whirring, the gears revolving, the klaxons producing their artificial mirth." Hollingsworth's sharp blue eyes look more and more like "identical daubs of pigment . . . opaque and lifeless." Seeing him straight on, Lovett notices Hollingsworth has the beaked face of a bird and "a black line between his gums and center incisors in his upper jaw" that gives "the impression of something artificial about his mouth" (pp. 38–41). These attributes of Hollingsworth become a sustained motif throughout *Barbary Shore*.

The first third of the novel moves gradually toward Hollingsworth's revelation of his insidious nature. But it is in the climax of Chapter 13 that Lovett feels the full impact of Hollingsworth's nature as Hollingsworth switches back and forth between his "divinity student" facade and the "shocking leer" of his hidden nature in a series of presto changes, which Lovett says "smacked of alchemy." The scene between Lovett, Hollingsworth, and the bar

6. I abstract considerable material from Paul Piehler in these two paragraphs to suggest the visionary qualities of *Barbary*. See Paul Piehler, *The Visionary Landscape*, especially pp. 4–5, 30–31, 38, 62–63, *passim*. Piehler argues that the therapeutic functions of the dialogue are suggested in its evolution from the classical impulse to arrive at "new intellectual truths to a psychodrama directed at the intuitive and emotional functions and shaped so as to promote healing and re-integration of a mind in spiritual turmoil."

waitress clearly illustrates Hollingsworth's double nature and exposes Hollingsworth as sadist, onanist, and bisexual voyeur.[7]

It is during this scene, while Hollingsworth demonstrates his capacity for mechanical cruelty, that he "triumphantly" insinuates his sexual relationship with Guinevere, who manages their rooming house and to whom Lovett is attracted. The whole experience frightens Lovett, who for the first time has "finally sensed the extent of his hatred for me." After assuring Lovett that he has nothing but sympathy for Guinevere, Hollingsworth takes Lovett back to their rooming house to prove to Lovett that Guinevere is his and to show Lovett who Guinevere's husband really is. Here the violent Hollingsworth, lashing out at Guinevere, comes into full light.

Beverly McLeod, or Guinevere, is the first to fall to Hollingsworth. She may have several meanings, depending on whether or not one stresses the political allegory, but her own hollowness is clear, and certainly she is false love and false life, a temptress endangering the hero. Everything about her suggests disorder and sterility. "Guinevere . . . had the basement apartment with its customary entrance . . . and a miniature plot whose stony soil was without even a weed" (p. 13). A personality in continual flux, she mimics the voices and actions of a telephone operator, a fishwife, a landlady, a Jehovah's Witness, a radio announcer, and a "cliché . . . blusterer with a heart of gold." To her, effect is everything, whether producing a "counterfeit simplicity" in her eyes or painting upon her real mouth a false one, "which was wide and curved in the sexual stereotype of a model on a magazine cover," but which "seemed to work in active opposition to the small mobile lips beneath." Lovett would "not have been startled if she had turned around and like the half-dressed queen in a girlie show: surprise! her buttocks are exposed" (pp. 13–14, 17–18, 28, 97). Guinevere cannot separate physical love from profit. "Now you and me could get toegther," she tells Lovett, "but what profit is there in it for me? You tell me" (p. 55). Though he realizes her motives and sees her facade, Lovett is obsessed with consummating his sexual desire for Guinevere. McLeod, Lovett, and Lannie are in turn attracted to her as a source of life, and each is betrayed. What Lannie sees in Guinevere is what McLeod did: her bigness, her beautiful coloring, her trumpeting "I'm full of life" (p. 103). How much Guinevere's past is another of her fantasies makes little difference. What is important is that by the time Lovett meets her she is deadened, existing in a world of Hollywood dreams fed by her hopes for her daughter Monina.

7. See Mailer's remarks on this in "The Homosexual Villain," *Ads*, p. 223. See also *Barbary Shore*, pp. 204, 206, where Hollingsworth's obsession with McLeod's sex life with Guinevere is evident.

Monina *is* Guinevere. Monina keeps the same hours as Guinevere, follows her everywhere ("more vivid than a shadow"), parodies her mother at every turn, and before mirrors kisses "her wrist with the absorbed self-admiration" Guinevere herself shows. Guinevere even argues that Monina is an immaculate conception. Monina acts as a foil to Guinevere and defines her death. Guinevere projects or creates Monina in an obsession to regain her "lost" fame, fortune, and youth. "You're all I got," she says to Monina, as a tear "which might have been genuine" falls down Guinevere's cheek and a compassion just "one degree from self-pity" shines in her face. As one in a parade of onanists in the novel, Guinevere has one channel of sympathy— toward herself. Monina is a stunted self. Guinevere says she wants "to keep her a baby" until they can get to Hollywood and make Monina a child star. After Chapter 13, Mailer accentuates Monina's role as Guinevere's conscience and youth. The split between Guinevere and Monina grows after Chapter 14 when Lovett sees Monina clutching McLeod "about the knees," and Monina begins returning to McLeod.[8] Even though the love between father and daughter is not one of total commitment, it is because of Monina's encourage-ment that McLeod begins to hope to establish a living connection with his wife. He accepts his own part in the disaster of their marriage, and he now sees Guinevere as a "possibility." That he hopes to return to her to "force a revolution into my life" is one mark of his coming defeat.

For as Guinevere becomes more alienated from her youth and conscience, she becomes more set on destroying McLeod. As she tells Lovett, "he stole my youth away," and he gave me "nothing." Though her obsession is her lost youth, she defines that youth only as Hollywood success and her vehicle to it as Hollingsworth. The paradox that traps Guinevere is that her true youth is not Hollywood success through Hollingsworth, but just the capacity for infatuation and devotion to another that Monina begins to demonstrate toward McLeod. Guinevere capitulates to Hollingsworth, and then to Lan-nie, not because she needs love, but because she desires things that channel love and desire back upon oneself, not out to others. Self-love, Lannie will tell her, is "the secret to everything."

Lannie Madison is another double, but she is "a duplicate" of Lovett himself. Lannie represents possibilities of defeat Lovett must

8. Monina as an allegorical figure is here obviously comparable to Hester's Pearl in *The Scarlet Letter.* One wonders, but cannot be sure, whether Mailer is in this novel borrowing techniques and ideas from Hawthorne, whether from *The Scarlet Letter* or from *The Blithedale Romance.* John Stark suggests that Mailer does draw on Hawthorne in the essay cited above. Laura Adams, *Existential Battles: The Growth of Norman Mailer,* p. 41, compares some aspects of *Barbary Shore* to *The Blithedale Romance* and *The Scarlet Letter.*

avoid; she makes a series of contacts and commitments the hero—
through luck, insight, and thwarted temptations—manages to escape. Lannie is an ambiguous figure at first; we do not know whether
she is a figure of Life or Death. "Somehow," Lovett says of her, "she
wove an obligation to accept her verdicts, to feel she had discovered
truths one had never discovered before" (pp. 102–3).

Lannie first appears to Lovett as an image from a dream. He sees a
stranger in a ragged violet suit when he awakens from a drowse; her
slender body balanced awkwardly, much "as though she would leap
into flight if I stirred too quickly." She seems to Lovett a narrow,
gentle, delicate, childish yet ageless sprite. Her background as
Trotskyite, her period of transformation at the hands of some medical institution, and her inability to distinguish fantasy from reality
associate her with Lovett all the more. But her case is more severe,
and between Chapters 14 and 17, she falls utterly to Hollingsworth.
The shock of Trotsky's death brought her to madness. In the asylum
her life was drained from her and placed in a green filing cabinet,
and she therefore sees herself as a sacrificial figure (pp. 151–52).

But Lannie, like Guinevere, is a false savior. She cries against the
absorption of her own life in the asylum, but she supports a very
similar absorption of McLeod's life and mind by Hollingsworth, who
would consign McLeod's life to a briefcase. Lannie tempts Lovett to
Hollingsworth's side. Lovett's escape is narrow. He begins by thinking he loves Lannie. But their lovemaking is mere onanism to him.
Lovett can but "perform" upon her, "remotely without tenderness
or desire or even incapacity." "She lay beneath me stiffly and suf-
fered it with a smile, her face calm and patient, sweet suffering
Jesus upon the cross. . . . All done now?" she asks (pp. 137, 153).

Lannie capitulates to Hollingsworth, first, because she believes
McLeod betrayed revolutionary socialism and must therefore suffer.
She will help effect his punishment by joining forces she once stood
against, since the world is hopeless now anyway and since it is the
Hollingsworths who have the power to punish. Second, but even
more important, is a certain magical power of influence Hollingsworth exerts over her. "I recognized," Lovett says of Lannie's
reaction to his warning that Hollingsworth is false, "that this performance was for Hollingsworth, and not a word of her speech, not
a gesture in the dance of her limbs was uninspired; she might have
been a geisha tracing the ritual of the tea ceremony." If she has a few
lucid intervals where she sees through Hollingsworth, she is always
somehow compelled to reject those perceptions. For example, when
Hollingsworth-as-divinity-student is bitten by Monina, he immediately blurts out, "When I see that kid again . . . I'll cut her fucking
heart out," and suddenly apologizes to "the lady" present with the

explanation that a child's bite can be poisonous. While Lovett and Lannie laugh at Hollingsworth, he sits motionless, but he finally asks, much as Lannie will ask Lovett, "Are you done now?" For "its effect upon her," Lovett tells us, "he might have pressed a button. Her laughter stopped. She quivered through every inch of her body, and I realized suddenly how close she was to hysteria." Hollingsworth taunts her further, and when Lovett threatens him, Lannie defends Hollingsworth. She is compelled to accept her false wise man (pp. 142–49).

Much of Hollingsworth's power over others lies in their strange fascination with the decreative force Hollingsworth represents, which is expressed here, as in so much of Mailer, as uncreative sexuality. It is in Hollingsworth's infertile sex and sadism that Lannie finds peace. He "looks at you as if you do not exist, so that slowly you're beaten beneath him . . . and love has finally come through the only way I want ever to see it when it is smoke and I am in the opium den and thugs beset me." "[H]e tells me what to do and then I do it, and so everything is very simple now" (pp. 156–57). Together, Lannie explains, they will punish McLeod.

But this McLeod, whom they seek to punish, is the novel's central image of Life. McLeod as the representative of Life struggles against the alliance of Death. The images of Life that cluster about McLeod project growth, movement, sympathy, and love, and suggest a kind of vision new to these characters. Until Monina leads Lovett to McLeod in Guinevere's bedroom in Chapter 13, Lovett is uncertain of him. McLeod's most striking difference from the others is his "mania about neatness" in both his room and appearance. But like the others, McLeod too is masquerading. He dresses in "anonymous clothing," keeps his marriage a secret, and works "in a department store as a window dresser." So far he has tested Lovett only in the most tentative way and has told Lovett he sees through his masquerade to pass himself off "like anyone else." By parodying Dinsmore's socialist cant, by probing Lovett to see whether he is a potential friend or enemy, McLeod guides their relationship into one of guarded trust in which McLeod begins to emerge as a teacher, guide, and confessor. "Characteristically," Lovett says of McLeod,

> he sat on his hard chair, arms folded upon his chest, his knees crossed, his eyes boring into me from behind his silver-rimmed spectacles. . . . I went on with my story, and under McLeod's scrutiny, so dispassionate, so balanced, I found myself admitting details which normally I would have found distasteful. In his presence I could find enthusiasm for the balm of confession as if nothing I might relate would ever provoke a dishonest reaction. (pp. 73–74)

When McLeod—"a pedagogue reaching his climax"—responds to his own question about what kind of man Guinevere's husband must be, he gives Lovett an important clue to Guinevere's and McLeod's particular kind of defeat. One chooses life as movement and growth, or one faces the defeat of stasis: "Why does he marry her? Because she gives out an emanation, call it what you will, that makes him think he's . . . *alive*. He knows he's *frozen*, and he wants to be laid against a body that's nice and warm. He sees it as an experiment on himself. That's the kind of man he is, I'm convinced. Only what he doesn't know is that *she's frozen too*" (my italics, p. 76). But after Chapter 13, Lovett and McLeod have a new truth upon which to base their relationship, and McLeod the teacher also becomes McLeod the father. "Once you've found a father, you'd better not to track him to a brothel," McLeod says to Lovett when discovered in Guinevere's bedroom. The revealed truth about Hollingsworth in Chapter 13 and about McLeod in Chapter 14 changes Lovett's perception of the world as the narrative moves into its second phase. Lovett's consciousness of the world and the people in it extends to a new dimension of irrationality and violence. The novel focuses more and more on this new dimension of consciousness; it is a consciousness that disrupts Lovett's tenuous balance.

> I was wretched, and if I had found a balance of sorts, the balance was lost now. . . . So I stood at my distance above the river, and watched a dirty moon yellow the water. Somewhere, today, I had read in the newspaper, a woman had killed her children, and a movie star had enplaned from the West to be wed in a tiny church upon some hill. A boy had been found starving on a roof, a loaded rifle in his hands. The trigger squeezed, the shot rang down the street, and I could have been holding the rifle. I could even hate the boy because he had missed. (p. 118)

The dialogue between Lovett and McLeod is the first "progress" in the allegory. This dialogue represents Mailer's no less than Lovett's movement beyond the muddle between politics and politics as metaphor, the emerging consciousness of hero as well as author. McLeod begins to guide the hero toward a verification of the images of Death. When Lovett and McLeod walk to the Brooklyn Bridge in Chapter 14, the setting of sea fog, murkiness, dull lights, and fog horns signifies the obscurity out of which the hero and his guide must travel. Here McLeod demonstrates his theoretical proclivities and tests Lovett's. McLeod hints at Hollingsworth's identity, at his own communist past, at the failure of his marriage. Tentatively approving Lovett's own assessment of the failure of Soviet Communism, "in the tone of a headmaster," McLeod establishes their alliance when he says: "You see, laddie, we're excrescences, and we're waiting for the stones to grind us between them. Let's not fight, you and I" (pp. 120– 25).

This dialogue has germinated Lovett's new consciousness of his past and his future. He recalls his adolescent dedication to Trotsky, with "the labor of parturition, a heartland of whole experience was separating itself to float toward the sea." The "sea" to which this heartland of past experience is floating is Lovett's mind. By recalling his past, Lovett is also revolutionizing his consciousness: "across my back scar tissue burned ever new circuits with its old pain. Things had altered this night" (pp. 125– 56). In chapters 16, 18, and 19, when McLeod reminds Lovett of the danger the other characters and the world represent—a danger McLeod calls "onanism"—Lovett increases his confused deliberations about the seemingly blameless disintegration of peace in and the economic structure of the modern world and is forced to use the "new circuits" McLeod is helping to burn into him. Lovett must act now upon his perceptions of the other people in the rooming house. He has, for example, less and less trouble turning from Lannie as another false life and toward McLeod. He has just seen Hollingsworth's interrogation chamber in McLeod's old room (p.162), and Guinevere, in her attempt to get Lovett to spy for her, has just told Lovett that the interrogation is about to begin (p. 168). So when McLeod now asks Lovett to leave, Lovett, responding to McLeod's questions, begins to see that he must commit himself to McLeod and accept the "consequences" of that commitment. Following Chapter 19 the ideological debate begins, and we move into the final and largest portion of the novel.

We can see at this point that *Barbary Shore* has a three-part structure. The first thirteen chapters establish a dream artifice, introduce the six main characters, and clarify the central polarization of character and image. This first division of the novel is static; that is, the thematic conflict and what little progress the novel will illustrate is yet to come. The second division of the novel, chapters 14 through 19, develops the relationships and tensions between the characters. In this section the hero is tested and makes limited progress toward increased consciousness, and in the chapters between the McLeod-Lovett dialogues, the other characters are increasingly clarified as onanistic forces of defeat. But the final portion of the novel, chapters 20 through 23, will present the debate between the forces of Life and those of Death, will illustrate the impact of that debate on the characters, and will show the transfer of power from the teacher to the narrator-hero.

As the central agents of Life and Death battle for supremacy in the long debate, Lovett, the witness of this battle, has four lessons impressed upon him. He gains further insight into what makes for

Life and what makes for Death as each side argues its case. He learns
that there are two kinds of consciousness, literal and metaphorical.
He learns that the true meaning of "revolutionary socialism" is the
latter kind of consciousness, which McLeod calls "metaphysical
vision." And he learns, finally, that an expansion of consciousness
makes necessary a personal commitment to the truth such consciousness reveals.

Superficially, the roles of Hollingsworth and McLeod are the
stereotyped roles of FBI agent questioning his subversive prey. But in
Chapter 20 as throughout the debate, Mailer heightens our view of
Hollingsworth as a stereotyped, deadened agent of a larger institution. And when Hollingsworth reads from his collection of McLeod's
writings in Chapter 24, we see that McLeod defines the barbarism
toward which mankind drifts as an example of Death. This barbarism is perpetuated equally by Soviet "State Capitalism" and
American "Monopoly Capitalism" by their exploitations of human
potential to produce wholly for war and by their techniques, developed during World War II, for swallowing all opposition.

Early in the debate (Chapter 20) the principals also illustrate their
sharp differences in consciousness. Hollingsworth is a factologist,
McLeod a metaphysician who sees and thinks metaphorically. Hollingsworth says he is "a simple fellow who concerns himself with the
facts," which he observes is no small matter because "I'm sitting
where I am, and you're sitting where you are." Toward the end of
their debate, Hollingsworth's charge against McLeod is that his
effort to change the world is the work of vanity and futility. After all,
only 98.3 people read each unit of propaganda. McLeod stresses that
he depends upon potentiality and that his work is for the future.
McLeod's repeated emphasis will be upon human potential, upon
the possibility of some new "circuit" that even another world war
may finally burn into our consciousness (pp. 237–86). To this
Hollingsworth can only respond that "we ain't equipped to deal with
big things."

But Chapter 20 also begins to illustrate a second kind of consciousness. Hollingsworth cannot understand what McLeod means
by "metaphysical." So through the examples of the tin can and a
"little object" that he has stolen from the American government,
McLeod tries in vain to make Hollingsworth understand his definition of revolutionary socialism as a way of life based on the capacity
to see objects, persons, and events metaphorically and to distinguish
between the evil (the "petrification of stolen labor," the "gore") and
the good ramifications of objects and events. When Hollingsworth
responds that McLeod is off the point, McLeod argues that there is
never any "point"; there is only "context."

"To begin with, the little object so-called, is completely a problem in context. What is it and where was it born?.... I want to take into account the vast structures which created it.... Supposing I possessed it. Where would it be? You assume woodenly that I've got it wrapped in brown paper, and it's in one of m' pants pockets. Or perhaps it's buried in the ground. But you've got no call to assume either. I might be keeping it here"—and he pointed to his head. "Or maybe nobody knows what it is. That's possible too. You don't have to know what something is to appreciate its value. You can still trace its relation to other things." (p. 192)

Hollingsworth's request for "practical examples" leads McLeod's speculations to the furthest reaches of the novel. " 'In the modern heavens what is the condition most unbearable for the Gods?' the question was answered with hardly a pause. 'Why it's a little object whose whereabouts is unknown. Something unaccounted for? No God can stomach that when he is collective' " (p. 193)—that is to say, totalitarian.

At several points, McLeod emphasizes the metaphorical nature of true socialist culture and consciousness that hounds him with his own insurmountable guilt and defeat. "I've covered that over for myself these many years," he says of his "sins," "oh, aware that I did, but none the less there is a certain crutch to the name of a thing, it all seems more reasonable and possible until you put it figuratively, until the metaphorical end, which is always the muzzle if you come down to it, blasts you in the face" (p. 239). The "metaphorical end" reveals to McLeod the connections between himself and the rest of the world; it reveals the meaning and malignance of his past actions as a Stalinist agent. If McLeod returned to the theoretical ideals of revolutionary socialism after his long support of the Soviet and after a year in the American government, if also he tried, as he says, to regain love through marriage to Guinevere because he believed she would bring him life, McLeod ultimately could not escape the self-defeat his metaphorical vision pressed on him:

in relentless turmoil each thought birthed its opposite, each object in the darkness swelled with connotation until a chair could contain his childhood, and the warm flaccid body of Guinevere . . . expanded its bulk to become all the women he had known, but in their negative aspect . . . the flesh of his wife . . . was the denominator of meat and all the corpses he had ever seen and some created.[9]

The one achievement McLeod grants of his life is his transformation from revolutionary to bureaucrat and back to revolutionary ("theoretician") again. In the end, however, the small success of

9. *Barbary Shore*, p. 240. McLeod perceives the same expansion of connotation in his small part in Trotsky's death and in his work for the U.S. government, which depends on "the misery of the rest of the world" (pp. 242, 243).

"theoretical retreat . . . grafting the little object into my flesh" cannot surmount McLeod's guilt. At the close of his defense, McLeod will separate his revolutionary hopes from his personal defeat.

It is McLeod's overwhelming guilt and his inescapable defeat that eventually lead Lovett to accept the responsibilities of his own increased consciousness, his awareness initiated by the battle of Life against Death that he witnesses. The progress of this allegory is the progress of the McLeod-Lovett relationship, for their dialogue amplifies and explains the McLeod-Hollingsworth debate and traces Lovett's expansion of awareness. As early as Chapter 21, McLeod expresses the difficulty of accepting the "responsibility." For the modern god of whom McLeod speaks here, and which will later become Mailer's Devil, is the devil that Hollingsworth represents: the devil of science-as-factology, of antimystery, of collectivism-as-totalitarianism. From lowest agent to Godhead, the totalitarian factologist is in power everywhere, and his power is overwhelming. "Yes," McLeod says, "I imagine a man could spend his life trying to find someone to pass it [the object] on to. Yet with what difficulty. For who could fulfill the specifications. . . . a man would be mad to accept such a responsibility" (p. 193). It is at just this point that Lovett moves closer to accepting "such a responsibility." Though McLeod says that Hollingsworth has whispered so tempting an offer that he is almost ready to give up the object, and though Lannie again tempts Lovett to their side, Lovett stands what little ground he has gained. He cannot yet be certain he is with McLeod, but he is sure he "can't be with them." By his mere presence, Lovett now becomes McLeod's conscience, and that transfer of roles is an initial transfer of power (p. 195).

In chapters 25 and 28, and in the final three chapters, Lovett's relationship to McLeod obviously grows more active. Lovett may be a "poor little friar," but he becomes the "confessor monk" to McLeod, who "carries his mortal illness with him, and [is] obsessed with the death he contains" (pp. 237, 244). McLeod reaffirms their friendship that began when Lovett's "theoretical equipment," however stunted, came to light (p. 245). And seeking desperately a source of healing, if not absolution, in love, McLeod inexplicably asks Lovett to judge Guinevere's potential for love. Lovett denies his power to judge, but McLeod, conferring it on him, again foreshadows the narrative's ultimate transfer of power. This last transfer will be made possible by Lovett's final acceptance of the responsibilities and commitments of consciousness when, in Chapter 28, the debate reaches an impasse and McLeod's defeat seems certain. McLeod's determination to transfer his ideas as existences (as powers or objects) is made clear when McLeod catches Lovett's eyes with his own and delivers a speech in his own defense to "transmit the intellectual conclusions of my life . . . and give dignity to my experience" (pp. 271–72). Lovett, who with Lannie has observed the entire debate, feels for the first time completely implicated in the struggle of the forces Hollingsworth and McLeod represent. "Behind us in the room, the battle over, the casualties counted, terms were being drawn. And it was I who felt the shame."

McLeod then performs two important events in the last two chapters; he actually transfers the object to Lovett, and he defies Hollingsworth. It had become clear in Chapter 25 that McLeod faces an existential choice. He can save himself by meeting Hollingsworth's offer and give up the object. Or, he can satisfy his "moral appetite" if he is willing to continue his theoretical work and die for it: "alive it's dead and dead I'm alive" (p. 246). By transferring the object to Lovett, who in the end has asked for it, McLeod chooses biological death but existential life. "The object" can now be recognized easily as a talisman of the hero. So Mailer uses the typical allegorical device of making the talismanic object the token of that power the hero seeks, expanded consciousness.

Angus Fletcher points out that the object is an image of power that fits the dualistic iconography the writer creates within the allegory, and it therefore plays a specific role in the dialectic form the allegory takes. In this novel, it is the object Life and Death battle to possess. And here, as it commonly is, the talisman is another example of what both Fletcher and Edwin Honig call the "Cosmic Image," by which they mean the relationship of images—whether as persons, events, or objects—to macrocosmic polarities.[10] Honig argues that it is the original function of allegory and its interpreters to sustain an explicit relationship between man and his divinities "by relating familiar archetypes to human aspirations" (p. 20). An object gains mana through its implied relationship to both natural and transcendental forces in a ceremony, dance, or allegorical text; the mana-power of the object transcends its merely physical properties. The "intangible" becomes an "energy working through the tangible and gives the object life and meaning" (pp. 22–23). Of course, this

10. See Edwin Honig, *Dark Conceit*, pp. 63, 81, and Angus Fletcher, *Allegory: The Theory of a Symbolic Mode*, pp. 88, 217, for the specific discussion of their points. In his analysis of cosmic image or Kosmos, Fletcher defines the allegorical image thusly: "It must imply a systematic part-whole relationship; second, it should be capable of including both metonymy and synecdoche; third, it should be capable of including 'personification'; fourth, it should suggest the daemonic nature of the image; fifth, it should allow an emphasis on the visual modality . . . finally, it should be such that large-scale double meanings would emerge if it were combined with other such images" (p. 109). Honig suggests that such external signs give the hero "something of the traditional authority of dramatis personae as well as sacred figures in myths" (p. 85).

sense of energy in objects also stimulates our perception that the object and the allegory have purposes requiring explanation.

McLeod—"the pedagogue again"—reminds Lovett of his new responsibility for this object with a quote from Lenin: "Study, little father, or you will lose your head." Unlike Lannie, Lovett manages to escape the FBI at the scene of McLeod's murder and enters that world from which he writes to us. "So the heritage passed on to me, poor hope, and the little object as well, and I went into the world. . . . I am obliged to live waiting for the signs which tell me I must move on again. . . . I work and study, and I keep my eye on the door. Meanwhile, vast armies mount themselves, the world re-volves, the traveller clutches his breast" (p. 311). He lives now in the time McLeod predicted, a time when one is no longer allowed even a corner in which to write a book, while "the storm approaches its thunderhead" and mankind drifts to barbarity. However limited Lovett's success as we see it, he has gained a new circuit of con-sciousness, a personal increase of force that is the kernel of human potential upon which McLeod placed his one hope.

> To Michael Lovett to whom, at the end
> of my life and for the first time within
> it, I find myself capable of the rudiments
> of selfless friendship, I bequeath in heritage
> the remnants of my socialist culture.
> . . . .
> And may he be alive to see the rising
> of the Phoenix. (p. 311)

Those critics who charge, as Irving Howe and Charles Rolo, that *Barbary Shore* is negative and nihilistic pay little attention to the transfer of power at the novel's conclusion. Clearly, this transfer expresses the hope of rebirth. I have said that the archetype of rebirth, of the discovery of Life through the regeneration of con-sciousness, is the central pattern of true allegory generally, just as it is the central pattern of the heroic quest throughout so many differ-ent cultures and epochs. With this novel, Mailer begins using the rebirth archetype as the basis for the structural and metaphorical design of his future allegories. Moreover, his use of this archetype suggests to me that Mailer succeeds early in adventuring into "the jungle of his unconscious" and finding there the materials of his art. In *Advertisements*, Mailer said that *Barbary* emerged "from the bombarded cellars of my unconscious" (p. 94). Carl Jung has em-phasized that "the symbolic process"—the manifestation of ar-chetypes as "active personalities in dreams and fantasies"—is "an experience *in images and of images*." And, like Mailer, in his theory of the dream, Jung considers this symbolic experience as a presentation to the dreamer not of fictitious dangers, but of real risks "upon which the fate of a whole life may depend."[11]

McLeod, the true savior or sacrificial figure of this novel, is a consummate example of the mythic "guide," a wise man who flourishes in dream as in literature when the times are out of joint and civilization is in danger of destroying itself. McLeod's impulse to sacrifice himself expresses the archetypal, the eternal impulse to "ransom creation," in Jung's words, "from death," to renounce "ego-hood" for a total rebirth.[12] In *Barbary Shore* it is through the death of the guide that both guide and hero are "reborn." Such sacrifice and rebirth are not evidence of nihilism; they are, as Jung says in "The Psychology of Rebirth," a "purely psychic reality" that is among the "primordial affirmations of mankind." If we look closer at the process of rebirth in *Barbary*, we find that such elements of that process as allegorical "progress" and "battle" are even more explicitly archetypal than they might seem. McLeod and Lovett participate in what Jung identifies as two "main groups" or patterns of rebirth. The first pattern is "the transcendence of life." In this case, the initiate

> takes part in a sacred rite which reveals to him the perpetual continuation of life through transformation and renewal. . . . [which] is usually represented by the fateful transformations—the death and rebirth—of a godlike hero. The initiate may either be a mere witness of the divine drama or take part in it or be moved by it, or he may see himself identified through the ritual action with the god. In this case, what really matters is that an objective substance or form is ritually transformed through some process going on independently, while the initiate is influenced, impressed, "consecrated," or granted "divine grace" on the mere ground of his presence or participation. . . . The initiate experiences . . . the permanence and continuity of life, which outlasts all changes of form and, phoenix-like, continually rises anew from its own ashes. (*Archetypes*, pp. 116–17)

The entire progress of the conflict between Hollingsworth and McLeod traces the defeat of the old hero or guide. Lovett is the witness of that conflict from beginning to end. During the debate specifically he is literally a mere observer, and it is through observation, enlivened to a new potential through his dialogues with

11. Carl Jung, *The Archetypes and the Collective Unconscious*, translated by R. F. C. Hull, Vol. 9, 1 (New Jersey: Princeton University Press, 1968), pp. 38–39. Future brief references are parenthetical.

12. See Carl Jung, *Symbols of Transformation*, translated by R. F. C. Hull, Vol. 5 (New Jersey: Princeton University Press, 1956), pp. 415, 421–35. In *Psychology and Religion*, translated by R. F. C. Hull, Vol. 11 (New Jersey: Princeton University Press, 1969), p. 272, Jung points out that the archetypal significance of "human sacrifice and ritual anthropophagy" strikes one of the "deepest chords" in the human psyche.

McLeod, that Lovett is led to make his eventual commitment. The whole drama of the novel's conflict traces the path of McLeod's existential defeat and his existential rebirth when he defies the forces of totalitarianism or Death by renewing his power in himself, by transferring it to Lovett, and by descending to Hollingsworth and his biological death. What is transformed by the long process of death and rebirth is the "object," the power of an intangible, expanded consciousness, implicitly embodied in tangible substance belonging to the old hero which is again made eternal. The important thing about any "transcendence rite," as Jung points out, is that the rite transcends life as it demonstrates eternal force in action rather than any particular historical fact or event. "It is a moment of eternity in time" (*Archetypes*, p. 118).

If the transcendence rite expresses a mythological significance to the novel's pattern of rebirth, the second "main group" of the rebirth archetype, which Jung calls "subjective transformation," suggests the psychological significance of rebirth. The McLeod-Lovett dialogues especially illustrate "subjective transformation." If at the beginning Lovett has undergone a "diminution of personality," a "loss of soul," or a "slackening of the tensity of consciousness," which Jung says is characteristic of "systematic amnesias," Lovett, by the novel's end, has undergone an "enlargement of personality." Such enlargement, Jung points out, depends upon the potential within, the potential that Mailer's later heroes will also exhibit. "Real increase of personality means consciousness of an enlargement that flows from inner sources. Without psychic depth we can never be adequately related to the magnitude of our object. . . . a man grows with the greatness of his task. But he must have within himself the capacity to grow. . . . More likely he will be shattered by it" (*Archetypes*, pp. 120–21).

It is in such subjective transformation that the greatest potential for growth lies. But of course this wise man himself is a psychic emanation "from within." He is, as Zarathustra is to Nietzsche, "the long expected friend of his soul" who will make "his life flow into that greater life." Subjective transformations of the dreamer, for example, typically depend upon the dialogue with the guide, the "certain other one, within." It is upon the colloquy that grace depends. In more clinical terms, the therapeutic value of any archetypal figure resides in the dialogue with the archetype.[13]

13. Jung, *Archetypes*, pp. 40, 121, 124–27, 130–33. Jung gives examples of the wise-man figure in its relation to sacrificial rebirth: Khidr to Moses, in which case Moses fails "to recognize a moment of crucial importance" and thereby fails to recognize the unconscious "source of life" until he has lost it (pp. 137–41); Osiris, who is disembodied by Antichrist, to the Egyptian pharaoh and nobility; Christ to the Christians (p. 141).

In this novel where "progress" and "battle" are determined by an archetypal pattern of sacrifice, the dangers besetting the hero are embodied as false sacrificial figures, such as Guinevere, Lannie, and Hollingsworth. They all represent the dangers of defeat and stasis to the hero. McLeod, the true wise man, is a master, enlightener, and savior "who symbolizes," as Jung writes of such a figure, "the preexisting meaning hidden in the chaos of life." He compensates for a "spiritual deficiency" in the hero by giving him knowledge and advice and by encouraging profound reflection for someone whose conscious resources are incapable of overcoming a "helpless and desperate situation." Mythologically, this figure often gives specific information to help the hero on his journey, but he is most notable for his moral qualities and for testing the moral qualities of others, which qualities, Jung argues, make his "spiritual character" plain. In myth, he usually represents the dynamic principle of life in battle against stasis and death. The wise man tests the hero's potential to receive the gifts of expanded consciousness.[14]

When we view *Barbary Shore* as true allegory and as a narrative representation of disembodied, archetypal elements of the self interacting with the narrator-hero, we see that the psychological implications of the sacrificial patterns and figures are not foreign to Mailer's expressed goals. For his work, as we will see, represents a continuous effort to integrate conscious and unconscious elements and perceptions in a way similar to Jung's description of the process of individuation: "the 'nourishing' influence of unconscious contents . . . maintains the vitality of consciousness by a continual influx of energy; for consciousness does not produce energy by itself" (*Archetypes*, p. 142). The energy of new perception the Mailer heroes seek is that energy of intuitive, prerational perception that can be integrated with rational and conscious perception. It is the mark of Lovett's potential, and hence of the Mailer hero, that through fortune, perception, and ultimately through choice, he accepts the source of regeneration and wisdom in a world of defeat and ignorance. It is the energy of metaphorical consciousness that not only reveals Lovett's own identity to himself but also reveals to him what makes for Life and what makes for Death in the modern world. The hero accepts his own potential at the novel's end, and that is *Barbary Shore*'s affirmation. But that the hero will himself be a source of regeneration to others, Mailer is not yet prepared to affirm.

14. Jung, *Archetypes*, pp. 35, 37. See especially "The Phenomenology of the Spirit in Fairy Tales," pp. 210– 14, 221, 239, and 253. Jung also points out that this figure typically warns the hero of dangers to come and supplies means of meeting those dangers.

3

The Deer Park

We know how, in the past, humanity has been able to endure the sufferings we have enumerated. . . . it was possible to accept them precisely because they had a metahistorical meaning, because, for the greater part of mankind, still clinging to the traditional viewpoint, history did not have, and could not have, value in itself. Every hero repeated the archetypal gesture, every war rehearsed the struggle between good and evil, every fresh social injustice was identified with the sufferings of the Savior. . . .

[W]e noted various recent orientations that tend to reconfer value upon the myth of cyclical periodicity, even the myth of the eternal return. Those orientations disregard not only historicism but even history as such. We believe we are justified in seeing in them, rather than a resistance to history, a revolt against historical *time*, an attempt to restore this historical time, freighted as it is with human experience, to a place in the time that is cosmic, cyclical, and infinite. . . . it is worth noting that the work of two of the most significant writers of our day—T. S. Eliot and James Joyce—is saturated with nostalgia for the myth of eternal repetition and, in the last analysis, for the abolition of time.

—Mircea Eliade, *The Myth of the Eternal Return*

Mailer conceived *The Deer Park* (1955) as the first installment of a large, eight-part work that was to be a "descendant of *Moby Dick*." The short story "The Man Who Studied Yoga" was to be the prologue to this large work and each book a dream of the story's hero, Sam Slavoda. These dreams, as Mailer phrased it in *Advertisements for Myself*, would "revolve around the adventures of a mythical hero, Sergius O'Shaugnessy, who would travel through many worlds." But Mailer's *Moby Dick* failed. All we have is *The Deer Park*, a much "simpler novel," Mailer tells us, that emerged from the characters themselves.[1]

The Deer Park itself fails. Its faults are those of a novel that was undergoing changes not only in style but in conception at the time of publication. In rewriting the Rinehart galleys, for example, Mailer began to develop the narrator's story further. Yet his story remains vague in the second half of the book. Mailer also began to develop further the Eitel-Elena story, the story that best focuses the novel's theme, into a larger and more complex relationship. And the novel's final "equation of sex and time" is an afterthought inserted at the

1. *Advertisements for Myself* (hereafter cited as *Ads*), pp. 153–55. Unless otherwise indicated, all citations are to works by Norman Mailer.

33

last minute before the printing deadline. The final Putnam edition,
therefore, represents only what was emerging from the characters
and ideas in the novel. Mailer admits that he simply did not have
"the guts to stop the machine, to give myself another two years and
write a book which would go a little further" (*Ads*, pp. 235–37,
242–43).

When we add the personal crises and the bouts with drugs Mailer
describes in *Advertisements* (beginning on page 228) to these problems of the novel's full development, it is a wonder the book ever saw
light in any form. And it is, therefore, a little unexpected that Mailer
should consider his central characters in this novel as among his
best and most fully developed. In an interview with Steven Marcus,
Mailer argues that these characters are "beings"; that is, a figure in
this novel is "someone whose nature keeps shifting," as opposed to
mere "characters," whose nature "you grasp as a whole."[2] This
implies he was dissatisfied with the effect of the manifest allegory in
Barbary Shore, and especially with the flatness of its characters. In
The Deer Park, Mailer does in fact heighten the realistic surface of his
novel. He also increases the complexity of the quest and hence of the
questers or beings. What the questers oppose, however, is still
expressed through flat characterizations.

Heightening the realistic surface of the allegory is a common
device allegorists use to soften the effect of their mechanical control
over a work. As the allegorist increases his external commentaries
on his symbolism or themes, as he typically does, such devices
softening the mechanical effect become even more necessary. Mailer
begins to demonstrate a distinctly allegorical attribute in the pieces
collected in *Advertisements*, and he continues to collect and publish
a growing body of commentary external to the novels through
interviews, explications, digressions, criticism, and journalism. The
shift to a heightened realism is the principal softening technique
Mailer uses in *The Deer Park*. In his later novels, we will see that
Mailer relies more on the opposite technique for lessening the effect
of mechanical control. For Mailer's novels of the sixties increase the
predominance of mythic patterns and figures already emerging in
the novels of the fifties. As Angus Fletcher has pointed out, we can
expect in true allegory a continual alternation between the explicit
emergence of the dominant idea and the emergence of either
mimesis or myth, which both cause the idea to recede. Fletcher
argues that such devices, whether employed consciously or unconsciously, do in fact loosen the boundaries of the allegorical mode,
and they provide the artist with the means to conceive and express

2. *Cannibals and Christians*, p. 212.

his ideas organically in art. The fluctuation in allegory between mimesis, myth, and idea, and the consequent multiple levels of meaning, suggest the inadequacy of any facile or ready interpretation, invite the reader to seek the "delayed message," and give the allegory its "translative value."[3]

The mythological patterns Mailer began in *Barbary Shore* are not obscured by the heightened realistic surface; realism and myth function reciprocally in the narrative. The fundamental pattern of the quest and rebirth continues, and the development of the narrator-hero's potential ends at the same point it did in the earlier novel. The hero's potential is, however, revealed in a slightly more affirmative light. And if this novel's major characters are more complex, more beings, than those of *Barbary Shore*, they nevertheless retain their power as archetypal figures. Eitel, for example, is a figure similar to McLeod. Both are fallen radicals whose struggles to regain the power of brave defiance are connected to their struggles to regain love. Both fail, admitting their own guilt in their failure and the failures of others. For the hero both older men are "fathers," confidants, and guides who tell the hero a truth he feels within himself. Through the dialogue with the hero, through advice and the example of his own battles and defeats, Eitel points the way for Sergius, just as McLeod does for Lovett. The only important differences in the two older men are that Eitel's radicalism is totally apolitical and his death is existential, not biological as McLeod's is. This increases the richness and the complexity of Eitel as a metaphorical figure. He cannot be mistaken for a misguided politician in a political allegory. Through the stories of Eitel and Elena, of himself and Lulu, and of Marion Faye, the narrator Sergius depicts a series of explorers who, except for himself, are defeated in their search for life in a dead world. By their words and their actions, these explorers become for Sergius a series of guiding intelligences or indicators of life and death, of growth and stasis.

With *The Deer Park* Mailer complicates his quest for what he calls "God the Life-Giver" by exploring three alternative paths to the same goal: the path of Love and Sex, the path of the Rebellious Artist, and the path of the Hipster. The true way remains unresolved in this novel though Sergius chooses the way of the rebellious artist. But the keystone of each alternative is rebellion. In his own life no less than in the life of his heroes, Mailer considers rebellion the foundation of creative growth. Especially in his columns for *The Village Voice* and in "The White Negro" (1957), Mailer expresses his own vision of

3. Compare this last point with Mailer's epigraph from Gide to *The Deer Park*: "Please do not understand me too quickly." My discussion here is based on Angus Fletcher's *Allegory: The Theory of a Symbolic Mode*, pp. 307–15, 321, 330.

himself as a "psychic outlaw" at war with his time and country. Mailer's answer to one of Lyle Stuart's "Sixty-Nine Questions and Answers" sums this view up best. "What advice would you give the young writer on the brink of fame?" Stuart asks. Mailer answers: "Try to keep the rebel artist in you alive, no matter how attractive or exhausting the temptations." He then adds that rebellion is "as healthy as the sense of life." For the hero and therefore for mankind, the chief resources for the encouragement of life in the world are bravery and defiance. For Mailer, "the instinct of rebellion" is the "foundation of man's consciousness, the source of his humanity and the vehicle of his evolution."[4] With a new emphasis on rebellion as the source of creative evolution, and with characters that are more complex than those of *Barbary Shore* but as much agents of forces larger than themselves, Mailer continues in *The Deer Park* to explore his theme of the struggle of Life against Death.

If Mailer continues the basic allegorical and mythological patterns he shaped in *Barbary Shore*, he also continues his search for the sources and effects of expanded or metaphysical consciousness. But he extends his previous quest for new consciousness to an investigation into the secrets of human energy and the relationships between energy and rebellion, growth, and "Time." Rebellion and growth must use some deep energy within us to take effect in the world. The relationship between energy and Time, to use Mailer's word, is more complex and obscure. As we will see, it is necessary to bring considerable outside material to the novel itself to understand that relationship. Throughout the 1950s Mailer engages in a personal quest for the sources of energy necessary to rebel and to create. His own sense of failed creative power did much to stimulate this search.[5] *Advertisements*, published in 1959, is the record of his search. The heroes and hipsters of his two succeeding novels will continue it.

In *The Deer Park*, Mailer explores the way of the lover and the artist through the story of Charles Eitel (pronounced "eye-TELL") and Elena Esposito. This story focuses on the dual nature of the pressures within the would-be rebel artist and lover: the impulse to live up to one's ideals and the demands of one's art and the impulse to capitulate to the demands of the dead world of commercialism, fake sentiment, hypocrisy, and falsehood. Eitel's story, most simply put,

---

4. See *Ads*, especially pp. 233, 269, and 305, where Mailer makes these points.

5. *Ads*, p. 240. As the "Fourth Advertisement" reveals, this quest is largely initiated by Mailer's fear of the dying of his own creative energies and talents. "The White Negro" is one of his "seeds" of new growth; it gives him the faith that he is making a fresh beginning (see especially p. 335).

is about a man whose ideals and actions are antithetical; it is the
central line of action upon which the other actions in the novel
depend. Eitel's potential and his best intentions are established
early; his ideals are clear.

Soon after Sergius arrives in the Hollywood resort of Desert D'Or,
he meets Eitel, a famous film director. The director quickly becomes
a source of strength and a "best friend" to Sergius because Eitel
seems to Sergius one of the few "honest men" left in the world.
Sergius founds his faith in the older man on the transcript, which
Marion Faye shows him, of Eitel's testimony before a Congressional
Committee investigating communists. Sergius recognizes Eitel's dialogue with the congressmen as an opportunity. It reawakens Sergius's consciousness of things he had vaguely awakened to in the
Korean War. From the beginning, this testimony serves him as a
touchstone of genuine courage and rebellion. In this case, it is
rebellion against those forces in the American government that
would homogenize individuals into a collective, deadening image of
itself. Sergius sees in Eitel's testimony the very sources of the power
to grow and to create that, we later see, he already believes to be in
himself. "I would always have a reaction from his words . . . I felt as
if I were speaking my own words."[6] For his defiance, Eitel is
blacklisted. Like McLeod, Eitel suffers "defeat" following bogus
success.

Eitel's commercial failure gives him his new opportunity to grow:
"I began to think that the reason I acted the way I did with the
Committee was to give myself another chance." Drinking, squander-
ing his days alone, Eitel futilely clings to his hope of writing a brave
and original script. It is while at the crossroads of growth and
existential death, beset with temptations and pressures, that Eitel
meets Sergius and confides in the younger man. The novel opens,
then, with Eitel's second chance, and most of what follows is Sergius's account of Eitel's struggle and failure to gain this power of
rebellious, creative energy.

Eitel fails because the temptations of the dead, unreal world
prove too much for him; his inner impulses are more in time with
the world than with his ideals. His earlier failure to maintain his
independent art is symptomatic; it foreshadows his ultimate failure. The world that defeats Eitel in his renewed quest for himself is
embodied in a series of tempters and temptations, and Eitel's former
assistant Nelson Nevins is the first. Nevins reaches to the heart of
Eitel's flaw. Elena tells Eitel that he depends too much on "what

6. *The Deer Park* (hereafter cited as *DP*), p. 24. Future brief references are
parenthetical.

other people think," on the standards of a false world rather than on what is genuine in himself. Though Eitel despises Nevins's work, he cannot help but envy Nevins's international commercial success.

The world comes to Eitel also as Collie Munshin, the son-in-law of Supreme's head, Herman Teppis. In chapters 15 and 16, Collie absorbs the last vestiges of integrity from Eitel's script. Boiling with "movie ingredients," the script becomes a "property" and "gold mine" with Collie's collaboration. The false script now offers Eitel little resistance: "what amazed him, annoyed him, and pleased him, was how easy the writing had become." He writes with "cynical speed." Collie's temptation proves more formidable and his "rehabilitation" of Eitel more thorough than Nevins's. In a whisper that "vibrates" through the room, Collie promises that if Eitel would share the script with him, he would bring Eitel to Supreme when Teppis dies and Collie takes command. Worse, Collie continues to insist that Eitel reverse his congressional testimony as part of the deal. So Eitel's final capitulation to Congressman Crane in Chapter 22 is especially defeating because Crane's own committee admits they were wrong about Eitel's party affiliation and betrays its promise of confidentiality by insisting that Eitel's congressional testimony be made public and that he run a personal statement of guilt in the newspapers. When Eitel agrees to such falsehoods, he gets his job with Supreme.

Eitel's failure is not so much a failure of vision as it is a failure of energy, a failure of his capacity to marshal his renewed sense of energy to conquer the forces of defeat in the world arrayed against him. Elena, in part, represents the buried nature in Eitel and this renewed energy. At first Eitel's relationship with Elena seems to presage victory for Eitel, but in fact it merely describes the potential that is doomed. Their affair began well. Eitel takes a first step toward renewed self-respect when he defies Teppis by taking Elena to Teppis's party. Sergius describes Eitel's act as a defiance "of no advantage to himself." Sergius's description of Elena at this party intimates what she will represent for Eitel. She is both defiance and strength. She is uneasy with and outside of the fantastic and absurd people and the atmosphere Sergius describes in the yacht club. Her strength, suggested by her voice, appears to Sergius to be a combination of delicacy, pride, and a "sense of her body." She is like "an animal, ready for flight."

Early in their affair Eitel repeatedly thinks of Elena as a "fresh beginning." The quality Elena brings to their sexual relationship is, in Eitel's words, her "odd capacity for love." By this, we learn, he means she gives so much of herself that both she and Eitel might "change together," and this giving of oneself is combined in Elena with her awareness that such change is always fragile (p. 123).

As long as he continues to discover his own deepest energies through Elena and as long as he is able to give himself over to her love, Eitel grows. But the growth is short-lived. While it lasts, this energy of renewed life creates new circuits of body and consciousness. "Eitel felt changes in his body race beyond the changes in his mind as though all those nerves and organs which had tired almost to death were coming back to life, carrying his mind in their path, as if Elena were not only his woman but his balm" (p. 122). This "blessed woman" Elena, he explains, causes him a pain that raises his whole sense of existence and potential. Sergius sees early that Eitel himself is on a quest for regeneration: "the trip he had begun so many times and quit as often and was now making again." Together, Eitel and Elena "would explore a little further."

In one late-night dialogue, Eitel tells Sergius that Elena is a source of growth not only because to choose her is to make his position more perilous, but because he now realizes, she will nourish him with "energy, flesh his courage and make him the man he had once believed himself to be" (p. 110). She is, in fact, a kind of primitive force or buried nature:

> the core of Eitel's theory was that people had a buried nature—"the noble savage" he called it—which was changed and whipped and trained by everything in life until it was almost dead. Yet if people were lucky and if they were brave, sometimes they would find a mate with the same buried nature and that could make them happy and strong. (p. 121)

Eitel's renewed awareness, through Elena, of his inner resources and energies reaches its height in Chapter 11.

> In betraying that love [filmmaking], he had betrayed himself. . . . The artist was always divided between his desire for power in the world and his desire for power over his work. With this girl it was impossible to thrive in the world except by his art . . . sitting beside her in the sun could give him a sense of strength . . . he would feel indifference to that world he had found so hard to leave. To quit it by the bottom—that was nice, it gave a feeling there was fruit to life. (p. 124)

Elena represents also the side of Eitel's nature that sees clearly just what is corrupt and false about his work and about Collie's temptations. She is at first lucid and strong, and her actions assert this strength. In her own art, flamenco dancing, she "scorns" commercialism and professional technique. "She could never grasp the first requirement for a professional. No matter one's mood, there was always a minimum to the performance. One was never terrible. . . . So he knew, although he hated to believe it, that the more he wanted to make of her, the less she would become" (p. 183).

Elena's wisdom has a power Eitel never quite gathers to himself. "Young as she was, he had heard experience in her voice which was beyond his own experience, and so if he stayed with her, he would be obliged to travel in her directions, and he had been fleeing that for all of his life." That she perceives and has the strength to act upon her perception of Eitel's character and defeat marks Elena as Mailer's first and one of his strongest heroines. Yet her heroism lies in a large potential defeated. For, more subtly, she moves to a defeat similar to Eitel's.

When Elena begins to separate herself from Eitel because his defeat is certain, it is his best self, his deepest nature and potential that Eitel is losing. As he works faster with the bogus energy of the professional, Elena grows depressed and loses vivacity. He now relies completely on "borrowed technique" rather than desire during sexual relations with her. He desperately tries infidelity with one of Faye's—the pimp and hipster—call girls, named Bobby, because his continual failure to sustain a genuine connection to his art and to Elena stimulates a desire for sex without emotional involvement, a kind of onanism that would be as "exciting as the pages of a pornographic text where one could read in safety and not grudge every emotion the woman felt for another man." Eitel sees such a move as an escape from Elena's love, but the experience only sickens him and increases his self-disgust. By the end of Chapter 17 Eitel has fallen a great distance in love as well as in his art. He realizes that the destruction of his "masterpiece" and of his love is "his own fault," but he helplessly continues the destruction. He maneuvers Elena out of his life with professional disinterest, like a "fish" on "slender tackle." He grants her, he says in helpless despair, "no life at all" (see pp. 203–4, 214). Destroying the good, the life, in her, he destroys the life in himself.

All along the path of capitulation to the world, Eitel sees his own guilt, his own limitations. This clarity of vision makes his defeat especially painful. Even after Elena leaves him and he has given up all struggle to be true to his best impulses, Eitel sees his own corruption, as he clearly does when he delivers to Sergius the meaning of his and Elena's separation. She left, Eitel says, not merely because she was no mate "for a commercial man," but because by killing the life in himself he "denied Elena a most valuable opportunity to grow." His personal failure to regain any power at Beda's orgy, which Eitel felt would open "a new life," leads him to discover a "hate" for Elena that is his hatred for "the life of everything." If the creative power he once hoped to achieve is forever dead, Eitel has gained the decreative power of "the world" (see pp. 297–98). He becomes a Collie Munshin at the end of Chapter 21, seeing Elena as Collie did. And when Sergius asks Eitel how it feels to be reconciled to the government and Supreme, Eitel sagaciously, if helplessly, sums up his defeat.

> You see, after a while, I knew they had me on my knees, and that if I wasn't ready to take an overdose of sleeping pills, I would have to let myself slide through the experience, and not try to resist it. So for the first time in my life I had the sensation of being a complete and total whore in the world, and I accepted every blow, every kick, and every gratuitous kindness. . . . And now I just feel tired, and if the truth be told, pleased with myself, because believe me, Sergius, it was *dirty* work. . . . In the end that's the only kind of self-respect you have. To be able to say to yourself that you're disgusting. (p. 306)

Eitel's defeat is defined by his failure of courage in art and in love. In both adventures, Eitel is unable to follow his own prescription for growth: "the essence of spirit . . . [is] to choose the thing which did not better one's position but made it more perilous." Even following his earliest sense of weakness before Nevins, Eitel realizes he is probably incapable of carrying forward the creative spirit of growth and defiance into the world. He senses that he must pass on his own legacy of creative rebellion and "dangerous work," an act that is clearly associated here with the world-renewing force of heroic mythologies, to a new person: "perhaps a young man was needed, someone so strong and simple as to believe the world was there for him to change it."

Mailer's "mythical hero" Sergius O'Shaugnessy is such a strong and simple young man. His own struggle for increased consciousness and growth parallels Eitel's. This struggle is told more briefly in a "doubling" of the plot through the story of Sergius and Lulu. Like his predecessor Mikey Lovett, Sergius is a hero moving from impotence and unconsciousness to potency and consciousness. He describes himself as "a young man who felt temporarily like an old man" and who believed in "many things" but was able to "do very little." He wears a mask to function in a world of masks and facades. In appearance he is the all-American, Hollywood war hero. Like an "actor who tries to interest a casting director by dressing for the role," however, he never feels convincing, or, as he says in Chapter 4, he "always felt like a spy or a fake."

Dissatisfied with his hollowness as an "impersonator," he is seeking some substance or power that will give him genuine identity. Since his childhood in an orphanage, he has fought to earn the heroic name his lost father fabricated for him. His father passed on one further legacy:

> he kept his little idea. There was something special about him. . . .
> Everybody has that, but my father had it more than most, and he
> slipped it on to me. I would never admit it to a soul, but I always
> thought there was going to be an extra destiny coming my direction.
> . . . But I was never sure of myself, I never felt as if I came from any
> particular place, or that I was like other people. (p. 21)

Sergius's belief in his destiny, his status as an orphan in search of a
father, and his heroic name are signs of the typical allegorical hero.
And like Lovett, Sergius discovers his heroic goal early in life: "I had
read a great many books . . . about English gentlemen, and knights,
and adventure stories, and about brave men and Robin Hood. It all
seemed very true to me. So I had the ambition that someday I would
be a brave writer" (pp. 22– 23). If Sergius duplicates Eitel's struggle
to learn "the way" of the rebel artist and the lover, the emphasis and
focus of Sergius's story are more upon the artist as rebel.

The prerequisite of the rebel writer here is vision, a vision that
penetrates false surfaces and sees the real connections between
things. This is the vision of a double reality Eitel experienced in the
Spanish Civil War and in World War II, especially in the concentration camps, described in Chapter 14. Eitel's and Sergius's stories
represent the similar opportunities of two generations, but the old
generation failed to accept and use its opportunity. This parallel
between the generations is clarified by the parallels in the two plots
and by the guide-novice relationship between the old man and the
young man. It is through Sergius's dialogues with the older man and
through his witnessing of the old man's death that he, just as Lovett
before him, learns to grow.

Sergius's awakening to a double reality during the Korean War is
the most significant mark of his potential. For the first time in his
life, Sergius was "happy" fighting the "impersonal" war in Korea. He
lived a life of simple comradery, danger, and action with his fellow
fliers, but he also lived in a world of such narrow vision that he did
not see the connection between his own participation in a war and
the lives and deaths of others. "Sometimes on tactical missions we
would lay fire bombs into Oriental villages. I did not mind that
particularly, but I would be busy with *technique,* and I would dive
my plane and drop the jellied gasoline into *my part of the pattern.* I
hardly thought of it any other way. From the air, a city in flames is
not a bad sight" (pp. 45– 46, my italics). But when Sergius's Japanese
K.P. burns his arm with a kettle of soup, he undergoes a change of
vision while giving the Oriental boy first aid.

> Suddenly, I realized that two hours ago I had been busy setting fire to
> a dozen people, or two dozen, or had it been a hundred? . . . I could
> never get rid of the Japanese boy with his arm and his smile. Nothing

sudden happened to me, but over a time, the thing I felt about most of the fliers went false. I began to look at them in a new way. . . . I was close to things I had forgotten, and it left me sick; I had a choice to make.

Sergius turns down an Air Force career and has a "small break-down." In the hospital he recalls his early heroic reading and returns to his "odd hope" that he may become a writer (pp. 46–47).

Sergius's vision of a double reality leads him to conclude that there is a "real world" in which the connections between oneself and others exist—the world of wars, of children's homes on back streets, a "world where orphans burned orphans." And there is another world of Teppis and Munshin—the world of narrow vision, facade, false sentiment, and hypocrisy. The other world is the setting for this novel, embodied in Hollywood and Palm Springs; it is the world of manufactured lies and of degenerate imagination, and a world in which one does not directly face the consequences of one's actions and one's life. It is the world most people live in.[7] The "real world" of true and frightening connections is not unlike McLeod's "metaphorical end." If one has the vision—what McLeod calls the metaphysical vision—to see the connections and to see, therefore, the true world below the false world, one must live according to these perceptions.

To live according to his best perceptions is precisely what Sergius must struggle to do, and it is precisely what Eitel fails to do. No sooner does Sergius tell us of his vision of two worlds then the false world begins to work against him. It comes to him first as Lulu Myers, and her power to tempt is enormous. Though there is some ambiguity about Lulu and though she has one moment of bravery, she essentially remains as Sergius first sees her during an armed forces tour, "like some fairy princess of sex who had flown across the Pacific to anoint us with tiny favors" (p. 35). Sergius soon discovers that sex for Lulu is a series of imaginary games, and he is willing to play. Her sex life is like her work; she assesses technique and employs gimmicks, tricks, and public show rather than private substance. Although Sergius sees her at once as "bigger than life" but "also without life," although he compares the excitement he feels with her to flying a jet in an impersonal war (both are like playing

7. Ibid., p. 45. Descriptions of this make-believe world abound, pp. 7–8, 29, 61–62, 184–85. It is the locus of the allegory. The opposition of the "imaginary world" of false vision and the real world becomes a fundamental, if obvious, theme in the novel. Numerous statements about this opposition express this theme; see, for example, pp. 65–67, 155–57, 192, 276. The juxtaposition of art as truth and commercialism as falsehood also expresses the same point; see, for example, pp. 88, 142, 151, 155–57. The epitome of the falsehood and hypocrisy of the "imaginary world" is in Chapter 20 in the long scene in Teppis's office.

"with magic," a "gimmick and a drug"), Sergius is caught. He and
Lulu stimulate the onanism in each other. "How I loved myself
then," he says. For Lulu, "the heart of her pleasure was to show
herself" (pp. 96, 136).

One facet of Lulu's temptation that captures Sergius is that she
offers him a sense of power in the dead, unreal world. The potency
she encourages in him is not the potency of the self, but the potency
of extrinsic considerations. That he takes this fairy princess of sex,
for example, "with the cheers of millions behind him" keeps Sergius's excitement high. As Sergius gives in to the temptations of such
extrinsic power in the world, his desire and energy to be a brave
writer diminish, as Eitel's did, "with a lack of ambition as cheerful
as a liver complaint." He mistakenly believes that making love to
Lulu puts him in a class with "the champ" Eitel, even though Eitel
has warned him that Lulu is no source of energy for one who seeks it:
"our marriage was the meeting of a zero and a zero."

In both Eitel's and Sergius's quests for growth, Mailer associates
creative sexual energy with creative artistic energy, both of which
oppose the absorption of the self by external forces in the unreal
world. The association between genuine sexual energy expressed
through love and genuine creative energy expressed through art is
nothing new in human thought, but Mailer binds both energies by
specifically depicting the common ground between them as disin-
terested choice, world defiance, and the "buried natures" of our
instinctual life. Although it will become more explicit as his work
develops, Mailer continually implies that biological and artistic
potency and creation have some vague if no less real connections to
common physiological and psychic sources of energy, which energy,
as we will see, has in turn roots in divine energy or Soul.

It is only when Sergius finds the inner force and the courage to
renounce the temptations of the world that he finally experiences
genuine love and renews the strength of his metaphorical vision.
Besides Lulu, Sergius's temptation by the extrinsic and the false
comes, as in Eitel's case, in the form of Munshin and Teppis, who
offer Sergius the opportunity to "fight" and to "grow" in the industry
and to meet people with power. Sergius saves himself when Munshin reveals the false sentiment, or "bullshit" as Sergius calls it, of a
planned movie where Sergius would play the hero as "war ace."

> I had been tempted . . . but it wasn't stubbornness alone which
> held me back. I kept thinking of the Japanese K.P. . . . and I could hear
> him say, "Am I going to be in the movie? Will they show the scabs and
> the pus?" The closer I came . . . the more he bothered me, and all the
> while Collie would go on or Lulu would go on . . . about the
> marvelous world, the real world, about all the good things which

would happen to me, and all the while I was thinking they were
wrong, and the real world was underground—a tangle of wild caves
where orphans burned orphans. (p. 224)

Eitel gives Sergius the necessary courage to surmount the temptation, by encouraging Sergius to follow his "instinct," to become a
brave artist. This advice leads Sergius to self-examination. "I had
one of those hints of what cold and violent ambition had been
stifling in me for so many years, and it was as if deep inside two
powerful hands fought each other forward and back, locked in a test
of strength which left room for little else." Sergius sees he shares a
"vanity" like Eitel's and a similarly conflicting inner life, but he
"somehow" had known "Eitel would help me to refuse the offer"
(pp. 225 and 228).

The courage of Sergius's choice is so awesome that it briefly
influences even Lulu, who stops tempting Sergius to Munshin's side.
Lulu and Sergius are then able to have their first experience of
genuine love. Staggered by the impact of his choice to redirect his life
and of their experience of love, Sergius undergoes a recurrence of
metaphorical vision, which is like McLeod's "expansion" of Guinevere's flesh, and suffers a relapse into impotency: "it was a tangible
fear, as if the moment I left her room the burned corpses of half the
world would be lying outside the door. We started to make love, and
I couldn't think of her or of myself or of anything but flesh . . . burst-
ing flesh, rotting flesh, flesh hung on spikes in butcher stalls, flesh
burning, flesh gone to blood." For the first time to anyone, Sergius
unburdens his guilt to Lulu, his portion of the guilt, as a human, in
the cruelty of mankind. The temptress becomes healer; it is Lulu's
finest moment, but it is brief. Lulu, once the horror of his guilt is
passed, restores Sergius, who is braced by his new sense of love, to
potency and to a faith in the beauty of the flesh. Yet they both realize
their love is something they cannot sustain. The next day, Lulu
leaves Sergius for two movie stars, a new movie, and her old self.
Sergius, on the other hand, retains his renewed potency and renews
his quest to become a brave writer.

But Sergius has passed only the first test, for by regaining his way,
he accepts new struggles and perils. Though he knows Lulu is lost to
him, her temptation lingers in his mind and raises new self-doubts
and feelings of guilt. Having passed, with Eitel's aid, the test of the
world, he must now pass the test of himself. He turns to penance
and purgation. Like a saint mortifying his flesh, Sergius takes the
worst possible job he can find and immerses himself in that side of
life most foreign to the world in which he has been living. He
becomes a dishwasher in an expensive restaurant where he had
often eaten with Lulu. The "steam and the grease and the heat" are

his "poor man's Turkish bath." It is a self-inflicted slavery to "a gargoyle of a machine" that teaches him "the most simple lesson of class," of life beneath the facade:

> after six years and eight months . . . I would earn back what I had lost in twelve days with Lulu, and this thought gave me a sort of melancholy glee, allowing me to relish like a saint counting his sores, how hard the work would be tommorrow.
> It was all my doing. I still had most of my three thousand dollars and I did not have to work, but with Lulu gone, there was no other choice than to sit down and begin the apprenticeship of learning to be a writer. . . . mortifying my *energy*, whipping my *spirit*, preparing myself for that other work I looked on with religious awe. (p. 289, my italics)

When Sergius, still uncertain of any change in himself, pays a final visit to Eitel, he finds strength in Eitel's record of defeat. And Sergius survives a last temptation; he turns down Eitel's offer to work for him as his assistant. Eitel admires Sergius for his strength and promises to send him Elena's letter, an act that, like McLeod's last message and the "object," represents a transfer of power from the old man to the new.

Strengthened by this success, by Elena's letter, and by his own self-examination, Sergius passes his final test of courage and defiance, echoing Eitel's original congressional testimony as he does so, when he defies the two FBI men who question him about his past associates. This final test leaves him on the edge of collapse, but his past successes generate in him the courage to go on. He embarks on a true rebirth as he begins his apprenticeship in earnest—studying, adventuring into his deepest self, writing, and renewing his determination to seek his goal.

> I began to think, at least I learned how to try to think, for to do that, one must be ready to live in a hunt for the most elusive game—our real motive or motives . . . and therefore I would have to look into myself. . . . knowing I was weak and wondering if I would ever be strong. For I touched the bottom myself. . . . I returned to it, I wallowed in it, I looked at myself, and the longer I looked the less terrifying it became and the more understandable. I began then to make those first painful efforts to acquire . . . the mind of the writer . . . until I ended with an idea that many men have had, and many will have again . . . but I knew that finally one must do, simply do, for we act in total ignorance and yet in honest ignorance we must act, or we can never learn for we can hardly believe what we are told, we can only measure what has happened inside ourselves. (pp. 325–26)

Elena's letter explaining her flight from Eitel to Faye helps Sergius begin his true apprenticeship and his journey within because her honesty of vision and self-awareness encourage him. Sergius now reads Elena's letter repeatedly, in the same way that he had read Eitel's testimony. He finds Elena's understanding of her own failure so genuine that he begins to believe he and Elena might "bring out the best in one another." But Elena's turn to Faye is a desperate effort to connect a new circuit as well as a gesture of defiance, like Beda's orgy, against an outraged community's opinion of her as "dirt." If it is an ineffectual defiance, it is at least honest. For unlike Munshin and Teppis, Elena would become an honest whore, not a whore in "the world" whose sentimentality and hypocrisy lead her to believe herself something more noble and creative. But her move to Faye is, ultimately, only another stop on the way to Elena's defeat.

Faye himself, as the critics agree, is Mailer's first fictional embodiment of the hipster. Faye represents Mailer's exploration into a third way of regeneration in a dead world in *The Deer Park*. What seems to confuse readers is that the way of the hipster appears alien to the ways of artist and lover. Yet the ends of all are the same. The hipster, like the artist and lover, engages in acts of defiance. Art, if anything, is pure defiance. But the hipster's defiance is physically destructive, not merely destroying ideas, concepts, and perceptions, but destroying the actual embodiments of falsehood, oppression, and homogeneity. It is, however, a phoenix-destruction.

As Mailer argues in "The White Negro," the hipster's quest is above all "a frantic search for potent change, for liberating energy" within the self. His individual acts of violence have the dignity at least, as Mailer sees it, of the creative potential in mankind's nature—the aspiration to act, live, love, and finally to destroy oneself "seeking to penetrate the mystery of existence."[8] The hipster seeks this self-creation by adventuring into "that inner unconscious life which will nourish" him because therein resides the dynamic energy of God Itself, of "life force" (*Ads*, p. 351). This search for the energy of life implies a further dignity to the hipster's quest and the reconciliation of self-creation and the re-creation of society. For in his search for divine energy, the hipster is a "vector" in "a network of forces" larger than himself. He can partake of those forces and in turn stimulate them. Seeking increase of divine energy for himself, the hipster engages in one side of the "primal battle" of divine energy against decreative energy and thereby opens the way to a creative future or a collective growth; he gives new birth to what we have lost through "the psychic havoc" of the twentieth century.[9]

8. See "The White Negro," in *Ads*, pp. 321, 325, 328.
9. See Mailer's columns in *Village Voice*, especially p. 325, and the introduction to "White Negro" for his specification of the "psychic havoc," in *Ads*, p. 338.

What haunts the middle of the twentieth century is that faith in man
has been lost, and the appeal of authority has been that it would
restrain us from ourselves. Hip, which would return us to ourselves,
at no matter what price in individual violence, is the affirmation of
the barbarian, for it requires a primitive passion about human nature
to believe that individual acts of violence are always to be preferred to
the collective violence of the State; it takes literal faith in the creative
possibilities of the human being to envisage acts of violence as the
catharsis which prepares growth. (*Ads*, p. 355)

Mailer is not facilely advocating all violence or the violence of the
hipster.[10] He is acknowledging the fact of individual acts of violence
in our time and exploring their meaning. Admitting that his concept
of the hipster in "The White Negro" is "no more than" a hypothesis
(p. 351), admitting too that hipsterism could as easily veer toward
fascism as toward a psychic preparation or source of some larger
re-creation of mankind and society (p. 355), Mailer still considers
the possibility, even the hope, that the hipster's acts of violence
represent the struggle of dynamic, divine energy to regain the power
to defeat a society that is "the assassin of us all." The hipster battles
society with the violent image of itself. And his confrontation with
society is heroic in the most primitive sense, for the hipster expresses
the primitive impulse to restore energy, being, and Time, to restore
what Mircea Eliade calls the "enormous present" against the rav-
ages of "historical time."[11] The hipster's efforts to restore to himself
the divine, the creative present is what Mailer means when he says
the hipster searches for "instantaneous existential states" that arise
from "the immediate apprehension and appreciation of existence."
Mailer believes, or hopes, that the individual's drive for the creative
or "existential" present will have a collective, creative effect upon
humanity. This sense and this expression of the dynamic energy or
"being" within the self is for Mailer "the new time coming."

Mailer said in his interview with Steven Marcus that Marion Faye
emerged after the first draft as an embodiment of the "dark pressure" or "evil genius" in the novel (*CC*, pp. 212–13). As a result, Faye
is as much outside the novel's world as Sergius is. Faye's role is to pass
judgment on the strengths, weaknesses, and defeats of the others.

10. See the 1958 interview by Richard Stern, *Ads*, p. 379, where Mailer makes this
point.
11. Mircea Eliade, *The Myth of the Eternal Return*, see especially pp. 3–4, 18,
85–86. The mythical hero's task is to imitate the heroic archetype of creation by
battling evil or decreation, p. 44. Mailer realizes that creation and violence are
opposites (see *Ads*, p. 363), but he also realizes the point Eliade makes repeatedly:
the return to chaos, destruction, orgy prepares the way for the creative act of
regeneration.

We see little, therefore, of his own quest. This may be why he is not very convincing as a "hipster." Though Marion Faye is himself defeated, the book ends with the promise of his return. But without reading the outside commentary on the hipster phenomenon, which Mailer wrote after the novel, one is hard pressed to see what Faye is learning and what his return will mean. Marion cannot say where his perception that "the whole world is bullshit" will take him, and neither can the reader.

Faye, however, is a "psychic outlaw" himself. He expresses Mailer's own rebellion against the unreal world that the movie capital and Desert D'Or represent. He is also another guiding intelligence for the hero, an indicator of courage and truth, an amateur in a world of professionals. He is, moreover, another face of Eitel, for artist and hipster are two faces of the same coin.[12] And, like Elena, Faye is a source of energy, an aid, to Eitel in his struggle. As long as Eitel displays courage, he has the support of Marion Faye. But as a measure of the power of the forces all three struggle against, Eitel drags Marion and Elena with him to defeat.

The narrator-hero also draws sustenance from Faye. Sergius cannot explain why he is drawn to him, but he feels that Faye's contempt for his affair with Lulu has something to do with it. Sergius is aware but helpless before Lulu; he sees himself as weakening from her "constant attacks." Contrastingly, Faye, by the example of his discipline, of his facing and mastering his repugnances and fears, maintains rebellious force. Faye hopes that such discipline will help him to "make it" so that he can "turn around and go the other way." Faye is, therefore, a potential healer and saint. He is "just a religious man turned inside out," who has turned "life on its head" to see the world that is anti-life more clearly (pp. 146–47, 150–51). Faye's dream of apocalypse suggests his role as a potential agent of regeneration.

> Even now, there were factories out there . . . and tons of ore in all the freight cars were being shuttled into the great mouth . . . it was even possible that at this moment soldiers were filing into trenches . . . while army officers explained their purpose in the words of newspaper stories, for the words belonged to the slobs, and the slobs hid the world with words.
>
> So let it come, Faye thought, let this explosion come, and then another, and all the others, until the Sun God burned the earth . . . let it come and clear the rot and the stench . . . let it come for all of

---

12. See *DP*, pp. 13–15, 27. Also Eitel's script, see pp. 126–27, clarifies that the "saint" is an impossible figure in the modern world because the predominant evil exists to destroy mankind, rather than mankind to destroy evil. The psychopathic hipster uses the very evil of the world as a source of its own destruction; he would "scathe the world with this mirror of itself."

everywhere, just so it comes and the world stands clear in the white dead dawn. (pp. 160–61)

Faye is both more and less than a hipster. He is more because he consciously, even intellectually, sees his quest as a metaphysical adventure. He thinks about things the real hipster only feels instinctively. He sees himself as a priest who will enlarge his darker, satanic potential. This potential, Faye believes, is a force he must learn to cultivate if he is truly to begin his search into the nature of God. Faye must stake everything on his hint that the true God is in exile, and that this true God-as-Life will regenerate the world. Faye believes, therefore, that he must use his satanic force to destroy what Satan has built in the world, for Satan, or God-as-Death, has now replaced God-as-Life. "For beyond, in the far beyond, was the heresy that God was the Devil and the One they called the Devil was God-in-banishment like a noble prince deprived of true Heaven, and God who was the Devil has conquered except for a few who saw the cheat that God was not God at all" (pp. 330–31). Simply put, Faye must fight fire with fire, must become satanic to destroy Satan's world of death.

In the fifties, Mailer began to assert his own belief, similar to Marion's, that the journey to God-as-Life is the human potential and, more importantly, that our destiny is "flesh and blood with God's." In his 1958 interview with Richard Stern, Mailer, a little more tentative about God's actual death or banishment, puts it this way:

> And I think there is one single burning pinpoint of the vision in Hip: it's that God is in danger of dying. In my very limited knowledge of theology, this never really has been expressed before. I believe Hip conceives of Man's fate being tied up with God's fate. God is no longer all-powerful. The moral consequences of this are not only staggering, but they're thrilling; because moral experience is intensified rather than diminished.

These "new moral complexities" Mailer feels are more interesting "than anything the novel has gotten into yet." If we are therefore the "seed-carriers" of God-as-Life's conception of creation, if we are explorers and battlers in God's behalf, then "we are engaged in a heroic activity, and not a mean one."[13]

Yet if Faye is more than a hipster, he is also less. He is a failed adventurer. He had not the strength to accept Elena's self-sacrifice. When she comes to live with him, he recognizes that his own failure parrallels hers. Just as Elena had failed to assert life through defiance, love, and compassion, Marion has failed to assert life

13. See *Ads*, pp. 380–81.

through the "black heroic safari" into his darkest nature. He has not maintained a necessary compassionless discipline, nor has he succeeded in beginning the necessary destruction. His life, he says, seems purposeless. It is at this point in the novel (Chapter 25) that Marion, as well as Mailer, faces his own ambiguous feelings about the sacrifice and violence of the hipster. It is as if while Elena tried to kill the love, the compassion, in herself, Marion increased the compassion in himself. One fails as lover, one as hipster. Elena's final defeat is that she returns to and marries Eitel; she loses her life in a labyrinthine suburb of big houses, adjusting analysts, and a husband who takes Lulu again as a mistress. Elena's defiance is reduced to a plea to Eitel to marry her so that she may "learn" the ways of the world "this time."

In this novel of failed adventurers—lovers, artists, and hipsters—only Sergius emerges with the renewed energy to carry forward a vision of life and defiance in a dead world. Like Lovett before him, he has passed the initiation; he has accepted the guidance of a series of sacrificial figures and sources of wisdom not strong enough to carry the spirit of regeneration into the world themselves. He too has received the power from the old man. But Sergius only begins his journey as a gatherer of forces and a hero of renewed life at the end of the novel. If we are left with only a hope rather than an actual redemption of the world, we are at least left, again, with Mailer's affirmation that it is such heroes alone who may ransom creation from death.

At the end of *The Deer Park*, Eitel has a vision of Sergius setting forth on his heroic journey. As one who has gained heroic consciousness, Sergius will have to burn new circuits of consciousness into the world, to redeem Time itself from God-as-Devil. Stopped in traffic, Eitel looks out beyond the shoddy neon signs, hamburger stands, and tourist camps to a freighter at sea "with its hold-lights and mast-lamps moving away to the horizon," and he wonders if Sergius is not one of this ship's adventurers. Eitel, despairing that he did not give to Sergius "the knowledge he wanted to give me," conducts an imaginary dialogue with the young hero, still hoping he can convey that knowledge to Sergius somehow. Eitel confesses to Sergius that the artist must show the real world against the "mummery" of what passes for life; with "the pride of the artist," Eitel says, you must "blow against the walls of every power that exists, the small trumpet of your defiance." Sergius accepts Eitel's message. The young hero asks God directly for the way to follow. He asks if perhaps sex is not "where philosophy begins." But God answers: "Rather think of Sex as Time, and Time as the connection of new circuits" (pp. 374–75).

Coming suddenly as it does at the end of the novel, this equation of
Sex and Time is too abrupt and isolated to mean very much to
Mailer's readers. The equation opens the way to more questions than
it answers. But if one views the equation as an extension of the third
way to the energy within, which is the way of the hipster, one sees
that by Time Mailer means one's immersion in the unconscious
through sexual orgasm. This immersion, to Mailer, may connect the
self with larger potential circuits. Mailer associates Time with a
kind of creative present that is simply the movement of unconscious
psychic energy in the self, in this case through sex. Sergius ends his
journey in this novel, then, not only with the message of artistic
defiance, but with the message of the energy-seeking hipster. To be
sure that we are supposed to view the equation of Sex and Time as an
equation of sex and the unconscious, however, we need to see
Mailer's subsequent development of the relationship between sex
and the unconscious.

We have seen, first, that Mailer's external commentary in "The
White Negro" represents his boldest adventure into the "psychic
wilds" of the unconscious in search of energy. But I should add that
Mailer desires to return somehow to the senses and the deepest
psychic contents without losing "the best parts of our civilized
being," by which he means the "capacity for mental organization
and construction, for logic." If the danger that Hip could destroy
civilization is real, however, there is a greater danger that "civilization is so strong itself, so divorced from the senses, that we have
come to the point where we can liquidate millions of people in
concentration camps by orderly process" (see *Ads*, p. 382).

The "final purpose" of art, for Mailer, is "to intensify, to exacerbate, the moral consciousness of people." Moral consciousness is the
consciousness that "the core of life cannot be cheated," that we live
in such a "dangerous moral condition" that each of us must realize
that every moment of our existence we grow into more or retreat
into less and that as we grow or retreat we take others with us
because we live in a "network" of forces, in an ecology and economy
of divine and cosmic energies (see *Ads*, pp. 384–85).

We need, further, to see that this adventure back into the bodily
senses and back into the unconscious psyche is, for both hipster and
artist, a fundamentally moral adventure, however destructive the
path to that end. Mailer associates the dynamic unconscious with
divine energy, the adventure to reach the unconscious, therefore,
with moral force. In his second column for *The Village Voice* he
argues:

> Thought begins somewhere deep in the unconscious—an
> unconscious which is conceivably divine—or if finite may still be vast

enough in its complexity to bear comparison to an ocean. Out of each human being's vast and mighty unconscious, perhaps from the depths of our life itself, up over all the forbiddingly powerful and subterranean mental mountain ranges which forbid expression, rises from the mysterious source of our knowledge, the small self-fertilization of thought, conscious thought. (*Ads*, p. 285)

In the fiction after *The Deer Park*, we also see an advance of the Sex-Time equation, especially in "The Time of Her Time" and "Advertisements for Myself on the Way Out," both fragments of that big, never-completed novel. In the former fragment, the same Sergius of *The Deer Park* continues the exploration, though here he goes less the way of the artist, more the way of the hipster. Sergius is a phallic figure who lives in a high, large, and white-washed Village studio, which he calls Mt. O'Shaugnessy. Women make their pilgrimages to this mountain and return with varying success. The sexual encounters are usually cold blooded and sterile, but this story focuses on one woman's experience of Time; that is, her immersion into the vast unconscious, "the sea," through orgasm. Denise Gondelman is a rational, educated, overanalyzed, pretentious young Jewess who has never made the journey. Sergius has numerous incapacities himself: he does not "make it" when Denise does; he withholds himself from the danger of emotional involvement; however, he finally takes Denise on her journey: "a first wave kissed, a second spilled, and a third and a fourth and a fifth came breaking over, and finally she was away, she was loose in the water for the first time in her life" (*Ads*, p. 502). Though Denise understandably despises Sergius because he takes her to a point of self-abandon that he was not himself prepared to experience, and though they separate, one assumes, forever, Denise at least becomes through her experience of Time — which is to say of the dynamic unconscious — a figure more heroic than Sergius himself. She is a person who might now be capable of returning the experience to help Sergius make a similar journey — "she was a hero fit for me" (p. 503).

Time is explored a little further in "Myself on the Way Out." Here the focus is on Marion Faye — just returned from prison — and on Faye's violence. The narrator is the ghost of a man Faye has killed. Faye and the ghost are on a journey to "capture Time" and the "illumination" the Prince of Darkness may furnish. The fragment is too discursive, even pretentiously theoretical. It is not difficult, therefore, to see why Mailer never finished it. I think here too Mailer may not yet have solved the problem he and Faye faced in *The Deer Park* — the inability to deal with compassion for the victims of violence. It will be only in *An American Dream* that Mailer comes to terms with the problem of violence through the effective embodiment of his ideas in symbolic allegory. Yet in this fragment we see another step, indeed a final step, in the author's discursive analysis of Time. In the discussion between the prostitute and the physicist, Mailer establishes three dimensions of time. "Passive Time" is Time on its way to death, which is dynamic energy extinguished. "Active Time" or "Dynamic Time" is the experience of growth, the movement of dynamic unconscious energy, whether elicited by sex, violence, or some creative act (p. 521). "Potential Time" is that latent psychic energy that, at the moment of orgasm or violence, for example, can leap the gap to "Active Time" and make a being grow rather than die (p. 523). The concept remains as abstract in the fragment as it does in my summary of it. But one thing is clear. Mailer's heroes and heroines are searching for the energy that will be the source of regeneration. And in this search they typify what Angus Fletcher has called the search for "pure power" that is "at the heart of allegorical quest." The adventurers seeking or momentarily grasping the power of creation and growth, on the one hand, and the tempters and temptresses using their power of the world to deny the adventurer this creative power, on the other, create the basic dialectic of the allegorical mode.[14]

As most of his readers know, Mailer's principal theoretical resource in his search for the secrets of human energy is Wilhelm Reich's psychological theories. Mailer admits as much in *Advertisements* (see, for example, p. 301), and a number of Mailer's critics use a Reichian viewpoint and nomenclature to interpret Mailer's novels and ideas. Robert Solotaroff provides the most thorough and perceptive analysis of what Mailer accepts and rejects of Reich. In the 1950s especially, Mailer does speak of energy as "orgone" and bioelectric force, and of the release of creative energies through orgasm. Yet, as Solotaroff wisely points out, Mailer reaches for something beyond Reichian energy theory too, and to see Mailer's "energetics" after the 1950s as merely Reichian is inadequate. Reich's orgone, to use Solotaroff's phrase, "belongs in its human manifestations to a closed system with an inner final cause." For Mailer, who is perhaps closer to George Bernard Shaw's concept of creative evolution and life force, human energy has transcendent purposes, potentials, and roots, just as reproduction can be a force of creative evolution toward some greater conception of civilization as well as of Being.[15]

On the other hand, the nearly complete absence of references to Jung in Mailer's theoretical discussions and investigations of human energy does not necessarily suggest that Mailer has not read Jung, but does suggest at least that Jung is far less a specific theoretical

14. See Angus Fletcher, *Allegory: The Theory of a Symbolic Mode*, pp. 47–49, 338.
15. See Robert Solotaroff, *Down Mailer's Way*, pp. 95–98, 270.

source for Mailer. One finds it difficult, however, especially reading the Mailer of the 1950s, to avoid considering the possibility that the similarities between Mailer's and Jung's theories of human energy are discoveries Mailer makes largely by adventures into his own unconscious life and being. The similarities between Jung and Mailer, therefore, tend more to take on the authenticity of independent discoveries about psychic experience and take on less the artificiality of a writer's mechanical appropriation of another's (Reich's) *ideas about* psychic experience.

But whether or not we are willing to accept this "apparent" difference as indicative of authenticity, Mailer seems to me to be closer to Jung than Reich in many ways as he searches for the sources and the meaning of human energy. Philosophically, the implications of the Jungian collective unconscious and psychic manifestations of the God-image indicate a substantially open system. Jung's hesitations to assert a psychic system open to the influxes of divine energy or the *élan vital* are practical necessities for the empirical investigator who hopes to make his scientific analyses and measurements credible. In his published, scientific work he avoided such "philosophical considerations" because he believed they were outside his scope. His personal beliefs, however, were a separate matter.[16]

Mailer's writings immediately after *The Deer Park* postulate a system of psychic energy like Jung's. We have seen that Mailer calls the potential for psychic processes "Potential Time"; Jung calls this potential "psychic force." We should keep in mind that Jung's theory of psychic energy is the foundation for his explanation of the emergence of archetypal patterns, which are the embodiments of that energy as *active* psychic processes. The actual, dynamic phenomena of the psyche that Mailer calls "Active Time," Jung calls "psychic energy." Art embodies these active phenomena as mythological motifs that are the record of the artist's psychic experiences in the act of creation. The hero archetype, which we have seen and

16. Carl Jung, *The Structure and Dynamics of the Psyche*, translated by R. F. C. Hull, Vol. 8 (New Jersey: Princeton University Press, 1968), pp. 6–7, 17. The title of this essay is "On Psychic Energy." Future references are parenthetical. Victor White, in *God and the Unconscious*, considers the theological implications of Jung's theories of the psyche at length. Although Jung never reached a definite position on the transcendental and metaphysical validity of religious images, the absence of religion was for Jung the root of adult psychological disease. Jung carries empiricism, according to White, to the very frontiers of theology (pp. 68–71, 81). Compare Jung's extra-professional letters in White's Appendix. Jung was eminently aware of the religious, even personally religious, implications of his work. "Self" may be "the receptacle for divine grace," Jung says, even though it will never "take the place of God" (p. 258). See also Jung, *The Structure and Dynamics of the Psyche*, pp. 265, 267, 269, 273. The self, for Jung, is "transcendental" because it is ultimately "indescribable and incomprehensible."

will see again in Mailer's work, is for Jung the symbol of the movement of "libido" energy to the unconscious for nourishment. Jung calls this movement "regression" and argues that it is "one of the most important energetic phenomena of psychic life." "Libido" is "life energy" within the psyche; it is not merely sexual but takes a multitude of forms; it may be spiritual as well, for example (see "On Psychic Energy," pp. 15, 17, 23, 32, 36). When Mailer reveals what his hipsters and heroes find in their journeys to the unconscious, he alienates many readers. Jung would have expected nothing less.

> What the regression brings to the surface certainly seems at first sight to be slime from the depths; but if one does not stop short at a superficial evalution and refrains from passing judgment on the basis of a preconceived dogma, it will be found that this "slime" contains not merely incompatible and rejected remnants of everyday life, or inconvenient and objectionable animal tendencies, but also germs of new life and vital possibilities for the future. ("On Psychic Energy," p. 35)

The dialectic of forces Mailer discovers in the inner life is the basis of psychic energy itself for Jung, and it is what Jung means by the psychic conflict of "Nature" and "Spirit" (p. 52). By "Nature" Jung means all the polymorphous instinctual nature of primitive man alive in the unconscious. By "Spirit" he means the opposing principle or tendency, also alive in the unconscious, to unify and integrate those instincts. For Jung, the universal experience of God is the experience of this tension, the influence of the instincts and the opposing influence of the aspiration for their unification, which is "Spirit." So, though Jung is an "empiricist" examining religious experience as a psychic phenomenon, he is able to postulate that this dynamic interplay in the psyche is precisely what mankind has always felt and believed to be God. Jung admits that from the "spiritual standpoint," this psychic energy is divine energy, the God within.[17] This "spiritual standpoint" is obviously the one from which Mailer speaks by 1959.

Jung also stresses, as does Mailer, that progress in life is made by

17. Ibid., p. 55. Compare Joseph Campbell, *The Hero with a Thousand Faces*, pp. 257–58. "[T]o grasp the full value of the mythological figures that have come down to us, we must understand that they are not only symptoms of the unconscious . . . but also controlled and intended statements of certain spiritual principles, which have remained as constant throughout the course of human history as the form and nervous structure of the human physique itself. Briefly formulated, the universal doctrine teaches that all the visible structures of the world—all things and beings—are the effects of a ubiquitous power out of which they rise, which supports and fills them during the period of their manifestation, and back into which they must ultimately dissolve. This is the power known to science as energy, to the Melanesians as *mana*, . . . and the Christians as the power of God. Its manifestation in the psyche is termed, by the psychoanalysts, *libido*. And its manifestation in the cosmos is the structure and flux of the universe itself."

individual acts of expanded consciousness—that is to say "the development of individuality" and the "growth of personality"—through one's return to what is essential in one's being. Whether one views such a progression of life as cyclical or linear, the return is always to the instinctual and spiritual essences of the unconscious, which will necessarily include the urges toward increased sexuality, murder, rage, and defiance (see especially pp. 56–57).

> Wherever the cultural process is moving forward, whether in single individuals or in groups, we find a shaking off of collective beliefs. Every advance in culture is, psychologically, an extension of consciousness, a coming to consciousness that can take place only through discrimination. Therefore an advance always begins with individuation, that is to say with the individual, conscious of his isolation, cutting a new path through hitherto untrodden territory. To do this he must first return to the fundamental facts of his own being, irrespective of all authority and tradition, and allow himself to become conscious of his distinctiveness. If he succeeds in giving collective validity to his widened consciousness, he creates a tension of opposites that provides the stimulation which culture needs for its further progress. (p. 59)

More explicitly than *Barbary Shore*, *The Deer Park* is ultimately a novel of attempted "regressions" to the sources of one's being, a novel of the death of the old man and the birth of the new, and a novel of the transfer of spirit as the dynamic principle of life and as the power within to survive and defy the incursions of a fallen, deadening world. When Mailer produced *The Deer Park* as a play more than ten years after the novel was published, he rewrote the closing imaginary dialogue between Sergius and Eitel to emphasize this transfer even more. In the play, Eitel's weariness kills him outright, and Sergius reflects over Eitel's corpse: "the poor man went of that disease which goes by so many names." Life itself had killed him, for the "law of life so cruel and so just" is that "we must grow or else pay more for remaining the same." Sergius continues, "And as he died, his spirit passed on to me, for to pass on one's spirit is the small gift we are allowed in Hell."[18]

18. *The Deer Park: A Play* (New York: The Dial Press, 1967), p. 189.

4

An American Dream

What shocked and astounded us at Belsen and Buchenwald was less their shaming inhumanity, than their manifestation of stark, ruthless, primitive devilry. They were inexplicable merely in terms of cynical, utilitarian power-politics. There was no use, no reason, not even a bad reason, in keeping thousands of people just alive, when they could have been so easily slain or just left to die, merely for their torture and affliction. Could it be that gods and demons, heavens and hells, are ineradicable from the nooks and crannies of the human mind, and that if the human mind is deprived of its heaven above and its hell beneath, then it must make its heaven and corresponding hell on earth? —Victor White, *God and the Unconscious*

MEPHISTOPHELES: This lofty mystery I must now unfold.
Goddesses throned in solitude, sublime,
Set in no place, still less in any time,
At the mere thought of them my blood runs cold.
They are the Mothers!
. . . .
Goddesses, unknown to mortal mind,
And named indeed with dread among our kind.
To reach them you must plumb earth's deepest vault,
That we have need of them is your own fault. —Goethe, *Faust*

An American Dream (1965) represents Mailer's boldest use of the allegorical mode. This boldness drew the sharpest negative criticism of any of Mailer's novels from those who read it as an attempt to portray realistically, in any ordinary sense, the hero's quest for energy and life. The negative criticism, in turn, led to a clear division in Mailer criticism, a division that clarifies the issues central to this study of Mailer's art and ideas. For it is after this novel was published in 1965 that several critics finally began to defend Mailer's work on the basis of criteria outside the realistic tradition. Richard Poirier, Leo Bersani, and John Aldridge were in the vanguard.[1] They stimulated other critics in the late sixties to examine Mailer in light of the

1. See, for example: Richard Poirier, "Morbid-Mindedness," *Commentary*, pp. 91–94; Leo Bersani, "Interpretation of Dreams," *Partisan Review*, pp. 603–8; John Aldridge, "The Energy of New Success," *Time to Murder and Create: The Contemporary Novel in Crisis*, pp. 149–63. All three articles are collected in Robert Lucid's *Norman Mailer: The Man and His Work* (Boston: Little, Brown and Company, 1971). Bersani also appears in Leo Braudy's collection, *Norman Mailer: A Collection of Critical Essays* (Englewood Cliffs, N. J.: Prentice-Hall, 1972).

American Romance tradition. That is to say, critics began to compare Mailer with those American writers who adventured into extraordinary areas of moral consciousness and self-realization. Richard Foster and Michael Cowan best represent the effort to place Mailer in the tradition of Cooper, Hawthorne, Melville, Emerson, Dickinson, Whitman, Fitzgerald, and Faulkner.[2]

The critical debate is important because it clarifies the peculiar difficulties of reading Mailer and emphasizes the need for a detailed assessment of what the narrative of *Dream* means. The debate also emphasizes the need for a clearer understanding of allegory. If, for example, one reads *Dream* as the negative critics have, one has to agree the novel is absurd. From the viewpoint of realism and the boundaries of understood consciousness, the novel is, as Elizabeth Hardwick charged, a collection of "vengeful murder, callous copulation and an assortment of dull cruelties," and Rojack's wife is a "poor unreal creature brought to rest in her own filth for reasons known only to the odor-and-anal-obsessed author." Like Gore Vidal, Hardwick believes Mailer's gifts lie in naturalistic technique and that to the extent Mailer deviates from such technique, he abuses his gifts and his readers. What little success Hardwick admits to *Dream*, she concludes must be merely unorganic, "brilliant diversions," such as the Shago Martin scene.[3]

While this novel is so easily made to seem ridiculous, however, as indeed novels of moral earnestness and absolute values can be by the merely literal eye, it can also be seen as a symbolic dream or allegory with an astonishing symbolic consistency that draws its power from mythological roots. The author guides us through stark, brutal, and intense experiences ranging from the horrible to the beatific. We are guided into the realities of the unconscious and the dream: sex, incest, masturbation, white and black magic, murder, love, creation, and painful acts of cowardice and courage. The novel is steeped in the violence and hallucinatory horror of the nightmare as much as in the visionary's dream of healing from disease and disorder.

As if to fuel the fires of negative criticism, Mailer engages his contemporaries on their own ground in this novel, much as he does in his television appearances. Mailer had mentioned in *Advertisements* that the writer must package himself for consumption like everything else in America today if he hopes even to be considered by

2. Richard Foster, "Mailer and the Fitzgerald Tradition," *Novel*, pp. 219–30, also in Braudy's collection. Michael Cowan, "The Americanness of Norman Mailer," from an unpublished manuscript excerpted in Braudy, pp. 143–57.

3. Elizabeth Hardwick, "Bad Boy," *Partisan Review*, pp. 291–94. Printed in Lucid as "A Nightmare by Norman Mailer." Gore Vidal, "The Norman Mailer Syndrome," *Nation*, pp. 13–16 (reprinted in Lucid). See also Tom Wolfe, "Son of Crime and Punishment," *Book Week*, pp. 1, 10, 12–13 (also reprinted in Lucid).

those he would reach. His allegory is cloaked in the conventions of the mystery and detective novel, the spy novel, and the supernatural tale. It appeals to our taste for exposés of international intrigue and of manipulation between the CIA and Mafia.

But just as this is a novel of something other than inflexible realism, it is also something more than a collection of bestseller tactics and superficial conventions. We might go so far as to read the novel as a rational allegory, and the commentary in *Cannibals* helps us to do this. But the symbolism of the novel is far too complex, shifting, and multivalent—as mythological symbolism is—to be read only as the iconography of a rational allegory. Something more is required still. Nothing could be clearer, from title to content, than that Mailer sees this novel as a journey into the unconscious. If Mailer views his responsibilities as a novelist to adventure into the unconscious and to replace the naturalistic novel and the novel of manners with the novel of intense experience and the dream, we should expect to find here, to the degree that this adventure is genuine, the recurring of complex symbols, situations, and trials that such adventurers have experienced throughout the recorded past.[4] Until we view the novel in such a way as to include its visionary material, we shall continue to err on the side of superficiality.

Robert Solotaroff misunderstands the novel, for example, when he remarks that he cannot keep *Dream* in "consistent focus" because of its multiple tones and levels of reality. He suggests that we cannot view this novel as conventional allegory because the forces in the novel are more than symbols in a clear-cut dualism; they are forces that are supposed to have relevance to causes in our own world.[5] This argument has merit if Solotaroff is really referring to "rational allegory" when he says "conventional allegory," and if one believes clear-cut dualism excludes the ambiguities of true allegory. Solotaroff seems to recognize the complexities of allegory when he

4. At the beginning of *Cannibals and Christians* (hereafter cited as *CC*), it is clear that Mailer intends us to see his faith that the resources of the unconscious may be our salvation. Questioning "absurd" art also, Mailer posits the alternatives. Absurd art is either the "patina of waste," part of the waste itself that will entertain us while we wait for apocalypse, or it has positive value, and we "are face to face with a desperate but most rational effort from the deepest resources of the unconscious of us all [that is, to say, collective] to rescue civilization from the pit and plague of its bedding, that swinish foul old bedding on which two centuries of imperialism, high finance, moral hypocrisy and horror have lain" (p. 2).

5. Robert Solotaroff, *Down Mailer's Way*, pp. 170–75. Unlike most of Mailer's sympathetic critics, Solotaroff is not particularly sympathetic to *An American Dream*; the whole chapter discussing the novel has about it the tone of tongue-in-cheek.

contrasts Dante to Mailer, and I agree Mailer is not Dante; nevertheless, we have to approach Mailer openly, by starting with a more flexible concept of allegory, if we would confront the complexities of *Dream*, and if we would understand where the novel succeeds and fails.

There are at least three levels of reality operating in *Dream*. First is the literal reality traditionally associated with realism—the detailed, conscious, and rational experience of such events as occur in the police-station episodes, in a series of telephone calls Rojack receives from the work-a-day world, in the autopsy scene, and, to some extent, in the Shago Martin episode. Behind this is the rational allegory, or that level of the narrative in which characters and events are directly translatable into the larger dualistic pattern of the novel as it portrays the battle between Life and Death. In this particular allegory the distinctions between Life and Death, at certain points, assume definite connotations of Good and Evil, often in the Christian sense of that dualism. Behind the rational allegory is the mythological level of the allegory in which images from the external world are used, in Piehler's words, to "shape a visionary world in which spiritual powers can be encountered and portrayed." These powers, one could call them psychic powers, are ever-shifting and ambiguous. At this level the writer's intuitive functions use "ancient and profound" images and symbols prior to their identification and control by rational functions. To discuss this novel in terms of such imagery, we will need the aid of those who have investigated the mythological patterns of world religions, literature, and art. This "reality" of *Dream* is intensely subjective, but as Carl Jung has argued, there is a point at which intensely subjective experience may become objective, or archetypal. We should recall also that true allegory functions on all levels simultaneously, not on separate levels exclusively. Just as in the midst of such enumerative or scientifically realistic scenes as those in the police station, Rojack receives a sign from God, which has numerous mythological antecedents. I will be concerned here with the second two levels of this novel; they predominate. Often both levels can and will be discussed together.

It will become obvious that there are many similarities between the heroic journey in *An American Dream* and the two previous novels. However, there are some important differences. The hero is middle-aged and has achieved, compared to the other heroes, a high level of success in the world. Rojack's tests are more extreme than those of the younger heroes, and, unlike Lovett and Sergius, Rojack must depend more upon the wisdom and courage he can find in himself than upon the wisdom and spirit passed on as a legacy from the old guide. There is, however, still one embodiment of creative force: Cherry, in whom the hero finds sustenance and with whom he must keep in touch. And, again, there are tempters everywhere.

Rojack dips below the surface of consciousness and confronts the four principal figures of his dream—Deborah, Ruta, Cherry, and Kelly. I will lend order to this novel by examining it as four successive stages of the mythical Night Sea Journey to rebirth. Each stage is heralded by a principal figure in the dream. Each stage is composed of the hero's confrontation with that principal figure and the testing situations and minor figures that cluster around the main figure.

Once Rojack has introduced himself as war-hero, ex-congressman, professor of existential psychology, and television personality who has engaged in the politics and public relations necessary to "manufacture" himself, he tells us that (like Mailer's earlier heroes) he is dissatisfied by his actor's hollowness, that the success he has achieved is really failure, and that his private obsession with death has reached the point where he must confront it. The extreme, dreamlike experiences begin when his obsession leads him to face either suicide—that "pale light" and call of something lonely, dreamlike, and dreadful—or murder—that release of rage and hatred that promises renewed strength.[6] Rojack is a hipster facing defeat or violence, but he is more. He must slay a Devouring Dragon before he can search for "love in another land." Deborah, his wife, is the dragon-guardian at the threshold to that other land. She is the "Great Bitch," the maimer and castrater, a figure mythical heroes have faced as long as their quests have been recorded. Once we see Deborah as a mythological figure in a visionary world, we will not be marooned on the literal issue of Mailer's sexist portrayal of women, as Kate Millet and Elizabeth Hardwick are. One could make a case against Mailer's sexism, but surely the least effective way of doing so would be to base it on a translation of mythic figures and allegorical agents into merely literal characters.

Rojack cannot separate himself from Deborah. Her hold is so great that she has forced him to confront his obsession with death by committing either suicide or murder. It is in facing suicide, that Rojack first sees the state of his own Being. He has lived his life and is dead with it, full of its rottenness (pp. 11–12). He misses the moment when he could have killed himself and returns to the nausea of his rotten existence, to the call of Deborah. By doing so, he takes a first step toward his rebirth without realizing it. Failing suicide, he returns to the sea. He feels at this point merely as if he has entered some indoor pool of steam and ultraviolet light.

6. *An American Dream* (hereafter cited as *AD*), pp. 8–9. Unless otherwise indicated, all citations are to works by Norman Mailer.

On the rational level, Deborah is the love of his "ego," the love of worldly power that has poisoned his inner life. Making love with Deborah, he tells us: "I always felt as if I had torn free some promise of my soul and paid it over in ransom." She has played a role in each personal loss. Returning to her now, he feels like an addict whose "substance" has fallen out of him returning for a fix. "Can you understand? I did not belong to myself any longer. Deborah had occupied my center" (pp. 27, 35).

When Rojack is most abject and fearful before her, she taunts him with the pleasures of her infidelities, and this taunting produces another vision of his dead self or Being. But it also kindles a fire in him, and impulsively he slaps her. This act makes Rojack feel a new power contrary to the feeling of Deborah's power within him, and when she charges him in turn, literally trying to castrate him, Rojack kills Deborah.

If Deborah were merely the egotistical infidel and the domineering wife who stifles her weak husband's chances of genuine success in the world, the murder would indeed be a ridiculous and gratuitous cruelty. But if in the rational allegory, Deborah represents one of the guardians of wealth and power as it functions in the world, she is something more still. Shago sums her up as Devourer: "I got a good look at her sitting with you in the front, eating me, man, I could feel the marrow oozing from my bones, *a cannibal*" (p. 190). Rojack describes her also as a queen with a "huge mass of black hair" and the "striking green eyes" of a serpent or dragon: "there was something so sly at the center of her, some snake, I used literally to conceive of a snake guarding the cave which opened to the treasure, the . . . filthy-lucred wealth of all the world." A "sullen poisonous fire, an oil on flame" goes out of Deborah to take Rojack in. She is also temptress and witch, her mouth shifting through many shapes, her voice "a masterwork of treachery." We later discover she is Kelly's incestuous witch, daughter in damnation, and rival for his satanic power in a network of international intrigue. Her powers are directed at the life in Rojack. "She had the power to lay a curse," and with this violent power, Deborah the huntress is as capable of murder as of curse. "But Deborah promised bad burial. One would go down in one's death, and muck would wash over the last of one's wind. She did not wish to tear the body, she was out to spoil the light . . .—that wide mouth, full-fleshed nose, and pointed green eyes, pointed as arrows—would be my first view of eternity."[7]

7. *AD*, pp. 19–20, 22, 26, 34. This motif of the huntress in touch with supernatural forces in the spiritual and animal world is another quality of the Terrible Mother (see *AD*, especially p. 35). Carl Jung makes this point in *Symbols of Transformation* (translated by R. F. C. Hull, Vol. 5 [New Jersey: Princeton Univer-

Carl Jung describes the "Great Bitch" Devouress as a fundamental symbol in the transformations of mythical heroes. Jung describes the Night Sea Journey as a return to, in Goethe's words, the "Realm of the Mothers"; that is, to the unconscious. For Jung, the devouring fish or whale and beast or dragon, the Helpful and Terrible Mothers, the Holy City and the Damned City, like the sea itself, are symbols depicting the dual aspects of the unconscious: the renewing and the devouring. Like the sea, the unconscious is the Primordial Mother, to which the hero periodically returns for nourishment and transformation. But rebirth is not guaranteed. The way is beset with danger and trial. As Joseph Campbell, in his own study of this journey, says: "the crossing of the threshold is the first step into the sacred zone of the universal source." The demons, temptresses, and witches the hero encounters are at once dangers and bestowers of power.[8] The first of these is the Terrible Mother, the whale, dragon, or beast who personifies devouring death.

For Jung the devouring figure represents the awesome demands of the unconscious, demands that can paralyze or enslave the hero and drain him of energy and resourcefulness like a hostile demon. She is his first view of the mysterious and awful unconscious that must be joined to the light of consciousness if rebirth is to follow, if consciousness is to be recharged with her energy. The battle against paralysis and absorption calls forth the hero's creative powers. The assault on the Mother becomes the source of future energy in the heroic conflict; the hero battles to gain his life, and if he succeeds, he descends to confront other figures of horror and regeneration. Here, in the deeper journey, the positive aspect of the Mother resides—the beloved, the divine child, the heavenly bride, the Nourishing Mother who is the unconscious source of life.[9]

---

sity Press, 1956]), pp. 369–70, identifying the huntress with Hecate and Artemis. "She is the mother of witchcraft and witches, the patron goddess of Medea, because the power of the Terrible Mother is irresistible, coming as it does from the unconscious." Jung also identifies this figure as the madness or "moonsickness" who sends invasions by the unconscious into consciousness. Mailer makes it clear that Deborah is "in touch with the moon" and aware of the moonsickness Rojack faced in facing his suicide and rotten Being alone (*AD*, see especially pp. 22, 26).

8. Joseph Campbell, *The Hero with a Thousand Faces*, pp. 81, 83. Campbell also notes the two aspects of the woman—the symbol of all that is Life and of all that is abominable, or Death.

9. In the last two paragraphs, I am condensing Jung's long and thoroughly documented discussion of principles found in countless myths in "The Origin of the Hero," "Symbols of the Mother and of Rebirth," "The Battle for Deliverance from the Mother," and "The Dual Mother," in *Symbols*, pp. 198, 235, 242, 245, 248, 272–93, 300–301, 314, 337, and 357.

Jung adds: "The teleological significance of the hero [is] as a symbolic figure who attracts libido [psychic energy] to himself . . . in order to lead it over the symbolic bridge of myth to higher uses" (p. 314). "Every obstacle that arises in his path and hampers his ascent wears the shadowy features of the Terrible Mother . . . and in

Deborah's ambiguities arise not only from the various levels of the narrative, but from the nature of the unconscious itself. She represents the evil in Rojack too. He tells us on the opening pages of the novel that he had seen Deborah first as an heiress, as a vehicle to the kind of power he will fight to transcend for the rest of the novel. The snake rustled in his own heart. We will see that each mythological figure gives Rojack and the reader a glimpse of his or her other nature, which, taken as the contents of a dream, or of the unconscious, is the dualistic nature of Rojack's unconscious as he journeys through it. It is an intensely subjective experience because it is Rojack's unconscious self that gives meaning and value to experiences, figures, omens, odors, and totems. Rojack's dream is, as much as anything, a dream of the self's struggle with the capacities for Life and Death within. Or, as Mailer phrases it in *The Presidential Papers*: "One has to keep coming back to one notion: How do you make life? How do you *not* make life" (p. 139). One difficulty of the novel is that of true allegory. We see clear divisions of light and dark forces on the rational level, but as archetypal figures, the representatives of these forces reveal an unsettling quality of mixed good and evil; that is, the unsettling quality of the self. The balance of good or evil for each figure in this novel is simply weighted on one side or the other as it represents potential snares or balms for the dreamer.

A further complication is that Rojack gains and uses two kinds of power to free himself from the death within. On one hand, each victory, beginning with victory over Deborah, gives Rojack the strength and calm of grace, the sense of passing from night to a morning of new life. Rojack describes the murder as a catharsis of hate and illness and as a floating into himself. This first infusion of grace brings a vision of a landscape of "oriental splendor" and of a heavenly city. Twice the scene that climaxes with the murder is described as a gathering of fire (pp. 29, 31). These are symbols promising regeneration.[10]

On the other hand, Deborah has led Rojack to his faith in black

every conquest he wins back again the smiling, loving and life-giving mother" (p. 390).

Campbell also sees the Night Sea Journey as a descent into psyche (*Hero*, p. 321). The central "monomyth" Campbell's book explores is the journey into the unconscious, the discovery of the deepest self. The hero as "life adventurer" makes a rite of rebirth that Campbell sees as the greatest overall pattern in mythology. The function of rite, myth, and dream is to carry the life energy across the "difficult thresholds of transformation" and change the "patterns of consciousness and unconscious life" (pp. 8, 10).

10. Fire is the archetypal sign of the hero. It expresses the grace or force within him of the sun, the visible God, itself. This is the universal source of life in mythology. The fire in the hero is the creative power of his soul, which Jung argues is the "libido" or life energy. The sun-hero's task is to canalize this energy for

magic, in witches, and in the Devil. The transformation of perception Rojack undergoes in this novel, which the reader experiences as Rojack's intense sensual and psychic awareness and associations, literally begins with Deborah too. Rojack had long ago, he tells us, cast off that world view of the positivist, the technocrat, and the liberal who believe in "the *New York Times*: Experts Divided on Fluoridation, Diplomat Attacks Council Text, Self-Rule Near for Bantu Province, Chancellor Outlines Purpose of Talks, New Drive for Health Care for Aged." He now swims in "the well of Deborah's intuitions" (p. 36). Part of this magic is the force Rojack gains from those he defeats. From Deborah's murder he gains the violence and black magic that will help him wage psychic battle against such Mafia types as Tony: "We avoided each other's eye and stood there side by side in a contest: his presence against my presence, two sea creatures buried deep in the ocean silt of a grotto, exuding the repellent communications of sea creatures. . . . So I called on Deborah" (pp. 116–17).

In *Cannibals and Christians* Mailer argues that messages from the unconscious, the "well of intuitions," the source of associative consciousness, can transform one's perception. In a second dialogue with himself, entitled "The Metaphysics of the Belly," Mailer argues that perception is both physiological and psychic. Psychic perceptions arise from the unconscious as it urges itself forward into consciousness and the external world (pp. 263–65). Rojack's deepest resources of perception emerge after he slays his wife. His intensified perceptions are essential to the first stage of Rojack's regeneration. His strange calm and sense of renewed life make him aware, with a hallucinatory intensity, of the life in his body, hair, and eyes. He sees molecules living and dying around him. His eyes seem, like those of the last German he killed in the war, to go all the way back to God. He does not know whether his delicate state is more good than evil, but he is quickly captured by some dark, primitive force, some touch that pushes him to descend to Ruta, to the door of a jungle rather than a celestial city: "I could have been in a magnetic field. . . . One kiss of flesh, one whiff of sweet was loose, sending life to the charnel house of my balls. Something fierce for pleasure was loose . . . I was near a swamp where butterflies and tropical birds went fanning up" (pp. 37–41). Ruta's intrigues, like Hollingsworth's, have an onanistic taint. Rojack catches her masturbating— "off in that bower of the libido where she was queen," her fingers

---

regeneration. In myth, the depiction of fire-making represents the killing of the dark state of the union with the Terrible Mother. See Jung, *Symbols*, pp. 121, 149, 170, 212. Compare Campbell on this same point in *Hero*, pp. 42, 69–71, 131–33, 146.

working "like maggots"—as a consequence of her spying on Deborah and Rojack. Ruta had mistaken their fight for lovemaking. Under the force that has sent him to Ruta, Rojack is as near to murdering her as to copulating with her. He battles her sexually for her powers. A mixture of hatred, anger, and lust gird him for the battle. He wins the Devil's gifts and treasures, which ride from her through him. The "Devil's kitchen," Ruta's anus, calls him, and his sodomy is a "theft" of satanic gifts. During his thievery, he is tempted to enter her vagina—"which, I could remind you, leads to creation"—but his excursions to the "tomb" of Ruta's vagina have not an adequate power. If he begins to enliven Ruta's womb briefly, even to make it into a modest "chapel," he still returns to the roar of the Devil's kitchen at the crisis. To Rojack's newly found perceptions, Ruta's womb had not "the glory and hot jungle wings" to keep him, her anus had the dangerous qualities and forces that he needed to confront other forces of defeat and pass other trials: "mendacity, guile, fine-edged cupidity, the wit to trick authority." "You know, at the end, you stole something from me," Ruta says. It will be the hero's test that he can channel the power of Ruta's gifts to succeed in later acts of renewal and, finally, to return to the Lord.

But as yet Rojack is unsure of his ability to use such gifts from Ruta's body, which are "now alive inside" him. Oppression gathers like a heavy force in the room, and he wonders if his seed "expiring" in Ruta's kitchen will be a curse rather than a power bestowed on him. Yet he conquers his doubts and fantasies and channels their power when a messenger from his unconscious slips "into the tower" of consciousness and tells him to use the new power for defiant confrontation. He returns to Ruta for another, if brief, rapacious sexual encounter. "I felt as fine and evil as a razor and just as content with myself. There was something further in her I'd needed, some bitter perfect salt" (p. 56). With this evil force and salt, Rojack strikes out into the street to face Deborah's corpse and to defy the police. Jung suggests that during the heroic struggle, the destructive aspect of the gods manifests itself as violent power, and it is with violence, "the violence of all unconscious dynamism," that the violence of these gods must be overcome (*Symbols*, p. 338).

When Rojack surmounts the test of Ruta, he completes the separation from the Devouress necessary for further descent, for Ruta is another aspect of Deborah, the bearer of Deborah's "gifts." Both are described as "witches" and "queens"; both are mistresses to Kelly, challenging him for power. Like Deborah, Ruta is a damned being whose little glimmer of life, or lost potential, cannot overcome the evil that imprisons it. And in a prevailing metaphor of both *Cannibals* and *Dream*, both women have a penchant for anal sex, which associates them with death. Scatological metaphors are becoming increasingly important at this point in Mailer's work. The scatological obsessions of some of his characters are based on the theories Mailer articulates in "The Metaphysics of the Belly" about the close relationship of one's being to one's deepest cellular functions. Persons or societies may be obsessed with scatology, Mailer argues, because the material of scatology contains some message from the unconscious that reveals a person's or society's disproportions or state of being. Mailer incorporates his theory in *An American Dream* that by airing one's obsessions, by confronting the messages of disease and waste, and by engaging death, perversion, and fear, one may help a disproportionate or stifled self to become a balanced self growing toward Life (see *CC*, pp. 274–86). Such messages of the unconscious are constantly urging themselves into consciousness in *Dream*. Rojack's rebirth depends upon a return to primitive states of consciousness in which the metaphorical connections between waste and being, for example, become real to Rojack. There is a clear similarity here between Mailer's assumption and the theory of the total self as a functional balance between body and psyche that Carl Jung develops in his introduction to *Aion*. And the similarity is even clearer when a post-Jungian, Erich Neumann, investigates the relationship between body and psyche further. Neumann points out that a sense of the functional relationship between the two is indeed a primitive, fundamental state of awareness or consciousness, as Mailer believes it is. In the primitive version of the body-psyche relationship, all parts and products of the body have significance because they are all products of the functioning of mana or soul-power in the self and between the self and the external world (for example, in food).[11]

At this point in the narrative of *Dream*, Rojack has separated himself from the Terrible Mother through Deborah's murder, which revealed the Celestial City, and through acquirement of Her gifts during the scatological encounter with Ruta, which revealed the Damned City. "I had a vision immediately after of a huge city in the desert . . . was it a place on the moon? For the colors had the unreal pastel of a plastic and the main street was flaming with light at five A.M." (p. 46). As Jung points out in his discussion of the role of the "dream city" in "Symbols of the Mother and of Rebirth," the maternal city harbors her inhabitants like children. Jerusalem and Babylon of the Old Testament are archetypal examples. The hero typically longs for the heavenly Jerusalem as he longs to be united with "the woman hard to attain." But the cursed city of Babylon is

11. Erich Neumann, *The Origins and History of Consciousness*, pp. 25–27, 288, 290–91.

"the mother of all abominations" and the "receptacle of all that is wicked and unclean," with whom "the kings of the earth" have fornicated. This image of the Terrible Mother (the Whore of Babylon) likewise threatens engulfment, the absorption of the grace of life, and damnation. At her center is the evil of unnatural fornication, of incest chiefly. By contrast, the city of healing, like the woman, is a river of life, described in images of beauty. Like the Heavenly Bride, this city represents a body of renewable life where "everything that incest would have made impossible now becomes possible" (*Symbols*, pp. 207–19).

In his own analysis of the Celestial City, Edwin Honig describes it as typically part of the allegorical "dream artifice." If the hero's goal promises to be attainable, the guiding intelligence may reveal a vision of paradise regained, the Celestial City. Even though the cosmic hierarchy of preromantic literature has dissipated, the ideal the modern allegorical hero seeks is, in Honig's words, some "good to which men need to be converted" or some "implied norm from which they have strayed." The ideal "gauges the spiritual or psychological distance that men have fallen," a distance the hero must cover in his quest and reveal to others. What the hero encounters in his quest tests the heroic stature of his consciousness and establishes a new mode of perception or a new pattern of consciousness for others to follow. The vision of the Heavenly City tells the hero his mission is nothing short of redemption in a world of sterility and defeat.[12] These are the symbols of life in the Night Sea Journey. It is toward this city and this bride that Rojack must now journey for rebirth.

The Heavenly Bride toward which Rojack moves in the third stage of his quest must not only be earned but also transformed along with the hero. Rojack's confrontation with the police leads to Cherry. Relying on what power and knowledge he has accrued, Rojack defies the police as Sergius defied the FBI. But Rojack is pushed to such physical and psychological extremity during the police interrogation that he begins to feel intimations of his coming transformation if he can hold out:

I felt just as some creature locked by fear to the border between earth and water (its grip the accumulated experience of a thousand generations) might feel on that second when its claw took hold, its body climbed up from the sea, and its impulse took a leap over the edge of mutation so that now and at last it was something new. . . . I felt as if I had crossed a chasm of time and was some new breed of man. (pp. 80–81)

A mixture of luck and destiny saves Rojack from defeat. After

12. See Edwin Honig, *Dark Conceit*, pp. 82, 152–53.

Lieutenant Leznicki has left him alone, he is finally too exhausted to call across the room and confess. And his prayer, "Oh, God, give me a sign," is answered by his sudden perception of Cherry's blonde hair across the room. "I felt a force in my body steering away from that back room, and a voice inside me said, 'Go to the girl'. . . . She looked a little like a child who has been anointed by the wing of a magical bird" (p. 89).

This "sign" is enough to make Rojack sustain his defiance and pursue a new level of his adventure: "I was like a wrecked mariner in the lull between two storms. Rather I was close to a strong old man dying now of his overwork, passing into death by way of going deeper to himself" (pp. 94–95). As Rojack goes deeper, Cherry becomes less a sign and more a source. The potential she represents must also be earned. She too is ambiguous, exhibiting the dual nature of the Mother figure. At first sight, Cherry appears to Rojack as at once a stereotype and "something better." Though she has the many empty masks of other actresses and singers, Cherry's touch has about it a "subtle hard-headed ever-so-guarded maternity." Rojack feels at times a balm in her voice. He feels in her "not one presence . . . but two," which at one point he identifies through a combination of tastes in her kiss, a health and "simplicity" mixed with "something compromised, inert, full of gas, something powerful and dull as her friends," which he calls her "taint" (see pp. 108–9). Cherry laughs "as if a silver witch and a black witch were beating their wings at one another," and she describes herself as both angel and whore. Her time with Kelly brought out the whore and "crazy killer" in her (pp. 114, 173). She represents the potential that can go either way; she is a "being" whose growth depends on Rojack's.

In Chapter 4 Rojack begins his attempt to understand and nourish this "sign" from God. In the bar where she sings, he turns his new power upon Cherry in order to protect and cleanse her.

> I shot one needle of an arrow into the center of Cherry's womb. . . . a sickness came off her, something broken and dead from the liver, stale, used-up, it drifted in a pestilence of mood toward my table, sickened me as it settled in. And there was a touch of regret in that exhalation from her, as if she had been saving such illness in the hope she might inflict it on no one, that her pride would be to keep her own ills to herself, rather than pass them on. (p. 100)

In the men's room, Rojack vomits, "as humble as a saint," the disease he has taken from Cherry upon himself. He describes this as a catharsis of the ills accumulated upon his soul for the past twenty years and as a "gathering wind which drew sickness . . . from others and passed them through me and up and out into the water." He knows he is drawing poison from Cherry when he hears her song "soaring like a golden bird free at last." Rojack's "minor" sainthood at this stage promises to grow into the sainthood of the hero-deliverer or scapegoat, "free at last to absorb the ills of others and regurgitate them forth." He finds peace and respite from "nausea," and, again, in the mirror his face and eyes partake of the new life of the "sea." But he knows that he has not completed his journey and that "insanity" is yet to be healer or destroyer; so he returns to the test (pp. 100–102). Rojack tests his courage and new psychic powers against the ex-prize fighter Romeo and the mafioso Tony to win Cherry from them. With each of Rojack's successes, Cherry draws closer and closer to him. He says she seems to be "using" him to free herself from the death that traps her. As a mythological figure, she is using the hero to transform her into the Nourishing Mother. She in turn defies Tony and the nightclub audience, mocking their fear "to go out and look at the sun," and, ironically, she sings to them her hope of deliverance: "Every day with Jesus/Is sweeter than the day before." Rojack's physical and psychic battles are both metaphors for battles between larger forces. The theoretical basis for this equation of physical tests with spiritual tests is explained in the dialogues from *Cannibals* entitled "The Metaphysics of the Belly" and "The Political Economy of Time," in which Mailer posits what he admits are tentative but sincere theories about the nature of and connections between Body and Soul. These dialogues, therefore, help us to see what Mailer believes to be the connections between the struggles of both Body and Soul in the world. Body is the vehicle of the Soul's progress in the world; we could call Body the present moment or embodiment of Soul. A "being" is a Body-and-Soul that has the potential to change and grow, both physically and morally (spiritually).

Mailer's theory of Body and Soul is important to our understanding of Rojack's quest because he is, at least potentially, an allegorical agent of divine force. For Rojack, as for Mailer, self-realization becomes Soul-realization, or Soul-growth. If Rojack's and Cherry's bodies are temporary "enlifements" of Soul, then these enlifements alter Soul (the divine force within) for better or worse, toward growth or death. Existence, in Mailer's belief, alters essence.

To Mailer, it is the Soul's instinct, once embodied, to grow beyond chaos, beyond absurdity, toward what he calls "Vision," by which he means God's mind and conception of Existence. What Mailer means by "new" or "greater proportions" of the self is this growth of Soul-in-enlifement toward God. A person's body and life may encourage such growth if that person chooses to keep in touch with the deepest requirements of his unconscious self, for ultimately in "The

Political Economy of Time," Mailer defines the Soul as the Unconscious. By a return to one's deepest instinctual life, which is precisely the journey Rojack is gradually making, a man would choose, as Rojack will choose, actions that will test the proportions of his Body and Soul. It is Mailer's basic conviction that actions which increase one's commitment to a feeling or an idea, which increase danger, which defy chaos, stasis, or death, test one's capacity to create life instead of death and prepare one's soul for growth toward God (see *CC*, pp. 287–97, 329, 342).

The union between Rojack and Cherry is a crucial test of Rojack's ability to defy chaos and stasis, to create life rather than make death: "when I was in bed with a woman, I rarely felt as if I were making life, but rather as if I were a pirate sharpening up a raid on life. . . . I had dread of the judgment which must rest behind the womb of a woman" (p. 119). The second "day" of the Night Sea Journey, then, begins with Chapter 5. It is a test of the hero more severe, closer to the edge of the abyss, than those which preceded it. And echoes of Ruta and Deborah remain. Rojack's and Cherry's first touch is merely sensual; they meet "like animals in a quiet mood, come across a track of the jungle to join in a clearing." Their "devotions" are first paid in a "church" no larger than themselves; their sex is a clash of wills. They pass the deadness within them back and forth like stale odors that "have nothing to do" with the part of them still alive.

But when they turn to sex as creation—metaphorically, when Rojack removes Cherry's diaphragm—their wills meet and "soften into some light. . . . like colored lanterns beneath the sea, a glimpse of that quiver of jeweled arrows, that heavenly city which had appeared as Deborah was expiring." They are prepared for love. "It was as if," Rojack tells us, "my voice had reached to its roots; and, 'Yes,' I said, 'of course I do, I want love' ":

> and some continent of dread speared wide in me, rising like a dragon, as if I knew the choice were real, and in the lift of terror I opened my eyes and her face was beautiful beneath me in that rainy morning, her eyes were golden with light, and she said, "Ah, honey, sure," and I said sure to the voice in me, and felt love fly in like some great winged bird, some beating of wings at my back, and felt her will dissolve into tears, and some great deep sorrow like roses drowned in the salt of the sea came flooding from her womb and washed into me like a sweet honey of balm for all the bitter sores of my soul. (p. 128)

This section of the novel repeatedly draws us to the words "dread," "choice," "sea," and "womb." Here Rojack faces the dread of the choice between death and life. That continent of dread is like a dragon, like the devouring Deborah, always threatening to rise again. Rojack again looks death in the face and must find the courage to choose. The womb of woman will judge him as he chooses death again or chooses the renewal of the "sea" in Cherry's womb in his act of love. The revelation of life, as he chooses it here, is again a brief washing out or catharsis of the death and nausea within. This is a brief revelation of the potential within each of them. The simple message of the moment of revelation, as Rojack awakens and comes up "like a diver" through successive levels of the sea, is that "everything was all right inside the room. Outside everything was wrong." Cherry's "special place," her slum tenement, becomes a center of healing surrounded by filth and disease. Their journey to the center of healing intensifies the contrast between what they find there and the outside world, the civilization rational consciousness has built. For the first time, Rojack faces the central fact of his new relationship to that world. He is a murderer and there is "ambush everywhere" (pp. 129, 131). The "pact" that Rojack and Cherry make is to be "good," which is to say to be strong and courageous, as courageous as Rojack was in choosing love by facing the Dragon of Death and his dread of Her. Rojack must now surmount the temptations of Ruta and the crutch of drink after he leaves Cherry's apartment. As he withstands these temptations for a time, he feels "back with the living" (p. 133). But the return to the "living" is precarious, ever to be renewed, for without the "courage" to win such a return, there can be no pact of love. *Dream* focuses more and more on this theme: acts of courage are acts of Being; love is the reward one is made capable of recovering by acts of courage.

The tests Rojack has yet to face require more acts of courage. Those forces he has tapped deep within himself threaten to overwhelm him. Such forces stimulate the dread he feels of psychosis "stretching behind" him. Rojack is facing dread in the way Mailer believes the primitive mind faced dread, for primitive dread arises from the belief that "one was caught in a dialogue with gods, devils, and spirits, and so was naturally consumed with awe, shame, and terror." And that terror is heightened by one's sense not only of impending death, but of dying "badly," of losing one's soul.[13]

The dread and trials Rojack must now face, he faces for Cherry as well, for their "pact," for what Jung has called "the stern Mistress Soul" who sets tests of preparedness before the would-be regenerate. Part of Rojack's pact is that he will have to face and "air" the worst in himself, to face, that is, his own guilt in the disease all

13. *The Presidential Papers* (hereafter cited as *PP*), p. 151. Compare with Neumann's discussion of primitive dread in *Consciousness*, pp. 40–41. The primitive mind facing the dread of the "dynamic" and "animistic" world represents the attempt of consciousness to overcome its fear, to continue to grow, and to bring the unconscious into greater balance with and within control of consciousness.

around him (*AD*, p. 162). His trials do include new onslaughts from the rational world depicted by a series of phone calls from his television and university employers who are threatened by public opinion. Detective Roberts again deploys the "evidence" and forces of the police against Rojack, which nearly make him crack. Again, Rojack is saved by luck, or, better, by destiny, when high-level powers (Barney Oswald Kelly) doctor the "official medical report." But when Rojack accepts Kelly's invitation to visit, he faces not the erosions of the fact-seeking world, but the ultimate test of his ability to face the "Mystery" itself. The mystery is the mystery at the heart of the disease — the plague and cancer of his time. The mystery has something to do with nature of mankind's Faustian (read "rational") efforts to gain the powers or fires of the Gods.[14] The mere idea of this confrontation fills Rojack with a dread as deep as "any invasion of the supernatural" to primitive man.

Rojack's "contract" with Cherry will not permit him to "flee the mystery." As his meeting with Kelly approaches, his fear grows in proportion to his expanding perceptions that the plague or sickness "revolved about me now," bringing with it a dread that washes over him like waves smashing through pilings on the shore (pp. 161–62). He returns to Cherry for strength and they renew the pact they made that morning, which renews Rojack's sense of the "new life . . . sweet and perilous and so hard to follow." Again the sea washes into Rojack like balm and "those wings" of love return. And again he realizes that love is to be earned by acts of goodness and bravery; love is not a "gift," like Ruta's gifts from the Devil, "but a vow" (pp. 163–64). Rojack's union which Cherry is his contract with the life within himself, the renewal of which he has had to earn every step of the way. He continually associates Cherry with birds, her love with wings. The bird, especially the golden-winged bird, is the mythological counterpart of the fire of life energy. The bird is the image of the soul, the spiritual messenger to the hero, and the harbinger of the resurrection of life energy.[15]

So the meaning of Cherry in the novel has three dimensions, which are also clear as she and Rojack discuss their pasts in Chapter 6. Here Rojack and Cherry carry on a dialogue, much to the annoyance of many critics, in the language of "The Political Economy

14. Compare "Professor" Rojack's lecture in *Dream*: "To the savage, dread was the natural result of any invasion of the supernatural: if man wished to steal the secrets of the gods, it was only to be supposed that the gods would defend themselves and destroy whichever man came too close. By this logic, civilization is the successful if imperfect theft of some cluster of these secrets, and the price we have paid is to accelerate our private sense of some enormous if not quite definable disaster which awaits us" (*AD*, p. 159). Compare Jung, *Symbols*, p. 170.

15. See Jung, *Symbols*, pp. 159, 170, 185, 215–19, 289, and 348.

of Time." They express their fear that their own souls are dying, that they have not escaped the entrapments of the Devil, by which Mailer means Anti-Soul or Soul-Defeator. The world, or civilization as mankind has evolved it, is for Mailer the Fall itself, the field in which Devil attempts to frustrate Soul or channel Soul-Energy to his own designs (see *CC*, pp. 329, 334). But Rojack and Cherry find hope (the hope of Soul renewal) in the "wings" of love and in Cherry's feeling that she is pregnant, has had her first orgasm, and is approaching biological death. This would be ridiculous and crass enough if the novel were functioning on the literal level alone, but Cherry is a figure in the hero's destiny and is a mythic figure alive in his "dream." As we have seen, orgasm represents for Mailer the movement of unconscious, instinctual energy (Soul) in the human being. Cherry's orgastic release, which we might call her "mythic destiny," represents the passing of the powers of the unconscious "sea" over to the hero, the integration of those powers into himself. As both real and mythic figures, man and woman have reached their greatest rapport and trust. They establish a "mood" that opens new unconscious perceptions. The "objects in the room" stand "like sentinels possessing some primitive property of radio."

It is this "mood" between Rojack and Cherry that Shago Martin interrupts. He is the herald of Rojack's final test; we could say he insures the test will be necessary. Shago is a defeated Soul and a double for Rojack who shows the hero the possibilities of defeat. Shago had come out of one of the worst gangs in Harlem to search for greater proportions for himself. Cherry had sought "something about him independent, something very fine." But instead of turning these qualities against the "society shit" that tried to mold him, he struggled and capitulated. His victory was small, but his defeats many. As the episode develops, Shago enumerates his defeats. He is not the heroic figure, "bearing his defeat with honor and pride," that Stanley T. Gutman suggests he is.[16]

Shago tries to put up a strong front, but admits, finally, the illness is upon him: "I'm a sick devil, no doubt of that." Like a defeated war veteran, Shago recalls his moment of strength when he spit in the face of the "Devil," Deborah. He tries to convince himself that he surmounted Deborah's temptations: "all that White House jazz, mow my grass, blackball," and the high governmental and Mafia connections. But he is without a self, marked now by the evil of protean masks and "tongues." His "big beat" now "comes from up High," from the powers of the "society" he pretends to mock: "it don't come from me, I'm a lily-white devil in a black ass. I'm just the

16. Stanley T. Gutman, *Mankind in Barbary*, p. 117.

future, in love with myself, that's the future. I got twenty faces, I talk the tongues. . . . I'm cut off from my own lines, I try to speak from my heart and it gets *snatched*" (p. 189).

Shago failed at love with Cherry. "We didn't make it. I could cry." This failure gives further definition to Rojack's earlier danger. To save face now, Shago argues that he is turning his devil's tongues against the Devil, but both Rojack and Cherry see through the ploy. "You're just an old dynamo out on the moon," says Cherry. Rojack says the same thing when he tells Shago: "Now *you're* on a television show." Shago is receding into the death Rojack is moving beyond. "I saw something in his eyes as the marijuana took hold," Rojack says of Shago when the black man realizes Cherry has "made it" with Rojack, "he had not been ready for this. He had the expression of a big fish just speared . . . something in the past had just been maimed forever" (pp. 190–91).

Rojack not only learns something about the possibilities of defeat in facing Shago, he gains a strength and violence in defeating the black singer. But by taking Shago from behind, Rojack also loses some part of what he has already gained—courage and love. "I had the choice to let him go, let him stand up, we would fight, but I had a fear of what I heard in his voice—it was like that wail from the end of the earth you hear in a baby's voice. . . . I was out of control, violence seemed to shake itself free from him . . . and shake itself into me" (pp. 192–93).

The manner of this victory contains a loss: "my body was like a cavern where deaths are stored [spirit]. Deborah's lone green eye stared up at me." Now Cherry's skin, like Shago's, goes dead to the touch; Rojack returns to whiskey for courage; Cherry compares Rojack's "victory" to the Mafia. A new falseness arises between them. So Rojack must renew his journey and regain this "child touched by an angel." He goes to his final test and the farthest point of his journey with two legacies: the gain of Shago's lost violence and strength, totemically symbolized by Shago's serpentlike umbrella, and the reaffirmation from Cherry that their love must be won anew through courage, that they may turn again to God if they can somehow "turn out well" (pp. 195–97).

In setting out on this final, fourth, stage of his heroic quest, Rojack realizes that "God is not love but courage. Love came only as a reward." At this point, Mailer is defining the failure of love in a deadening world, which he began in *Barbary Shore*, as the failure of the self to define its existence. If Rojack chooses to face some final test, it is destiny that chooses what that test will be. He cannot choose between facing Shago again and Harlem or facing Kelly. He deliberates so long that the taxi drives him to the address he first gave, Kelly's Waldorf Towers.

There is no ambiguity, finally, about the kind of power Kelly represents, but there is some ambiguity about the magnitude of Kelly's power. Rojack approaches Kelly as if he were the Devil himself. The description of the Towers as the "ante-chamber of Hell" is too obvious to need repetition here. Rojack's psychic perceptions are so acute now that he tells us he has entered "an architecture to eternity which housed us as we dreamed." And Kelly is surrounded by subservient figures notorious for their evil—Ganucci who is "an essence of disease, some moldering from the tree of death"; Bess, who is the most evil woman in Europe; and Ruta, whose hair is now a "soft lick of flame" and "rich clay."

But when Kelly confesses his history to Rojack, it becomes clear that Kelly is not the Devil, the Plague, the Mystery itself, but rather its greatest possible incarnation in this world. By raising our expectations that Kelly is "the Big Guy" himself, and by making him a kind of phenomenal epitome of satanic power, Mailer simply embodies its destructive force and demonstrates the huge, inexplicable proportions of the Mystery against which the Soul must struggle. Kelly's motto, *Victoria in Caelo Terraque*, is especially apt, "Victory on Heaven and Earth." In the rational allegory, Kelly is another damned being, possessed by some greater power that he struggled to possess himself. He is "solicitor for the Devil," as he says, the Devil in microcosm. This is not to say Rojack does not, on the psychological or mythological level, face the heart of darkness within himself and in the world, for he clearly does, so far as it can be portrayed. Knowing the face of the enemy, Mailer has said in both *Papers* and *Cannibals*, might give death "dimension" and might allow us to "leave a curse" (*CC*, p. 41). Kelly is one effort to depict the face of the enemy, to suggest the kind of power it is, to suggest what kind of power can be employed against it. Kelly is not the courageous hero Gutman would have him; he is the supreme Mailer anti-hero; the Anti-Soul who cowers before the demands of his own soul and defeats the soul of others. Kelly is that darkness, that ultimate devouring power of evil Deborah threatened to be.[17] Kelly's "presence," says Rojack, was "more real to me as an embodiment of Deborah than of himself"; it "was all of Deborah for me" (p. 217).

Rojack is sorely tempted by Kelly's seductiveness. Or, as Kelly puts it, "We're closer than you expect." But Rojack still has the power to

17. Contrast Gutman, *Barbary*, pp. 120, 122, 126. Compare Jung, *Symbols*, p. 338, on the Devil as devourer. He is another face, perhaps the ultimate face, of the Devouring Mother.

associate that seductiveness with the emptiness in himself, and he rejects it (see especially p. 217). To stave off capitulation, which would make Rojack himself embody evil, he performs a ritual of purification, which has an appropriate psychological and symbolic significance. The compulsive rite is a metaphorical test of Rojack's courage and a preparation for his passage, beyond the evil that binds Kelly, into freedom. When Kelly compulsively confesses the long and detailed story of his fall, or his own evil, it is clear that the power he sought and gained is the power to manipulate the processes of human life, of civilization, and of nature to slake his own greed, a power that by its nature denies the enlargement of souls on their journey toward Vision.

For example, to gain the power of Sicilian connections, Kelly damned his own child at her conception. "I took a dive deep down into a vow, I said in my mind; [*sic*] 'Satan, if it takes your pitchfork up my gut, let me blast a child into this bitch.' And something happened . . . Leonora and I met way down there in some bog, some place awful, and I felt something take hold in her. . . . Deborah was conceived" (p. 240). Though Kelly tried to renege on his vow, the Devil "collected" by giving him Bess, witch of the Riviera, who ended up stealing every last part of Kelly's soul and leaving him "carrion." But he gained, at every stage of his fall, immense manipulatory power in the world. "I decided," Kelly says of his temptation and damnation, "the only explanation is that God and the Devil are very attentive to the people at the summit. . . . That's why men with power sometimes act so silly. . . . There's nothing but magic at the top. . . . you have to be ready to deal with One or the Other" (p. 246).

Kelly, like Deborah and Rojack, has looked to both suicide and courageous action as a way out of damnation. Like Deborah, Cherry, and even Ruta, Kelly has literally faced the Devil within and without and made his choice to follow the easiest way. This is what Rojack faces when Kelly, as an "agent" of Deborah's "fury" and of "death," tempts him. "I floated out on the liquor to a promise of power, some icy majesty of intelligence, a fired heat of lust . . . between us now the way there had been heat between Ruta and me . . . and knew what it had been like with Deborah and him, what a hot burning two-backed beast." Kelly offers to bring Ruta forth, the "three of us to pitch and tear and squat and lick, swill and grovel on that Lucchese bed . . . where he went out with Deborah to the tar pits of the moon" (p. 254). Kelly's offer perfectly fits one prevailing metaphor of *Cannibals* and *Dream*; it emphasizes the polarities of Mailer's dualisms. "Shall we get shitty?" Kelly tempts.

When Rojack realizes the incest between Kelly and Deborah, which has grown into a metaphor of evil and death, he is compelled to face that death, that disease, which has threatened to engulf him since the start of the novel. He feels himself slip "off the lip of sanity" and into "some deep waters." He wants "to be free of magic, the tongue of the Devil, the dread of the Lord, I wanted to be some sort of rational man again, nailed tight to details, promiscuous, reasonable, blind to the reach of seas. But I could not move" (p. 255). Rojack has journeyed too far, must capitulate or face his fear and dread to express his soul's proportions before he can return to the rational, conscious world, which will then be filled with new meaning and with new dimensions of perception. It is in facing the fear, challenging the adversary that threatens engulfment, that the hero gains deliverance from his fear and integration of the conscious and unconscious mind.[18] Facing the danger of an overwhelming darkness—of insanity, in short—Rojack reaches his deepest level of inner experience and must make his greatest commitment to be restored.

Another unconscious "messenger" shows him the task he must perform to free himself from the overwhelming "sea": "Walk the parapet or Cherry is dead." Encountering the last trial alone, without the aid of totem (umbrella) or anyone else, Rojack feels "death come up like the shadow which is waiting as one slips past the first sentinels of consciousness into the islands of sleep." He makes one journey around the parapet. He realizes that journey was for his own salvation; he must walk the parapet again, says the messenger, if he would save Cherry. "Each step I took, something good was coming in, I could do this. . . . There was the hint of when I would finally be done—some bliss from infancy moved through the lock of my lungs." Kelly says he was never able to try the parapet, and Deborah "got off midway." And when Kelly sees Rojack is going to make it, he tries to push Rojack off with Shago's umbrella, with that old power of totem Rojack no longer needs. Rojack has reached his deliverance, and he leaps down to strike Kelly unconscious, but Rojack is unable to return for a second trip around the parapet for Cherry (pp. 256, 259–60).

Cherry dies violently at the hand of Shago's friend. Rojack returns to her just before her death, saying, just as he did of Deborah, "She's my wife, officer." We really have to reach the mythological level of the novel to see what this means most fully. The hero's deliverance is incomplete. He has delivered himself from Satan, from the devouring maw of death, and from insanity, but he has not yet won the Heavenly Bride and the Celestial City. If he has been delivered from the "whale," he has yet to achieve that Vision himself.

18. Jung, *Symbols*, especially pp. 156, 259, 354, 419.

The novel's epilogue, entitled "The Harbors of the Moon Again," confirms this. In the daylight world of "Super-America," Rojack faces the "mystery" in a scientific light, in the autopsy of a cancer patient. He then emphasizes one lesson of his "dream." The plague or cancer arises from the exploitation of our organs and our selves. If one does not face and battle the "madness" that enters the self from our exploitations, one "locks" the madness inside and "denies" it, the madness grows and usurps the body and soul, the cells take the leap toward cancer. Rojack's salvation from the madness is his immersion in it, his airing of it, and his struggle to defeat it during his journey within.

Another lesson of the quest he has endured is that he must continue his search for life and growth in the phenomenal world. In the epilogue Rojack travels to South America, but he stops in the literal City of the Damned, Las Vegas, which he compares to "the chambers of the moon." He realizes he cannot defeat this city alone; he is not "good enough to climb up and pull down" the electric and neon "jewels." His journey must continue, this time to the jungles of Guatemala and Yucatán.

On the rational level of the allegory, the phone call to Cherry, which ends the novel fantastically, reaffirms that Cherry's death means Rojack has not yet reached the point where he can save others by bringing his own salvation into the world. But in the mythological sense, the phone call shows that the salvation of the hero is only partial because the Heavenly City and Bride are not yet his. To be clear on this we have to look briefly at the moon as a recurring symbol. The moon is another dual symbol, associated with Deborah's psychic powers as well as Cherry's healing balm. Cherry is several times compared to the moon as a "Silver Lady." So the moon has the ambiguity and dual quality of the Mother symbol itself in this novel as well as in myth.[19]

In *Dream*, the closer the hero moves to his salvation, the more terrible the moon becomes. It is Rojack's "appreciation" for the moon that has singled him out for the challenge to his soul the novel describes. He has looked into the "abyss" by facing death in the war. Then the moon's "stain" led him to surpass danger and acquire grace and force ("it") so that he could begin his attack on the machine-gun nest. Through the deaths of the first three Germans, Rojack faced death with the help of the moon. But facing the fourth German, he was on his own, the moonlight had turned "clear as ice."

19. Jung, for example, points out mythological comparisons of the sun with fertile seed and the moon with woman or uterus. The moon is also the gathering place of departed souls, the guardian of the seed of life. See *Symbols*, pp. 203, 307–18.

Here Rojack faced the other side of death in the German's eyes and saw that it was a migration more dangerous than life for which one had to prepare. The experience began his private obsession with death because it began his "perception of death" as a possibility rather than a "void" (*AD*, pp. 3–6, 40).

Once Rojack's "dream" begins, the moon, both tender and not too innocent, calls him to suicide. His soul is called to give up its enlifement and cast whatever is left to the moon. She is a "shimmer of past death and new madness," and it is her "madness" that may lead Rojack's soul to a growth rather than lead it in its diminished state to the moon's caverns. When he misses this moment of diminished migration, the moon retaliates and "cancer" sets in. But Rojack faces the moon's madness and the cancer within. That is his heroic potential and destiny. The moon symbol undergoes a transformation. It turns from being an "assassin" who offers clean death and free passage of a diminished soul to being more like Deborah, "the charnel house" (p. 162).

When in Chapter 8 the moon again calls Rojack to suicide at Kelly's, she also offers him a way out of this death or diminished migration; he may walk the parapet. That other face of the moon, the "tar-pits" of incest, had shown itself in Kelly's confession, but in walking the parapet solely under his own power, Rojack realizes that the moon of death can also be the "silvery whale," as he calls her, the Mother of Deliverance surfacing "in a midnight sea." He can "earn" his release from the moon's "cage," from his murder, and from his death. As he walks the parapet, Rojack gradually feels himself come alive (see pp. 223–24, 254, 259).

The important point for the regeneration theme is that Cherry is not, as many critics suggest, in "heaven." She is in a limbo, in some "safety chamber" of the moon not unlike the hollow spaces of Las Vegas. Her soul is clean but static; it is the "spirit" she feared she would become in the collective harbors of the moon, which is now, she says, her "mother" (pp. 259, 263, 269). This mother is "the mother of pain and loss" as Mailer described the moon in *Cannibals* (p. 248). Cherry's soul is at peace; it has "escaped" the confrontations of life, but its journey has ended. By the equations established in *Cannibals*, the moon is "Spirit-as-Function," ruling over the souls it harbors. By Spirit-as-Function, Mailer appears to mean any sort of static substance than can collect and harbor Souls diminished to a state of non-growth and therefore alienated from existence or Being. The Spirit-as-collective cannot grow or make the Soul's journey, only Soul-as-individual can. If one allows one's Soul to realize itself and to live out the Soul's impulses, Mailer argues in "The Political Economy of Time," then one's Soul after death passes *through* Spirit and back into Being or Existence (see *CC*, pp. 336–38, 358, 371–73). The reader of *Dream* can only assume that if Cherry is ever to gain her deliverance from the "cage" of the moon, if her soul is to return to an enlifement that will give it the opportunity to grow toward Vision, the deliverance will depend upon Rojack; he will have to complete some ritual of courage and atonement that he left unfulfilled on Kelly's parapet. We can conclude only that the hero's quest has returned to him his soul and potential, but his quest is incomplete at the novel's end. The journey to Yucatán and "the old friend" is the opportunity Rojack has earned to continue his quest for growth of his soul or being. His soul may reach heroic proportions equal to the salvation of others and to the destruction of the Damned City. But if Rojack's potential seems greater and more deeply won than that of his predecessors, he is not yet a hero who actually returns from the quest with the legacy of regeneration for the world.

In *Advertisements*, Mailer made it clear that during the composition of *The Deer Park* and afterwards he felt his life and his work had reached a crucial and desperate point. His sense of frustration and failure was acute. The tone of crisis is repeated in his collection of "poems" *Deaths for the Ladies (and other disasters)*, published in 1962. Here the despair of failing marriage and his flirtations with suicide add to the tone of personal crisis.[20] This tone is somewhat mitigated in *The Presidential Papers* because the subject matter is focused differently; it is the beginning of his "new journalism." The tone of crisis, however, is still alive in *Papers*, published in 1963, as is the mixture of "defiance and self-hatred," to borrow Solotaroff's phrase. That year Mailer began *An American Dream*. The failure of Mailer's second and third marriages could only exacerbate his desperate self-examinations. In November of 1960, as his readers know, Mailer stabbed his second wife Adele. He regretted it as an ungenuine act. As Brock Brower suggests, the incident was part of the "personal hell" Mailer dropped into, resulting from his long flirtation with "the burning question of violence," with hip-dares, and with drugs. Mailer had been fighting with party crashers at his pre-mayoralty campaign party just before the stabbing. Daniel

20. In *Existential Errands: Twenty-Six Pieces Selected by the Author from the Body of All His Writings*, Mailer describes the poems as existential exercises during one of the lowest points of his life. Kierkegaard, Mailer suggests, came back from such a "Christian" experience—hearing inspiration from an angel while kissing the flames—with the knowledge "that such moments not only existed but indeed were the characteristic way modern man found a knowledge of his soul—which is to say he found it by the act of perceiving that he was most certainly losing it." It was the *Time* review of *Deaths for the Ladies (and other disasters)* that made Mailer more certain that "the enemy was more alive than ever, and dirtier in the alley," and that he must mend, gird himself, and return to battle (see pp. 198–204).

Wolf, who introduced Mailer and Adele, knew them during the Village years, and was an editor on the *Voice*, suggests the incident was part and parcel of the Mailers' "distortions" as Norman "moved out with her to the pot scene and the sexual anomy of mere orgiastic linkage." Mailer and Adele were competing to live up to Norman's hip code; and he was sliding into a profound depression from Seconal. "Let me say," Mailer said of the assault, "that what I did was by any measure awful. It still wasn't insane." He pleaded with the court to go to prison rather than Bellevue, because if he was believed insane, "for the rest of my life my work will be considered as the work of a man with a disordered mind." He ended briefly in Bellevue and came out of it "judged responsible—even if criminally responsible—for his own acts." He continued his work and married Lady Jeanne Campbell. But he worried that he had destroyed "forever the possibility of being the Jeremiah of our time."[21] When he wrote *Dream*, his marriage to Campbell had collapsed and he had married actress Beverly Bentley, who looks not unlike the physical descriptions of Cherry.

But when Mailer composed *Dream* serially for *Esquire* to insure he would write the book in a year and to earn some badly needed money, he did not turn back to himself merely because it was the closest and easiest subject at hand. The numerous parallels between Mailer's life and the novel that Solotaroff lists are less gratuitous and artless borrowings than self-explorations in a time of crisis intended to reveal as much about the fallen world as the fallen hero. The novel is a response to the crises he had passed through as well as to the external crises and failures of his country catalogued in *Advertisements*, *Deaths*, and *Papers*. Rojack's situation is close to Mailer's. Mailer is speaking of himself as well as of his compatriots when, in *Cannibals*, he says:

> Postulate a modern soul marooned in constipation, emptiness, boredom and a flat dull terror of death. A soul which takes antibiotics when ill, smokes filter cigarettes, drinks proteins . . . takes seconal to go to sleep, benzedrine to awake, and tranquilizers for poise. It is a deadened existence, afraid precisely of violence, cannibalism, loneliness, insanity, libidinousness, hell, perversion, and mess, because these are the states which must in some way be passed through, digested, transcended, if one is to make one's way back to life. (pp. 269–70)

An American Dream is Mailer's dream of healing, of finding the knowledge of his soul by the "act of perceiving that he was most certainly losing it."

21. I use here Brock Brower's account in his article on Mailer's career, "Always the Challenger," *Life*, pp. 100, 111, 112.

We should, moreover, have little trouble recognizing that Mailer continues in *Dream* what he described in *Advertisements* as his extension of the theological and moral possibilities of the novel. He has obviously continued and expanded the resources of the allegorical mode as a dialogue between spiritual forces depicting "man caught in a dialogue with gods, devils, and spirits." The "primitive lore," this dialogue with dynamic spiritual forces, which he invokes is to Mailer one of the best weapons to subvert the foundations of modern civilization's "malignancies," whether communist or capitalist (see *CC*, p. 87). The pattern of myth, another kind of primitive lore, established in the previous two novels is used again and intensified here: the death of the old man and the birth of the new. But in *Dream* these figures are even more clearly embodiments of the hero's "dream." Rojack himself "dies" and is reborn. At the farthest point of the inward journey, Rojack faces Kelly, who, like McLeod and Eitel, is a fallen old man who "confesses" the story of his fall. It is by facing the dead man in all his horror and by defeating him that the hero of *Dream* attains the power to pursue Life, or Being, which Mailer also calls "Time" in his dialogues.[22]

Though physical courage is one metaphor for the "courage" Mailer's heroes must gain to pursue Life, and though Mailer himself clearly values physical courage as somehow actually connected to or symptomatic of larger courage, we should not take courage in these novels to be only physical courage or a display of *machismo*.[23] Mailer defines courage otherwise, in this novel and in his commentaries, as we have seen, first, as making one's death meaningful through facing, and therefore knowing, the enemy before us and within us. Mailer believes that if a person would restore a lost authenticity, he or she may have to search for extreme situations because in them the conscious mind is turned "back upon its natural subservience to the instinct." Instinct is the Unconscious, or, as we have seen in *Cannibals*, the Soul itself. The return to instinct breaks down the insulation of the human being from his or her deepest psychic life as well as from nature itself. The imbalance Mailer seeks to correct is the

22. Compare Jung again in *Symbols*, pp. 280–81: "Time is thus defined by the rising and setting sun, by the death and renewal of libido, the dawning and extinction of consciousness. . . . So time, this empty and purely formal concept, is expressed in the mysteries through transformations of the creative force, libido, just as time in physics is identical with the flow of the energetic process."

23. Gutman, in effect, makes such a charge in his assessment of *Dream*, see pp. 110, 119, 131. Gutman goes so far as to suggest Mailer is engaged in "a futile embrace with *machismo*" at the conclusion of his assessment. He lumps Ruta and Cherry together as objects that Rojack must sexually dominate, and, then, nine pages later inexplicably writes about Cherry and Rojack's sexual encounter as a "mutual surrender."

imbalance of consciousness "alienated from instinct," which causes consciousness to construct "intellectual formulations over a void."[24] The confrontation with the truth within is itself enough to give the Soul power to "voyage" out to "where whatever created us wishes us to be" (*CC*, pp. 348, 369–73).

There is still one more kind of courage Mailer requires of his heroes, the courage to face the Vision toward which one journeys. In its present state, Vision is also the "dread of the Lord." For given the decline of Vision—that is, God's Existence—one faces the horrible dread of apprehending the truth that God is dying. Such an awesome recognition includes "the vision of God's fear" and of his wrath. Mailer's commentaries on Buber's *Tales of Hasidim* make this point in *Cannibals* (pp. 376–79). So courage also prepares the Soul for its Vision.

Mailer's concept of courage is important to an understanding of his novels because he believes the forces arrayed against Soul are greater in the postwar world than ever before. The "signs" of defeat are in the "forms"—these records of Soul struggle—of contemporary civilization. The mightier the struggle of the Soul and the greater a whole human's endurance and courage, the more extraordinary the form (*CC*, pp. 371–73).

> Objective criteria overwhelm us. The signs are everywhere. . . .
> They show themselves in every crack of every detail in our lives, in the processing of our food . . . in the plastic commodities we handle, the odor of vaginal jelly, the dead character of public communication, the pollution of air, the collective assaults upon human nerve. . . .
>
> Look to the forms. The forms of the modern world break down. . . . in the art of the twentieth century, above all in the architecture, in the empty monotonous interchageable statements of our modern buildings. (*CC*, pp. 366–67)
>
> . . . When the soul is mighty and the environment resists mightily, the form is exceptional and extraordinary. . . . Stone hoisted up ramps by men became the pyramids. Cut by crude iron tools and harder stone, shaped over years by sculptors who attacked the rock out of the stone of their own being, one had Chartres, Notre Dame. Today the stones are made from liquid cooked in vats and rolled into blocks or sheets. Fiberglas [*sic*], polyethylene, bakelite, styrene, styronware. The environment has less resistance than a river of milk. And the houses and objects built from these liquids are the record of a strifeless war, a liquidation of possibilities. (*CC*,p. 371)

Since Mailer believes that Soul in the world is dying and God is dying with the death of Soul, he argues that at the prospect of death modern humanity experiences a dread and nausea unlike any ever

24. *PP*, pp. 128, 198.

experienced before. Modern life, therefore, comes to represent for Mailer a final battle between Soul and Anti-Soul: "existence approaches a climax" (*CC*, pp. 363–64, 367). The extent to which we (or, in the instance of *Dream*, Rojack) insulate ourselves from the experiences of awe, terror, beatitude, and the courageous defiance of Anti-Soul, is the extent to which we do not prepare ourselves for growth, to which we deny God and our own Soul, and to which we seek to capture Life by a series of "cheats." Courage, therefore, becomes for Mailer both a physical and an existential attribute; something one accrues by separate acts of courage.

Kelly, in contrast, had sought not to earn his power but to receive it as a gift, and as a gift he received tremendous power. The cost of the gift was the alienation of his Soul from existence. He ransomed his Soul to that which opposes divine or creative energy. Neither he nor Deborah could reverse the loss. But Rojack reversed his loss. He too had "pirated" the Devil's gifts. He used that power to fight it in other embodiments. Such power was the first stage of his encouragement. But he went beyond these gifts and, with Cherry's guidance and "balm," transformed them so that he could "go the other way," as Marion Faye once put it. To do this Rojack had to choose love; he had to choose Cherry at the moment he faced the dread of his death. In the mythic and psychological sense, he had to choose his own best innocence, the nourishing maid or child within, the healing resources of the unconscious. The allegorical progress of the hero is toward gradual, expanding revelation and power.

In one way Mailer's concern with "power" carries forward D. H. Lawrence's concern with two kinds of power. Both authors express this concern through the sexual activity in their narratives—the power to control and to dominate others (Kelly's manipulatory power) and the power to fulfill oneself, to increase one's Being. This latter power, the power of self-fulfillment, is what Lawrence ultimately calls, in *The Man Who Died*, "the greater power" and the "larger life." When in a 1961 *Playboy* interview, excerpted in *Cannibals*, Mailer said he hoped to achieve something "between" D. H. Lawrence and Henry Miller (p. 198), Mailer was referring especially to his hope to combine somehow what Lawrence said, especially in *Lady Chatterley*, about the beauty and tenderness of sex, with what Miller said about the violence of sex and the complications that impinge upon the lovers, but Mailer is closest to Lawrence in the quest for "the greater power."

Mailer associates this greater power with *his* definition of existentialism. The authenticity Mailer's heroes seek is in part the integrity of self-hood and self-created values in a chaotic world that existential fiction traditionally depicts. But Mailer carries his "existentialism" beyond phenomenal and relative authenticity or value. By positing an "existential" God whose self-hood, Vision, and authenticity depend upon the state of humanity's authenticity and Soul, Mailer leaps the bounds traditionally associated with existentialism. Authenticity of self and God becomes his chief concern.[25] I don't think it particularly important whether Mailer's "existentialism" is or is not derived from or consistent with European existentialists. Any number of critics have argued whether Mailer's existentialism is so derived or consistent.[26] What is important is that Mailer is on his own "existential" quest. Since *Advertisements* he has argued that his "American Existentialism" is something else. Mailer charges "modern European existentialism" with a reluctance "to take on the logical conclusion of the existential vision": that the "life" after death is as existential as life on earth. European existentialism, Mailer feels, brings itself to a halt on "the uninhabitable terrain of the absurd" as a result.

> The German philosopher [Heidegger] runs aground trying to demonstrate the necessity for man to discover an authentic life. Heidegger can give no deeper explanation why man should bother to be authentic than to state in effect that man should be authentic in order to be free. Sartre's advocacy of the existential commitment is always in danger of dwindling into the minor aristocratic advocacy of leading one's life with style for the sake of style. Existentialism is rootless unless one dares the hypothesis that death is an existential continuation of life, that the soul may either pass through migrations, or cease to exist in the continuum of nature. . . . But accepting this hypothesis, authenticity and commitment return to the center of ethics, for man then faces no peril so huge as alienation from his own soul. (*PP*, pp. 213–14)

We could argue that Mailer is wrong about Heidegger, who is perhaps closer to him than he thinks. But it is Mailer's view of Heidegger and Sartre that provides him with the impetus and energy to strike out and enlarge his own concept of existentialism, to combine psychology and metaphysics through an eclectic view of what the existence of the self is.

Mailer, like Rojack and even like Jung, is an "existential psychologist" in the sense that his emphasis is always on becoming, on self-growth as soul-growth.[27] In his commentary on dread in 1963,

25. See *CC*, pp. 321, 323, and 326–27, where Being equals Soul, and p. 342, where Soul equals the Unconscious.

26. See, for example, George Schrader, "Norman Mailer and the Despair of Defiance," *Yale Review*, pp. 267–80 (reprinted in Braudy). Gutman argues that Mailer is a branch of Martin Heidegger's tree.

27. Compare Victor White, *God and the Unconscious*, p. 76. White demonstrates the relationship of Jung's emphasis on "becoming" to a "view of religion" that is existential as much as it is inconsistent with reductive Freudian analysis.

Mailer similarly asserts that the modern failure to see a relationship between dread, existential psychology, and ethics, as Jung and Reich did, is at the heart of the modern failure of consciousness.

> What is never discussed: the possibility that we feel anxiety because we are in danger of losing some part or quality of our soul unless we act, and act dangerously; or the likelihood that we feel dread when intimations of our death inspire us with disproportionate terror, a horror not merely because we are going to die, but . . . because we are going to die badly and suffer some unendurable stricture of eternity. These explanations are altogether outside the close focus of the psychological sciences in the Twentieth Century. . . .
>
> Faced with our failure . . . the investigators of the intellect have taken to intellectual tranquilizers. It is logical positivism, logicians, and language analysts who dominate Anglo-American philosophy rather than existentialists; it is Freudians instead of Reichians or Jungians who rule psychoanalysis; and it is journalism rather than art which forges the apathetic conscience of our time. (*PP*, pp. 151–52)

Rojack's intense and associative sense perceptions are intended to demonstrate the possibilities of associative mental processes, of metaphorical or primitive vision, and of expanded consciousness in our world, as indeed one's dreams might or one's "vibrations," as we say, might. The hero Rojack's experiences arise from his journey to his deepest Being or Unconscious life to find there a power of perception that sustains an ever-increasing growth of the self.

5

Why Are We in Vietnam?

"I came not to send peace, but a sword. For I am come to set a man at variance against his father, and the daughter against her mother, and the daughter-in-law against her mother-in-law. And a man's foes shall be they of his own household. He that loveth father or mother more than me is not worthy of me: and he that loveth son or daughter more than me is not worthy of me."   —Matthew, 10:34–37

Why Are We in Vietnam? (1967) is Mailer's most economical narrative. Though this economy is reminiscent of *Barbary Shore*, the story of *Why* is told through a narrative consciousness of a complexity unparalleled in the previous fiction. Ostensibly, the novel consists of the narrator D.J.'s remembrance of a hunting expedition in Alaska with his father, two of his father's business underlings, and D.J.'s best friend "Tex" Hyde. As he sits "grassed out" at a dinner party held in his honor at his parents' Texas "Manse," D.J. recalls actions that took place two years ago. D.J. and Tex, eighteen and nineteen years old, are about to leave for the Vietnam War, which is not mentioned until the last page of the novel. Below the ostensible action, however, is a complicated tale of a young man's journey into self. D.J.'s particular journey illustrates that despite the hero's successive acts of regeneration, he can be defeated. D.J. is Mailer's first defeated hero and his last fictional hero to date. The narrator-hero's defeat expresses in turn the triumph of Death over Life.

The many misreadings of this novel seem to stem not only from the usual misunderstandings of allegory but also from the failure to recognize both the significance of the setting in this novel and the nature of the hero's guilt.[1] The setting, Alaska, becomes an intense

1. Critics differ widely on D.J.'s nature as a narrator, and therefore on the effectiveness of the novel. As representative examples, Stanley T. Gutman sees D.J. as the novel's greatest weakness; D.J. is unbelievable and too unreliable in his multiple identities. See *Mankind in Barbary*, p. 134. In his chater on *Why Are We in Vietnam?* in *The Structured Vision of Norman Mailer*, Barry Leeds finds the novel a retrogression and believes the narrative voice evinces Mailer's loss of control. Donald L. Kaufmann sees the novel as a mere "cross between a leftist polemic and a political novel," and considers it "yesterday's wisdom" filtered through "pop art." See Donald L. Kaufmann, "Catch-23: The Mystery of Fact (Norman Mailer's Final Novel)," *Twentieth-Century Literature*, pp. 247–56. The opposing view is that the narrative voice reflects the madness in America itself; see Robert Solotaroff, *Down*

force field. Beginning with the "fact" of the electromagnetic force of the earth's poles, Mailer metaphorically extends the fact to make Alaska above the Arctic Circle a collector of impulses from the "psycho-magnetic" field of southern civilizations. Rusty's safari is the physical presence of these fragmenting forces from the south that cause a "fission" of the electromagnetic field (the e.m.f.) and the psychomagnetic "mood" (the collective "magnetic-electro fief" of the dream, or M.E.F.): "Cop Turds are exploding psychic ecology all over the place, and this is above the *Circle*, man, every mind, human, animal, even vegetable, certainly mineral (crystal mineral) is tuned into the same place. . . . Big Luke knows he's getting away with too much, he's violating the divine economy which presides over hunters . . . this is Yukon, man, heroes fall" (*Why*, p. 115).[2]

As Alaskan cities are looking more like "the high technological nexus and overdeveloped civilization of a megacity like the Dallas-Fort Worth complex," so is the wilderness looking more like a dude ranch preparing for some kind of surrealistic military invasion. All nature is on edge with the corruption and fragmentation of its mood and economy. So when Tex gut shoots a wolf or M.A. Pete blows the rectum off a caribou with an elephant gun, the whole of surrounding nature stirs. Hills clap together, air moves, and the trees of the forest shift and fill with "awe" as they watch "one of their own take a wasting." Because the setting is the frontier, it becomes a place of intensely conflicting forces. Like the dream itself, Alaska becomes a heightened battleground for God and Devil, a place of extreme possibilities of contagion and beatitude.[3]

A second cause of misunderstanding seems to be the failure to recognize the nature of the hero's guilt. D.J. feels guilty about the wastes of his past, both the wastes of his life as the son of a

---

Mailer's Way, p. 180 and *passim*. Richard Poirier argues that D.J. simply represents another of Mailer's favorite theories: the multitude of selves within each self. See Richard Poirier, *Norman Mailer*, p. 129.

2. *Why Are We in Vietnam?* (hereafter cited as *Why*). Unless otherwise indicated, all citations are to works by Norman Mailer.

3. *Why*, chapters 9 and 10 of "Intro Beep." Future references are parenthetical. See also Mailer's speculations in *Existential Errands: Twenty-Six Pieces Selected by the Author from the Body of All His Writings*. Here the dream fiefs of the heroic, of those who test themselves and expand their existence, are "theatrical revues" that dramatize dangers one has or will have to encounter. The "Navigator" at the seat of the heroic mind therefore becomes increasingly able to "chart a course through the possible rapids soon to be encountered in his life," making, in short, the dreamer a greater warrior in God's army of Being. The degree to which one's deepest mind is influenced by the "misconceptions" of society—Hollywood, television, and modern communications—is the degree to which the Navigator may be thwarted and misdirected in his quest and the degree to which the human psyche is disrupted (pp. 112–14). See also *Cannibals and Christians* (hereafter cited as *CC*), pp. 246–47, 280, where Mailer argues that the interruption and annoyance of mass communications are "the foundation of modern existence."

corporation chief and the wastes of his father's safari two years ago. In fact, the wastes of D.J.'s adolescence are simply epitomized in his safari experience. "D.J. has wasted his adolescence," he says in "Chap Three," "in their purlieus and company mansions and has eaten off their expense accounts all his days, D.J. knows them asshole to appetite . . . they are not all that dumb. . . .They can all swim uphill through shit face first although in fact corporate faces are never seen to move" (pp. 50–51). The waste of the safari is the massive "animal murder" D.J. says he has committed as the novel opens, a murder that gives him the "bloods," or the guilt, he is about to recall for the reader. All of this waste is "shit," and his return to it and his immersion in it are what cause much of the scatological profanity in the novel. As D.J. puts it, he is "marooned" in the shit or on the "balmy tropical isle of Anal Referent Metaphor" (p. 150). This "shit" is like the waste that Mailer himself has often returned to since he introduced the metaphor in "The Twelfth Presidential Paper," entitled "On Waste." Mailer argues here, as he will in *Cannibals*, that examining the wastes of the individual and of our industrial production will reveal "the root" of our growth—whether our growth is insufficient, or genuine, or disproportionate and cancerous. The "shit" like the "cancer" Mailer discovers in our civilization is, he argues, no "scientific image" but a "precise metaphor" for the state of society and the individual.[4] D.J. is searching for the root of his growth, or, more accurately, for the cause of his loss of growth, by examining his wastes.

D.J.'s obscenity is a reflection of his own waste and guilt; the obscenity expresses his irreverence for all establishment authority and reminds us of Mailer's continuing belief that the real obscenity in American life is the violence done to humanity and nature by, for example, those politicians and corporation executives who are "perfectly capable of burning unseen women and children in the Vietnamese jungles, yet [feel] a large displeasure . . . at the generous use of obscenity in literature and in public."[5] D.J.'s obscenity spews out as if to purge the speaker of the experience and guilt as much as if to affront the deadened souls who have some responsibility for the experience. As D.J. says of his and Tex's language during their hike: "they so full of love and adventure and in such a haste to get all the mixed glut and sludge out of their systems that they're heating up all the foul talk to get rid of it in a hurry like bad air going up the flue

4. *The Presidential Papers* (hereafter cited as *PP*), p. 272.
5. On this point see especially Mailer's *The Armies of the Night*, pp. 47, 49. Of his own army experience, Mailer says of common man's language: "that noble common man was as obscene as an old goat, and his obscenity was what saved him. The sanity of said common democratic man was in his humor, and his humor was in his obscenity."

and so be ready to enjoy good air and nature, cause don't forget they up in God's attic" (p. 180). On the other hand, when D.J. remembers the experiences of purgation and potential transformation, the language becomes sensitive and lyrical, suggesting a wistfulness for the opportunity that has been lost. "Memory," D.J. reminds us, "is the seed of narrative." D.J.'s memories possess him. His obsessive need to return to his sins or wastes and to his opportunity for purgation directs the stream of his consciousness, as if the mind's return to and identification of the evil and the good in one's life could somehow purge one of guilt. The entire tale could be seen as D.J.'s prayer to the Lord to obtain purgation. The tale-as-prayer is clearly a sinner's prayer, a hopeless desperate prayer for salvation. And the difficulty of the prayer increases as D.J.'s tale approaches his failed transformation and the loss of his soul: "D.J. is hung because the events now to be recounted in his private tape being made for the private ear of the Lord . . . are hung up on a moment of the profoundest personal disclosure" (p. 174).

That D.J.'s quest and the structure of his tale are determined by his obsessional anxieties is, as Angus Fletcher argues, typical of the compulsive nature of the allegorical hero's quest. The self-imposed duties, compulsive rituals and repetitions, and the hero's continual ruminations about his own desires keep his anxieties in bounds and suggest the impulse of expiation and ritual atonement. The narrative tendencies to "encapsulate" agents and isolate episodes into particular moments of contagion and beatitude express the compulsive quest for expiation in allegory and "prophetic literature" generally.[6]

D.J.'s profane language, then, is not purposeless; it is satirically directed against all that D.J. hoped to surmount: Rusty, the corporation, and the supercharged "animal murder" and "fission" in Alaska. D.J.'s description of the corporation is an example of his comically profane approach, which gains the reader's confidence, to a subject otherwise frightening, grotesque, and ultimately tragic.

> Central Consolidated Chemical and Plastic . . . till they found out the Red-ass Russians had their Communist Party initials CCCP, so they changed the name—look into the difficulties—an approval vote of the stockholders 1,179,008 to 241,642, change of listing on the stock market, reams of pure shit, reprinting of stationery, invoices, packages, loading, relettering boxcars—they a bunch of tight assholes running the inner mills of the mills, so . . . they called it Central Consolidated *Combined* Chemical and Plastic, the new coagulation of title now being CCCCP or as the team began to say, 4C and P. . . . and he [Rusty] was brought back in to head a new division for Four C-ing the cancer market—big lung subsidiary. . . . they

6. See Angus Fletcher, *Allegory: The Theory of a Symbolic Mode*, pp. 284–98, 302.

come up with a plastic filter for cigarettes . . . trade name Pure
Pores—is the most absorptive substance devised ever in a vat—traps
all the nicotine, sucks up every bit of your spit. Pure Pores also causes
cancer of the lip but the surveys are inconclusive, and besides, fuck
you! (*Why*, pp. 29–31)

As if to strike out for his loss of soul and life, D.J. strikes out at
everything that might have caused the loss, at everyone who might
perpetuate the psychic fragmentation of our time. Even the reader is
implicated. If D.J. calls the reader relatively innocuous, playful
names such as Horace, Henry, son, fellow Americans, Fergus, dear
clients, little punsters out in fun land, Pericles, Newton, and the like,
he as often expresses his contempt for the reader as one more
member of the death alliance, as one more perpetrator of the death
D.J. describes. The reader becomes a contemptuous "statistics per-
vert" out in "implosion land," whom D.J. will make "fly up your own
asshole before you read him right." D.J. sees himself in the role of a
vernacular prophet to his time and country, a modern "Huckleberry
Finn . . . here to set you straight" and teach you "how to live in this
Electrox Edison world." His mixed address to the reader, like his lack
of sympathy for those he satirizes, is the strategy of satire. The
humorous playfulness encourages the reader to come into the narrator's confidence and be sympathetic to his vision of the evil the
narrator points out. But the confrontation with the reader is intended to make the reader suddenly realize that he or she too is the
foe, is implicated in the guilt and waste that both narrator and
reader, the satirist hopes, have seen. The degree to which D.J., as a
fragmented personality, is himself in control of this strategy is an
open question, but the satirist Mailer is clearly behind D.J., manipulating the confidences and confrontations with the reader to
expose the reader's participation in the waste. But in this novel,
Rusty and the corporation are at the center of the waste.

As in *Barbary Shore*, the struggle of Life-potential against the
Death-alliance expresses the theme of *Why Are We in Vietnam?* The
characters, like the setting, are highly symbolic. They are "agents,"
as D.J. tells us we all are, "of Satan and the Lord." A "heroic looking"
Texan, the cream of "corporation corporateness," David Rutherford
Jethroe Jellicoe Jethroe, or "Rusty" as D. J.'s father is known, is, like
Hollingsworth before him, the central image of Death toward which
the dead and dying move.

Rusty and his "opposite number" in the corporation, Big Al Percy
Cunningham, initiated the safari as a part of their drive to assert
status and prove corporate power. But when Big Al has to go to Cape
Canaveral to make "big power space decisions" and argue the merits
of his corporation's "plastic Univar valve and plug" for the as-

tronauts' space-suit toilet, Rusty is forced to invite two lower-level extensions of himself, whom D.J. calls M.A. (Medium Asshole) Pete and M.A. Bill. Rusty sees the safari as an extension of his corporate power; the safari defines the nature of the corporation. Because Rusty no longer has "Wise Ass Cunningham" to compete with and trip seems "downgraded," Rusty begins the safari as a struggle to test himself and see how he "shapes up in a contest against a man who is not an asshole, Mr. Luke Fellinka," Indian guide. But Rusty's safari ends as one more quest to increase the power of the material and the people he manipulates—corporate power—not as a quest to increase the power of his self. "He got a corporation mind. He don't believe in nature; he puts his trust and distrust in man. 5% trust 295% distrust." He is another of Mailer's fictional devils, or a grand, Kelly-like devil's solicitor. The "open war" that Rusty ("Jet Throne") and his corporate extensions declare on the animals is a metaphor for corporate power. At great length in "Chap Five," D.J. contrasts a true hunter's single, all-purpose weapon to the corporate arsenal and the Apache Helicopter "vomiting big equipment out of its guts."

Yet the ethical questions D.J.'s tale raises do not come simply from the battle between men with machines and the animals, but, more accurately, from the battle between two kinds of power—corporate or Rusty power, which is the power of external accoutrements, and self or authentic power, which is the intrinsic power of increased consciousness and self-definition. As in *An American Dream*, courageous acts develop the power of authenticity, which is a power D.J. and Tex seek in chapters 7 through 11. The exchange between Rusty and Big Luke initiates the novel's explicit reference to this ethical conflict. Rusty asks Luke "about the fine difference in ethics between using Ollie's 30.06 and my Special .404, or your .375." Rusty continues, "Yes, it may be our animals will die a degree more from shock and a hint less from vital execution. But of what final ethical consequence is that?" (pp. 85–86). Tex's practical reply that "your meat tastes better when you're executed," is shortly verified. The pragmatic difference is clear enough when the safari party eats caribou steak blown to "jelly" and "blood pudding" by Pete's Nitro Express: "it tasted loud and clear of nothing but fresh venison steeped in bile, shit, and the half-digested contents of a caribou's stomach—it was so bad you were living on the other side of existence, down in poverty and stink wallow with your nose beneath the fever—that was Luke's message to us" (p. 98). As the novel progresses, the ethical difference between "vital execution" and "massive shock" grows larger and larger. Rusty's Moe Henry and Obungekat Safari is a cheat of existence and of oneself. The guilt these "hunters" accrue is the guilt, the "cheat," that Mailer has

charged twentieth-century humanity with generally, as he did in
The Presidential Papers.

> We gave our freedom away a long time ago. . . . in all the
> revolutions we did not make, all the acts of courage, we found a way
> to avoid, all the roots we destroyed. . . . There had been a vast
> collective social effort in the twentieth century—each of us had tried
> to take back a critical bit more from existence than we had given to
> it. . . . Was it not possible that we were sent out of eternity to become
> more than we had been? (p. 159)

> In our flight from the consequence of our lives, in our flight from
> adventure, from danger, and from the natural ravages of disease, in
> our burial of the primitive, it is death the Twentieth Century is
> seeking to avoid. (p. 176)

The guilt from the cheat and the loss of the self is what D.J. fears.
Rusty and Luke both serve as warnings to D.J., as reminders of what
he may become. An important reason for D.J.'s "delinquencies"—
why he has to grass-out at family dinners, for example—is that he
cannot bear to see himself in his father. His father is a false guide, a
betrayer. He sees in Rusty's eyes the cause of his own dread -the
chasm of the empty tomb, and the power on which America now
runs, which D.J. compares to some mysterious creature with a
plastic asshole installed in his brain (the G.P.A.) to "shit out all his
corporate management of thoughts," his waste, across the landscape. In his father's eyes, D.J. sees "voids, man, and gleams of yellow
fire . . . fifty thousand fucking miles of marble floor down those eyes,
and you got to walk over that to get to The Man" (p. 36). D.J. fears
that his "success" will be to become like Rusty, and in this fear D.J.
represents a generation of disaffected youth. Such "success," D.J.
warns us, stimulates "you to suffocate," to abandon the power of the
authentic self, to become one more Medium or Highgrade Asshole
working for the G.P.A., or the Devil. Big Luke is another sign or
warning. As a heroic figure he retains an ambiguity, but ultimately
he is a failure, another unauthentic man. D.J. and Tex begin to
realize that Big Luke is a fallen hero as he daily becomes more like
the executives he guides.

> Big Luke now got his kicks with the helicopter. He was forever enough
> of a pro not to use it with real hunters . . . but he had us, gaggle of
> goose fat and asshole, killers of bile-soaked venison, so the rest of the
> hunt . . . he gave what was secretly wanted, which was helicopter
> heaven, and it was curious shit. . . . so we broke open a war between
> us and the animals . . . hopping to the top of a mountain in copter
> wings to shoot down on goats . . . . and it was a haul of big-ass game
> getting. (*Why*, pp. 98–100)

Big Luke, on the other hand, also serves as an introduction for D.J.
and Tex, through one of several blood rituals in the novel, to the old

magic and ways of the hunter and to the primordial telepathies of the natural world as soon as D.J. and Tex begin to sense their own inadequacies as hunters early in the safari. This is their first positive lesson in the qualities of authenticity and the powers within the self, but it reveals to them another sign or warning that, like the other warnings, has a certain ambiguity. As they begin to experience the telepathies between hunters, animals, and trees, D.J. and Tex make contact with an order, economy, and instinctual life below the safari's surface that prepares them for a true hunt. The drink of wolf's blood puts D.J. "on" to the instinctual, wild, and brutal animal nature, but he also sees something of the "insanity," the "anger" like a "burnt electric wire," of the wolf as he faced his own death. The instinctual nature and wildness D.J. sees in the world are like an "eye looking at you in the center of a midnight fire," and like "looking up the belly of a whale." This wildness in the "guts of things" is not the "animal insanity" of the mangled, over-hunted beasts. The animal insanity is a disproportion, a distortion of that wildness; it is another distortion of one's deepest, authentic life. This is an important point, for critics have often confused the two and thereby misread the final pages of the book. Kenneth Easterly first hints at this insanity when he says the wild animals have changed their psychology as a result of the overkilling and maiming of animals by "hunters" who are excited by greed and a terror of being cheated. Then Big Ollie makes an important distinction when Rusty misses the significance behind Easterly's remark. The wilderness is gone, Ollie says; the hunters and helicopters are driving the animals insane ("animal no wild no more, now crazy"), and the animals are gaining the dangerous revelations of insanity (p. 65). Mailer, therefore, makes the distinction between *wildness* (animal instinctual nature) and *bestiality* (animal insanity).[7] It is the same distinction Mailer is making between the part of D.J. that is a reflection of the disease and the part that D.J. hopes to gain—the wild, instinctual nature that Tex represents for him. The devouring bestiality is the insanity D.J. and Tex must face. It is something different than the genuine lust to hunt, kill, and eat, a lust that D.J. feels from the "black-shit fuel" of the wolf's blood. The insanity reflects not the

---

7. This insanity is the bestiality (as opposed to the wildness of animal nature) Mailer obviously had in mind when in *CC* he said that as the spirit dies, "the buried animal in American life grew bestial," pp. 78–79. He is referring to the failure of the "Great Society" and the nature of that society as encouraging purge or war. Mailer's principal argument against the war is the form it takes—the impersonal violence—rather than the war itself. He might have been less vocal about the Vietnam War had we fought the Vietnamese "man to man" rather than through a huge, impersonal, technological violence. But one cannot be sure, for Mailer has little sympathy with the motives of American imperialism in any form or shade. See, for example, *CC*, pp. 80–81.

wildness of the hunting animal, but the animal's response to the explosion of "psychic ecology" in the North, an insanity D.J. himself also begins to see.

This danger of insanity provides an important lesson for D.J., for it helps him to see which side of the battle he must be on and where his potential authenticity lies. Once his consciousness is stimulated by the telepathies in the natural world and by the insanity around him, he faces the loss of his self as it is absorbed and controlled by the machine, and he faces the dread of his existence as an ever-diminishing self or soul. He first encounters "Herr Dread" when he looks into the eyes of a mountain goat that he has killed, essentially, by helicopter. He realizes the machine has "hypnotized" him as much as it had hypnotized, in a different way, the terrorized animals. He sees in the goat's death his own dying, his own waste. D.J. did not have to work, to hunt, for that kill; he did not have to test himself against the terrain and the goat. Two years later, during the dinner party, D.J. sees that it is the dread he discovered in Rusty's eyes, in the goat's eyes, in the nature of his family and his whole life, and in the consciousness of his own loss that causes him to rebel and to desire the restoration of his lost self.

> Whyfor does Doctor Jekyll have such a total rejection of all the positive elements in his rich secure successful environmental scene including social backing, strong sentiment, national roots, loci of power, happy physical endowment . . . and clearly individualistic and highly articulated parents?
> And D.J. says in answer: ever read *The Concept of Dread* by . . . Kierkegaard? . . .
> D.J. is up tight with the concept of dread. He don't have to read S.K. S.K. can stick dread up his own ass. . . . D.J. has ideas like nobody else. He sees through to the stinking roots of things, contemplate Eternity the poets might say. (*Why*, pp. 34–35)

D.J. sums up his guilt, his dread of a tremendous loss on the third page of the novel. It is intended to be our guilt and loss as much as his: "God has always wanted more from man than man has wished to give him. Zig a zig a zig. That is why we live in dread of God. Make me another invention, Edison. Bring in the electric come machine." Like Hemingway's Francis Macomber, D.J. and Tex are beginning to learn, just before they abandon the safari, that it does matter how one hunts or performs any act, that one's "life" or existence depends upon recognizing the ethical difference between authentic action and the "cheat."

If it is D.J.'s new awareness of instinctual telepathies that causes him to wake in the night recalling the manner of the animals' deaths, "his sixteen-year-old heart racing through the first spooks of an encounter with Herr Dread," it is his obsession with this dread, with the loss of his soul, and with his consequent quest for purgation and wholeness that drives the narrative forward to the center of the novel's ethic. In the first two hundred pages of the novel, Mailer draws the progress of D.J.'s drive to find wholeness, a drive that increases the more it is frustrated by the safari's events. D.J. tells us that the frustration of an impulse leads to its crystallization as well as to increased "telepathy." The more D.J. is frustrated, crystallized, in his search for identity or for an authentic and whole self, the greater his telepathy becomes. The greater his telepathy—his consciousness of all the impulses and messages that surround him—the greater his desire to purge his guilt. "So call for the flushing waters. . . . gather here, kiss this crystal, dissolve its form. Unloose my stasis" (p. 153). When the frustration and drive for wholeness reach an unendurable point, D.J. and Tex cut loose for the mountains in a final attempt to purge themselves, to loosen their stasis. In short, the relationship between authenticity and dread is reciprocal. A heightened awareness or dread of what one is about to lose stimulates the drive for authenticity.

But before D.J. and Tex escape to search for their authenticity, Mailer further polarizes the conflict between Rusty-as-Death and the Life-potential in D.J. through the episode of the bear hunt, in which Rusty and D.J. venture out alone. The potential in the hunt, its importance, is that it is a "test" of motives and heroic potential, consciousness and courage. D.J.'s and Rusty's motives for attempting this hunt are explicitly opposed. Their motives foreshadow the outcome of the hunt as much as they exacerbate the opposition of father and son as symbolic figures.

Rusty's deepest motive to hunt is the same that has operated throughout the safari—corporate power. However close Rusty may come to loosening his own stasis, he cannot transcend this motive. He is "half-insane" with his obsession not to be outdone by Pete, so insane that he gets the "guts" to go out for a "grizzer" himself: "if he don't get a bear now, he can transfer to Japan." This potential loss of his corporate power feeds Rusty's mind as he lies awake, like D.J., contemplating the recent bear kills. Rusty fears emerging threats against white civilization, organized religion, traditional authority, white men generally, and America; he feels betrayed by his own weaknesses: "Rusty's secret is that he sees himself as one of the pillars of the firmament, yeah, man—he reads the world's doom in his own fuckup. If he is less great than God intended him to be, then America is in Trouble" (p. 111).

We see in Rusty's "large thoughts" the germ of Mailer's own philosophy, but the germ grows to distortion. Who is Rusty's god but the "biggest corporation of them all." The hunt and Rusty's deepest motives for it will emphasize his role as a figure already beyond redemption and as the incarnation of the modern disease. Rusty is a monstrosity, a disproportion, a cancer.[8] He has distorted a fundamental need in the individual to assert his or her existence, distorted it into the cannibalistic absorption and manipulation of other men. And Rusty's larger problem is that to make his "philosophy" work, however distorted the emphasis of the first twelve "thoughts," he, Rusty, has to be "an honest son of a bitch," because if you are a "fulcrum of the Lord"—and Mailer has always argued that such is the human *potential*—then the Lord takes "his reading off you." But Rusty cannot be honest "by definition." What he has become, what he *is*, is consummate dishonesty, the type of ungenuine existence or "cheat." Rusty has reversed the field, to use Mailer's metaphor, and it is not the divine but the satanic conception that takes its reading off him. It will be Rusty's final action that will show D.J. what he must do to save himself.

D.J.'s motives for the hunt as well as his actions during it conflict with Rusty's. D.J. wants to conquer the "dread" he feels about his existential death in the safari. He also wants to prove himself in a true hunt by conquering his fear of the bear and by shooting as cleanly as Tex, a "natural hunter" who has just taken a bear with one clean shot to its brain with his .270. What D.J. wants to prove most at this point is that he is closer to Tex than to M.A. Pete who, with his Nitro Express, has just received credit for another bear that dies from the "bomb and superblast" of "General Luke's" collective "military" operation in "Chap Seven." And D.J. now has the instincts of the true hunt to slake, which were awakened by his first drink of wolf's blood (pp. 118–19).

When father and son strike out on their own, D.J. feels his first love for his father: "he don't know if he's going to be a hero or dead, but he loves his daddy this instant, what a fuck of a stud, they will take off together, they will make their own way back to camp, and Big Luke will sweat a huge drop." As Rusty and D.J. penetrate the forest, Rusty begins to shed his corporation layers, giving off the old rot as he does, which is the smell of "many a hero." Father and son, "like two combat wolves," slowly sweep into the "mood" of everything around

---

8. Mailer said in his "Speech at Berkeley on Vietnam Day" "that the ill of civilization is that it is removed from nature—disproportions thrive everywhere. The war in Vietnam is just such a monstrous disproportion. We are present at a mystery. All monstrous disproportion conceals a mystery or an insanity. . . . Most strong motives are finally psychological—money or power is required to satisfy some imbalance in ourselves." The violence of the war is an attempt to purge the psychic "disease." That the purgation takes the form of massive, technological, and impersonal violence rather than direct confrontation is the measure of the disease's hold upon us. See *CC*, pp. 73–79.

them and begin to feel the "good" or grace that they are earning by their effort and by the danger they face. They enter the mood of the genuine hunt: "there's fine cool in them now, they're off the *fever* of hunting and into the *heart* of it" (p. 135, my italics). Rusty briefly reveals the other face of the father; he becomes the true father and teacher. He points out curiosities of flora and fauna. He delivers three parables to his son that teach the necessity of seeking one's roots, of adventure and courage, and of taking what one needs from nature cleanly, economically, and with one's intrinsic rather than extrinsic powers. But there is an important irony in these parables. For finally, Rusty cannot act in accordance with the intentions they express, a fact that is presaged by the dimness of vision Rusty expresses in his explication of the third parable. In this parable Rusty explains that the eagle is a false symbol of America's greatness. Rusty once saw an eagle killing a wounded deer by plucking out one eye at a time and then going for the deer's testicles. This "most miserable of scavengers," Rusty says, betrays the country it symbolizes. What Rusty does not see is the appropriateness of the "miserable scavenger" symbol to his country as it now is, as it proliferates malignancies across the landscape and engages in an obscene war. It is Rusty's way of life that has made his country become a "miserable scavenger."

Though D.J. briefly sees another side of his father in the hunt and dares to hope that this side of Rusty may sustain him in his own quest, there are times even in the hunt when D.J.'s old anger against Rusty returns. D.J. is reminded of Rusty's betrayer face, for example, when D.J., tracking the bear, realizes that this devouring beast is the foe they must conquer through alertness, skill, and force. Thrown back on his own resources, D.J. becomes aware of a "hole in his center," of some possibly irreparable loss. He senses Rusty's role in that loss and recalls a series of smaller betrayals. Rusty has provided as a model for courageous self-expansion only a corporate hollow. Each of the old instances of betrayal that D.J. recalls in "Chap 8" as in "Intro Beep 3" is in turn a lesser but symptomatic betrayal of the more serious betrayal yet to come. At those moments during the hunt when D.J. portentously sees the actual face of Rusty again, the face of the father who will "suffocate" the son and frustrate the son's quest for authenticity, D.J. wants to kill Rusty, and he nearly does.

But D.J. does not slay the father-betrayer because "the beast's" presence is so imminent that he must concentrate on the task at hand, the hunt itself. And surely Rusty's revelations suggesting another potential, of the helpful and true father, weaken D.J.'s sense of the real danger the false father represents. Facing the immediate danger of the beast, father and son regain their "cool" and the "heart" of the hunt. They stalk this beast as if going deeper into themselves, as if entering a calm flat sea, as D.J. describes it, going "in deeper on every step . . . a rock God laid on water" (p. 138). D.J. is ready when the grizzly, "Mr. Death," charges out of the brush.

> D.J. in some sweet cool of rest below all panic and paralysis dropped to one knee, threw up Remington, had a sail of light at the top of his head of far-gone tree and sky, and pulled off the trigger to smash a shot into that wall of fur, almost leisurely, like shot-putting a rock into a barrel. . . . it kept coming down like a twelve-foot surf of comber bamming right for your head, and D.J.'s heart and his soul sweet angel bird went up the elevator of his body . . . before he slammed bolt and fired again. (*Why*, p. 141)

Sounding like the "foghorn" of the bear that died from massive shock and like "the crazy wild ass moan of every animal they'd gunned down and the tear and blast of all flesh," the bear comes on like the violated beast it is—the accumulated rage of all the violated animals in the North, "with affiliates down to the Equator," as D.J. in a moment of heightened metaphorical vision sees the bear. The bear is also the Nemesis of the violated self in our century. This animal, like any true symbol, functions on more than one level of meaning in D.J.'s tale. The literal devouring beast of the forest, though now himself "insane," is also the symbolic devourer of myth and dream. As we saw in *An American Dream*, literal and symbolic beasts are the same for Mailer. By facing the mythic beast, which represents an overwhelming insanity, D.J. faces psychological and existential death. This psychological and existential death is the loss of D.J.'s self, of the opportunity to integrate instinctual and conscious life, and of control over his now fragmented consciousness. As a symbol of a distorted, uncontrollable unconscious life that threatens to devour D.J., this bear must be faced and overcome if D.J., or indeed life in general, is to progress and triumph. This bear also prepares us for the climactic symbol of the book: the cosmic devourer, the insane beast or devil that the disintegration of psychic life in our time has unleashed upon the world.

By facing this beast, D.J. momentarily earns the grace he describes as the flight of his soul bird. The grizzly's charge shows D.J. that the center of things is now insane and insane with force. This lesson is "like a stroke across the strings and nerve in his life—say, it will come back and back again." But he will return to this moment of perception into the heart of things as something sacred because it also reveals to him the other essence of Nature, a nearly lost potential in Nature. This beast, finally, offers D.J. an absolution, a forgiveness, beyond the bestial insanity in the world and in oneself.

It is important to see that the center of things is not only insane, as many of Mailer's critics seem to believe. There is still some ethical, divine order and some regenerative force in nature, however far away now, that a few might reach. But the more this ethical order is disturbed, the greater the imbalance grows and the more the insane violence erupts.[9] The forgiveness is offered in a moment of self-transcendence that begins as Rusty and D.J. work to approach the dying bear who looks "like a tabby cat on its stomach, forelegs tucked under him, peaceful, looking to be stuffed bear served on a red plate ten feet in diameter, for that blood beneath was monumental in its pool" (p. 145). This stage of the hunt has no such meaning for Rusty as it does for D.J. Rusty would kill the bear outright. But D.J. holds his father off and gets close to the bear so that he might enter "the peace" coming off the animal "like the moment a gull sets on water." The animal's eyes now seem to D.J. like "transparent eyes" revealing Nature's message. In those eyes Nature is a "fellow, an intelligence of something very fine and far away"; the eyes "brand" some part of D.J.'s "future."[10] Fluctuating between the message from the depth of Nature and the "shattering message" of pain from the animal's "shattered" organs, the bear's eyes respond to D.J. as he makes a first step toward his return to grace. The eyes promise D.J. an excruciating struggle if he would complete his return: "Baby, you haven't begun." But just as D.J. initiates his return, Rusty inflicts the ultimate betrayal; he denies D.J.'s communion with the deep-seated soul of Nature, so "very fine and far away" in the bear's eyes.

> And when D.J. smiled, the eyes reacted, they shifted, they looked like they were about to slide off the last face of this presence, they looked to be drawing in the peace of the forest preserved for all animals as they die, the unspoken cool on tap in the veins of every tree, yes, griz

9. Compare my point here with Mailer's discussion of violence in "Talking of Violence," *Twentieth Century* 173 (Winter, 1964–65): 109–12. Mailer distinguishes between social and personal violence. Social violence creates personal violence, which is the "antithesis" of social violence. Our "institutional deadenings," for example, force juvenile delinquency to flourish, and such delinquency, as personal violence, is an expression of "social suffocation."

10. One cannot be sure Mailer has been reading his Emerson, but compare Emerson's description of transcendence in a similar passage from *Nature.* "The lover of Nature is he whose inward and outward senses are still truly adjusted to each other; who has retained the spirit of infancy. . . . His intercourse with heaven and earth becomes part of his daily food. In the presence of nature a wild delight runs through the man, in spite of real sorrows. Nature says,—he is my creature. . . . In the woods . . . a man casts off his years, as a snake his slough. . . . In the woods we return to reason and faith. There I feel that nothing can befall me in life . . . which nature cannot repair. Standing on bare ground,—my head bathed by the blithe air and uplifted into infinite space,—all mean egotism vanishes. I become a transparent eyeball; I am nothing; I see all; the currents of the Universal Being circulate through me; I am part or parcel of God." From Stephen E. Whicher's, *Selections from Ralph Waldo Emerson,* pp. 23–24.

was drawing in some music of the unheard burial march, and Rusty
. . . chose that moment to shoot, and griz went up to death in one last
paroxysm, legs thrashing, brain exploding from new galvanizings
and overloadings of massive damage report, and one last final
heuuuuuu, *all forgiveness gone.* And coughed blood out of his throat
as he died. (p. 147, my italics)

Mailer's bear-hunting tale has generally been compared with
Faulkner's "The Bear," and there are specific similarities and differences worth emphasis at this point to clarify Mailer's tale. Ike
McCaslin sees in Old Ben's death some hint of nature's eternal
essence, much as D.J. does in the dying grizzly's "transparent" eye.
In abandoning the powers of civilization to approach the bear, Ike
and D.J. both trade the power of the extrinsic for the power of the
self, and both boys place themselves before the bear in a kind of
humility that leads to moral insights that the extrinsic powers of
civilization seem only to obscure. The wilderness and nature that
both Faulkner's and Mailer's bears represent, therefore, are potential
sources of moral and spiritual knowledge. Such knowledge is at-
tained by suffering, endurance, courage, humility, and the awaken
ing of sensibilities. Both Mailer and Faulkner oppose this moral
knowledge and strength to the power of civilization because it is the
wilderness, this root and source, that civilized man destroys in his
greed and through the misused resources of his technology. This
wilderness may be either the actual wilderness of nature or the
primordial wilderness of the psyche, or it may be both. Both are
obvious and traditional sources of mankind's deepest experiences
and roots. R. W. B. Lewis hints that Faulkner's Old Ben possesses the
characteristics of the Terrible Mother in heroic mythology. The same
is true of Mailer's bear. The bear D.J. faces has the two aspects of this
figure: the dark upwellings of the violated unconscious and the face
of the healer and protectoress who represents the nourishing potential of Goddess Nature and creative unconscious. She can aid the
hero in subduing the Terrible Father, and thereby may help the hero
reach his atonement with the True Father (the enlightener) and
carry redemption into the world.[11]
There are, however, significant differences between Faulkner's
and Mailer's bear hunts, especially if we consider Faulkner's Ike only
in the hunting tale itself.[12] If both Ike and D.J. attempt retribution

11. See R. W. B. Lewis, "William Faulkner: The Hero in the New World," in R. P.
Warren's *Faulkner: A Collection of Critical Essays*, p. 212. Compare Joseph
Campbell, *The Hero with a Thousand Faces*, pp. 131, 155.
12. For a reading exactly the opposite of my points in this paragraph, see Richard
Pearce, "Norman Mailer's *Why Are We in Vietnam?* A Radical Critique of Frontier
Values," *MFS*, pp. 409–14. Pearce reverses my contrast of Ike and D.J. Considering
not only Faulkner's "The Bear" but also "Delta Autumn," Pearce sees Ike as the

for the sins of their fathers, D.J. has no Sam Fathers, no true guide, to aid him on his journey to "manhood" in the primitive sense of the word—in the sense of proven "valor" and "virtue." Unlike the annual "pageant-rite," as it has been called, of Ike's hunt, D.J.'s safari is utterly corrupt. The Indian guides' attenuated rituals are mocked by their corrupt actions. The father is no source of enlightenment, but the satanic avatar of a frenetic, corporate-power-hungry civilization. In this role, Rusty contributes to the cumulative patterns of myth and ritual in the novel. As with the symbolic bear and the later "purification ceremony," the mythic level of the novel confirms the literal. As much as Rusty reveals his nature as an agent of Death in Mailer's allegory, his role as the archetypal "Terrible Father," to use Erich Neumann's phrase, extends the mythic dimension of the novel. His characteristics and actions repeat a central pattern in primitive, classical, and modern literature. Rusty's final betrayal of D.J. denies D.J.'s potential renewal of heroic consciousness through the nourishing aspect of the Mother. This nourishing aspect is revealed in the promise of the bear's "transparent" eye. Rusty, like the mythic Terrible Father, symbolizes the negative and satanic image of a "castrating patriarch" who is the old and rigid consciousness, the stifling ego, and the old ways and systems in their suffocating deadness.[13] When Rusty adds to his betrayal the insult of taking credit for the kill before the Indian guides and his corporate extensions, D.J. separates himself from the father he failed to slay: "Whew. Final end of love of one son for one father."

D.J. separates from his father so that he, D.J., may prepare a second attempt to gain the communion with and forgiveness of that

---

failure and D.J. as the success. I find it curious how many critics either believe that D.J. represents some kind of moral rebirth in the end or are simply confused by his apparent effort at moral rebirth and the apparent failure of that effort.

13. See Carl Jung, *The Archetypes and the Collective Unconscious*, translated by R. F. C. Hull, Vol. 9 (New Jersey: Princeton University Press, 1968), especially pp. 214–15; and Erich Neumann, *The Origins and History of Consciousness*, especially pp. 184–87, 190–91. Joseph Campbell summarizes the issue in his subchapter, "The Hero as World Redeemer": "the work of the hero is to slay the tenacious aspect of the father (dragon, tester, ogre king) and release from its ban the vital energies that will feed the universe." See *Hero*, p. 352. Campbell describes the various aspects of this Terrible Father throughout his work as Mephistopheles, as the devourer in primitive initiation rites, and as the old and rigid system of tribe or society; see pp. 73, 138, 155.

Joseph DeFalco is particularly thorough on the role of the archetypal father figure and the father as betrayer in Ernest Hemingway's heroes. See DeFalco's, *The Hero in Hemingway's Short Stories*, especially pp. 23, 31, 52, 56–62, and *passim*. DeFalco would be useful in pointing out other relevant parallels between Hemingway's fictional heroes and Mailer's: for example, Hemingway's archetypal motifs of the heroic journey and initiation, of death and rebirth, and of the struggle of mankind, particularly in our time, toward individuation. We do well to remember that Hemingway is one of Mailer's chief literary heroes.

Nature which lies beyond the "bestial insanity" of things. This second attempt, which again recalls Ike McCaslin, D.J. frankly calls his "purification ceremony." D.J.'s "ceremonial" acts move toward a restoration of certain eternal values that are, for example, typically expressed in primitive initiation rites of manhood.[14] In this novel, the values are humility and endurance, self-awareness and intrinsic power, and the knowledge and acceptance of the divine economy in Nature. Loss of Life, Mailer says in *The Presidential Papers*, is the loss of contact with the past, with the earth, and with courage (p. 159). The acts that encourage such values in the "ceremony" are: hiking into the wilderness of "God's attic" in the Brooks Range, leaving the accouterments of civilization behind, and immersing themselves in the life and "messages" of the surrounding wilds. Such acts, as D.J. says of the hike, are intended to purge the hero of the "mixed shit" and "glut" of civilization, by which D.J. means the insulating, extrinsic powers of the corporation and the safari thoroughly depicted in the previous chapters. D.J. himself points out that the relationship between the acts and the values he and Tex seek are based on the "equations" of "celestial mechanics."

Mailer's "celestial mechanics" here are clearly related to the kind of metaphysic Eliade calls "primitive ontology." The mechanics of primitive ontology, which traditionally operate in archaic ritual, are based on the faith that the value of objects, humans, and acts resides in their participation in a transcendent reality that gives them eternal existence and "saturates" them with "being." Through such mechanics, concrete existence becomes a receptacle of eternal, divine force, and the meaning and value of acts come from their reproduction of primordial acts or archetypes of regeneration. Formula and ritual, as vehicles to ceremonial time, express a "reality" that corresponds to a desperate effort "not to lose contact with

14. Joseph Campbell gives numerous examples of such rites in *Hero*. See for example the Navaho myth of the "Twin Gods" who journey to the true father through tests of endurance, pp. 69–71; and the myth of Minos and Daedalus in which the hero's self-achieved submission to the sources of rebirth expresses the necessity of ritual humility, pp. 13–17. In the rites of initiation for the Australian Murngin tribe, the boys are ritually passed from the world of the mother to the world of the father, and the male phallus becomes the central point of the initiate's imagination instead of the mother's breast; it is this movement from mother to father that D.J. calls the "phallic" catapult of future "virility," pp. 138–47.

Campbell points out that the second stage of the hero's journey is the stage of purification in which the "senses are cleansed and humbled" and the "energies and interests" of the hero "concentrated upon transcendental things," p. 101. Mircea Eliade, in *The Myth of the Eternal Return*, also points out that the regenerate aspiring to transform the profane to the sacred traditionally tests his endurance against difficulties. And in the case of Tex and D.J. they are enduring a trial typical of primitive religion—the ascent of the Sacred Mountain. The mountain as an archetypal "symbol of the center" confers "being" upon he who journeys to find it (pp. 5–10, 12–15, 18).

being" and to restore to concrete time or history the spiritual energy of divine Time and Being. D.J. intends his ritual purification to abolish his past time and sin as much as primitive ritual purification does. The hero's duty is to restore "pure Time" to the degenerations of historical time. The ritualistic gesture is the gesture of the eternal return, the existential act of urging becoming toward being, and the psychological act of restoring integral wholeness and union with created existence.[15]

The mere "idea" of the hike into the Brooks Range begins to clean D.J. and Tex out. But the narrative specifies a series of purifying actions. Lashing their weapons and unessential gear to a tree, D.J. and Tex feel a "clean fear" and a genuine awe of nature and of the task before them. On the hike, D.J. and Tex pass through the same stages of purification and awakening consciousness that D.J. and Rusty passed through on the hunt. D.J. and Tex enter the mood of the life around them as they slough their civilized corruptions. They see again, in nearly the same order, the kinds of animals they slaughtered on the safari: wolf, caribou, and grizzly. But now they enter each animal's mood and make some discovery, about themselves or the animals, to which they were blind before. They face down a hunting wolf by entering his "psychic field," an act that charges their own valor enough to threaten the wolf into running away. And the boys completely understand every sound of the wolf's howl when he regains his own energy by fending off the attack of an eagle. The grizzly they watch is specifically contrasted to the dying bear D.J. faced earlier. D.J. wonders if this animal that just devoured a baby caribou could also reveal to him "the big eye" of the dying bear—the other side of nature—"as if the center of all significant knowledge" would thereby be revealed to him (p. 193).

When D.J. and Tex enter the mood of the animals, and when they are fascinated by the return of the mother caribou to her dead, half-devoured baby, by their view of a Dall ram on an opposite peak, and by the migrations of cranes and animal herds, they begin to penetrate the surface of life. Mailer likens such penetrations to extracting a "supernatural equivalent" from concrete experience in his commentary on Buber's *Tales of the Hasidim* in *The Presidential*

---

15. Eliade, *The Myth of the Eternal Return*, pp. 3–4, 25, 35–42, 52–55, 90–92. Compare Campbell in *Hero*: the rites of purgation are ultimately affirmations of celestial or cosmic time against the dissolutions of the phenomenal world. Before the clean terror of his trial, the hero is prepared to understand the "majesty of Being" opposed to the "sickening and insane tragedies" of life, pp. 146–47. Neumann suggests that the telepathies of the primitive hunt and magic are a primitive truth that might well be restored, and that these telepathies are also a primitive truth of ceremony or ceremonial "time"; see *Consciousness*, pp. 268–69, 284.

Papers. When one penetrates concrete experience, Mailer argues, it is "almost as if a key is given up from the underworld to unlock the surface of reality," to show a realm of real events "whose connection is never absurd" (*CC*, p. 153). As D.J. and Tex come to sense the beauty, awe, and the connections between their sights and experiences, they approach the mystery in Nature—its economy and dreadfulness, its "ambush and reward," as Mailer called it in 1964.[16]

> Whoo-ee! whoo-ee; they can hardly hold it in, cause this mother nature is as big and dangerous and mysterious as a beautiful castrating cunt when she's on the edge between murder and love, forgive the lecture, Pericles, but the smell is everywhere, the boys are moving on smell. . . . Man, it's terrifying to be free of mixed shit. And they got the unfucked heaven of seeing twelve Dall ram on an outcropping of snow . . . heading into valleys for winter and for feed . . . they are so white and their horns, oh, man, the underside is yellow golden rosy color that gives D.J. twiddles in the gut . . . and the sun is on that snow and space! man. (*Why*, pp. 184–85)

As for Rojack in *Dream*, there is a creative potential in D.J.'s entering the deeper truths, connections, harmonies, and "telepathies" of the life about him. It is this element or action of the purification ceremony that leads to the knowledge and acceptance of the divine economy of Nature and prepares the initiate to become a part of that economy. Once the process of perception has begun, it stimulates subsequent perceptions. As they contemplate their experiences on the hike later that evening, for example, D.J.'s and Tex's "charged" memories seem about to reveal some greater truth or essence in the mysterious underworld of Nature. "D.J. full of iron and *fire* and *faith* was nonetheless *afraid* of sleep, *afraid* of wolves, full of *beauty*, *afraid* of sleep, full of *beauty*, yeah, he unashamed . . . and D.J. could have wept for a secret was near, some mystery in the secret of things" (p. 196, my italics). In *Papers*, Mailer writes that the essence of biology "seems to be challenge and response, risk and survival, war and the lessons of war." In the biological connections of life, Mailer suggests, beauty and danger are inseparable companions (p. 167).

For the boys, now, concrete experience is transfigured in a way similar to that in which the dying bear's eye transfigured the experience of the hunt for D.J. Concrete experiences now seem supernatural; separate physical perceptions are filled with implications and connections to other perceptions. Part of the mystery D.J. now senses is the "dominion" of the trees, which bear their message of some great sorrow up in the North, some crystallization and frag-

16. See Mailer in "Talking of Violence," p. 112.

mentation, some "speechless electric gathering of woe," some disruption of the peace and the terrible economy of Nature. When they
see the King Moose they see the beauty and terror (the moonlight
and blood) of Nature as well as the fragmenting, wounding incursions from civilization. King Moose comes down to them now

> with his dewlap and his knobby knees and dumb red little eyes across
> the snow to lick at salt on the other side of the pond, and sunlight in
> the blood of its drying caught him, lit him, left him gilded red on one
> side as he chomped at mud and salt . . . the full new moon now up
> before the sun was final and down silvering the other side of this King
> Moose up to the moon silhouettes of platinum on his antlers and hide.
> And the water was black, and moose dug from it and ate, and ate
> some more until the sun was gone and only the moon for light and the
> fire of the boys and he looked up and studied the fire . . . and gave a
> deep caw pulling in by some resonance of this grunt a herd of
> memories of animals at work and on the march and something gruff
> in the sharp wounded heart of things bleeding somewhere in the
> night, a sound somewhere in that voice in the North which spoke
> beneath all else to Ranald Jethroe Jellicoe Jethroe and his friend . . .
> "Texas" Hyde. (*Why*, p. 197)

But at the very moment when D.J. and Tex are about to penetrate
to the heart of the mystery in Nature and transform their consciousness, the symbolic setting of this purification ceremony takes on the
greatest importance. I have said that the setting is a metaphorical
battleground of intensely conflicting electronic and psychic forces.
The Brooks Range itself is the "Crystal," the field of receiving nodes
and needles, that stores and emanates civilization's "Encyclopedia
of Cataclysmic Knowledge." If the purification ceremony has revealed to D.J. and Tex something of the dreadful and beautiful
essence of God in Nature, then immersion in the "cataclysmic" field
of civilization's electronic and unconscious impulses reveals still
more of the Devil whose force exists in those impulses from the
south. The forces of contagion reveal their dominance now, as they
have throughout the safari and the hunt.

Just when D.J.'s and Tex's potential is at its height, when the
purgations and the accumulated "good" of the ceremony charge the
boys with a restlessness and energy that pushes them to the edge of
some commitment and communion with nature and one another,
the aurora borealis flashes into the sky with an opposing message.
D.J. recalls that the northern lights are a "mountain of heavenly
light" scientifically certified to be a reflection of magnetic disturbance, and the lights speak to the boys of the satanic south, of
something agitated and crackling in the heavens like static and
sparks. The "God" of the aurora borealis is here in the North. But he
is no "man"; he is a "beast of a giant jaw and cavernous mouth with

a full cave's breath and fangs, and secret call: come to me" (p. 202). This God-turned Devourer is Mailer's Devil or Anti-Soul. Whether we see this Devil from the psychological or metaphysical view, it is Death. This Devil is fulfilled by ourselves and set loose upon the world as a mad devouring beast; It "hates nature," deadens "the soul of all of us, invite[s] it to surrender" (see *CC*, pp. 334, 364).

The question of whether this bestial god is God or Devil has caused the greatest confusion among critics of *Why* and has resulted in the most divergent readings of any of Mailer's books. As always, Mailer's external commentaries help.[17] We have in this novel itself, however, a continuous portrait of opposed conceptions and states of being. On one hand is Rusty and his safari, the fragmentation or fission of electro- and psychomagnetic fields, the extrinsic and manipulatory powers of the corporate machine and civilization, and the insanity of devouring men and beasts. On the other hand, we have the ethical order in the transparent eye, the divine economies of animal instinct and migration, the intrinsic power of the true hunt, and the self-realization and penetrating perception that emerge during the ceremonial test. It is quite clear which is the Good and which the Evil. We can add to this opposition Mailer's distinction in *Why* between animal wildness and animal insanity or bestiality, and we can add the juxtaposition of D.J.'s diseased language and consciousness and his desire for wholeness, for connecting his instinctual or wild self with his conscious self. This search for wholeness of self is one of the earliest motifs in the novel. In the chapters before the narrative begins, D.J. imagines his mother talking to her psychiatrist, Dr. Fixit, about her desire to keep D.J. ("Jekyll") and Tex

17. In *An American Dream* no less than in *CC* and *PP*, as in mythology generally, the devouring aspect of cosmic or psychic force is associated with the Devil. In *PP*, for example, the Devil-as-Plague is continually compared to a great Devouring Goat. Yet both Solotaroff and Gutman, to take two recent critics, see this Beast as the true heart of Nature and as "God." Gutman's analysis of the violence in nature somewhat mitigates this simplification in his book; see Gutman, *Mankind in Barbary*, pp. 131, 138–39, 150–51. Solotaroff begins his chapter on *Why* with the revealing suggestion that D.J.'s flaw is that he confuses God with the Devil. But in the end, Solotaroff does not follow this insight and argues that the "Cannibal Emperor of Nature's Psyche" is God himself. Solotaroff admits he quite possibly misread the ending of the novel, but he offers in hope that he did not misread it, only the general statement that the details of the safari lead us to believe the Devourer is God. I confess Solotaroff confuses me, and I believe him to be far more accurate when he says he could have misread Mailer here. For finally it is both D.J. and Solotaroff who confuse God and Devil. See Solotaroff, *Down Mailer's Way*, pp. 196, 200, 205–6. Perhaps John Aldridge started these misreadings in his "From Vietnam to Obscenity," *Harper's*, pp. 91–97. Aldridge sees *Why* as a novel of absolution in the sense that *Moby Dick* and *Huckleberry Finn* are. All of these critics pass over Mailer's distinction between animal nature (including natural, direct violence) and bestial madness. For a representative opposing view of the novel as a defeat of the hero rather than an absolution see Roger Ramsey's "Current and Recurrent," in *MFS* (Autumn 1971), pp. 415–31.

("Hyde") separate, to keep D.J. wholly within the corporate norms. Tex is too much the wild one, the "panther," the one close to instincts, passions, and the realities of death. Though each boy has some attributes of the other, D.J., who represents the influences of technology and intellectual or accrued knowledge, seeks something in Tex that he needs to break through the technological surface of America.

To interpret the final pages of this novel we have only to ask ourselves which way the boys turn: toward the disease or toward the wholeness and expanded consciousness epitomized by the potential in the ceremonial purification and test? They are unable to reap the promises of the purification ceremony. The influence of the beast in this center of "apocalyptic messages" is too great. The love D.J. feels for Tex and the desire to be one with the instinctual "brother," a love and desire that hang suspended like "an intensity" and "purgation" above them as they nearly reach across to one another, cannot be free of the satanic presence—the cumulative forces and messages from their civilization and, perhaps, the accumulated wastes of their lives. Their failure is not that heroic, authentic act and existence are, as Stanley T. Gutman puts it, "irrelevant," but that satanic existence is so overwhelming now that they cannot be authentic. D.J. and Tex end in a lust for perverted power, which D.J. calls the "lust" to own one another, to dominate the other, literally, through homosexual assault: "something went into them, and owned their fear, some communion of telepathies and new powers" that captures the love between the boys.[18] They know not *what* "owns" them—"Prince of darkness, Lord of light." They know only that they are owned and "touched forever." Now they are "killer" brothers who reach across not in love but in a pact of killers, "blood to blood." They have become the tools of the Devourer. When they return to base camp, they reenter the dead, predictable ways of corporate consciousness, but they bring with them a new power and increase of "electrified mind." They are in total communion now with the "electrified telepathies" of a Devouring, satanic civilization, not in communion with the rigorous economies of Nature or the essence of a fellow "intelligence of something very fine and far away."

The purification ritual that the boys underwent, and to which D.J. returns, is potentially the ultimate compulsive action intended to stay the threats of anxiety, dread, waste, and death in their lives. It would be an example of what Fletcher has called "visionary ritual" or the "higher function" of ritual in allegory, which traditionally leads to some "positive moment of exuberance and delight." The

18. *Why*, p. 219. Compare *PP*, p. 277, where Mailer argues that God must "raid" Evil to recover his existence and that Devil lusts to capture love.

climax of D.J.'s "ceremony" is one of those final moments of vision that, as Fletcher puts it, causes particular allegories to become a "closed climactic form," by its introduction of apocalyptic images, which promote "mere allegory" to "the higher order of mysterious language" we generally call mythical. Unlike the promise of fruitfulness and the triumph of love and creation traditionally associated with the apocalyptic vision—such as that in *Moby Dick* or Eliot's *Ash Wednesday*, to use Fletcher's examples—*Why Are We in Vietnam?* suggests the opposite triumph, the triumph of Antichrist and the destruction of order, the archetypal "catastrophic vision" like that of Orwell or Samuel Beckett (see Fletcher, pp. 353–55).

D.J. has lost his soul to the collective disasters of the e.m.f. and the M.E.F., of his civilization, and has gained a satanic consciousness, has been hypnotized by the Beast, will feed Him messages now, perform His "will" to "go forth and kill." D.J. has reached no atonement with the Father, no nourishment from the Mother. He has not rejected the Tyrant father and Vietnam, as some critics suggest. Betrayed by the corporate consciousness and the electrified mind of their homeland, D.J. and Tex have become that mind. They surface from the safari, the hunt, and the hike more like Mailer's portrait in *Cannibals* of Lyndon Johnson and the general American insanity: ready to go forth as statisticians and deny Nature, to kill, and to revel in the power of an extrinsic mechanistic force by burying the inhabitants of a faraway land, as Rusty put it, in "fire, shit, and fury." This thoroughly defeated hero "signs off" in the words Mailer ascribes to President Johnson in Mailer's Berkeley Vietnam Day speech: "Vietnam, hot damn."

If, finally, D.J. is defeated, if he has gained satanic consciousness, he is also doomed to the obsessive guilt of a sinner. For his narrative, by its manner and structure, reveals a defeated self who returns, painfully, chaotically, digressively, to a moment in his past when he struggled for expiation and failed. His tale is an imaginative return to "ceremony." And Mailer has compared ceremony, in *Existential Errands*, to a prayer, a repetition of invocation and propitiation to the gods (p. 104). The narrator-hero of *Why* is unable to combine his original intention—purgation, expiation, wholeness—with his final actions: his lust to "own" Tex, his enthusiastic acceptance of the war, his return to the world of his fathers, his fragmented speech, his demonological impulses or "freaks." *Why Are We in Vietnam?* is a record of the victory of the satanic act and the defeat of expiation and rebirth. This victory marks the death of Mailer's fictional hero: it also marks the darkest moment of Mailer's vision.

Perhaps this novel is an expression of the author's own sense of defeat by the catastrophic events of the late sixties and an admission of his helplessness and failure before those events. Speaking of his fear of helplessness amidst the events of his time in *Advertisements*, Mailer writes: "How poor to go to death with no more than the notes of a good intention. It is the actions of men and not their sentiments which make history" (p. 477). It is only through the emergence of the nonfiction hero, of that protean persona called "Mailer," in the year following *Why* and throughout the 1970s that Mailer again engages in the battle for Life, in the effort to make his sentiments real, and in his hope of expiation and rebirth.

6

Heroic Consciousness and the Origins of the Nonfiction

Already . . . we can discern, in single individuals, where the synthetic possibilities of the future lie, and almost how it will look. The turning of the mind from the conscious to the unconscious, the responsible *rapprochement* of human consciousness with the powers of the collective psyche, that is the task of the future. No outward tinkerings with the world and no social ameliorations can give the quietus to the daemon, to the gods and devils of the human soul, or prevent them from tearing down again and again what consciousness has built. Unless they are assigned their place in consciousness and culture they will never leave mankind in peace. But the preparation for this *rapprochement* lies, as always, with the hero, the individual; he and his transformation are the great human prototypes; he is the testing ground of the collective, just as consciousness is the testing ground of the unconscious.　　—Erich Neumann, *The Origins and History of Consciousness*

This is a chapter of retrospection, but also of synthesis and definition. Before turning to Mailer's nonfiction, we need to be clear on two aspects of his fiction: the nature of the Mailer hero and the attributes of heroic consciousness. We will then be prepared to trace Mailer's gradual transition from fiction to nonfiction and to understand how Mailer sees himself before the years of his major nonfiction works.

Following World War II, American fiction reflects a search for the modern hero. Among many of Mailer's contemporaries, this search produced what has come to be known as the absurd hero or the anti-hero. But Mailer is anxious to establish the differences between his own goals and heroes and those of Updike, Styron, Bellow, and Salinger, to name a few. In "Some Children of the Goddess," reprinted from *Esquire* in *Cannibals*, Mailer analyzes the differences between himself and, as he sees them, his competitors. Chief among his points is that the anti-hero is too weak a figure to reflect the revolution in consciousness Mailer deems necessary for human survival and growth. The other writers and their heroes, Mailer argues, are too often evasive, retreating before the mysteries they would explore. A second difference is in part the cause of the first. Mailer believes his contemporaries' attempts to return to the self and the pscyhe are bogged in the "cancerous debilitation" of the reductive intellectual structure and language of psychoanalysis. Although

113

Mailer's own work is not free of the language of psychoanalysis, he would have us believe that his journey within is free of any conscious, reductive structure. He believes the weight of such an external structure gives to much of his competitors' work the taint of the artificial and the unauthentic. As a result, Mailer continues, the journey into self that in the Middle Ages or the Renaissance would "come closer to a vision of God or some dictate from eternity" is thwarted today (*CC*, see especially pp. 129–30). Much as he admires some aspects of Saul Bellow's art, for example, Mailer argues that in Bellow the necessary, rebellious urge of the power to advance one's own life is enervated by a timid quest.

> Frank Cowperwood once amassed an empire. Herzog, his bastard
> great-nephew, diddled in the ruins of an intellectual warehouse.
> Where once the realistic novel cut a swath across the face of society,
> now its reality was concentrated into moral seriousness. Where the
> original heroes of naturalism had been active, bold, self-centered,
> close to tragic, and up to their nostrils in their exertions to advance
> their own life and force the webs of society, so the hero of moral
> earnestness, the hero Herzog and the hero Levin in Malamud's *A New
> Life*, are men who represent the contrary—passive, timid,
> other-directed, pathetic, up to their nostrils in anguish: the world is
> stronger than they are; suicide calls. (*CC*, p. 100)

In the context of his essay and the "argument" that prefaces it, Mailer is being contradictory and a little unfair. He compares apples and oranges: the realistic novel and the writer of the journey into self. Later in the essay he will establish these as two separate categories. Of course suicide calls Mailer's own heroes, and Mailer's novels are nothing if not novels of moral earnestness. But Mailer's charge against the anti-hero is nonetheless important: "Herzog was defeated, Herzog was an unoriginal man, Herzog was a fool—not an attractive God-anointed fool like Gimpel the Fool, . . . but a sodden fool, over-educated and inept, unable to fight, able to love only when love presented itself as a gift" (*CC*, p. 100). If *Herzog* still succeeds, Mailer suggests, it succeeds only by compassion, not by making us recognize our guilt.

If Mailer is oblivious to the similarities between his heroes and the anti-heroes and if he is somewhat confused rather than consistent and precise in his charges against his "competitors," he does draw an essential distinction. His heroes are different. They are "up to their nostrils" in their exertions to advance their own lives and to pursue growth. The anti-heroes tend to stumble or retreat merely toward a code of survival in an absurd world. But if we amplify the real similarities as well as the differences before going further, we may approach a clearer definition of the Mailer hero. In his *The Absurd Hero in American Fiction*, David Galloway considers Updike,

Styron, Bellow, and Salinger and offers useful insights that should help us avoid some of the oversimplifications Mailer himself commits as he takes on his contemporaries.

The similarities between the absurd hero, as Galloway has concisely defined him, and the Mailer hero seem striking at first. Both are exiles, outlaws of their respective cultures. Both are on a "religious" quest, as Mailer himself acknowledges in the final pages of his "Goddess" essay. But a further definition is needed here. The religious quest of the absurd hero is limited to man's hunger for unity (his intention) in a disordered universe (the reality). Using Albert Camus's conception of the absurd man as he presented it in *The Myth of Sisyphus*, Galloway points out that this quest is religious simply because it seeks to fulfill a spiritual need in man for order against an omnipresent disorder. Both the absurd heroes and the Mailer heroes deny that conventional value systems and rationalism can resolve the conflict between intention and reality, and both, to the extent that they succeed, reject suicide as a solution to mankind's absurd situation. The absurd man is as wedded to life as the Mailer hero.

Also to both heroes, consciousness is of the greatest importance. Consciousness for the absurd hero is the awareness of his situation, of the absurdity of it. Absurd consciousness is therefore by its nature an abnormal expansion of awareness and an extraordinary act of the individual amongst the mass of his or her species. Camus calls this consciousness the "weariness tinged with amazement." The absurd hero's vision of the irrationality and the spiritual sterility of his environment is the fundamental fact of his awareness. The hero's refusal to avoid either his intention to seek unity or to deny the chaotic, sterile reality is the basis of his heroism (his heroic endurance) and the essence of his "absurd" position.[1]

Unlike the absurd novelists that Galloway discusses, Mailer envisions a reality that reflects his intention. And this difference is crucial. Mailer and his heroes are on a quest for absolute value or truth, which Mailer calls variously Life, Vision, or God. The chaos and directionless force in the cosmos are not for Mailer the whole cosmos but one element of it. The opposing element is Life, or the order and purpose of creation. As we have seen, chaos and order, Devil and God, are at war on the smallest and grandest of scales. And for Mailer, right and wrong have not entirely lost their ancient names and become meaningless. On the basis of his faith that God's vision gives purpose to life, Mailer disavows the absurdity of disease

1. I am summarizing in these paragraphs the conclusions of David Galloway's complete study that represent points of convergence with my own study of Mailer. See *The Absurd Hero in American Fiction*, especially pp. 5–17.

and death and, therefore, of life (see *CC*, p. 311). God is not all-powerful but at war. Only if he were all-powerful, Mailer argues in *Existential Errands*, would the "monumental disproportions and injustices" of life be absurd (p. 252).

The absurd novelists and their heroes face the lack of meaning and hope in a world without God; their victories and defeats are restricted to the personal sphere. Updike's heroes, like "Rabbit" Angstrom, find value for living in love as a communion of the flesh. But Rabbit's fulfillment arises from fleeing the sterile environment. As Mailer puts it: "his character bolts." David Galloway points out that as Bellow's heroes develop, their quest for life or value is restricted to the individual, not expanded to God-in-the-individual. Herzog's final peace, what he calls his "human life," is that he can accept what he despises and still live. If his sin was a pedantic detachment from life, his salvation is merely "to be," to accept a chaotic reality *and* his own life, and to hope for future engagement. But Mailer defines Life differently.

If the absurd hero portrays man finally appealing to himself, as Mailer's heroes do, to find Life, the absurd hero does not find in himself the divine energy or the eternal, purposive, creative, and transpersonal force of some élan vital or, to use Mailer's word, It. The affirmation of the self in a godless world is the defiance of the absurd hero and the goal of his religious quest. Unlike the absurd man, Mailer boldly directs his defiance against Death and disorder, and Mailer's and his heroes' defiance supply the energy for the quest for God and for the quest to establish a new order beyond the self.

Mailer's quest and the quests of his heroes have moved closer to the quests of the mythological heroes of the past. For more than a century, those who have specifically studied the hero phenomenon in the heroic literature, mythology, and history of many epochs and cultures consider the heroic journey an inward quest for something larger than the self. Thomas Carlyle, Carl Jung, Joseph Campbell, and Erich Neumann, to name a few, see the heroic adventure as the archetypal return to the life-source within the individual. But the goal of that return into the self is the hero's reappearance in the world bearing the source—the divine source—of expansion, enlightenment, and nourishment of consciousness.

In the postindustrial nineteenth century, the hero and the heroic self are obvious concerns of a number of writers other than Carlyle—Emerson and Whitman, for example. But Carlyle, in particular, is studying precisely the same phenomenon as those twentieth-century writers: the nature of the hero throughout history. Carlyle's discoveries have a great deal in common with the discoveries of the twentieth-century mythologists, and by abstracting what is fundamental to them all and to Mailer, we can more precisely define the kind of heroism Mailer seeks. In particular, Mailer carries the concern with a special kind of consciousness into the late twentieth century. Jung and the post-Jungians not only illuminate Mailer's work, they are interested in the same issue as Mailer—the human urge to transcendence and expanded consciousness in the postindustrial world. For all of these writers the urge to transcendence has a larger foundation and a greater potential than it does for twentieth-century existentialists. In his study of this "monomyth" in *The Hero with a Thousand Faces*, Joseph Campbell summarizes the nature of this archetypal heroic journey. Once the hero, voluntarily or not, passes the "threshold of adventure," he has dipped into the realm of the unconscious life-source.

> There he encounters a shadow presence that guards the passage. The hero may defeat or conciliate this power and go alive into the kingdom of the dark (brother-battle, dragon-battle; offering, charm), or be slain by the opponent and descend in death (dismemberment, crucifixion). Beyond the threshold, then, the hero journeys through a world of unfamiliar yet strangely intimate forces, some of which severely threaten him (tests), some of which give magical aid (helpers). When he arrives at the nadir of the mythological round, he undergoes a supreme ordeal and gains his reward. The triumph may be represented as the hero's sexual union with the goddess-mother of the world (sacred marriage), his recognition by the father-creator (father atonement), his divinization (apotheosis), or again—if the powers have remained unfriendly to him—his theft of the boon he came to gain (bride-theft, fire theft); intrinsically it is an expansion of consciousness and therewith of being (illumination, transfiguration, freedom). The final work is that of the return. . . . At the return threshold the transcendental powers must remain behind; the hero reemerges from the kingdom of dread (return, resurrection). The boon that he brings restores the world (elixir). (pp. 245–46)

"The changes," Campbell continues, "rung on the simple scale of the monomyth defy description." A tale may isolate and enlarge one or two steps of the heroic cycle, for example. But always the hero turns to the source of life and undergoes a test or battle to regain life. Above all in importance is the boon of expanded consciousness won from the unconscious kingdom of dread, for that is the elixir to change the self and the world. This is the heroic boon sought throughout "revolutionary history," in Carlyle's words. We could generally define *heroic consciousness* as that consciousness which synthesizes the resources both of the conscious and unconscious psyche. But as Mailer depicts and describes it, heroic consciousness has five principal qualities. The first two qualities are components of heroic consciousness in itself: metaphorical perception and divine energy. The other three qualities define the relationship of heroic consciousness to society. Heroic consciousness is revolutionary, it redresses the imbalance between conscious and unconscious pscyhe in contemporary mankind, and it is discovered and carried into the world by the extraordinary individual.

The immediate goal Mailer's heroes seek is metaphorical perception, which is to say, a perception that has the capacity to see relations, connections, and telepathies between things, people, actions, and between parts and wholes. Metaphorical consciousness is a result of the fusion of the unconscious or intuitive organs of perception with those that are conscious or rational. In *Barbary Shore*, McLeod calls this perception "metaphorical vision," and that novel represents Mailer's first step in defining the metaphorical quality of a new consciousness. McLeod's perception of his own guilt in the decreativeness of the postwar world is the metaphorical end that reveals to him his true relationship with that world, the context in which to see himself and others. Death in *Barbary Shore* is loss of metaphorical perception, a loss characterized by Hollingsworth's realism—the rational consciousness of only isolated facts and statistics.

In *The Deer Park*, Sergius also discovers his real potential by observing the rise and fall of the old man. And we have seen that Sergius seeks a potential or consciousness that penetrates the surface of an unreal world, sees the connections between things in the "real" world beneath, and faces the consequences of one's actions and life as a result of such vision. Mailer, like Thomas Carlyle, defines the chief attribute of the hero in *The Deer Park* as the capacity to look beyond the visible facade of things and into them. The "seeing eye" is the basis of Carlyle's and Mailer's heroic consciousness, which Carlyle believes to be "not the result of habits or accidents, but the gift of Nature herself; the primary outfit for a Heroic Man." For both Mailer and Carlyle, the hero's imagination or "Power of Insight" is the effect of the "vital Force which dwells in him" and the source of his "moral quality." Carlyle also argues that this power of insight, heroic consciousness, integrates the rational and prerational, the moral and the courageous, in a single act of perception.[2]

In the 1950s and early 1960s Mailer continuously emphasized a similar point about the moral quality of the seeing eye that realizes

2. Thomas Carlyle, *On Heroes, Hero-Worship and the Heroic in History*, see especially pp. 55–56, 105–7. Carl Jung and Victor White associate expanded (heroic) consciousness with prophetic revelation and the prophet-hero. They also define "intuition" as the integration of unconscious and conscious psyche. See White's *God and the Unconscious*, pp. 178, 210.

the truths in the connections between things, connections which Mailer, in *Advertisements*, called "the quick flesh of associations." Notably in "The White Negro," Mailer argued that we live in a "dangerous moral condition" or "network of forces." It is the perception of this network that leads to the hero's perception that the "core of Life cannot be cheated." In *The Presidential Papers* he argued that the moral quality of heroic perception was that it draws sustenance from instinct (the vital force within) and that instinct comes from God.[3] Though Rojack's salvation is obviously bound up in such a network of forces and perceptions, Mailer uses D.J. the defeated hero to give fullest expression to his convictions about the moral economy and ecology of the divine forces and energies that connect all things below the surface of life. The health D.J. seeks is the "primitive health" that Joseph Campbell, in *Hero*, calls the perception of and belief in the relationships, the divine ecology, of all things animate and inanimate (p. 169).

Mailer's theories and his artistic practice often work toward the same goal of increasing metaphorical perceptions and awakening unconscious energy. We have seen in *An American Dream* especially how symbols function, often simultaneously, on diverse levels—the realistic, the rationally allegorical, and the mythic or visionary. When an image has timeless, mythological properties—as allegorical *potentiae* might—it is no longer a mere picture but, as both Campbell and Neumann point out, a "psychological image" or a "symbol" from the psyche. Mythological images are symbols that act as a bridge between the conscious and unconscious, that make unconscious energy available for conscious activity. If the symbol has a side that accords with rational consciousness, it also has a side that is inaccessible to rational consciousness. Because certain primordial images have latent meaning for the unconscious and because they appeal to the whole human, not just the rational elements of a being, they have always been used as metaphors for truths that cannot be discursively articulated by great teachers who seek to reach the whole human being, who seek to charge their readers or pupils with renewed psychic energies. Campbell calls such timeless images "psychological metaphors."[4] By comparing a woman to a goddess, and by defining her goddesslike attributes through various mythic images, Mailer uses mythic images as

3. *Advertisements for Myself* (hereafter cited as *Ads*), p. 385; *The Presidential Papers*, p. 194. Unless otherwise indicated, all citations are to works by Norman Mailer.
4. See Joseph Campbell's *The Hero with a Thousand Faces*, pp. 173–78; Erich Neumann's *The Origins and History of Consciousness*, pp. 7, 365–69; and Carl Jung's *Symbols of Transformation*, translated by R. F. C. Hull, Vol. 5 (New Jersey: Princeton University Press, 1956), pp. 124, 232.

psychological metaphors to give the largest possible connotations and associations to his work and to awaken latent unconscious energies that a simply literal realism might not.

The second quality of heroic consciousness is just this awakening of psychic energies, which Mailer associates with divine energy. With the publication of *The Deer Park* and the external commentary that begins in *Advertisements,* Mailer's quest for heroic consciousness shifts slightly in emphasis toward an exploration into the secrets of human energy. I argued that we could see *The Deer Park* as a series of attempted "regressions" to the source of one's being. Eitel's failure is not so much a failure of vision as a failure to tap the inner resources necessary to sustain his vision and live by it.

While it is true that for both Lovett and Sergius the effect of increased consciousness is metaphorical vision and penetrating perception, the lessons Sergius draws from what he observes and from his parallel temptations depend more upon his search for some substance or power within. The potency of the self is continually opposed to the potency of "the world" in *The Deer Park.* Self-potency is the basis of Marion's and, finally, Sergius's defiance of the forces of restricted consciousness and falsehood, and self-potency is the basis of Sergius's personal growth. *The Deer Park,* then, begins to explore the reciprocal relationship between energy and vision. Sergius's courage and his choice to forego the rewards of "the world" depend upon his vision of the truth of real connections below the facade. Each time Sergius sees or is reminded of this truth, he regains the energy necessary to continue penetrating the facade and to rebel against it.

But if Mailer begins to suggest the energetic qualities of sustained, expanded consciousness and its consequences in *The Deer Park,* he depicts merely tentative and failed acts of defiance. It is only after this novel, beginning with *Advertisements,* that unconscious or instinctual energy, which will be the source of self-creation and rebellion, clearly becomes the divine energy within. We saw Mailer propose that the unconscious is "conceivably" divine in *Advertisements.* And, consciously or not, Mailer's hipsters in "The White Negro," "The Time of Her Time," and "Advertisements on The Way Out" view or feel their destinies to be "flesh and blood" with God's. Their search for energy is the search for divine energy. By the time Mailer writes the "dialogues" collected in *The Presidential Papers* and in *Cannibals,* he defines unconscious perceptions as agencies of associative truth and divine energy. He frankly calls the unconscious the "soul."

Yet until Rojack appears in *Dream,* Mailer does not demonstrate how the hero's journey into his deepest energies results in specific acts of self-creation. Lovett and Sergius are relatively passive. With Rojack, however, the quest for energy, depicted through the myth-ological imagery of the Night Sea Journey and the Nourishing Mother, combines with the consequences of the quest: expanded vision, self-creation, and defiance. Rojack channels instinctual energy into will through the authenticity he gains. When he faces the judgment of Cherry's womb or faces the awful temptations and powers of Kelly, or when he walks the parapet alone, Rojack engages in successive acts of courage that free the power of unconscious energy ("grace") and expand the proportions of his soul or being.

Since, as we have seen, this novel is an allegory containing numer-ous mythological motifs or archetypes, it is especially appropriate that Mailer should personify soul-energy in the anima-figure Cherry. She is the culmination of two other tentative and less vividly drawn female *potentiae*. As another indication that Mailer combines the journey into self with specific resultant acts of self-creation, Cherry is not ancillary but central to the hero's quest. Rojack's bride-winning is a clear point at which Rojack and the mythic heroes of the past converge. Erich Neumann has argued that the winning of the soul is the fundamental mythological act of reuniting unconscious life and "ego-consciousness." The hero must conquer his fear of the soul's power and turn that fear to joy; he must "snatch new territory from the unconscious" and place it within the power of consciousness; he must join two ways of perceiving the world—the rational and the prerational. And it is in separating the light anima from the dark mother that the hero perceives and acts to attain his goal of nourishment through soul-energy. The symbolic marriage of hero and bride, as of Rojack and Cherry, is the marriage of inner and outer worlds.[5] Perhaps the most important point for this discussion is that we can now see *Dream* as a fusion of Mailer's avowed goal of creating a new consciousness and his embodiment of the processes of that consciousness in his art. It is by portraying the hero's quest for his soul or divine energy, which is our second quality of heroic consciousness, that Mailer connects his narrative with ancient and timeless heroic mythology and, as we have seen, with allegory generally. A century before the modern mythologists and psy-

5. Carl Jung, *Aion: Researches into the Phenomenology of the Self*, translated by R. F. C. Hull, Vol. 9 (New Jersey: Princeton University Press, 1951), p. 35. Compare Mailer's hypothesis in *Cannibals and Christians* that each of us has male and female principles within, and that the male principle is primitively defined as virility and strength of the ego which stands against that which threatens the self from within and without. See Erich Neumann, *Consciousness*, especially pp. 137, 204, 208, 210–13, 269, 318, 343, 379.

chologists, Carlyle described the heroic quest as the quest for soul-energy on the basis of his research as much as his faith.[6] And twentieth-century depth psychology and mythology both conclude, as Campbell and White point out, that the "sacred zone of the universal source" in which the exploits of heroes take place is both psychic and cosmic. In their intercourse with psychic images as *potentiae*, the heroes have always sought not the gods or goddesses themselves, but the "grace," the "the power," the "miraculous energy substance" they incarnate.[7]

This search for divine energy is inseparable from our third quality of heroic consciousness, which defines one aspect of the relationship of heroic consciousness to society. For Mailer's heroes, heroic consciousness is revolutionary consciousness, just as it was for the "historical" and mythological heroes of the past. From McLeod's "metaphysical" version of "revolutionary socialism," to Sergius's rebellious trumpet of defiance and Faye's cataclysmic hipsterism, to Rojack's dream of tearing down the city of the damned, and D.J.'s thwarted desire to slay and transcend the tyrant father and the bestial civilization he represents, Mailer's fictional heroes are revolutionaries in the sense that founders of cultures and religions are always "creative" revolutionaries. Such heroes are at once conservative and radical, as Mailer frankly believes he is himself, and as he stresses in the nonfiction of the late sixties and early seventies. These heroes are conservative in the sense that they would return humanity to fundamental truths even if it means reversing a "progress" that is mechanistic. The principal truth is that divine energy is the animating force behind the phenomenal world. They are radical in the sense that they are committed to the destruction of a civilization that has become static and/or mechanistic and that restricts conscious perception so that it sees the human being only as one mechanism or fact-in-itself within a larger world-machine. A point

6. Carlyle, *On Heroes*, pp. 8, 80, 108–12, 115.
7. See Campbell's *Hero*, pp. 81, 181, 243, 258–60. Compare Campbell with Victor White's study of Jungian psychology in *God and the Unconscious*, pp. 46, 72, 98, 135. White argues that depth psychology—by which he means analytical psychology—again and again exposes the "gods" we thought dead. They seem to be ineluctable, pervasive powers within. White compares Jungian *libido* energy with the God-as-formless-energy in traditional metaphysics. Revelation and beatific vision, White argues, are the expression of God in the unconscious. Compare also Erich Neumann's point that the gods themselves change as the energy is transformed and tapped more and more by consciousness. See Neumann, *Consciousness*, pp. 324–26. Paul Piehler also expresses the view that if we make full allowance for the differences of approach appropriate to the Christian mystic and the modern depth-psychologist, the visionary experiences both described are "about the same phenomena," i.e., "individuation." See *The Visionary Landscape*, especially pp. 159–60.

central to both Carlyle's and Mailer's conception of the hero, for
example, is that the hero would turn the World-Machine into the
living Tree Igdrasil. In his "Open Letter to Richard Nixon," Mailer
emphasizes the mechanistic disproportions of the contemporary
world: "There is a crisis in the world today which comes out of the
massive over-development of the machine before we have com-
prehended its excesses, or even how to dispose of its wastes."[8] The
hero's practical task has always been to subvert the status quo so that
an influx of divine energy can make the world live and grow again, as
Mailer has said, out toward whatever created us wishes us to be. If
the hero is the agent of violence, destruction, and chaos, Mircea
Eliade argues, he is also the agent of creation. Eliade's mythic hero is
a cosmic figure engaged in battle with Evil, with what is ultimately
De-creative. The hero's duty as an imitator of the heroic archetype is
to "regenerate time."[9] In *Cannibals* Mailer says that he does not
want to be disruptive for "the sake of disruption," but that his
function as a novelist is to be dangerous to the status quo. "Actually," he adds, "I have a fondness for order" (p. 220).

Though we have seen that *The Deer Park* tentatively explored
rebellion, violence, and cataclysmic destruction as ways of self and
world renewal, it is only in *Advertisements* that Mailer explicitly
argues that the instinct to rebel against the existing order is fundamental to life and evolution. Particularly in his discussion of
psychologist Robert Lidner's *Must You Conform*, Mailer argues in the
Village Voice that:

> It is this instinct that underwrites his survival, this instinct from
> which he derives his nature: a great and powerful dynamic that
> makes him what he is—restless, seeking, curious, forever unsatisfied,
> eternally struggling and eventually victorious. Because of the instinct

8. Carlyle, *On Heroes*, p. 173. The Mailer quotation is from *Existential Errands:
Twenty-Six Pieces Selected by the Author from the Body of All His Writings*, p. 319.
Neumann, agreeing with Jung's view of the artist, points out that the hero is both
progressive and conservative. The artist as hero seeks to restore a balance to his age
by compensating for the one-sidedness in the "spirit of the age." By doing so he
shatters the existing values and establishes new provinces of consciousness. As
with Carlyle, sincerity and intensity are the prime criteria of the revolutionary's
value: "The depth of the unconscious layer from which the new springs, and the
intensity with which this layer seizes upon the individual, are the real criteria of
this summons by the voice, and not the ideology of the conscious mind," see
Consciousness, p. 377.
9. Mircea Eliade, *The Myth of the Eternal Return*, pp. 35–47, 55–57, 69, 87–88.
Compare Neumann, *Consciousness*, p. 381. The hero engages the "toils of his
culture" with "creative assault," destroys the old canon to build the new. Compare
also Carlyle, *On Heroes*, pp. 119, 122, 127, 135. Carlyle sees this repeated theme:
heroic history is revolutionary history. Times of unbelief are ever becoming times
of revolution and belief. For Carlyle the "revolutionary nation" would be a nation
of heroes and a believing nation.

of rebellion man has never been content with the limits of his mind. . . . Man is a rebel. He is committed by his biology *not* to conform, and herein lies the paramount reason for the awful tension he experiences in relation to Society. (*Ads*, p. 305)

An American Dream is, as we have seen, a further step in the fictional portrayal of rebellion and violence as vehicles of death and rebirth. And though later D.J. even fails at personal rebirth, Mailer does distinguish between satanic and divine violence in *Why Are We in Vietnam?* by juxtaposing the large, mechanistic, and impersonal violence of the safari to the primordial violence of the hunt and to the ceremonial test of endurance and growth. To whatever degree Mailer's heroes succeed or fail, they are all would-be revolutionaries. They come forth like the mythic heroes of the past to change the world, not to sustain it.[10] For both Campbell and Neumann the warning of violent change is characterized by the words of Jesus as much as it is by the violence of the archaic, heroic cycles, and for Carlyle by Mahomet, Dante, Luther, Rousseau, and Cromwell.

From the view of modern depth psychology, Jung, Campbell, and Neumann describe the hero's journey in the monomyth as an effort to restore a balance between ego and unconscious, to place some of the unconscious under the control, within the grasp, of conscious life. This impulse to restore a "wholeness" and balance to the self and society is our fourth quality of heroic consciousness. This fourth quality also helps define the relationship of heroic consciousness to society. We have seen that Mailer's program for turning Death into Life contains a number of elements that would readjust the balance between instinctual and rational life. And Mailer, like Carlyle and Campbell, emphasizes the spiritual dimension of the journey. As Campbell explains it, this regression is a source of regeneration because it represents man's return to his spiritual potential and restores spiritual significance to a dead world (*Hero*, p. 16).

If Mailer's "way" and the ways of his heroes to reestablish a balance in favor of unconscious experience and impulse, as the "way" does, say, in "The White Negro," are iconoclastic, often violent, or filled with what seems at first "slime from the depths," to borrow Jung's phrase, the goal is still balance. Mailer tends to see his unconscious emphasis as a necessary gathering of force to overcome

10. See Neumann, *Consciousness*, pp. 161, 252. The mythic and the allegorical heroes converge here, as in many ways allegory and myth converge. Both are embattled heroes dramatizing the soul's struggle for salvation through the fundamental pattern of rebirth. The allegorical hero, like the mythic hero, shows mankind how far it has fallen from what is taken to be fundamental truth, how great the spiritual and pscyhological distance is between that truth and man's present state. The mission of both heroes is redemption in a fallen world. See Edwin Honig, *Dark Conceit*, pp. 82, 99, 152.

the inertia of an unbalanced civilization. We have seen in *Cannibals* and in *Existential Errands*, that Mailer believes the dream to be one vehicle that can restore this balance to the two systems of psyche. This belief in the dream is a tenet of depth psychology espoused most clearly by Erich Neumann, in *The Origins and History of Consciousness* (see especially p. 372). And Rojack's "dream" is the best fictional incorporation of this tenet.

Mailer's concern with the relationship of the individual and expanded consciousness to society places him in an important tradition of literary and social thought. Wherever the spirit is dying, wherever one or another element of the self thrives at the expense of the whole self, the mythic hero emerges seeking to restore a balance. We have seen that this theme runs through the work of Jung, White, Eliade, Campbell, and Neumann—all of whom draw from multicultural sources. But since the end of the eighteenth century, when rationalism reached its apex and the scientific and industrial revolutions began to change the shape of human life, writers have continually sought to articulate the dangers of a disproportionate rationalism. Blake, who opposes the god of rationalism to a god of irrationality and human potential (living in bondage), is a fountainhead of this prevailing theme in Western thought. Carlyle is another source of the idea. His influence upon such writers as Emerson, Thoreau, and Ruskin, to name a few others in the tradition, is commonly known. All of these writers from the eighteenth through the twentieth centuries warn humanity of the dangers of its drift toward spiritual impoverishment, toward loss of unconscious life and soul, toward mechanization and totalitarianism. This is Mailer's warning, too. It is the central idea of his work. And it is upon this idea that he will have to base his claims to be a Jeremiah of his time.

Erich Neumann's post-Jungian work in mythology and psychology represents a kind of culmination of this warning and tradition in social and psychological thought, just as Mailer's work represents the twentieth-century culmination of a similar tradition in English and American literature. That the message of this tradition, as voiced by Erich Neumann, is both central and external to Mailer's work is the significant point. This point lends a certain credibility to Mailer's view of the imbalance and crisis of modern consciousness. Like Mailer, Neumann is especially interested in the psychic dynamics of this crisis. In a chapter entitled "The Balance and Crisis of Consciousness," Neumann examines the problems emerging from the separation of the conscious and unconscious systems. The evolutionary theme of his work is that such separation is a necessary product of evolution. But Neumann's consideration of the state of that evolution as reflected in contemporary history and life leads him to warn that the separation has degenerated to a schism at a time when we most need a rapprochement. Like Mailer, Neumann considers the "degeneration of the group into the mass" as symptomatic of the crisis.

To return from the mass collective to the group is also the goal of Mailer's political ambitions. One is easily tempted to see Mailer dreaming of the presidency—as he first tells us he has in the opening lines of *Advertisements*—or Mailer announcing his candidacy for mayor in 1960 and running a hard campaign for mayor of New York City in 1969, as mere exercises in megalomania. But Mailer specifically argues that his candidacy is a real chance for him to actively repay his "debt to society." His goal is not to gain power for himself, but quite clearly to restore it to others, and to restore vitality and power specifically to the group and to take it away from the deadening mass. Giving autonomous political power to the neighborhoods and to ideological communities is the basis of his program for restoring power to the group. This program is Mailer's brand of pluralism, which he suggested in his campaign as an immediate solution to the city's political and economic disasters. "We might begin to discover which political ideas had validity, the power to continue themselves, and those ideas which, finally, were surrealistic, nihilistic, excessive, and destructive to the ultimate aims of society, which is finally to find some balance in the lives of men and women." The specifics of his proposal and the argument for it are collected in *Existential Errands* in "An Instrument for the City," "Two Mayorality Speeches," and "To the *Time-Life* Staff"(pp. 322–62).

The degeneration of the group into the mass, Neumann points out, throws the claims of individual and society out of balance everywhere. Neumann, like Jung as well as Mailer, sees the artist's function as restoring the balance between individual and society by restoring the balance between ego and unconscious. Though the evolutionary movement of man in history as well as in each individual is ever away from the bonds of the unconscious, the ego must never lose touch with instinctual life. "Like all differentiation," Neumann writes, "it runs the risk of becoming overdifferentiated and perverse." If the hero loses his nourishing link to instinctual life, he deteriorates. This deterioration is what Neumann means by "patriarchal castration," which is true megalomania and which Rusty's relationship to D J. and to Nature archetypally depicts. Neumann characterizes such "megalomania" as ego-inflation, loss of connection with one's body or instincts, inflation of the intellect or of rationalism, inflation of the status quo, inability to react to sense-images, and the "hypertrophied consciousness" or spiritual sterility of the age of the machine and of mass man. This degeneration of the self, Neumann calls "sclerosis of consciousness."[11] Near the end of his study of the evolutionary rise of "heroic consciousness" and the dangers of its fall, Neumann specifies the character of the modern crisis of consciousness in words and examples familiar to Mailer's readers, especially to those who have read *Why*.

> Typical . . . is the state of affairs in America, though the same holds good for practically the whole Western hemisphere. Every conceivable sort of dominant rules the personality, which is personality only in name. The grotesque fact that murderers, brigands, gangsters, thieves, forgers, tyrants and swindlers, in a guise that deceives nobody, have seized control of collective life is characteristic of our time. . . . Worship of the "beast" is by no means confined to Germany; it prevails wherever one-sidedness, push, and moral blindness are applauded; i.e., wherever the aggravating complexities of civilized behavior are swept away in favor of bestial rapacity. . . .
>
> The possessed character of our financial and industrial magnates, for instance, is pscychologically evident from the very fact that they are at the mercy of a suprapersonal factor—"work," "power," "money," or whatever they like to call it—which . . . "consumes" them. . . . Coupled with a nihilistic attitude towards civilization and humanity there goes a puffing up of the ego-sphere which expresses itself with brutish egotism in a total disregard for the common good and in the attempt to lead an egocentric existence, where personal power, money, and "experiences"—unbelievably trivial, but plentiful—occupy every hour of the day. . . . and "isms" of every description take possession of the masses and destroy the individual. . . . The disintegration caused by an idea is no less dangerous than the disintegration caused by the empty, personalistic power-strivings. . . . we have attempted to show the connection between depth psychology and the new ethos. One of the most important consequences of the new ethos is that integration of the personality, its wholeness, becomes the supreme ethical goal upon which the fate of humanity depends. (*Consciousness*, pp. 391–92)

Mailer is close to Neumann here: true civilization is a civilization

11. Neumann, *Consciousness*, especially pp. 88, 220–21, 262, 286, 382–93. Compare Honig, *Dark Conceit*, p. 173. The heroic ordeal of allegory is the quest for "integration" and for the affirmation by which societies hope to survive. Victor White in *God and the Unconscious* suggests that the most advanced physics and science are preparing us now to sacrifice the very intellect we thought alone could save us. For White the Fall is the loss of unconscious nourishment or of God's grace, a loss which leads to the disintegration of self and society, pp. 32, 98. Compare Campbell also, *Hero*, pp. 258–60.

of "life." Life for the individual is the wholeness and balance of the total self. In *Papers*, Mailer says that to be open to the unconscious is to be "enormously civilized" (p. 130). And in *Existential Errands*, he adds that the first spiritual problem of the twentieth century is alienation from the self. Authentic action, even if dangerous, extreme, or violent, may be necessary to return us to our selves (p. 334). True power is the power of the self, not the manipulating power of the totalitarian. This is the lesson Rojack learns in his success, and the lesson the reader sees in D.J.'s defeat. Mailer continually depicts totalitarianism's disproportionate power-strivings and opposes it with the power of the authentic, whole self. Against such agents of disproportion as Hollingsworth, Teppis, Kelly, and Rusty, Mailer places McLeod and Lovett, Sergius, Rojack, and the defeated D.J. In the context of his own warning, Neumann explains that he is not "glorifying the past" but describing the "symptoms of an upheaval," of which the "predatory industrial man" and the "power politician" are but a few. Neumann's optimism, which perhaps is more consistently buoyant than Mailer's, is that the collapse of Western civilization is a preparation for a new order, but, like Mailer's, Neumann's affirmation is guarded. Whether the way beyond the collapse, our "fate," leads to life or to death depends upon our capacity for a rapprochement between our conscious and unconscious life. Standing between an inner world that threatens to overwhelm him and an outer world that threatens to "suffocate" him, the hero today may need to be as extraordinary an individual as the hero of myth or history (*Consciousness*, especially pp. 380–81).

Considering how many of Mailer's contemporaries see him, and considering how Mailer will increasingly play the heroic role himself in his nonfiction, we should distinguish between the necessarily strong ego stability or self-assertion of the embattled hero and the megalomania of "hypertrophied consciousness." Even Carlyle, in the years before depth psychology, makes a similar distinction. It is not the sugar plums of power and luxury in the world, Carlyle points out, that lead the hero to speak his truth or do his deed, but his vision of the worthiness of his call, the challenge of danger, difficulty, agony, and expulsion that lead him forward to his task. Carlyle argues simply that he who is open to the divine significance of life must speak of it; the hero's goal of leading others toward that significance is the end in itself. This goal Carlyle specifically opposes to the pride of "ego consciousness" embodied in the mechanistic science of his day: "Knowledge without worship is pedantry" (see *On Heroes*, pp. 69–70, 115). Campbell makes the same distinction. He agrees with Arnold Toynbee that the assertion of the hero is not simply the assertion of "egotism," for egotism is the assertion of the tyrant Holdfast. Heroic assertion is, rather, a submission to the power and necessity of rebirth through the return to the sources of life. The hero does not, like the ego-tyrant, seek to control life and nature, but, as an extraordinary individual, seeks to realize what is, and to show what is to others (see *Hero*, pp. 16, 383–86).

In his novels and throughout *Papers* and *Cannibals*, Mailer has sought to distinguish between the egocentricity of heroic types necessary for a dynamic society and the arrogant separation of mankind from nature and the lust to control nature (*CC*, pp. 3, 79). In *Existential Errands* Mailer defines megalomania best when he describes *Why Are We in Vietnam?* as the depiction of twentieth-century arrogance, which is the Faustian desire to control nature (pp. 221, 292). So self-confidence in the hero or artist is faith in what Mailer has called one's "vision of existence"; it is a prerequisite of heroic action and valor and a necessary attribute of any ambitious writer.

This faith in the extraordinary individual is the fifth quality of heroic consciousness. There is something fundamentally "romantic" as well as archetypal about Mailer's faith in the intensity, power, and truth of the subjective perceptions of heroic or tested individuals. Mailer sustains the paradox—perhaps we should say dialectic—of the hierarchic and democratic impulses of romanticism as well as myth. Mailer does not deny the potential in men and women to achieve expanded consciousness, but he feels dubious about the capacity of each person alone to realize this potential against the onslaughts of the deadening world. His novels are saturated with defeats, often with the defeat of considerable potential, as in the case of Elena or D.J., and his heroes' successes are provisional and earned by severe trial. In his commentaries no less than his novels, Mailer expresses little doubt about the necessity of a hero for his time. His candidates for heroism are as apparently diverse as Ernest Hemingway, John Kennedy, and Fidel Castro.

In *Papers*, Mailer most specifically discusses the hero and the myth that the modern hero must awaken. His essay on the existential hero, entitled "Superman Comes to the Supermarket," argues that the frontier that remains to be conquered is the psychological frontier. This frontier is "still alive with possibilities." To lead his people on the exploration of that frontier, a hero, such as John Kennedy may become, has to create a new psychological reality by giving a new direction to his time, by encouraging his nation to discover the "deepest colors of its character," and by altering the nature of history (pp. 41–42). Mailer is committed to the hope that every living impulse of our instinctual life, which he calls our "underground river," will struggle against the degeneration of individual man to mass man.[12]

America was also the country in which the dynamic myth of the Renaissance—that every man was potentially extraordinary—knew its most passionate persistence. Simply, America was the land where people believed in heroes. . . . It was a country which had grown by the leap of one hero past another. . . . And when the West was filled, the expansion turned inward, became part of an agitated, overexcited, superheated dream life. . . . the romantic possibilities of the old conquest of land turned into a vertical myth, trapped within the skull, of a new kind of heroic life, each choosing his own archetype of a neo-Renaissance man. . . . And this myth, that each of us was born to be free, to wander, to have adventure and to grow on the waves of the violent, the perfumed, and the unexpected, had a force which could not be tamed no matter how the nation's regulators—politicians, medicos, policemen, professors, priests, rabbis, ministers, *idéologues*, psychoanalysts, builders, executives and endless communicators—would brick-in modern life with hygiene upon sanity, and middle-brow homily over platitude; the myth would not die. . . . as if the message in the labyrinth of the genes would insist that violence was locked with creativity, and adventure was the secret of love. (*PP*, pp. 39–40)

Mailer consistently argues that after World War II misguided social legislating and psychological engineering have exacerbated the schism between instinctual life and the public mind of the nation. In particular, the politics of the nation have too far separated from the myth of expansion, freedom, and individual growth. Mailer maintains that the period of Kennedy's rise to power was a period of the nation's collective search for a man who could capture the "secret imagination" of a people. The first quality of Mailer's personal heroes is that they embody the people's fantasy of freedom, adventure, and growth. Like Carlyle, Mailer is deeply suspicious of the machinery of progress and far more likely to found his hope of making a whole people "more extraordinary" on the extraordinary

12. Neumann is subtle and complicated on the nature of the Fall to the "mass collective" and on mankind's recovery. He sees in the "psychologically reactionary massing together of modern man" the possible birth throes of a "new canon." His central point is, however, not far from Mailer's view as expressed in the quotation that follows in my text. Neumann writes that "the sanctity of the individual soul which asserted itself throughout the Middle Ages in spite of all orthodoxy and all burnings of heretics, has become secularized since the Renaissance, though it was in existence long before that. It is the same with the accentuation of individual consciousness . . . . there must inevitably be a temporary leveling down of consciousness and of individual culture in comparison with the single individual as the end product of Western Civilization since the Renaissance.

"The four phenomena—aggregation of masses, decay of the old canon, the schism between conscious and the unconscious, and the divorce between the individual and the collective—run parallel to one another" (pp. 382–83).

individual who is fit for courageous, adventurous action and battle in a time of crisis and schism. "At bottom the concept of the hero is antagonistic to impersonal social progress, to the belief that social ills can be solved by social legislating, for it sees a country as all-but-trapped in its character until it has a hero who reveals the character of the country to itself" (PP, p. 42). Carlyle phrased the idea more extremely: "We shall either learn to know a Hero, a true Governor and Captain, somewhat better, when we see him; or else go on to be for ever governed by the Unheroic;—had we ballot-boxes clattering at every street corner, there were no remedy in these."[13] The hero is at the root of Mailer's "existential politics," for it is he who battles the faceless disproportions of our time through a "consecutive set of brave and witty self-creations." As he captures our secret imagination, as he bravely creates himself and promotes our growth, the hero leads his nation toward a healing beyond schism and plague (PP, pp. 5–7). Consciousness is in effect, Neumann points out, one of Life's experimental organs, and the Great Individual as a bearer of greater consciousness promotes cultural evolution and individual development (see Consciousness, pp. 35–36).

Gradually, however, in Papers, it becomes clear that, for Mailer, such men as Hemingway, Kennedy, and Castro are in all probability unequal to the task of becoming heroes for their time. Mailer has had more difficulty finding real heroes than fictional heroes. But as early as 1955 we begin to see Mailer himself preparing, for lack of another hero, to enter the lists. He helped found the Village Voice, a landmark of "alternative journalism," in 1954, and his column appeared in that paper from 1955 to 1956. In his column Mailer articulates his decision to go to war with mass media. This column, much of it collected in Advertisements, is often shrill and, as Mailer admits, poorly written, but it announces his candidacy as an embattled, existential hero at war with the weaknesses in himself and the defeating forces in contemporary society. He hopes "above all else to change a hundred self-defeating habits which locked my character into a space too narrow for what I wanted to become," but, Mailer

13. Carlyle, On Heroes, p. 217. Campbell says essentially the same thing in Hero, p. 16. Schism in soul and society cannot be resolved by the manipulation of secondary effects. "Only birth can conquer death—the birth, not of the old thing again, but of something new. Within the soul, within the body social, there must be—if we are to experience long survival—a continuous 'recurrence of birth' . . . to nullify the unremitting recurrences of death." For Campbell, also, this is the job of the hero today as ever: "a transmutation of the whole order is necessary, so that through every detail and act of secular life the vitalizing image of the universal god-man who is actually immanent and effective in all of us may be somehow made known to consciousness." A people's yearning for a hero is its yearning beyond a fallen life, beyond a life that is a depthless, flat world of the ego alone (pp. 308, 388–89).

writes, "at heart, I wanted war." The *Voice* is to be his field of battle.
His column is to be a "first lick of fire in a new American consciousness." He adds in an "advertisement" that writing for the *Voice* leads
him to "rediscover" his desire to be "a hero of my time" because the
one "noble emotion" rising from the frantic prose is his "rage
against the national conformity which smothered creativity, for it
delayed the self-creation of the race."[14] If Marcus Klein's argument is
correct that in postwar America the "we" and the "they" have been
obscured or have disappeared, if the enemy is no longer "high" and
"low" as it appeared to be for the writers of the twenties and thirties,
and if the postwar novel has tended merely to express "the state of
nerves" of the individual in a faceless, mass society, Mailer's original-
ity as a writer may be in his efforts to define the enemy.[15] Mailer's
early forays into enemy territory in the 1950s as the zany, outraged
"General Marijuana" represent the most outrageous portion of his
career. The bad-boy image, suggesting disruption for its own sake,
promoted by his "warrior's" antics during this decade has stayed
with him in the popular mind, and it too often obscures the issue of
just what Mailer is saying about the civilization in which he lives.

From the *Voice* onward, Mailer continues to see his work as war.
He defines war as the quest for the mysteries of existence and self
which oppose the totalitarian culture that would destroy all mystery. Just as he described "form" as the "record of a war" in *Cannibals*, he describes it here as the study of "energy and entropy." The
"Evil" in his novels has been stasis and those characters and forces
attempting to make everything static, and the "Evil" in his nonfiction is also stasis. "My passion," he writes, "is to destroy stereotype,
categories, and labels" (*Ads*, pp. 310, 325, 428). In this statement
Mailer refers to the specific persons, institutions, and forces that
either are static or that promote stasis and make "stereotypes"
active agents in our culture. It is clear that this passion to destroy
specific stereotypes and to depict fictionally the stereotype as a
negative person or force exists in a somewhat paradoxical relation-

14. *Ads*, pp. 277–78, 283, 284. Future references are parenthetical. Compare
Emerson's "Self-Reliance": "Society everywhere is in conspiracy against the manhood of every one of its members. Society is a joint-stock company, in which the
members agree, for the better securing of his bread to each shareholder, to
surrender the liberty and culture of the eater. The virtue most in request is
conformity. Self-reliance is its aversion. It loves not realities and creators, but
names and customs. Whoso would be a man, must be a nonconformist . . . .
Nothing is at last sacred but the integrity of your own mind." See Stephen Whicher,
Selections from Ralph Waldo Emerson, p. 149. Mailer's contrast between security
and self-integrity is a repeated theme, but Emerson of course emphasizes the
benign self-creation of transcendentalism, not the violence of revolutionary consciousness in mythic heroes.
15. See Marcus Klein's introduction to *The American Novel Since World War II*,
pp. 11, 14–15, 20–21.

ship to the larger themes of his novels. For by discovering what promotes Life and what Death, his heroes learn to perceive, which is to "label" in an ethic of ultimate values, the Good and Evil in institutions and others. This juxtaposition of finite stereotypes and ultimate values is not a blatant contradiction when we consider that God or Life is defined as anti-stasis or growth, but the juxtaposition presents a difficulty in Mailer's work that the nonfiction will approach with greater subtlety.

With Mailer's attention turned full-time to the production of nonfiction in the late sixties and the seventies, we see a reflection of the writer's own doubts about the capacity of purely imaginative writing to stimulate the actions necessitated by the extremity of the moral choices, dilemmas, and disproportions facing contemporary humanity. And the desire to stimulate action is the root of allegorical didacticism. It is as if the gap between fictional art and real action continually and dangerously widens for Mailer and forces him to make ever bolder and more difficult personal moral choices as he reassesses the relationship of his art to his life and to ours.

On one side we see Mailer's convictions about the function of art and the artist. Writing in the *Voice* of Beckett's *Godot*, Mailer asserts that the role of the artist is to increase consciousness and, as he does so, to "accelerate historical time itself." For Mailer, history is the progress of consciousness as it alters society. The velocity of history is directly related to the velocity of expanding consciousness (*Ads*, p. 324). The writer or hero who increases consciousness, therefore, accelerates history itself. In *Papers* Mailer defines history as God's creative power taking form (p. 193). In *Cannibals*, what Mailer means by history is the progress of God's vision. So redeemed time or history is the only true history for Mailer; the rest is stasis and Fall. The point to see here is that in the 1950s Mailer already viewed the writer as a potential hero for his time who might accelerate consciousness and redeem time.

In the 1960s the artist again emerges as a potential generator of expanded consciousness. Against the "moral poltroons" in political life, Mailer contrasts the artist who, through the exercise of his talent, embodies what is best in a nation, its dreams. It is the duty of culture, which is an expression of the artist's talent rather than his character, "to enrich the psyche, not just part of us." Art, he goes on to argue, is at least as necessary to civilization as any of our technology. If art is "dangerous," we still cannot afford to give up its enrichment (*PP*, pp. 69, 91–92). And in *Cannibals*, Mailer presents himself as an artist-hero and "physician" who tries to communicate his "vision of existence" as an antidote to the plague of his time (pp. 5, 218).

But on the other side we see Mailer's concern with the difficulty, perhaps the impossibility, of insuring that art becomes action, that art and action are one. *Advertisements*, as Laura Adams has pointed out, is Mailer's literary manifesto.[16] Though Mailer placed his hopes for new action and work on the "seed" of "The White Negro" (p. 331), the final note he strikes in his manifesto is a note of self-doubt. He is questioning here whether his work through *The Deer Park* is a large enough and dangerous enough act. "Fitzgerald was an indifferent caretaker of his talent, and I have been a cheap gambler with mine."

The Presidential Papers continues to be a curious blend of assertion (or hope) and doubt about his ability to act dangerously enough to gain his "soul" and to help others gain theirs (p. 151). His public appearances, his political campaign, his public actions that generate his most important nonfiction of the late sixties and early seventies are clearly attempts at least to match and occasionally to combine bold actions in his life and his art. More and more in the sixties, Mailer comes to believe that the rights and freedoms of the existential life, no less than of existential politics, are "best won by face-to-face confrontation" (p. 269). His nonfiction will be the record of a war.

Mailer's work of the early sixties begins to give shape to the possibility that some new kind of journalism or nonfiction may hold for him the means of combining art and action. As we trace the development of Mailer's nonfiction in these last three chapters, we will see that in shifting from fiction to historical events, Mailer allows his own personality to play a gradually increasing and then a gradually diminishing artistic role. This rising and falling curve of ego-assertion reaches its greatest height in the early parts of *Armies of the Night* (1968) and begins its decline in the latter portions of that book. The writer's self diminishes gradually through *Of a Fire on the Moon* (1970) and *The Fight* (1975) and ends in his complete self-effacement in his last nonfiction work, *The Executioner's Song* (1979). It is almost as if Mailer's nonfiction period provides the writer with the opportunity not only to try to become the artist-hero he found absent in his time, but to become, through a cathartic process of self-assertion, the objective, mature artist who is prepared to write his final fictions in the last decade or so of his creative life.

But it is in the earliest nonfiction, that written during the sixties, that Mailer's personality rises in his work toward the fullest expression of selfhood and personal vision. From the start, the center of

16. Laura Adams, *Existential Battles: The Growth of Norman Mailer*, p. 27.

Mailer's antijournalism is his own personality. The war with conventional journalism begins in the *Voice* as a purge of his own weaknesses and as a personal indicator of whether he was daily growing into more or retreating into less (*Ads*, pp. 282–83). In Mailer's pieces about the Kennedys and in his coverage of public events, such as that of the Patterson–Liston fight for *Esquire* from 1960 to 1962, the perceptions, intuitions, and ruminations of the interviewer and journalist take on an unprecedented importance and become essential to the kind of truth Mailer intends to reveal in his journalistic work.

His earliest journalism admittedly distorts "reality" in an effort to create a new "psychological reality" that would affect the status quo and stimulate his compatriots to pursue a creative evolution. "I was bending reality like a field of space to curve the time I wished to create," he says in his "Superman" essay (*PP*, p. 60). Mailer uses about twenty pages of this essay preparing for its subject—John Kennedy. In these twenty pages, Mailer discusses the supermarket as a symbol of disease, analyzes the shortcomings of political conventions and delegates, and argues the need for a new American hero. He only vaguely describes the convention in Los Angeles which he was to cover, and he admits that he watches most of the routine proceedings on television. When Kennedy finally appears in this essay, Mailer carefully molds him into the psychological reality of heroism that Mailer is trying to establish. Kennedy has performed the acts Mailer deems necessary to regeneration and heroism, and it is upon these acts that Mailer dwells. Kennedy has faced death and dread, courted political suicide (i.e., endangered his position rather than bettered it), and responded to pressure with coolness and grace. He is a man who has found in the trial and agony of death the energy to remake his psyche: "heroism is the first Doctor." Kennedy, a certified war hero, emerges more than a little, as a fellow writer first suggested to Mailer, like "Sergius O'Shaugnessy born rich." In a separate article, Mailer again draws forth one essential feature of his heroine, Jackie Kennedy, as he depicts the meeting of his personality and hers: she "disturbs the American need to believe that political life is as concrete and reasonable as the kind of engineering which produces bridges" (*PP*, p. 82).

What we see even in these early journalistic ventures is the play of a consciousness similar to Rojack's. It is an expanded, associative consciousness in which the impact of the subjective mind upon what is assumed to be the objective world is all-important. This consciousness illustrates Mailer's belief that intensity and wholeness of perceptions more closely approach the truth, or the most important truth, of the thing perceived than objective reporting. And the tendency of such consciousness to universalize naturalistic detail, to see the macrocosmic in the microcosmic, is typical of the allegorist.

Mailer's coverage of the 1962 Patterson—Liston fight more clearly reveals his discovery of the possibilities within journalism and nonfiction of shaping from the most unlikely circumstances implications of moral and metaphysical dimensions. Mailer has laid a claim to boxing similar to the claim Hemingway laid to bullfighting, but Mailer is more explicit about the universal proportions of the contest. Mailer views champions as "prodigies of will" and of "the urge to endure" through agony and crisis. In "Ten Thousand Words a Minute," collected from *Esquire* in *Papers*, Mailer draws a portrait of two boxers who represent much more than they would if seen simply as two individual men doing their jobs. Through the details of Patterson's and Liston's past lives, the description of the people who surround and support each champion, and the delineation of the ways in which each man is connected to his embattled predecessors. Liston and Patterson become colliding "ideal archetypes," to use Mailer's phrase, or agents who battle to shift the "wealth of the universe" toward the Lord or the Devil, the authentic or the inauthentic, through their private struggles (pp. 255–61). In Patterson's defeat before a representative of inauthentic power—an agent of the Mafia, Las Vegas, the gimmick—Mailer discovers a regeneration of his own commitment to try to play a greater role himself in determining which way the "wealth of the universe" will shift. Out of the surprise and despair that Mailer and James Baldwin share over Patterson's defeat, Mailer discovers a meaning emerging out of that defeat. Patterson's loss is connected somehow with Mailer's own, with our own, loss of authentic power before the inauthentic.

> Now, after the knockout, in some fatigue-ridden, feverish whole vision of one's guilt and of Patterson's defeat . . . out of a desire to end some war in myself . . . I began in the plot-ridden, romantic dungeons of my mind . . . to see myself as some sort of center about which all that had been lost must rally. It was not simple egomania nor simple drunkenness, it was not even simple insanity: it was a kind of metaphorical leap. . . . To believe the impossible may be won creates a strength from which the impossible may indeed be attacked. (p. 261)

In short, Mailer reenlists as an active archetype himself in a world of conflicting forces.

If this reenlistment determines the kind of nonfiction Mailer will later write, we have not yet focused adequately on less important factors that influenced Mailer's turn to nonfiction and to a new kind of journalism in particular. Like some of the journalists of the sixties, Mailer addressed himself particularly to what seemed to be the pernicious influence of conventional journalism. So Mailer's new journalism becomes a reflection of other forces operating in journalism at about the same time. Since Mailer, however, was considering the question of a new journalism in the 1950s and exploring its rudimentary forms from 1960 to 1962, he is clearly in the vanguard of the movement known as the new journalism. Tom Wolfe, for example, dates its start at about 1962–1963, with Gay Talese's piece on Joe Louis, written for *Esquire* in 1962, and with Jimmy Breslin's feature column in the *Herald Tribune* in 1963. Wolfe himself tried his own wings with an article on dragsters in *Esquire* that same year.

Mailer's antijournalism, then, is less an isolated phenomenon than one might expect. By new journalism I am not referring to one specific technique. As Tom Wolfe points out, the new journalism was a force or an excitement that particularly in magazine journalism during the 1960s began to supplant the conventional formulas of objectivity and factual presentation. Wolfe, the chief proselyte of the new force, calls it a more ambitious, more intense, more detailed, and more time-consuming type of journalism than that of the previous decades. He adds that the first concern of the new journalists is to write journalism that will read like a novel, and "excite the reader intellectually and emotionally." He is not far from Mailer on this point. Everette Dennis and William Rivers argue that if the new journalist uses verifiable facts, he or she does not stop there but seeks a truth larger than the mere facts in themselves. He or she emphasizes the more imaginative potential in an event or in a character and, for example, freely depicts the subjective and emotional life of characters. This depiction may be executed through the use of dialogue, authorial speculation, or interior monologue. By completely immersing oneself in the event or the life of his character(s), the new journalist discovers the mood, experiences the atmosphere, of the event and the people he or she writes about. Such a journalist may be a participant in the event, as Mailer is in the Pentagon March, or as Hunter Thompson is in the revels of the Hell's Angels. But for Wolfe the new journalism above all reconnects twentieth-century art with what he believes to be literature's "main circuit" of "detailed realism," rediscovers the "joys" and "strange powers" of realism, and restores a sense of immediacy and life to, in Wolfe's view, a postwar fiction that has atrophied in an artificial and academic mythicism.[17] This power of realism, even if one does not agree with Wolfe's assessment of postwar mythicism, will be an important discovery for Mailer. But Mailer's new journalism before

17. Tom Wolfe and E. W. Johnson, *The New Journalism*, pp. 9, 10–15, 20–21, 23, 28, 31, 50; Everette E. Dennis and William L. Rivers, *Other Voices: The New Journalism in America*, pp. 1–2, 5–6, 11, 15–17, 27–28.

Armies of the Night emphasizes the universality of the specific and
the speculative penetration of his character's minds.

Mailer makes three specific charges against conventional journalism. His first charge, clearly stated in "Ten Thousand Words a
Minute," is that journalism distorts the essential truth about the
events it pretends to present as objective truth. It is difficult for a
reporter to be true to precise detail because his story, his details, and
his readership ride "the stocks" of public opinion and current interest. "There is a logic to news—on a given day with a certain
meteorological drift to the winds in the mass media, a story can ride
along certain currents." But if details are askew to ride such drifts,
readers are given an unreal view of an event and of life. Especially
today, the unreal view makes American life seem easier, less complex, more rewarding than it is. "A nation which forms detailed
opinions on the basis of detailed fact which is askew from the subtle
reality becomes a nation of citizens whose psyches are askewed,
item by detailed item, away from *any* reality."

Mailer's second criticism is that the mass media too often develop
a parasitic relationship to the institutions they are supposed to be
reporting about and upon which they depend for news. The journalistic medium, therefore, easily becomes the handmaiden, rather
than the nemesis, of those institutions. In "Ten Thousand Words a
Minute," Mailer analyzes at length, for example, the relationship of
political reporting to the government in the 1950s and early 1960s.
He sets the mood of his discussion by describing a political press
headquarters as having the odor of "cancer gulch," which is a little
"like the smell of left-wing meeting halls, except it is worse . . . for
there is no poverty to put a guilt-free iron into the nose. . . . everybody is getting free drinks, free sandwiches, free news releases." The
releases especially erode the reporters' desire to battle for the truth;
the release is a free list of facts, figures, and statistics "with a little
love from the Welfare State." One manifestation of this marriage
between politics and press is the curious phenomenon that the "only
institutions which remain alive in American life are those which can
afford a press representative." The papers stop reporting history and
begin making it along with the establishment's press representatives, "so the newspapers help to create institutions which will
supply them with news." Mailer's most developed example of the
phenomenon of controlled or institutionalized news is the "leaks" to
the *Times* during the Truman–Eisenhower years.

Mailer's third specific charge against conventional journalism is
that the people who work in the media are encouraged to lust after
power and money, and not the power of any particular idea or goal
worth fighting for, but a power that, like Rusty-power, is "the only

thing which will relieve the profound illness which has seized them. Which has seized all of us" (p. 129).

On the other hand, Mailer has always been aware of the potential in journalism for a reporter of perception, endurance, and courage. And the honest reporter does have an excuse for unfinished writing and for confronting the "enemy" with a mere holding action. "Writing for a newspaper is like running a revolutionary war, you go into battle not when you are ready but when the action offers itself" (PP, p. 199). In this fact lies the strength of reporting for a writer: it has what Mailer considers existential possibilities. You enter the lists unprepared and in doubt of the outcome; you test your proportions against larger forces. In his interview with Steven Marcus, included in Cannibals, Mailer says that though he doesn't want "to be caught justifying journalism as a major activity," it can nonetheless be a "venture of one's ability to keep in shape" and not necessarily "an essential betrayal of the chalice of your literary art." Mailer argues that if one writes under every conceivable mood and condition, as a good journalist must, one can exercise consciousness. Journalism, therefore, Mailer continues, can be a reflection and measure of one's consciousness (pp. 218– 19). Mailer is again implying an important point for understanding his nonfiction work: a "psychological reality" can be changed by an event itself if the event is strong and startling enough. Changing psychological reality is changing consciousness, and it is the first job of the writer as a consciousness in the center of an event to charge the reality of the event with sufficient strength to create a new psychological reality.

That Mailer turned to nonfiction or new journalism in the 1960s to express his consciousness is therefore a reflection of both the times and the man. As Tom Wolfe points out, we see in Mailer and Truman Capote not conventional journalists who are suddenly, in the 1960s, writing nonfiction with fictional techniques, but novelists turning from the novel to write a nonfiction that uses novelistic techniques as well as those associated with journalism: factual research, interviews, and the observation of contemporary events. And in the process, both Capote and Mailer, as Wolfe notes, tremendously revive waning careers and deteriorating reputations.[18] The impetus for the new journalism was largely in that decade itself, as Dennis and Rivers point out. "In a time when old values are crumbling, when the miracle of advancing technology is suddenly seen to create as many problems as it solves, when disorder, turmoil, and violence become hallmarks of a nation . . . it cannot be surprising that the mass media . . . should feel the shock waves of change." If we add to

18. Wolfe and Johnson, New Journalism, pp. 15, 26– 29.

the shock waves, Dennis and Rivers go on, "an affluence that allows Americans to pause and consider how one's head was put together instead of where the next meal was coming from," larger elements of the society begin to reconsider what in another time might have been left unquestioned (pp. 1, 4–5, 16). Novelists and journalists began to meet the shock waves with new techniques. In an article in *Commentary* in 1961, Philip Roth suggests the inadequacy of traditional genres to meet the experiences of the mid-twentieth century: "the American writer in the middle of the twentieth century has his hands full in trying to understand, and then describe, and then make *credible* much of the American reality. It stupefies, it sickens, it infuriates, and finally it is even a kind of embarrassment to one's own meager imagination."[19]

Mailer was struck by the events of the sixties in the same way that most people were. But his personal convictions, which he expressed early in the fifties, were heightened by the subsequent decade. Mailer said in *Existential Errands* that none of us knows "what reality is" now, and that we spend most of our lives looking for it (p. 360). By turning more and more to the new journalistic mode, Mailer is able, therefore, to become a hero in his own work. But what is more important, he is able to test his own consciousness not only by confronting larger forces and defining his own proportions, but by using journalism, as he earlier said it could be used, as a measure of his ability to find and report the truth of an event in such a way that the psychological reality, the consciousness of his time, may be changed. Such change, after all, is the goal of heroes and heroic consciousness in all times. Mailer's nonfiction becomes a vehicle for discovering the largest moral and metaphysical dimensions in contemporary events, for affecting the status quo by going to war with forces of defeat, for uniting art with action, and for uniting the consciousness of a hero with the psychological reality of his nation and time.

19. Klein, *The American Novel*, p. 144.

7

The Armies of the Night

I am not a critic of the West. I am a critic of the weaknesses of the West. I am a critic of a fact which we can't comprehend: how one can lose one's spiritual strength, one's willpower, and, possessing freedom, not to value it, not to be willing to make sacrifices for it. . . . Those people who have lived in the most terrible conditions, on the frontier between life and death . . . they all understand that between good and evil there is an irreconcilable contradiction, that it is not the same thing—good or evil—that one cannot build one's life without regard to this distinction. I am surprised that pragmatic philosophy consistently scorns moral consideration.

—Alexander Solzhenitsyn (from a BBC interview with Michael Charlton: March 1, 1976)

You see, what Solzhenitsyn has said is on an entirely different level from the comments that go on about our world on television, by politicians. It's in terms of truth. It's in terms of good and evil. . . . from a man who . . . chose to jeopardize his life, his work, everything, and to give us in the West a last chance by telling us what the world situation is *really* about, which is *not* energy, *not* inflation . . . *not* who gets into power, but good and evil.

—Malcolm Muggeridge (response to Solzhenitsyn's interview: March 10, 1976)

In *The Armies of the Night* (1968), Mailer begins a full decade of nonfiction by exploring the concerns and doubts he expressed earlier about his fiction, about his role as an actor in the events of his time, and about the possibilities for some new kind of journalism that would initiate a war against the stifling forces in the media and society. Mailer attempts here to fulfill the desire he discovered in the fifties and sixties to be a hero for his time and to become a writer who will help accelerate consciousness. Mailer's primary achievement in *Armies* is that he discovers and communicates large implications and hope for a human renaissance in an event full of absurdity, compromise, human weakness, and mass movements. And he makes this discovery in a time and country he had recently portrayed as hopelessly defeated. This book is clearly a record of a war, a war between a dead world and a living one.

Armies is, first, a continuation of Mailer's response to conventional journalism. Mailer, like so many new journalists of the sixties, will present a meaning or a truth of an event without pretending to be objective, but by comparing, or indeed fusing, the personal truths of the experience with the events themselves. The emphasis of Book

141

One, entitled "History as a Novel," is upon the narrator as an actor *and* observer, upon the personal truths of larger events. The emphasis of Book Two, entitled "The Novel as History," is upon the event itself and the other participants. Though this larger structural division juxtaposes the personal with the larger truth, neither kind of truth is entirely exclusive to either book. The lively narrative consciousness, as we will see, insures a fusion of the personal and the larger truths throughout the entire book.

Mailer opens Book One with a *Time* magazine account of himself and the Pentagon March. That account clearly illustrates the biases of *Time* in favor of the Establishment cause, against the demonstrators, and against Mailer personally. *Time* uses every adjective, pun, and turn of phrase it can to perpetuate a public image of Mailer as only a mad dog who "staggers" drunkenly about the stage of the Ambassador Theater the night before the March. Mailer performs a "scatological solo," *Time* assures us, for an audience ("mostly students") in the "scruffy" theater, a place of "psychedelic frolics" and "capers." *Time* also pronounces *Why Are We in Vietnam?* useless for answering the question in its title. Mailer uses this *Time* account to launch himself into the book: "Now we may leave *Time* in order to find out what really happened." The argument that the press is "the silent assassin of the republic" becomes a recurring motif, with comparisons of eye-witness and media accounts throughout. Mailer is, cumulatively, more than a little convincing on this issue of the inadequacies of the media, and at one point Robert Lowell, another participant in the March, similarly scolds the press for its facile misrepresentations. Mailer could see that even Lowell, a man of high reputation and a relatively innocuous public image, suffers from the "great wall of total misrepresentation" the press builds between a writer "and the audience reached by a newspaper," which is most of the country. Mailer admits that he has done much to create his own bad image, which he drags around like a sarcophagus. Yet all the examples of misrepresentation about himself or the events are mere symptoms of a large problem—a continual misrepresentation of events and people that divorces the public from any reality.

Mailer explains his own approach to the event at the outset of Book Two with the metaphor of the tower. Book One, he explains, is a tower he built in a forest of mass media inaccuracy so that we might better see where we are and see our own horizons.[1] The tower is built by a narrator who acts as a novelist and as a historian.

The narrator builds his tower with various techniques skillfully

---

1. *The Armies of the Night* (hereafter cited as *Armies*), p. 219. Unless otherwise indicated, all citations are to works by Norman Mailer.

employed. He rapidly fluctuates between narrative and digression. He may digress in the very midst of the narrative or, like Swift, in separate blocks of digression, such as the long digression opening Part IV of Book One. Each large or small digression either enlarges our knowledge of the event or allows the narrator to make important associations through speculations, explications, or asides. In Book Two, especially, the narrator compares and analyzes as many facts, accounts, and statistics as he possesses. The narrator imaginatively penetrates other people's thoughts. He ruminates on events in long sections of interior monologue. He fluctuates between comedy and serious meditation. He gives ample realistic details to describe specific characters or episodes. And he sometimes carefully delineates a point or argument with well-developed dramatic scenes. But one central technique determines the nature of all the others— the creation of a lively, ambiguous consciousness at the center of events in Book One. This consciousness is a persona for Mailer himself, whom the author treats with both distance and intimacy in a third person autobiographical point of view. The most remarkable aspect of this hero, whom Mailer variously calls Mailer, the Novelist, the Participant, the Ruminant, the Historian, and the Existentialist, is that he is a comic hero. In this regard also Mailer's journalism is not as outrageous as it might appear if considered in isolation. The device of the narrator-observer as a crazed hero or fool seems to be one aspect of the larger ferment in the new journalism of the late sixties and early seventies. Two fellow journalists whom Mailer will describe in *The Fight* use a somewhat similar technique. Hunter Thompson, whom Mailer sees as a writer whose strength is the sensational repudiation of organized madness, uses a crazed-citizen persona as the narrative consciousness of his *Fear and Loathing in Las Vegas* (1971), for example. Here Thompson's "Gonzo journalism" represents the extreme emphasis on narrative consciousness. He loads himself up with drugs and careens about Las Vegas in search of the American Dream. With a mixture of outrage, buffoonery, and madness, the Thompson persona observes events he is on assignment to cover, such as the Mint-400 off-the-road race and the National District Attorney's Conference on Dangerous Drugs in Vegas. He witnesses such events only long enough to get a sense of their grotesqueness, but actually writes about himself and the impact on him of such bizarre Vegas institutions as the Circus-Circus club, which provides a picture of what the "whole hep world would be doing on Saturday night if the Nazis had won the war."

George Plimpton, whom Mailer also portrays in *The Fight*, is certainly less outrageous. But the center of his book *Paper Lion* (1966) is his own ridiculous five-play performance in an exhibition

game in Pontiac, Michigan — at the end of a long period of training
with the Detroit Lions. The purpose of his personal humiliation
before the "massive attention" of a stadium crowd is to demonstrate
his theme—that professional athletes are extraordinary men.
Plimpton specifically compares himself to such sports clowns as
baseball's Al Schacht and the Charlie Chaplin buffoons of bullfighting as he plays "the fool in Pontiac."

Mailer's narrator-hero in *Armies* is also absurd; but more than
this, he is an inspired, prophetic figure. The hero is, first, as humanly
fallible as any of us and a chief resource for the humor in the book.
Describing himself as a man who had given his own head "the
texture of Swiss Cheese" and had made all sorts of "erosions in his
intellectual firmament," which erosions had given him the illusion
of being a genius, Mailer is most relentless on the subject of his own
fantasies, illusions, and vanities. His vanity clearly emerges, for
example, when he reports that his glee and sense of triumph at
getting the job as master of ceremonies at the theater—over Lowell,
Paul Goodman, and Dwight Macdonald—created such a disproportionate sense of his own importance and "incandescence of purpose"
that he neglects to notify his fellow notables of a trip to the men's
room, which itself is described in comic detail, and thereby throws
his "first gig as Master of Ceremonies" into a confusion from which
it never recovers. Instead of captivating the audience with succinct
and witty speeches and introductions, as he had fantasized on his
way to the theater, he cranks up a vaudeville clown. "He had
betrayed himself again. The end of the introduction belonged in a
burlesque house—he worked his own worst veins, like a man on the
edge of bankruptcy trying to collect hopeless debts" (pp. 43–44).
The actor in his personality takes over and, playing a favorite part of
Southern demagogue, hobbles about the stage as Lyndon Johnson's
"dwarf alter ego" answering all criticism of the war and Adminis-
tration with a "fuck you!" Even Robert Lowell, who, as Mailer
reminds us, has accomplishments suitable to greater vanity than
Mailer, is not spared from the hero-fool's wit. Indeed, all the characters are somewhat absurd. The episode of Mailer's and Lowell's
conversations, their literary logrolling and "headmastermanship,"
is as concise a scene as any in the book. The episode, as Lowell was to
say later of *Armies* itself, does not miss a trick, which is to say,
Mailer's portrayal of the details and absurdities of the events and
other actors is complete.[2]

2. See Dwight Macdonald's account of Lowell's conversation about *Armies* with
Macdonald in "Politics," *Esquire*, p. 42. " 'Curious,' Lowell said to me after reading
it, 'when you're with another novelist, you think he's so sensitive and alert and you
find later he wasn't taking in anything, while Norman seems not to pay attention

The comic hero himself is, then, in some ways a microcosm of his compatriots and his time. He suffers the disease of disproportion and of multiple, uncontrolled personalities, as he tells us in detail during his opening phone conversation with Mitch Goodman (p. 8). And over all of his personalities is a division between the "modest everyday fellow of his daily round" and the "absolute egomaniac, a Beast" who seizes control of the everyday fellow quickly and with "little warning." He compares the architecture of his personality to a "provincial cathedral" designed over several centuries by warring orders of the church. If he has the desire to lead a nation toward God, he is "sufficiently devil-ridden to need action." He tells us near the end of Book One that he cannot tell "whether he was fundamentally criminal, a devil indeed."

The same Mailer who believes (who does not?) that he could better serve as president than any holder of the office since Kennedy, who fantasizes about bending the bars of a prison bus and making a dramatic escape, who dreams of leading revolutionaries with a gun in the hills, is also the Mailer who chides himself as a "philosophical monomaniac," a "sexologue," and a "surrogate Hemingway" or "poor man's Papa" who must continually face his own fear, whether it be for life and limb or for inconveniences and disruptions of his daily life. Confronting his fear of a lengthy term in jail, Mailer is appalled by his inability to keep principles first, his breaking of his own maxims: "but Mailer! with his apocalyptic visions at Lincoln Memorial and again on the March, his readiness to throw himself, breast against breast, in any charge on the foe, why now in such a rush [to go home]? Did he not respect his visions?" (p. 118).

If he is not in complete control of himself, however, he is still a hero-fool who would seek Life in an insane world, who is compelled by the force within him to speak his truths as an inspired prophet might. He cannot give up the impulse to educate his country, though his own self-doubts and shortcomings are very real. As a novelist, he feels compelled to take on the heroic role of educator on a grand scale, and in this regard he compares himself to Fitzgerald, Hemingway, and Thomas Wolfe. The responsibilities of these novelists arise from their perceptions of their country's potential and loss, and they accept these responsibilities despite a preference, as Mailer suggests, for a safe place, security, and a nice wine cellar. But Fitzgerald, Hemingway, and Wolfe all failed to reach out beyond the brainwashings of bestsellers, Hollywood, *Time*, and now television

---

but now it seems he didn't miss a trick—and what a memory!' " Macdonald agrees and goes on to explain it all *is* memory, no notes and so forth, yet Mailer reproduces whole scenes and dialogues, to Macdonald's mind, exactly, reconstructing them "by ear."

to show to the nation its best self. In the absence of a greater hero, Mailer offers his comic hero as a philosopher-fool, "Prince of Bourbon," a "mountebank actor" and "crazed citizen" who nonetheless feels some depth of truth he must utter.

> While the audience was recovering from the existential anxiety of encountering an orator who confessed to such a crime [urinating on the floor of a dark men's room] he would be able . . . to bring them up to a contemplation of deeper problems, of, indeed, the deepest problems, the most chilling alternatives, and would from there seek to bring them back to a restorative view of man. Man [i.e., Mailer] might be a fool who peed in the wrong pot, man was also a scrupulous servant of the self-damaging admission; man was therefore a philosopher . . . ; he could turn loss to philosophical gain . . . his most special fool's garden: *satori*, incandescence, and the hard gem-like flame of bourbon burning in the furnaces of metabolism. (*Armies*, pp. 31–32)

This persona "Mailer" is in part an outraged self at war with his culture, but he would still bring to his culture deep and disquieting insights. His lot will be to reveal the absurdity of his comic flaws and disproportions, to suffer persecution and humiliation by larger forces, and to travel a pilgrim's progress from egotism through humiliation and suffering, and eventually to knowledge and affirmation. He is both actor and sufferer. His grace will manifest itself as his best self. That best self is the instinctual drive for freedom, growth, and Life, a drive that Mailer will associate with God and with the assertion of one's soul, of one's creative and moral potential as a human being. The persona is, therefore, at once an absurd fool, a holy fool, and a hero.

The heroism of Mailer-the-fool is, as the fictional heroes are, part of a larger tradition. As Enid Welsford points out in *The Fool*, the fool, when he succeeds, represents the human emancipation from the stifling law or order, from the leviathan state and its representatives who threaten to swallow the individual's original personality and freedom. The fool is in this sense a hero because he embodies the cause of the stupid against the clever, the weak against the strong, David against Goliath. As a successful underdog, he can turn the tables on the authority and outwit the "wise" by his physical, moral, and spiritual resilience. His wisdom is not of the intellect, but of the spirit; he draws forth from mankind its inner antagonism between the impulse to free the self from restriction and the impulse to preserve the social order.[3]

In one of his longest digressions, Mailer presents his technical

---

3. Enid Welsford, *The Fool*, pp. 315, 317, 319.

rationale for using a hero-fool as the central narrative vehicle of his book. Since the March on the Pentagon was an ambiguous "event whose essential value or absurdity may not be established for ten or twenty years, or indeed ever," Mailer argues, it would be misleading and not resolve the ambiguity if he were to focus on the real principals—as in fact he will briefly in Book Two—such as Dellinger, Rubin, or high government officials. Mailer argues further that the monumental disproportions of the event might be resolved or imaginatively perceived and captured best by an eye-witness participant who is himself ambiguous, absurd, disproportionate, and comic. The buffoon figure traditionally breaks down the distinctions not only between wisdom and folly, but between life and art. He is equally at home in reality or imagination. He is an educator, as Welsford has suggested, who draws out the latent folly of his audience, or shows folly for what it is, and who attunes us to the possibility that at any moment life threatens to turn into a farce (*The Fool*, pp. xii, 28). Whether Mailer's hero is ludicrous with mock-heroic associations, or whether heroic and tragic, each reader must decide, he tells us. But as we will see, the hero-fool is both. Such a persona serves as a bridge to the "crazy time" of history when symbolic warfare (medieval and primitive) was reinvigorated against the avatar and high church of technological civilization— the Pentagon. Playing upon his public image as an outrageous egotist, which he cannot escape and which the media will amplify, the Mailer persona is at once self-assertive and capable of "a detachment classic in severity." These qualities equip him to act and to regard himself and others in action against the enemy. "Once History inhabits a crazy house," he tells us, "egotism may be the last tool left to History" (p. 54).

The narrator as both historian and fool will seek to find and interpret for us the timeless in the historical event. He records a war that reveals the timeless pattern of a rite of passage, which implies the potential renaissance of a people in the grip of Death. The enemy has representatives high and low, and though no single face of the enemy is the enemy itself, each literal and symbolic agent reveals a face of the enemy. The enemy is both obvious and ambiguous, both without and within. Mailer attaches chief importance to the event as an opportunity to confront the enemy for those who, in all their human confusion, are seeking some passage to the conduits of Life.

Throughout Book One, Mailer continually prepares us to recognize the sight and the feel of the enemy in its various guises from innocence and humanitarianism to obvious malignancies upon nature and life. The last test of malignancy left to each of us now may be to "trust the authority of our senses" and to "look to the feel of the phenomenon": if it feels bad, it is bad.[4] The many faces of the enemy may be real or symbolic or both. The enemy may emerge as that consensus of the most powerful middle-aged WASPs after World War II, who pledged intellectual troth to the idea that Communism was the deadly foe of Christian culture and had to be fought by a series of overt and cold wars mixed with periods of "modest collaboration" (p. 181). Or the enemy may be any number of corporations who are more guilty than the Communists of debasing nature, our goods, and our sense of a meaningful work and life (pp. 72, 152). Or the literal enemy may wear the mask of the liberal. Even with the best intentions, the liberal has difficulty in doing good because the liberal cannot go to the root of the problem — to the technology that divorces humanity from real, precise, and deep experience, from metaphor, from nature, and from challenge and growth. Mailer argues here, as indeed Aldous Huxley did in his 1946 preface to *Brave New World*, that the modern liberal's faith is not in humanity but in the "Great Society's supermachine" and its managers.

> If the republic was now managing to convert the citizenry to a plastic mass, ready to be attached to any manipulative gung ho, the author was ready to cast much of the blame for such success into the undernourished lap, the overpsychologized loins, of the liberal academic intelligentsia. . . . They were servants of that social machine of the future in which all irrational human conflict would be resolved, all conflict of interest negotiated, and nature's resonance condensed into frequencies which could comfortably phase nature in or out as you please. So they were servants of the moon. . . . they were ready to move to the moon and build Utope cities there. (*Armies*, pp. 15–16)

During the protest, the enemy materializes as the law enforcer, particularly the U.S. marshals to whom Mailer devotes a great deal of descriptive space. Their faces have a "low cunning mixed with a stroke of rectitude"; many look like ex-first sergeants, "the toes run out; the belly struts"; they emit a collective spirit of "apathy rising to fanaticism only to subside in apathy" (Mailer remarked in *Canni-*

4. Mailer repeats this twice in *Armies*, pp. 25 and 90–91, and thanks Aquinas, Hemingway, and Macdonald for giving him this clue, which is enough, he tells us, to "enable a man to become a good working amateur philosopher" and not just "an embittered entertainer . . . a John O'Hara!" Part of what Mailer expresses here is his belief that sensual, intuitive, and instinctual perceptions inform consciousness with greater truth than consciousness alone can command (see *Armies*, p. 28). Stanley T. Gutman was correct, it seems to me, in assessing Mailer's faith in one's total immersion in experience as a means of deriving values, and this is one point of Mailer's affinity with existential thought in general. See *Mankind in Barbary*, p. 167. But of course the values Mailer seeks are ultimately larger and more selfless than the self-contained values of existential fiction, as I pointed out in the previous chapter.

bals, p. 196, that this attitude leads to violence); their eyes speak of hollows in the soul in places like Las Vegas, "where the fevers of America go livid . . . and Grandmother," the churchgoer with orange hair, drives half-dollars into a slot machine while "gooks" burn in Vietnam. These marshals are like men Mailer had known in the army, but the dignity and humor had gone out of them and something "rabid and toothless" had come in. As we see later, by eye-witness accounts, these marshals beat the women protestors with special enthusiasm. Applicants to work in the garrisons and future concentration camps would come not only from "a hundred American novels," but from "half the Marshals outside this bus, simple, honest, hardworking government law-enforcement agents." Something is loose in America, Mailer ponders; technology had driven some wildness and nightmare out from secret primitive places and into the fevers of the air and blood. Vegas, race riots, suburban orgies were not enough to contain the fever—this "poet's beast slinking to the market place"—the country had to go to Vietnam and unleash the fever in the "nozzle tip of the flame thrower."

The protean enemy emerges in symbolic as well as in literal agents. Chief among these symbols is the Pentagon itself, a concrete entity to be sure, but in its architecture and function a representative of the disease itself: "chalice and anus of corporation land, smug, enclosed, morally blind . . . destroying the future of its own nation with each day it augmented its strength." It speaks of "oppressive Faustian lusts," entraps the nation's own innocence—just as it traps the soul of a boy (i.e., D.J.) hot out of high school before he knows he has a soul—and reminds the hero of the "technological excrement all over the conduits of nature." The Pentagon is a symbol, a paradigm with very real effects.

By writing in a journalistic-historical medium, Mailer is able to suggest the reality of his metaphors to a reader.[5] But he finds only a grim pleasure in the verification in his metaphors. As the marchers approach it, the Pentagon looks first like an "anomaly of the sea," then like a plastic plug in a hole made in flesh by "some unmentionable operation." Closer, it looks like a "five-sided tip on the spout" of a giant deodorant spray can, or like a "cluster of barnacles" whose cancerous proliferation is its own defense. A first reconnaissance by the leaders of the demonstrators' coalition reveals the building's subtle strength: they could find no objective in the monotonous corridors. "What could one do inside?" Mailer asks. It is one of the

5. By "journalistic" I refer literally to the fact that Book One of *Armies* was first published in *Harper's* as "The Steps of the Pentagon" (March 1968). It was written with great energy and speed in about three months.

"anonymous, monotonous, monstrous, massive interchangeable" signs of totalitarianism, reflecting an image of our highways, architecture, food, and communications (see pp. 113–16, 154–55, 158, 176, 226–28).

If the enemy is a technology grown cancerous and a machine man talking technologese or using a billy club or a rifle, it is also, in its most subtle and insidious face, the enemy within, the machine man in all of us. Mailer's Crusaders are not glorious heroes, but the smallest, most oppressed representatives of some dim flame left in the core of life. General Mailer's troops are none other than the confused escapees of the urban middle class who harbor a "secret slavish love for the oncoming hegemony of the computer and the suburb," but who also are pressed by the most outrageous occurrences into increasingly militant stands.

What is the nature of this enemy within? What shortcomings must the protestors surmount in Mailer's view? They have, first, indiscriminately consumed chemical drugs. Mailer tells us he now believes that promiscuous drug use exploits the present at the expense of consuming the past ("whether traceable in the flesh, or merely palpable in the collective underworld of the dream") and demolishing "whole territories of the future." The drugs continue what Mailer sees as the technocracy's lobotomy of the mind, which separates the human from a sense of responsibility and of guilt. The young people in the March seemed indifferent to waste. Second, they automatically accepted technology land. When Mailer sees, for example, that most of the black demonstrators keep themselves separate from the white demonstrators, he believes this separation to be a reflection of the denial of technology land by the Black Left, which sought to fulfill its "unruly jungle intuitions that technology land and corporation land were the same."[6]

But these youthful "villains" display qualities that give the narrator hope. He sees beyond their worst selves another potential that the other villains from corporation land did not display. These other

6. Later in *Existential Errands: Twenty-Six Pieces Selected by the Author from the Body of All His Writings* Mailer develops this theme. He contrasts middle-class youth disaffected by war and Black Power. He believes Black Power expresses the truly conservative ethic and passion, "for any real conservation is founded on regard for the animal, the oak and the field; it has instinctive detestation of science, or creation-by-machine." The basis of primitive life is the tradition that God resides in, sanctifies, nature. Contrastingly, what white civilization has come to see as its "wealth" is a corporate production that poisons "the wellsprings, avatars, and conduits of nature." Mailer sees in Vietnam and Africa the rejection of technological culture by a primitive, exploited world (pp. 293–94, 300–301, 321). The conflict between primitive life and exploitative technology is also the subject of his essay accompanying Kurlansky and Naar's photography of the graffiti of urban minorities in New York City. See *The Faith of Graffiti* (New York: Praeger, 1974).

villains were, after all, utterly destroying their sons and daughters and the future of their country in a "self-righteousness and greed and secret lust (often unknown to themselves) for some sexo-technological variety of neo-fascism" (p. 93). If the New Left represented a generation born to technology and a generation embracing technology as no generation had before, the New Left still had awakened another consciousness closed to the five preceding generations of the middle class. Some of this new generation could see that the authority had lied, that people in high places were corrupt, that somehow the authority had deadened the life of everyone, had created one disaster after another for which the authority always had "the subtlest apologies." At times this new generation also demonstrated promising élan and freedom epitomized for Mailer in their variety of battle costume. Finally, this new generation of protestors returned a sense of mystery and symbol to politics. They believed in witches, magic, tribal knowledge, orgy, and revolution. And, of course, they would never have tried to blow their minds with easy visions of heaven had not the authority so sterilized the present.[7]

Since the disproportion between the forces of the government and the marchers was so great, the marchers had to create a symbolic warfare. But it was the government itself that first closed the gap between the symbolic and the literal. The government troops acted as if a symbolic wound were literal and mortal. Of course from the first a symbolic march held literal potential. The New Left learned to probe the heart of the government's fear of image, of what Mailer calls a "concrete disaster of international publicity." For everyone involved in the March and arrests, however, the dangers and discomforts were real. For Mailer, arrest was both a symbolic act of defiance of governmental policy in Vietnam and an opportunity to see the faces and operations of the other side.

Mailer's principal discovery, however, is the meaning of the event. It is the purpose of Book Two, "The Novel as History," to clarify the meaning of Book One and the whole protest. In the process of writing Book One for *Harper's* Mailer "was delivered of a discovery of what the March . . . had finally meant, and what had been won, and what had been lost, and so found himself ready at last to write a most concise Short History" (p. 216). Although Mailer argues perversely and ironically that Book Two is more novelistic, by which he means it required more imagination because it covers incidents Mailer did not participate in, it is an attempt to objectify parts of the event through the reporting of facts by a comparison of accounts

7. I am summarizing the points Mailer makes throughout *Armies*, see especially pp. 33–34, 86–88, 92–93, 268–69.

and by guarded speculations. The meaning is ultimately that the March is both symbolically and actually a rite of passage and one of the most promising acts of regeneration since World War II. But this rite of passage is two-fold: personal and transpersonal. Despite the Mailer persona's early doubt, which he expressed to Mitch Goodman, about the value of his participation in the protest, this hero-fool experiences a lesser passage that foreshadows and prepares him to explain the larger rite.

It is, first, as a witness of some of the ceremonies in the protest that he faces certain truths about himself. In a somber, ceremonial burning of draft cards, young men perform what for Mailer is a basic existential act. They defy a large power, and the outcome of their acts is uncertain. They face a promise of trial and danger and make a "moral leap" that requires a faith in "some kind of grace." Mailer wonders if he could do as much in their place. These young men appear to have "souls of interesting dimension" and a "surprising individuality." And when faculty members, swept along "this moral stream," repeat the acts of the younger men, Mailer recognizes that the same liberal academics and technologues he had criticized the night before were still capable of perhaps greater moral leaps than the young men. For these older protesters placed themselves in a more precise danger; they were acutely aware of just how their lives, their families, and their careers were most jeopardized; they were abdicating "from the machines they had chosen for life" (pp. 76–77). Mailer also devotes seven pages to describing as a theatrical event the exorcism of the Pentagon led by the Fugs. Shouting, noise, rock music, incantations in the name of every conceivable archaic god ("Out, demons, out—back to the darkness, ye servants of Satan—out demons out!"), and a rite of sexual love intended, in the name of Priapus and Life, to rid the Pentagon, in the words of the exorcists, of "the cancerous tumors of the war generals"—all are pure grist for Mailer's Manichean mills.

> On which acidic journeys had the hippies met the witches and the devils and the cutting edge of all primitive awe, the savage's sense of explosion. . . . Now, here, . . . suddenly an entire generation of acid-heads seemed to have said goodbye to easy visions of heaven, no, now the witches were here, and rites of exorcism, and black terrors of the night. . . . Yes, the hippies had gone from Tibet to Christ to the Middle Ages, now they were Revolutionary Alchemists. Well, thought Mailer, that was all right, he was a Left Conservative himself. "Out demons out!"

> "You know I like this," he said to Lowell.[8]

8. *Armies*, pp. 123–24. Compare the ceremonial elements in the larger rite to Mircea Eliade's description of primitive rites of initiation in *The Myth of the Eternal Return*, which are also clearly associated with purgation as well as renewal. The

The Mailer persona is a little like the writer's earliest heroes in that he is a mere witness who finds himself "being steeped in a new psychical condition." The courage of others forces him to face his own fear, to face the possibility that to act himself could disrupt his own life and work. He begins to feel an uncomfortable modesty, and after the draft card ceremonies near the end of Part II of Book One, the emphasis of the narrative and description of Book One changes gradually from the narrator's sense of self-importance to his sense of self-recognition and humility. He casts aside his life-long fantasy of heroically leading a revolution; he sees that he will be too old, too imcompetent, too "showboat," and too lacking in essential judgment to play such a role. His role is rather to be a hero-fool and a figurehead, a scapegoat: "not a future leader, but a future victim: *there* would be his real value" (pp. 77–78).

In this role of the holy-fool-as-a-scapegoat, Mailer's hero again becomes a figure of greater universality. The traditional scapegoat, of which Frazer provided so many examples in *The Golden Bough*, merges with certain traditional fools throughout history and myth, folklore and religion. Enid Welsford's third chapter in *The Fool*, entitled "Origins: The Fool as Mascot and Scapegoat," is a thorough study of the fusion of the fool and scapegoat in Indian, Eastern, Arabic, and European seasonal festivals and fertility ceremonies. Fool-scapegoats ruled for ritually determined periods as pariahs who scorned and rebuked the existent systems of society and culture until they were driven into exile. Before the regeneration of order or the renewal of the agricultural seasons could begin, such fools encouraged every excess, chaos, and breaking of the law. In the great seasonal festivals of Christian Europe, for example, the ceremonies were occasions for both worship and wild feasting, lawlessness, and buffoonery. At times the dances and games and general Saturnalia were carried into the cathedrals themselves. Fools, like the ancient scapegoats, belabored bystanders for their sins and folly and created an atmosphere in which all revelers became fools themselves.

Like Mailer's hero-fool, the festival fools, by their ritual roles as actors, sufferers, and observers, were endowed with holiness. The fool's usual distance from the revelers also indicated his status as an excommunicate from his culture and as a mock king. But the holy fool is also part of the prophetic tradition, from the primitive

---

scapegoat-clown figure is often at the center of such rites, and the ceremonial expulsions of the demons and diseases consist of fastings and ablutions; ceremonial extinguishings and kindlings of fire; group incantations, noises, and hullabaloo; collective orgies; ceremonial combats; and the interpenetration or intermingling of the souls of the dead and the living. All such ceremonies seek the abolition of corrupted past time (historical time) and the creation of a new, sanctified time (pp. 53–54).

shaman, to the Hebrew prophets and the Greek oracles. In the subsequent chapter, entitled "Origins: The Fool as Poet and Clairvoyant," Welsford discusses the attribution of divine and demonic inspiration to the mad fool, especially in Irish legend and history. The holy fool in this tradition most clearly represents the receding of the "logical soul" or psyche and the advancing of the inspired, irrational soul. This shift in the balance of the logical and the irrational has always been a goal of Mailer and his heroes. The inspired fool's satire was considered a kind of magical utterance, and satire, which began to emerge in *The Deer Park* and erupted furiously in *Why Are We in Vietnam?*, returns with greater restraint and effect in *Armies*, especially where Mailer satirizes the foolishness and vanities of others and himself. Though, in this light, the clowning and coarse ridicule of D.J. might be seen as the ravings of an ultimately defeated fool, the hero-fool of *Armies* will be a triumphant fool—a fool who embodies in the oldest traditions of inspired rantings and ruminations the power of information, eloquence, and abusive raillery.[9]

Mailer's hero-fool is both actor and observer, combines in fact both attributes of the previous heroes in one. He is the focus of others' attention, one who is the actor at the center of events, but he is also a witness, or a self who is a center of perception and whose greater role will be to reveal the meaning in the events he observes. His first duty to this role of symbolic figure and real victim is to get himself arrested. And as he begins to participate in the March and in the active demonstrations, he feels the promise of purgations and renewals just beginning. Such promise is even in the absurd comedy of the March from the Lincoln Memorial to the Pentagon, which Mailer describes in detail. As he and the distraught notables struggle against the "upstarts and arrivistes" immediately behind them, who are pushed in turn by the billowing ranks and masses in the parade, as the parade monitors bellow orders at the chaotic ranks, as motorcylces roar and jockey with television cars for position, Mailer feels some timeless warrior's experience awaiting them beyond the comedy. In the front line of battle he feels "a promise of swift transit— one's soul feels clean; as we have gathered, he was not used much

---

9. See Welsford, *The Fool*, pp. 65–76, 78–80, 87–88, 111–12. Welsford points out,·in her long discussion of the Irish *fili* or poet-wizard traditions, that the holy-fool's supernatural gifts of insight and prophecy were not only valued as prophetic powers but also as powers to ward off malignant influences and to satirize enemies with a magical potency. The divine fool is a particularly primitive form of the fool. As the modern ages approached, the fool generally became more and more a simple grotesque, until, of course, he was revived as a prophetic figure in Renaissance theater.

more than any other American politician, litterateur, or racketeer to the sentiment that his soul was not unclean . . . in some part of himself at least, he had grown" (p. 113).

When Mailer breaks through the police lines at the Pentagon and is arrested, he takes the first tangible step in his own change. The symbolic protest converges with real actions for a real cause. His senses charged by the confrontation, he compares his feeling at the moment of arrest to being confirmed; he discovers some initial stage of wholeness and a new kind of importance. "He felt his own age, forty-four, felt it as if he were finally one age, not seven, felt as if he were a solid embodiment of bone, muscle, flesh, and vested substance, rather than the will, heart, mind, and sentiment to be a man . . . as if this picayune arrest had been his Rubicon" (p. 138). If his trials are not fantastically heroic, they are real. When he is thrust into a police wagon with a counterdemonstrator who is an American Nazi, Mailer faces down the Nazi in a Rojacklike contest where each man's eyes becomes the focus of his soul, and where Mailer, "obliged not to lose," holds his own. Imprisonment itself is a test, a series of erosions of strength and integrity for the twenty-four hours Mailer endures it. He is forced into a self-discipline in jail that he had tried to avoid earlier. To keep his strength he must learn to cast aside personal interests—returning to wife and children, going to a party in New York. Again in prison he is encouraged by the integrity of some of the young men and of such notables as Noam Chomsky and Yale chaplain John Boyle. And at his own trial he is helpless before the bureaucracy that singles him out for special punishment until a bright young lawyer named Hirschkop battles cleverly to earn Mailer's release.

Through such experiences, the narrator-hero is himself being tested throughout Book One. As actor and sufferer, he is being made aware of his own strengths and weaknesses, and he has opportunities to compare himself to others. As we have seen, the way in which the narrator sees people at first, or imagines them to be, at times contrasts with what he discovers about them in the midst of real events. To some extent, therefore, the way Mailer as a new journalist will shape his events is less under his total control than the shape of events in his novels. Imagination and reality are uniting in *Armies* to produce a new foundation for narrative structure and theme and a new complication in Mailer's relationship to his characters and material. Aware of these new elements in his material, Mailer-the-writer observes with some distance the changes in Mailer-the-persona's vision that such complications encourage.

Upon his release from prison, the final effect of all the ceremonies and trials is the hero's sense of humility and elation, a sense that completes the comic hero's movement from brawling self-assertion to a new modesty. The comic hero's development from Beast to modest participant is important because it can better foreshadow one direction of Mailer's future work than would a hero of supernatural strengths and perceptions. Still, extraordinary consciousness is clearly important, and it is the goal. But since 1967 Mailer has increasingly sounded a note of self-doubt, of wondering if anyone can tell if he or she is finally more good than evil. Mailer's previous work suggests that some may attain the perception of good and evil in oneself and others, but that faith is now being called into doubt.[10] In *Armies* this note of doubt may be a function of the author's move from fiction to journalism where the raw material is more resistant to a writer's attempts to give it shape and heroes are few.

Mailer describes his deliverance in terms of celebration and rebirth. His renewed sense of the possibilities of life and the importance of freedom make him unusually magnanimous about the possibilities in humanity and America. He associates the potential in humanity and America with the Christ within: "standing on the grass, he felt one suspicion of a whole man closer to that freedom from dread which occupied the inner drama of his years, yes, one image closer than when he had come to Washington four days ago" (pp. 212–13).[11] The discovery of Christ is the discovery of "this nice anticipation of the very next moves of life itself," of the wholeness of the self, and of compassion. It is the discovery of a god-in-man quite different from Mailer's embattled, banished, dread-inspiring God, but closer to some hint of the ethical order and absolution that D.J. glimpsed in the bear's eye. If the "Christian" god and the god of protean power are not entirely reconciled in *Armies,* neither are the

10. Seven years later, in 1975, Mailer addressed this problem specifically. He abdicated his power to determine finally the good and evil in others and in oneself. Kierkegaard has, he admits, helped him to this position. But Mailer does not abdicate the capacity to feel sensations of the good and evil from the experience of an event he is participating in and reporting on. Rather than imposing categories on experience, Mailer argues that he is attracted to events in which polarities are obviously at war. I agree with the note of skepticism in Laura Adams's questions on this point. It is problematic to what degree the categories arise from the experience or are brought to the experience. It is certainly true that Mailer has made it his study to seek out the elements of each side of the dualism. At least Mailer is increasingly aware of complexities that his work to this point does not convincingly demonstrate. See Laura Adams, "Existential Aesthetics: An Interview with Norman Mailer," *Partisan Review,* pp. 197–214. I merely introduce an issue here that I will return to later.

11. For Jung's own study of the archetypal association of Christ and wholeness of self, see "Christ, a Symbol of the Self," *Aion,* pp. 36–71, and Jung's Foreword, pp. 3–23.

pagan and Christian metaphors of the book. Part of Mailer's discovery here would appear to be that the Christian and pagan gods are not entirely irreconcilable but may coexist as different manifestations of the God of Life itself.

It is not that Mailer gives up his existential god, but that he discovers another possibility of God. As wholeness, this Christ within is the opposite of that schism between body and soul and between the conscious and the unconscious that Mailer has been warning about in America since *Advertisements*. Just before he is released from prison, Mailer, in a digression, has speculated again that the average American at midcentury believes in, serves, "two opposites"—mystery, which is at the center of Christianity, and the detestation of mystery, which is at the center of the corporation and technology. The modern schism in the Christian soul, Mailer argues, is unequaled by any schism before it. Vietnam, he continues, is a result and manifestation of the schism. This schism Mailer loosely calls schizophrenia, because "the expression of brutality" offers the schizophrenic a "definite if temporary relief." Against the mystery of Christ the corporation offers security, television, the unspoken promise that the judgment of one's soul will be "no worse than the empty spaces of the Tonight Show" (p. 189). When Mailer, seeking salience rather than profundity, tells the waiting reporters upon his release that Christians have somehow become cannibals consuming Christ by technological fire in Vietnam, he confuses them. They report, therefore, only in terms of what they do understand— Mailer's public image as an anarchic fool. Mailer ends the narrative of events in Book One by quoting a press report that accuses him of being a Jew who grandstands a Sunday sermon in a court of law.

If Book One illustrates the observations and personal experiences that led to Mailer's passage through the "long dark night of the soul" in America, and if his passage illustrates the growth of the protagonist from his worst self (the Beast and vaudeville clown at the Ambassador Theater) to his best self (the humbled convict who recognizes the meaning of the Christ within), Book Two illustrates the darker passage and greater change for others. Book Two is Mailer's analysis of as many accounts as he could find of the events he did not witness, but that analysis is charged with the consciousness of a participant in ancillary events.

> It is terribly important who the observer is. That's why I always try to put myself into these works of journalism so the reader can have his sense of me. It's important to be able to decide whether I'm perceiving well or where I'm perceiving badly. Whereas, if I attempt to present to readers what I consider the end product of objective truth, it's likely

> to be nothing more than the harshly digested conclusions I came up
> with in my somewhat unbalanced soul. (What else is most
> journalism?) Whereas I believe the fun in reading comes from
> observing the observer. (Adams interview, pp. 209– 10)

At least, Mailer continues in the interview, he gives even disagreeing
readers a chance to approach truth by comparing lies. The synthesis
of two antitheses may, in other words, lead to a higher level of
consciousness in the reader-observer.

It is obvious even from the title adopted from Arnold's "Dover
Beach" that Mailer will portray two ignorant armies, two antitheses,
clashing by night, in this case the night of the American soul. But one
ignorant army undergoes a positive rite of passage. It is with this
army that Mailer will cast his lot. Mailer compares the rite of the
working-class soldiers and marshals and the government officials
with a negative rite of passage. "Men learn in a negative rite to give
up the best things they were born with," he says of an official
speaking in "totalitarianese" who has stripped his speech of moral
content. "How much must a spokesman suffer in a negative rite to
be able to learn to speak in such a way?" (p. 285). In contrast,
wherever there were ceremonial acts and direct confrontations in
Book One, there were remarkable young people emerging out of
their past lives and the dimming force of all their organizations,
programs, and speeches. In Book Two the actual battles between
police and protestors continually narrowed the army of demonstrators down to what Mailer calls "the best." As for Rojack and
D.J., the essence of the rite of passage resides in tests of endurance
and courage. From the thousands who marched, to the few
thousand who stayed to protest, to the final two hundred who
resisted until the end, and to the last resisting Quakers, the movement from Book One through Book Two is toward the gradual
revelation of the essential form or soul, the hardest core, or protest
for moral obligations.

Mailer's description of the "Battle of the Wedge" near the end of
Book Two illustrates the climax of this "passage through the night."
For the demonstrators who stayed, this battle is a final act of
defiance and courage, an act Mailer describes as outshining his own
battles. These demonstrators face successively dangerous choices on
the moral ladder that Mailer himself could not when imprisoned (p.
195). I disagree with the gist of those critics who believe Mailer sees
his decision not to resist the sentence as a rejection of the moral
ladder. Upon his release, Mailer simply suggests that ejecting oneself
from the guilt one feels if one refuses to climb the ladder might be
worth it if one could see the possibilities in a new freedom and
reduce the nausea of guilt enough to go on with one's work. He

obviously admires the strength of the last resisters and even the martyrs; they represent Mailer's own chief hope. [12]

In the Battle of the Wedge, seasoned paratroopers and marshals move into the last group of demonstrators as they sit beside the Pentagon. Here Mailer sees that the rite of passage these young people endure is connected, in some timeless way, to such rites everywhere and especially in American history.

> . . . the light reflected from the radiance of greater more heroic hours may have come nonetheless to shine along *the inner space* and caverns of the freaks, some hint of a glorious future . . ., some refrain from all the great American rites of passage when men and women manacled themselves to a lost and painful principle and survived a day, a night, a week, a month, a year, a celebration of Thanksgiving—the country had been founded on a rite of passage . . . Very few had not emigrated here without the echo of that rite . . . each generation of Americans had forged their own rite, in the forest of the Alleghenies and the Adirondacks, at Valley Forge, at New Orleans in 1812, with Rogers and Clark or at Sutter's Mill, at Gettysburg, the Alamo, the Klondike, the Argonne, Normandy, Pusan. (*Armies*, p. 280)

If this rite is pale beside some of those in our past, it is still, Mailer reminds us, a true rite for each of those resisters who, though "drug-ridden," "jargon-mired," and spoiled, faced his or her own resources of endurance and courage in a "painful spiritual test" where "some part of the man has been born again, and is better" (pp. 280–81).

In retrospect at the end of Book Two, Mailer reaffirms the timelessness of the event through recalling two continuing motifs in *Armies*: the presence of the ghosts and the esprit of the Union Dead and the spawning rites of the chinook salmon in Robert Lowell's lines from *Near the Ocean*.

> O to break loose, like the chinook
> salmon jumping and falling back,

12. Compare, for example, pp. 179–81, where Mailer is aware of his "unholy desire" to be released, and pp. 280–81, where the basis of the greatest rite and promise for Life is in "the incomprehensible mysteries of moral choice," of facing the moral ladder until one's last strength or sanity gives out. I agree, for example, with Adams that Mailer discovers in prison that the linear view of moral development is replaced by a cumulative view: that is, if one's cumulative acts have more good than bad, then moral progress is made. See Laura Adams, *Existential Battles: The Growth of Norman Mailer*, pp. 132–33. But the conflict between worst and best selves is ultimately always linear; that is, progressive if one approaches Life more than Death, and the moral commitments of the most-daring demonstrators are the basis of Mailer's whole new "modesty." Robert Solotaroff, in essence, agrees with Adams but is more aware of the striking "secularity" of Mailer's position in choosing not to engage the certain defeats of prison. But Mailer argues finally, Solotaroff sees, that cumulative good amidst one's bad is still a linear, that is, a Life-approaching, moral progress. See *Down Mailer's Way*, pp. 230–31.

nosing up to the impossible
stone and bone-crushing waterfall—
raw-jawed, weak-fleshed there, stopped by ten
steps of the roaring ladder, and then
to clear the top on the last try,
alive enough to spawn and die.

The meaning of the Pentagon protest is that thousands of people underwent rites of passage that changed their inner lives, that regenerated Life to some part of body and soul. Mailer, a microcosm, a lesser initiate, was among them. What counts for Mailer, first, is that each person goes from the March and resistance with some inner victory. What Mailer admires most about Jerry Rubin, for example, is his revolutionary mysticism which sees that beyond the endless negotiations between coalition and government and beyond all the compromises in the revolutionary aesthetic or image, a war of publicity is still far subordinate to an inner victory, a transformation of the psychological reality of the initiates. This inner change is caused by the rigors of moral choice and moral action that test one's courage and endurance (one's proportions) for a point of belief. The negative rite of passage strips moral content from one's words and actions and shapes public opinion into an amoral position.

"There are places no history can reach," Mailer admits as he prepares to deliver his speculations on the last throes, the final private rigors, of the rite for those extraordinary few who choose to stay in prison and climb the moral ladder to its end. Mailer imagines for us the group of Quakers from Voluntown, Connecticut, suffering the fevers and visions of fasting and dehydration—some force-fed, some thrown in "the Hole"—dreaming of a "long column of Vietnamese dead, Vietnamese walking a column of flame, eyes on fire, nose on fire, mouth speaking flame, did they pray, 'O Lord, forgive our people for they do not know' " (p. 287). These few had struggled to the "thin source" of Lowell's chinook river, had given up that nice anticipation of life that Mailer associates with the Christ within, to bear a Christlike penance for their people. The modern crisis of Christianity, like the crisis of consciousness, is illustrated for Mailer in the opposition of military heroes in Vietnam and the last Christian heroes in prison who chose passive resistance and martyrdom.

In the final brief chapter, entitled "The Metaphor Delivered," Mailer describes America as God-in-Bondage. This country, a light to the world—born of the idea, Mailer repeats, that God as both compassion (Christ) and power (embattled creature) lives within each of us—has locked God's Life in some dreadful curse. This curse has come to reflect the will of the people, a diseased people. If the people can but find some key to turn the locks of Life, their will may become God's will, but if they cannot, those locks must remain the will of a Devil, of a Death, whose liars now control the locks and distract us, insulate us, from seeing where lies the will of One or the Other. Whether the labor of birth that Mailer sees America undergoing will produce "the most fearsome totalitarianism the world has ever known" or "a babe of a new world" that will be tender, artful, and brave, depends upon the capacity of America's people to find the key to the locks of Life. "Rush to the locks," Mailer implores in closing, "God writhes in his bonds. Rush to the locks. Deliver us from our curse" (p. 288).

The closing prayer for deliverance suggests some of the answers to our general question about Mailer's turn to nonfiction. What does he gain in *Armies* over his past work? He gains, first, what he frankly tells us he does: new energy. The entire Vietnam experience gave Mailer the necessary impetus to express his rebellion, just as his participation in the protest of the war renewed his rebellious energy. The war and protest gave him the grim satisfaction of seeing some of his ideas and metaphors confirmed, for the awakening consciousness of the demonstrators also preceived the country as diseased, the war generals as cancerous tumors, the Pentagon as both the symbol and reality of evil. Secondly, *Armies*, obviously, and all of Mailer's journalism since then, is a workout for the main event, the big novel Mailer is finally writing under contract with Little, Brown for a reported million dollars over several years. In his preface to *Existential Errands,* Mailer describes the nonfiction as a preparation and a discovery of material and ideas for that main event (pp. ix–x). The National Book Award and Pulitzer Prize for *Armies* made Mailer credible enough to a commerical publisher that he now has an opportunity to enter the main event. A third gain is that Mailer discovered the value of a new approach to a postwar world so absurd, so chaotic, and so dangerous that, as Marcus Klein argues, "clear social fact" has disappeared and writers no longer have a sense of a civilization "against which and within which fiction might act."[13]

Fourth, Mailer has faced the problem Hawthorne faced working in the allegorical mode: the problem of making the writer's allegorical conceptions (plot, character) more warmly, complexly human. In his prefaces to *The Blithedale Romance* and *Rappaccini's Daughter*, Hawthorne attributed part of the problem to his attempt to write romance in a country without a native tradition of mystery, enchantment, and romantic atmosphere. Had there ever been less a feeling of mystery and enchantment than in our midcentury

13. Klein, *The American Novel Since World War II,* p. 15.

America, at least until the upheavals of the late sixties? Edwin Honig
suggests, however, that Hawthorne's problem may well be a problem with all allegory and that Melville alone made the first real and
effective attempt to resolve the problem of creating "vigorous moral
and aesthetic authority" in fiction while retaining life and truth.
Melville, first, removed *Moby Dick* from the world of "landlocked
Christians," and then he introduced an unprecedented amount of
factual material, which, Honig argues, created a "new sort of literal
dimension for his allegorical narrative." Melville incorporated a
natural history of whaling, immense in its detail, from which his
allegory explicitly drew its effects, and by which the symbolic and
literal truths were interfused. A sustained literal dimension can
create a convincing realism without separating the literal and symbolic levels of the allegory. One level contains the other, as a whole
contains its parts, as Melville's avalanche of facts contains "the
overwhelming idea of the whale." There would be some truth in a
comparison of Hawthorne's fiction to Mailer's fiction and of Melville's
Moby Dick to Mailer's nonfiction. Hawthorne's characters are ever
approaching "some dream of purpose from which the full glow of
reality and self-determination has faded." But Melville, at least in
Moby Dick, is ever "moving simultaneously on both planes," meeting the metaphysical problem head on. The impact of such an
organic work as Melville's is that it expresses, to continue Honig's
observations, "as comprehensive a definition of phenomenal reality
as it is possible to get in allegory: a reality that is both contained in its
own manifest self sufficiency and fluid and chanceful as the sea." [14]
    Mailer increases the literal dimension of his work by approaching
a real experience in which opposing polarities are already clear and
by depicting a number of real people with whom he is somewhat in
sympathy and somewhat in opposition. The nature of the experience
itself in Book One recasts Mailer's symbolic and metaphorical concerns and enables him to give to them a viable, more convincing,
more complexly human literal dimension than ever before. We have
seen examples of this complexity in Mailer's description of the marshals as real men, not unlike his former army buddies, who had
undergone some rabid change, or when Mailer portrays Lowell as
both heroic and foolish himself, both admirable and vain, strong
and humanly weak. We have seen such complexity when Mailer
argues that there is an enemy within us all, and when he realizes
that the moral capacity of others whom he had damned is greater

---

14. Edwin Honig, *Dark Conceit*, pp. 101–4, 144. Honig notes that Kafka does
much the same with the bureaucracy of law and institutions, the realistic facts and
details of which support the allegorical content as Melville's facts and details on
whaling do.

than his own, as Chomsky and Boyle in particular suggest to him. We have also seen it when the narrator-hero is both wise and foolish, both inspired and schizophrenic, both actor and sufferer. In Book Two Mailer presents as many facts and eye-witness accounts as he has in order to give a further validity. And in the end, the facts return us to, indeed tend to substantiate, the metaphorical battle between Life and Death. Whether or not Mailer learned from Melville, one of his acknowledged masters, his ability to increase the literal dimension of his allegory, we cannot say for sure, but the overall effect is similar. Mailer seems, however, to have been more satisfied with the lessons of realism. After *Moby Dick* Melville becomes more allegorical, less factual. And both Mailer and Melville retire from fiction after their attempts to create an archetypal consciousness in *Why Are We in Vietnam?* and in *The Confidence-Man*. Yet unlike his literary hero Melville, Mailer does not retire altogether; Mailer becomes more public, more the moralizer, more a seeker of some order behind the seemingly fragmented, purposeless world of his time. Mailer turns directly to historical events to pursue his vision of a primitive, meaningful order amidst chaos.

There is, however, in *Armies* a tension between the author's allegorical, didactic purposes and the greater complexity and humanity of the literal dimension. There is often a seeming lack of complexity and human warmth, as when the forces of the enemy are defined and attached to the evils of corporate technology, or even when, one must admit, the emphasis on the marshals is more on their mechanical functioning as tools of malignant powers. It is of course possible that this tension between the real and the unreal (or the complex and the purely allegorical) is a literally and historically valid depiction of contemporary America; that when events become "sufficiently emotional, spiritual, psychical, moral, existential, or supernatural,"the instincts of the novelist and the egocentric may be required to capture the event. For history itself is turning novelistic.

Stanley T. Gutman has associated Mailer's ego assertion with the romantic faith in the subjective perceptions of the artist's primary imagination.[15] It is true that this romantic faith, which Mailer calls in *Armies* his "Emersonian" faith in the "incandescence" of powerful subjective states, is the starting point of the narrator's view of events. But ultimately the event itself will color Mailer's subjective consciousness of it. The allegorist traditionally creates not simply historical truth but, as Edwin Honig puts it, autonomous truth. Autonomous truth is distinguished by the artist's exploitation of what is most important to him, which becomes the "imaginative

15. *Armies*, pp. 28–29, and Gutman, *Mankind in Barbary*, pp. 189–92.

center of the action." The allegorical truth becomes autonomous because the artist creates his own authority and because the work itself proves the credibility of that authority and the value of its report. The allegorist, therefore, transforms "history and action and frees them from the bondage of time." He creates a new order and a new time—a permanent present where things past confront, in Spenser's words, "all things to come." [16] Mailer's allegorical journalism does lead him to rediscover the strange powers of realism and of experience. He does begin with the allegorical or artistic assumption that by exploiting the imaginative center of the action he frees history from time. But he reverses the process by immersing himself in the experience of the event, by observing himself and others, and by finding *in the experience itself* the real center and meaning of the action. The direction and shape of his book are determined by what actually happened to him and by what he observed. The new journalism thereby becomes for Mailer a vehicle for discovering as well as for portraying the timeless in the historical, the mythic and symbolic in the literal, and the complex in the polarized. In *Armies* he goes further than ever before in dissolving the barriers between fiction and history, between ceremonial Time and historical time, between art and act. Mailer begins here a definite return to the largest possibilities within experience itself and he moves away from the tendency in allegorical art to limit the allegorical or archetypal as a purely imagined existence. It is in historical experience that Mailer discovers the primitive order of the archetypes, finds wholeness and purpose in a world apparently without wholeness and purpose, and discovers that through the unifying force of art he can demonstrate this order and thereby give meaning to the chaotic events of his time. These discoveries apparently gave him the impetus to spend the next decade of his career in the historical arena of nonfiction. In this arena, Mailer sees that an archetypal order operates through events, and that allegory still serves the ends of social criticism.

Mailer's final gain *Armies* is that he is able to show what he has meant by our worst and best selves. Both selves are embodied in Mailer and in the demonstrators as coexisting antitheses. Since Mailer believes that our hope for growth and life resides in our best selves (again echoing Matthew Arnold), if only we can learn to turn the best that is in us against the worst that is in us, he makes another important gain by an historical illustration of our best and worst selves. If as a number of critics have said, Henry Adams, whom Mailer mentions in *Armies*, is the spiritual progenitor of this book

16. Honig, *Dark Conceit*, pp. 95, 109.

depicting the hero's journey to humility, Mailer is, unlike Adams, arguing that blind power, power stripped of moral content, power void of humanity, power unleashed as chaos, has not yet triumphed. Such power has yet to defeat an opposing power of our deepest human unconscious life, which may, Mailer is saying, be undergoing a renaissance. In the hands of a blind power, the protestors pass through the trials that lead to self-discovery and inner victory. As Mailer said in *The Presidential Papers*, only self-discovery can lead one to know how one is good or how one is evil (pp. 172–73). In *Advertisements* Mailer maintained that "communication that does not lead to action is not communication" (p. 286). By illustrating how we once turned our losses to gain, Mailer is able to plea for continued, increased action; he can plead that his compatriots continue the movement they began when they waged symbolic warfare on the Pentagon, a movement to free a banished God and release the locks of Life.

8

Conclusion: A Decade of Nonfiction, Women, and Promise

All true science is "savior vivre." But all your modern science is the contrary of that. It is "savoir mourir."   —John Ruskin, *Fors Clavigera*

Man is not order of nature . . . nor any ignominious baggage; but a stupendous antagonism, a dragging together of the poles of the Universe. . .here they are, side by side, god and devil,mind and matter,king and conspirator, belt and spasm, riding peacefully together in the eye and brain of every man.
                        —Ralph Waldo Emerson, "Fate"

Extra vagance! . . . I desire to speak somewhere *without* bounds; like a man in a waking moment, to men in their waking moments; for I am convinced that I cannot exaggerate enough even to lay the foundation of a true expression.
                        —Henry David Thoreau, *Walden*

Between *The Armies of the Night* and *The Executioner's Song* (1979), Mailer published eight more nonfiction books: *Miami and the Siege of Chicago* (1968), *Of a Fire on the Moon* (1970), *"The King of the Hill"* (1971), *The Prisoner of Sex* (1971), *St. George and the Godfather* (1972), and *Marilyn* (1973). He also published the script of his third film entitled *Maidstone: A Mystery* (1971), another collection of prose on various subjects entitled *Existential Errands* (1972), and a long essay accompanying the photography of Mervyn Kurlansky and Jon Naar in a book entitled *The Faith of Graffiti* (1974). During this time Mailer also published critical and journalistic pieces for periodicals and made a number of speaking engagements and television appearances. *The Fight*, which first appeared in *Playboy*, was published in book form in 1975. Then Mailer produced a critical anthology on Henry Miller, entitled *Genius and Lust* (1976), continued his political journalism in an article on Jimmy Carter in the *New York Times Magazine* (September 26, 1976), and published a screenplay in *Playboy* (December 1976) entitled "The Trial of the Warlock" and based on J.K. Huysman's novel *Là-Bas*. That same year, a collection of political writings, *Some Honorable Men*, appeared. And of course with the publication in October 1979, of *The Executioner's Song*, Mailer capped his decade of nonfiction with a final work that may prove to be a major nonfictional achievement on the order of *Armies*. *The Executioner's Song* appears

166

to be not only the capstone of the nonfiction period, but a point of departure for a third distinct period in Mailer's career, the period of Mailer's final fictions.

We cannot possibly do justice to all of Mailer's later works in one chapter. However, the differences between the presidential journalism, which certainly is interesting in its own right, and *Armies* suggest why we may look at the convention coverage only briefly to keep within the particular limits in this study. Mailer shapes the March on the Pentagon into a eternal battle and a timeless rite in which he participated. The convention coverage is frequently concise and revealing, but most of this material will surely date in a way that *Armies* will not. The 1968 and 1972 conventions in *Miami and the Siege of Chicago* and in *St. George and the Godfather* are described as conventions, with digressions and ruminations. If the convention coverage is in many ways acute, perceptive, and lively in *Miami*, the coverage is not clearly part of a larger artistic purpose; the author does very little to shape and emphasize the event as a timeless moment in history. In *Armies*, Mailer develops the greatest commitment to the event; he executes his subject matter most effectively into a whole. In *Miami* nothing arises from the writer's engagement with his material like the final declaration in *Armies* that God's life (and therefore humanity's) is on the line. Mailer's last note in *Miami* is that he probably will not vote, that as for the revolution, well, "we may yet win, the others are so stupid. Heaven help us when we do" (p. 223).

One important thing about Mailer's disengagement in *Miami* is that it typifies increasing self-doubt throughout the late sixties and early seventies. Mailer's ruminations are mostly concerned with his own sense of confusion over who he is and just what he or anyone can now know. It is not so much that he loses all the convictions of his life's work, but that the Jeremiah edge is off the rhetoric and the prophetic view of himself, and a relative peace settles in, a moment of fitful rest as Mailer surveys what appear to be new complexities in the landscape of Super-America.

But Mailer also specifically stresses that the time itself, or the confusion of the sixties, contributes to his self-doubt and his disengaged reporting in *Miami*. He tells us early in his coverage of the Chicago convention that he did not find the justifications for participation he had found in the March. Until the end of the convention, he saw no definite symbol against which he could act, no bastion of the military-industrial complex that had remained impervious to the scrutiny of the press and the people. As the convention progresses, Mailer does grow more and more concerned about the demonstrators and the police violence, and he steps into the action two or three times. He makes two speeches. He tries to mobilize two hundred delegates into a protest against the police-state tactics inside and outside the convention hall, but he fails. He is forced by shame to ruminate, mostly alone over drinks, about his own reasons for staying aloof and about his own fears. He will, finally, go so far as to confront the National Guard and come close to getting himself jailed again, but he ends up going to a party at Hugh Hefner's mansion with fellow journalists Pete Hamill and Doug Kiker. His later ruminations will force him to face the fact that in middle age he is ever moving further from Marx and closer to Edmund Burke; he is unsure of his readiness to give up his life and work for the chaos of the Yippie revolution and the alternative police state. It is only clear, finally, that Mailer is more sympathetic toward the demonstrators than toward the police. "The children were crazy, but they developed honor every year, they had a vision not void of beauty; the other side had no vision, only a nightmare of smashing a brain with a brick." [1]

During the seventies, however, Mailer published three books that require our careful scrutiny because they are more directly concerned with Mailer's largest themes and more clearly represent the continuation of his allegorical art into his nonfiction period. The books are *Of a Fire on the Moon* (1971), *The Fight* (1975), and *The Executioner's Song* (1979). These texts also exemplify the movement of Mailer's work and mind in the seventies.

Fire stands between the convention reportage and the nonfiction art of *Armies*. Like *Armies*, *Fire* opens with the narrator's light-hearted irony and self-mockery: "His fury that the world was not run so well as he could run it encouraged him to speak." The narrator is rather humble and modest throughout the later book; he is weary with himself, his voice, and his sense of importance. He feels in fact disembodied or separated from his ego. But this loss of ego he hopes to turn to gain. He argues that since he is "a little shunted to the side" of the spirit of the age, he may be in the best position to observe this age. [2]

Yet the narrator is, as in *Armies*, also a microcosm of his time and country. "What did we know of what we did?" (p. 466). He continually calls himself a man adrift, a guideless explorer searching for clues and signs. Again the confusion of the sixties generally has considerable impact upon the narrator himself. He is part of the schism and lunacy of the decade, which he began by stabbing his second wife and ended by running for mayor of New York. He feels

---

1. *Miami and the Siege of Chicago* (hereafter cited as *Miami*), p. 214. Unless otherwise indicated, all citations are to works by Norman Mailer.
2. *Of a Fire on the Moon* (hereafter cited as *Fire*), pp. 3–4, 51, 56–57, 63.

an ambiguity, a hopefulness and emptiness, about the flight to the moon that he believes the rest of the world shares. Vaguely recalling the hero-victim of *Armies*, he promises to pass judgments only after passing through his own torments: his dread of the conquest of the moon, his inability to comprehend the material he is assigned to cover, his failure in a fourth marriage. Near the end of *Fire*, he will invite his readers to judge the narrator for themselves. "The question is whether it is better to trust a judge who travels through his own desolations before passing sentence, or a jurist who has a good meal, a romp with his mistress, a fine night of sleep, and a penalty of death in the morning for the highwayman" (p. 435).

Like *Armies* again, *Fire* is a kind of journalism that is explicitly reacting to conventional journalism, even though this emphasis in *Fire* is relatively mild. Mailer complains that journalists covering the events in the conventional ways lose what is best in their talent because they are constantly stripping their facts of nuance. He then adds that in a time when events themselves are developing "a style and structure that [makes] them almost impossible to write about," journalists are becoming obsolete, and Mailer is beginning to wonder at this point if even the unconventional journalist can discover and report the meanings of events. Perhaps the technicalities are becoming too great, the confrontations too masked in superficiality, the nature of men and machines too ambiguous. One of his principal difficulties as a reporter is finding a way to make the astronauts seem real to him; they seem so devoid of human emotion and so machinelike (pp. 88–89, 96).

But unlike the author of *Armies* and closer to the author of *Miami*, Mailer is now employed as a journalist to cover a specific assignment for *Life*. If he retains the third person point of view, he is always shifting his emphasis away from autobiography. He plays no personal role in the events he reports. He promises to be a modest, quiet observer who will not take root, who will only occasionally pull in his ego to help him criticize what he observes. He self-consciously employs such journalistic tools as the interview (i.e., NASA officials, the astronauts), the press conference, and the informant, but he finds these tools essentialy useless. The one tool Mailer finds useful in writing his book is research, hard factual research. Never has the sheer onslaught of facts, statistics, and scientific analyses played so large a role in a Mailer book.

It is as if Mailer's sense of the power of fact and reportorial realism discovered in *Armies* assumes a much larger influence in *Fire*. A look at the overall pattern of *Fire* would indeed reveal Mailer's continuous alternation of large sections of detailed descriptions and factual data and smaller, digressive commentaries on what the narrator

observes. Part I, "Aquarius," introduces the narrator, but most of its
five chapters describe press conferences, NASA, Cape Kennedy, and
the blast-off and flight of Apollo 11. Part II, "Apollo," accounts for at
least two-thirds of the book. Here Mailer retraces the entire flight to
the moon and back, and the event itself takes over almost entirely.
We understand through the exhaustive details the magnitude of
Mailer's research. But Aquarius is far in the background, only on
occasion commenting or digressing to guide and increase the meaning of his long descriptions. Finally, however, in the brief Part III,
"The Age of Aquarius," the narrator reemerges fully and his speculations become bold enough to recall the narrator of *Armies*.

But this heightened use of detail and realism should not obscure
an allegorical purpose in *Fire* that is in some ways similar to the
allegorical purpose of *Armies*. If *Fire* is not a strong call to action, if
it is perhaps a less successful embodiment of an idea, it still has
didactic allegorical intentions consistent with the central development of Mailer's work. The first of these intentions, he tells us, is to
begin "a reconnaissance into the possibility of restoring magic,
psyche, and the spirits of the underworld to the spookiest venture in
history," despite the thick layer of "technologese" that shrouds the
event, and despite "the resolute lack of poetic immortality in the
astronauts' communications with the earth" (p. 293). The moon
itself has always been an important symbol for Mailer, and in *Fire* he
is particularly anxious to restore our sense of the mystery of the
moon. He emphasizes her eerie presence, her importance as a form
whose surface reveals some existential meaning about the cosmic
blasts and struggles of outer space from which the earth is pro-
tected, and her vast if mysterious connection to earth life, and
possibly the human psyche, especially the connection between the
interval of completion of the moon's phases and the cycles of fertility
of women on earth—a connection that Mailer sees as an example of
"a hieroglyph from the deep."[3]

Mailer uses his observations to demonstrate the existence of the
inexplicable. He tries to emphasize that we cannot discover any final
knowledge through science alone and that even technology is never
free of magic and irrationality. Modern physics, the previous NASA
flights, and even the astronauts all testify to these points.[4] His piling
up of instances of the irrational behavior of machines is one example. His emphasis on the dreams and deeper levels of emotion and
thought that now and again appear through the astronauts' dehumanized facade, as we will see, is another.

If the largest allegorical intention of *Fire*, then, is to penetrate the

3. Ibid., pp. 278–79, 281, 286, 293, 300–302.
4. The best examples of these points occur in *Fire* on pages 160–75, 268, 331,
351, 371, 375, 429, and 430.

bland, technological surface of the moon flight and to restore mystery to that event, the profound ambiguity Mailer-as-journalist feels about what he perceives is fundamental to the discovery of the mystery. To suggest that the ambiguous forces at work in the flight are larger than the men and events themselves, Mailer develops two predominant themes. The first theme is that the central actors, the astronauts, are microcosms of a divided American consciousness. The second theme is that good cohabitates with evil in the space program as in contemporary life.

The astronauts themselves appear ambiguous to Mailer. Because they seem both noble and insane to the journalist, he views their divided nature as a microcosm of the colossal ambiguities and the "schizophrenia" of modern America. If one side of their personalities seems heroic and life-enhancing, the other side seems mechanical, damned, life-denying. They have, for example, cultivated a deadened, machinelike surface personality. In their news conferences as well as their flight performances, the astronauts try to reduce all chance, every inexplicable phenomenon, and all hint of menace into meaninglessness by, in Mailer's phrase, their "logical positivism": "Interpret the problem properly, then attack it." They talk about their adventure in a self-effacing, impersonal way. Their language develops into the interchangeable, generalized, and emotionless language of the computer, as if, Mailer says, the more natural forms of English are too primitive, direct, and frightening. Their language is incapable of matching the grandeur of their endeavor. Like the NASA officials themselves, the astronauts take every opportunity to erect an impenetrable shining surface about them; they seek to divide heroism from fear, awe, and romance.

Yet hints of a deeper, more intense life in these men do appear. If they had spent endless hours of physical inactivity adjusting their responses to a machine and "plunking all [their] ambition, avarice, charity, pluck, discipline, and education into an electrical set of brains which will give back nothing but firm answers," they had once lived lives that were athletic, adventurous, and "near-violent" (p. 252). Collins reveals a sense of humor and, relatively speaking, a tendency to be flamboyant. During the flight he is the one most likely to demonstrate a sensitivity to what Mailer endlessly documents as "the psychology of machines." Following a long exchange of numbers and technical terms between Apollo and Houston on the matter of malfunctioning fuel cells, Collins will say: "Those fuel cells . . . are funny things. . . . They are like human beings; they have their little ups and downs." He will go on to speak of the cells' "bad days," hypochondrias, and their spitefulness (pp. 268–69). Armstrong, when pressed by frustrated reporters for some clue of an inner life and a human response to his challenge, is capable of admitting that

men are flying to the moon because it is in "the nature of his [man's]
deep inner soul" to face challenges as much as it is in the instinct of
the salmon to swim upstream (p. 42). Armstrong thereby expresses
Mailer's own ideas about the forces at work in the human soul and
about the potential in large events to become rites of passage that
change the inner life. And Armstrong expresses his point with a
simile that no less a poet than Robert Lowell has used. Aldrin, a
doctor of science and the astronaut who even admits he is "a sort of
mechanical man," is capable of an intensely religious attitude
toward his mission. He will quietly take bread and wine aboard and
celebrate communion on the moon. More, Aldrin will write a
monograph with his minister Dean Woodruff on the symbolic meaning of the flight to the moon, entitled *The Myth of Apollo 11: The
Effects of the Lunar Landing on the Mythic Dimension of Man*. This
paper searches for a symbol "of man's expanding search," as Aldrin
puts it, to demonstrate that the human's "capacity to symbolize and
to respond to symbols is the central fact of human existence." Apollo
11 may be such a symbol. Taking the words out of Mailer's mouth,
Aldrin and Woodruff will write: "Science has created a worldwide
technical civilization, and, as yet, has not given birth to any cultural
symbols by which man can live. . . . We need now a paradigm of the
'experience of the whole' " (p. 339). Does not Aldrin, Mailer asks,
illuminate something of the dichotomy of the WASP, a dichotomy
visible in the long line from "Calvin, Luther, Knox and Wesley to
Edison, Ford, and IBM's own Watson?" (p. 338).

Mailer can only explain the nature of the astronauts as divided
personalities who have learned by years of training to separate "the
depths of their character" from their daily lives. Their surface
personalities reflect America's Faustian pole: the rationalist, the
machine, and the willing absorption into the corporate mill. But
hints of their deeper lives reflect irrational, religious forces that are
also beginning to emerge in American life, through what Mailer
calls America's Oriental pole, a pole evident, for example, in the
group ecstacies of the rock festival (pp. 315– 16). "From their conscious mind to their unconscious depth, what a spectrum could be
covered. . . . their personality might begin to speak, for better or
worse, of some new psychological constitution to man" (p. 46).
Mailer will later write of Armstrong as a twin-souled figure: a bona
fide devil or Faustian, a "cat-technician" prepared to "tamper with
the rain," but also a mystic who has dreams of hovering in space and
who is obsessed by his instinctual drive to engage in a large and
dangerous adventure to a new frontier.

Mailer is also struck by a profound ambiguity in the space program itself. Is it "the noblest expression of the Twentieth Century or

the quintessential statement of our fundamental insanity?" (p. 15). Like the astronauts, the entire Apollo program seems to be characterized by a mixture of the heroic and the dull, the mysterious and the technological, the good and the evil. The evil in the event is the same decreative evil that Mailer has consistently argued is evident in our corporate technology. On one hand, the flight to the moon is an exercise in a consciousness and lust most clearly embodied in Rusty. Saturn V is a chariot of fire to the heavens, but it enters the heavens more like the shocking and glaring of static and electricity than like the royal spectacle and mystery of flame in the sun. The huge, three-stage rocket suggests a brute, headless power and achievement. At NASA, Mailer had never seen such "a modest purr of efficiency" in people so delighted with being cogs in a machine. Their apparent facelessness and interchangeability are emphasized by the depersonalization and monotony of their speech and behavior. The architecture of their place of work and their homes suffers the similar monotony of environments sterilized of nature. They view a machine not, like the true scientist or artist, as a tool to be used for communicating and exploring ideas, but as an end in itself. The machine is the communication. In the NASA program, Mailer continually finds reflections of a Herculean feat about to be executed with half a brain.

NASA, which Mailer argues was conceived by Kennedy's advisers to prime the economic pump as much as to insure a technological status equal to the Russians, would color and shape everything it touched. NASA would usher in the wholly technological age, "bloated with waiting," and all the phenomena of the age from the new prefabricated housing, to monotonous plants of higher education, to the computer; in short, would usher in what Mailer has long called technological totalitarianism. By depicting the actions and words of corporation chiefs and NASA officials, Mailer continually reminds us that their collective view of their adventure is totalitarian. They view their adventure as an exercise in removing contradiction and mystery from the earth, in subduing contradictory ideologies, in extricating irrationality (that counterforce growing across the land in the sixties), and in removing humanity from a sense of responsibility for its acts and from the sense that one's soul may be judged. The black professor Mailer meets in the home of Texas friends corroborates Mailer's arguments and intuitions. "Technology begins," the black man says, "when men are ready to believe that the sins of the fathers are not visited on the sons. Remission of sin—that's what it's all about" (p. 140). This statement returns Mailer to Kierkegaard: in a time without guides, anyone can lose his or her soul without knowing it.

But sin and guilt are inextricable from corporate life to Mailer, not only because a massive technology has created as many problems as it has "solved," and not only because we have made machines faster than we can control them, but because we have lied about the nature of our work. Mailer concludes, for example, that the guilt of such a lie is the real force behind a dinner conference, which he attends, celebrating the cooperative successes between NASA and the corporation. Each corporation executive must have felt some guilt over the disparity between what he said and wanted to think he was doing and what he actually was doing. The space program promised some relief from guilt because the activities of the corporation were

> at once immense and petty, like the manufacture of toothpaste, immense and noxious, like the production of cigarettes or poisons for war, or immense and depressing, like the shoddy production of slovenly functioning automobiles, or even immense and scandalizing, like the ways in which aviation contracts were garnered, the corporation not only gave security but engendered [the] loneliness and woe. . . . of meaningless effort: here at last was American capitalism attached to a corporate activity which was momentous, dangerous, awesome. . . . [which] gave sentiments of nobility to corporation executives looking to find a line of connection between their work and the vault of this endeavor. (*Fire*, pp. 186–87)

Taking his lead from Collins's reference to the command ship as a mini-cathedral, Mailer will say, indeed, the ship is a mini-cathedral of corporate technology, and the astronauts are its high priests.

On the other hand, the space program seemed to have great potential, too. The flight to the moon did after all speak of some new leap in creation, even as Von Braun and Armstrong said it did. Indeed, a Leviathan was certainly ascending the heavens with men aboard. Mailer will not only describe Saturn V as electronic fire, but as a "white stone Madonna," and as a Moby Dick slowly rising into some new element like a surfacing whale. The most repeated metaphor in the book compares the moon ship and the astronauts to the womb and seed of new growth, to newborns and toddlers. Their task is compared to the delivery of a babe, of some new conception of humanity out across the universe.

This apparent congruity of life-enhancing and life-denying potentials in the space program leads Mailer to extend some of his previous ideas. At the end of Part I, and in Part II, for example, he wonders if God might be using humanity to carry his seed, his will. his conception out to other systems in the universe. If he is, then this stripping of humanity from men and this turning them largely into machines may be a measure of God's desperation in his long battle to fulfill his Vision. Mailer at first believes that the alternative to this speculation is to view the Apollo project as "a species of sublimation for profoundly unmanageable violence in man" and as a meaningless journey undertaken because mankind had not the wit, goodness, or charity to solve its real problems. Mailer has consistently given large significance to human activity, so he struggles to see this flight as part of some great, even divine design, or as a clear blasphemy against God and humanity.

But Mailer is simply uncertain about which view to sustain. This uncertainty may indicate that with *Fire* he is approaching a crucial point in his development. He had said in Book One that the positive effect of journalism, and especially this assignment, might be that one is forced to make adjustments in one's world picture. And in Part III, one scene encapsulates Mailer's uncertain fluctuations between outrage and doubt in the whole book. Aquarius prepares himself to seek the last meanings in the event. Returned to Provincetown to begin writing for his deadlines, he takes his wife and a friend named Eddie Bonetti (a poet and novelist from South Boston) to a "Wasp spa" for dinner. Bonetti is a raucous, eccentric character who is capable of jumping over the handle bars of his bike while riding down the main street in Provincetown to give his friends a laugh, of growing the best tomatoes in town by playing his flute to them in the middle of the night, or of writing a novel so chaste no publisher will touch it. In the "spa" Eddie plays a drunken fugitive from the unwashed masses: "Norman, this place is filled with drunken assholes. Fucking drunken assholes," Eddie bellows. Though Aquarius quiets Eddie down, Aquarius is himself silently outraged when he thinks of all the "friends of his generation" and the next who have used up their years of alienation with alcohol and drugs and with a sexual revolution they sought to usher in as spoiled fools bellowing "obscenity like the turmoil of cattle." This "unholy stew of fanatics, far-outs, and fuck-outs" who had "roared at the blind imbecility of the Square, and his insulation from life," had "dropped out, goofed off and left the goose to their enemies." Aquarius berates Eddie for being drunk all summer while "*they* have taken the moon" by "prodigies of discipline." [5] Yet despite his feelings of outrage, Aquarius again returns to his intellectual doubts. Looking at the outraged restaurant patrons at the opposite table, Aquarius cannot say for sure that these "sturdy worthy" people with "red righteous ire" and "beauty parlor lacquer" are not, or had not become, the

5. Mailer was not alone in seeing the moon-shot as a contest between "we" and "they." I recall a NASA official saying on television, after the LEM landed safely, "That's one for the Squares!" If we would believe Mailer's black friend in *Fire*, many black people would see the whole space program as another unnecessary venture in WASP self-aggrandizement. Mailer, of course, agrees with the anti-WASP sentiment but can't help seeing something larger in the moon flight too.

vehicle of God's Vision however compromised the Vision may at present be (pp. 440–41).

But the final mood of *Fire*, which Mailer evokes in two more brief scenes, is a mood of hope. In the last chapter, "A Burial at Sea," he depicts a symbolic act of regeneration. The Bankos, friends of Mailer, ceremoniously bury an automobile in Provincetown as Labor Day approaches. Friends and nieghbors joyously crowd around; there are several readings of poetry and scripture. The sacrificial carcass of mechanism ("conceived in cynicism and sold in exhortation") is defiled, partially buried, and gradually transformed into a work of art by a metal sculptor named Kearney. Clearly the implication of the scene is that regeneration may yet reside in turning mechanism into life and art.

The potential for regeneration is, again, what Aquarius discovers as he shuttles back and forth between Provincetown and Houston "like a man looking for the smallest sign" while writing his piece. His small sign turns up in the Manned Spacecraft Center at Houston—a two-inch piece of moon rock encased in double vacuums of glass. Looking at the moonstone, Aquarius must finally return to his beginnings, to the authority of his senses and intuitions. All the factuality of *Fire* has only indicated the mysterious ambiguity of men and events, which is no mean accomplishment given the nature of the event. If this moonstone is a warning like the stone Aquarius had seen earlier in a Magritte painting, the moonstone is also a sign or a promise. The promise, first, comes from Aquarius's sense that there was "something young about her, tender as the smell of the cleanest hay, it was like the subtle lift of love which comes up from the cradle of the newborn" (p. 472). This small promise suggests that "before three and a half billion more years were lost and gone" the smell of this rock would work its way through two panes of glass. But the promise of the emerging moon rock implies a larger promise for humanity too. Might not there be, Aquarius asks looking at the stone, some divine design in this conquest of the moon by "Waspitude" and mechanism? Such space voyages, he begins to believe, may at last open the way for us to discover the "metaphysical pits" of our technological world. "Yes, we might have to go out in space until the mystery of new discovery would force us to regard the world once again as poets, behold it as savages who knew that if the universe was a lock, its key was metaphor rather than measure" (p. 471). Had not Aldrin, that self-admitted mechanical man, after all, returned from his flight seeking to restore to science and "technical civilization" a "mythic dimension," to restore cultural symbols that would give humanity an "experience of the whole"?

Fire ends on a note of hope founded less upon the kind of

thoroughly integrated and demonstrable acts of regeneration we observed in *Armies* than upon the author's positive intuitions. It is, as a result, a far less convincing and less engaging book. And some of Mailer's critics have argued that *Fire* demonstrates that Mailer is so locked in his tired dualisms (technology versus life, God versus Devil, etc.) that he seems at this point incapable of reporting anything without shuffling his material into worn-out categories.[6] I would agree that, especially after *Armies*, there are times in Mailer's journalism when a loyal reader must wonder if the dualisms are not wearing a bit thin, becoming a bit automatic. But certainly Mailer's dualistic vision is becoming more complex than it was in, for example, *An American Dream* or *Why Are We in Vietnam?* In fact, there is every reason to suggest that the journalism represents a gradual shift in his vision. That vision may not, probably will not, exclude Mailer's long obsession with Life and Death, but surely a growing complexity and self-doubt are becoming more and more obvious in the journalism since *Armies*. Were it not that such half-human, half-machine men were in control of the events described in *Fire*, Mailer could have written about it with an easy shuffling of dualisms. But his greatest difficulties arose from the recognition that, to use his own conceptions, modern humanity's enterprises seemed to be so inextricably tangled in both the divine and the satanic. The dualisms of *Fire* are not automatic or even clearly in conflict. What Mailer succeeds in doing is to restore ambiguity and mystery to a large event and complex men who made themselves and their acts so flat and dull. But Aquarius has learned that he, like his compatriots, can no longer say for sure what is distinctly good and distinctly evil in what we do.

The Fight (1975) continues Mailer's search for mysteries and large meanings in the events of his time. This book is, for one thing, part of

6. See Richard Poirier, *Norman Mailer*, especially pp. 160–62. See Robert Solotaroff, *Down Mailer's Way*, pp. 243, 245–48. Solotaroff is correct in suggesting that Mailer oversteps his bounds as a credible writer when, in the interest of penetrating the mysteries and potentials of the astronauts and the moon trip, he expects his readers to believe he knows what the astronauts are thinking and dreaming. But Solotaroff ignores a number of real instances when the astronauts do reveal a "psychology" not easily reconcilable with their technological selves. Both Poirier and Solotaroff, rightly I think, suggest that the strength of the book is in its detailed descriptions and cogent characterizations. Laura Adams, in *Existential Battles: The Growth of Norman Mailer*, p. 160, also takes Mailer to task. There are times, as she points out, when Mailer is so heavily researched and so bent on getting at mysteries and profundities that he misses more simple and obvious explanations. Her example of Mailer's fanciful application of astrological data to prove that the common water signs reflect the astronauts' personal preferences for water sports and perhaps the future of evolution is a good case in point. Mailer misses the obvious influence of the Houston climate on the astronauts' preferences.

Mailer's continuing quest for a hero. Contrary to one line of movement in his journalism of the fifties and sixties, *The Fight* leads Mailer to a hero beyond himself. Finding such a hero, the writer clearly transcends the bounds of his own ego even more than the writer and the hero of *Armies* ultimately did. The new hero will not simply embody Mailer's own will but the will of others, will not only act out Mailer's own obsessions and beliefs, his own conceptions of good and evil, but the beliefs and conceptions of others as well. This shaping of his material into a form consistent with other world pictures is important because it is the fruit of Mailer's impulse, which began in *Armies*, to combine the verification of his essential ideas with the complication of his world picture. *The Fight* focuses on two men as heroes in conflict. The question becomes not so much who represents good and who evil, but who is the greatest hero, who is the greatest gatherer of forces. This is a book about boxing as a twentieth-century art, when viewed at its best, and as a religion, in the case of the Ali–Foreman fight. By exploring the art and religion of a championship fight, Mailer continues to explore a central preoccupation of his work—Vital Force, a force that to Mailer is one of the clearest signs of the divine roots of the phenomenal world.

Mailer went to Africa to cover the fight between Muhammad Ali and George Foreman for *Playboy*; he was a working journalist covering his favorite sport. Yet he was also drawn to Africa because he believed Africa had something to teach him. He wanted to "look a little more into his own outsized feelings" of love and possibly hate for black people and black movements.[7] Mailer's first impressions of Zaire, especially Kinshasa where the fight would take place, were not good. From the view of a reporter struck by "some viral disruption in Cairo," Kinshasa looked like nothing so much as a depressing mixture of Hoboken and jungle, or a "Levittown-on-the-Zaire." When the fight was canceled because Foreman was cut in training, Mailer returned to New York and studied two books on Africa while he recuperated from his illness. These books, in order of importance to Mailer's book, are *Bantu Philosophy*, by a Dutch priest named Father Tempels, and *Muntu, The New African Culture*, by Janheinz Jahn. These books and apparently his recuperation prepared Mailer to see Africa in a fresh way.

Mailer tells us that the first thing he noticed in Africa upon his return was "what everyone had been trying to say about Africa for a hundred years, big Papa first on the line: the place was so fucking sensitive! No horror failed to stir its echo a thousand miles away, no

7. *The Fight* (New York: Bantam Books, 1976), p. 37. Mailer raised his ambiguous feelings about the black movement in America in *Miami*, see pp. 53–56. Future references are parenthetical.

sneeze was ever free of the leaf that fell on the other side of the hill"
(p. 36). Mailer began to see Africa as an exemplary setting to
explore his own conceptions of physical and spiritual ecology. Africa, the fight, and the two books on Africa helped confirm and
extend Mailer's idea of the human being as one force in a universe of
communicating and warring forces. In Mailer's and the Bantu's
view, all humans are servants as well as gatherers of larger forces,
including the forces of the dead. One has to be bold, therefore, to live
amidst "all the magical forces at loose" as one tries to learn to bend
some of them to one's own strength. And one always has to be
humble before God. The whole web of forces between beings and
things, whether alive or dead, is the karma Mailer will speak of so
often.

Mailer approaches major heavyweight boxing matches, dominated as they are by black fighters, as one key to the deepest black
experience, especially the experience of karma-force. He admits that
as a white observer he is limited in what he can learn about black
people and about Foreman and Ali, even though he is armed with
his African books and a vast knowledge of boxing. Yet Mailer does
bring readers an entirely different view of the sport than other fight
journalists. What began in *Esquire* in 1962 and *Life* in 1971 as boxing
reportage that introduced collective and supernatural dimensions
of the boxer as hero becomes in *The Fight* Mailer's boldest voyage into
the possibilities of organized combat between two men who represent the culminations of the esprit and force of those who support
and apotheosize them.[8] "A Heavyweight Championship [is] a vortex," Mailer writes, and he later describes the people and events
surrounding the fight as "a charged magnetic field" that takes on the
"logic" of "magical equations" (pp. 124–25). If we place any credibility upon the narrator as an observer, we discover that such
speculative comments are not simply the author's own fantasies, for
everyone intimately involved in the fight, as well as millions of
Africans, share Mailer's perception of the fight as a vortex of forces.
To both contestants the fight is a kind of religious war: Ali prays

---

8. Ali, as the clearest example of the hero of his people, embodies a theme Mailer
introduced in "The King of the Hill," published in *Life* in 1971 and collected in
Existential Errands. Ali has "taken all the lessons of his curious life and . . . the
deep comprehension of his own people . . . and elaborated them into a technique
for boxing." Mailer suggests that one might begin a "psychology of blacks" with
Ali. Ali's first trip through Muslim Africa led him to his personal commitment to
become a world leader for black people. Mailer views the prizefighter as a human
being who speaks with his body with all the detachment, subtlety, and comprehension at his command as Henry Kissinger or Herman Kahn have when they
speak using their minds. Boxing is to Mailer a "dialogue between bodies," a rapid
"debate between two sets of intelligence . . . conducted with the body." See
Existential Errands, pp. 6–8, 14–16.

from the Koran with Elijah Muhammad's son just before entering the ring; Foreman prays in a circle of special supporters. Ali's manager Drew Bundini boasts of using magic against Foreman and sees the fight as a conflict prepared by "God." Mailer describes Bundini as a man of metaphor. Bundini clearly believes in the reality of his sexual and celestial boxing metaphors. Like most men at the fight, Bundini readily admits an awareness of the magic and force God gave him to help bring the fight about. He is delighted when he discoveres his name "in African" means "something like dark" or black, a meaning Bundini sees as connecting him with African roots and "black juice." Don King, the central promoter and mover of this fight, lives his life according to similar beliefs. King's chief satisfaction as a fight entrepreneur is that he becomes for a time "an instrument of eternal forces" by organizing and promoting championship bouts (pp. 117–18). Even President Mobutu of Zaire, who worked with King in arranging the fight, views the fight as one more vehicle for the unification of his people into one nation, one consciousness, and one source of power.

What the two champions represent from a religious perspective is not always clear. At times the dualism represented by the two contenders seems to be a simple opposition of good and evil, especially when Mailer focuses on the fight from Ali's point of view. But at other times the opposition is more a conflict of ideologies, of perceptions of life, and of religions. Mailer feels ambiguous about the fighters. Though he favors Ali, he admires Foreman's strength and discipline and expects him to win. Unlike Patterson and Liston, the fighters seem less ideal archetypes of good and evil, and more two different "embodiments of divine inspiration" (p. 47). When Mailer is most objective, he reduces the fight to a simple principle: he who gathers and makes useful the greater collective force will win.

During most of Mailer's coverage, however, Ali especially embodies a particular kind a heroism as "pugilism's master of the occult." Through the inner disciplines of his entire life, his audacious actions, and his bizarre training practices, Ali will seek to bend to his arena "all forces of the living and the dead." He will seek, therefore, to mobilize the collective *muntu* (the Bantu word for the amount of vital force in human beings) and *kuntu* (the force within things, characterized by audacity and beauty) of Zaire's hundreds of tribes and groups of languages, for Zaire is struggling to unify itself after a complete social upheaval and the breakdown of ancient tribal systems. Ali's success in uniting black people is clear before the fight and incredible afterward. He is a heroic figure to black people in the Third World. In conversations with Mailer, some will refer to Ali as a genius and a god. The people of Zaire adulate Ali as their hero and redeemer.

At twilight, he took a walk on the banks of the river, and was surrounded by hundreds of Zairois men, women, and children. He kissed babies and had his picture taken with numbers of black and jubilant housewives in African Sunday dress, and with shy adolescent girls, and little boys who glared at the camera with machismo equal to the significance of these historic events. All the while Ali kissed babies with deliberation, slowly savoring their skin, as if he could divine which infants would grow up healthy. (*The Fight*, pp. 133–34)

This description shows Ali's relation to the Zairois before the fight. After it, the crowds are so dense and enthusiastic he cannot even go out for a walk. Ali is also a diplomat for the black world. If he wins, he says, he will become a black Kissinger, a true symbol who, as Ali now freely admits, has used his boxing for larger purposes—"to change a lot of things" rather than only for the "glory of fighting" (pp. 78–79). Maybe, Mailer ruminates, Ali's craziness is not so crazy. Ali has been living with a vision of himself as the leader of half the Western World, of future black and Arab republics, and his vision is given substantial reality by people around the world.

The champion's stature is indicated by his name too. Father Tempels wrote that "the name is not a simple external courtesy" to Africans, it "is the very reality of the individual" (p. 216). And after the fight, Mailer will compare another sentence from *Bantu Philosophy* with Ali's reality. " 'On the occasion of his investiture,' writes Father Tempels, the chief 'receives a (new) name. . . . His former name may no longer be uttered, lest by so doing his new vital force be harmed' " (p. 222). The Muslims had bestowed on Ali a name of great weight, for the original Ali was the adopted son of the Prophet Muhammad. Mailer will realize on the flight home that Ali is wholly a Black Muslim and that being one "might be the core of Ali's existence and the center of his strength" (p. 218). Mailer now sees that Ali's beliefs are not whims and contradictions but are built on "the firm principles of a collective idea," which is to say, on national (Islamic) and tribal (African) traditions.

After the fight, African media people will gather around Ali with the awe, "solemnity and respect they might once have offered to Gandhi." And Ali assumes his role as leader and embodiment of collective will and force. He will tell the press of his admiration and love for modern Africans and guide their direction (pp. 221–22). Ali will try to make everyone see, and to some degree convince Mailer of, the essential difference between himself and Foreman, which we could say is the difference between a true hero and a pretender. Foreman, Ali aruges, does not recognize the need to attach ego to larger forces, even to the largest forces, to be an instrument of God rather than of one's own vanity. Ali says that beating George Foreman and conquering the world with his fists "does not bring freedom to my people," and that he, Ali, must now "enter a new arena." Ali implies that Foreman could not surmount the idea of winning for himself, and to the extent that Foreman saw his role as a part of something larger, he was a part of white power, of technology and America, of the white gimmick and vanity. "I got to beat this guy," Ali says. "I saw him at Salt Lake City. He was wearing pink and orange shoes with platforms and high heels. I wear brogans. When I saw his fly shoes, I said to myself, 'I'm going to win' " (p. 214). Ali is getting at the difference between true *kuntu* and the white man's gimmickry, a gimmickry of which, in Ali's eyes, Foreman was the tool and fool, a gimmickry that speaks of ego separated from the largest collective force and the dignity of black people and the Muslim philosophy.

Although Mailer is not as certain as Ali about what Foreman represents, Mailer has prepared us for an essential distinction between heroism and egotism. He is more inclined than ever to let the men and events speak for themselves. But he reminds us at the beginning that the whole purpose of training is to strengthen the ego of the fighter, to turn the raw material of his body and his anxieties into ego, to connect his ego with his will. The fighter who would be a servant of God, however, as Ali would, must also connect his ego with vital force, with libido and *N'golo* (another expression for *muntu*). Defeat then becomes a loss of vital force or *muntu*, which to the black man, Mailer believes, is "pure loss," loss of ego and status and beauty, loss of communication with other forces, loss that is tantamount to disease. [9] He who achieves the greatest *muntu* will be the victor.

It is in Mailer's twenty-seven-page description of the fight itself, in his insight into it, that he reveals his own discovery of just how Ali has the heroic edge over Foreman. Here Mailer is at his journalistic best — fast, concise, vivid. A true aficionado, he is able to make rapid assessments of technique and comparisons with past championships. He has so prepared us for the fight throughout the first one hundred and fifty pages with the details of prefight training and events that we are indeed prepared to see the championship as a collision of opposing worlds or conceptions of existence. As we watch the fight we begin to understand the meaning of numerous details and hints in Mailer's prefight coverage. We come to understand, for example, why Ali spent so much time in training against

9. I am summarizing Mailer's points in *The Fight* on pp. 16–17, 42–43, 75, 215.

the ropes, why Angelo Dundee quietly adjusts the ropes to their greatest resilience just before the fight, why Ali chided the press as ignorant of boxing and described himself as a "boxing scientist" and artist who knew he would win despite the opposite convictions of the press. The sports writers, and Mailer includes himself, are mere engineers, Mailer argues as he continues a metaphor from *Fire*. Ali is a theorist, a physicist, and artist of pugilism. Ali revolutionizes the sport as he fights, Mailer realizes, and that is Ali's great creative potential; his heroism is demonstrated by his ability always to balance "on the edge of the possible" and to turn weaknesses and losses to strengths, as when Ali repeatedly reverses the classic maxims of boxing during the fight.

Mailer's description of the fight is a combination of blow-by-blow and running, concise commentary. If the metaphysics is subdued, it is still implicit through the preceding one hundred and forty pages of Bantu philosophy, training-camp voodoo, and all that talk about African force. Watching Foreman is, for one thing, watching a failed hero, a hero who has a failure of wit. He is convinced that he can beat Ali in the way he trained to beat him no matter what surprises the actual fight holds. Foreman is not capable of existential confrontation by Mailer's definition; Foreman prepares only for a preordained pattern of combat, which he would determine. If physical force has not yet been enough, then more physical force must be the answer. One of the best examples of Mailer's rapid, precise, metaphorical descriptions focuses on the climax of Ali's strategy in the historic fifth round. Ali's creative wit, as he uses the ropes as shock conductors, and Foreman's dogged attack are clearly opposing extremes in a conflict between two physically heroic men. Mailer's description is worth quoting at length because it also gives the flavor of the full range of his powers as a reporter of the real conflicts he observes.

> Then the barrage began. With Ali braced on the ropes, as far back on the ropes as a deep-sea fisherman is braced back in his chair when setting the hook on a big strike, so Ali got ready and Foreman came on to blast him out. . . . Foreman threw punches in barrages of four and six and eight and nine, heavy maniacal slamming punches, heavy as the boom of oaken doors . . . punching until he could not breathe, backing off to breathe again and come in again . . . great earthmover he must have sobbed to himself, kill this mad and bouncing goat.
>
> And Ali, gloves to his head, elbows to his ribs, stood and swayed and was rattled and banged and shaken like a grasshopper at the top of a reed when a wind whips, and the ropes shook and swung like sheets in a storm, and Foreman would lunge with his right at Ali's chin and Ali go flying back out of reach by a half-inch and half out of the ring and . . . back into the ropes with all the calm of a man

swinging in the rigging. All the while, he used his eyes. They looked like stars, and he feinted Foreman out with his eyes, flashing white eyeballs of panic he did not feel which pulled Foreman through into the trick of lurching after him on the wrong move, Ali darting his expression in one direction while cocking his head in another, then staring at Foreman expression to expression . . . muntu to muntu . . . teasing Foreman just a little too long . . . somebody in Ali's corner screamed, "Careful! Careful! Careful!" and Ali flew back just in time . . . Foreman threw six of his most powerful left hooks in a row and then a right, it was the center of his fight and the heart of his best charge, a left to the belly, a left to the head, a left to the belly, a left to the head, a left to the belly, another to the belly and Ali blocked them all, elbow for the belly, glove for the head, and the ropes flew like snakes. . . . Foreman hit him a powerful punch. The ringbolts screamed. Ali shouted, "Didn't hurt a bit." Was it the best punch he took all night? He had to ride through ten more after that. . . . Something may have finally begun to go from Foreman's n'golo, some departure of the essence of absolute rage, and Ali reaching over the barrage would give a prod now and again to Foreman's neck like a housewife sticking a toothpick in a cake to see if it was ready. . . . Ali finally came off the ropes and in the last thirty seconds of the round threw his own punches, twenty at least. Almost all hit. Some of the hardest punches of the night were driven in. Four rights, a left hook and a right came in one stupendous combination. One punch turned Foreman's head through ninety degrees, a right cross of glove and forearm. . . . Foreman staggered and lurched and glared at Ali and got hit again, Zing-bing! two more. When it [round five] was all over, Ali caught Foreman by the neck like a big brother chastizing an enormous and stupid kid brother, and looked out to someone in the audience.

"I really don't believe it," said Jim Brown. . . . "He came back. He hit Foreman with everything. And he winked at *me!*" (*The Fight*, pp. 196–98)

Mailer describes rounds six through eight as "the third act" of a heroic drama, and as a drama that reveals just how much the perfection of Ali's art is based on the principle of "no wanton waste." "Back in America," Mailer writes, after Foreman falls in the eighth round "like a six-foot sixty-year-old-butler who has just heard tragic news," "everybody was saying the fight was fixed. Yes. So was *The Night Watch* and *Portrait of the Artist as a Young Man.*"

Mailer's phrase "muntu to muntu" is at the heart of his coverage. Which man's physically heroic proportions come to represent something larger than the physical, just as Rojack's physical tests come to represent something larger than machismo? On the physical level, Ali's victory is the defeat of a witless if enormous strength by a creative wit translated into physical movement and power. From the philosophical view also employed throughout *The Fight*, Ali's victory is the defeat of vital force limited by ego and lack of wit. Ali is a hero who can apparently allow vital force both unlimited play and precise focus. Which is to say that Ali had best succeeded in bending the greatest collective force to his own energies and powers. But these powers, if focused in the hero during his trial, remain transpersonal too. This is how Mailer sees it; it is obviously how black Africa sees it. Outside the arena Mailer feels the crazy air of liberation in the streets, the air of revolution and renewed potential in life. He is the butt of catcalls from exuberant blacks who assume that he, as a white man, must have been for Foreman. Before leaving Zaire, Mailer sees young boys everywhere jogging along roadsides. And when his return flight to America stops over at Dakar before leaving Africa, thousands of black people rush and immobilize the plane to get a view of Muhammad Ali, whom they mistakenly believe to be aboard. Ali has undergone a species of apotheosis; he is the embodiment of the black people's will, their vital force, their dreams. As an embodiment also of their best selves who promulgates the principles of black freedom, work and discipline, and the community of resources in the Black Muslim religion, Ali has succeeded in awakening black people around the world to their own powers, and to the recognition of heroism for which Louis Farrakhan had pleaded in his speech on Black Family Day. "How come," Farrakhan had asked, "we can't recognize the greatness of men while they live? How come we have to wait until a man is dead and gone before we recognize what kind of man we have?" (p. 229). If the black world has at last recognized a living hero, Mailer too has at last found one. But this hero is no simple embodiment of Good or Evil; he is, rather, a collector of force in a world of communicating and warring forces.

   We have seen *The Fight* as a late journalistic effort in which Mailer continues to develop his philosophical position. As in *Armies*, the narrator's relationship to the greater heroism he views is often comic by comparison. Indeed, the narrator's heroism is minute in *The Fight*. If he succeeds in being the only reporter to push his way into Ali's dressing room after the bout, he is unable to use the opportunity for an interview because he is so awed before the victor. If he faces the challenge of a run with Ali, his poor living and eating habits bring the narrator to the brink of a heart attack. If he overcomes his fear by gliding like Rojack along a parapet, he is a little drunk and is too unsure of whether his relation to such magic produces good or perverse effects, or whether he can really help Ali win by being a little more honest and brave himself. He only knows that if bravery triumphs a little here and there, Ali might somehow triumph for "everything which did not fit into the computer: for audacity, inventiveness, even art" (p. 162).[10] At this point in his career, Mailer's journalism shows the writer discovering personal inadequacies that lead to a position that is for the most part contrary to his earlier professed aim to be a hero for his time. It is not Mailer himself, but another man, a fighter, who actually embodies many of the characteristics of Mailer's heroes and of heroic consciousness. By focusing on the fight in light of what he learned about black Africa, Mailer is able to depict Ali as an instrument of eternal and divine force, as a man who perceives the workings of divine energy in himself and the world, as a unifying force of his people and their best potential, as a figure of collective consciousness or projection, and as a being who is able to turn loss to gain and to live on the existential edge of possibility in such a way that he can adapt himself to the fluid nature (to the experience) of a profound confrontation itself.

But both *Fire* and *The Fight* do continue Mailer's professed aim of restoring mystery and divine significance to humanity and nature. In his latest work of nonfiction, *The Executioner's Song* (1979), Mailer continues his pursuit of large significances, his fascination with the conflicting elements of personality, and his interest in the way extraordinary people can act out the eternal drama of the soul's struggle for salvation through ancient patterns of rebirth. And true to the evolving line of Mailer's nonfiction period, this long book about Gary Gilmore culminates Mailer's increasing self-effacement through his art and continues his focus upon the events and personalities of his time. *The Executioner's Song* is the capstone of his nonfiction period; writing the book seems, in the matters of point of view, style, and distance, to have prepared him for his final fictions. Mailer has come full circle since *The Naked and the Dead*. For the first time since that war novel, he is now writing again in the third person and shifting between numerous points of view. There is in *The Executioner's Song* neither narrator-hero, as in the fiction of the fifties and sixties, nor Mailer-persona (by Aquarius or any other name) to serve as the guiding consciousness of the book.

The theme of *Song* is familiar. "You cannot escape yourself," Gilmore says. "You have to meet yourself." Mailer comes to his subject, Gilmore, with a special understanding, even sympathy, because the challenge to meet one's self is at the heart of the quest of every hero from Mikey Lovett to D.J. And in the new journalism from the *Village Voice* to *The Armies of the Night* and beyond, Mailer has been on a similar personal quest. To face yourself, your own good and evil, your dreams, rational and irrational mind, your best and

10. Compare also pp. 85, 220–21, where Mailer again emphasizes "Norman's" fatigue with his own image, voice, and ideas. He is a "master of bad timing," a being losing force, a writer trying to improve his style.

worst impulses and motives, your own life and your own death—
that has long been "Dr." Mailer's prescription for an ailing American
people and culture. Mailer interrupted his work on the trilogy he is
under contract to write for Little, Brown to devote fifteen valuable
months to Gilmore, a flesh-and-blood man who is the kind of
character Mailer has always pursued.

Gary Gilmore, it turns out in *The Executioner's Song*, might have
sat for Mailer's incomplete portrait of Marion Faye in *The Deer Park*
or sat partially for Stephen Rojack in *An American Dream*, or even,
much earlier, for Sergeant Croft in *The Naked and the Dead*. Mailer's
portrait of Gilmore answers our obvious question: Who was this
Gary Gilmore that so fascinated the public, the media, and finally
Mailer himself? There is more than a little of Mailer—and Mailer
would probably add "of us all"—in Gary Gilmore.

Flawed, confused, frustrated, possessing large passions and designs as both man and artist, Gary Gilmore was both murderer and
philosopher, both psychopath and saint, both chameleon actor and
Middle American. He was the kind of man who could kill two young
men in cold blood to vent his rage over lost love and then by the sheer
force of his intelligence, integrity, and wit make fools of the judicial
system, the media, and the whole "liberal" money-making machine. There was much in his personality that was crass and drab,
and much that was brilliant and exciting.

Gilmore was, above all, a divided personality, a personality full of
contradictions. On the one hand is Gilmore's prison record, which is
enough to intimidate the most hardened con. On the other hand is
Gilmore's painting and drawing, his writing of poetry and—largely
through his love letters and interviews—self-educated philosophical
tracts. Like the "Mailer" of *The Armies of the Night,* Gilmore is a
"peculiar mélange of right-wing ideas and left-wing emotions." He
is at times the ultimate macho man, arm wrestling or fighting for
his male pride, but he is at other times a creature of huge self-doubt:
"I am one of those people that probably shouldn't exist."[11]

With his divided self go his many masks of the actor—confidence
man. Gilmore's father, we are told, was a con artist, a man of several
identities, and that father in turn may have been the illegitimate son
of the great shape-shifter Houdini. In each photograph, Mailer
notices, Gilmore shows a different face. Before the "theocratic"
courts of Mormon Utah, the confessed murderer "might have been a
graduate student going for his orals before a faculty of whom he was
slightly contemptuous" (p. 674). And Mailer extends the metaphor
of the masked actor right through to the end. During the postexecu-

11. *The Executioner's Song,* p. 160. Future references are parenthetical.

tion autopsy, the doctors peel Gilmore's face off his skull like a "rubber mask" and later return the flesh to its proper position so that the corpse "looked like Gary Gilmore again."

What must have fascinated Mailer especially was that Gilmore was deeply involved with theories about the supernatural. Like Mailer himself, Gilmore is a primitive mind born into our modern factologists' world. Gilmore's interviews on karma and reincarnation read like Mailer's own philosophical "dialogues"—"The Metaphysics of the Belly" and "The Political Economy of Time." Synchronicity is a repeated motif in the book, sometimes veering toward Gilmore's more faddish obsessions with numerology, sometimes toward that quasi-Eastern, Maileresque philosophy of karmic debts, burdens, and interconnections. Mailer and Gilmore both associate karma with an intangible force field, as well with the underworld of the psyche, that ties men and women not only to one another but to the men and women who came before them, and even to the other life forms.

Gilmore's choice of death, futhermore, is typical of Mailer's "American existentialism": a choice to accept one's best and worst, one's life and death, in an effort to get closer to one's own soul and to God. In a letter from prison, for example, Gary writes to Nicole:

> But I might be further from God than I am from the devil. Which is not a good thing. It seems that I know evil more intimately than I know goodness and that's not a good thing either. I want to get even, to be made even, whole, my debts paid. . . . I'd like to stand in the sight of God. To know that I'm just and right and clean. When you're this way you know it. And when you're not, you know that too. It's all inside of us, each of us. (pp. 305–6)

Later, Gilmore will comment on his murders and on his own desire for death in turn: "and if you kill somebody, it could be that you just assume their karmic debts . . . thereby you might be relieving them of a debt. But I think that to make somebody go on living in a lessened state of existence, I think that could be worse than killing 'em" (p. 833).

It is Gilmore speaking here, but it might have been Mailer. We have seen that whenever Mailer has had his fictional characters talk like this—whatever we may personally think of the philosophy— critics have hounded him for a lack of realism, as they did when Cherry and Rojack spoke similar words in *An American Dream*. In Utah, Mailer finds a real con, Gilmore, and his girlfriend Nicole, a young uneducated divorcée, talking such words in letters to one another and in interviews.

It is, however, not simply the fact of the thoughts and words spoken and written by Gilmore that interests us or Mailer. What interests us and Mailer is the personality and mind of Gilmore. He is a kind of archetypal figure who relives the old quest for deepest self and soul, and he does so in the most unlikely conditions. The masked confidence man, the many-faced hero, the divided, fluid self that is ever creating new selves to meet the ambushes and rewards of the life he lives, in the time he lives it, is here the questing self, the self searching for a life, for some deep-rootedness and stability, in a place and time where stability and deep-rootedness can be little more than a hope or a dream. Nicole, Gilmore's chief hope, is herself a drifter, obsessively promiscuous, searching for something she never finds.

The environment in which Gilmore acts out his drama is clearly the modern social condition of rootlessness, instability, and fragmentation. Mormon Utah is a kind of focal point of Mailer's Super-America. The hundreds of ranch bungalows like a picture in a supermarket magazine where Nicole lives, the synthetic decor of Holiday Inns, the "media monkeys" crawling all over one another to get their Gilmore scoop, psychopharmacology in prisons, the dealings of the influential and rich—David Susskind, ABC, CBS, NBC, *Playboy*, *The National Enquirer*, Bill Moyers, and Jimmy Breslin all jockeying for a piece of the story—and the endless liberal justifications denying a guilty man the choice of his own death—it is all here; it is Mailer's America as "Cancer Gulch," the backdrop for his tale. It is the environment that would turn one man's struggle to meet himself and his fate into a circus and diminished experience, just as the Utah desert, which Mailer reminds us once had a beauty like Palestine's, has been turned into a smog-ridden, mini–Los Angeles: "Mormon . . . Moroni . . . More Money." Set in this environment, the archetypal quest is again used as social criticism, just as Mailer has always used that quest.

And like Mailer's previous heroes, Gilmore is a modern man in search of his soul, wondering whether he might be closer to God or Devil, wanting to make himself whole, willing to pay his debts until he is right and clean and able to "stand in the sight of God." Gilmore reenacts the essentially religious quest that has always characterized heroic effort. The appeal to the self becomes ultimately a quest for divine energy and eternal, purposive, creative force. And of course the more enormous the hero's guilt is, the more forceful and dramatic the quest becomes. It is in prison that Gilmore faces himself, by accepting his guilt and facing his death. What he finds in himself—the continuing dream of the severed head, the "Oldness," and "the darkness" that all come to represent previous lives and debts; the guilt of the murderer; his own death—he accepts and pursues to the end. He chooses expiation and death in the face of that vast machinery a twentieth-century liberal democracy marshals against such a choice. He takes responsibility for his actions, and he acts accordingly and with little hesitancy. "Let's do it," he says before the firing squad. His last words are: "May the Lord be with you all." Only possible reunion with Nicole ever tempted him from that path.

Once again Mailer, in his nonfiction, has gravitated toward subjects and events that reveal, give life to, his own preoccupations. Yet if Mailer is still writing the book he has always been writing, if familiar images of soul-birds, tales of magic forces, descriptions of severe and dangerous tests of the self return here as in the previous books, *The Executioner's Song* does offer a significant departure too. One does not find here the voice we have come to expect, the discursive, self-conscious, intrusive narrator who, in the case of the journalism especially, finds his own response to events as important as the events themselves. Nor do we find the baroque, eccentric, energized prose that sweeps the reader along with the force of its verbal and philosophical waves and contortions. It is as if, suddenly, the old master of tumultuous prose has passed on, as if Mailer's first literary hero, Melville, has been laid to rest, and as if Mailer's second literary hero, Hemingway, is emerging as the guiding genius of Mailer's later years. The prose is hard and lean: "Right outside the door was a lot of open space. Beyond the background were orchards and fields and then mountains. A dirt road went past the house and up the slope of the valley into the canyon." Mailer now uses images and metaphors so sparingly that when they do come, they come, like Hemingway's, with renewed power. "Outside the prison, night had come, and the ridge of mountain came down to the Interstate like a big dark animal laying out its paw." The author is removed; the prose is clean.

Yet this new prose and this distance from his subject are a source of Mailer's greatest weakness in the book. For what Mailer hoped to do by letting the characters tell their own stories and by staying out of the story himself is to let the characters themselves act as myriad centers of consciousness or points of view. That idea in itself is fine; sometimes Mailer succeeds in translating the idea into effective technique; and the grace and rapidity with which points of view sometimes shift is an admirable technical achievement. But if Mailer succeeds in switching our attention from one vision of events to another, he most often fails in giving adequate dimension to the individual qualities of voice, and voice embodies consciousness. Too often the reader finds separateness of consciousness obscured by uniformity of voice.

The tapestry of figures and visions is vast: relatives, lawyers, journalists, friends, and the principals of the murder case. Yet in presenting all these different points of view, Mailer resorts to only a few devices to capture the rhythms of individual language. Double negatives, appositive phrases in place of sentences, *like* in place of *as*, and current slang expressions are among the chief devices used. Used selectively, such devices work effectively; they may seize the quirks of unique voice and thought. But used indiscriminately, monotonously, they confuse, dissolve the qualities of personality, do nothing to convince readers of the separateness of inner selves. The same structural and grammatical devices are used, for example, to express the points of view of deadbeats and uneducated relatives as to express the views of lawyers, journalists, and law student Max Jensen. In Jensen's case we have a particular lack of necessary distinction because with Jensen Mailer is trying precisely to establish the contrast between the Mormon, college-educated, hardworking, middle-class victim and Gary Gilmore and his most subterranean associates. Mailer has done much to strike the balance he has sought in the stories of both victims and assassins—his portraits of the Jensens and the Bushnells is as sympathetic yet honest as his portraits of Gilmore and Nicole—but his blurring of voice does little to forward that balance.

Mailer's new, clean style, however, marks a definite point in his creative development. Mailer himself sees his new style and techniques of objectivity as a point in his development too. In an interview with Ted Morgan, Mailer said that he was trying to be little more than a "transmission belt" for the characters to tell their stories, and that it took him thirty years of writing "to be willing to relinquish his ego" enough to allow characters that freedom. "I couldn't have done it 15 years ago," Mailer commented.[12] The increased objectivity through which the archetypal drama is told strikes me as a definite gain in style and technique after a decade of self-oriented nonfiction. Perhaps it is gain, among other qualities, that the Pulitzer Prize Committee recognized in awarding the Prize to this book. If Mailer can only overcome his weakness—the blurring of the voices of individual selves—his new, promised fictions may gain much from the lessons and developments of the nonfiction period. What he actually produces later will remain to be seen, but he is, up until now, still seeking large, even the largest, significances in humanity and nature as he restores mystery to the events and personalities of our time.

It is this goal in all of his writing that has led to so much opposition. We have seen that Mailer's allegorical impulse has led many critics to take what they consider to be the literal unreality of

12. Ted Morgan, "Last Rights," *Saturday Review*, pp. 57–58.

Mailer's work as grounds for seeing his work as a simple failure of
verisimilitude. My principal goal in this study has been to restore
Mailer to himself, to discover what Mailer as an artist and a thinker
is and what he wishes to be, and to suggest that it is by seeing Mailer
himself and not the categories of certain critics that his work must
be criticized, or even approached. It is precisely this same impulse to
restore mystery and to work in the allegorical mode that has led
feminist criticism and the women's movement generally to voice
strong opposition similar to that (and often on the same grounds) of
the "realistic" critics. Here, again, we need to restore Mailer to
himself.

The feminist opposition has, first, failed to take into account the
allegorical nature of Mailer's work. We have seen that Mailer speaks
in his novels and nonfiction in symbolic and archetypal, as well as in
realistic, modes. He has protrayed most of his women as the embodiments of light or dark forces, as mythic figures, as soul-energy and
mystery as well as satanic power. To many women, Mailer's tendency to portray women as beasts at their worst and goddesses at
their best is exactly, as Gloria Steinem once told Mailer in a luncheon
interview, where Mailer goes astray for many readers. [13] This is a
just criticism insofar as we consider only the literal dimension of
Mailer's books. But we can hardly speak of continuing, ancient,
profound, cross-cultural, cross-temporal images as *simply* sexist,
any more than we can label as *simply* sexist a writer who attributes
to women not only huge potentials for destructive evil but huge
potentials for creative good. [14] Yet this dualistic tendency in Mailer is
the basic cause of his problems with many women readers, espe-

13. See *The Prisoner of Sex* (hereafter cited as *Prisoner*), p. 19.
14. While we can argue reasonably that culture, epoch, and upbringing affect
the dispositions of an artist as of any man or woman, there is no final evidence that
every act, image, and behavior of the individual is determined by nothing but
environmental factors, nor that everything a man associates with his masculinity
or a woman with her femininity is a mere environmental effect. For every
behavioristic-materialist, there are, if not necessarily in the American academy,
mythologists, psychologists, and socio-biologists who present evidence for an
opposing view; that is, not all psychic experiences or images or patterns of behavior are culturally taught responses. Many responses, or predispositions to
patterns of behavior and image-making, may be inherited and transpersonal. We
would do well to recall, considering the nature of this study, that Jung continually
defined the archetype as an inherited disposition to the formation of images in the
human psyche (not as inherited images themselves), which can be indirectly
encountered through symbols. See, for example, Carl Jung's *Symbols of Transformation*, translated by R. F. C. Hull, Vol. 5 (New Jersey: Princeton University Press,
1956), pp. 158, 181, 313. Victor White defends the basic concept of the archetypal
predisposition on the grounds that comparative studies of motifs and myths
existed long before Jung ever mentioned "archetypes" and that the widespread use
of related images proves Jung's point. The evidence is quite "empirical." From the
archetypal view, the mind that turns a woman into a devourer or into a goddess is

cially since women critics have held up for attack the literal Rutas and Deborahs of the fiction to the exclusion of the literal and symbolic Cherrys. [15] If Steinem and Kate Millet are indicative, many modern women wish men writers to make no extraordinary or mysterious claims for women at all, but would prefer women to be seen as merely ordinary people in an ordinary world. We might accept it as a given that in America in the 1960s and '70s, a symbolic writer will run afoul of one group of interests or another. Nothing seems more abhorrent to women in the feminist movement than to be endowed with extraordinary power and mystery by the male, unless it is, to take a more extreme case, the abhorrence Millet feels for every female figure in Mailer's novels who is not a paragon of positive human potential. We could of course quibble endlessly with Millet over the evidence that no male figures are such paragons in Mailer's fiction either and that there are as many women endowed with large evil and good as there are men. But Millet's criticism is always in danger of falling into the fallacy of a woman who, to make a simple analogy, might consider Flaubert a male chauvinist pig simply because Madame Bovary is not a paragon of sagacious womanhood, and who would necessarily have to ignore in making such a charge the considerable human frailties of Dr. Bovary and the male lovers. If one is to make a case for Mailer's sexism, one will have to make it on other grounds. One may, in fact, have to redefine sexism, at least in the way that term has been used to categorize Mailer. For if Mailer is a sexist, he is one in no superficial sense, but in a profoundly radical and conservative sense because of the way he views the forces in women's lives with which women must deal and find some balance. He has said as much of men and the forces in their lives, but he views these forces as different if as potentially restrictive. We have only to think of Ali and Foreman and of the many male characters in his novels who represent failures of human potential. The point is that a critic or a reader must go to the level of Mailer's fundamental beliefs and values before he or she can honestly assess his weaknesses and strengths.

---

not necessarily a sexist mind, but may be a mind functioning on the mythic, transpersonal level. In such a case, the woman does not represent only a woman, but the unconscious itself, a transpersonal symbol revealing a timeless threat and a timeless promise.

The gist of my point here about cultural conditioning versus instinctual impulse and disposition is precisely Mailer's point as he grapples with Millet's reductive behaviorism throughout *Prisoner*, see, for example, pp. 168–69.

15. We have seen an example of this in Elizabeth Hardwick in Chapter 4. Kate Millet's *Sexual Politics* provides another. Vivian Gornick's "Why Do These Men Hate Women?" in the *Village Voice*, pp. 12–15, takes on Mailer, Henry Miller, Philip Roth, and Saul Bellow in a similar manner.

In *The Prisoner of Sex* Mailer points out a number of ways in which he agrees with the women's movement. He is not a sexist who wants women confined to the home, to be manipulated by a superior male class, to be stifled politically, economically, and socially. But this is the charge leveled against him by Millet and other feminists. He specifically emphasizes that he is encouraged by the movement's "fundamentally radical" idea that men have proved themselves incapable of administering the world with an ounce of humanity (p. 43). He agrees that to the extent that we see women only as social and economic beings, they are indeed a class exploited by the ruling male class. He is looking for a cultural and sexual revolution too. He favors the ERA. He agrees with Linda Phelps's position that women cannot afford merely to emulate men, to live in positions of power in a man's world, or to live men's lives, but that the society males have created has to be changed before a human world can be built (pp. 48–57). He disavows Freud's sexist, reductive theories of penis envy and the castration complex (pp. 82–84) and is quite in line with Millet on this point. He denies that he is a sexual reactionary in the sense that he wants women stifled in their roles in "the ranch house and plastic horizon." His enthusiasm for the mysteries of the womb are not simply a ploy to "squeeze women back into that old insane shoe" (p. 179).

But Mailer's actual oppositions to certain implications in the women's movement certainly have led and will continue to lead him into trouble with many women. What Mailer will not give up is his conviction that human beings and human activity have great, even supernatural, significance, a significance always larger and more mysterious than the agents or actors in events themselves. To feminists such as Millet who take a wholly behavioristic and materialistic approach to human phenomena, this conviction of Mailer's will not do. Millet, for instance, is a woman who endlessly documents the male expression of the experience of "phallic power" across all cultures and times and offers no explanation, especially no instinctual explanation, for the phenomenon's origins other than suggesting that it somehow must be culturally conditioned. If there are areas of female experience men cannot be expected to understand, is it not possible there are areas of male experience that women cannot understand? Mailer, for example, searches in vain among female writers for any attempt on their part to understand a male's sense of phallic, sexual force. And there is probably no reason why women should be expected to know or understand a male's experience of his phallus.

Mailer has agreed that the culturally sustained misapplication of male sexual force against women is abhorrent. But he is not as willing as Millet to ignore the possibility that there are psychic and biological roots to man's experience of phallic force, or even the experience of a certain sexual antagonism between males and females. Mailer is exploring instinctual factors of male sexuality; he is not condoning the use of that sexuality in a way that enlarges an already disproportionate, oppressive culture. It has always been Mailer's argument that by facing the reality of an instinctual drive or experience, we may come to accept it and use it with some less destructive balance in our lives. Indeed, if we follow the logic of Mailer's argument about instinctual behavior, we see that by facing their sexual experience of women—which Mailer has always described as both lustful and loving, both violent and tender—men might come to separate the realities of phallic force from their disproportionate technological society, a society that rapes nature of its economies and ecologies as much as it rapes women of fundamental human rights.

But what does Mailer believe about women? One must first ask what does he believe about humans. He believes they are agents of larger forces, which to some degree they can control, in a mysterious universe. He believes that human sex has significance far beyond the participants in the sexual acts themselves. His "reasonable point" is simply that "the fuck either had meaning which went to the root of existence, or it did not," that if humans "embody a particular Intent," if we can "assume just for once that there is some kind of destiny intended" and that we are not simply absurd, not totally, then "sex cannot comfortably prove absurd." Sex without larger meaning, or "absurd" sex, is best "shunted over to semen banks and the extra-uterine receptacles" (pp. 190–92). Mailer is not so much asserting that he knows the destiny of all women (i.e., the womb and the creation of life) as he is suggesting the significance of the womb's existence. It is at least probable, he says, that the significance of the womb is larger than the organs of sexual pleasure alone. He does not say that bearing children is the *whole* destiny of women; he argues that the functioning of the womb in a fertile woman is a large part of her natural existence. The womb attaches woman to a force larger than the individual, a force with which she may learn to live in balance. In fact, the specific charge Mailer makes against Henry Miller is not that he is a sexist, but that Miller's work never developed to the point where he presented a woman of moral and creative strength and integrity equal to his men. Miller never created a Nora like Ibsen, a woman who can say to the man, "I am a human being as much as you," and who will strike some balance between her "sacred" duty to herself as a human being and her "sacred" duty to her sexuality and womb (see p. 123).

Men are prisoners of their sexuality to a large extent too. A man's phallus, first, sets him in some polarity to woman, at least in the sense that phallus and womb are not the same thing and that womb has some "psychic tendrils" or closer connection to the creation of life. Mailer also suggests that there is something about a male's sexuality that tends to increase his drive toward another kind of creation than the woman, a creation that tends to separate men from nature. This too is a force in men's lives with which they must learn to live in balance. Male ego assertion has led so far only to imbalance, for its crowning achievement is our grotesque technological and industrial world. Mailer's point is not that men and women have no choice, but that their choices as individual humans must operate within a larger arena of forces. Ali, for example, is an instrument of larger forces, but he is effective as an individual *and* as a hero because he has learned to balance God's force and destiny with his own powers, to serve as a unifying center for the collective force of his people, to sense the vital force within himself and the connection between that force and larger forces, and to adapt to trial and confrontation. To balance one's destiny *and* one's will, to balance biology *and* one's wishes, to balance collective *and* individual force—these are the trials besetting all men and women.

Mailer is vulnerable to the criticism that he places too large a share of woman's destiny in one place, her womb, which limits her choice. But we have to acknowledge his actual position again. His position is not that men naturally have a greater choice or freedom from destiny or larger forces, but that, because they have no womb, men face more kinds of forces than women. The total pull of destiny or force upon men and women is roughly equal.

His principal argument with the women's liberation movement is with that tendency in it which he believes encourages women to separate themselves from their wombs. Unlike men, women are in full possession of a "mysterious space within" that, in Mailer's view, not only places them a step closer to the "creation of existence," but probably exists in women for that particular purpose—the creation of life—which purpose is larger than the individual woman herself. In technologyland, women carrying around this creative space have to compete for power, economic status, and self-expression on a technological basis; that is, on the basis of efficiency, finely tooled labor, uniform behavior, and mechanical dependability. Technologyland has no time or room for the realities of the womb, of pregnancy and birth, all of which technocratic man sees as an interruption of mechanical labor. To compete in this world, women, Mailer argues, have accepted, or have had to accept, such a world's terms. They reacted with rage against a strange, mystical communion with creation (the womb) and saw it as a burden rather than an advantage. The result is a technological attempt to solve the woman's "disadvantage" in a technological world: birth control, abortion, the uprearing of children by professionals. Rather than denying our technology as a blasphemy against nature, women embraced it, looked to technology, as Dana Densmore hopefully depicts it, to control nature. Densmore unabashedly argues for a Huxleylike world of total technological control of the processes of impregnation, gestation, and birth (pp. 64–65), looks to rid herself and women of their wombs by technology so that they might compete in and perpetuate a world where technology has already dehumanized life. She is not, by Mailer's evidence at least, a single instance. And nothing could be clearer in Mailer's work than that he argues that men too must reject technologyland. He is not suggesting that *only* women reject it. But Mailer believes that as long as you seek solutions in technology, as long as technology is your faith, you *are* a part of the oppressive, inhumane system. Technology *is* the system.

Mailer's second complaint is that there is a tendency in the feminist movement to technologize the sexual revolution, which revolution, on the contrary, should be a force against technology. The issue rests on the controversy over the female orgasm. Some feminist writers have taken the conclusions of modern sex research that the female orgasm is stimulated by and limited to the clitoris alone as reason to believe that, finally, men are unnecessary to sexual fulfillment. Mailer's counterargument is that, even if based on "facts," such conclusions are still only half-truths because the evidence derives from laboratory procedures as unnatural, sterile, and mechanically probing as the tendency of such evidence to promote the contemporary drive toward the technological and onanistic sex of "plastic pricks," "laboratory dildoes," and electronic vibrators, and is about as close to the human realities of sexual love. Mailer is, here, at least consistent with the general movement of his life's work. He offers Germaine Greer and his personal sexual experience of women as counter evidence to argue for the great variety of female orgastic response and the "qualitatively different" orgasms, to use Greer's words, between clitoral stimulation and male penetration (see pp. 77–82).

Mailer has assumed the debatable premise throughout his life that nature depends upon the dialectic of polarities and the diversity of existence. So he argues from that premise, or faith, that the more pernicious ramification of sexual technology is that it shapes the sexual revolution into unnatural, totalitarian forms, into a unisexuality and bisexuality that homogenizes male-female sexual polarity.

It "might be more natural to believe that God had established man and woman in some asymmetry of forces" (p. 83). He is by definition reactionary because he views sex as something larger than the pleasure of the participants; he

> preferred to believe that the Lord, Master of Existential Reason, was not thus devoted to the absurd as to put the orgasm in the midst of the act of creation without cause of the profoundest sort, for when a man and woman conceive, would it not be best that they be able to see one another for a transcendent instant, as if the soul of what would then be conceived might live with more light later?

Sexual technology measured orgasms by "periodicity and count," but, for Mailer, it is not technology but "the eye of your life" looking back at you at the moment of orgasm (pp. 87–88). In our age we look not for large meaning and responsibility in our acts. We are more willing to accept Dr. Shettles techniques of swabbing "vinegar or baking soda up one's love" to determine the sex of a child, or to believe that the child we create "with an eye on the alkalinity factor" is the same as the child we create in "the juices of an unencumbered fuck" (p. 214). Mailer's general point in all this is that to some extent we *are* prisoners of our male or female sexuality and that to attempt to blur all distinctions between male and female is one more example of the modern forms of totalitarianism. The second part of Mailer's argument with Millet is over just this issue of the totalitarian disintegration of sexual polarity. Millet insists that men and women are exactly alike except for reproductive systems. Mailer's reply is that "reproductive systems are better than half of it!" Millet's propensity to view the sexual apparatus as purely material and isolated from the whole self simply astounds Mailer (as if ten cubic inches of penis opposed to the 3,000 cubic inches of the body meant that male sexuality is 1/300th of the self). It is as if Mailer, who has spent his life portraying the fictional factologist-materialist as an agent of evil, found one in the flesh who outdid his own powers to imagine one.

If Mailer is to be attacked honestly for his sexual theories, it is upon such premises and theories as these that he must be criticized, or even upon his more extravagant assertions in passing that birth control was in the primitive state probably a function of the female psyche, or that women are differentiated from men by the differences in their inner lives: their closeness to nature, their irrational propensities, their mysterious associations with the moon (all positive associations for Mailer himself).

But his negative critics among women have not addressed themselves to these issues; they have, like their male counterparts, misunderstood the mode of Mailer's art. In the case of Kate Millet the

misunderstandings and misrepresentations are more serious because what she has done to Mailer is exactly what she has done to
Henry Miller and D. H. Lawrence. She has written a sexual polemic
in which her lack of fidelity to her material is so egregious as to
embarrass a reader familiar with the texts and the life work of the
writers she deplores. A male critic, of course, risks the chauvinist
label himself in making such a suggestion. But it may help to point
out that a woman, Laura Adams, has said the same thing about
Millet's *Sexual Politics*, even though Adams personally disagrees at
several points with Mailer's sexual theories.[16] At any rate, the evidence of Mailer's best restorations of Miller and Lawrence is indis-
putable. Mailer simply places full quotations beside Millet's excised
quotes and false insinuations. Mailer's full quotations from Miller's
and Lawrence's texts clearly reveal that the authors are often saying
something the very opposite of what Millet says they are saying.
Again and again Mailer catches Millet in the act of quoting grossly
out of context, making fallacious and biased summaries, and even
attributing false quotations. However admirable her desire to subvert a grostesquely exploitative male-dominated society may be,
Millet is still, as Mailer puts it, a "thesis monger with an axe." In
Mailer's case, Millet not only mistakes the symbolic for the literal,
not only focuses on the satanic women to the exclusion of the divine
"vessels," she distorts even the bare literal material of his books to
peddle her thesis.[17]

Only when men and women free themselves from a life-denying
technology, Mailer has been saying for thirty years now, will they
subvert the gross imbalances in our culture. So Mailer's view of the
role of the womb in woman's destiny is not in line with American
postwar culture because he does not define that destiny as his
culture does (i.e., the ranch house, plastic horizon, corporation, and
the institutions of the ruling male class), but specifically refutes it.

16. See Laura Adams, *Existential Battles: The Growth of Norman Mailer*, p. 165.
17. The point should be clear by now, but a few examples of such misrepresentations follow: Millet misreads such a simple detail as the police letting
Rojack go. She sees it as a blind comradery among men, when, in fact, it is clearly
the result of the evil and power of Kelly in the world. She talks of Elena's suicide as if
it were a fait accompli, which it never is, and the suicide is no more than an
automobile accident that is the direct result of Faye's suicidal impulse, not Elena's.
She sees Rojack's pilgrimage as an argument for promoting the "American way of
life," when nothing could be more obvious about *An American Dream* than that
everything Rojack aspires to promotes just the opposite. And Millet is careless
enough not to investigate and understand Mailer's distinctions about personal and
impersonal violence, or to see that he most certainly is not recommending can-
nibalism, or to see that D.J.'s rite is not "successful" by any measure of Mailer's
approach to Rusty-power, Vietnam, and technology. To Millet, *An American Dream*
is nothing but "an exercise in how to kill your wife and live happily ever after"; see
Millet, *Sexual Politics*, especially pp. 15, 46–47.

What Mailer is suggesting in *The Prisoner of Sex* is that a woman's life may be as open as that of Ibsen's Nora, but with this stipulation: it is equally possible that God's Intent in giving women wombs is that their lives (their "destinies," if you will) are somehow connected with the creation of new life to a larger degree than man's.

If Mailer fails women in his work and in *Prisoner*, he fails them not because he thinks women should be recast into an oppressive society. He fails them because he is too much the nay-sayer. He does not attempt to suggest a feasible alternative for a woman's tech-nological separation from her womb if she hopes to gain any semblance of equality in our sexual, political, and economic life. If he argues that humans must reject technology and begin to find new lives on other foundations, that is little compensation for a woman facing gigantic disproportions against which she cannot effectively struggle alone. And it is on this point especially that feminist critics might readily and honestly take Mailer to task.

One is bound to assume that Mailer's war with technology and with certain implications, as he sees it, in the women's movement will continue to place him very much in the role of an adversary to his civilization and his time. But that is where he obviously wishes to be; he has always drawn enormous, if not always effectively chan-neled, energy from his view of himself as an adversary of the predominant culture. And whether a reader can sympathize with and enjoy Mailer's work will in large part depend upon his or her real relationship to dominant values in that culture, whether or not the reader *thinks* he or she is in opposition to those values. Mailer opposes those values that favor the technological over the natural, that rely solely upon facts and statistics rather than upon feelings and intuitions, that view the processes of nature and human phenomena as ends in themselves rather than as playing lesser roles in a universal or even divine drama, that explain human behavior in materialistic terms rather than in terms of the human struggle to balance the influences of ageless, conflicting, dynamic forces in oneself and in the world. The center of the difference between Mailer and the culture in which he lives is best expressed in *Why* . Here Mailer argues through metaphor that all life exists in a physical and divine economy and ecology, an economy and ecology that mankind (especially masculine industrial culture) violates at its peril, that no waste is acceptable, that waste is the clue to our disease, that insofar as we seek to adjust the imbalances in ourselves through external (industrial and technological) power we endanger Life and God itself.

Mailer's opposition to the dominant values of our culture during his lifetime is precisely what places him in a major American literary tradition. He has joined the long lineage of writers who have sought to awaken the moral consciousness of their people, who have sought to attach words, through image and symbol, as Emerson said, to visible things, who have allegorically depicted the journey of the individual soul as somehow connected to the journey of America — as both an existence and an ideal — itself. In the works of the Puritans, of Emerson, Thoreau, Hawthorne, Melville, Twain, Fitzgerald, and Faulkner, the pilgram soul confronts extremes of good and evil, at times divided as God and Devil. The pilgrim often undergoes an apocalyptic voyage in which the expansion of self and soul, and the intergration of nature and God and self, are all part of the same process of growth and the same possibilities of defeat.[18] It is in describing such journeys that Mailer is most American and most in the literary tradition that seeks to define America's best, most liberated, most creative self. And it is in describing such journeys that Mailer is most repetitious. Yet as Richard Poirier has said, great writers are repetitious writers, and if Mailer can only expand while he repeats, he may yet produce a work of greatness.[19]

Will a work of greatness be forthcoming? We can only say that, finally, in middle age, Mailer has been given the rare opportunity to write one.

Whether he seizes the chance, we will have to wait to discover. In 1975, he had submitted a 120,000-word manuscript to Little, Brown as the first installment of his "big novel," a novel that will appear in several volumes. In late 1979 in an interview with Dick Cavett, Mailer said the work was about half completed. Laura Adams has said that those who have read the manuscript describe it as "epic, Jungian, Tolstoian, dealing with a racial theme." His latest book, *The Executioner's Song*, which has ended a decade and perhaps a period of nonfiction, holds some promise of creative development. That book ends the line of his development that started most clearly in *Armies* in 1968. Throughout his nonfiction period, Mailer has turned more and more to reality as it is in his time to seek the allegorical and archetypal order in apparently fragmented events and people. In doing so, Mailer has at the same time increased his use of realistic techniques and become ever-more objective and self-effacing. The greater balance he is striking between realism and allegory points up the continued potential of allegory and archetype as social criticism. For Mailer found in Gilmore a type of modern hero. Like

18. Compare Thomas Werge, "An Apocalyptic Voyage: God and Satan, and the American Tradition in Norman Mailer's *Of a Fire on the Moon*," *Review of Politics*, pp. 108–28. Werge makes the same point about *Fire* specifically, but his point is, of course, applicable to the entire Mailer canon. Werge specifically compares Mailer to John Winthrop, Emerson, Hawthorne, Thoreau, Whitman, and Twain.

19. Richard Poirier, *Norman Mailer*, pp. 57, 160.

Lovett, Rojack, or Mailer himself, Gilmore is a man whose life when
we meet him is base; he is a man psychologically and physically
adrift in a fragmented world, a guideless explorer looking for clues,
signs, and guides; he is a man searching—if at times ignorantly—for
meaning, action, and self-definition. But in the end, as he looks into
himself, Gilmore begins to grow toward some greater life, or soul,
rather than to die toward some meaningless death. It is as if the
resources within the self and the archetypal order of the quest still
hold value for Mailer, still may serve as the symbolic stage for
individual acts of regeneration and patterns of existential growth. It
is this regeneration that Mailer holds up for twentieth-century humanity to witness as our world becomes increasingly fragmented, as
we drift farther apart, and as society (the center of the old order)
veers either toward totalitarianism or toward disintegration.

If Mailer has learned from his years of writing nonfiction more
about himself, about the powers of realism (which do not exclude
allegory), about the necessity of making one's material more complexly and warmly human, he may produce the work he has promised. But I doubt that he will transform the foundation on which he
has built his themes—his life-long obsession with the discovery of
the deepest self. D. H. Lawrence has described this drive as also a
part of the American literary tradition, as part of the conflicting
claims of the self in the works of Franklin, Crèvecoeur, Cooper, Poe,
Hawthorne, Dana, Melville, and Whitman, and as a manifestation
of the deep split in Western consciousness between intellect and
body, love and sex, spirit and matter, the white industrial ego and
the archaic soul, and between the conscious and unconscious
psyche. "The true liberty will only begin," writes Lawrence, "when
Americans discover IT, and proceed to fulfill IT. IT being the deepest
whole self of man, the self in its wholeness, not idealistic halfness."[20]
It is doubtful, too, that Mailer will jettison the power of the symbols
with which he has worked, that his work will become nonsymbolic
and nonallegorical.

If Yeats said that a reader need not believe his particular systems
of mythology and supernatural time to understand his images and
to see how his systems offered correlatives in his poetry, the Mailer
critic might ask as much for Mailer, whether or not he wishes the
dispensation himself. Mailer may believe in his systems; he may
even ask us to believe them, but belief is not necessary to an understanding of his metaphors or to an appreciation, even a distant
appreciation, of the power and timelessness of some of his values
and ideas. It has been my purpose to demonstrate how the idea is

20. D. H. Lawrence, *Studies in Classic American Literature*, p. 7.

related to the art, both conscious and unconscious art, in Mailer's allegorical work. What seems certain is that Mailer's future writings, whatever else they may be, will continue to seek their place in the literature of ideas. The ideas are not yet necessarily set forever. In fact they increasingly raise new questions. They continue to seek fulfillment and form, just as they continue to express the outrage of a man who, however uncertain of himself, still possesses a huge, baleful uncertainty about where the human race is headed and about the disintegration of human potential. "If brooding over unanswered questions was the root of the mad . . . and sanity was the settling of dilemmas," Mailer writes in *Of a Fire on the Moon*, "then with how many questions could one live? He would answer that it was better to live with too many than with too few. Rave on, he would. He would rave on" (p. 458).

Bibliography

I. Books by Norman Mailer

Advertisements for Myself. New York: G. P. Putnam's Sons, 1959.
An American Dream. New York: The Dial Press, 1964, 1965.
The Armies of the Night. New York: The New American Library, Inc., 1968.
Barbary Shore. New York: Rinehart and Company, Inc., 1951.
The Bullfight: A Photographic Narrative with Text by Norman Mailer. New York: CBS Legacy Book, 1967.
Cannibals and Christians. New York: The Dial Press, 1966.
Deaths for the Ladies (and other disasters). New York: G. P. Putnam's Sons, 1962.
The Deer Park. New York: G. P. Putnam's Sons, 1955.
Existential Errands: Twenty-Six Pieces Selected by the Author from the Body of All His Writings. Boston: Little, Brown & Company, 1972.
The Executioner's Song. Boston: Little, Brown & Company, 1979.
The Faith of Graffiti. New York: Praeger Publishers, Inc., 1974.
The Fight. Boston: Little, Brown & Company, 1975.
Genius and Lust: A Journey through the Major Writings of Henry Miller. New York: Grove Press, Inc., 1976.
The Idol and the Octopus: Political Writings on the Kennedy and Johnson Administrations. New York: Dell Publishing Company, 1968.
Marilyn. New York: Grosset & Dunlap, Inc., 1973.
Miami and the Siege of Chicago. New York: World Publishing Company, 1968.
The Naked and the Dead. New York and Toronto: Rinehart and Company, Inc., 1948.
Of a Fire on the Moon. New York: Little, Brown & Company, 1971.
The Presidential Papers. New York: G. P. Putnam's Sons, 1963.
The Prisoner of Sex. Boston and Toronto: Little, Brown & Company, 1971.
St. George and the Godfather. New York: The New American Library, Inc., 1972.
Some Honorable Men: Political Conventions, 1960–1972. Boston: Little, Brown & Company, 1976.
Why Are We in Vietnam? New York: G. P. Putnam's Sons, 1967.

II. Other Sources Cited

Adams, Laura. "Existential Aesthetics: An Interview with Norman Mailer." *Partisan Review* 42 (1975): 197–214.
——. *Existential Battles: The Growth of Norman Mailer.* Athens: Ohio University Press, 1976.
Aldridge, John. "From Vietnam to Obscenity." *Harper's* (February 1968): 91–97.
——. *Time to Murder and Create: The Contemporary Novel in Crisis.* New York: David McKay Co., Inc., 1966.

204

Bersani, Leo. "Interpretation of Dreams." *Partisan Review* 32 (Fall 1965): 603–8.

Brower, Brock. "Always the Challenger." *Life* 59 (24 September 1965): 100, 111, 112.

Campbell, Joseph. *The Hero with a Thousand Faces*. New Jersey: Princeton University Press, 1968.

Carlyle, Thomas. *On Heroes, Hero-Worship, and the Heroic in History*. Edited by Carl Niemeyer. Lincoln: University of Nebraska Press, 1966.

Cowan, Michael. "The Americanness of Norman Mailer." *Norman Mailer: A Collection of Critical Essays*, edited by Leo Braudy, pp. 143–57. Englewood Cliffs, N.J.: Prentice-Hall, Inc., 1972.

Current Biography, 1948. Edited by Anna Rothe. New York: The H. W. Wilson Company, 1948.

DeFalco, Joseph. *The Hero in Hemingway's Short Stories*. Pennsylvania: University of Pittsburgh Press, 1963.

Dennis, Everette E., and Rivers, William L. *Other Voices: The New Journalism in America*. San Francisco: Canfield Press, 1974.

Eliade, Mircea. *The Myth of the Eternal Return*. New York: Bollingen Foundation, 1954.

Fletcher, Angus. *Allegory: The Theory of a Symbolic Mode*. Ithaca: Cornell University Press, 1964.

Foster, Richard. "Mailer and the Fitzgerald Tradition." *Novel* 1 (Spring 1965): 219–30.

Galloway, David. *The Absurd Hero in American Fiction*. Austin: University of Texas Press, 1970.

Geismar, Maxwell. "Frustrations, Neuroses, and History." *Saturday Review* (26 May 1951): 15–16.

Gornick, Vivian. "Why Do These Men Hate Women?" *Village Voice* (6 December 1976): 12–15.

Gutman, Stanley T. *Mankind in Barbary*. Hanover: The Univeristy Press of New England, 1975.

Hardwick, Elizabeth. "Bad Boy." *Partisan Review* 32 (Spring 1965): 291–94.

Honig, Edwin. *Dark Conceit*. Evanston: Northwestern University Press, 1959.

Howe, Irving. "Some Political Novels." *Nation* 172 (16 June 1951): 568.

Jung, Carl. *The Collected Works of Carl Jung*. Edited by Sir Herbert Read, Michael Fordham, and Gerhard Adler. 19 vols. New Jersey: Princeton University Press, 1957–1976.

Kaufmann, Donald L. "Catch-23: The Mystery of Fact (Norman Mailer's Final Novel)." *Twentieth-Century Literature* 17 (October 1971): 247–56.

Klein, Marcus, ed. *The American Novel Since World War II*. Greenwich, Conn.: Fawcett Books, 1969.

Lawrence, D. H. *Studies in Classic American Literature*. New York: The Viking Press, 1961.

Leeds, Barry. *The Structured Vision of Norman Mailer*. New York: New York University Press, 1969.

Lewis, R. W. B. "William Faulkner: The Hero in the New World." *Faulkner: A Collection of Critical Essays*, edited by R. P. Warren, pp. 208–18. Englewood Cliffs, N.J.: Prentice-Hall, Inc., 1966.

Macdonald, Dwight. "Politics." *Esquire* (May 1968): 42.

Marcus, Steven. "The Art of Fiction: Norman Mailer, an Interview."*Paris Review* 8:31 (1964): 28–58.

Millet, Kate. *Sexual Politics.* New York: Doubleday & Co., Inc., 1970.

Morgan, Ted. "Last Rights." *Saturday Review* (10 November 1979): 57–58.

Neumann, Erich. *The Origins and History of Consciousness.* New Jersey: Princeton University Press, 1973.

Pearce, Richard. "Norman Mailer's *Why Are We in Vietnam?* A Radical Critique of Frontier Values." *Modern Fiction Studies* 17 (Autumn 1971): 409–14.

Piehler, Paul. *The Visionary Landscape.* Montreal: McGill-Queen's University Press, 1971.

Poirier, Richard. "Morbid-Mindedness." *Commentary* (June 1965): 91–94.
———. *Norman Mailer.* New York: The Viking Press, 1972.

Radford, Jean. *Norman Mailer: A Critical Study.* New York: Harper & Row Publishers, Inc., 1975.

Rolo, Charles. "A House in Brooklyn." *Atlantic* 187 (June 1951): 82–83.

Schrader, George. "Norman Mailer and the Despair of Defiance." *Yale Review* 51 (December 1961): 267–80.

Solotaroff, Robert. *Down Mailer's Way.* Urbana: University of Illinois Press, 1974.

Stark, John. *"Barbary Shore:* The Basis of Mailer's Best Work." *Modern Fiction Studies* 17 (Autumn 1971): 403–13.

Vidal, Gore. "The Norman Mailer Syndrome." *Nation* 190 (January 1960): 13–16.

Weatherby, W. J. "Talking of Violence." *Twentieth Century* 173 (Winter 1964–1965): 109–14.

Welsford, Enid. *The Fool.* New York: Farrar and Rinehart, 1935.

Werge, Thomas. "An Apocalyptic Voyage: God and Satan, and the American Tradition in Norman Mailer's *Of a Fire on the Moon.*" *Review of Politics* 34 (October 1972): 108–28.

Whicher, Stephen E., ed. *Selections from Ralph Waldo Emerson.* Boston: Houghton Mifflin Company, 1957.

White, Victor. *God and the Unconscious.* New York: Meridian, 1961.

Wolfe, Tom. "Son of Crime and Punishment." *Book Week* (14 March 1965): 1, 10, 12–13.

Wolfe, Tom, and Johnson, E. W. *The New Journalism.* New York: Harper & Row Publishers, Inc., 1973.

Index

A

Absurd hero: in existential fiction, 113–16; compared to Mailer's heroes, 115–17

Allegory: types and elements defined, 5–12; use of realism or myth in, 34

B

Bantu philosophy: compared to Mailer's, 3; Mailer's sources of, 178

Barth, John, 5n

Bellow, Saul: Mailer's criticism of, 114–15; heroes, 116

Brown, Norman O., 3n

Buber, Martin: Mailer's use and analysis of, 85, 106

C

Campbell, Joseph: 7; spiritual elements of hero, 56n; summary of hero myth, 117; theory of divine ecology, 119, 124; heroic ego-assertion versus egotism, 128–29. See also Jung, Carl

Camus, Albert, 115. See also Absurd hero

Carlyle, Thomas: theory of heroic in history, 116–18, 124; heroic quest, 122–23; compared to Joseph Campbell and Victor White, 122; "revolutionary history," 123; "World Machine," 123; ego-assertion versus egotism, 128; political processes versus hero, 131

D

Devourer archetype: devil and mother as, 77n, 109; beast as, 101–3. See also Mother archetype

Dos Passos, John, 12

E

Eliade, Mircea: being versus historical time, 48; ceremonial time and primitive ontology, 105–6; hero as agent of creative violence, 123, 152n

Emerson, Ralph Waldo: "Self-Reliance," 132n; compared to Mailer, 201

Energy, psychic: as unconscious and divine, 47–48, 52–54; heroic search for, 54

Existentialism: hipster philosophy as, 48; Mailer's theological dimension of, 71; as courage, 86; Mailer's definition of, 86–87; Mailer compared to Heidegger and Sartre, 87; Mailer compared to Eliade, 106; "American" existentialism, 188

F

Farrell, James T., 12

Father archetype: as guide, 35; as healer, 100; as Terrible Father, 95, 100–105. See also Old man archetype

Faulkner, William: compared to Mailer, 103–5

Feminist movement: criticism of Mailer, 192–200; sexual and cultural theories, 194, 197. See also Millet, Kate

Fitzgerald, F. Scott, 145

Fletcher, Angus: definition of allegory, 6, 9, 10, 11–12, 28; myth and realism in allegory, 34–35; search for power, 54; compulsive ritual, 92; visionary ritual, 110

Fool, The: in history compared to Mailer, 146–47; as scapegoat, 153–54

Frazer, James George, 12, 153

H

Hawthorne, Nathaniel, 161–62

Hemingway, Ernest: heroes compared to Mailer's, 145, 148; as Mailer's literary model, 190

Hero: signs of in allegory, 42; hero as quester, 51; as symbol of psychic energy, 56; as deliverer, 71; Mailer's definition of, 117–30; ego-assertion versus megalomania, 128–29, 182

S

Shaw, George Bernard: creative evolution, 54

Soul: symbols of, 74, 101; transformation of, 74; Mailer's theories of connection with body, 71–72; as unconscious, 72, 87n

T

Thompson, Hunter S., 143

U

Unconscious: as divine energy, 52–53; Mailer's theories of, 66, 68; as instinct, 84. *See also* Energy; Soul

Updike, John, 116

W

White, Victor: on Jungian theory, 55n; on the archetypal image, 192n

Wolfe, Tom, 137, 139, 145. *See also* New journalism

Permissions

Advertisements for Myself by Norman Mailer, copyright © 1959 by Norman Mailer. Reprinted by permission of G. P. Putnam's Sons.

An American Dream by Norman Mailer, copyright © 1964, 1965 by Norman Mailer. Reprinted by permission of The Dial Press, and Scott Meredith Literary Agency, Inc.

The Armies of the Night by Norman Mailer, copyright © 1968 by Norman Mailer. Reprinted by permission of The New American Library, Inc., and Scott Meredith Literary Agency, Inc.

Barbary Shore by Norman Mailer, copyright © 1951 by Norman Mailer. Reprinted by permission of author and his agents, Scott Meredith Literary Agency, Inc.

Cannibals and Christians by Norman Mailer, copyright © 1966 by Norman Mailer. Reprinted by permission of author and his agents, Scott Meredith Literary Agency, Inc.

The Deer Park by Norman Mailer, copyright © 1955 by Norman Mailer. Reprinted by permission of G. P. Putnam's Sons.

The Fight by Norman Mailer, copyright © 1975 by Norman Mailer. Rprinted by permission of Little, Brown and Company.

The Presidential Papers by Norman Mailer, copyright © 1963 by Norman Mailer. Reprinted by permission of G. P. Putnam's Sons.

Why Are We in Vietnam? by Norman Mailer, copyright © 1967 by Norman Mailer. Reprinted by permission of G. P. Putnam's Sons.

The Hero with a Thousand Faces by Joseph Campbell, Bollingen Series XVII, copyright © 1949 by Princeton University Press, copyright © renewed 1976 by Princeton University Press. Reprinted by permission of Princeton University Press.

Near the Ocean by Robert Lowell, copyright © 1967 by Robert Lowell. Reprinted by permission of Farrar, Straus & Giroux, Inc., and Faber & Faber, London.

"Norman Mailer's *Why Are We in Vietnam?*: The Ritual of Regeneration," by Robert J. Begiebing, appeared as an article in *American Imago* (Spring 1980). Reprinted by permission of *American Imago*.

The Origins and History of Consciousness by Erich Neumann, translated by R. F. Hull, Bollingen Series XLII, copyright © 1954 by Princeton University Press. Reprinted by permission of Princeton University Press, and Routledge & Kegan Paul, London.